K. 62. The oth...
   freedom - 63

Corpus mysticum and varium
   page 43

96 - Comm and Irony - Solitude

   love kills - 253

   love and law - 279
   foundling time - 315

   In the imagination that Devil
   produces devil 349

   writing and sex 399

   Hegel, God is dead - 618 note 6

   Kenosis - 404

) / through writing the other
   ceases to be forbidden, ceases to
   be separate 434

Teresa, My Love

Teresa, My Love

An Imagined Life of the Saint of Avila

a novel by

Julia Kristeva

TRANSLATED BY LORNA SCOTT FOX

COLUMBIA UNIVERSITY PRESS | NEW YORK

Columbia University Press
Publishers Since 1893
New York   Chichester, West Sussex
cup.columbia.edu

Copyright © 2008 Librairie Arthème Fayard
Translation copyright © 2015 Columbia University Press
All rights reserved

This work, published as part of a program providing publication assistance, received financial support from the French Ministry of Foreign Affairs, the Cultural Services of the French Embassy in the United States, and FACE (French American Cultural Exchange).

Columbia University Press wishes to express its appreciation for assistance given by the Pushkin Fund toward the cost of publishing this book.

Library of Congress Cataloging-in-Publication Data
Kristeva, Julia, 1941– author.
    [Thérèse mon amour. English]
Teresa, my love : an imagined life of the saint of Avila / Julia Kristeva ;
    translated by Lorna Scott Fox.
        pages cm
    Includes bibliographical references.
    ISBN 978-0-231-14960-0 (cloth : acid-free paper)
    ISBN 978-0-231-52046-1 (ebook)
    1. Teresa, of Avila, Saint, 1515-1582. 2. Christian saints—Spain—Avila—
Biography. I. Fox, Lorna Scott, translator. II. Title.
    BX4700.T4K7513 2014
    282.092—dc23
    [B]
                                                        2014007011

Columbia University Press books are printed on permanent and durable acid-free paper.
This book is printed on paper with recycled content.
Printed in the United States of America
c 10 9 8 7 6 5 4 3 2 1

Cover image: *Teresa of Ávila* (detail), 1827, Françoise Gerard/
Infirmerie Marie-Thérèse, Paris
Cover design: Jennifer Heuer
Book design: Lisa Hamm

DeAgostini/Leemage.

For my father

Contents

Abbreviations and Chronology   *xiii*

Part 1: The Nothingness of All Things

1. Present by Default   3

2. Mystical Seduction   29

3. Dreaming, Music, Ocean   51

4. *Homo Viator*   61

Part 2: Understanding Through Fiction

5. Prayer, Writing, Politics   77

6. How to Write Sensible Experience, or, of Water as the Fiction of Touch   87

7. The Imaginary of an Unfindable Sense Curled into a God Findable in Me   105

Part 3: The Wanderer

8. Everything So Constrained Me   121

9. Her Lovesickness   151

10. The Ideal Father and the Host   171

Part 4: Extreme Letters, Extremes of Being

11. Bombs and Ramparts 189

12. "Cristo como hombre" 203

13. Image, Vision, and Rapture 207

14. "The soul isn't in possession of its senses, but it rejoices" 215

15. A Clinical Lucidity 225

16. The Minx and the Sage 233

17. Better to Hide . . .? 239

18. ". . . Or 'to do what lies within my power'"? 249

19. From Hell to Foundation 261

Part 5: From Ecstasy to Action

20. The Great Tide 269

21. Saint Joseph, the Virgin Mary, and His Majesty 277

22. The Maternal Vocation 289

23. Constituting Time 313

24. Tutti a cavallo 331

Part 6: Foundation—Persecution

25. The Mystic and the Jester 377

26. A Father Is Beaten to Death 387

27. A Runaway Girl 407

28. "Give me trials, Lord; give me persecutions" 421

29. "With the ears of the soul" 437

Part 7: Dialogues from Beyond the Grave

30. Act I. Her Women   453

      Act I, Scene 1   455
      Act I, Scene 2   468
      Act I, Scene 3   476

31. Act II. Her Eliseus   493

      Act II, Scene 1   494
      Act II, Scene 2   508

32. Act III: Her "Little Seneca"   517

      Act III, Scene 1   517
      Act III, Scene 2   530
      Act III, Scene 3   540

33. Act IV. The Analyst's Farewell   547

Part 8: Postscript

34. Letter to Denis Diderot on the Infinitesimal Subversion
of a Nun   567

      Notes   *597*
      Sources   *631*

Abbreviations and Chronology

ABBREVIATIONS

The Book of Her Foundations: *Found.*, followed by number and paragraph

The Book of Her Life: *Life*, followed by chapter and paragraph

The Constitutions: *Const.*, followed by the paragraph number

Letters: *Letter*, followed by letter number

Meditations on the Song of Songs: *Medit.*, followed by chapter and paragraph

On Making the Visitation: *Visitation*, followed by number and paragraph

Poems: *Poems*, followed by title

A Satirical Critique (Vejamen): *Critique*

Soliloquies (Exclamations): *Sol.*, followed by number and paragraph

Spiritual Testimonies (Relations): *Testimonies*, followed by number and paragraph

The Interior Castle: Roman numeral, followed by D (*Dwelling Places*), chapter, and paragraph

The Way of Perfection: *Way*, followed by chapter and paragraph

CHRONOLOGY OF WORKS

1560–1563	*Testimonies 1–3*
1562	First draft of *The Book of Her Life*
1563	First draft of the *Constitutions*
1565	*The Book of Her Life*

1566–1567	*The Way of Perfection*
1567	*The Constitutions* of the Discalced Nuns
1569	New series of lesser *Testimonies*: 8–27
1573	*The Book of Her Foundations*, chaps. 1–26
1575–1576	*Testimonies* 4–5
1576	*Manner of Visiting Monasteries*; continuation of *Foundations*, chaps. 21–27
1577	*The Interior Castle*
1577–1580	*Letters* (almost 200)
1581	*Testimonies* 6
1580–1582	Completion of *Foundations* (chaps. 28–31)
1581–1582	Final letters (around 100)

The *Soliloquies*, the *Meditations on the Song of Songs* (predating *The Interior Castle*), and the *Poems* are difficult to date with accuracy.

REFERENCES

The English translations used for all quotations from Teresa of Avila come from the following sources.

The Collected Works of St. Teresa of Avila. trans. Kieran Kavanaugh and Otilio Rodríguez. 3 vols. Washington, D.C.: ICS, 1976–1985.

The Collected Letters of St. Teresa of Avila. trans. Kieran Kavanaugh. 2 vols. Washington, D.C.: ICS, 2001–2007.

Any italics in quotations have been added by Julia Kristeva.

Teresa, My Love

Part 1

The
Nothingness
of
All Things

Chapter 1

PRESENT BY DEFAULT

We are not angels, but we have a body.

Teresa of Avila, *The Book of Her Life*

Or perhaps there is only a single mind, in which everybody has a share, a mind to which all of us look, isolated though each of us is within a private body, just as at the theater.

Marcel Proust, *Within a Budding Grove*

The flung-back face of a woman asleep, or perhaps she has already died of pleasure, her open mouth the avid door to an empty body that fills before our eyes with a boiling of marble folds . . . You must recall that sculpture by Bernini, *The Ecstasy of Saint Teresa*?[1] The artist's inspiration was Teresa de Cepeda y Ahumada (1515–1582), whose religious name was Teresa of Jesus, better known as Saint Teresa of Avila. At the height of the Renaissance, her love of God quivered with the intensity of the *beatus venter* that Meister Eckhart knew so well. Her ecstatic convulsions made her into a sumptuous icon of the Counter-Reformation. Though she was, in Dostoyevsky's sense, possessed, she was bathed in the waters of desire rather than, like Mary Magdalene, in tears—for her body and soul were fused with the absent body of the Other. "Where is He, where have they taken Him?" fretted the holy women at Golgotha.[2]

Teresa loved to read; they made her write. In a style quick with emotion, yet firm and precise, she portrayed the blend of pain and jubilation she felt with an emphasis on the deft agent of her undoing: Eros, armed with a spear, the iron tip of God Himself. "*Prudentia carnis inimica Deo*" (Prudence of the flesh is inimical to the Lord), so the Church Fathers taught. In this spiritual, illusory marriage to the Other, the unreachable Father is relayed in the praying woman's fantasy by a heavenly stripling, an undefiled brother, a male mirage of Teresa herself, whose voluptuous pride will never pierce her hymen.

Oh, how many times when I am in this state do I recall that verse of David: Que-madmodum desiderat cervus ad fontes aquarum [As the hart panteth after the water brooks, so panteth my soul after thee, O God. (Ps. 42:2)] . . . When this thirst is not too severe, it seems it can be appeased somewhat; at least the soul seeks some remedy. . . . At other times the pain becomes so severe that the soul can do neither penance *nor anything else,* for the whole body is paralyzed. One is unable to stir with either the feet or the arms. Rather, if one is standing, one sits down, like a person being carried from one place to another, unable even to breathe. . . . The Lord wanted me while in this state to see sometimes *the following vision: I saw close to me toward my left side an angel in bodily form. . . . the angel was not large but small; he was very beautiful, and his face was so aflame that he seemed to be one of those very sublime angels that appear to be all afire.* They must belong to those they call the cherubim. . . . I saw in his hands *a large golden dart and at the end of the iron tip there appeared to be a little fire. It seemed to me that this angel plunged the dart several times into my heart and that it reached deep within me. When he drew it out, I thought he was carrying off with him the deepest part of me; and he left me all on fire with great love of God.* The pain was so great that it made me moan, and *the sweetness this greatest pain caused me was so superabundant that* there is no desire capable of taking it away; nor is the soul content with less than God. The pain is not bodily but *spiritual, although the body doesn't fail to share in some of it, and even a great deal. . . .* But when this pain I'm now speaking of begins, *it seems the Lord carries the soul away and places it in ecstasy;* thus there is no room for pain or suffering, *because joy soon enters in* [*así no hay lugar de tener pena ni de padecer, porque viene luego el gozar*].[3]

Desire existed before she did, and this woman knows it. Nevertheless she is consumed: a burning wound, a delightful pain. In the key of the Song of Songs, but by the hand for the first time of a European woman, pleasure unto death is conveyed with a sensual exactitude that defies decorum. Make no mistake: the fire that "carries off" the deepest part of her suggests that rather than capture the potency of the "large dart," as in the male fantasy of the castrating female, Teresa gifts it to the angel. It is in dispossession and exile that she joins with the Other and becomes divine. In the same vein, at once a shooting star and a clap of thunder, she resumes her account in the "Sixth Dwelling Places" of *The Interior Castle*, her spiritual testament:

> The soul dissolves with desire, and yet it doesn't know what to ask for since clearly it thinks that its God is with it.
>
> You will ask me: Well, if it knows this, what does it desire or what pains it? What greater good does it want? I don't know. I do know that it seems *this pain reaches to the soul's very depths and that when He who wounds it draws out the arrow, it indeed seems, in accord with the deep love the soul feels, that God is drawing these very depths after Him.* I was thinking now that it's as though, from this fire enkindled in the brazier that is my God, a spark leapt forth and so struck the soul that the flaming fire was felt by it. And since the spark was not enough to set the soul on fire, and the fire is so delightful, the soul is left with that pain; but the spark *merely by touching the soul produces that effect.* It seems to me this is the best *comparison* I have come up with. *This delightful pain—and it is not pain—*is not continuous, although sometimes it lasts a long while; at other times it goes away quickly. This depends on the way the Lord wishes to communicate it, for it is not something that can be procured in any human way. But even though it sometimes lasts for a long while, it comes and goes. To sum up, it is never permanent. For this reason it doesn't set the soul on fire; but just as the fire is about to start, the spark goes out and the soul is left with the desire to suffer again that loving pain the spark causes.[4]

Teresa's body—as passionate and amorous as David's or Esther's, or that of the Sulamitess in the Song of Songs—falls back upon the Word. A gem of European memory, her text is steeped in Scripture, while her fiery verve rhythms a great movement in Catholic history: the baroque revolution. Might she also, unlikely as it may seem, be our contemporary?

Teresa's "torment" is "beatific," she experiences its ambivalence as "spiritual joy." Such a fabulous autoeroticism, strained through Old Testament passions and sublimated by New Testament ideals, does not eschew "corporeal form." "Christ's humanity" was a theme of sixteenth-century piety; Erasmists, *alumbrados* (Spanish Illuminati), Jewish converts, and plenty of believing women embraced it. Thus Teresa's ecstasies were immediately and indiscriminately formed of words, images, and physical sensations pertaining to both the spirit and the flesh: "the body doesn't fail to share in some of it, and even a great deal," she admitted. The experience, too, is a double one straightaway: while being the passive "object" of her transports, the nun is also the penetrating "subject," who approaches "graces" and "raptures" with an astounding, unprecedented lucidity. Lost and found, inside and out and vice versa, this woman was a flux, a constant stream, and water would be the undulating metaphor of her thought: "I . . . am so fond of this element that I have observed it more attentively than other things."[5]

* * *

I ran into her again on the cover of a Lacan *Seminar*, while doing my MA in psychology.[6] I'd already admired Bernini's sculpture, whose voluptuousness so stirred the susceptible Stendhal,[7] in Santa Maria della Vittoria in Rome—long before this learned publication promised to tell us everything about female *jouissance* and its insatiable cry for "More!" Every summer, docile cultural tourists that we were, my small family spent vacations plowing up and down the Italian peninsula. I didn't know very much in those days about the illustrious Carmelite nun, but at the La Procure bookshop, opposite the church of Saint-Sulpice, I had purchased her *Collected Works*—two onion-leafed volumes fat with unreadable prose. The kind of impulse buy you commit on the eve of a solitary weekend, instantly banished to the top of the bookcase and as soon forgotten.

I may as well tell you right away, I'm not a believer. I was christened as a matter of course, but Jesus was never a dinner-table topic at our house. My father was a general practitioner in the 13th arrondissement, and my mother taught literature at the lycée in Sceaux. Everyone worked too hard to see much of one another or to talk; it was a standard secular family of a kind very common in France, efficient and rational. Any discussions revolved, on Mother's side, around literary prizes and the horrors of the world—much the same thing, perhaps. Whereas my father, who purported to be a left-leaning Gaullist, was forever grumbling about how France would never recover from the Algerian war, or how beggars were ruining the city center, or how some people believed in nothing but their doctor: a big mistake, as he was in a position to know. Anxious to spare Mother and me the "trials of life," he'd made sure to give us "nothing but the best, my darlings." That was his hobbyhorse, being more of an elitist than a republican, to put it mildly; he was proud of his success at providing for us, as he saw it. Meanwhile Mother, a fan of Colette and Françoise Sagan, was forever feeling let down by the latest Goncourt, Renaudot, or Femina book prizes, whose standards were so "dreadfully mediocre," and pushing for the three of us to travel abroad, preferably to Italy, which was not a common destination in those days. I would listen with half an ear. I was pretty independent for an only child. It was May 1968, and my mind was elsewhere.

I love the night. I'm not an insomniac, but I've been regularly waking up around 2 A.M. ever since my father passed away, ten years ago this September. My mother faded away barely fifteen months after that, that's apparently how it is when people love each other—not that love had been particularly noticeable in their case. I had never found them terribly interesting; you don't when you're a child, so it hadn't occurred to me they might seem interesting to each other. Nowadays I listen to France Info and Jazz 89.9 or 88.2 as a cuddly toy substitute. Rocked by the sounds of the world, I doze without really dropping off, until the alarm clock rings.

I love the night, its furtive, underwater life of news flashes and rhythmic beats snagging memories at random, or semidreams, because a no-body opens up to nothing, and I only feel good when I'm rid of myself. Was my brain saturated by the latest dreary debate on the clash of civilizations, secularism versus head scarves? Or was it some dream that still escapes me? Anyhow, one night I fished up a word from my chance dives into the murky depths, the word "mystical," which gave me such a stomach cramp that I rolled out of bed at first light. Where had that popped up from? I was hardly likely to have heard the word "mystical" on France Info, or Jazz point something.

I drank my tea over the first volume of the saint's works, which I retrieved like a sleepwalker from the top of the bookcase, where I couldn't remember having put it. It was quite an encounter. The kind of thing that gets under your skin and no one can figure out why. Teresa of what? Sylvia Leclercq reading Teresa of Avila, you're kidding! After that sharp little book on Duras? No way! Maybe the silly goose thinks mysticism's due for a revival, like she's happened on a money-spinner!

They've got me all wrong. I'm not sharing my saint with anyone; I'm keeping her all to myself. She will be the roommate of my submarine nights, her name is Teresa of Avila.

* * *

Should conspicuous tokens of faith be allowed in schools, yes or no? Yet another committee that can't manage without a psychologist, this time to discuss France's constitutional secularism. Representatives of every brand of sensibility, profession, gender, and politics had been convened to guide a lawmaker through the issues. Unsurprisingly, we were at odds: some, like me, felt that religion is a private matter and public space shouldn't be an arena for the contest of beliefs; others took our rigorous stance for an assault on the very right to believe, a disgraceful mark of intolerance. A young woman in a head scarf suddenly raised her voice above the noise: an IT engineer, pretty, clever, and adamant. She explained to us very forcefully that she and her God were *one* and that the veil was the immovable sign of this "union," which she wished to publicize in order to definitively "fix it" in herself and in the eyes of others. Her desperate need to be fixed, defined, seen, was immediately obvious to the rest of us, especially the psychologists. Furthermore, should we deny her this "identity," she was quite prepared to sacrifice herself—like those female suicide bombers on the other side of the world, and soon, perhaps, in our own suburbs. We had been warned. Hot-faced, voice spiking shrilly but full of eloquent resolve, she informed us that her veil was also a protective barrier, shielding her body from the lust of men, and visible proof "that I'm devoted to my work, that I'm a serious person, and that I don't have the slightest interest in sex."

"'Neither whores nor submissives*'!" cried the woman on my left, incensed, and I clapped. [*Ni putes ni soumises: women's rights movement founded by French Muslim women in 2002.—Trans.]

"She wears her veil like Saint Teresa wore a habit, she'll get over it in a few hundred years," snickered the man on my right.

"But that's completely different!" Reproving stares pierced me from every side. Trapped, I said meekly: "Well, *I* think it is, anyway." It was no time to be splitting hairs.

The spontaneity of my outburst surprised me. As if Teresa had just installed herself inside me, suddenly, *by default*, as the software manuals call it: from now on, automatically, as soon as your mental programs are booted up, before you've thought to modify this ineluctable presence by recustomizing your habits or traditions of thought, there something or someone *is*. In my case, there was Teresa, finally turning me away from a pointless, pretentious debate whose speakers were simply regurgitating the usual arguments and counterarguments as heard on TV. Should have expected it.

I fell into a kind of stupor, sucked into the abyss that separates the IT jihadi—protected from everything and then some by a scarf that strangles her worse than a convict's neck iron—from the Golden Age visionary attempting to reconcile the faith of her desires with her loquacious reason. Was it really such an abyss? Sure. Not sure. Let's see.

* * *

Teresa, as I read her, was able, by entering into ecstasy and writing down her raptures, not only to feel suffering and joy in both body and soul, but also to heal herself—almost—of her most salient symptoms: anorexia, fatigue, insomnia, fainting fits (*desmayos*), epilepsy (*gota coral* and *mal de corazón*), paralysis, strange bleedings, and terrible migraines. What is more, she succeeded in imposing her policies on the Church by reforming the Carmelite order. She founded seventeen monasteries in twenty years: Avila, Medina del Campo, Malagón, Valladolid, Toledo, Pastrana, Salamanca, Alba de Tormes, Segovia, Beas, Seville, Caravaca, Villanueva de la Jara, Palencia, Soria, Granada, and Burgos. In addition she wrote prolifically (her *Collected Works* run to nine volumes in the Spanish critical edition by Fr. Silverio de Santa Teresa); showed herself to be a most skillful metapsychologist, well before Freud, obviously; and emerged as a canny "businesswoman" within a Church that hadn't asked for it. Unrepentantly carnal, she was moved by an insatiable desire for men and women, and naturally for the God-man Jesus Christ, never troubling to conceal her passions, even though she had taken vows, gone into seclusion, and hidden herself in a prickly woolen robe. Teresa used on the contrary to stoke her ecstasies to the limit, the better to savor their delights—sadomasochistic, of course—while analyzing them. And she bequeathed to us a masterpiece of self-observation and baroque rhetoric, not so much a *Castle of the Soul*, as it may be too hastily translated, but rather a kaleidoscope of "dwelling places," *moradas* in Spanish: a "psychic apparatus" composed of multiple facets, plural transitions, in which the writer's identity slips its moorings, is lost, is freed . . . with apologies to the head-scarfed engineer. Enough to make my colleagues, were they to go out of their way to visit this unlikely "castle," turn green with envy.

Ever since she surfaced in the vagrancy of my submarine nights and imposed herself "by default" upon my discourse, Teresa hasn't left me alone for a moment. This can be irritating, especially during the psychotherapy sessions with my analysands. For they are, male and female, one and all, sick with love, like Teresa, like Marguerite Duras, like the IT engineer, and plenty more. Like me, except that I have spent so many years analyzing myself and others that I lost the capacity for passion and it's no longer that simple. Teresa wasn't fooled either, in a way; at any rate she was far less gullible than some of my patients of either sex who revel in lovesickness and close their ears to my interpretations, no doubt because they love me too much.

But Teresa had no qualms about delving to the "root" of her "sins," of her "boiling desires," those "galloping horses" as she called them, nor about attacking the incompetence of her confessors, who did not understand her.

> The whole trouble lay in not getting at *the root of the occasions* and with my confessors who were of little help. For had they told me of the danger I was in and that I had the obligation to avoid those friendships, without a doubt I believe that I would have remedied the matter. . . .
>
> All these signs of fear of God came to me during prayer; *and the greatest sign was that they were enveloped in love,* for punishment did not enter my mind. This carefulness of conscience with respect to mortal sins lasted all during my illness. Oh, God help me, how I desired my health so as to serve Him more, and this health was the cause of all my harm.[8]

I take it that Teresa was implicating certain "friendships" and more precisely "prayer," the practice of mental prayer for fusion with God: both of these presumably lay behind her "sins" and her indispositions. But I also see her as decomposing the internal shifts of her way of believing in God. If she, Teresa, loves God so much, it's because she fears Him—punishment being the solidary inverse of love. Can love be a ruthless demand that punishes one to the point of illness? "These signs of fear of God . . . were enveloped in love." Teresa points to the central knot of her malaise, a pernicious knot that the lovely engineer, fixed to her identity along with so many lovesick analysands, will take years to unpick. The earthly "punishment," her symptoms but also her penances, derive from a *mixture of love and fear, sex and terror.* This weave that constitutes desire itself—desire for the Creator, as well as for His creatures—had hitherto eluded her, insightful though she was. In the sentence I am now reading, Teresa expresses herself like an analyst, or at least that is how I translate her. I feared, she says, that loving would be either meaningless or forbidden, and hence always culpable; and I contented myself with mobilizing all of my "conscience" (my moral sense, my superego). I remained "careful of conscience" so as to combat those unworthy desires, those sins. My very illnesses were punishments that I inflicted on myself out of fear of the Beloved, fear of not measuring up to Love. But by the time of writing these lines, she concludes, I've gone beyond that point: I have understood that such a conscientious longing for "health" in order to "serve," were it even to serve God, can only cause me "harm."

The future saint has just discovered what the superego enjoins: "Delight in suffering!" What to do? Without relinquishing that feminine stance— "A female I was and, for better or worse [*pour en souffrir et pour en jouir*], a female I find myself to be," as Colette put it[9]—the Carmelite nun transforms it into a different position, for which she finds plenty of justifications in Scripture: as a garden lets itself be watered, so Teresa lets herself be loved, abandoning herself to the mingled waters of pleasure, sublimation, and a kind of self-analysis that she discovers as she writes. With no resistance or dread— no tyrannical superego, as my colleagues of the Parisian Psychoanalytic Society would interpret it.

Offered up, passive, defenseless, Teresa embraced the rite of prayer as preached by the Franciscan Francisco de Osuna[10] in his *Third Spiritual Alphabet*, and passed down to her by her paternal uncle, Pedro Sánchez de Cepeda: silent rather than spoken prayer, submersion of the self in an infinite longing for the other, the absolute Other, the divine, as penetrating as a Spouse. This amorous state, heightened by the nun's very account of it, engulfs its author and infects the reader with an imaginary pleasure so potent it makes itself felt and is embodied in each of the senses (mouth, skin, ears, eyes, guts). Teresa is a well, a Persian wheel, an underground stream, a downpour, the beloved Being impregnates her with His grace.

* * *

Delirium? Inebriation? That may well be, she doesn't care, she prefers *that* to the love-fear that hounded her before. How dismal it is, that anxiety in which melancholics love to wallow! Their black bile can be left to the Lutherans, because La Madre wants no part of it, ever again! Unknown to herself Teresa is preparing a miracle, and she succeeds where Judge Schreber will fail. This celebrated jurist believed himself to be persecuted by a God who cared little for the living, the instigator of a plot to turn him into a woman who would redeem the human race. Fit to haunt the body and soul of any self-respecting psychology student! You know the case I mean? That's right. Even outside psychology

circles, it's well known that the "Schreber Case" prompted the first psychoanalytic investigation into psychosis.[11] Teresa's God, by contrast, has managed to
split off from the vengeful Creator God of judgment and damnation, and His
rays, notwithstanding their omnipotence, are wholly beneficial: He cannot do
other than love and be loved, even when He is not responding. Over a few
decades of monastic experience Teresa rewrote, after her fashion, the thousand-
year-old story of God the Father, which Jesus had already done much to trans-
figure; but now the Spaniard will die of bliss in Him without dying. In her
visions, through her pen, the tyrannical Beloved, the stern Father, *Père-sévère*,
softens into a Father so tender as to become an ideal alter ego, kind and rewarding, who draws the ego out of itself: ek-static. Does He put her to the test?
Teresa knows that He adores her, because He speaks to her, assures her of His
unfailing presence by her side. What's more, He is in her, He is her as she is
Him. God, God-man, his body marked by five wounds, who suffered and rose
again, whom Teresa embraces as he hangs on the Cross. An angel's body, too,
equipped with a long dart that can penetrate you, inflame you, then slake your
thirst with water and sometimes, indeed, with mother's milk:

> Let us come now to speak of the third water by which this garden is irrigated, that
> is, the water flowing from a river or spring. By this means the garden is irrigated
> with much less labor, although some labor is required to direct the flow of the
> water. The Lord so desires to help the gardener here that He Himself becomes
> practically the gardener and the one who does everything.
>
> This prayer is a sleep of the faculties; the faculties neither fail entirely to func-
> tion nor understand how they function. The consolation, the sweetness, and the
> delight are incomparably greater than that experienced in the previous prayer.
> The water of grace rises up to the throat of this soul since such a soul can no
> longer move forward; nor does it know how; nor can it move backward. *It would
> desire to enjoy this greatest glory* [to revel in it: *querría gozar de esta grandísima
> gloria*]. It is like a person who is already holding the candle and for whom little
> is left before dying the death that is desired: *such a one rejoices in that agony with
> the greatest delight describable*. This experience doesn't seem to me anything else
> than an almost complete death to all earthly things and *an enjoyment of God*
> [*estar gozando de Dios*].
>
> I don't know any other terms for describing it or how to explain it. Nor does
> the soul then know what to do because it doesn't know whether to speak or to be
> silent, whether to laugh or to weep. This prayer is *a glorious foolishness, a heavenly*

*madness [Es un glorioso desatino, una celestial locura] where the true wisdom is
learned; and it is for the soul a most delightful way of enjoying.*

Often I had been as though bewildered and inebriated in this love, and never
was I able to understand its nature. . . .

*The soul would desire to cry out praises, and it is beside itself—a delightful dis-
quiet.* Now the flowers are blossoming; they are beginning to spread their fragrance. The soul would desire here that everyone could see and understand and
understand its glory. . . .

It would want to be all tongues so as to praise the Lord. . . .

While I write this I am not freed from such holy, heavenly madness. . . .

Since [this soul] desires to live no longer in itself but in You, it seems that its
life is unnatural.

. . . There is no reason sufficient to prevent me from this excess when the Lord
carries me out of myself—nor since this morning when I received Communion
do I think it is I who am speaking. It seems that what I see is a dream, and I would
desire to see no other persons than those who are sick with this sickness I now
have. I beg your Reverence that we may all be mad for love of Him who for love
of us was called mad.[12]

My parents are dead, my partner left me, I don't have children: I don't have
anyone. Nature is beautiful; the world situation is beyond help; life makes
me laugh, because I never could do tears. My colleagues at the MPH (for
the uninitiated, the Medical-Psychological House, my official base where I
practice as a psychologist) think well of me: "Everything works out for Sylvia
Leclercq, what a dynamo!" Not particularly discerning, as assessments go, but
I'll settle for it. What the ladies mean by that (and I say "ladies," because in
such an institution, the staff is invariably 99 percent female) is that they don't
resent me, that I do my job well enough. I socialize with them just as often as it
takes to maintain my image, for I don't look for truth in human contacts, apart
from those undefinable relations that attach me to our inpatients and my own
cases. Whether or not they can be called "bonds," these are my greatest weakness, at any rate.

Paul is a "compensated autistic," according to his medical records. He seldom
speaks, his gaze wanders, and what sound like sentences from him are often
no more than TV advertising slogans or snatches of a fable by La Fontaine.
Paul's memory and ear are faultless. He is an excellent piano player and spends
much time listening to cassettes. He's a teenager going on thirty, tall and lanky,

slightly stooped, prone to losing his balance and passing out. Paul also likes hugging girls, who willingly reciprocate, having fallen for those feline eyes, which never rest on anyone. Yesterday, out of the blue, he came and flung his skinny arms round me and rocked me hard. "I don't want you to die." I must have looked pretty stupid, because for once he stared me straight in the eye. He went on repeating the same thing all day long. Was it in response to another sentence running through his head that he wasn't telling me, along the lines of "You should die, I want you to die"? That evening, he decreed: "All things considered, I need you for my life. Understand?" I left the building under his catlike gaze, cheered by that "all things considered." I hadn't understood that Paul had understood everything, after all.

Élise is a tougher nut to crack. She is fifteen and incontinent, which people find quite trying. She has to be changed, dressed, the works. But she can't stand nurses or nurses' aides. "Not touch!" she shrieks in anguish. Furious outburst, dose of tranquilizers, and it starts all over again. Nobody wants to look after her. "Mrs. Leclercq, I *know* it's not your responsibility, really I do, but as Élise seems to get along with you so well . . . " Dr. Toutbon, our director, can always be trusted to light upon the cheapest solution. "Don't worry, I'll see to her." Because the life of the psyche lodges in unexpected places, there's no reason a therapist shouldn't change Élise's diapers. I soap her, I scent her, I've found out she likes lavender. She draws fields of lavender for me, and I bring back fragrant blue armfuls of the stuff from my garden at Île de Ré.

"Quit acting like one of those old-school analysts: lavatory/lavender, is that it?"

Marianne Baruch, the MPH psychiatrist, my only friend in here or anywhere, sticks to prescribing slews of pills. She loathes all that Freudian–Lacanian mumbo jumbo, which it amuses her to attribute to me. Parapeted behind thick glasses, encased in faded jeans like a fifty-something teen, she's a gruff character whose affection, on its rare outings, is mostly for me. But I was talking about Élise. Any exchanges between the young girl and myself serve only to help us arrive at the things that begin (with all due respect to Dr. Baruch) in the sphere of sensation. Lavender is odorous and tactile, it dampens and lubricates, it caresses. *It* does these things, not me. I improvise: I bring flowers, I play, she plays, savors, sniffs. And one thing leading to the next, Élise brings out some pieces of her ragged story. Her mother hasn't been to see her for five years. She remarried and left Paris, she's probably got other worries now. Only her father still takes my Élise out for the odd weekend. He is a sad, shriveled little man, impossible to seduce, no matter how much supermarket cologne or lavender essence his daughter pours over herself.

Nothing had predisposed me to do this job. I drifted for years between the couch and the library, but I was not cut out to teach, still less to teach literature. My salvation was Marguerite Duras: I never completed my thesis on her, because the more I thought about her the more depressed I got, but I did turn it into a slim volume, *Duras, or the White Apocalypse*, published by Zone.

"You're a shrewd psychologist, Sylvia, and one might also spot a streak of theology in that apocalypse of yours," remarked my publisher, Bruno Zonabend. This was hardly a compliment to the literary type I thought myself to be. Theology meant nothing to me in those days. I ditched my thesis and went back to school, this time to study psychology, and here I am: Sylvia Leclercq, clinical psychologist. Practicing part-time at the MPH, the rest with private patients. And, more lately, sharing my nights with Teresa of Avila.

* * *

On March 28, 1515, in the province of Avila, a third child was born to don Alonso Sánchez de Cepeda and his wife, doña Beatriz de Ahumada. It was a girl. Don Alonso was the son of Juan Sánchez, a "reconciled" convert from Judaism also known as Juan de Toledo, a wealthy tax collector and draper, and of doña Inés de Cepeda, from an Old Christian family of minor aristocratic rank. At her christening on April 4 in Avila, the infant was given the name of Teresa after her maternal grandmother, doña Teresa de las Cuevas, and her paternal great-grandmother, Teresa Sánchez. Her family name was a composite of her parents' surnames: de Cepeda y Ahumada. The patronym Sánchez, perceived as Jewish, was gradually dropped in favor of the stalwart Catholicism of the Cepeda stock. Thus Teresa bore just one first name plus the last names of her only Catholic forbears (the Cepedas and the Ahumadas), all on the female side. Such an onomastic apparatus strikes me as perfectly tailored to the person in question.

But what of the Marrano status of her father's line, the forced conversion to Catholicism? Had it become diluted, or did it, on the contrary, persist like an invisible magnet attracting Teresa's faith to the inner, exploratory life, rather than to the facile schemas of established religion? Some scholars make much of the humiliation suffered by her merchant grandfather Juan Sánchez, condemned to wear the *sambenito*—the infamous yellow ruff that denoted a converted "swine" (Marrano) who had secretly relapsed into the old faith—for seven Fridays in a row, jeered by the Toledans who were not so fastidious when it came to using his financial services. Others cite the incident as evidence that Teresa's ancestor could not have been a serious backslider, let alone a heretic, because the penance assigned by the Inquisition to obtain his "reconciliation" was distinctly moderate for a period when death sentences were handed out by the thousand. Besides, Alonso, Teresa's father, regarded himself simply as a good Catholic. Could it be that this dissolution of Judaism into the intimacy of a new, ardent faith, rebelling against the exhaustion of tradition, provides a key to Teresa's uncompromising, reforming spirit?

This view is taken by Michel de Certeau, who finds that a "strange alliance joins the 'mystic' spoken word to 'impure blood.'"[13] The crossing of two religious traditions, one repressed and hidden in the private realm, the other triumphant but "corrupt," undoubtedly helped the "New Christians" to create a new discourse, freed from dogmatic reiteration and structured—like a spiritual *marranismo*—by the opposition of internal "purity" and external "falsehood."

If on the one hand Teresa inherited, albeit unconsciously, this spiritual *marranismo*, it merged on the other hand with a sensibility dominated by Catholicism . . . in the feminine. For better or worse, for suffering or pleasure. Did that alone persuade the future saint that God was more generous to women, that women "make much more progress along this path [of mystical experience] than men do"?[14]

Teresa was four years old when the municipal authorities brought a fiscal suit against the Sánchez de Cepeda family, requiring them to prove in court that they possessed the rank of hidalgos, without fiefs or titles perhaps, but exempt from tax. In fact, they already enjoyed this privilege. Juan Sánchez and then his sons had earned it by their social success; they lived like nobles and served the king. Formal hidalgo status was legally granted four years later. Was this how Teresa learned that she was the granddaughter of a converso? Her writings give no indication of it. Nevertheless, the suspicion of a lack of *honra*, "honor," tormented the future saint all her life. She harps tirelessly on this "point of honor," this obligation to "*sustentar la honra*," uphold the burden of honor and preserve one's rank. It was a constant worry for the Sánchez de Cepeda family, as much when they were rich as when they were poor: could it be due to their *marranismo*? Most theologians and other interpreters of Teresa have studiously ignored the sociohistorical and political dimensions of this particular obsession.

* * *

In 1528 Alonso Sánchez de Cepeda was left with twelve children on his hands—two from a first marriage (María and Juan), ten from the second (Fernando, Rodrigo, Teresa, Juan, Lorenzo, Antonio, Pedro, Jerónimo, Agustín, and Juana)—when Teresa's mother Beatriz de Ahumada died, possibly in the course of her tenth and final delivery. In July 1531, aged sixteen, Teresa entered the small Augustinian Convent of Our Lady of Grace in Avila. All of her brothers became soldiers, except for Juan. They emigrated: Fernando was the first to sail for the Indies (America), and the favorite, Rodrigo, embarked for the Plate estuary in 1535. Antonio, Pedro, Jerónimo, Lorenzo, and Agustín followed in their wake between 1540 and 1543, eager to acquire wealth and honors in the New World now that their father's money had almost run out. Living exclusively off the land as a hidalgo was less profitable than selling silks or collecting taxes, and before long the Cepeda y Ahumada family was ruined.

On November 2, 1535, Teresa ran away from her father's home to join the Carmel of the Incarnation. There she took her vows, after spending a year as a postulant. She was twenty years old. Her father died in December 1543, leaving considerable debts, over which some of his heirs would quarrel for two decades.

Teresa's "conversion," the beginning of her deep surrender to religion, dates from 1555. Her contemplative life intensified. A devotee of the orisons of the *alumbrados*, Teresa nonetheless strove to understand and elucidate them. Two years later she heard her first heavenly "words."

In 1559, the Inquisition placed on its Index of Prohibited Books many of the spiritual books and chivalrous novels in Castilian that Teresa's mother had taught her to enjoy. Christ appeared and reassured her: "Don't be sad, for I shall give you a living book."[15] A vision of Christ in 1559, a vision of Hell the following year. First raptures. Disillusioned by the worldliness of the "calced" Carmelite order, she planned to found, with her fellow nuns, a convent that would reinstate the order's original rule, the "discalced" Carmel. She would replace shoes with canvas sandals.

At the request of her confessor, the Dominican Pedro Ibáñez, in 1560–1561 she undertook to write her life story. Already in 1554, following the advice of her confessors Gaspar Daza and Francisco de Salcedo, she had embarked on an autobiographical work, marking in her copy of *Ascent of Mount Zion*, by Bernardino de Laredo, the passages that mirrored her experience.[16] The confessors, somewhat skeptical, suggested she make confession to the Jesuit Diego de Cetina. It was for him that Teresa set down "as clear an account of my life as I knew how to give, without leaving anything out."[17] But no trace remains of that early text; Teresa or her confessors must have destroyed it. In 1562 Teresa finished the first version of the *Book of Her Life*, delivered to the Dominican García de Toledo and subsequently lost, and founded the first reformed Carmelite convent, Saint Joseph of Avila, thanks to, amongst other donations, 200 ducats sent from Peru by her younger brother, Lorenzo. She took the name *Teresa of Jesus*. García de Toledo and the inquisitor Francisco de Soto Salazar asked her to resume and complete her account, which she did between 1563 and 1565: this is the version that has come down to us. It testifies to the way in which Teresa's experience was influenced by the spiritual teachers of her time: Juan de Ávila, the "Andalusian apostle" acknowledged by Ignatius Loyola as his sole spiritual father; and in the lineage of the Franciscan Francisco de Osuna, Bernabé de Palma; but also Bernardino de Laredo and Alonso de Madrid (*The Art of Serving God*). These practiced the mysticism of recollection and were regarded as *recogidos*, or contemplatives, but they were not ignorant of scholasticism. Such readings calmed the anguish provoked by the silent prayer of Francisco de Osuna and guided the nun toward a vocal prayer that began with reading, before turning into ecstatic meditation. Teresa met numerous Church dignitaries of various orders (Jesuits, Dominicans, Franciscans, Carthusians) who supported or challenged her, criticized or guided her. Her mysticism gained authority under the notable influence of the Franciscan and future saint Pedro de Alcántara, whose kindliness toward women and special trust in her she commends in a 1576 letter to her brother Lorenzo.[18]

* * *

Teresa of Jesus wrote *The Book of Her Life* at the age of fifty: a sum of familial and amorous memories that bares, without the least coyness, a body sick with desire and exultant in its affliction. If Teresa's faith asserts itself as an expression of love, the coiling of this lover's discourse upon itself would infuse her writing with devastating lucidity, continually redoubling the lover's illusion without ever breaking away from it altogether. Doubtful, skeptical, frequently hostile, at last won over, her confessors instructed her to record the strange raptures she spoke of, those half mad, half rational states that so fascinated the *letrados*, learned churchmen of rank. Under their supervision the ecstatic seer became a writer: theologians pored over her notebooks, revising and correcting, while the ardent author, whose humility veiled a certain astuteness, soon got into her stride and, while never less than self-deprecating, poured out more and more onto the page. Self-analyses, constitutions, counsels, letters, poems: syncopated, in spurts and gusts, Teresa's writing grew mentally and physically incessant. This scriptorial therapy deepened the confessional analysis of raptures and agonies—sensations that were appeased, if not effaced, beneath the torrent of texts and monastic foundations. Teresa *founded herself* in writing at the same time as she founded the Discalced Carmelite order.

A writer? She demurred, waved it away, forgot about it. Her confessors were the ones who got her started, after all; they supervised her output, they edited it, and now and then they censored it. Only one work was to be formally signed and authenticated by her, *The Way of Perfection* (1573).

A woman possessed by the devil? More than once Teresa doubted her visions, and took care to obtain endorsement from her spiritual guides. When she was suspected of Illuminism during the 1560s, the Dominican Pedro Ibáñez came to her defense with a highly favorable report. But matters were not always so simple. In February 1575, Teresa was the happiest of women: she had just met her "angel," her "Elysium," her "darling son," Fr. Jerome Gratian of the Mother of God,* [*I have used the English version of Jerónimo Gracián's name, as I have done with John of the Cross. Elsewhere I have kept the Spanish names.—Trans.] the apostolic visitor for Andalusia. He was thirty, she was sixty. They made up coded names for each other and loved under the Inquisition's very nose: "I will never have better days than those I had there with my Paul." As it happened, the Inquisition got onto La Madre's case in 1575–1576. Thanks to the support of her confessor and spiritual director, the Dominican Domingo Báñez, doctor of theology and advisor to the Inquisition in Valladolid, they left Teresa alone but placed *The Book of Her Life* under lock and key: it could not be allowed to circulate among the populace. Recovering it in 1580, the next year she titled it, with wry humor, *The Book of God's Mercies*. She no doubt held laughter to be next to love, and radiated both.

Although she was a great friend and accomplice of Saint John of the Cross (they met in 1567, when he was twenty-five and she was fifty-two) in both the Carmelite reformation and the life of the soul, Teresa eschewed the purgative asceticism of her "little Seneca"; she shared neither his endurance under flagellation nor his "privation of every kind of pleasure which belongs to the desire" (*Ascent of Mount Carmel*).[19] The author of the *Living Flame of Love* would ultimately burn every single letter addressed to him by the sensual reformer.

After her death on October 4, 1582, in Alba de Tormes, Teresa was interred in the chapel of the dukes of Alba, under a heap of soil, stones, and lime. When her body was exhumed in 1586, its wondrously preserved state naturally encouraged the publication of the books. While she was alive, successive popes were at the very least wary of her: Paul IV, Pius V, and Gregory XIII (who recast the calendar) had no time for febrile mystics, especially female ones. La Madre was beatified a century after her birth, in 1614, in a festive Madrid of serpents, ships, and blazing castles. King Philip IV, the ambassadors, and the nobles paid homage to her in the cathedral adorned with her portrait: this depicted her holding a palm frond in one hand, the symbol of virginity, and a quill in the other, to represent literary genius. Lope de Vega himself presided over the poetic joust of sonnets composed in her honor. The Blessed Teresa was canonized by Gregory XV in 1622, in recognition of her "divine wisdom." The Jesuits had supported her in life: Francisco Borgia, Baltasar Álvarez, Ripalda . . . The Council of Trent, inaugurating a new epoch for the Catholic faith, had need of someone like Teresa, whose experience fitted so well with the new outlook without being reducible to it.[20] For La Madre had patently prefigured, indeed embodied, the baroque. She had led the way in balancing ascetic rigor, rehabilitated by the Carmelite reformation, with the wonders of supernatural spiritual contemplation, legitimized by her genius. It was in this spirit that Luis de León and Jerome Gratian posthumously published and commented upon her works, to consecrate Teresa of Avila as *the* saint of the Counter-Reformation.

* * *

Why do I feel so sure that this Carmelite nun has slipped the leash of her time and her world, and stands beside us in the third millennium? Is Teresa the diarist a modern sensibility, revealing that the secrets of baroque civilization are female? Or is she a novelist who weaves romantic plots, the necessary love interest, around the mystical subject—man or woman, man and woman? Or perhaps the maverick thinker of the Self outside the Self? A Montaigne of extreme, borderline states? The first person to theorize the imaginary with the aid of its own specific tools?

Master of triumphant narcissism inasmuch as she was loving/loved, Teresa was not content to develop the Christ-centered revolution introduced into Judaism by a God-man of love, whose *madness*—lately called *sadomasochistic* passion—had touched Mary Magdalene, Saint Paul, Saint Augustine, and been passed on. Mel Gibson's 2004 film *The Passion of the Christ* is simply the cinematographic mise-en-scène of these rejoicings, these shades of pleasure and pain that glimmer throughout the Bible and, for anyone still unenlightened, through Christ's Calvary. But the ecstatic Madre was no less possessed of a rational mind, capable of paring down her extravagant but therapeutic "visions" and coupling the convulsions of the body with the shifting infinity of thought. Ten years after *The Book of Her Life* (whose definitive version was completed in 1565), *The Dwelling Places of the Soul* (1577) feels its way toward a "spiritual marriage" that is not so much a hallucinatory "vision" as a carnal thought, a pure joy of the mind inseparable from the body. It allows her to assess with considerable philosophical precision the difference between thought in motion, a turmoil of the *imaginary*, and the *intellect* loosed from the body:

> The important thing is not to think much but to love much . . . I have been very afflicted at times in the midst of this turmoil of mind. A little more than four years ago I came to understand through experience that *the mind* [*pensamiento*] (or imagination, to put it more clearly) is not *the intellect*. I asked a learned man and he told me that this was so; which brought me no small consolation. For since *the intellect* is one of the soul's faculties, it was an arduous thing for me that it should be so restless at times. Ordinarily the mind flies about quickly, *for only God can hold it fast in such a way as to make it seem that we are somehow loosed from this body.* I have seen, I think, that the faculties of my soul were occupied and recollected in God while my mind on the other hand was distracted. This distraction puzzled me. . . . It seems I myself wanted to take vengeance on myself. . . . And since our reading and the counsels we receive (that is, to pay no attention to these thoughts) don't suffice, I don't think that the time spent in explaining these things for those of you with little knowledge and consoling you in this matter is time lost. . . . Yet, it is necessary and His Majesty wishes us to take the means and understand ourselves; and let's not blame the soul for what a weak imagination, human nature, and the devil cause.[21]

On the one hand, moral judgment, on the other, the imagination of the Bride, desirous without fear of being judged for it: "I would kiss thee, yea, I should not be despised" (Song of Songs 8:1). Teresa recognizes the legitimacy and advantage of the former, but nothing could induce her to give up the harrowing desires without which there is no path to the Beloved: "It isn't good for us to be disturbed by our thoughts, nor should we be concerned"; "the pain is felt when suspension does not accompany the prayer. *When suspension does accompany prayer*, no pain is felt until the suspension passes."[22]

The point is neither to submit to the intellect, nor to substitute it with restless thought and imagination, but to construct a new expression that constitutes the Teresian discourse: suspension of the intellect, while also eluding that illusory, misleading, mystificatory imagination. A *different* imagination—let's call it the *imaginary*—is ready to "fly about," to soar free of Teresa, to free her in turn, to deliver her even from God; since God is in "the very deep and intimate part" of her, and it's this that she seeks to liberate and be liberated from.

My sandal-wearer, who claimed to be so unschooled as not to "know who the Assyrians are,"[23] didn't feel at all inferior to the learned doctors who guided her soul; she even took them down a peg in a burlesque homage of a type called *vejamen*, a comic-satirical critique penned in response to a solemn symposium (that's right!) held in 1577.[24] The perplexing title of her riposte, "Seek Yourself in Me"—words the Other once addressed to her as she prayed—would have left Socrates,[25] Montaigne, and Descartes confounded. For Teresa's formula has nothing to do with the Socratic "Know yourself," that injunction to "Be wise!" that could have been engraved on the Delphic pediment like a greeting from Apollo to his devotees, which Plato examines in the *Phaedrus* and the *Critias*.[26] Nor must it be confused with the motto of her contemporary, Montaigne: "What do I know?" Because, although he did not lose his Christian faith, even while suspecting it of bounding "the power of God . . . by the rules of human language," the sage of Bordeaux was happier rehabilitating the Pyrrhonian skeptics and replacing every affirmative proposition by doubts.[27] He chose the symbol of a pair of scales to represent this doubting Self, poles apart from Teresa's ravished transports. Lastly, having arisen in dialogue and being derived from transference to the Other, Teresa's phrase is equally unrelated to the "I think, therefore I am" reached by Descartes in his *Discourse on the Method*, because the latter is based on solipsistic certainty.[28]

Not rationalistic, not skeptical, not isolated, not even "balanced," and yet drawing on knowldge as much as on unknowing, Teresa's Self is a twofold knowing from the start, born in the Other's love and for the Other* [*"Le Moi de Thérèse est d'emblée co-naissant dans l'amour de l'Autre et pour l'Autre." The author makes a pun on *connaissant*, knowing, and *co-naissant*, co-being born.—Trans.], ceaselessly inscribing itself in the spiral of call and response from *I* to *you*, between *you* and *me*. After the dialogical Socrates, before the doubting Montaigne and the cogitating Descartes, this woman had the idea—a biblical idea? baroque? psychoanalytical?—to invent a self-knowledge that can only be realized on condition of an inherent duplication: "you in me" and "me in you." Her castle is *interior* inasmuch as it is infiltrated by the *exterior* Other, irreducible and yet included, body and soul; sensible and signifiable. This double knowing is a long way, too, from Rimbaud's "illumination" ("I is another")[29] and more an intuition of something close to Freudian transference: a clarified passion for seeking a self that is grounded in the bond with another, inevitably poignant and definitively jubilant. Does Teresa posit this "third kind of knowledge" in muffled resonance with Spinoza the Marrano?[30] Maybe, but from there to celebrating her as a scholar in theology was quite a step—one finally taken in 1970, in the aftermath of Vatican Council II, almost five centuries after she was born. Teresa of Avila and Catherine of Siena were proclaimed by Pope Paul VI the first women "Doctors of the Universal Church."

* * *

On hearing me enthuse about the droll letters Teresa sent to her confessors (those secret or semiavowed loves, who no matter how erudite she often chided for their lack of what she called "experience") my friend Dr. Baruch teases me: "Our Freudian Sylvia, lapsing into Catholicism, eh?"

Not a bit. Or no more so than Leibniz, whose company is nothing to be ashamed of. Indeed, the great rationalist who aspired to overcome the rifts within Christianity took La Madre seriously in his *Discourse on Metaphysics*, describing her as "a person of noble mind whose sanctity is greatly revered [and who] used to say that the soul must often think as if there were only God and it in the world. Now nothing makes immortality more completely comprehensible."[31] In a letter to André Morell, he is explicit about his debt to her: "And as for St. Teresa, you are right to esteem her works. One day I found in them this fine thought: that the soul ought to conceive things as if there were only God and itself in the world. This thought gives rise to an idea which is significant even in philosophy, and I have made good use of it in one of my hypotheses."[32]

Teresa's soul incorporating its God, consubstantial with the Other: might this be the only possible immortality? Enough, surely, to mark down the Carmelite saint, the inspirer of Bernini, as the precursor of the infinite monad and Leibniz's infinitesimal calculus!

* * *

Did I mention my former partner? I finally erased him altogether, it's true. It's all so long ago. We were fifteen in May 1968, we manned the barricades on rue Claude-Bernard, discovered sex and drugs at the Odéon, experimented with the whole gamut of erotic fantasy and power games. His name? Can't remember, not a clue. Honestly. My friends, the few I still have from those days, are the same: they say "your ex," "her ex." My ex left no trace of himself in me, good or bad, which might seem strange for a psychologist, or perhaps it just shows how thoroughly I was psychoanalyzed. He claimed to like women and hate children; he made love like—and with—anybody else, but preferred me for sleeping with. When we were together he'd cross the road to avoid greeting an acquaintance, male or female. Was he ashamed of me? Ashamed of himself? Given that everything was or ought to be transparent, this hole-and-corner stuff made no sense to me, I couldn't see why we had to play at secret lovers. So I asked him, I nagged him about it, and he'd fly into a temper and disappear for days. We carried on that way for ten years or so, I wanted to be up to date, but I was just a masochist. One day he didn't come back. One of *our* friends, mine that is, I never met his, got some news via a mutual contact. "Seems your ex opened a holiday club in Thailand, can't you just picture it! Did you know? I always thought he was in computing." I could picture it alright, but I hadn't believed in anything for quite a while. I'd been depressed. A spell in the Sainte-Anne psychiatric hospital, a lengthy analysis, the Duras book, the psychology degree, I did whatever it took to delete the whole thing. You can hiss as much as you like, the fact is that I came out unscathed, smooth as a pebble.

Love, the tritest business of our whole lives, as my mother used to say in evocation of her favorite authoress—Colette or Sagan?—love had ditched me for good. Free of it at last, I find life nicely open and varied, full of surprises. My patients offer unexpected gifts, my dear colleague Baruch buoys me up with her businesslike approval, and occasional affinities with the male of the species afford me occasional pleasures of the kind known as physical. With 9/11 and the rise of Islamic terrorism, I realized that religion is the only world—besides those of Paul and Élise—that can still rouse me to passion. For better and for worse.

It's late, I'm in my apartment on Place d'Italie gazing out at the city lights. My father always loved this great window; the view would relax him after a strenuous day. I'm getting supper ready and listening to the news: from one folly to the next, Sky News, CNN, on goes the world.

The phone rings. It's Zone Books.

* * *

Bruno doesn't call very often, and why should he: sales of my Duras book were modest, except abroad. "There's a Duras cult in the States, what do you expect, all those depressed women sucked in by feminism . . . Sorry, did I upset you?" Of course not: I wouldn't kick up a fuss with my publisher. All he's asked after that is to meet for a drink every two or three years, in case there's something to be got out of the dingbat psychology circles I now move in, and which include Zone customers. Invariably he draws a blank: I'm not the mole he's after. Let's do it again soon? I'll call you. That would be lovely . . .

Meanwhile, Zone switched niches. Seeing as everybody else was writing and publishing fiction, Zonabend slashed the literary list to the bone and went into contemporary nonfiction. "Essays are such a catch-all, ever since Montaigne and Rousseau, you know, essays have been great sellers." But without spurning his old flames.

"The time has come for you to take up your pen once more, my dear! I need you, yes I do, I'm serious, surely you realize you're cutting-edge? Come now, I've always known you had flair. Value crisis! Apocalypse now! The new sicknesses of the soul! How to become a suicide bomber so as not to go crazy when you're crazy already! You are at the total front line of all that, my dear Sylvia, and plus you've got the inside story, with those fruitcakes of yours! You hold the key to the enigma, on the deep-down intimate level, I mean."

Bruno is trying to flatter me: he dreams of a *White Apocalypse* Mark 2. I'm thrown, I'm not on the same wavelength as when he published me.

"Do you hear what I'm saying? Today's Anne-Marie Stretters, Lol V. Steins, what are they doing? In France they're singing on shows like *Star Academy*, or making a fortune as high-end escorts, like the one who tripped up Daniel Stern, what was her name? Anyway. So, think about it: suppose those same rather sordid heroines are Muslims, what choices do they have, between the Pill and the chador? Suicide bombers in the making. I'm rushing the transitions, ok, but here's your theme: apocalypse, feminine case. What say you?"

"You mean the Hiroshima of love would only get more devastating?" I'm alluding to the subtitle of my book, which Zonabend has evidently forgotten. "And I'm supposed to be the expert in the field?" I say, feigning jokiness.

"The Hiroshima of love, excellent!" Bruno can already see me on TV, guesting on the Guillaume Durand show, or, why think small, on prime time with Patrick Poivre d'Arvor.

"I don't know, but I do think there can be religious women in love. I happen to be reading one now who talks about nothing else." Teresa, *by default*, again.

"Really? Well, why not . . . Let's see. Not Diderot's nun, she's been done. A fundamentalist? A mystic?"

"A writer."

"Not another writer! Ok, do me a synopsis." My publisher goes quiet all of a sudden. He doesn't seem very excited about my saint. "Religion is always a mystery for you psychologists as well, isn't it? So that's it . . . I'll trust you. I want it. I'll send the contract. And get your skates on."

Bruno's such a bore. I don't feel like ticking boxes. I am steeped in Teresa, her faith and madness speak to me, and the faith I never had may not be so far distant. As for madness, well . . . A bonfire under my white apocalypse?

* * *

Hail Teresa, borderless woman, physical hysterical erotic epileptic, made word, made flesh, who unravels inside and outside herself, tides of images without pictures, tumults of words, cascades of florescence, a thousand tongues listening out for whom for what, listening to time etched in stone, eardrum larynx cry out write out, night and brightness, too much body yet disembodied, beyond matter, empty gaping matrix throbbing for the Beloved ever-present and yet never there, but there's *presence* and *presence*, His in her, hers in Him, sensed felt buried, sensation without perception, dart or glass, pierced or transparent, that is the question, transverberated instead, and again inundated, La Madre being the most virile of monks,[33] most canny of the herders of souls, a veritable twin of Christ, she is He, He is she, the Truth is me, or Him in the deepest part of me, me Teresa, a successful paranoiac, God is myself and what of it, what's the matter? A free-for-all, who can beat that? Certainly not Schreber, not even Freud, awfully serious chap from Vienna, gloomy rather, a woman finds it easier to talk about these things, what things, well, her of course, her beside herself, obviously, in the throes of dread and delight, little butterfly expiring with indelible joy because Jesus has become it or rather her, butterfly-Jesus, woman-Jesus, I know someone who though she's not a poet composes poems without trying, novels that are poems with an extra something, extra movements, I wonder whether it is really I, Teresa, speaking, the path that is pain, the Nothingness of everything, that everything which is nothing, do what is in you to do, but gaily, be cheerful, my daughters, for twenty years I vomited every morning, now it's in the evenings and it's harder to bring up, I have to provoke it with a feather or some such thing, like a baby a baby girl if you prefer latched on to the Other's teat, mystic or is it spiritual marriage, young John of the Cross[34] says there's a difference, I don't really see it, more like two sides of a coin, or like the Song of Songs, as always as ever she sings off-key but she writes true and carries on founding her convents, her girls, her Church, her own gestation, her game, a game of chess, games are allowed, oh yes, even in a cloister, especially in a cloister, God loves us to be playful, believe me, girls, Jesus loved women, what are the Doctors so scared of in us, yes, checkmate to God too, oh yes, Teresa or Molly Bloom, I am numb at last, I flow into the water of the garden, flow on by, all we do is feel pleasure, souls that love can see all the way into atoms, that's right, for yes is all there is to souls like mine, mine sees as far as the infinite atoms that are atoms of love, the philosophers don't have a clue, they become scholars, they recoil from your sensations, the best of them are mathematicians, tamers of infinity, and yet it's as simple as that, oh yes, metaphors mutating into metamorphoses, or possibly the other way around, oh yes, Teresa, my sister, invisible, ecstatic, eccentric, beside yourself in you, beside myself in me, yes, Teresa, my love, yes.

Chapter 2

MYSTICAL SEDUCTION

Besides obeying it is my intention to attract souls [entice souls: *engolosinar las almas*] to so high a blessing.

Teresa of Avila, *The Book of Her Life*

Transforming the beloved in her Lover.

Saint John of the Cross, *Dark Night of the Soul*

It's Christmas. People are buying trees, foie gras, oysters, gifts. Some will go to midnight Mass, millions are already clogging the freeways, apparently London is paralyzed by the weather (shame that the one destination that could tempt me is off limits due to global warming); there's been a deadly pile-up in Gironde, three young people carjacked by a drunk in the 13th arrondissement, two dead, one critically injured. I'm staying put. The MPH ladies are of one mind for the vacation: they are trooping off for some thalassotherapy in Ouarzazate. For some unfathomable reason Morocco at Xmas is a magnet for the political class ("Of a right-wing bent," my friend Dr. Marianne Baruch points out) and for women of a certain age.

Marianne is going as well, not looking forward to it much—but the alternative is "Not been there, not done that," already the favorite expression of this Prozac-popping chronic depressive and proud of it. Ouarzazate wins: "Cheaper than Biarritz or Quiberon, and sure to be sunny, you know?" I do.

"So I guess Mme Leclercq will be staying put, as is her wont?" Our psychiatrist's intent sympathy is trained on me. I must be looking even more oblivious than is my wont; Marianne is fishing for a smile.

"Don't worry, I'm fine."

"I'm not the kind who says, 'it's nothing, just a woman drowning.'"

★ ★ ★

She doesn't miss a trick, that one. When Dr. Baruch wants to please me, she fires off one of those Exocets I myself taught her to use, in this case a line from La Fontaine. We are supposed to chortle together. Not me so much, because I don't agree with her in the slightest. For the moment Teresa is my entertainment, she's a great deal more engaging than anything else, including thalassotherapy, and since my one vice is curiosity I'm currently devouring all I can get hold of that has to do with my saint in particular and mystics in general. I feel well within my rights to fire back: "I'm not drowning, darling, I'm allowing myself to be seduced!"

But I've underestimated her again.

"Not Bruno, is it?" she says, with a censorious sniff.

Well I never! Has she overheard a phone call, or gone into my e-mails? Unlikely, it's not her style. Did she spot that old exhibition catalog of works by the Beguines, which Zonabend found in an antique bookshop and gave to me the other day?[1] "For company on your journey toward Teresa. Love, Bruno." That surplus word "love" did not escape my notice. But Marianne can't have seen the catalog or its inscription; I keep it at home, where I consult it religiously.

Got it: Bruno had Freud's complete works delivered to me at the MPH address. The standard edition in English, twenty-four volumes accompanied by an "affectionate" note. A generous if somewhat ostentatious gift, and a peculiar one, because not only do I read English poorly, the MPH is also growing increasingly cognitivist, in line with the rest of our globalized planet, and disdainful of psychoanalysis. Zonabend decided to defy the international trend, he claimed, simply to "please me."

Point noted. I got the message, and couldn't help feeling a consequent twinge. My colleagues rapidly forgot about the anachronistic offering, except, as I now realize, for Dr. Baruch. In love and therefore jealous, my friend saw the whole thing in a flash, well before I woke up to the pickle I was in with my funny old publisher. Who has, sure enough, become rather more than that in recent days.

"Oh, stop fantasizing!" I stand up, to cut the conversation short. "Happy Christmas, happy hydrotherapy, happy New Year! Send me a card I might get before Easter!" I give her a warm, close hug, but I can sense that she's not fooled.

* * *

Did I really seduce Bruno with my talk of saints? Or does mystical seduction itself make straight for its human target, publishers included, without need of assistance from me? Having lost, as the reader will recall, my faith in human relationships, I am inclined to favor the second hypothesis. Be that as it may, Bruno is a changed man since I mentioned Teresa to him. The Beguines catalog, the complete Freud; my middle-aged publisher is getting adventurous.

For he did not stop at "love" and efforts "to please me" with gifts of books. We were at the dinner-date stage. I accepted the invitation, just to see what he was after. Never in our long and intermittent history had I thought of him in any but a professional capacity, but pieces of his story started coming back to me as I sat opposite him, nursing my drink, in the Café Marly overlooking the sculpture courtyard at the Louvre. The erstwhile handsome rogue and shameless philanderer had been kicked out by his wife—what, five years ago?—because she couldn't stand any more of his Monster Baby scenes. To the surprise of tout-Paris, that microcosm of media-savvy glitterati, his wife went and married a great but obscure biologist at the INSERM medical research institute, without either celebrity status or private income—not much of a playboy either, at best a boat in the marina of La Rochelle, thanks to which I numbered him among my summer acquaintances. As expected, the diffident scientist had found safe haven in the arms of Stéphanie formerly Zonabend, henceforth Coblence. He has found happiness, actually, if the beaming face of their little girl, nearly three, is anything to go by. She skips along the strand at the Île de Ré under the frankly spiteful glances of the readers—mostly women—who feign an interest in the output of Zone Books.

So Bruno found himself alone, not really noticing, rapidly swamped by feminine attentions as calculating as they were tiresome. At length, having escaped this enterprising harem "for the sake of liberty and the Enlightenment," as he put it, he settled into a comfortable, carefree celibacy. His only ambition now, his great priority, was to consolidate his position as a tough businessman. "The only publisher who doesn't lose money by reading books": quite a feat, I must say, in our times of runaway illiteracy. It won him respect across the board in the trade. Meanwhile he kept a proud eye from afar on the education of his twin sons, students at a prestigious business school across the Atlantic.

* * *

I thought he seemed shy, for once. His soulful eyes, like those of a romantic youth, slid surreptitiously from my lips to my cleavage and back, but sought more often to plumb my own gaze in search of goodness knows what depths. He had not, however, shed his old go-getting energy, his knack for knowing when to push. On this occasion he made bold to tell me about his boys, signaling intimacy. They had jointly won the sought-after Humboldt Prize, involving a training course in India related to the famous microcredits system that had earned its deviser a Nobel Prize. At the same time ("and this, Sylvia, is what matters!") the experience had led the pair to discover Buddhism.

"You see, Thomas and Michaël are staunch rationalists, like their father, whose agnosticism you can rely on." He took a long sip of Château-Lagune, closing his eyes beatifically. "But then they get to visit all kinds of holy places, temples, and monasteries. They talk to gurus, how about that? They even met up with one of their Israeli cousins, the son of my aunt in Haifa. The guy's living in an ashram in Pondicherry, for goodness sakes! Mind you, what with those violent God-squad crazies in the Middle East not to mention our precious ally Bush and his neocons, I don't blame the Israelis for getting hung up on Eastern spirituality, do you? First India, then Japan, it'll be China next . . . Not your field, you say? Sure, it's not mine either, but I've started learning Sanskrit, did I tell you? Absolutely, been doing it for a while now. No, I didn't rediscover my faith, the future belongs to ecumenism, it's just a matter of intellectual curiosity. At the same time I'm keeping up my Hebrew, in order to follow the teaching of a spiritual master who looks at the great currents within Judaism and knows how to put them across to people like me . . . So when I hear you talk about mysticism . . . Do you know that book by Gershom Scholem, *Major Trends in Jewish Mysticism*?[2] Absolutely essential, my dear . . . Of course you have, but allow me to suggest you read it again, you know how these things mature with every reading, however many, in my experience . . . How about his *Zohar*? No? But that's the very pinnacle, the *ne plus ultra*, you absolutely must, it's all in there . . . Excuse me? I'm being ridiculous? But I thought you were letting me know that . . . well, that all that was important to you, and so I thought to myself I wasn't so alone after all." It was my turn to drain another glass of wine.

Bruno wasn't alluding merely to an exchange of spiritual intimations. "Of course, I mean, you approach the issue from a Christian perspective, and that interests me too . . . You must agree that Agamben's book on Saint Paul is his best by far? *I* should have published that, don't you think? . . . Oh, I can't tell you anything, you're so much more knowledgeable than I am, with your training and your female sensibility, goes without saying. And yet, how can I put this, a complicity between you and me *is* worth saying . . . I think so. A new alliance, if you like, in Hebrew they call it *akeda*, sacrificial alliance, or *berit*, over circumcision . . . Now you mustn't feel that I'm trying to influence you, far from it, you write it your way, like you always have. For me it's the diversity of approaches that counts, you know me, Mister Multi-pronged Attack . . ."

He floundered and flailed, absurdly and endearingly, and I felt he was being genuine. Was this really the same Bruno I had known ever since my Duras book? The cynical big shot with his marketing jargon, the wizard of publishing scoops with an air of the *soixante-huitard* recycled into a credible CEO? He wanted to talk and talk, certainly not to listen to me; his outpourings were rambling rather than erudite. I liked him better that way; I let him ramble on. When finally he got around to his Charolais steak I managed to slip in edgewise some details of Teresa's life. Her Marrano grandfather, the court case over her father and uncles' right to call themselves hidalgos, her ambiguous friendship with John of the Cross, her dalliance with Fr. Gratian. I'd unplugged my "Sigmund" antenna, it seemed more appropriate to bolster his male yearning for complicity.

"Absolutely, absolutely," he nodded absently, as if in a dream, "that's it, our subject. You don't mind me calling it *ours*? But look here: what exactly did 'love' mean, to these people? We don't know anymore, do we? And that's the problem. The 'Hiroshima of love,' you said the other day, if I remember rightly? There you are: we don't know the first thing about it, we've lost the taste for it . . . I hope you're enjoying your fish?"

✶ ✶ ✶

We had gone out into the Tuileries court. A biting wind drove snow against the steep glass of Pei's *Pyramid*, blew white flakes into my hair, my shoes, in a giddy vortex of lights. Bruno drew me close to shield me from the blizzard breaking over Paris. Then he slowly turned my face toward his, found my lips, and I lost consciousness of all but the taste of his mouth. Fragrance of blond tobacco, enveloping saliva that dilates me. A burning sap creeps through my chest, flows into my belly, floods my sex, my thighs. My legs have gone. I want to gulp down everything, this man, the wind, the wine, the museum and its auspicious scars, I am pleasure open wide. Bruno feels it, feels me, comes closer still, his face vanishes, now the whirlwind of memory that raked it vaporizes it into a mist of sleet. His tongue is still inhabiting me, I am fluid, I will not cry out, I will not fall, I strain, I melt, he licks the roof of my mouth, my cheeks, he holds me back, we start again. Not me, not him, it isn't us, this kiss belongs to nobody; someone or something beyond ourselves courses through it. Who is kissing whom? The Louvre itself participates in this exorbitant desire, and Notre Dame as well perhaps, and the Bernini sculpture of Louis XIV on horseback nearby, and the *Pyramid*, and definitely the Carrousel mall, and why not the Great Architect while we're about it; and then there's the Ganges, and my readings of La Madre, and the complete Freud, and Gershom Scholem, and Agamben, and the installations crafted by the Beguines—everything and nothing, in this snowstorm that's painting the city white.

Unplanned and futureless, that strange, long embrace, outside of time, outside of place, had the tang of impossibility, and we both knew it. All the more reason not to let go, to cling on, with bodies on fire and bellies throbbing, in a weightless suspense that was neither erotic nor antierotic: more than perfect, pluperfect. As the pluperfect tense indicates an action completed before another action in the past, so must our ancient histories, Bruno's and mine, have crossed in the far distant past, around follies and temerities that had been lived and left behind by others long before us. For a quick moment this past made as if to snatch us out of our skins before bringing us back, inevitably but undramatically, for once, to those pleasures we still call physical—according to Mother, Colette, or Sagan, I'm not sure which. All of a sudden our bodies felt pneumatic, impalpably light, drained of passion. Just a smile and a swarm of symbols and memories, a trail of exploding grenades.

Silence, taxi, "Take care of yourself," "Work well," "I'll call you," "I'm going away tomorrow." Serenity.

He's going away, I don't know where or with whom, and I don't care. Attempting to decipher Teresa's experiences is pride and exhilaration enough. Now Bruno's effervescent kiss makes me think that the headiness of it might be shared, like lonelinesses are shared that do not communicate but walk side by side into infinity. And it reminds me, if need be, that the most ideal quests keep me enthralled only insofar as they are wedded to the body. Alright, it's my job to know that, I knew that. The extraordinary thing is that it took that silly, infuriating Bruno to remind me of it!

Build up a little database gleaned from the history of mysticism—now there's an idea. After the Café Marly kiss plus the sensual details provided by my Teresa and avidly drunk in by me, I've lost my ability to classify, systemize, and synthesize. The useful oddments I come across in the works of theologians and other religious historians keep breaking up and scattering, before adhering like magnets to one another at the whim of my moods and fancies. I rearrange, I draw my *Carte de Tendre*,* my topography of feeling, in Teresa country. [*La Carte de Tendre*: map of the emotions engraved in Madeleine de Scudéry's *Clélie*, 1655–1661.—Trans.] Did I say country? "Continent" is a better word for that mystical universe that Teresa may not necessarily have understood or truly explored, but which precedes her, surrounds her, and nourishes her unawares. Yesterday it made her more intelligible to me; today, however, I feel it muddying her singular, boundless, scandalous trail.

* * *

Whereas in canonical faith all souls are divine and by the same token immortal, I use the word "mystical" to denote a psychosomatic experience that reveals the erotic secrets of that faith in a parlance that it either constructs or silently refuses. In the mystical experience an extraordinary union comes about—while the speaker is in life—between the soul and his or her God, the finite cleaving to the infinite in order to consummate its true eternity, "alone with God" in the most immediate, intimate sense of a successful incarnation and indwelling. The body wounded by desire experiences and signifies its unspeakable union with the "fundamental principle of being" (Lalande),[3] with the Other (Lacan),[4] with "Christ's humanity" (Saint Teresa of Avila). The figures of this hierogamy, this sexual and sublimated osmosis with the absent Beloved may vary, but each inscribes a fracture in the sacral community to which they pertain, and by derivation often touch upon the social and political pact itself. Maximal singularity, rupture of links, recasting of the religious, or of the a-theological quest: mysticism is regarded by "ordinary people" as a form of inner, albeit extravagant, wisdom at odds with the official knowledge, whether ecclesiastic or secular, that so readily reveres it when unable to recuperate it retrospectively.

The impossible desire for a lacking love object is exaltation and pain that are hidden, reticent, at once thrilling and morbid. Excess or emptiness? Or both? The word *mystery*, from the Greek μυω, "to conceal," to be closed up (like lips or eyes or sores) goes back to the Sanskrit *mukham*, "face," "mouth," "entrance." But the mystics, nurturers of this most inner of interiorities inhabited by the All-Other (*le Tout Autre*), transmute it to the outside—and hiddenness becomes a path. Life bursts into fullness, absence into genuine presence, suffering into bliss, mortification into delight, Nothingness into ecstasy, and vice versa. Religious space is thus transformed into a stage for love, while the search for truth becomes a matter of body-to-body, spirit-to-spirit, body-to-spirit encounters. Mysticism, without distinction of "categories," embarks on a genuine recasting of metaphysics.

★ ★ ★

The earliest instances of the word "mystic" appear during the first century, in Pseudo-Denys the Areopagite,[5] sharpened to a fine point of Neoplatonism with Plotinus's *aphelepanta* ("Leave everything behind!")[6] and even Aristotle's *theôria* in contemplation of the One,[7] separate from what can be apprehended by the senses.

And yet, far predating this lexical appearance, hints of "mysticism" abound throughout the Bible. Moses finding God in the midst of the burning bush,[8] Ezekiel with a vision of God's chariot, receiving a scroll he must eat in order to deliver its message;[9] these are scenes in which reason is overturned in the clearest light of day. Indeed, mysticism filters into the apocalyptic scriptures (the books of Enoch and Esdras), into Essenian convents, the Pharisee world, and the thought of the Jewish Mishnah masters—all these being focused on the knowledge and contemplation of God and his throne (*Merkabah*), goal of the mystical progress through the heavenly palaces. Various aspects of the Torah (oral revelation) and the Talmud contain mystical tendencies. Thus the subtle reasonings, like "mountains hanging from a hair," of the Torah's inspired scribes; the thirty-two logical rules defining the ways of acceding to Talmudic wisdom and developing the dialectics of reason, aim to elicit visions with the supreme goal of man's identification with God. Then, from the first century B.C.E. to the tenth C.E., the Kabbalah comes to swell this biblical and Talmudic initiation. It calls the earthly world into being through the operation of twenty-two originary letters in the air, creative entities whose permutations express every idea and every thing. Pharisees, Essenians, the journey through the *Hekhalot*—palaces of Heaven, which Teresa will call *moradas*, the seven dwelling places of her Castle—the mystical impulse reemerges in thirteenth-century Spain and Germany. Contemplation, based on a scriptorial combination and practiced by means of techniques recalling those of yoga (breathing, positions of the body, musical notes), culminates in prophetic ecstasy, supernatural illumination, identifying man with the Torah, with the Word, and with God. Cross-fertilization with Islam and Christianity enriches these mystical currents, while Islam and Christianity in turn absorb the wisdom of visionary Kabbalists, despite and throughout the vicious persecutions, expulsions, and exterminations suffered by the Jews.

During the Middle Ages, a full-blown "medieval Jewish philosophy" flourishes in counterpoint to Arab philosophy. Unacquainted with Greek metaphysics, Talmudic thought that could be described as a monism of thought and action nonetheless developed a rich ambivalence between abstract speculation and mystical experience. Theological ignorance of God, who is undefinable by definition, does not rule out a loving knowledge of Him based on the Alliance: through the concept of *shekhinah*, God accompanies the exiled Jew on earth. The medieval *gaon*—a spiritual master such as Saadia Gaon, the political leader of the eastern diaspora—links rationalistic interpretation with enthusiasm for revelation; the commentary on the *Sefer Yetzirah*,[10] that germ of the Kabbalah, with the moderate religious philosophy followed by the Muslim Kalâm. As part of the same opening toward philosophical reflection, Jewish mysticism evolves with Judah Halevi[11] and Maimonides,[12] preceded by Ben Joseph of Fayum,[13] Solomon Ibn Gabirol,[14] who looks deep into his affinities with Plato,[15] Philo of Alexandria,[16] and Gnosticism. Not forgetting Bahya Ibn Paquda,[17] who stands at the intersection of these tendencies, or Abraham Abulafia,[18] who takes up the theory of the mystical power of the alphabet to explore the "unknotting of the soul" by means of musical experiments with arpeggios, transpositions, canons, and fugues. At last comes the surpassing step that is the *Zohar*, in the second half of the thirteenth century: the *Sefer ha-Zohar*, or *Book of Splendor*, whose presumed author, Moisés de León, insisted on attributing it to a second-century Mishnah scholar.[19] Reprising the *Sefer Yetzirah*, the *Zohar* drops the distinction between "spirit" and "letter," condensing them instead into an indivisible unit. And gathering the diverse components of Jewish mysticism into one harmonious structure, it graces the exile of Israel with the ultimate meaning of releasing the "divine sparks" and completing the work of redemption.[20] Translated into French by Jean de Pauly,[21] the *Zohar* went on to influence no less a figure than Marcel Proust![22]

Such a wealth of tendencies, however, can never overshadow the Torah and the Talmud, writings that destined the Jewish people—committed to biblical exegesis and free of major mystical interferences—to a ceaseless study of the texts, so as to imbue themselves with the spirit of God's Law and put it into practice, thus assuring the salvation of the chosen community.

* * *

Bruno is far away, it would be untrue to say I ever think about him, and yet I feel him alongside me, inside me, for example when I'm leafing through the Beguines catalog. My readings of the past few weeks are arranged in my mind like the surrealist collages of those bygone pious women who piled bits of string and handfuls of rose petals around the figure of Baby Jesus. The Sovereign Infant was liable to disappear altogether under the cumulative passion of those tender sisters. He merged with the huge heart they embroidered for him in cross-stitch or molded out of crushed, colorful butterfly wings, a heart that was the real theme and focus of the work. Was it Jesus's heart, or was it theirs?

It would be wrong to assume that contemporary artists have transcended this kind of reiterative, magpie accumulation. I see a lot of it in the galleries, and most often the artist is a woman. One, Annette B., trusted me enough to lie down on my couch. Her wary, piercing eyes seem cloned from Picasso's. As a rule her words do not get past her lips, or only in spurts of dulled, futile complaint, abruptly doused. A long, frozen silence ensues. When the artist can no longer bear her own speechlessness, she brings me some "beguinesques," as she calls her confections of twisted threads, mounted letters, screws of paper, beads, buttons, leaves, and a series of tiny cut-up photographs, skillfully embedded in the vortices of this kaleidoscope of mega-significant nothings. Photographs of her dead children. Impossible icons of impossible loves. Annette's "beguinesques" succeed in making such impossibilities visible. At least to people who enjoy looking. And who've been through a vortex like hers.

I cut out my data, I sort, I glue, I amass. My canvas is taking shape. No, it's lost me. Later on I will set Teresa into it and she will resorb the picture, all that will be left is her very own heart, her style, her beat.

* * *

Might it be because Muslim mysticism slumbers in the form of "Koranic seeds" within the values, if not the formulations, of the dogma? Or is it down to the Neoplatonic influence? In any case, the first mystics appeared in eighth-century Iraq, as bands of ascetics who cultivated trust in God (*tawakkol*). They "repeated" God's name and began to believe in a prior communication between God and His creature. A little later, clad in white woolen garments (*suf*), the Sufis gathered into spiritual circles and concerts, bent on a loving union with God. Schools sprang up in the cities of Basora and Baghdad, then across Afghanistan, India, and Egypt, until the advent of the Master, al-Hallaj, a mystic who was martyred in 922 C.E.[23] The Hellenic origins of this mystical experience, which took the form of a poetic quest, are not in doubt. It was a "science of the heart" that sought to transform the sensible body into pure "spirit" (in philosophical terminology) through the burning love that consumes the saint, disposed to "isolate himself before the One." "Legal war" thus mutates into "inner war," and the Seal of Saints embodied by Jesus is set against Muhammad's Seal of Prophets; God is henceforth to be sought within, and the mystic, rather than overthrow the Law, transcends it. "I have become the One I love and the One I love has become me. We are two spirits infused in a single body," wrote al-Hallaj.

Whether focused on reciprocal love (al-Nuri), private inspiration (Ibn Karram), or union with God (al-Hallaj), Sufism borrowed the spiritual methods of Christian monachism while influencing that movement in return. It also appropriated Hindu and Persian techniques.

Accused of heresy and impiety, stigmatized for its incompatibility with the Law of Islam, Sufism finally found a direction: the compromise between juridical authority and ecstasy paved the way for its esoteric brotherhoods. Notwithstanding some serious deviations that degenerated into opium clubs and sham whirling dervishes with dodgy morals, in the eighteenth century, philosophical Sufism became an "existential monism," with the Andalusian Ibn al-Arabi: no distinction between the soul and God any longer subsists in the mystical union.[24] Committed to immanentism, eschewing neither literal meaning (anathema to the Shi'a) nor sacred meaning, this current believed that the Absolute cannot become conscious of itself other than through Man in the image of God. In Sufi thought, then, immanence and transcendence are not mutually exclusive, and opposite meanings (as in the "primitive words" studied by Freud) coincide, since the Unique is manifest in the All. "I mean that you absolutely do not exist, and never will exist by yourself alone, any more than by Him, in Him or with Him. You cannot cease to exist, because you do not exist. You are Him and He is you, without dependence or causality. If you accept that quality of your existence (which is to say, Nothingness), then you shall know Allah. Otherwise you shall not." As a result, "the prayers of lovers are blasphemous." There are five steps leading to this revelation of Being at the same time as the impossibility of Being: "there is of him only Him"; "there is of you only You"; "there is of me only Me"; "I-ness, you-ness, he-ness, all these are viewpoints that add to the eternal essence of the One." Set in motion by God, the experience soars into the "limitless," where it is vividly clear that only "he who is not in love sees his own face in a pool."

Meanwhile, as of the eleventh century, mystical poetry had put down roots and thrived, feeding off profane, erotic, and bacchic poetry. The "sultan of lovers," Ibn al-Farid was one such,[25] along with the Persian mystic Jalal ad-Din Rumi, founder of the whirling dervishes brotherhood,[26] and the Turkish poets Nesimi and Niyazi.

This *adogmatic* Muslim mysticism resisted integration into the Islamic mainstream, until the Sufi theologian and philosopher al-Ghazali proposed a "mystical orthodoxy" that would complete traditional knowledge with a "taste" or realization of God: an intimate knowledge that was gained through tempered asceticism.[27] Sufism went on to spread the cult of thaumaturgical saints—including al-Hallaj,[28] the most revered of all despite his excommunication—and became a "popular religion," treating the Muslim faithful to that "taste" the jurists had denied them and so reinvigorating the moderate morality of that faith.[29]

* * *

"Hello? Can you hear me, Sylvia? Where am I, I'm in Thailand! Told you, didn't I? Okay, my mistake. The Phuket beaches, crawling with tourists . . . Fantastic. No sign of the tsunami . . . at least not around here . . . Me, scared? . . . Of course people have short memories, what do you expect, that's life . . . Oh, the usual, swimming and sleeping. And I've been going to this Buddhist temple . . . Sylvia, please, the Muslims are in Indonesia . . . Actually no, I haven't converted, or not yet. But I'm great chums with one of the bonzes. I'm approaching the Void. Go ahead, laugh! If you're not wise to Nothingness, my dear, you may as well give up the mysticism game. Even your baroque saint must have known that . . . The Void is at the bottom of everything, you dig? . . . How do you mean, compatible with my lifestyle? These Buddhists are highly pragmatic fellows . . . Tomorrow I go to Banda Aceh with this NGO, old friends of mine, they're building boats for the fishermen who lost everything in 2004, you know. We're going to walk the sandbank in Lhoong . . . really beautiful . . . So you're surprised to see me doing something humanitarian? That's right, it's got a lot to do with the boys and their gurus . . . They're fine, thanks . . . And so's Stéphanie, why do you ask. You know it's finished . . . Just a stop-off in India . . . Yes, of course we'll do a book, with photographs, it's the trend, and besides it's my job . . . That's right, everything is connected. I don't have to explain that to you of all people . . . Ciao, take care . . . kisses and all that, you know."

Do I know or am I forgetting? Inimitable Bruno! He's far away, and he's who he is. Let him make his own discoveries in his own way. He can sort out his syncretism however he wants, I'm all for the great leap from Paris glitz to global compassion, but I'd rather he went into analysis, it would save so much time . . . Oh well. I guess I don't always take the shortcuts either, I follow my own detours. With Teresa, for instance.

⋆ ⋆ ⋆

So, while it's true that Judaism contains veins of mysticism, that the Upanishads relish sensual joys and annihilation in the sounds of the language, that Muslim Sufism reveals Being and its impossibility together, and that Zen koans are peerless propagators of the Void, it was in Christianity that mystics male and female were to find their royal road. Like Saul on the road to Damascus.

Are the mystical currents that flow through the three monotheisms the result of interferences, contaminations, influences, or structural coincidences? Did the Hassidim sway Meister Eckhart, Suso, and Tauler after introducing the thought of Maimonides into the ghetto of Worms? Or was it the other way around? Did the Arab peripatetics in the wake of al-Kindi[30] transmit the symphony of the two great philosophies of antiquity, Platonism and Aristotelianism, via Albert the Great[31] to Eckhart himself? And in particular the theory of *analogia entis* that posits the paradoxical nature of creation as at once Being and Nothingness? The ebullience of Being as the negation of negation? Nobility as humility and detachment?

Whatever the channels and facets of this convergent experience, all of whose manifestations are regarded as "mystical," it has to be acknowledged that the true "deification of the Christian," or "theogenesis," was the doing of Greek patristics and its thinkers such as Origen,[32] Gregory of Nyssa,[33] and Pseudo-Denys the Areopagite. What Saint Augustine called *abditum mentis*, the "hidden place" of the soul, and its sequence of *conversio/reformatio/conformatio*, became tools for attaining ecstasy. Thus began a complex history during which the Church would bestow two complementary meanings on the expression *corpus mysticum*, the union with impossible, indispensable Love.

On the one hand the Eucharist invites each believer to incorporate the Body of God, for Christ is the one true love object: "This is my body, this is my blood." Eat me, I am in you, and you can form part of the body of this ideal Subject, this single being who redeemed every member of humanity. A modest event during the early years, the Mass grew ever more sumptuous, performing its osmosis under cupolas ringing with music and naves lined with sculptures and frescoes: an erotic, purified, intense osmosis whereby men and women alike identified with the Body of Christ and its mortifications, death and resurrection. In *Communion* I swallow the bread and wine, Jesus's flesh and blood, I introject the Christ, I am Him and He is me, we fuse in hierogamic union. I do not participate in, I *partake of* His Passion and resurrection, of Hell and Heaven, of Nothingness and bliss.

On the other hand and at the same time, the community of the faithful, which is to say the Church, is born of this sacramental communion and assures its continued social and political relevance.

Faced with those Christians who still take communion—scarcer in the West than on other continents—I follow Freud in wondering whether the Eucharist does not perhaps constitute a necessary psychodrama, one which allows participants to experience in a "closed space," in the recondite security of the service, the ravages of desire in order to quench them and as far as possible preserve the community from them. I would like to think so. Or perhaps on the contrary, this sacrament slyly authorizes, if not brutally imposes, the sadomasochistic truth of human passions at the very heart of community and intercommunity relations. Persecutions, pogroms, purges, roundups of heretics, inquisitorial trials, all were unfailingly sealed by the sacrament of Communion . . . Christianity's two thousand years of history bear witness to the vertiginous effects of this pendulum. Today, at last, we are surely justified in hoping that the time for stillness has arrived. Pope Benedict XVI plays Mozart, after all, while certain other faith leaders trumpet holy war. Not that this defuses the tensions of identity politics, or prevents the reaction against real or supposed aggressors from poisoning the very discourses that most flaunt their commitment to helping the less fortunate, or to defending human rights. Murderous violence answers violence, intolerance combats intolerance, and mindless fundamentalists, both Muslim and Christian, plan massacres bloodier than the Saint Bartholomew of Voltaire's nightmares.

Throughout these vicissitudes, it is none other than the bodies of the mystics of both sexes, delivered through their writings, that offer themselves as the secret laboratory in which human beings have been able to reach maximum lucidity about the physical and psychic excesses of their fantasy-induced transports. In the wake of this solitary, perilous experimentation, reforms, foundations, and schisms arose to ensure, over the long term, the vitality of illusions and the renewal of both doctrine and institutions.[34]

* * *

From the middle of the twelfth century on, the phrase *corpus mysticum* no longer denoted the Eucharist but simply the Church, and *corpus verum* was used for the osmosis with Jesus through Communion. The adjectives *mysticum* ("hidden") and *verum* ("knowably real") changed places, and a chiasmus appeared: from now on it was the Church, the social body of Christ, that would enclose the "hidden meaning" of the sacramental "true body," rendered visible in the form of consecrated bread and wine. This meant that nothing in Catholicism was now hidden! With the Church presenting itself as ever more universal and inclusive, the mystery it celebrated and enshrined could no longer be a secret for anyone. It follows that the transubstantiation of the God-man into bread and wine was no longer a mystery properly speaking, but a "knowable reality" that invites communicants to immerse themselves in it, body and soul, desire and reason; to each his or her own journey within a truth susceptible of being universally acknowledged. The appeal to extreme individual experience was henceforth coupled to a wholesale communitarian, not to say pragmatic, concern.

The revolution undergone by the *corpus mysticum* entailed momentous consequences. Before, the body of Christ signified by the hidden sacrament (the mysterious, mystic Eucharist) linked apostolic history to the present Church. Now, the Church was the hidden signified of the visible signifier that is Christ's body. Christian history *and* the sacrament stood connected to, yet separate from, the Church, which was entirely their extension: mysterious, mystical, and yet open to all. This curious topology could not but inscribe itself within the subjects who shared in it, for it was in the social and political *reality* of the present Church that the mystical third (the union) must be produced. The Church was therefore summoned to reform itself, its mystical body had to be constructed as a fusion of community *and* communion, of the social bond *and* the bond of desire for the Other. At that point two movements became possible: the Reformation, with its social imperatives, which was already underway (fourteenth to fifteenth centuries); but also, in a parallel counterpoint, the supernatural excesses, the fervid amorous transports, the ever more bizarre extremes that enacted the risks of subjective freedom and prefigured from afar the baroque faith of the Counter-Reformation (late sixteenth to late eighteenth centuries).

* * *

It was during the thirteenth century, then, that the peculiar profile of Christian mysticism took shape. Just as Thomas Aquinas[35] was applying Aristotelian philosophy to biblical and evangelical revelation in order to show that the unity of God was accessible to reason, a galaxy of mystics prepared to sound out and diffract this same reason. They infiltrated it with the logics of love and Nothingness, giving the Greek Logos a pre-Socratic slant, and, rather than seek to prove God's existence philosophically, they anticipated the contemporary investigation into the very *need to believe* in the form of a polymorphous experience of love, excessive and inescapable.

Among the figures who illustrated these various currents and left a profound mark on European culture, I would underline—as does Teresa, my guide in this research—the "modern" devotion of the Flemish school, especially the lovelorn Jan van Ruysbroek[36] and the great poetess Hadewijch of Antwerp;[37] but above all the Rhenish mystics, first among them Meister Eckhart, the "unborn" (*ungeboren*), who begged God to leave him "free of God." A "deep calling unto deep,"[38] "free of all things," "creating emptiness," the soul "begets God from within itself, where it has the color of God; there is the image of God." The soul of the "nobleman" is, according to Eckhart, negative as much as unitive; a supreme Intellect, but also a superessential Nothingness.[39] It reaches the mystical state in *Gelassenheit*, the "abandonment" sung by Angelus Silesius in his *The Cherubic Pilgrim*,[40] after Henry Suso[41] and John Tauler,[42] Eckhart's direct continuators, had managed to smuggle his message as far as Nicholas Krebs of Cusa[43] and into the stream of "speculative" mysticism that culminates in Jakob Böhme.[44]

The mystical theology thus created, having fertilized Christianity with late classical thought and Neoplatonic techniques of spiritual purification, would furnish the whole vocabulary of German philosophy. "Here is what we were looking for!" exclaims Hegel[45] upon reading parts of Eckhart's sermons 12 and 52, while Schopenhauer writes that Buddha, Eckhart, and himself "teach substantially the same thing." Heidegger, for his part, constantly abandoning himself to the "abandonment" of Silesius,[46] modulates the *analogia entis* that enables the conception of Being and Nothingness.

Fanned by the Salamanca student, John of the Cross, did the Rheno-Flemish wind blow as far as Teresa of Avila? It takes nothing away from La Madre's originality to admit that the answer is *yes*.

Indeed, women are the foremost architects of this new dwelling-place of the soul we call mystical experience: an erotic, lethal escalation propels them to the summit of *excessus*. In Hildegarde of Bingen, this takes the form of a fabulous anatomical perception of her own body.[47] It is enfeebled but sovereign in the cult of "nothing," the apophatic thinking expressed by the "severed, immobile tongue" of Angela of Foligno.[48] It inflames the anorexic Catherine of Siena with sacrificial devotion when she licks the pus from a cancerous breast:[49] this fervent Dominican became the patron saint of Italy alongside Saint Francis of Assisi[50] and Saint Thomas Aquinas. She was made a doctor of the Church by Pope Paul VI, at the same time as Teresa of Avila.

Why is there such a female infatuation with mysticism? Modern scholars have outdone one another in fascinated hypotheses. Is it because a woman's *whole body* is a sexual organ, because desire scorches her skin, her eyes, her ears, her tongue, her clitoris, her vagina, and her anus alike, and all her senses sweep her toward the object of her desire while he, like the Beloved in the Song of Songs, is always eluding her, a fleeing spouse or hidden God, absent, invisible, imaginary, unimaginable? If a woman's whole body is a sexual organ, it can just as thoroughly repress desire to the point of sickness or vacate it into daydreams, words, sublimity.

The reasoned Protestant faith was quick to pour scorn on such deviations: "Visionen will ich nicht!" declared Luther.[51] But the Golden Age Spanish Illuminati did not hesitate to draw on reformed humanism, and the Counter-Reformation seeded in its turn a new flowering of mysticism.

* * *

While reformed congregations put the accent on Scripture and the charitable vocation of a Christian community whose moral rigor was intended to quell and resorb the excesses of the desiring body, the Catholics, whose resistance to this formula was empowered by the Counter-Reformation, strove to make the secluded meanders of faith plain to see within the actual space of the Church—to infiltrate the *corpus mysticum* via the *corpus verum*.[52] From then on, the more modulated meaning of the word *mystic* exhibited itself with forceful brilliance: it no longer denoted an inaccessible concealment, but beckoned what is concealed to come forth; it summoned the torments of flesh and spirit to emerge into the light and to seduce us. The *corpus verum*—Christ's Passion, of which the subject partakes—was no longer a protected secret. By the grace of the mystics and of the Church that consecrated them, the seduction became universal.[53] Such was the context of Teresa's experience.

This mutation would unfold through a long and patient labor of theology, ritual, and aesthetics, tending to invent an ecclesial mystical body to link the present of the ecclesial institution (the hierarchy) to its history (textual, scriptural), but also to couple the boundless intimacy of mystical experiences to the visibility of religious society. The hearing of confession had already broken down some social opaqueness. The elevation of the Host accompanied by its observed consumption made a spectacle of the sacramental body itself, exhibiting the mystery in public. All this contributed to manufacturing the paradox of a *transparent intimate body*. Private life was "individualized" by highly customized "spiritual guidance" and other "confidential" dialogues, leading to the dissemination of "Exemplary Lives" or "Exercises" for the edification of a fascinated populace. A radical transformation took place via this process of *visualization of the sacred*, which today we might call the *mediatization of the sacred*, in and through the new conception of the Church promoted by the third[54] and fourth Lateran councils[55] and given a radical twist by the Council of Trent[56] and the ensuing Counter-Reformation. Even prior to that, however, as the hidden became progressively "mediatized," so the new mysticism became "epiphanic": the *corpus mysticum* would be a placing in common, a transparent solidarity with the wretchedness of the "exiled" creatures that we are, and beyond: "Omnes . . . habebant omnia communia" (All the faithful together place everything in common).

The brilliant novelty of the Counter-Reformation, whose signature saint Teresa became, was its way of placing the turbulence of desire in full view and in common, thanks to the transparency at work since the twelfth century: a turbulence that was sacred inasmuch as it was representable, secret inasmuch as sensual, and, not least, rhetorical. Erotic, tortured carnality would be magnified by composers and painters, Vivaldi[57] and Tintoretto.[58] And the city of Venice turned *corpus mysticum* in its entirety would deploy its perpetual therapy, the real presence of the desiring body indefinitely reborn, a *renaissance* in every painting and at every concert. It has been labeled an aesthetic religion. But it's more than that: the "mystical body" *and* the "real body" come together in the art of the Counter-Reformation into an unprecedented blossoming of *representation* alive to the infinity of bodies. Inside-outside bodies, supple, mobile, baroque, transitive, contagious, the very bodies conjured up by Teresa of Avila; a sacred apprehension of God's presence in that part of the soul where the sensible melds with the highest spirit. The mystical experience (Teresa's experience, the one that intrigues me here), whether it lets itself be influenced by the mutations of the *corpus mysticum* while influencing them, or whether it is also subject to the course of secular history, never fails to cultivate, steadily and tirelessly, that third place, that mystical third consistent in union with the divine, *hic et nunc.*

Imperceptibly, however, the content of this mystical union also mutated, in such a way that its protagonists (for me, here, Teresa) appear to us as the inventors of brand-new psychic spaces. Mysticism is the crucible of subjective diversities produced by the history of Christianity. With hindsight, several types of "interior castles" can be glimpsed, among which Teresa's construction stands out for its extravagant originality: an unprecedented combination of total exile from self in the love match with the Other, acute lucidity, rhetorical exuberance, and staggering levels of social activity. This was before seventeenth-century medicine and investigative reason had neutered those firebrand negativists, those insurgents of the concept, those oxymoronic maniacs, the mystics, in order to install the empire of the cogito. Before eighteenth-century libertinism had cynically desecrated the innocent erotomania of nuns. Before today's calculating mentality had stopped it up and shrunk it down, in benefit of the new maladies of the soul and the antipsychotics industry.

★ ★ ★

Turned into a laughingstock, jeered at on church squares during medieval car-
nivals, mysticism retreated for good as soon as Renaissance and Enlightenment
eroticism prised the sexual body away from its secret enclave in the shadow of
cathedrals and let it loose to gambol in drawing rooms and boudoirs, in paintings, music, and books. The libertine consciousness definitively silenced the
mystics who had opened the gates of desire. By dint of overrefining physical
delights alongside those of words, colors, and sounds, the incipient sexual liberation whose apogee was reached in the French eighteenth century was impatient to cut free from the polychromatic journeys Otherward of the soul, and
soon began to shut the numberless doors of the interior castle.

Nowadays we might read the mystics much as we sniff the opium waft of
moldy parchments, for they are merely the vestiges of a vanished humanity, fit
to inspire some atavistic poet or a man like Heidegger,[59] that deconstructor of
metaphysics who saw himself reflected in Meister Eckhart: "Pure Being and
pure Nothing are therefore the same." But in that case, why is it mysticism that
attracts me, that attracts us, when we attempt to break free of instrumental
rationality, or to loosen the vise of fundamentalist manipulation and analyze
the insane logic of the terrorist's ecstatic drive?

As he was finishing the *Critique of Pure Reason*, Kant hoped for, and glimpsed
in a flash, the possibility of a world in compliance with moral law.[60] But the proclaimed universality of the rights of man has still not given our global village
an exemplary code of ethics, and the rolling news of the postmodern age brings
home the persistence of barbarity more cruelly than ever. Perhaps this is because
the Kantian promise was not to be imagined as the fruit of some inconceivable
"intelligible intuition"; it could only be that of the "world of sense" linked to
"practical reason," and more precisely, of the "*corpus mysticum* of rational beings
in it." By *corpus mysticum* Kant understood a universal "systematic unity" (that
"unity-union" again!) informing "the *liber arbitrum* of the individual . . . under
and by virtue of moral laws"; a systematic unity "both with itself, and with the
freedom of all others." "This is the answer to the first of the two questions of
pure reason which relate to its practical interest: —*Do that which will render
thee worthy of happiness.*"

There is nothing to connect Kant with Teresa of Avila. And yet, notwithstanding the gulf between their times, cultures, vocabularies, and projects,
this *corpus mysticum* appearing in the last pages of the *Critique of Pure Reason*
doesn't strike me as foreign to the saint's experience, or even to my submarine
nights. Where does this resonance come from?

If Kant's ultimate aspiration to "reunite" morality and freedom speaks so strongly to me, it's because the final metaphor of unity—the union with the self and with *all others*, the All-Other—cannot be understood merely in the present trite and bankrupt sense of solidarity, or even fraternity. Such a diminishment not only clips the wings of the adventure; too many heads have also rolled along the way. If freedom is synonymous with desire, how can I enter into union with the centrifugal, centripetal forces of my own desires, let alone with those of others? This question is still searching for an answer. "Seek yourself in Me," said the Other to Teresa, and they never ceased answering each other. How? On the analyst's couch? At a meeting of the UN Security Council? At a rock concert? At the Beijing Olympics? At a Gay Pride march? By playing Mozart operas at Ground Zero, in Tel Aviv, in Baghdad? Contrary to all rational expectation, Kant invites us to update an ancient European experience, the theology of the *corpus mysticum*. Is this possible? What if it were?

It would seem that at the dawn of the third millennium we are still waiting for this new "*corpus mysticum* of rational beings" to show up. But perhaps the old *corpus mysticum* of inordinate and excessive beings, *alumbrados*, lovers of the Absolute and of nothing, has not said its final word . . . Perhaps Teresa keeps some surprises up her sleeve.

Chapter 3

DREAMING, MUSIC, OCEAN

Mysticism is the obscure self-perception of the realm outside the ego,
of the id.

Sigmund Freud, *Findings, Ideas, Problems*

At the start of the twenty-first century, under the drones of the new crusades brought to us by globalized satellite TV, that Old Continent of godly lunatics whose memory Teresa is reawakening for me, far from disappearing into abstruse mists, appears strangely contemporary. The commodification of the sacred by various sects, alongside that of hard-core porn DVDs by an industry that does not blush to seek spiritual endorsement from the Moonies, Scientology, or Soka Gakkai, fail to discredit, for me, the *regressus animae* in search of true interiority. The language I inhabit like a curious foreigner bids to seep into the folds of the disparate writings known as "mystical" texts. My first move is to unify their polysemy under the generic term *mysticism*, ignoring the plural of its outlandish singularities for the time being. A common logic subtends those bodies in their exultant "meditations," those "poems" and "narratives" unintelligible to today's profane culture-mart and beyond the scope of religious competition. Later I will discern the suns and skies, the hills and gullies, the rivers and deserts, the plants and animals of this promised land of sacred lunacies: Teresa will guide me to them. For now, I survey the terrain from afar: another time, another space. My viewpoint is not that of a bird or the stars but chiefly that of psychoanalysis.

* * *

"The mystics, eh? You know the score, don't you. A bunch of narcissists who get off on *manque à être*, on lack of being itself!" The speaker is a colleague who might be my alter ego on a guided tour of Mystic Country. He's far more solid, intellectually speaking, than Bruno. I haven't seen Bruno since he came back from Aceh. He sends me kisses by e-mail and over the phone but devotes most of his time to the NGO that helps tsunami-hit fishermen to build new boats, neglecting his editorial duties at Zone. Jérôme Tristan, on the other hand, has just published a piece in a journal specializing in the contemporary vicissitudes of mystical thought. I'm impressed!

"Hold on, slow down. Narcissists, yes, clearly they are: the withdrawal from the world of other people, the denial of external reality, the retreat into traumatic, therefore unnameable, desire. And the refusal of language—again, I'm with you—following hurt, separation, or bereavement. Unhappy Narcissus invents imaginary nuptials with lost Object, transformed into an ideal but just as imaginary Object, not even by now an 'object' separate from the 'subject,' but the Great Totality in which loser and lost are both subsumed. Whether you want to call it 'fundamental principle of Being,' Being, Other, God, Cosmos, Mother Goddess, Tao, God-man, who cares, it's about 'unbridled *jouissance*,' as we used to say in '68 on the way out of our Lacan seminar. No me, no you, communicating vessels, denial of separation, the interior swallowing the exterior in one gigantic orgasm. I know that stuff. And you? Vaguely, okay, but it rings a bell. Now. My problem is with the way you assume that they obtain *jouissance* from separation itself. You'd have to be more than ordinarily masochistic, wouldn't you?" I try to sound naive.

"Think about it. To counter the fear of death, and the tiny deaths and losses of every kind that are the milestones of life, religions invented a major consolation: the afterlife, in a Beyond where the ideal Father awaits. More subtly, a space both radiant and eternal. This mystical location, we'll call it Heaven, contains Daddy and Mommy reconciled at long last and granting me permission to enjoy immortal pleasure, because this is the point: pleasure for ever. Others prefer the cosmic breath of yin and yang, in their equally harmonious cohabitation. Why, people can reunite what they like, to stop the flight of time . . . But the mystics, you see, weren't satisfied with this promise. Too easy. Not that they rejected it, either. You will concur, oh dearest"—my colleague can be a little precious at times; there are still plenty of his sort who want to sound like Lacan—"that they were given to piling up the most with the least, the same with its opposite. Refusing to choose, you see. 'Apophatic' thought, to use a fancy word, was extremely common among mystics, as the experts in the field will tell you. Because, not content with the mirage of Heaven, our seekers after the Holy Grail identify with separation itself, which Heaven will heal, even when they are not into death as such. As if lack, absence, Nothingness were the final, most secret and precious legacy offered by the elusive love-Object, the lost or inaccessible partner. Sinuous Nothingness is the absolute essence of the desire they felt, feel and always will feel for this unknown, unknowable, impossible object of desire, the Beloved."

"You make them sound like psychoanalysts *avant la lettre*!" I'm being provocative here, I haven't read his piece; he may as well explain it to me face to face.

"They were, in a way . . ." A meditative pause. "At any rate they never ceased to utter the insatiable truth of desire. That's it: they knew that death or Nothingness make pleasure, tireless as it is, work harder, and unlike ordinary believers they weren't content with the promise of a Beyond that would negate this negative machinery. What's more they never failed to thoroughly annihilate themselves in death and Nothingness, against and because of which the promise of Heaven was constituted. But since they were apt to think in paradoxes, they didn't miss out on the benefits of the promise, either. In short, the mystical perspective is nothing less than the corpse, which is no different from Nirvana! A splendid paradox! That's why all their insights are built on antithesis. Like this outstanding phrase, wouldn't you agree, from the Koran: 'He is the First and the Last, the Manifest and the Hidden.'"[1]

"All very interesting, but to get back to business, what are the psychic advantages for them in all this?" I have to remain pragmatic: our job as mind doctors is to treat people.

"Elementary, oh dearest! Man's access to nonbeing is what achieves his divinization, according to theologians and to some philosophers, because the creature has got to be put to death so as to clear a space for reaching the Creator and dissolving into Him. But that's not all. Let me explain the relevance to your everyday practice, although I suspect you've worked it out already and you're just letting me talk: ah, women, flatterers vile! Where was I. Seen from our analytical bubble, this psychic disturbance, which reacts to the anguish of separation and death by identifying with the death that threatens it, is a way of *detaching oneself from the Mother*—because we all agree, yes, that the mother is the first object of separation?—*without fixating exclusively on the ideal Father.* Neither father nor mother: I settle on *nothing,* to preserve my desire for *both.* This trick of indefinitely prolonging the 'depressive position,' as Klein calls it— whom you've just discovered, and about time, too—allows the child to distance itself indefinitely from the mother while postponing, indefinitely, the merger with the father . . . You're not vexed, I trust, you're still on board? Delights of infantile omnipotence, perverse* [*French *père-vers*: Lacanian pun meaning toward-the-father.—Trans.] traps of a regression that only indulges in infantile behavior the better to merit the grace and power of the father! Well, then, the mystical solution is similar, but goes further. It succeeds in inhabiting, psychically and physically, the extreme tension that binds the subject to her and to him, the Mother and the Father, the feminine and the masculine, until the annihilation of that tension and with it of the loved objects and of the subject itself. They called it 'peace.' Or 'serenity,' if you prefer."

"Of course I do . . ." I put on a compassionate smile.

★ ★ ★

I find myself wondering how Jérôme Tristan handles Mrs. Tristan, Aude Tristan to be precise, also a therapist, and a militant feminist. Couples in general are a mystery to me, I grant, but a couple of analysts defies comprehension. Shared monomania, complementary neuroses, hetero gender gap filled by some alleged "homo" harmony . . . Wisdom or tedium? My colleague looks uneasy and somewhat glum. Back to the mystics.

"Come on, Jérôme, these men and women must have been awfully vulnerable, besides possessing amazing psychic plasticity and towering strength of soul, in order to wrestle the terror of death into a triumph like that!"

"Yes, but the triumph is dogged by setbacks, from way-out mental derangement to being literally put to death, not to mention a paranoid hatred for the world that plainly overtakes many visionary individuals and groups whose ritual practices accentuate passivity, resentment, dolorism; in a word, castration. The Nazis themselves attempted to recruit the German mystics to 'resist' the 'Syrian Yahweh'—on whom they blamed all Europe's 'misfortunes'—and launch a new religion stripped of every alien concept from Syria, Egypt, and Rome, as the National Socialist ideologue Alfred Rosenberg would have it.[2] Rosenberg actually claimed, in horribly twisted fashion, to be an admirer of Meister Eckhart!"

"But this loving exaltation of their status, as they see it, of chosen ones, how is it not downright hysterical erotomania, rather than narcissistic regression? If you'll pardon my crudeness. Remember that eighteenth-century saint who projected herself so entirely into Christ's holy foreskin that she experienced feverish fondlings, a burning in her breasts, and even the sensation of being fellated . . ."

"As you know, oh dearest, male mystical subjects perceive themselves as feminine. Look at Saint Bernard, who starts lactating beneath the loving rays of God. Whereas female mystics become masculinized, like Hildegarde of Bingen, Elisabeth von Schönau, Teresa of Avila herself . . . well, to a degree, correct me if I'm wrong . . . This psychic bisexuality, avowed and paraded, appears to me instead as a clear-eyed acceptance, also a traversing, of the common instability of the hysteric, always wondering which sex she belongs to. More than a common or garden hysteria, I'd say this is a hysteria mounted on a psychosis—mounted as befits these Amazons for God!—and prompting the outbreak of body symptoms like stigmata, convulsions, hallucinations, levitations, comas, and 'resurrections.'"

My colleague's admiration for the intrepid horsewomen is plain, as is his appreciation of their rare "hysterical" panache. Aude Tristan must be an ace at such defenses and illustrations of bisexuality! She must stalk him into every last recess of virility. I raise the stakes.

"Some practitioners manage to slow down their heartbeats and respiration, like in the heart prayer of the Orthodox Church, and even more clearly in yogic meditations. Subjects who have a long history of meditation can lower their metabolic rate, you know, carbon dioxide and oxygen, and alter an EEG reading of alpha rhythms—nine to seventeen cycles per second—to theta rhythms, six to seven cycles per second." It's my turn to impress him, with a flourish of very recently acquired knowledge.

"Without reducing mysticism to pathology—let's be more nuanced, shall we?—you know as well as I do that the 'unifying' impulse of the mystic toward the Object, an effect that feels 'obvious' or like a 'revelation' to him or her, is also present in psychosis." (Nothing doing. My scientific tidbits have only encouraged him to labor his point.) "And every self-respecting psychiatrist knows that this feeling of 'union' marks the symptomatic moment that in schizophrenics can herald either a cure or—should the feeling repeat itself—an aggravation of psychosis. In the same way, these modified perceptions, searing instants of an 'altered' consciousness of mystical experience, remind us of temporal seizures in epileptics. Allow me, however, to contradict you: neurological 'diagnoses' of pathogeny are of limited usefulness, because such states can only become mystical on condition of a background theological culture, or at the very least a mythological infrastructure, to lend them meaning over and above the pathological. I remain the analyst, you understand. And only on that condition can marginality—fruitful or destructive—become culturally transmissible, and museums, libraries, or churches start replacing hospitals. Do you see what I mean?"

"You're right. The arts do seem to belong with those experiences, pathology included. Perhaps the only ones of their kind to survive in the modern world, however shakily, I agree. There's no doubt about music and poetry, at least . . . What are they but sublimated transpositions of orgasmic sex, mutual penetrations of the artist's universe and the world of the senses, encouraging further interpenetrations with the audience? Al-Hallaj said the same thing: 'The eye with which you see me is the eye with which I see you.'"

I can tell Jérôme suspects me of overestimating the positive role of sublimation in these "extreme" cases. Aren't I also being slightly hasty with countertransference?

"If you ask me, oh dearest, in our culture it's the Song of Songs that provides the secret dramaturgy of great aesthetic adventures and mystical raptures. That said, merely to acknowledge the amorous dynamic that underlies artistic achievement explains nothing about how a particular individual actually got there! That remains an unknown, you see. A gap that scientific reason may never succeed in filling, no matter whether we're talking about Mozart's music or the very different but no less mysterious works of your Teresa. Ah, the unknown! Therein resides the tremendous pull we feel toward artists and mystics . . ." Phew, my colleague hasn't taken against me. He drifts, almost humbly, into reverie.

★ ★ ★

To announce a method is to announce its limits. Tristan is happy to leave it at that, but I'm not. His generalizations about the mystic continent are so unsatisfactory that I've no choice but to gird myself for the patient auscultation of a text, a body. I don't insist, there'd be no point. My colleague has just admitted that psychoanalysis, albeit more enlightening than other commentaries on the amorous logic of "God's lunatics," is a long way from flushing out its secrets. It edges nearer to them, though. Getting warmer, burning! Is not the *unconscious* a dynamic that breaches classical rationality and operates through the contradictory or "apophatic" logics with which mystical experience is studded? Or am I going too far, too fast?

First Bruno, now Jérôme. "You're a man-eater," snarled my ex before he disappeared. Not really. An eater of ideas, more like. I listen, read, absorb, appropriate, I tend my patch. There's no denying I enjoy it. But I don't steal, I steal away, at my own risk. Both faithful and unfaithful, and rather the latter. I linger in the company of the charming, the knowledgeable Jérôme Tristan during Parisian Psychoanalytical Society meetings and other after-dinner events. We are always the last to leave, sometime after midnight. He reassures me that I'm not the only one who thinks psychoanalysis could be poised, today, to recapture Freud's audacity, the daring of his take on Moses, on monotheism, on civilization and its discontents . . .

"Thanks, but I really don't need a lift, place d'Italie is very close and I feel like a walk."

I pick up the morning papers at the kiosk in boulevard Saint-Michel, the moon is full, thin mist blurs the bare horse chestnuts of the Luxembourg gardens and wets my face. I veer toward Les Gobelins, different neighborhood, different style, different world, Paris is an always possible journey. No, I won't follow the trail blazed by my colleague, I shall travel in my own way. A more personal way? Not only that, as we will see.

* * *

Freud knew how indebted he was to German philosophy and psychiatry, to Hartmann and Goethe, as much as to his hysterical female patients. Duchamp's *Bride Stripped Bare by Her Bachelors, Even.*[3] Wasn't Freud the Dadaist of lovesickness? The analytical process that "perlaborates," as he put it, the symptoms generated by the accidents of erotic and thanatic attachments, resembles the mystic "path"—or so said some caustic black book or other. It does? Only if you ignore the want of any transcendental consolation, as well as the elucidation of the sexual motive, both of which are pretty major differences. The analytic "path" remains amorous, that is, transferential. It involves silence and the verbalization of desire, certainly, but it does not "lead anywhere." Except to the dissolution of the transferential bond itself, of that loving bond at last stripped bare, and to an understanding of the immemorial traditions of totem, taboo, and other disturbing oddities of a more or less devilish nature. Quite extraordinary, surely? Certain mystics got there too, in their fashion, when they confessed to being "free of God," breaking with the religious community, or when they exposed themselves to Nothingness in all serenity.

And yet, if like David Bakan I can detect resonances between Freud's discovery of the unconscious and Jewish mysticism, the founder of psychoanalysis refers more often to Judaism than to its mystical currents.[4] In his rare allusions to mysticism at large, Freud is worse than suspicious: he is impervious. While identifying similarities between the logic of dreams and that of mystical discourse, he makes this abrupt confession to Romain Rolland: "To me mysticism is just as closed a book as music."[5] And at the very beginning of the twentieth century he writes to his friend Wilhelm Fliess,[6] about Dionysiac lyricism in Nietzsche, "in whom I hope to find words for much that remains mute in me."[7]

Could such reticence stem from the fact that the mystical outlook seeks to "restore unlimited narcissism,"[8] which Freud compares to the "oceanic feeling" (*ozeanische Gefühl*) connected to the infantile need to depend, to be protected, indeed to be archaically alienated in the mother;[9] a need he was careful to guard himself from, if not to cast off altogether? And might it also reflect his justified concern to shield the nascent science of psychoanalysis from the "black tide of mud of occultism"? His watchful rationality led him to classify mysticism as a branch of "falsehood,"[10] to which he spontaneously opposed "*logos* and *ananke*, inflexible reason and necessary destiny." He reiterated the point in 1932: "Mysticism, occultism—what is meant by these words? You must not expect me to make any attempt at embracing this ill-circumscribed region with definitions."[11] And again: "Our god λόγος may not be particularly omnipotent, not able to perform more than a fraction of what his predecessors promised," but "what would be an illusion would be to think we might obtain elsewhere that [which science] cannot give us."[12]

Be that as it may, Freud's reaction reveals a denial of oceanity that goes hand in hand with the denial of sensorial, preverbal dependency on the mother. And the logical consequence of this avoidance will be the return to an archaic experience of the mother–child bond conducted by Freud's dissident successors, from Groddeck to Winnicott via Melanie Klein, the matricidal Orestian: all of them except Lacan! Against the Freudian model of an unconscious solely governed by the Law of the Father, a varyingly anti-Freudian "antimodel" appears, haunted by motherly *jouissance* and mystical *apeiron* . . .

In the course of his dispute with Jung (the occasion of dizzy spells and passionate swoonings when relations were severed for good), Freud wrote Jung a long letter on April 16, 1909, in which, after a long riff on numbers and death, he declared: "You will see in this another confirmation of the specifically Jewish nature of my mysticism."[13] We can read this to mean: I am not a mystic in the way you are, *I have my own*: my mysticism has to do with Judaism, which is "the temporal conception of life and the conquest of magic thought, the rejection of mysticism, both of which can be traced back to Moses himself."[14] Was Freud right or wrong about this? Notwithstanding his "resistance" to the "oceanic dream," the ultimate developments of his theory of the unconscious betray some brilliant appropriations of mystical experience.

$$\star \;\; \star \;\; \star$$

The founder of psychoanalysis, *Aufklärer* that he was, had nothing but contempt for the *Schwärmer*, the enthusiastic dreamer; but he did not reject "superstition" out of hand, as the French Enlightenment did, for he regarded mysticism as an intriguing intersection between knowledge, sense experience, and the suprasensible. He erected his own conception of psychic life as a *rationalistic dualism*, and his entire oeuvre opposes the "dark monsters" that abolish the difference between the spiritual and the corporeal. Freud was at once hostile to "conscientialist" rationalism, which refuses to deal with unconscious phenomena, and wary of the "elusive, intangible unconscious" of philosophers such as Eduard von Hartmann. After the turn his thinking took during the 1920s, however, the Viennese bequeathed to us an exploration of the psychic apparatus that, long after him and beyond his personal limitations, brings peerless insights to bear upon the mysteries of desire, including mystical desire.[15]

Without lowering their guard against the insanity of telepathy or occultism, the *New Introductory Lectures on Psychoanalysis* suggest that mysticism and psychoanalysis attack the "same point": the "deep ego's perception of the id"; and share the same goal: to expand the domain of the ego (and of language) by giving it access to the drives of the id, so that it may "translate" them and make them conscious, free of censorship by the superego, and thus able to be shared.

Are we therefore to understand that psychoanalysis is a "metapsychology of mysticism," linking by means of transference the "unconscious representations of things" to the "representations of words," or deeply buried unconscious desire (the mysterious id) to the deep ego?

There is no denying the affinities between mysticism and psychoanalysis. In both experiences, a reshuffle of schemas takes place, to borrow the language of the learned Jérôme Tristan; the psychic authorities id/ego/superego change places, and their functions are transformed. But these reshuffles differ radically. Freud takes great care to avoid any confusion, and remains watchful to the end.

Thus, analytical perlaboration allows that "where id was, there ego shall be," and reinforces the ego by elucidating the logics of the desire that is peculiar to the id. In a lengthy meditation upon the goals of psychoanalysis, Freud grants with reference to mysticism that "It is easy to imagine, too, that certain mystical practices may succeed in upsetting the normal relations between the different regions of the mind, so that, for instance, perception may be able to grasp happenings in the depth of the ego and in the id which were otherwise inaccessible to it." But he goes straight on to say: "It may safely be doubted, however, whether this road will lead us to the ultimate truths from which salvation is to be expected. Nevertheless it may be admitted that the therapeutic efforts of psycho-analysis have chosen a similar line of approach. Its intention is, indeed, to strengthen the ego, to make it more independent of the superego, to widen its field of perception and enlarge its organization, so that it can appropriate fresh portions of the id. Where id was, there ego shall be. It is a work of culture—not unlike the draining of the Zuider Zee."[16] It could not have been stated more clearly.

The mystical path, by contrast, plunges the ego into the id by a kind of sensorial autoeroticism ("obscure self-perception") that confers a certain omnipotence upon the id, which lies "outside" the ego, and by the same token underwrites the collapse of the knowing ego, in thrall to the darkness of the realm of the id: revelation and absence, *jouissance* and Nothingness. The mystic, then, revels in the visual or aural representation of the Thing or Object of desire, and this unspeakable delight can turn into a perverse or psychotic impasse. The final apophthegm of 1938 runs as follows: "Mysticism is the obscure self-perception of the realm outside the ego, of the id."

The psychoanalytic cure, for its part, addresses the same pleasurable tryst between the ego and the id, but through uttering the transference allows them both to circulate, from id to ego and from ego to id. Even so, how many analytic cures have ever facilitated the full blooming of such states of grace? On the other hand, Teresa's "reports" to her confessors, texts written in a situation of transference with their addressees, do allow a certain perlaboration of unspeakable delight: an elucidation of the "obscure self-perception of the id," or, as she is fond of saying, a clarification of "imagination" by "understanding"?

Freud's genius, marking the decomposition and recomposition of psychic personality, does not spare the mystical personality. Dream, music, ocean; neither cleaving to experience nor ignoring it, analytical listening gives meaning to its *jouissance.*

"Sylvia Leclercq, what a dynamo." People notice a kind of optimism about me. Does that bother you?

Chapter 4

HOMO VIATOR

All the things of God made me happy; those of the world held me bound.

Teresa of Avila, *The Book of Her Life*

Some five hundred years stand between us, Teresa; your Catholic culture is foreign to me, and I have difficulty in reading your language, Castilian. But none of this is an obstacle. The two French editions of your works, by Marcelle Auclair and by the Carmelites of Clamart, are available to me, along with a wealth of scholarly works harking back to the Spanish source.[1]

Across the centuries and languages and cultures you "speak" to me, because I translate you in my own way. Your moments of illumination, Teresa, my love, your raptures, your hallucinations, your deliriums, your style, your "thinking" that claims not to be an "understanding," that wants no truck with that—I receive them through my filters, I gather them into meditations of my own, I shelter them in my body, I penetrate them with my own desires. Transformation, journey. *Homo viator*, wandering in search of sense and sensations in the language of psychoanalysis and fiction. My telescope (a seeing from afar), which is my microscope (magnifying the infinitesimal), brings you to me as an anguished, laughing woman whose harshness is born of generosity, a woman morbid and yet cheerful, a crazed but surprisingly lucid nun, who imposed on all the world the metamorphoses of her amorous body on the pretext of its desire for "Christ's humanity."

And you accomplished this at the height of the Golden Age, when Spain was discovering Erasmus, fearing and fighting the Lutherans, and enriching itself by sending fleets to the antipodes. Humbly I take the liberty of addressing you: for I know what store you set by your girls' "effacement" or "dominion" of self, you, the practitioner of "abandonment" (*dejamiento*), and I will try simply to abandon myself to your pages and let your word be heard.

I am the kind of unbeliever who won't accept that your body remained uncorrupted by death, as the Spanish king's confessor thought when, at Alba de Tormes, on January 1, 1586, he found your remains intact—for their preservation was the less than miraculous work of stone and lime. However, I am convinced that your texts can and indeed must be read today and, why not, for centuries to come. And because your body had already been wholly decanted into your writings and monastic foundations—as I shall attempt to show in what follows—and since this apparent exterior, those external objects, those tools of battle are the one and only testimony to your most secret interior, that which sometimes you called "my jewel," sometimes "divine center," sometimes "bruised heart"—well, all things considered, I can't really disagree with those who hold you to be immortal.

* * *

Your work seems deathless to me in the here and now, because through your faith, circumscribed by a particular civilization at one historical moment, you underwent an experience and developed a knowledge of human desire (male and female) that have a message for every speaking creature. Christianity made this knowledge and experience possible, no doubt, through the exorbitant hypostasis of loving passion that is its genius. After many a fantasy-infused wandering that encouraged, if not provoked, some grave pathologies, but without straying from the "illuminated" prayer inspired by the *alumbrados*, you finally clung fast to the plumb line of biblical, evangelical, and theological texts the better to deploy the freedom of your own desire, while elucidating its perils and joys.

Dare I appeal to your good cheer, your restless energy, your sparkling sense of mischief for the license to retrace your journey from the standpoint of my irreconcilable foreignness? Before anything else I have a major infidelity to confess, an impediment that may prove to be a handicap in your eyes: since God is unconscious and the unconscious shadows us, I contend that the Other dwells within, not in the Beyond, and that the transcendence you yearn for is an immanence. Indeed, I find evidence in your own writings to support this hypothesis, for that is where you get to in the end, isn't it? God dwells inside you; you say so yourself.

Your path through the mansions of the interior castle is not a dead end, as in Kafka; this castle's walls are permeable, and there is no closed door to bar access to the Master lodged in the innermost chamber of intimacy. You move through a maze of crossings, a stream of spaces, facets, and questions. The Other suffuses the opaque depths of body and soul, generating a real vaporization of the traveler, no less than of her Beloved. Your scandalous appropriation of the divine, the megalomania of your fantasy of being God's spouse and moreover a polymorphous creature, indissociable from God Himself, whom you ingest and swallow with feigned humility while proclaiming to be "dying of not dying" in Him, when it is none other than He who faints into you in this unchaste embrace, well, is all this strictly Catholic on your part? It's certainly baroque. It would be more exact to say that you both swoon at once, like two lovers possessed, who can only thus discard their proud identities. And that earthy, ardent Song of Songs that you push to its logical limit, what is it but a way, the only way, to end up . . . free of God? You don't pray to God to leave you "free of God," as Meister Eckhart does.[2] Out of love for Christ's humanity, you receive your freedom from Him continually. Continually, without solution, without end, infinitely free. What if that was the definition of humanism?

* * *

Follow me. It was thought that there was another way to emancipate oneself from the supreme Being, the Creator God, supreme in majesty and in power of command: it sufficed to apply the equality principle, making others into our fellows and placing a "point of honor" on charming, serving, and helping them (you dislike that "point of honor" that ensnared you for so long, Teresa, you hate it in fact, you, a saint!). Compassion, in the guise of political solidarity, would eradicate faith for the benefit of short-haul democracy. This juridical humanism, whose great feat was to promise an existential collaboration between the various "social actors," ran to ground in the impotence of the welfare state, when it did not degenerate into an atheist terror that was, sadly, just as bad as the wars and inquisitions of religion. Today, however, a new humanism seeks to emerge, one that cannot avoid paying attention to your delusions and bedazzlements.

For this humanism, interaction with others, all the others—socially marginalized, racially discriminated, politically, sexually, biologically, or psychically persecuted others—is only possible on condition of immersing oneself in a new idea that I shall formulate as follows, translating into my language the ancient experience you took to its height: *an irreducible otherness is conceivable, which, being plural, and the blazing pole of singular desires, makes us speak, reflect, enjoy: therefore it exists.*

The self-perception of this otherness, as the founding moment of humanity, is what gradually transformed gangs of "great apes" into speaking, thinking societies. All religions celebrate this otherness in the form of a sacred figure or limit (a deity), ruling the desires of the vital flow while remaining separate from it or else by associating with it (as in the Chinese Tao, for example). To discover the frontier where that otherness dawns in me, to nurture and respect it in my dealings with other people will finally allow me, perhaps, to approach these others as beings of desire, rather than objects of need.

Your nuptials with God, that joyous reversal of your fears, your revulsions, like the horror of toads and sundry serpents of sexual-political persecution forever assailing you, this reconciliation with the impossible—not with this or that ideal, law, or institution, but with the impossibility of desire for the Other in other people—all of this seems to me to converge, like rippling watercourses (that was your element, was it not?), mingled in the mighty, troubled waters of that humanism in search of itself, a tide the earth is thirsting for, of which I dream.

Just one quibble, though: your effusive love for Christ's wounds and the mortifications you inflicted on yourself rather obstruct the current that interests me, if I may insist on that point. Actually, had you lived two centuries later, reading the Marquis de Sade might have delivered your imaginary from its crudest and most morbid fantasies—the ones you dared not articulate but instead embodied, literally, until you almost died of epilepsy.

I will grant, however, that you were never the most assiduous at those exercises, and advised against them altogether, you wrote, for the more "nervous" and "melancholy" of your girls. John of the Cross himself went too far for your taste in terms of purgative zeal when he lived in the mountains at Duruelo. The Passion, by all means; Calvary, of course; but all of it cheerfully, if possible. "Be merry, my daughters": may I take those words to sum up your vision of "Christ's humanity" and . . . your own?

* * *

I am far from suggesting that only the Catholic Church is capable of realizing the *corpus mysticum* of modern humanity, unlike those theologians convinced that their own tradition meets all the requirements for ministering to humans without exception—whether they believe in the Eucharist, like the pope, or in nothing, whether they be Taoists in China, rabbis in Jerusalem, Buddhists in India, or psychoanalysts at the MPH who occasionally publish with Zone Books, like yours truly, Sylvia Leclercq. Extrapolating from your experience, Teresa, which led you from ecstasy into a blossoming that was political, pragmatic, and often downright humorous, despite its travails, I imagine a humanity that cares about the desire for the Other in every other, seeking itself through and in all our histories, Jews, Christians, Muslims, Confucians, Shintoists, the lot—without being blind to their antagonisms, or reduced to their divergences, or compliant with their institutions.

A pious hope? Perhaps; but then again, perhaps not. Because we agree that *Otherness exists*, don't we, Teresa; such is the biblical message with which you, a Marrana in denial, tacitly keep faith. And if the principle that *Otherness exists* resides in us in various forms—Jewish, Catholic, Muslim, Confucian, Buddhist, Shintoist, and the rest—then our discourses are not necessarily prayers but certainly hopes and wishes, wagers, sharings-out.

I have to confess to another, even more radical infidelity that estranges me from your experience, and I say so "in all humility" (using this expression in the same way you do, I believe, to wit, with a hint of cheekiness, am I right?) I am out of love with love. After years of listening to my analysands, not to mention everybody else, I've come to the conclusion that crazy love is a disease if ever there was one. A sickness that the three monotheisms, much more explicitly than other religions, revealed to be the hidden core of wisdom as well as of the bellicose passions. It was Freud's brain wave, once he had grasped this, to make his patient relive his or her malady on the couch, while he interpreted it by probing into the way "it" spoke.

Not only did he find that "yearning" or "craving" in love (*Sehnsucht*), whether thwarted or joyful, is the condition of all speech, but also that the listening that is able to receive its truth is the most disengaged and rational of all experiences.[3] Listen to love, and you will hear a sickness the human brotherhood cannot dispense with. We psychoanalysts call it *transference*: lover melts into loved and loved into lover; you know all about that, Teresa. That is why there is no way to treat the lovesick except by listening lovingly, a response known as *countertrans-ference*. The therapist in love with her patient embarks on it because only thus can she pick up the other's truths. Now she must tell those truths back, return them to the patient, before disengaging from this countertransferential love (you know all about that too, Teresa, as we will see). And then she will start all over again, because there's no end to this lovesickness, only eternal beginnings, for as long as "it" is speaking.

Thus felt and understood, not only is Eros (your cherub, the angel with the dart sculpted by Bernini) a self-analyzing *jouissance*, it also reveals its insepa-rable double, Thanatos, alias hate, alias the death drive that your "little Seneca" explored more deeply than you did, in Duruelo. Yet he forbade himself your sensuality, as you were quick to point out. How well he understood you all the same, your friend John of the Cross; we shall have much to say about him.

* * *

If we too unfold the speech of love for years on the couch, if we unearth its "carrier wave," which is the death wish (remember the threat uttered by that young, veiled engineer at the secularism debate, eager to be a kamikaze, the Islamic brand today and tomorrow sold on any fundamentalism you care to name, for it's not about Islam, you understand), what do we have left? I can see you coming, my honorable prioress. Who said anything to you about "left"? It's not a question of getting rid of love and its twin, hate, in order to escape to the heights of "pure noetic joy" or into the grave of a spiritual marriage stripped of the scoria of sensation. In psychoanalysis there is no retreat into Nothingness, that bleached lining of Being, but simply (so to speak) a journeying through the *self*: not settling into any one dwelling place, but passing through them all, there being no other way to become infinitely familiar with the plasticity of the soul, of its peculiar "wax," "flame," or "fragrance," its malleable desires and inconstant identities, the unbearable lightness of being and of the being; scatterbrained freedom. But you'd said all this already, Teresa, perhaps without knowing. Still, I like to believe that you weren't fooled, given how restless, obstinate, and droll you were.

You relied on the sacred texts and on the counsel of your confessors. These doctors of the faith, while sensibly curbing the prayers, visions, and raptures that were making you so ill, were determined to guide you in your transports and hallucinations. The most inspired of them, in tune with you, the ones you loved the best, advised you to follow the teaching of Ignatius of Loyola: never overdo the praying, and above all pin it on Christ's example—preferably during the Passion—as the best way to avoid an always dangerous surfeit of personal emotion.

To tell of your raptures, or better still, to write them down came to you with disconcerting ease, with amazing felicity, a success that startled you as much as it impressed your supervisors. And yet for them to confess sensitive women in the grip of demonic desires and channel their hysteria into writing was common in those days. Priestly wakes were aswirl with female lives, feelings, and secrets. In the twentieth century Freud could still inquire: "What do women want?" But he did not wonder about the wants of men. Maybe because, like the priest, he already knew the answer: female souls and bodies to guide.

* * *

But your genius was not only to make the most of that ecclesial strategy to restore your health. You took possession of the writerly space thus constituted, and your discourse was forged in perfect accord with that scriptorial dynamic whose quintessence you had extracted and into which you drew your scholarly directors of conscience. You confected a mobile idiom that took shape on the page at the same time as in your body.

Hence you were less intent upon what might make a book, and more concerned with the actual transformations this writing worked in your physiology and your relationships with other people: "I shall give you a living book," as the Lord told you. That "living book" was yourself and your monastic foundations, in the wash of a text made incarnate in actions. Between the loss of your selfhood in a drive whose very frustration was gratifying, and the thought that absented itself from that regression at the moment of the event, only to join it again a moment later: such was the oscillation of your life in writing, a thinking that immersed itself in desire and nevertheless gained mastery over it.

You deployed the whole gamut of psychic capabilities. And you named the sufferings and the pleasures embedded in the palette of sensations—visual, aural, olfactory, tactile, motor—without omitting to bracket them with the intellect, that is, with the ideals of your family and religious upbringing. On the wings of exaltation or in the abyss of despond, you were illusion itself, and yet without illusions. Outside yourself, ek-static, you caught and recentered yourself once more by talking about it, sure that whatever you might have to report was better than the unspeakable. For it has not merely to do with Nothingness, and has certainly nothing to do with death, but rather concerns a "to die," in the infinitive. Your infinitive dying endures in the range of perceptions that separate the Self from its Self in order to pour it into the Other, to make it become Other. It mutates into rebirth in this Other, but never once and for all, because this infinitive dying is spoken and written indefinitely, in the flux of time and waters. And so your written word paradoxically imbues Truth itself: a floating Truth, programmed but indefinite, infinite.

Such an ambition was folly in the sixteenth century, when many were burnt at the stake for far less. You dodged the Inquisition by persuading the Church that in order to comply, both with the reformed branch's call for cleansing and with the yearning for miracles proper to an economically and sexually deprived congregation—in order to trim reason to fit faith, in other words—what this era of Lutheran heresy required was an ascetic, ideally female, who happened also to be a supernatural wonder.

You alone could satisfy this double requirement. You—that is to say, the talking and writing that refurbished your body and in which you yourself became embodied. Skillful, astute, indefatigable, energetic, you lobbied the entire Church hierarchy: *alumbrados*, Franciscans, Dominicans, Jesuits, Carmelites, naturally, the Vatican, obviously—nobody escaped, including the Spanish monarchy and its satellite nobles.

Transcending historical eras to beguile me today, your writing reaches us in the manner of that liquid matter you adored, in watery spurts and streams. The Spanish word *agua* flows freely from your pen. Water is not so much a metaphor as a sign for the metamorphoses of your supposed identity in the very act of writing: you cascade from one state into another, from convulsion to jubilation, from sensations to their comprehension, from Gospel stories and characters to the virtuosity of the next overwhelming insight, from disclaiming the understanding to claiming knowledge, from looking to listening, from savor to skin and thence to so delicate an intellectuality that it barely brushes the mind before eclipsing it. Movement, flux, dipping and diving, all the facets of a butterfly forever returning to its chrysalis are folded into the dwelling places of the garden: fragments of everything, flashes of nothing.

As a child you evoked "the nothingness of all things [*todo nada*],"[4] now you say *yes* to this all which is nothing, this nothing which is all. *Yes* to your visionary opus, which is not an *obra*, an object, thing, or product, but a continual metamorphosis. Your writing, which prefigures and accompanies your commitment as a founder, is really an infiltration of words into things and things into words without collapsing the difference between them. By writing, you hold psychosis in suspense. Your love madness is nuanced, filtered through a mesh of perspicacity in the very midst of swoons and comas, with a clarity that's infectious.

* * *

For all their subtleties, your interior and exterior experiences do not by any means make you into a precursor of psychoanalysis. Still, the precision with which you record your visions of the Beloved, that blend of sexual sensation and fragmentary thought, all dissected by the scalpel of your watchful intelligence and wit, have much to teach the stalkers of the unconscious. It could even instruct Lacanians, who already know a thing or two about those excesses of yours that defeat, I fear, most other colleagues—including Jérôme Tristan, if he will excuse me for saying so.

Indeed it was Jacques Lacan, himself born into the Roman and Apostolic Church, who first extolled the *jouissance* he thought he detected in you and defined it as *other*. For it twines around the paternal phallic axis a novel way of being aroused: sensory, forever unsatisfied, and for that very reason outside time, on a cosmic scale. You not only experienced this female *jouissance* but also, and more importantly, recorded it. Otherwise how should we have known? Your great exploit was not so much to feel rapture as to tell it; to write it. Lacan saw you less as a "case" than as the intrepid explorer of that desired, desiring otherness that used to be called the divine and is at work, according to psychoanalysts, in all human beings, believers and unbelievers alike, as soon as they speak or refrain from speaking.

Nevertheless, unlike some academic critics (such as the great Jean Baruzi) for whom the mystics were forerunners, giants- *manqué* of the metaphysics to come,[5] I do not regard you as agiant- *manqué* of future psychoanalysis. In your "I live without living in myself," the "psychic domains"—those constitutive spaces of the soul you so elegantly laid out into seven dwelling places of your "metapsychology"—were in reality more often crushed on top of one other.[6] But though this *collapsus* plunged you into great mental confusion, catatonia, or coma, you proved capable of making your way through and lifting it up as a thought-body, in an unprecedented, exceptional body-thought. You rose there to a grandiose sublimation that most of us have only known in fragments, faltering words, hazy approximations. Few have ever achieved so complete a convergence of regression and reason.

You knew that sexuality is the carrier wave of love, especially the love of God, even if you only said so indirectly, through fiction, fable, and metaphor. You heard the Other whisper: "Seek yourself in Me." This certainty, this truth was so enthralling that you no longer dared to think outside of Him, in your own name, alone: *ego Teresa*. Except for a handful of pages (that you cut from the final draft of *The Way of Perfection*), your thinking was always to unfold with Him and from Him, and that is why it is a love thinking, rather than reasoning pure and simple. You are not quite a Cartesian, God forbid, but your lucidity prefigures the love in transference and countertransference. And if the narrative of the moods of your soul hardly constitutes a novelistic plot, it is nonetheless a novel about the consciousness/unconsciousness of love.

I understand your qualms about thinking for yourself, as if no *I* could exist apart from *Him*. Anyone with the presumption to say "I think, therefore I am" (but only after 1637, with Descartes) is too apt to forget the Other whom *I* desire in thought, and who splits the thinker's very being in two. The ego's audacity risks turning into a simplification: highly convenient for purposes of cogitation but inadequate to tease out the delicious, pernicious unison of body and mind that it is the business of psychoanalysis to complicate, in its best moments taking a cue from your vow, Teresa, that there shall be no *me* without *thee*.

Never to cut the umbilical bond with the Other—such was your right, your frailty, and your charm. It's also what enabled you to remake your body at the same time as you were fashioning your life's work. You are neither a philosopher nor a psychoanalyst, Teresa, you are a writer, and writers are revealed by their propensity to be physically altered by the bare fact of writing. With one difference: I've never known a writer who brought off anything like the fakir's tricks, if I may so describe them, attributed to you by the Carmelites (such as levitating upright, inches above the ground). Despite your vaunted humility you granted live performances in this vein to extramural audiences, too.

* * *

This metamorphosis troubles me a bit, so I shall try to approach it more closely by reading you. Reading the fabulous space of your body, between death (they were so sure you were dead, one time, they sealed your eyelids with wax and wrapped you in a shroud) and laughter (even the Inquisition, you wrote, "makes me laugh"), between paralysis and agitation, between suckling the Godhead and fleeing from toads, between plumbing inner depths with exquisite skill and manipulating your superiors, between the foundation of the Discalced Carmelite order and the invention of a way to be "outside oneself." Not forgetting your bold, funny, forceful style in Castilian, the language Cervantes was to magnify a few years later and that engulfed Catholicism itself.

Your body is a paradoxical place, at once inward and outward, flesh *and* word, desire *and* Nothingness; a nonplace where *I* merges into *you* and is then referred in the third person, *she*, a nonperson in the feminine. A vision? Perhaps; but one that "sees" with something other than "the eyes of the body." An inner, metaphorical vision, which turns you into Him:

> She saw some visions and experienced revelations. She never saw anything, nor has seen anything, of these visions with her bodily eyes. Rather, *the representation came like a lightning flash*, but it left as great an impression upon her and as many effects as it would if she had seen it with her bodily eyes, and more so.[7]

A suffering–jubilant body turns into characters and visions, a cascade of third persons brought about by the grace of the Other, the better to know oneself in losing oneself.

You are attracted by the "jewel" whose sparkle is attenuated by a fold of fine linen, you say, and which lies in a reliquary as in an impenetrable stronghold.

> But we do not dare look at it [the inner vision of the divine] or open the reliquary, nor can we, because the manner of opening this reliquary is known solely by the one to whom the jewel belongs. . . .
>
> Well, let us say now that sometimes he wants to open the reliquary suddenly in order to do good to the one to whom he has lent it. Clearly, a person will afterward be much happier when he remembers the admirable splendor of the stone, and hence it will remain more deeply engrained in his memory. . . . And even though the vision happens so quickly that we could compare it to *a streak of lightning*, this most glorious image remains so engraved on the imagination . . .
>
> *Although I say "image" let it be understood that, in the opinion of the one who sees it, it is not a painting but truly alive* . . . But you must understand that even though the soul is detained by this vision for some while, it can no more fix its gaze on the vision than it can on the sun. Hence this vision always passes very

quickly, but not because its brilliance is painful, like the sun's, to the inner eye. It is the inner eye that sees all of this. . . . The brilliance of this inner vision is like that of an infused light coming from a sun covered by something as transparent as a properly cut diamond. The garment seems made of a fine Dutch linen. Almost every time God grants this favor the soul is in rapture, for in its lowliness it cannot suffer so frightening a sight.[8]

You stumble against that nameless threshold where the erotic drive becomes *meaning*. You pass over to the other side, even though the third person, the non-person, *she*, has no idea of what this could possibly mean, because the sensorial meaning has not yet hardened into conceptual meaning. You stand on the edge of the originary repression, a psychoanalytic dictionary would say. Hovering in the place at which "most people" go *mad*. But not you, Teresa, for you seize on that dazzlement, the brilliance of the jewel, and dim it beneath a gauze of written language. And in the telling, the writing, your body changes.

* * *

Since your humanity is what fascinates me, as you might guess, and with apologies to your worshippers in the Lord, I shall begin by nosing into your background, your family, your friends, your loves: things you yourself bring up only to subordinate them to the events of your faith. Discreet to begin with, these epiphanies become steadily amplified in step with your metamorphoses. This is the subject matter of *The Book of Her Life*. You practice *writing as a power of regression proper to desire, and as a power of desire over regression*: this is, I consider, the experience in which you're dying of not dying.

Being a busy woman, you weren't always ready or able to commit your experience to paper, and this omission often pitched you into painful distress, rather than the death to self that would let you curl into the Other. In the end, the written word—as you explain it in the "Fourth Dwelling Places" of *The Interior Castle*—replaces suffering by the transubstantiation of sensual desire into the desire to formulate ideas. Yet the text as it has come down to us today (in a 1588 first edition of the *Life* revised by Ana de Jesús and Luis de León) seems to interest you less than the actual movement of writing. You write in a rush, seldom bothering to correct, caring more for the exploration than for its traces. What better proof than this lack of perfectionism of how little—while aspiring to simplicity and depth, like the humanists—you care about creating a "work"?

Instead you avidly pursue transmutation in a stream of images that overwhelms you, overwhelms us! I hear you, and I hear us. *It is written* in the relish of your mother tongue, which in your hands sounds lively, cadenced, and muscular while being also dreamy, negligent, and relaxed. You keep an eye on your language, revisiting and correcting it. But this is far from the obsessive rituals of the professional writer, and I can well believe that the making of your books was spurred onward by the same élan with which you wrote to your brother: "You shouldn't make the effort to read over [the letters] you send me. I never reread mine. If some word is missing, put it in, and I will do the same here with yours. The meaning is at once clear [*que luego se entiende lo que quiere decir*], and it is a waste of time to reread them unnecessarily."[9]

* * *

Proud voluptuousness forbade you to engage in sexual intercourse, so far as we know, even though your letters and writings are oddly spiced with mild erotomania. But you were not a modern, by any stretch. Belying the ostentatious way you were clothed by the baroque spirit of Bernini's sculpture, the writhing of your body and soul convey but one, infinite, possession: that of you by your own self, that of I by her own other. Your boudoir needs the Eucharist, but it is only in writing that you taste all the flavors of the divine and are drenched in all the waters of the Other.

Nevertheless, psychoanalysis maintains that the Heavenly Gardener who floods through you is unquestionably the heavenly Father, relayed in life by your father Alonso Sánchez de Cepeda, whose *hidalguía* court case turned him for you into a negative of Christ. I will suggest that the paternal image was reinforced by the far more internalized faith of your uncle, Pedro Sánchez de Cepeda, whose love of courtly novels and Franciscan—perhaps indeed Erasmist—manners perturbed your adolescent body.

But the Other was already locked into your own psychic virility by osmosis with a beloved brother, like a twin but two years older, the one you played at martyrs with: "*Para siempre, Teresa—para siempre, Rodrigo.*" Forever. And the four celestial waters you so avidly imbibe in the pages of your *Life*, what are they but allusions to an "idle seed" (Klossowski), *their* idle seeds, as much as to your intense and lonely pleasure inundated by the fantasy of the human masculinity of the divine? A great big masturbation session: some have not hesitated to say so in writing. The "spurts" of the Heavenly Youth are yours, it's your body melting, relaxing from nun-like stiffness as your convulsive-hysterical juddering softens and trickles away through your nib. It's the only way to appease your sexual tension while womb and vagina remain unnamed and unnameable, amid a bright ripple of words.

To modern consumers of guilt-free sex, to sadomasochistic role models who would rather beat themselves than know themselves, to fundamentalists swathed in hypocritical prudishness, to the casualties of the new soul sickness— if they have not already been destroyed by deadly enactments of fantasies or toxic psychosomatic pathologies—you offer the sumptuous halls of a flesh that throbs to imagined perceptions, embodied images, in an insatiable orgasm of impossibility. Is this spiritual wedding night anything but the peak of delusion? Indeed it is, for your successive rebirths, Teresa, my love, testify to the vivifying powers of the imaginary when it truly inhabits the desires that brought it forth.

Have your seasons and your castles* [*A reference to Arthur Rimbaud's poem, "Ô saisons, Ô châteaux . . ."—Trans.] since been drowned? I fear they have, now that the imaginary has been killed off by the Spectacle: nothing is impossible in this increasingly virtual world, and so there's nothing to desire. And yet my wager is to lift a corner of your habit—not just to display your body and works before the fetishistic curiosity of jaded spectators, but to invite them to a tryst with your metamorphic intensities. We are in want of such a thing, let's take the risk.

Part 2

Understanding Through Fiction

This image I've used in order to explain . . .

[this fiction: *hacer esta ficción para darlo a entender*]

Teresa of Avila, *The Way of Perfection*

Chapter 5

PRAYER, WRITING, POLITICS

Between us and other people there exists a barrier of contingencies, just as
. . . in all perception there exists a barrier as a result of which there is never
absolute contact between reality and our intelligence.

Marcel Proust, *Time Regained*

Whatever the wellspring of her writing, internal urgency or external urging, Teresa clearly knows that she writes in order to be: to
encounter herself, to encounter and understand others, to "serve"
as a conduit for "words" so as to "seek herself" and hopefully "find herself."
She writes "almost stealing time, and regretfully because it prevents me from
spinning";[1] "[Saint Martin] had works and I have only words, because I'm
not good for anything else!"[2] And again, "I don't understand myself . . .
So that when I find my misery awake, my God, and my reason blind, I might
see whether this reason can be found in what I write" (*pueda ver si la hallo aquí
en esto escrito de mi mano*).[3] None of this diffidence prevents her from holding
her imagery, or *fiction*, in high esteem—not least when noting the appreciation
of the Inquisition.

Thus she tells Fr. Gaspar de Salazar that *The Book of Her Life*, then under
examination by the Grand Inquisitor Gaspar de Quiroga, bishop of Toledo,
is a "jewel" in the latter's hands. He "praises it highly. So until he tires of it
he will not give it over. He said that he wants to examine it carefully." Teresa
champions her fiction with mixed anxiety and irony. She affects a swagger when

announcing that "another" gem awaits her detractors, with "many advantages over the previous one. It deals with nothing else but who [Christ] is; and it does so with more exquisite enameling and decoration. The jeweler did not know as much at that time, and the gold is of a finer quality, although the precious stones do not stand out as they did in the previous piece."[4]

Indeed, while not as straightforwardly autobiographical as the *Life*, *The Interior Castle* chisels in its Dwelling Places a faceted itinerary of the mystical journey, revealing Teresa as the master craftsperson of a rarefied genre: theological psychology. The poems of John of the Cross, such as the *Dark Night of the Soul*, the *Living Flame of Love*, or the *Spiritual Canticle*, are accompanied by explanatory "spiritual treatises" both short and long. More intersubjective and physical than the prose of the man she called her "little Seneca," less elliptical than his verse, might Teresa's fiction constitute that gemstone, that crystal, condensing theopathic states and expounding them so thoroughly as to rule out any future hermeneutics or philosophy of stature in the Castilian tongue?[5] Contrast with the Rhenish case, whose densely intellectual mysticism, of an Albertino-Thomist cast, cried out to be conceptualized—as it would be by German philosophy. In reality the two Avilan mystics, John and Teresa, invented bridging genres that passed between theopathy and theology on the one hand and the psychology of extreme creative states on the other. The writing produced by these "ungenred" genres appears to us, at this distance, as the crucible of the continent in gestation that was European literature; its fiery quality remains unequaled, with rare exceptions.

Teresa suspects that she thinks like a novelist, and comes close to saying so, with a proud twinkle. And sure enough I see a novel of introspection, appropriating Chrétien de Troye's *Grail*, to be decoded in the "precious gems" of her greatest texts, just as there is a picaresque novel lurking in her letters.[6]

In all these forms, however, and given that it traces the begetting of the self, writing seems to be an essential stage, foundational but not final, of the experience of the "love of God" according to Teresa. Is this "mystical theology, which I believe it is called"?[7] But "I am speaking about what has happened to me, as I have been ordered to do [*yo digo lo que ha pasado por mí como me lo mandan*]."[8] Precaution, irony, disclaimers: Teresa frames her fiction from the outset by defining it as the "account" of a complex "sensorial experience" whose initial station was prayer. The act of re-founding the Carmelites, which would mark the history of the Catholic Church in general and Spanish society in particular, would be its political counterpart.

⋆ ⋆ ⋆

Regardless of her epileptic seizures, in these writing states, on their twin pillars of prayer and foundation, the Carmelite nun exhibits a remarkable capacity for observation, bolstered by an unprecedented rhetorical elaboration of what it is to lose and to reconstitute oneself through amorous transference onto the other. These writings cannot be reduced to the discharge of a duty; they refashion in depth the complexity of a whole person, along with her relationships. First in the verbalization of Confession, then in the still more intimate act of writing, the ground covered mentally and physically, emotionally and culturally, biographically and historically takes over the subjective state of distress, be it neuronal or existential, and moves aside from it—when not independent of it—to transform it at last into a being-in-the-world that re-founds both self and others. From that point on, prayer-writing-politics are lived and restored as the three indissociable panels of a single process of ceaseless re-foundation of the self, of the *subject*, continually open to its own otherness, thanks to the call of the Being-Other ("Seek yourself in Me"). They trigger the spiraling re-creation of the woman who prays, and writes, and is metamorphosed: "When the soul [in the form of a silkworm] is, in this prayer, truly dead to the world, a little white butterfly comes forth."[9]

⋆ ⋆ ⋆

Teresa begins her "search" with a "suspension of the faculties"—in scholastic terms, the intellect, the will, and the imagination—in order to regress to that state in which the thinking individual loses the contours of his or her identity and, beneath the threshold of consciousness and indeed of the unconscious, becomes what Winnicott calls a "psyche-soma."[10] In that state, which for psychoanalysis is a reversion to the archaic osmosis between mother and infant (or fetus), the tenuous link to the self and the other is maintained solely by that infralinguistic sensibility whose acuteness is the greater in proportion to the relinquishment of the faculty for abstract judgment. A different thought results, an a-thought, a dive into the deeps that terms like *sensorial representation* or *psyche-soma* convey better than any notion of mind. It is as if the reasoning mind had passed the baton of being-in-the-world to a fantastic fabrication domiciled in the entire body, touching-feeling outside and inside, its own physiological processes and the external world, without the protection of intellectual work or the help of a judging consciousness. Winnicott wondered why we locate the mind in the brain, when the regressive states entered by some of his patients testified, he thought, to how all the senses and organs play a part in self-perception and perception of the outside world: his observation suggested that the psyche is the body, or soma, and the body is the psyche.

UNIVERSAL SEPARATION

After the work of *repentance, quiet,* and *union,* Teresa describes the fourth degree of prayer, which is *rapture*: this shows how the destitution of the self in the psyche-soma begins with the sense of "being distant from all things."[11] In an acute state of melancholic loneliness, the soul desires "only to die," feeling bereft of consolation and not finding "a creature on earth that might accompany it." And yet this low mood does not lead it to complain:

> Now, I understand clearly that all this help [from others] is like little sticks of dry rosemary and that in being attached to it there is no security; for when some weight of contradiction or criticism comes along, these little sticks break. So I have experience that the true remedy against a fall is to be attached to the cross and trust in Him who placed Himself upon it.[12]

For there is not a "creature on earth" who is consistent, lovable or kind; people invariably let one down; and this primary frustration has me cloistered in a convent as if to embody, confirm and perpetuate my isolation. My longing for love is not however quelled by this universal separation, this "distance from all things": in a last-ditch erotic impulse, I invest it in an imaginary Object who is the absolute Subject, the God-man who bestowed divinity upon human suffering (and vice versa) to the point of fusion with it, a merging of the two. Is Christ the last of the gods? Did He betray divinity? Or perhaps, by revolutionizing the one God of the Bible, He incarnates an ultimate anthropological truth: it is imperative to divinize the universal separation and turn it into a Great Other, this being the only way to mend the distance and mend ourselves in the union with Him, our fellow, the Crucified One who rose again. If you wish to be "saved" from universal separation, if you believe in the possibility of rapture, go in for regressions as delightful as they are excruciating, because the price of salvation is to cross that distance (a process later known as masochism—albeit the friars of Duruelo, supporters of Teresa's reforms, could have shown a thing or two to that scandalous Sacher-Masoch).

Teresa's trajectory is a descent into the doloristic depths of the religion of salvation to uncover its intrapsychical operations. But she also transcends these, as no one had done before, by opening body and soul to the joys of the love of the Other and reasserting His presence on earth with the creation of an innovative religious institution: "I have become so adept at bargaining and managing business affairs."[13] Is she adumbrating an exit from voluntary servitude? Or locking it into a new and exalted impasse?

✶ ✶ ✶

For the early Christians, as for Teresa de Cepeda y Ahumada in the sixteenth century, Jesus and His powers were in no sense the "fantasy" the coming humanism would label them as (shortly echoed by psychoanalysts, including myself). Christ was convincing. He imposed himself as an absolute truth because He managed to project everybody's pain into His own "masochism," to inscribe our grief into His Passion, if only we believe that this loving sacrifice on the Cross will also open the Heaven of resurrection to us. Thus Jesus Christ became a subtle antidepressant for abandoned, unhappy humanity.

The black sun of melancholia that weighs on "separated" humanity then split into its parts. On one side, the sun: the God-man, the Light, the Word, Who loves and saves us; the exultant denial of separation, sorrow, violence, death. On the other, the black shadow that overhangs believers in the grip of solitude: the body of the tortured Christ, in which men and women can immerse their own. Either side, heads or tails, when through prayer the osmosis with the crucified-resurrected Christ is realized, it can only be paroxystic—annihilation and rebirth—and, on that condition, gratifying. The consolation that results does not suspend sorrow, let alone get through it. It is content to maintain or stoke it up, the better to reward it.

Is this a reparation, or a stimulation of the "pleasure unto death" diagnosed by Nietzsche well before the Freudians got hold of it?[14] Teresa is sharply aware of the issue, enticingly so for future analysts. In this properly vicious circle, the melancholic pain of separation from one's loved ones becomes vastly more poignant when the Beloved is God Himself, as she points out:

It seems to me that God is then exceedingly far away. . . . This communication is given not to console but to show *the reason the soul has* for becoming weary in the absence of a blessing that in itself contains all blessings.

With this communication *the desire increases* and also the extreme sense of solitude in which, even though the soul is in that desert, it sees with a pain so delicate and penetrating that it can, I think, literally say: *Vigilavi, et factus sum sicut passer solitarius in tecto* [I watch, and am as a sparrow alone upon the housetop. Ps. 102:7].[15]

By identifying with the wounds of Christ, who is God, desolation compressed becomes a glorious pain, absolute doloristic bliss in lieu of the absolute Body: unhappiness cries out, but in flight, over the housetop and far away.

"I LIVE WITHOUT LIVING IN MYSELF"

Before long, the descent into the underworld is qualified by the inordinate gratification of being *Him*: inhabiting a man's body, of course, which is far preferable to a woman's, let alone that of a pretty, cloistered girl without a dowry! In addition the man on the Cross is a God-man, the Son of God, and a potential lover of the praying woman, as the Song of Songs joyfully proclaims. The Bride undertakes penances, but her desire for the imaginary Object–absolute Subject is so overwhelming that the pain—"little felt" as such, however intensely mentalized and interiorized—is on the contrary a "special favor," because it is mingled with His pain, shared with Him.

Exhibiting a rare gift for psychological self-observation, introspection, and retrospection, Teresa depicts the initial stages of prayer in terms of anorexia: her worship of the ideal Man obliterates elementary desires, beginning with the appetite for food. She wants to annihilate herself the better to deserve Him, in the suspension of every sensation. She will let the tears flow, she's good at that, but almost without noticing; above all she will not complain, for that is a female trait. The praying woman, unable to eat, feverishly cleaving to her ideal Object, is lifted up by fasting and hovers beside Him, beyond the scope of sexual difference:

The impulses to do penance that come upon me sometimes, and have come upon me, are great. And if I do penance, *I feel it so little* on account of that strong desire that sometimes it seems to me—or almost always—that penance is a very *special favor....*

It is the greatest pain for me sometimes, and now more extreme, to have to go to eat, especially when I'm in prayer. This pain must be great because it makes me weep a good deal and utter words of distress, almost without being aware of it, which I usually do not do. However great the trials I have experienced in this life, I don't recall having said these words. I am not at all like a woman in such matters, for I have a robust spirit.[16]

Here Teresa's account adopts, as it often does, the precision of a clinical description. She reconstitutes in writing the body paralyzed by cold acceptance of her separation from the One who, nevertheless, remains present in mind by the strength of the union she has thought and felt. This rigid body will be succeeded by a body blown on the air, carried away in a whirlwind of energetic release. The radiant phase climaxes in a feeling of hollowing out, weightlessness, elevation, levitation—so many states of grace that are recaptured by the racing pen and brim over in abundance of writing. And then, a final reversal: the nocturnal phase returns. She plummets into revulsion and refusal: refusal to eat, denial of pain, intense pleasure of self-dominion that harshly abrogates the gendered experience: "I am not at all like a woman in such matters, for I have a robust spirit." The merciless precision of this clinical semiology cannot, beneath its ironic scalpel, conceal the writer's pride at escaping the feminine condition.

* * *

The catatonia that accompanies manic-depressive psychosis or states of comatose epilepsy, as diagnosed by modern neurology, assuredly overtakes this soul as it strains for fusion with the imaginary Object with all the verve of its psyche-soma, aspiring only to "rise" toward the All-Other, the "exterior agent" of her "interior castle," the missing second person, the *thou* of love. And the abolishment of the self in the suffering-delighting body remains the goal, if one is to attain the grace of dissolution into the fervors of medieval faith that transcend the life of all mystical practitioners.

But what distinguishes Teresa from other adepts of prayer is the way she couples this suspension of reason to an astonishing clear-sightedness, which notes, if transiently, its own befuddlement:

Everything is almost fading away through a kind of swoon in which breathing and all the bodily energies gradually fail . . . one cannot even stir the hands without a lot of effort. . . . [The persons in this state] see the letter; but since the intellect gives no help, they don't know how to read it, even though they may desire to do so. . . . In vain do they try to speak, because they don't succeed in forming a word, nor if they do succeed is there the strength left to be able to pronounce it. . . . The exterior delight that is felt is great and very distinct.

It is true that in the beginning this prayer passes so quickly . . . that neither these exterior signs nor the failure of the senses are very noticeable. . . . The longest space of time in my opinion in which the soul remains in this suspension of all the faculties [*esta suspensión de todas las potencias*] is very short; should it remain suspended for a half hour, this would be a very long time. . . . It is true that since there is no sensory consciousness one finds it hard to know what is happening. . . . It is the will that holds high the banner [as one side in a joust: *mantiene la tela*];[17] the other two faculties quickly go back to being a bother. . . .

But I say this loss of them all and suspension of the imagination . . . lasts only a short while; yet these faculties don't return to themselves so completely that they are incapable of remaining for several hours *as though bewildered* [confused, befuddled: *como desatinadas*], while God gradually gathers them again to Himself.[18]

Sensory regression, exile from self, installation of Him within me in the fourth prayer; the intellect and the ego are abolished for the sake of the contact, shortly to become capture, of the psyche-soma and the Being-Other:

The Lord spoke these words to me: "It detaches itself from everything, daughter, so as to abide more in me. It is no longer the soul that lives but I. Since it cannot comprehend what it understands, there is an understanding by not understanding. . . ."

If a person is reflecting upon some scriptural event, it becomes as lost to the memory. . . . If the person reads, there is no remembrance of what was read; nor is there any remembrance if one prays vocally. Thus this bothersome little moth, which is the memory, gets its wings burnt here; it can no longer move. The will is fully occupied in loving, but it doesn't understand how it loves. *The intellect, if it understands, doesn't understand how it understands; at least it can't comprehend anything of what it understands.* It doesn't seem to me that it understands, because, as I say, it doesn't understand—I really can't understand this![19]

Even more incisively, Teresa describes the paradoxical "joust" of this deconstruction as if it were another life, one consisting of an uninterrupted death of the self exiled beyond the frontiers of identity: "I live without living in myself";

"I already live outside myself" (*vivo ya fuera de mí*). One must enter a *continual* state of "dying of love," in which "sensitive betterment" is felt as infinitely preferable to being locked into conscious, self-protective life. For "dying of love" is an alternative way of living, in opposition to that biological life, which represses the risk of regression and stubbornly wants "not to die." Only thus, only on condition of dying of love, can Teresa's soul make "her God her captive." But in a further paradox of apophatic thought, shutting oneself away with one's God in the prison of the living body here below might come down to a tedious wait, a postponement of the plenitude of bliss in Him, the Pauline face to face in the Beyond after death. Therefore, it is crucial that, in the meantime, the passion for the "captive God" is soothed in sweet abandon to the Lord:

I live without living in myself,
And in such a way I hope,
I die because I do not die.
Since I die of love,
Living apart from love,
I live now in the Lord
Who has desired me for Himself.
He inscribed on my heart
When I gave it to Him:
I die because I do not die.
Within this divine prison
Of love in which I live,
My God my captive is.
My heart is free
To behold my prisoner-God,
Passion welling in my heart,
I die because I do not die.
Ah, how weary this life!
These exiles so hard!
This jail and these shackles
By which the soul is fettered!
Longing only to go forth
Brings such terrible sorrow,
I die because I do not die.
Ah, how bitter a life

When the Lord is not enjoyed![20]
While love is sweet,
Long awaiting is not.
Oh God, take away this burden
Heavier than steel,
I die because I do not die.[21]

This poem, the most successful of Teresa's verse pieces, sums up the states of *rapture* described in *The Book of Her Life*.[22] However, it is in her fiction—itself inherently poetic and meditative—that the saint's writing comes into its own.

Chapter 6

HOW TO WRITE SENSIBLE EXPERIENCE, OR, OF WATER AS THE FICTION OF TOUCH

> [The soul] will feel Jesus Christ. . . . Yet, it does not see Him,
> either with the eyes of the body or with those of the soul.
>
> Teresa of Avila, *The Interior Castle*

TACTILE VISIONS

Teresa began writing for the first time between 1560 and 1562. The *Relations* or *Spiritual Testimonies* (1–3) date from 1560–1563; the first draft of *The Book of Her Life*, now lost, is from 1562.[1] By now, aged between thirty-five and thirty-seven, her second "conversion" (1555) was behind her, and the silent and vocal praying that accompanied her early monastic life had become very intense. She meditated on Francisco de Osuna and Juan de Ávila, and in 1562 she met Pedro de Alcántara; her vision of Hell (1560) came to her at much the same time as her decision to found a convent based on the Primitive Rule. As a spiritual, physical, and political activity, writing was a necessity for her. The act of writing was the element that allowed her to keep contact with regression in prayer (itself induced and spurred on by theological and evangelical texts: Teresa was an avid reader), while at the same time elucidating it and making it shareable— by tying it to her own memory, culture, and will, as well as to the judgment of her confessors and, beyond the domain of the Church, to the social and political life of Renaissance Spain.

The writings of La Madre (first published in 1588 thanks to the offices of Luis de León and Ana de Jesús, and completed later) bear witness to her itinerary and to the many strands of her personality. As we have seen, *The Book of Her Life* (final draft, 1565) braids autobiography into the meticulous description of the constant self-deconstruction inherent in spiritual experience and essential to its clarification. *The Way of Perfection*, the one text Teresa was minded to publish, stresses the exactions of monastic life with a view to fortifying her fellow nuns and ushering them along the path of prayer.[2] The *Foundations* record the foundress's social experiences, intermixed with her spiritual life.[3] Finally, *The Interior Castle*, also known as the *Mansions* or *Dwelling Places of the Interior Castle* (*Moradas del castillo interior*, 1577), recomposes the plural space that had constituted and sustained the complex movements of Teresa's love for Jesus, internalizing into a single but shifting emplacement—the "castle" of many abodes—her three aspects: prayer, writing, and foundation.

Across the range of themes and intentions, secret aims, and foundational ambitions, Teresa's style is stamped with an indelible seal: it works to translate the psyche-soma into imagery, images that in turn are designed to convey visions that are not a function of sight (at least, not of eyesight alone), but indwell the whole body. They make themselves felt first and foremost in terms of touch, taste, or hearing, only afterward involving the gaze. The psychical or physiological descriptions of her states, cumulatively presented, are thus products of a *sensorial imaginary* rather than of any imagery, imagination, or images in the visual sense. This sensorial, or sensible, imaginary in writing demands to be read by the psyche-soma as much as by the intellect. Are contemporary readers capable of adjusting to this requirement? If so, they may have access to this experience, in which the words on the page render sensual perceptions, the author's sentience. Again, for La Madre it was not a question of creating an oeuvre but of calling into play (into the jousting lists?) the felt experience of her addressees, from the confessors who requested and approved her texts, the sisters who looked up to her, and the believers who followed her, to the readers of today and tomorrow.

Metaphors, similes, or metamorphoses in words? How did Teresa take possession of the Castilian language to say that the love bond between a secluded nun and the other-being—both the other in oneself, and the Other outside oneself—is a tournament of the senses? How did she express so recognizably the otherness impressed on her in the experience of separation magnetized by rapturous union? A separation, which albeit radical, is bridgeable by words, by a certain utterance; a separation that does not set itself up as an abstract law, or goad itself into a spiritual vocation, or fret over metaphysical conundrums.

Instead it finds a balm in the reciprocal, if not symmetrical, calls and responses between two living bodies in desirous contact with each other; two infectious desires gently appeased in the *moradas*, the mansions of writing.

* * *

What guided the flow of Teresa's silent prayers? Was it her deep intuition, or the resurgence of the evangelical theme of baptism, or again her devotion to Francisco de Osuna's *Third Spiritual Alphabet*? Osuna's text, which proved seminal for her development, abounds with *images* of *water* and *oil* to suggest the state of abandonment (*dejamiento*) cherished by the Illuminati or *alumbrados*, and compares this to the infant suckling at its mother's breast. Likewise Teresa wrote: "This path of self-knowledge must never be abandoned, nor is there on this journey a soul so much a giant that it has no need to return often to the stage of an infant and a suckling [*tornar a ser niño y a mamar*]."[4] La Madre was also prone to regressing, more consciously than not, to the state of an embryo touched-bathed-fed by the amniotic fluid. For the hydraulic technique narrated by Teresa is intended to gratify the skin, that first, constant frontier of the self, rather than the eyes. Moreover it "easily and gently" carries away the trusting, abandoned soul, like a "straw" or "little bark" in a "trough of water" fed by springs—before "with a powerful impulse, a huge wave rises up."[5]

And yet the bather, for all her blissful abandon, is well acquainted with the "dryness" that necessitates the "tedious work" of the gardeners. These "need to get accustomed to caring nothing at all about seeing or hearing," and "to solitude and withdrawal"; sometimes they will feel "very little desire to come and draw water," frequently "they will be unable even to lift their arms for this work." A case of boredom or distaste? Open your eyes, water is everywhere. "Here by 'water' I am referring to tears and when there are no tears to interior tenderness and feelings of devotion."[6] It's enough to lighten the yoke of God himself ("For my yoke is easy" [Matt. 11:30]; "*suave es su yugo*"),[7] amid surprise at "obtaining this liberty."[8]

The *comparison* with water practically forces itself on Teresa, not without arousing her misgivings:

> I shall have to make use of some *comparison*, although I should like to excuse myself from this since I am a woman and write simply what they ordered me to write. But these spiritual matters for anyone who like myself has not gone through studies are so difficult to explain. I shall have to find some mode of explaining myself, and it may be less often that I hit upon a good comparison....

Beginners must realize that in order to give delight to the Lord they are starting to cultivate a garden on very barren soil, full of abominable weeds. His Majesty pulls up the weeds and plants good seed. Now let us keep in mind that all
of this is already done by the time a soul is determined to practice prayer and
has begun to make use of it. And with the help of God we must strive like good
gardeners to get these plants to grow and take pains to water them so that they
don't wither but come to bud and flower and give forth a most pleasant fragrance
to provide refreshment for this Lord of ours. Then He will often come to take
delight [*deleitar*] in this garden and find His joy [*holgarse*] among these virtues.[9]

Is she embarrassed by the sensuality of this watering, which might seem to
overstep a strictly spiritual contact? She disowns the image: "It seems now to
me that I read or heard of this *comparison*—though since I have a bad memory,
I don't know where or for what reason it was used." She goes on to distinguish
the four degrees of prayer by comparing them to the "four waters" that may
irrigate a garden:

It seems to me the garden can be watered in four ways. You may draw water from
a well (which is for us a *lot of work*). Or you may get it by means of a *water wheel*
and aqueducts in such a way that it is obtained by turning the crank of the water
wheel. (I have drawn it this way sometimes—the method involves less work than
the other, and you get more water.) Or it may flow *from a river or stream*. (The
garden is watered much better by this means because the ground is more fully
soaked, and there is no need to water so frequently—and much less work for
the gardener.) Or the water may be provided by *a great deal of rain*. For the Lord
waters the garden without any work on our part—and this way is incomparably
better than all the others mentioned.[10]

RHETORICAL FIGURES OR WORD-THINGS?

Always ready to laugh at herself, Teresa pretended not to know the first thing
about rhetoric, when in fact she was highly proficient in this art. As Dominique
de Courcelles has shown, she is highly likely to have read Miguel de Salinas's
Retórica en lengua castellana (1541), as well as the *Libro de la abundancia de
las palabras*.[11]

Sixteenth-century Europe was richly endowed with courtly literature. Beatriz de Ahumada, Teresa's mother—like Ignatius Loyola—was a great fan of *Amadis of Gaul* and its sequel *Esplandian*. She passed down this taste to her daughter, despite the reservations of her husband Alonso Sánchez de Cepeda, who, as befits a second-generation converted Jew, made it a badge of honor to prefer Seneca, Boetius, and spiritually edifying "good books" such as hagiographies. Meanwhile the popular surge of vernacular literature was spawning, even then, a science devoted to studying its allure: the various "discourses" came under intense scrutiny in the light of the rediscovery of Greco-Roman grammar and rhetoric, which scholars rapidly adapted to the new profane registers. Sifting the novels everyone was talking about through the screen of his erudition, Salinas stressed the importance of comparison for their narrative structure. "The third manner of amplifying a story is comparison: whether by similarity or inversion, it permits all circumstances to be taken into account." *Inventio*, the author insists, is built of images; and "do not the Latins use *imago* to denote both comparison and parable without distinction?"

There is every reason to suppose, then, that Teresa was familiar with Salinas's works. So what prevented her from citing her source? Was it, as she claimed, her "bad memory"? Or is the water she evoked not really a rhetorical figure like comparison or metaphor? In that case, what is it?

Let us go back to the account of the water that comes between the lover and the Beloved.

Water *is*, for the writer, the soul's link to the divine: the amorous link that puts them into contact. Springing from outside or inside, active and passive at once, or neither, and not to be confused with the gardener's labor, water transcends the earth whence it emanates and on which it falls. I, earth, says Teresa (*tierra*: terrestrial, Teresa), can only become a garden by the grace of contact with the life-giving medium of water, which bubbles from my entrails up to the surface, and/or showers down and soaks into me from on high. Water I am not, for I am earth; nor is God water, since He is the Creator. *Water is the fiction of our encounter*, that is, the sensible narrative representation of it. This representation figures the space and time of an interaction that can only be expressed in narrative, resorting to comparisons and *metaphors* that narrative converts into *metamorphoses*. At the moment when fiction *utters* the interaction between *I* and *He*, it also *accomplishes* it: an erotic cleaving body to body, a co-presence and co-penetration that convince me I exist, I'm alive.

This *written water* is a crucial moment in the event we refer to as "Teresa of Avila"; I would even say it constitutes Teresa's own brand of ecstasy. The fact is that before being whispered abroad by sisters who had witnessed her raptures, before being put into words in the aquatic fictions of the protagonist, this ecstasy was basically an epileptic fit, as modern physicians like Esteban García-Albea and Pierre Vercelletto have diagnosed.[12] Only fiction, first speechless, then spoken, and finally written, and above all the fiction of water, could transform what had been undergone, but was unnameable, into an experience. For the water fiction maintains the tension between God and myself; it fills me with the divine but does not subordinate it; it saves me from the madness of confusing myself with Him, while allowing me to claim an association. Water is my living protection, therefore my vital element. As a figure of the mutual contact between God and his creature, water preserves agency, the Other's action, but it also demotes God from his suprasensible status and brings Him down, if not exactly to the role of a gardener (though didn't Mary Magdalene take the resurrected Jesus for a gardener at the Holy Sepulcher?), then at least to that of a cosmic element I can taste and which feeds me, that touches me and which I can touch.

⋆ ⋆ ⋆

Husserl wrote that "the element which makes up the life of phenomenology as of all eidetical science is 'fiction.'"[13] In other words, fiction "fructifies" abstractions by resorting to rich, precise sensory data, transposed into clear images. Never has this value of fiction as the "vital element" for the knowledge of "eternal truths" been more justified, perhaps, than it is in Teresa's water fiction, used to describe her states of prayer and to figure the meeting between the earthling and her Heaven, her Beyond.

The fable of the four waters severs Teresa from the faculties (intellect, will, imagination) to plunge her below the barrier of word-signs, into the psyche-soma. So what remains of "words" in the economy of this kind of writing as fiction? Assuredly not signs (signifier–signified) independent of external reality (referents, things), as is habitual in everyday language and understanding. Prayer, which amalgamates self and Other, likewise and inescapably amalgamates word and thing. The speaking subject then comes dangerously close, when she does not succumb, to catastrophic speechlessness: the self "is undone," "liquefies," becomes "bewildered." "Exile from self" is a psychosis: I am the other, words are objects. Nevertheless, through the novel of her liquefaction, Teresa balances her experience at a point halfway between these two extremes, on one side the faculties and on the other a delirious befuddlement (between consciousness and psyche-soma), without falling into the vacuum of asymbolia. Here lies her genius, in that ability to go back over the loss and to designate it with the mot juste. In her prayer fictions, what separates the word *water* from the thing *water* is not so much a "bar" as a fine and permeable membrane through which they alternately overlap and separate, as the self is lost and recovered, stricken and jubilant, forever between two waters. Annihilation/sublimation: the fluidity of the aquatic touch exactly translates this rapturous to-and-fro. And the penchant for "greatest ease and delight" (*grandísima suavidad y deleite*) leads Teresa to set water's thirst-quenching properties above its capacity to drown, its cleansing above its siltiness; she also prefers water's coolness to fires of pitch— the black desire that even water is apt to be enkindled by, inflaming too the woman at prayer.

> Let us consider now that the last water we spoke of is so plentiful that, if it were not for the fact that the earth doesn't allow it, we could believe that this cloud of His great Majesty is with us here on earth. . . .
>
> There is a very strong feeling that the natural bodily heat is failing. The body gradually grows cold, although this happens with the greatest ease and delight. . . . In the union, since we are upon our earth, there is a remedy; though it may take pain and effort one can almost always resist. But in these raptures most often there is no remedy; rather, *without any forethought or any help* there frequently comes a force *so swift and powerful* that one sees and feels this cloud or mighty eagle raise one up and carry one aloft on its wings.
>
> I say that one understands and sees oneself carried away and does not know where. Although this experience is delightful, our natural weakness causes fear in the beginning. . . . Like it or not, one is taken away. . . . Many times I wanted to resist . . . especially sometimes when it happened in public. . . . It carried off my soul and usually, too, my head along with it, without my being able to hold back—and sometimes the whole body until it was raised from the ground.[14]

By the end there is no longer violence in the *raptus* (from Latin *rapere*, "to seize or abduct"). The abruptness of *rapto* and *vuelo* (flight) gives way to euphoric transports (*traspasos*), subtilized by entrancement or *arrobamiento*, and Teresa's rapture dispels into clouds, mists, serried raindrops, billows of vaporized spray. Or into a "mighty eagle" (viene un ímpetu tan acelerado y fuerte, que veis y sentís levantarse esta nube o este águila caudaloso y cogeros con sus alas). Isn't that so, my apophatic Teresa?

Had these written waters been sensed during the epileptic seizure itself, or were they subsequently reconstituted in the act of writing? We cannot know. But Teresa's intellectual honesty, the vivid detail of her chills, frights, and swoons, suggest that verbalization was not part of the shock of the experience. It seems likely that the aquatic narrative emerged later in a written reconstitution, with its cortege of physical, psychological, and spiritual comments giving rise (or place, literally) to ecstasy. Therefore I confidently maintain that Teresa's ecstasy, as it has come down to us, is the doing of her writing. By returning to the "tournament" of the fantasy incarnate that is prayer, writing recreates the theopathic state, and only then does ecstasy exist. In this very real sense, Teresa only found *jouissance* in writing.

* * *

In this fiction of a soul's romance with its Other, it would be pointless to ask whether Teresa's water image is a simile (a figure comparing "two homogeneous realities belonging to the same ontological kind") or rather a metaphor (a figure establishing a resemblance between two heterogeneous realities). Doubtless the infant science of rhetoric as expounded by Salinas was more or less directly of assistance to the writer-nun, who shared that author's fondness for the vernacular. But, like all the "disciplines" that sprang from the fragmentation of metaphysics, rhetoric, with its elaborate figures, was ultimately irrelevant to the experience Teresa was attempting to translate in terms of water.

In Teresa's hands, the referent water is not just an object—and one of the four cosmic elements—but the very practice of prayer: the psyche-soma induced by the state of love, that generator of sublimated visions. Language is not a vehicle, for her, but the very terrain of the mystical act. To discourse, the object of study for rhetoric and other recently rediscovered stylistics at the time, Teresa adds the ingredient of a savory, tactile, sensual, overwhelming passion—to the point of annihilating herself in it, the better to dodge both discourse and passion. But it is also a sovereign, imperious passion, as God's captive captures God to make Him her pleasure-giving prisoner.

Unschooled in Latin, and lamenting this ignorance with a certain coyness, Teresa finds great relish in Castilian. But unlike a linguist concerned with dissecting a language by uncoupling its signs from their objects, the better to analyze them, Teresa plunges into her mother tongue as into a bath consubstantial with the experience of engendering a new Self, coiled in the Other: a Self that loves the Other, whom the Self resorbs and the Other absorbs. Her "water story,"* [*histoire d'eau*, pun on *Histoire d'O*, the mystico-erotic novel published in 1954 under the pen name Pauline Réage.—Trans.] if I may call it that, imposes itself as the absolute, inescapable fiction of the loving touch, in which *I* am touched by the other's touch who touches me, whom I touch back. *Water* is the fiction of the decantation between the other-being and what is intimate and unnameable, between the external milieu and the "organ" of an interior empty of organs, between the Heaven of the Word and the greedy void of a woman's body.

What language could possibly accommodate such porosity? None could satisfy the writing of this woman. She presses on with it, not rereading very much, so that her fiction will always be the outpouring of herself into manifold streams of subjective positions, sites of utterance, *moradas*. It will be her delirium and her rebirth. Her soul "would want to be all tongues so as to praise the Lord" (*toda ella querría que fuesen lenguas para alabar al Señor*).[15]

BEGUINES

I leaf through the Beguines catalog Bruno gave me. As time goes on I find myself accepting the truth: it wasn't Bruno I was hugging in the courtyard of the Louvre, it was the life of these women, among other experiences and higher things of the mind that were dancing through my head that Christmas Eve. Or at least the novel I was building around them, the stories I still can't stop weaving around "all that," as my publisher calls it.

These paintings, covering a span from the fifteenth to the seventeenth centuries, were part of the everyday life of the lay Beguine communities of the southern Netherlands. They were anonymous commissions, most likely designed by the Beguines rather than painted by them; only the reliquaries and the "installations" they called "secret gardens" seem to have been made by their own hands. Their vows were not for life, and they did not give up their property; they worked to support themselves, and celebrated Saint Begga as their patroness. A world away from Teresa and her Carmelite reforms—except perhaps as regards solitude.

Here, look at this woman with her luminous face, framed by a black wimple and crowned by a circlet of thorns. She loves just one man. He is her God. It is absolutely indispensable for this man to have suffered and died. Jesus's martyrdom, the Nothingness He walked through, is proof for this woman of what her subconscious experience has already taught her, what the males of this world stubbornly deny: no man is not castrated, no father is not dead. While lavishing this sadistic assurance on her, the depiction of the Passion and the skull in the right-hand corner reconcile the woman to her own melancholic passion—the passion for suffering, for becoming gradually frozen into indifference, for dying. In love, this man, this death's head, *is* her. And yet He came back from Nothingness into life. His loving heart delights the earth, fulfills her to overflowing. She will stroke Him with an infinite, maternal, absentminded tenderness. Is it the male sex she is saving from damnation? Or the germ of life, their reciprocal immersion, her own fertilized womb? In another painting, the crucified Christ's breast is cut open to show a heart in which nestles the embryo of Jesus, as if in a uterus of its own.

A woman is fundamentally alone. By leaving her mother to enter into language and the father(s), she has no other choice: either she attempts to love the man, that stranger, with the aid of a few children and a dash of sublimation (daydreams, embroidery, reading, and faith); or, she returns to the mother via a homosexual affair or a sisterly community of mutually idealized women. The shadow of an incomplete separation always hangs over her. Alternating between frustration and euphoria, female solitude removes us from (provisional) communities and casts us out into the black sun of melancholy; on our good days, it furnishes us with all the masks of irony.

How does this female condition differ from that of all other humans? Men, too, have to give up the mother in order to become speakers, but variants of incest remain open to them; men can regain, in sexual encounters and even in the *fleurs du mal*, the fragrant Paradise of yore. More radically, women share this common condition, and yet they are (with rare exceptions) debarred from regaining via eroticism the safe haven of primary oneness—even the original relationship is often refused to them, because mothers are liable to reject their daughters for the sake of more dependable values. Female loneliness simply adds pathos to the common condition of both sexes, one that in given historical circumstances has relegated women to silence, isolation, or repression. The nun or Beguine constructs an experience that is at once imaginary (a series of fantasies), symbolic (adherence to sacred law), and real (modulation of her body, her existence, her entire being), allowing her to sidestep this choice, or better said, to reconcile the two options. Thus she loves the absolute Man (Jesus), devotes herself to ordinary men (by treating their symptoms), and appeases her female passions (through solitude and proximity in the fabric of collective work and prayers).

And of what did the secret garden consist? What images, what reveries, what fantasies fed into these women's forsaking of all things in order to nurture and enhance that vital energy, self-command, and mischievous slyness that come through so clearly in these old portraits? Materialized in the *hortus conclusus* of the Beguinage, their "apartness" from the world touched off a profusion of naive confections and unselfconscious pieces of exuberance, cruelty, and love crafted by the weavers, spinners, embroiderers, tapestry-makers, gardeners, jewelers, and apprentice sculptors that they were. Voluntary seclusion was reversed into symbolic power. Women whose bodies had never "opened up to any creature" open themselves up here to unsuspected delights of the mind, which in turn will nourish the body. Frontiers are breached: those that surround the Beguinage, those that stand between man and woman, and between the Beguine and her God. It's heaven to be cloistered in this secret garden amid such excesses.

* * *

I admire the Beguines, but I admire Teresa more, because my nocturnal companion cultivates the seclusion of her soul nowhere else but in the folds of language, in the pungent beats of her rocky yet fluid Castilian, dreamy yet incisive. She, too, is into making and crafting, but when she speaks of *hacer esta ficción*, her materials are words. And suddenly I comprehend, no, I perceive with all the fibers of my body, with all the shades and glimmers of my mind, that it's the power of language, handled with her own peculiar craft, that permits her to saturate the "cloister of the soul" differently from the Beguines, in order to escape it. Deployed in speech and writing, the same amorous loneliness as that cultivated by the followers of Saint Begga steps back from the signs of the unspeakable to become transformed, across La Madre's pages, into subjective lucidity: as the captive of the Other, she is sure to capture this Beloved herself, and thus sure of existing. The sensual, manual, cosmic, biblical, and evangelical bricolage displayed by the Beguines' installations is turned by Teresa's pen into a new world: the thought of an aloneness (a lone Self) that encompasses the Infinite. The a-thinking of extreme singularity is on the way to being constituted, in and through fiction.

NARRATIVE, OR THE SURPRISES OF WATER

Neither simile nor metaphor, but both at once, playing one against the other as symmetrical opposites, Teresa's fiction is a paradox: controlled yet wayward, serious and fantastical, imperious and docile. But these ambiguities are not due to mental laxity so much as to the bipolarity of the experience itself, at once impairment and conjunction, inventing an undecidable enunciation in which water will be the fiction par excellence. An enunciation in which water itself is trumped by fire, and vice versa, while the narrative goes on to lose the logical thread of these multiple inversions to create that perceptible ductility of Teresa's writing, which infects us with its stylistic, psychological, physical, and theological metamorphoses.

I say *metamorphosis* rather than *metaphor*, using the word in Baudelaire's sense, when he refused to be taken for a poet "comparing himself" to a tree, for he *was* the tree, he took on its reality, rather than picturing himself as *like* a tree.[16] Water, says Teresa, is not *like* divine love; water is divine love, which is water. And we form part of it: me, you, and God Himself. The watery image Teresa lights on shifts us from stylistics to the tactile nature of the psyche-soma, which the writer conveys through the sensory, tirelessly elucidated metamorphoses that are the fabric of her texts.

In the eyes of the unbelieving denizens of the third millennium, the mystical experience equates to this recomposition of the speaking being by means of metamorphic writing. Teresa transcribes the dissolution (*análusis* or *diálusis* in Greek) of her intellectual-psychical-physical identity in the amorous transference toward the All-Other-Being: God, the father figure of our childhood dreams, the Sulamitess's unpindownable Spouse. A lethal, blissful metamorphosis, this writing heals the melancholy of separation by appropriating the Other-Being in an infracognitive and psychosomatic yet infinitely nameable encounter.

When regression, edged by masochistic pleasure, succeeds in adjusting to the Word, it is not rhetoric that helps us to read this elevation of the speaking subject, recomposed in the begetting of its speech, but Aristotle. In *On the Soul* and *Metaphysics*, he defines *touch* as the most fundamental property of being and the most universal of all the senses. To tell of touch, to touch by telling: might the inception of the incarnation myth lie here? Does Jesus's "*Noli me tangere*" only prohibit the act as an invitation to the word to become touch, tact: delicate presence, subtle reciprocity?

If it's true that every animate body is by that token a tactile body, the sense of touch possessed by living things is also "that by which I enter into contact with myself," as Jean-Louis Chrétien reminds us.[17] On a naive level, touch appears as unmediated contact. But there always remains a hiatus between the toucher and the touch: sheath, air, blade; and therefore the impression of direct touch, with no mediating element, implies "a concealment of mediation from sensation itself." Teresa, by contrast—aware of herself as being touched-bathed by and in the Other—far from concealing the mediation, grants it the status of a third element: the mystic third party of her immersion in the Spouse.

The fiction further outlines a narrative that does not confine itself to naming the mediation as "water," but refracts the water into a story involving God, the gardener, and the four ways of watering the garden. This ingenious procedure allows for an implicit critique of the immediacy of osmosis with the divine: Teresa distances herself from it and attempts to unfold the autoeroticism, painful and joyful in equal measure, of her nuptials with the Other into a series of physical, psychic, and logical actions, neatly figured by the four registers of water. It is not the water so much as the "narrateme," the story, the novel of waters, that diffuses the fantasy of an absolute touch via a sequence of ancillary parables (the well, the water wheel, the rain, the gardener, the earth, the nun).

★ ★ ★

In *The Way of Perfection*, the writer continues to relate the adventures of these waters, to which she now ascribes three properties: cooling, purifying, and thirst quenching. The soap opera of divine touch is compounded and amplified as Teresa proceeds to couple water with its opposite, fire, making these contrary elements vehicles for the contradictory states of amorous passion. Having distinguished the waters, she evokes the variants of fire, and compares the two elements while also mixing them up, undaunted by the risk of contradicting herself: "Oh, God help me, what marvels there are in *this greater enkindling of the fire by water . . .* !" Fire and water: on closer inspection, are they really so opposed? The story eventually reconciles its opposites in the realm of passion, the passion for writing the unnameable. Then it loses interest in images, words, writing; it pulls out of the exchange; it bows out of love itself to contemplate the brilliance of the diamond alone, petrified liquid in the cache of the "Seventh Dwelling Places." Is water, then, as much the fiction of the sensory impact on Teresa of the divine, as a critique—unconscious, implicit, ironical—of that impact? Touched by the Other, I am diluted into Him, who Himself is diluted and then condensed in me.

Let us follow the metamorphic adventures of water.

The first [property] is that it *refreshes*; for, no matter how much heat we may experience, as soon as we approach the water *the heat goes away*. If there is a great *fire*, it is *extinguished* by water—unless the fire burns from *pitch*; then it is *enkindled* more. . . . For this water doesn't impede the fire, though it is fire's contrary, but rather makes the fire increase! . . .

Those of you, Sisters, who drink this water and you others, once the Lord brings you to drink, will enjoy it and understand how the true love of God—if it is strong, completely free of earthly things, and if it flies above them—is lord of all the elements and of the world. And since water flows from the earth, don't fear that it will extinguish this fire of the love of God; such a thing does not lie within its power. Even though the two are contraries, this fire is absolute lord: it isn't subject to water. . . .

There are other little fires of love of God, that any event will extinguish. But extinguish this fire? . . .

Well, if it is water that rains from heaven, so much less will it extinguish this fire: the two are not contraries but from the same land.[18]

If water provides a privileged link to the Beloved in the *Life*, in the *Way* it sometimes proves helpless in the face of fire, the "absolute lord" that is not "subject to water." Here Teresa's experience turns before our eyes into an "ignitiation," to borrow Philippe Sollers's coinage regarding Dante. And now a fresh reversal causes water to itself become fire: an antithetical figure, apophatic par excellence. Does this suggest poor reasoning? On the contrary, it betrays an outsized attempt to control everything, negating difference in a bid to obtain, in the process of writing, total dominion over all the things of this world, and find an absolute remedy for separation and loneliness:

Isn't it wonderful that a poor nun of Saint Joseph's can attain *dominion over all the earth and the elements*? . . . Fire and water obeyed Saint Martin; even the birds and the fish, Saint Francis; and so it was with many other saints. There was clear evidence that they had dominion over all worldly things because they labored to take little account of them and were truly subject with all their strength to the Lord of the world. So, as I say, the water that rises from the earth has no power over the love of God; the flames of this love are very high, and the source of it is not found in anything so lowly.[19]

Teresa's water, cleansing and refreshing, can just as easily cease to be "living water" and turn into a parable of *understanding*. For when it comes to "reasoning with the intellect" it is "not so pure and clean," but muddied by "running on the ground" and soiled by our "natural lowliness." We must wait for the sublimity of the Other to "bring us to the end of the journey":

> Living water is not what I call this prayer in which, as I say, there is reasoning with the intellect. . . .
>
> Let me explain myself further: suppose that in order to despise the world we are thinking about its nature and how all things come to an end. Almost without our realizing it we find ourselves thinking about the things we like in the world [things we love about the world: *cosas que amamos de él*] . . . [20]

Wondrous Teresa, unearthing in every utterance—like Freud—the counter-meaning that is pleasure's secret lair!

* * *

Lastly, water douses the fire of mortal desire, because the pleasure of slaked thirst is a "relief" that deflects the praying woman from the "desire to possess God"—from sexual, and hence lethal, passion: "and so sometimes it kills"—and nudges her toward an "enjoyment" depicted as a slackening of tension. Thus metamorphosed in this last water, love overwhelms the experimenter, leaving her without defenses or initiative, offered up, passive, deprived of her *I*. Teresa alludes to herself in the third person here, as a *she* delivered from "desires" and "devils," whose ravishment has her "almost carried out of herself with raptures."[21] But since nothing is simple in this labyrinthine fiction with its multiple detours and switchbacks, her desires continue to pain her—a welcome pain, for it comes from Him, although one can never be quite sure of that: the devil's stratagems are unpredictable. The very thirst for God, insofar as it is "indiscreet" and violent, is a desire verging on "derangement." Witness the derangement of the hermit who threw himself into a well in order to see God sooner, not realizing he had been deceived by the devil.[22]

As the *princeps* figure of metamorphosis, according to Teresa, water holds a last surprise for us: it will need the diversion of thought in order to "cut short" desire, if not to take it away altogether, thus helping the lover/beloved, who touches/is touched, to "enjoy God more."

There is always some fault, since the desire comes from ourselves. . . . But we are so indiscreet that since *the pain is sweet* and delightful, we never think we can have enough of this pain. We eat without measure, we *foster this desire* as much as we can, and so sometimes *it kills*. . . . And I believe *the devil* causes this desire for death, for he understands the harm that can be done by such a person while alive. . . . Anyone who reaches the experience of this thirst that is so impelling should be very careful.[23]

Do you mean yourself, Teresa, my love? You continue, with razor-sharp intelligence:

For I do not say that the desire be taken away, but that it be cut short. . . . Sometimes the pain [in itself . . . very delightful] is seen to afflict so much that it almost takes away one's reason. Not long ago I saw a person of an impetuous nature who . . . was *deranged* for a while by the great pain and the effort that was made to conceal this pain. . . .

I wouldn't consider it wrong if [a person] were *to remove the desire by the thought* [*que mude el deseo pensando*] that if he lives he will serve God more . . . he will merit the capacity to enjoy God more.[24]

That's right, Teresa, the only resort we have left is to transmute desire by thinking (*que mude el deseo pensando*). You knew it, and you wrote it 440 years ago.

THE TRIUMPH OF THE WORK, THAT GREAT FLOWER

Let's consider [let's imagine: *hagamos cuenta*], for a better understanding . . .
Teresa of Avila, *The Interior Castle*[25]

Gardens. The Paradise of dreamers, of Persian astronomers, of lovelorn poets, of seekers of the Grail, of Beatrice, of Molly Bloom, of flowers . . . and yours, too, Teresa? "And all my spring-time blossoms rent and torn" (Omar Khayyam);[26] "O perpetual flowers / Of the eternal joy, that only one / Make me perceive your odors manifold" (Dante);[27] "Sweetheart, let's see if the rose . . ." (Ronsard);[28] "I pray thee, give it me. / I know a bank where the wild thyme blows, / Where oxlips and the nodding violet grows" (Shakespeare);[29] "I have punished a flower for the insolence of Nature" (Baudelaire);[30] "Oh rose, pure puzzlement in your desire to not be anyone's sleep beneath so many eyelids" (Rilke);[31] "Though haunted by telephones, newspapers, computers, radios, televisions, I can watch right here, right away, dozens of white butterflies visiting roses against a backdrop of sea. The Work alone triumphs, that great Flower" (Sollers).[32]

I return to the garden of the Beguines, which really was a garden: joy, bliss, mystical rose, triumph of ecstasy beyond words. But above all a secret, silent garden—on the other side of human passion, a simple craft of blooms, enamels, cameos, colored yarns tressed into figures. A geometry of the senses, metaphors of the fragmented body seized by a thought preceding thought. Red drops of your blood, my blood, intimate fluttering of my being, beacons of Being. Nature or abstraction, no matter, this ornamentation transcends human quibbles: whether pre- or postanthropomorphic, it exudes the simplicity of its communion with culture and the cosmos at their most rudimentary, most resistant to interpretation. The simplicity of these flowers, pebbles, tapestries is far from mean, but its wealth has an obvious immediacy that preempts comment. It does not argue with happiness or misery, it is content to appear, to exhibit what converts into a string of questions for you, visitors and interpreters: "What does this nosegay mean?" "Where did that stone come from?" "Whose is this coat of arms?" "What is that disembodied shower of blood about?" Here, face to face with the carpet of flowers, something remains undisclosed, not because it seeks to hide, but because the rose, for Angelus Silesius, has no why or wherefore.

Still, as the reliquaries fill up with little flasks and pouches, and the secret garden begins to burst with buds and blossoms, the secret may betray itself: it comes within a hair of acknowledging its sexual underside, the image of a body that parades itself or, on the contrary, punishes itself in order to merit the Garden of Eden at long last.

Judging from the paintings and objects shown in the catalog that will be my sole souvenir of Bruno, the mystical adoration of these far-distant women was prone to paroxysms of passion, unendurable splinterings, intimacies that stayed intact despite being shared. These lay sisters discovered, in mystical love, a continent—a continent-container, external and internal to the lay and religious communities of their time. They stood apart from both, not as a way to escape exclusion, horror, or evil, but the better to confront them, to consume them in self-consummation. Such was their path to happiness.

Teresa's garden is quite different. It is not exactly poetic, as in the works of the masters of floral eroticism, nor does it contain, as in the enclosures of the

Beguines. Flowers are mentioned in passing, they have no fecund names; there are no petals, no feathers, no wings, no pearls, no agricultural or horticultural bric-a-brac, no household accessories. A precociously intellectual outlook? A reflection of Castilian aridity? Maybe, but it is also more. In Teresa's garden, we read about—she only desires—two things, an abundance of water and a solitary flower, which is her body. Drowned in the electric waves of her epileptic brain or soaked through and through by the mist of the divine Spouse, this woman wrote but a single garden to remember, the garden of sensation elucidated; the garden of her infinite introspection with the Infinite. The flower then becomes a way of perfection forever wending through the dwelling places of the translucid castle, which it also is. Once ensconced—inside the flower, the way, the castle—and quill in hand, Teresa will climb into carriages and carts, take the reins of horses, donkeys, whatever she must. She will set forth to conquer austere Spain and turn it into another garden, physical and political this time, the garden of the reformed Carmelite order.

Chapter 7

THE IMAGINARY OF AN UNFINDABLE SENSE CURLED INTO A GOD FINDABLE IN ME

> Turn your eyes toward the center.
>
> Teresa of Avila, *The Interior Castle*

UNFINDABLE OR OMNIPRESENT: TOUCH

And so I arrived at this conclusion: Teresa's ecstasy is no more or less than a writerly effect! Spinning-weaving the fiction of these ecstasies to transmute her ill-being into a new being-in-the-world, Teresa seeks to "convey," to "give to understand" the link with the Other-Being as one between two living entities: a tactile link, about contact and touching, by which the divine gifts itself to the sensitive soul of a woman, rather than to the metaphysical mind of a theologian or philosopher. To sense the sense, to render meaning sensible: in Castilian, Teresa's writing and her ecstasy overlap.

Perceived by the mouth and the skin, essentially gustative and tactile, water is the fiction par excellence of a body thought-touched by the Other, thinking-touching the Other. It is the privileged element of an unsymmetrical reciprocity that realizes the contact between outer environment and inner depths. Water also reveals that the praying body is an orifice-body, a skin-body, that operates through proximity and is perpetually in vibration with everything that affects it.

Normally, sight and hearing tend not to be invaded by what is seen or heard. In the case of mystics and artists, however, the senses may be so overwhelmed by perceptions that they all work like the sense of touch. With Teresa, this incessant exposure is no bar to lucidity, but rather a royal road, the divine road to a more nuanced apprehension of that Self reborn in the link to the Other.

In Greek (*aisthesis*) as in German (*Gefühl*), the same term designates both touch and sensitivity, as though to insist that touch—understood as the generic for all the senses—transcends the senses; it founds them and exceeds them. That is why touch is not confined to any particular organ; it is not exclusive to the skin, or the mouth, or the hand, or the flesh.

Teresa seeks in vain, all through her body, for this enigmatic agent of contact and sensibility. After journeying through the multiple dwelling places piled up in her castle, she finally withdraws to the deepest retreat of inner space, a provisional, elusive place of shifting levels that liquefies at the very instant when the writer—and with her the reader—tries to stabilize it within fixed contours. Is it some cavity (vaginal, gastric, pulmonary)? A ceaselessly pulsating cardiac muscle? Where should the nameless site of self-perception of one's own insides be located, when a touch from outside filters through into one's heart of hearts? Teresian theology, echoing the Aristotelian idea that intelligence becomes intelligible "by contact with the intelligible," "for "thought does think itself,"[1] is a psychosomatic intelligence engaged in a permanent act of deconstruction–reconstruction; it perceives and traverses itself by constantly destabilizing and restabilizing the contact between contingency and the intelligible: to-ing and fro-ing, crossings, ripples.

Hunting for the mots justes, for an exact image of the touching-touched body thrown open to the plenitude of the Other-Being, Teresa adds to the water fiction of the *Life* and later works the fiction of overlapping *dwelling places* inside a *castle*: heaped, penetrable, ostensibly numbering seven but consisting of a host of doorless rooms and cellars, porous spaces separated as if by stretches of translucent film. Is it an allusion to the Sheva Hekhalot, the seven palaces of Jewish mysticism?[2] Or to the parable of the palace in Maimonides' *Guide for the Perplexed*?[3] No testimony survives, whether from Teresa, her associates, or her exegetists, to settle the question. At any rate the echoes are striking.

From the very beginning of the *Dwelling Places*, Teresa admits to her lack of a "basis" for what she is preparing to write. "While beseeching our Lord to speak for me because I wasn't able to think of anything to say nor did I know how to begin to carry out this obedience," it occurs to her to ground her account in a vision of frozen water, a diamond: "We consider our soul to be like a castle made entirely out of a diamond or of very clear crystal, in which there are many rooms, just as in heaven there are many dwelling places." The castle of the soul or the palace of the Lord? *Both*, of course, for however wide the gap between them, the creature is in the image of the Creator. Here we have it: interpreted in masterly fashion by Saint Augustine,[4] the *image* experienced by Teresa, in which she experiences herself, is consubstantial with the Creator, and, again, she will apply herself to conjuring "visions" (representations) in order to cast light on how "the very secret exchanges between God and the soul take place."[5]

Straightaway the image-visions start proliferating, contaminating one another, changing places, blurring together, always touching-touched: a castle, but made of glass; a stone building, but transparent; an earthly work, and yet celestial; a single castle, but many rooms. The habitat thus designed is not out of bounds, barred and fortified against trespassers; on the contrary, it can be entered at will: "I think it will be a consolation for you to delight in this inner castle, since without permission from the prioress *you can enter and take a walk through it at any time*."[6]

It would be no good trying to delineate this topography, although many still attempt to do so, for the chief property of imaginary vision is to baffle our eyesight. We catch barely a glimpse of the jewel's brilliance, only a rapid "streak of lightning" is left "engraved on the imagination" should we try to open the reliquary, that hiding-place of the Other in the Self. If any sort of image transpires, it's not so much a painting as a bedazzlement, always sensory and implicitly tactile: like a "sun covered by something transparent," the Beloved's body is nothing but a draped form, in a garment like "a fine Dutch linen."

* * *

Bernardino de Laredo, whom Teresa had read, expresses the closeness to God in tactile terms: "Thus was God's will touched . . . without the mediation of reason or thought."[7] The "application of the senses," for Luis de la Palma among other Jesuits, was after all a higher method of prayer than verbal orisons.[8] The beginning of contemplation? The prerogative of perfect men? Ignatius Loyola's *Spiritual Exercises*, whose coincidences with Teresa's practice cannot be overstated, urge the meditator to "realize and relish things interiorly" (*el sentir y gustar de las cosas internamente*), in imitation of Christ.[9] The ecclesiastical authorities jumped at that: did he mean imagined or spiritual senses? There loomed the danger of heresy, the specter of an excessive fleshliness: such lack of rigor could open the door to those Illuminati, already in the Church's sights, or to the misplaced fervor of overemotional women. Aristotelo-Thomism was always on its guard, and rightly so. The Jesuits' riposte showed them to be more knowledgeable and prudent than Teresa. Are not sense impressions, they argued, always-already molded by the spiritual virtues, at least among the faithful? Theological reason was saved, and Fr. Jerónimo Nadal, who had great insight into the founder of the Society of Jesus, could proclaim, in a sublime prayer: "From the conviction of faith comes hearing, and from its intelligence comes sight. From hope comes the sense of smell. From the bond of charity comes touch; and from the joy of charity comes taste."[10]

The aesthetic profusion of the Counter-Reformation imbues this cenesthesia of virtues and senses governed by . . . the virtues themselves. It could equally be a synesthesia of Teresa's glorious body as she wrote her *Dwelling Places*.

* * *

A cascade of sensible and ephemeral images, in fluid movement: the partitions between the dwelling places seem as yielding as hymens, and to pass through them unleashes such an intensity of emotion that these "intellectual visions" obliterate ordinary cares and feelings. Is this to say they petrify the woman as she prays? Make her into a fortress? No, they turn her rather into a crystal hive whose cells enclose the invisible, the searing flash, the imprint . . . God's touch is forever diffracted into warmth, flavor, fragrance, and sound, and sometimes it whips up a storm: a babble of parables orchestrates the polyphony of sensations around this unfindable sense, the most human and sublime of all. Not to touch, while yet touching: isn't that the definition of *tact*?

What Teresa sets out is a delicately mobile approach to God. First He is "this sun that gives warmth to our works";[11] he is also the "center" toward which all eyes turn, likened to the tender heart of a "palmetto" whose outer bark is "covering the tasty part."[12] This mystical desert does not prevent the writer from gulping in the divine "touch" with a great longing of the soul to enjoy that "spiritual delight in God [pleasures, in Spanish the same word as tastes: *gustos de Dios*]."[13]

Taste, that olfactory contact that ensures our survival and inspires the refinements of cooking, seals the Teresian link to the divine in what she calls "the prayer of *quiet*." In the Fourth Dwelling Places, "two founts" overflow "through all the dwelling places and faculties until reaching the body," for "the delight

. . . begins in God and ends in ourselves."[14] But the union of the Lover to the lover can just as easily smolder away like a "brazier giving off sweet-smelling perfumes," and this "swells and expands our whole interior being."[15] Not forgetting the eardrums, tickled by a "whistle so gentle that they themselves [the senses and the faculties] almost fail to hear it."[16] A flurry of parables relates the lover's metamorphoses: Teresa calls them comparisons, again, and blushes for them: "I am laughing to myself over these comparisons for they do not satisfy me, but I don't know any others. You may think what you want; what I have said is true."[17] What is truth? A cataract of metamorphic fictions telling of the perceptions anchored in the touched and touching body, which thrill the flesh like a "delightful tempest" (*tempestad sabrosa*).[18]

The castle curves in on itself, and its partitions give way when the soul's love touches the mercy of the King. Just as the hedgehog and the tortoise retract into themselves (according to Francisco de Osuna in the *Third Spiritual Alphabet*, which Teresa knows by heart), so the soul pulls the Other inside before rising to float above itself.[19] Should its senses and faculties "have gone outside and have walked for days and years with strangers—enemies of the well-being of the castle," they need only to have "seen their perdition" and, abashed but "not traitors," "begun to approach the castle," for the Monarch to call out to them, like the shepherd he is, "with a whistle so gentle that even they themselves almost fail to hear it," before they "enter the castle" once more.[20] They enter it differently, for the ever-malleable doors are absorbed into the state of "suspension" that overtakes the soul: there is no closed door between the Sixth and Seventh Dwelling Places.[21] Only thus can the ductility of the dwelling places touched by the supreme Good deal with "enemies," wretchedness, and every "symptom."

★ ★ ★

Was Teresa anorexic, bulimic, or both? That cluster of disorders being so fashionable just now, my friend Dr. Baruch and even Bruno has asked me about it, all agog. I dodge the question: "Read her and see!" But I have my suspicions. Teresa, anorexic? Maybe, at times, not always. She was certainly keen on "experiences that are both painful and delightful [delicious: *sabrosas*]",[22] and strove to defend herself against her own hearty appetite for tasting, feeling, knowing, listening, seeing: against the blooming of all the senses together in *aiesthesis-Gefühl*. As a novice it disturbed her, and she'd make herself vomit, empty herself out in order to meet the high standards of her heart's Elect. Later, she learned to convey conaesthesia in words. Desire, experienced as a delectation of all the senses triggered by suffering, would then become equal to its object, and ultimately be assuaged in the "spiritual marriage" of the Seventh Dwelling Places. With the strange, asymmetrical parity that obtains between the Bridegroom and his Bride, this spiritual soaring also finds expression in sensible or sensory terms—metamorphic terms, in Baudelaire's sense: "When our Lord is pleased to have pity on this soul that He has already taken spiritually as His Spouse because of what it suffers and has suffered through its desires, He brings it, before the spiritual marriage is consummated, into His dwelling place which is this seventh. . . . Let us call it another heaven."[23] On reaching this point, the writer ceases to defend herself. For speaking and writing for the Spouse about their mutual truth, touching and touched, is proof in itself for Teresa that the divine, not the devil, has entered into her.[24]

But can we be so sure? No appeasement of Teresa's spirit can be read in her account, no matter how serene she tries to sound: the story goes in circles, and the comparison—yes, that again—links Jesus and the one who prays, sets off again, contradicts itself, asserts itself by dint of repetition. Teresa is aware of it, she scolds herself: "Indeed, sometimes I take up the paper like a simpleton [idiota], for I don't know what to say or how to begin."[25] Or is this perhaps a scrupulous loyalty of the pen to the psyche-soma that will be transmitted—drowning the visible in the sensible—by tracing the very loss of intellectual understanding in ek-stasy, where the conscientious silkworm is annulled and there is only the dancing butterfly of the imaginary incarnate?

"IMAGINARY VISIONS"

Teresa's visions dictating her experience of the divine have nothing in common with a painting, as I've already said. For by sensorializing to extremes her contact with the All-Other via the fiction of water and its multiple conaesthetic transformations, La Madre inscribes it into the cosmos. But in the fiction of the castle, whose walls turn into nets, her experience relates to the constructions of men—oppressive fortresses in contrast to her own crystalline mansions—which can only be justified by being perpetually rewritten. In so doing, Teresa of Avila is not content with humanizing the Creator. Against Lutheranism, she rehabilitates images . . . and becomes a Counter-Reformation saint.

I read in a book that it was an imperfection to have ornate paintings.... And ...
I heard the following: that *what I wanted to do was not a good mortification* (what
was better, *poverty or charity?*); that since *love was the better*, I shouldn't renounce
anything that awakened my love, not should I take such a thing away from my
nuns; that the book was talking about the many carvings and adornments surrounding the picture and not about the picture itself; that *what the devil did
among the Lutherans* was take away all the means for awakening love, and so they
went astray. "My Christians, daughter, must now more than ever do the opposite
of what they do."[26]

Suspected at one time of Illuminism, then anointed a Catholic saint, perhaps Teresa is inviting us to temper our resistance and raise the portcullis of our
defenses. Her apologia for an interior body and soul fully exposed to the Other,
inhaling the Other, is certainly not given to everyone. But what a demonstra-
tion of the therapeutic powers of the imaginary! What openness toward the
possible metamorphoses of the divine itself, under the impact of the fiction
Teresa managed to found upon ... an unfindable sense!

★ ★ ★

The water parable and the permeable castle lay the groundwork for the recur-
rent fable of the silkworm that evolves into a butterfly, which to my mind marks
the climax of Teresa's metamorphic fiction.

You must have already heard about His marvels manifested in the way silk originates, for only He could have invented something like that. The silkworms come
from *seeds* about the size of little grains of pepper. (I have *never seen this* but only
heard of it ...) When the warm weather comes and the leaves begin to appear
on the mulberry tree, the seeds start to live ... The *worms nourish themselves on
mulberry leaves* until, having grown to full size, they settle on some twigs. There
with their *little mouths* they ... go about spinning the silk [out of their own selves:
van de sí mismos hilando la seda] and making some very *thick little cocoons* in which
they enclose themselves. The silkworm, which is *fat and ugly*, then dies, and a little
white *butterfly*, which is *very pretty*, comes forth from the cocoon.... The silkworm,
then, starts to live when by the heat of the Holy Spirit it begins to benefit through
the general help given to us all by God and through the remedies left by Him to
His Church ... It then begins to live and to sustain itself by these things ...

Well, once this silkworm is grown . . . it begins to spin the silk and build the house wherein it will die. . . . This house is Christ. . . . It seems I'm saying that we can build up God and take Him away, since I say that He is the dwelling place and we ourselves can build it so as to place ourselves in it. . . . *Not that we can take God away or build Him up, but we can take away from ourselves and build up*, as do these little silkworms.[27]

Where the hysteric fails—in defying the Master, in seducing Him, in being unable to dispense with Him—the metamorphic soul (seed, silkworm, silk, butterfly, and seed once more, and silkworm . . . eternal return) succeeds, by merging into oneness with Him. He, the "intellectual vision," the "flight of the spirit," the "Giant" with "milky breasts." A feminine sensibility, with typically extravagant, immoderate drives? Absolutely. Accompanied by a terrific super-consciousness, it sets off an unexpected biblical and Hellenic return to shake up the austere, Albertino-Thomist interpretation of the Areopagite corpus.

Touching and touched, this fiction is still, of course, an act that requires the full vigilance of her own judgment, according to La Madre. Nothing "automatic" about Teresa's writing: laxness and torrential fancies, keep out! Stiffened by her experience as founder, she was critical of postulants whom she felt did "not have good judgment." Not only would such girls not be accepted by the Discalced Order, they must be discouraged from writing about prayer: "Even though doing this amounts to nothing but a waste of time, it impedes freedom of soul and allows one to imagine all kinds of things. . . . and if something could do them harm, it would be for them to give importance to what they see and hear. . . . I understand the trouble they will run into from thinking about what they should write."[28] For cloistered little Bovarys like these—a breed Teresa disliked—it was quite sufficient to talk to their confessor. In the same dismissive vein she calls one overschooled woman a *letrera*, rather than *letrada*, or "lettered": she is a mere bluestocking, more at home with facts than with experience. And the rapture goes on . . . in writing.

* * *

In the "Sixth Dwelling Places," "another kind of rapture" appears, which she calls "flight of the spirit." Here it is no "small disturbance for a person to be very much in his senses and see his soul carried off (and . . . even the body with the soul)."[29] And so on to the Seventh Dwelling Places, where the "spiritual marriage" comes to pass, "not in an imaginative vision but in an intellectual one, although more delicate than those mentioned" before; "I don't know what to compare it to," and yet there will be no shortage of metamorphic comparisons.[30] The more high-minded are gratified here to see Teresa revert to the "core experience" of the likes of John of the Cross, purged of "imaginative visions." However, I invite them to read the lines that surround the moment, finally regarded as authentic, of Teresa's elevation.[31] In this text the "flight of the spirit" mutates into a "straw" being snatched up by a "great and powerful Giant," then into a "little bark" being lifted high by a "huge wave" (the waters, again) let loose by "this great God."[32] As for the "spiritual marriage" whose glory is revealed "in a more sublime manner than through any spiritual vision or taste," is it really quite relieved of imaginative comparisons when God can appear as "divine breasts" from which "flow streams of milk bringing comfort to all the people of the castle"?[33]

Consistently and to the end, Teresa stages an intimacy that is secret and yet without secrecy, in a continuous state of budding emergence, alluring and infectious: in a word, baroque. Devoid of sensation, it seems, during the final ecstatic trance, and yet always supraconscious of what makes her swoon with pleasure, the writing of rapture "touches" the theopathic state to the point of "divine touch." At this point too, dispossession and destitution can only be described in a flow that is more denuded than ever, admittedly, and yet still incandescent with metaphors and metamorphoses.

Was this not a peerless exposition in plastic terms of the very principle of the Incarnation? The Church, and the world, were impressed.

The fiction produced by this paradoxical theologian, at the intersection of flesh and spirit, of subconscious drives and conscious meanings, triggered a theological revolution. Not only did Teresa fully earn her title of "Doctor of the Universal Church," she also bequeathed us a mission that would otherwise be impossible to fulfill: to solve the enigma of that embodied imaginary—of sublimation, Freud would say—as the prerequisite for going further, or indeed in a different direction.

And here am I, Sylvia Leclercq, knowing nothing about faith but embarking on that very mission! Oh, why did it have to be me—when all I care for is young Paul, that misfit teenager who could be my son, and that frail and crumpled flower-bud called Élise?

I DREAM, THEREFORE I AM

"If I didn't dream, I wouldn't exist. I dream, so I'm alive."

Paul has just unleashed one of his breathtaking aphorisms. Where did he get that from?

"But it's true, isn't it? I dream, so I'm alive." Here we go: he's going to keep on repeating it until I say something.

Eventually I figure out that the source is our director, Dr. Toutbon. Paul had just told him that he wasn't planning to join in with any more MPH activities until Ghislaine came back. Ghislaine, his best friend, the one he used to kiss the most, left the home over a year ago when she moved with her parents to the United States. Paul knows perfectly well she's not coming back. Toutbon, for some reason that escapes me and must relate to his personal hang-ups, decided that our young in-patient needed bringing down to earth. "He shall place his finger on the borderline between the real and the imaginary!" Our dear director loves to talk in such terms.

"In your dreams, Paul! Quit dreaming!"

It was thanks to this inspired phrase of Toutbon's, whose first blunder it wasn't, that Paul hit on the formula he has just recited, and which is already doing the rounds of the home. Every one of my colleagues is raving about it from a philosophical and, need I say, therapeutic angle. At the director's expense, and serve him right!

Paul hands me the milky tea he's brought from the dispenser and sits down next to me, holding an espresso, visibly itching to develop his idea. I adore him. Oh no: here comes Marianne like a whirlwind into my office.

"Am I interrupting? Yes I am, I see." She only hesitates for a second. I shoot a meaningful glance in Paul's direction, but nothing doing. Ker-pow.

"You idealize your patients and your books in the exact same way your saint idealized her divine Spouse. What's the difference? Do you see a difference?"

She looks badly upset. I ask Paul to go wait in the games room, this won't take long, there's an emergency Dr. Baruch needs to discuss with me. His wide green eyes empty out, rake me blindly as he turns to leave. I don't know how I'm going to repair the damage done by this sudden separation Baruch has provoked.

"I'm going on a trip," says Marianne more soberly. She sits down, removes her glasses and rubs her eyes.

I sip my tea. I'm waiting.

"I'm going to Spain!"

"Really!?" I know she hates flying, is scared of trains, and refuses to drive.

"Nothing to do with you or your precious Teresa." I deduce the contrary. Silence.

"I'm going with my father, who's doing some research into our family background, you know."

I don't know. Marianne never talks about her family, and I've even wondered whether her attachment to me wasn't a way of detaching from them.

"Well, you see, Dad's gone back to the expulsion of the Jews from Spain in 1492. Our ancestors lived in Cuenca, right in the middle of Castilla-La Mancha. He's set his heart on going there, to find out something or other important in the local archives. Looking for himself, I guess. So, seeing as he's not exactly young or fit any more, I felt I couldn't let him do it on his own. That's why I'm going along."

I understand now. Marianne is letting me know that this journey is her way of going into analysis, without admitting it to herself or lying on a couch. Today I'll listen to whatever Dr. Baruch can or wants to tell me. Too bad about Paul, I'll pick up that thread tomorrow.

* * *

Marianne's father (whom I've seen a couple of times at her house: faint smile, elaborate politeness) is the youngest son of wealthy Jewish parents. Haïm Baruch was born by the Danube, in Ruse, Bulgaria. His family spoke Ladino and Bulgarian at home, but could communicate in every European language. They held the faith of their forebears in moderate respect, its observances reduced over time to a few culinary traditions and keeping of holidays. The sons were packed off to universities abroad—one to Austria, one to Germany, one to Russia, one to France. Haïm, the mother's favorite, was sent to live with some cousins of hers in Nancy. He entered law school under the innocuous French name of Aimé, "Beloved"—a whim Marianne had not forgiven him. "Just because the French pronounce it 'Em' instead of Haïm, dropping the aspirated aitch and the diaeresis, Dad couldn't find anything stupider than to call himself Aimé!"

As luck would have it, Aimé was on vacation in Bulgaria when Vichy ordered the first roundups of Jews. Since Bulgaria was the only country besides Holland to oppose the Nazis' deportation drives (or that's what they say), he escaped the Holocaust. During the war years he married Maria, a Bulgarian childhood friend, and took her back to Nancy, where she would give birth to Marianne.

I still couldn't see the Teresa connection, but Marianne said it was coming. Firstly, my psychiatrist chum had always been at odds with her "Beloved" progenitor, aware of his disappointment at getting a girl when he'd wanted a boy. He had named her Marianne in honor of the Republic, despite the darkness of the Occupation years. Secondly, this great Francophile, who had wept for the German destruction of Oradour but was forgiving of collaboration, felt increasingly less beloved in his adopted land as he grew older. Though a staunch secularist, he began to study Hebrew, and on retirement he decided to reconstruct the family tree.

Now, having traced the itinerary of his ancestors, he wanted to look into the sources. Aimé Baruch knew too much about the history of his people, and history in general, to expect to find reliable archive material this side of 1492 relating to such a modest merchant household. He did, however, hope to glean some earlier data about a family that had, from the twelfth century, been well-integrated and indeed respected in Cuenca—until finding itself summarily expelled by the Inquisition. Cuenca appeared to him now as the golden age of integration, the diaspora's Eden in Europe. But was it? This is what he sought to know.

"He dreams of finding proof of the peaceful coexistence of Jews, Christians, and Muslims in Spain on the eve of the expulsion, which would imply that it could happen again, sooner or later." Marianne has softened, she seems positively tender toward her father. Is she telling me that she harbors dreams of a peaceful coexistence with Aimé?

The first effect of the research undertaken by Baruch senior was to make him re-adopt his old name, Haïm; before long the good jurist had become a fount of expertise on Spanish Jewry before the expulsion and their survival after it. He was particularly interested in the diaspora of southern Europe, where his family ended up: Greece, Turkey, Bulgaria—not forgetting the conversos, the Marranos who stayed in Spain.

"Converts such as Teresa's paternal family, the families of Ignatius Loyola and John of Avila and maybe even Cervantes." I'm chucking twigs on the fire of Marianne's newfound erudition, just to show that I understand, in my own way, her rapprochement with Haïm.

"Well, that's the trouble. Some Jews were expelled and went elsewhere, like our ancestors. Others were collaborators, basically. Or pretended they were, but even so! Teresa betrayed her people, just as her forebears did by converting. Except she went further still by becoming a Catholic saint. Do you see what I'm getting at? She betrayed her father to side with her mother, didn't she?"

It's not the right time to say that matters are considerably more complex, in my view. But Marianne isn't asking for my view, she carries on without a break:

"Anyhow, Haïm wonders whether all those mystics Spain claims such credit for weren't simply the craziest among the Jews who stayed behind. People who could come up with nothing better than to annoy the Church, then in the pits of decadence, with the exaltation of their constricted little souls. He calls it 'delirium,' he doesn't mince words, unlike some . . . You know he calls himself a rationalist. Or used to . . . Can you see it?"

I can see that Marianne is the one feeling guilty of betraying her people by her silly war against her father, by her tomboy—or is it bachelor—existence. I see that she's taking on Haïm's guilt as he attempts to pick up the threads of tradition in his own enlightened style. As for Teresa . . .

Marianne doesn't let my silence last.

"Guess what? My dad now knows as much as you do about your blessed saint! He's just read a book, a study or something, by a Professor Yovel, do you know him? A Spinoza specialist who's into Marrano mystics, very original![34] So, Haïm is impressed by Teresa's hallucinations, of course he is. But of course he doesn't believe in them either. He's a man of reason, he doesn't make the allowances you do, right?" Or wrong; I wait. "So, he says that the more she tried to integrate, the more Teresa de Cepeda y Ahumada was humiliated by all those Spanish grandees and prelates around her. The more she played at being the crafty diplomat, the more they used her raptures for their own ends, if they didn't just make fun of her. Even when they saved her from the Inquisition and let her start her gang of barefoot Carmelites, they went on undermining her to the end."

"Is Mr. Baruch retraining as a theologian?" I'm trying to jolly this courtroom drama along, uncertain whether it's Teresa or myself standing in the dock.

"You're kidding! Haïm has only looked into the *Foundations* texts, Teresa's business end, if you will, and all the bad karma she got from her delusions of grandeur. He says the hierarchy treated her like a Jew, until they realized it would be more profitable to make her a saint. What do you think of that?"

* * *

How should *I* know? Her father, her mother . . . a Jew, a Christian . . . Is Christianity a refutation or a continuation of the biblical message? Was Teresa an *alumbrada* recruited by the Counter-Reformation to close down the Christian faith, or on the contrary to open it up? And open it up to what? True enough, she was marked by inquisitorial Spain. And rehabilitated by the Council of Trent, that's true, too. Maybe she did profit from the decline of royal power in the wake of the conquests, which only benefited the Golden Age—a flamboyant moniker and a fair description of the era's arts and letters. But what if Teresa's experience had rendered Marianne's claims downright obsolete all the same? Obsolete at the time, and more so today, even when such claims about identity are making themselves heard again in the context of the Middle Eastern conflict or 9/11? Teresa was far from dealing with such issues, simply displacing them in the mad intensity of her singular quest. But surely there's no other way of moving beyond identity politics, which are necessarily conflictive, than by displacement—toward this amazing, unprecedented singularity that somehow succeeded (but how?) in living in an open, shareable, foundational way. How did she do it? That's what I want to find out: concretely, step by step, how did she know, how did she manage? With what gains and what losses?

"You're right to go with him." (I'm evading, dodging backward.) "This trip will teach us a lot, to me too, I mean. When do you leave?"

"Tomorrow."

"What!"

"I know, I should have told you. I've been preparing it for a while, I didn't know how to tell you . . ."

"No harm done. See you in two weeks!"

★ ★ ★

I spend the vacation alone in Paris, as is my wont, with my roommate. I gaze at the city lights through the great window my father loved so much, et cetera. And I haven't forgotten Paul, who still resents me, I know, for putting Marianne before him the other day, but he'll wait for me. "If you don't dream, you don't exist. I dream, therefore I'm alive." Certain journeys are dreams. Certain readings, too.

Part 3

The Wanderer

It is very important for any soul that practices prayer . . . not to hold itself back and stay in one corner. Let it walk through those dwelling places which are up above, down below, and to the sides, since God has given it such great dignity. Don't force it to stay a long time in one room alone. Oh, but if it is in the room of self-knowledge!

Teresa of Avila, *The Interior Castle*

Teresa of Avila at sixty-one. Juan de la Miseria, 1576. Carmel of Seville. © Gianni Dagli Orti/
Art Archive at Art Resource, New York.

Chapter 8

EVERYTHING SO CONSTRAINED ME

> This true Lover [*verdadero Amador*] never leaves it. . . . it should avoid going
> about to strange houses . . . to avoid going astray like the prodigal son and
> eating the husks of swine [*comiendo manjar de puercos*].
>
> Teresa of Avila, *The Interior Castle*

"**G**od forgive you, Brother John, you have made me look ugly and blear-eyed [*me habéis pintado fea y legañosa*]!" La Madre, at sixty-one years old, doesn't think much of the portrait which fray Juan de la Miseria painted from life in 1576.[1] She would doubtless have preferred herself in the version attributed to Velázquez: refined, pensive, quite the "young intellectual." But all is well: she has just "made a foundation" in Seville, celebrated in the streets with flower-strewn processions, music, and canticles. Her conquistador brother Lorenzo, back from the Indies, helped to purchase the house for the new convent and has entrusted her with his youngest daughter, nine-year-old Teresita. Her major clashes with the Church are still in the future, and there is as yet no question of a grateful posterity.

Whatever the Carmelite's attachment to her interior castle, she was not one to neglect outward appearances. I think she was unfair to her portraitist, all the same. Framed by a white wimple under a black veil, her rosy face reflects her liking for fine fare. A long narrow nose balances the soft sag of the sixty-something jawline, while the pursed mouth conveys the strong will of the foundress and the authority of the "businesswoman," skilled at real-estate operations and negotiating with Church bodies. The large, somewhat asymmetrical eyes shine with an insatiable, inquisitive intelligence. Teresa explodes on the painter's canvas like modern stars explode on the screen. There is no sign of abandonment, that lascivious *dejamiento* for which she was alternately envied and denounced, and to which she herself laid claim, at times, in describing her union with the Spouse. This is obviously a nun with a mind: her gaze is quizzical and were it not for the prayerfully joined hands, I might almost have read recrimination or mistrust in the look she directs at the Beyond. To me her eyes are saying: "What's going to fall on me next? Suffering for suffering's sake, that'll be the day!" A robust woman despite her ailments, she seems well acquainted with One who is invisible to me as I contemplate the scene here and now, excluded from their exchange. She looks at Him not without apprehension, yet ready to stand up for herself. This was the attitude captured by Velázquez (or an anonymous disciple) when he gave the saint that charcoal gaze that seems to hear and write more than it sees. On the other hand, there's something sensual about the grave mouth depicted by Juan de la Miseria. Could that be why the dove of the Holy Spirit concentrates its attention upon the praying hands? How many women were there, inside Teresa of Jesus?

The portrait was commissioned by her very dear friend, Jerome Gratian; its author was an oddball born with the name of Giovanni Narducci. A peasant hermit from the Abruzzi mountains, he had been expelled from the minor orders, made a pilgrimage to Santiago de Compostela, became a sculptor's apprentice at Palermo, and spent a year in the workshop of Spanish portraitist Alonso Sánchez Coello. He was good friends with Mariano de Azzaro, a brilliant diplomat falsely accused of murder and jailed before being put in charge of hydraulic works by King Philip II. Eventually Mariano retired as a hermit to the Tardón desert near Seville. Both friars became enthused by Teresa's ambitious project to reform the Carmelite order, which at first only numbered two discalced White Friars: Antonio de Jesús and John of the Cross. In July 1569, Mariano, renamed Ambrosio Mariano de San Benito, and Narducci, now Juan de la Miseria, founded the second monastery for discalced friars at Pastrana, where they would produce silk. If these characters don't seem entirely wholesome, well, everyone knows that the most proper folks don't necessarily make the best reformers, and Teresa knew it too. She described the artist as a "great servant of God and very simple with regard to the things of the world."[2] Posterity would note the casual detachment, for La Madre made use of the humble as well as the exalted—but never with her eyes closed. The profound kinship linking hermits, Carthusians, and Carmelites may also account for the ease with which the first were persuaded to sign up to the reformed Carmel.

* * *

Wholly taken up by her visions and foundations, Teresa would never have dreamed that more than four centuries after her death, people would be scrutinizing her portrait and trying to find her in the pages she saw fit to write about her life. No doubt it gratified her to imagine the Discalced Carmelites, as an institution, continuing down the centuries—for fulfilled though she was by that Other residing within, she was not immune to vanity. But from there to fancying that women who might doubt the existence of the divine Spouse, or deny it outright, could one day be fascinated by her far from cloistered life, crisscrossing Spain on a donkey to the outrage of the Inquisition, which nonetheless hesitated to burn her at the stake—never! Not a chance. For Teresa's imaginings—entirely real to her, unseen by her eyes but felt with all her heart, which is to say her body, despite the fear of being a victim of holy madness— were indifferent to passing time, let alone therefore to modern times, and certainly wouldn't care what we might think.

I say "we," because I am not the only one puzzling over the portrait painted by Giovanni Narducci, alias Juan de la Miseria. Beyond Carmelite or pilgrim circles, where Teresian relics are prized as part of popular tours (run by Catholic business interests like memory trails, the Mysteries of Faith package), her writings have attracted a range of contemporary "sisters" as diverse and improbable as I am: Marcelle Auclair, Rosa Rossi, Dominique de Courcelles, Mercedes Allendesalazar, Alison Weber, Gillian T. W. Ahlgren, Mary Frohlich . . . These unlikely exegetes came as a surprise to me. Teresa infuses them, infuses us, with her taste for the union with the Other in oneself. All of a sudden these modern women, perfectly at ease in the epoch of the Pill and raunchy sex, began to haunt the waters, paths, and castles of the Spanish nun. They became theologians, interpreters, or writers in order to follow the thread of her raptures, comas, and foundations. Men, too, men like Michel de Certeau, Denis Vasse, Jean-Noël Vuarnet, Américo Castro, Antonio Márquez, Joseph Pérez, and others, as lacking in circumspection as their female counterparts, have trodden the labyrinth of our philosophical sorority.[3]

It is my turn to travel through Teresa country, in the variegated company of these passionate loners who are not always acquainted with one another, don't necessarily get along, may or may not know one another's books, and have nothing in common but the writings of Teresa of Jesus. Could the saint's texts provide a key to the enigma that is faith, the last stronghold of secrecy in our see-through, mediatized globalization, where everything is instantaneously divulged?

I bathe in the liquid imaginary of La Madre. I drink it in, filtered by the tastes and notions of the "specialists" on her, I glimpse it through the tracery of their interpretive ruminations. I build my own castle out of their dwelling places, I cultivate my dreaming garden in order to bring you a Teresa alive in us, coming alive again in you.

* * *

Buried at Alba de Tormes beneath a heap of soil, lime, and stones after her death on October 4, 1582 (or October 15, due to the switch to the Gregorian calendar that year), Teresa's body was later exhumed in secret at the request of Jerome Gratian, who wanted very much to look at it. Her garments were moldy, but her flesh was intact. The body was taken to Avila and examined by Fr. Diego de Yepes, prior of the Hieronymites of Madrid, alongside legal advisers Laguana, of the Council of State, and Francisco Contreras, of the chancellery of Granada; both men had been dispatched from Madrid. Also present were two physicians, a handful of notables, and the bishop of Avila. Each witness concurred that the body was incorrupt. According to the medical report, "It was impossible that this be a natural occurrence, rather than truly miraculous . . . for, after three years, never having been opened or embalmed, so whole was it that nothing thereof was missing, and an admirable fragrance wafted from it."[4]

With apologies to the pilgrims, I should say that I much prefer the vision of Teresa's living body always traveling toward us to that of her uncorrupted corpse. I seek that body in her books—of which she herself only edited one, *The Way of Perfection*, helped by the archbishop of Evora, Teutonio de Braganza; it was published in 1583, a year after her death. I visualize that other incorruptible body through the commentaries of her recent interpreters; I appropriate it, dream it up, and restore it back it to you.

First of all, she was a *wanderer*. The apostolic nuncio Felipe Sega, hostile to her work as a foundress of monasteries, accused her of being a "restless vagabond, rebellious and headstrong, who invented twisted doctrines she called devotions and gave herself license to teach, which the apostle Paul had forbidden to women." A woman, restless and wandering, that's what you are, Teresa, and it's a compliment in my eyes. But where does a life begin? And how many beginnings make up a lifetime?

* * *

The novel of Teresa of Jesus, suffering and sovereign, was slowly plotted in the destiny of Teresa de Cepeda y Ahumada; but it was crystallized in a crucial event of 1533. I picture a young girl of around eighteen, pretty, elegantly dressed, enchanting—no portrait exists, but there are many testimonies to that effect, and she herself often mentions her good looks. Many pages written in a painstakingly pungent Castilian for the benefit of her confessors, thirty years after the fact, retrace this youthful period. Indeed, Teresa only completed the first draft of *The Book of Her Life* in June 1562, when she was forty-seven.

The young lady had just spent a year and a half at the Augustinian school of Our Lady of Grace, where her father, don Alonso Sánchez de Cepeda, had sent her in hopes of safeguarding the honor of his bright, too-bright child. Her mother Beatriz had been dead for some years and her elder half-sister, María de Cepeda, was now married, after playing chaperone to the little one as best she could. Don Alonso, that loving, too-loving father, knew just how cute and seductive she was, better than anyone—except perhaps her cousin Pedro, one of the three sons of don Francisco Álvarez de Cepeda. Or perhaps Vasco, or Francisco, or Diego, one of Elvira de Cepeda and Hernando Mejía's boys? A plotline takes shape. We don't know the name of the elect, but Teresa was said to be dangerously in love.

In love, maybe, though without a dowry. The young beauty hesitated to take the plunge: "I also feared marriage."[5] Was she reluctant to share the fate of the countless women who passed away, sad and young, their bodies wrecked by an unbroken string of childbirths—her own mother's fate? Teresa liked to have fun. She read novels about knights and ladies, like her mother, and adored masked balls, parties, flirting, and conversation. Her favorite interlocutors were the servant women, bent on improving this spotless soul with salacious stories, and her cousin Elvira, reputed to be vain and an airhead.

"I must warn you, Father, that Teresa is receiving instruction in wickedness from the servants. I can't prevent it, she's obstinate and won't listen to sense." María's accusation only upsets the widower more, for he already suspects it.

"But what if I were to get engaged?" Teresa cautiously brings up the mirage of marriage, family honor *oblige*. María weighs in crossly:

"Don't even think about it! I mean, you don't seem to be thinking about it."

"We are proud but of modest condition, increasingly modest, understand me, child." Teresa frowns. Don Alonso cannot get his favorite daughter to see that a father has the right to expect strict decorum and total obedience from a young girl of such a condition.

Teresa shuts herself away with her secrets.

★ ★ ★

It's the same old story: fathers have always relied far too much on convents or marriage to calm their daughters' lusts. Don Alonso had no idea how easily love notes passed through the walls of the Augustinian school, via keyholes, furtive meetings in the parlor, the mediation of the airhead cousin . . .

The girl was on fire, and concealment being the rule, her young body soon fell sick. Palpitations, depression, continual weeping. Oh, to be free like Cousin Pedro, to sport velvet doublets slashed with gold, and buoyant ruffs, to twirl one's cape and sword . . . Let him take her in his arms, let him be her and she be him, let them waft together from ball to ball, or sail away to the antipodes. They could follow Rodrigo and his New World dreams, Rodrigo her favorite brother, two years older and born on the same day, whom she overtook in maturity long ago. Wasn't she cleverer, quicker, more intrepid than other little girls her age? The whole Cepeda-Ahumada clan agreed on that. The things they got up to together! Hardly surprising, when she stuck like a shadow to her likeness, her double, and he, although a boy, followed her lead in the peculiar games that so dismayed their parents.

One day, while reading the *Lives of the Saints* together, Teresa informs her brother that she aspires to be a martyr, like Saint Catherine or Saint Ursula.

"Or Saint Andrew or Saint Sebastian," says Rodrigo.

"For the love of God!" cries Teresa, in imitation of her mother, the godly doña Beatriz.

It was after the sack of Rhodes by the Turks—an event that had all Christendom quaking, Spain above all. But not these two children, who resolved to go and get their heads chopped off in the land of the Moors, across the Strait of Gibraltar, where menacing foreigners lived who were completely unlike the Spaniards. They set off—for the love of God!—and were caught up with on the Adaja bridge, still inside the city walls. Phew.

"It was her idea!" Rodrigo opts for shameful betrayal, rather than undergo the father's anger and the mother's sorrow.

Teresa did not hold this against him: her masculine double had at last admitted that *she* was the brains and the heart of their partnership. Closer now than ever, the runaway pair turned into a pair of writers: their amazed family was very soon presented with a chivalric novel, *The Knight of Avila*, by Teresa de Ahumada and Rodrigo de Cepeda. In this osmosis between brother and sister, might the virtuous knight be a foreshadowing of that "virile soul of a monk" that some detected in Saint Teresa? In any case, here began her writer's path.

But boys have a future ahead of them. If adolescence is excruciating for girls, it's largely because it brings home to them that they don't have such a future. This is not easy to stomach, especially for one who like Teresa has grown up among male siblings: coming after Fernando and Rodrigo into the world, she was followed by Juan, Lorenzo, Antonio, Pedro, Jerónimo, and Agustín, before the advent of another girl, Juana. How she longed to be a man, to set sail for the Americas like Fernando, the eldest, or like Rodrigo himself, who enlisted in Pedro de Mendoza's expedition! All her brothers, except for Juan, became conquistadors. In reality, Teresa had no need to be jealous. She could make people laugh, she could beat them at chess, and she produced superlative embroidery—the last was less unusual, being an Avilan specialty. The family, bewitched, would celebrate the child's witty sallies while fearing for her, given the impetuousness of her nature. "Our little charmer makes the most of herself, tastefully to be sure, but she overdoes it a bit: what a passion for baths and perfumes and jewels . . ."

Were you quite sure, Teresa, of what you later claimed: that you enjoyed yourself wherever you went, and that the least rag looked like a queen's raiment on you? No doubt you were, since you sought out "pastimes" and "pleasant conversation," indeed you were "strikingly shrewd when it came to mischief," as you later wrote, with stern self-reproof. There's nothing wrong with being at once the knife and the wound, and I guess this made you feel better. Your half-sister María's marriage to Martín Guzmán de Barrientos was an opportunity to engage in "vanities" for the full three months of the event. How embarrassing! How shameful! All this "could not be achieved so secretly as to prevent me from suffering much loss of reputation."[6] Checked by your confessors, you said no more about it, Teresa, my love, but not because you, a connoisseur of mortification, were loath to flagellate yourself. Marcelle Auclair thinks your discretion was due, not to the wickedness of the alleged frivolities, but to their innocence. That's plausible. I would also point out, though, that the honor of the Church forbade you to be more candid:

> Since my confessors commanded me and gave me plenty of leeway to write about the favors and the kind of prayer the Lord has granted me, I wish they would also have allowed me to tell very clearly and minutely about my great sins and wretched life. This would be a consolation. But they didn't want me to. In fact I was very much restricted in those matters. And so I ask, for the love of God, whoever reads this account to bear in mind that my life has been so wretched...[7]

* * *

Don Alonso knew that his favorite daughter was a magnet for the young and not so young people revolving around her—women and men both, needless to say. All the more reason to protect her, but how? Mysterious Teresa.

Her father did not know, however, that she had already come to terms with a fatal, irrevocable reality: the transitory nature of human love. "*Para siempre,* forever," she and Rodrigo had sworn it: and now he was getting ready to start on his man's life, away from her. Away from that role as her double, which he played so well under her direction—menial parts, it must be said, as an extra in the runaway scene and then as quill-carrier, all to his sister's advantage. The word "forever" does not exist, there is no forever between men and women, neither with Rodrigo nor with Cousin Pedro. Nor between don Alonso and doña Beatriz, who died of love, poor thing, her belly swelling up again and again, her children being the death of her until she really did depart to the Beyond, and forever. So does "forever" apply solely to separation and death and Nothingness? Her mother was only saved by leaving them all behind, bequeathing nothing to Teresa but a passion for courtly novels and a holy picture of the Virgin in a bright blue cloak. Mothers are cruel. So are the men who drop you, who never love you enough, who've always got somebody else to love.

> My father was fond of reading good books, and thus he also had books in Spanish for his children to read. These good books together with the care my mother took to have us pray and be devoted to our Lady and some of the saints began to awaken me when, I think, six or seven years old, to the practice of virtue....

My father was a man very charitable with the poor and compassionate toward the sick, and even toward servants. So great was his compassion that nobody was ever able to convince him to accept slaves . . .

My mother also had many virtues. And she suffered such sickness during her life. She was extremely modest. Although very beautiful, she never gave occasion to anyone to think she paid any attention to her beauty. For at the time of her death at the age of thirty-three, *her clothes were already those of a much older person*. She was gentle and very intelligent. Great were the trials she suffered during her life. Her death was a truly Christian one.

We were in all three sisters and nine brothers. All resembled their parents in being virtuous, through the goodness of God, with the exception of myself— although *I was the most loved of my father. And it seemed he was right—before I began to offend God.* For I am ashamed when I recall the good inclinations the Lord gave me and how poorly I knew how to profit by them.[8]

* * *

Doña Beatriz de Ahumada was don Alonso's second wife. The first, Catalina del Peso y Henao, who succumbed to the plague, was proud to be an Old Christian with connections to the Dávila family, a prestigious line of Castilian nobles whose coat of arms displayed thirteen golden bezants. Beatriz was Catalina's cousin thrice removed; she was barely fifteen when she wed this widower of thirty. By the time Teresa arrived, she had already borne two sons and was taking care of her two stepchildren, María de Cepeda and Juan Vásquez. Seven more children were still to come. Exhausted by so many childbeds, the fine and delicate Beatriz commended her soul to Almighty God at the age of thirty-three: a Christlike sacrifice in female mode.

Nuns who complain of the monastic life "do not recognize the great favor God has granted them in . . . freeing them from being subject to a man." You wrote this much later, Teresa, my love. Unfair, carried away, too much in love with Mother? With Simone de Beauvoir, the revolt of the "second sex" ought to acknowledge a precursor in you, who continued angrily: "a man who is often the death of them and who could also be, God forbid, the death of their souls."[9] An angel passes: it is the soul of Beatriz de Ahumada.

You were thirteen and a half when your mother died, and the only woman of the line accompanying your father, except for your half-sister María, the firstborn of the previous union. Surrounded by servants but responsible for the youngest children, you were probably tempted to become the center of this domestic circle, now that the mistress of the household was no longer around and the master was doubly appreciative of his daughter's looks and brains. But was it possible? Not when one has imbibed, at the departed mother's knee, so many tales of knights and martyrs. Doña Beatriz thus managed to instill in her eldest daughter the sense of another world, not in so many words, of course, simply by reading novels—as if there was no difference between such love stories and the lives of the saints, which her husband preferred. There is an elsewhere, my girl, innocent of childbirth and domestic drudgery, and that's where salvation surely lies, beyond this earthly plane, beyond my bleeding maternal body, beyond bodies, beyond everything . . .

Teresa absorbed the message in her own way. Not only was she as beguiled by these knightly and saintly adventures as by the feminine charms of her aristocratic progenitor, but she had also developed a taste for freedom in the company of boys to whom she never felt inferior. After all, she'd reigned supreme over the Ahumada siblings.

As far back as she could remember, Teresa's playmates had been boys, and she had been the domineering one. Look at how she dragged her darling Rodrigo, the best of them all, to be decapitated in the land of the Antichrist: no one ever tired of that story. She herself sounded tickled to recall it in her autobiography, years after the event. At the time, though, love unto death and a saintly end were in deadly earnest: cross my heart and hope to die.

She loved her mother, of course she did, and she prayed feelingly to the Holy Virgin, doña Beatriz's beloved patroness, and kept the picture of her in a blue veil, with those large white hands crossed over her breast, until the day she died. But was the Virgin really a woman? Or was she a creature unique to her sex, as someone had suggested? In any case, the mischievous tomboy was not keen to be mothered. She preferred playing chess, she had no desire to spend her own life gestating, and one may wonder if she ever needed a mother at all, such was her individuality and independence.

"What a handsome girl she is, and prouder than a boy!" The neighbors either admire or deplore her for it.

* * *

A young woman afraid of woman's destiny as exemplified by her own mother: it's a rare phenomenon, but not unique. The fear is stifled, opaque, inescapable.

Even the queens of the Golden Age were little more than wombs in the service of a monarchy and its political ends. From the birth of Philip II in 1527 to that of Charles II in 1661, the queens of Spain produced thirty-four heirs, infantes and infantas—not counting miscarriages. That's to say one child every four years, seventeen of whom (exactly half) did not live to see their tenth birthday! Some queens died in labor, as did countless women who were not queens and did not play chess: it was their destiny. In 1532, girls had little choice in the matter. Since 1525, however, the *alumbradas* or "illuminated" women had been advocating celibacy, a state far superior to the indignity and enclosure of marriage, against which any freedom-loving spirit chafes. Women who were unwilling to be just another link in a dynastic chain, or who had no dowry, or whom no one wanted, did what the Ahumada girl did: they entered a nunnery. Their bodies sick with desire, often without a religious vocation, they took the veil. What else could they do?[10]

* * *

Now, if Teresa preferred the company of boys, it was also to turn their heads with the scent of her skin through layers of silk and velvet while she fantasized, just like those haughty males, of being a knight or a sailor or a conquistador across the sea: a combination which her cousin Pedro found alluring and alarming at once. I shouldn't be surprised if Pedro shrank from her, maybe attracted to a different, more submissive girl, or maybe heading for the El Dorado that galvanized the whole of Spain at its apogee, a place known as Peru. That's right, the boys will be *peruleros*, and the girls, well, they won't be anything. "Too bad," the schoolgirl said to herself, but her heart started racing, and the tears gushed all over again . . .

She likes this torrent, she drowns in tears, it's so lovely to cry, as well as shameful! "Too bad," don Alonso's best girl doesn't see herself wasting to death in one confinement after another. "Always bedded, always pregnant, always birthing," was how Louis XV's queen described herself. Teresa will be as worthy as any son, free and independent. Impossible for a woman, of course, but the family honor will be saved. Father is always so preoccupied with that: honor must be saved! She will do as her father asks, but in makebelieve, that's all that's expected of a girl. All that's expected of mothers, women, families. She's one of them and she adores them, mothers, women, families. How else could she feel? It would be a long time before Teresa

admitted to herself that the paradise of women, sisters, and mothers is also
a kind of hell.

* * *

In the evening of her life, well past sixty and busy writing the *Foundations*,
Teresa projects herself into a rather strange sister, Beatriz de la Madre de Dios.
Now known as La Madre herself, she evinces a curious closeness to her subject
when relating the story of this other Beatriz. A victim or a monster? It's hard
to tell. She was illiterate, and her mother used to beat her. She was variously
accused of poisoning her aunt and seducing her confessor Garciálvarez, whom
she saw alone, or even Father Gratian, that special friend of Teresa's . . . She fancied herself on the road to sainthood, and reported visions and spiritual favors
aplenty. Manipulated by another sister, Isabel de San Jerónimo, who was both
crazy and in league with the calced Carmelites, who had it in for the reforming
nun, Sister Beatriz accused Teresa—to the Inquisition—of maintaining sinful
relations with the same Fr. Gratian and bearing several children by him, whom
she slyly dispatched to the New World . . . What a scandal! But Beatriz retracted
her story, Seville simmered down, and the Inquisition did not even open a file
on the case.

Does Teresa's concern for this abused and abusive child suggest an emotional affinity with a possible rival for Gratian's affections? Or does it cast
light, for the nosy posterity that we are, on just how hard it was to be a young
girl or a young woman caught up in the vortex of desires and horrors that
made up the world of other people, and how even harder this was in the ruthless ambit of female desires? A terrifying mother has a vile daughter. Which
is the murderess, and which the manipulator? Who are these passages of
the *Foundations* about—Beatriz de la Madre de Dios, Beatriz de Ahumada,
or Teresa de Cepeda y Ahumada herself? The "novel" left to us by Teresa of
Avila muses on the crossed destinies of love unto death. How can one not be
involved? And how does one cope?

* * *

On the whole Teresa preferred the company of women: she liked being under
their spell, before imposing her sovereignty. Frivolous Cousin Elvira, for instance,
the one execrated by don Alonso and his solemn daughter María—how sensual

she seemed, how free, how different from the misery-guts who slunk about in corners, sniveling! Teresa also fell for the charms of María de Briceño, mistress of the young seculars at Our Lady of Grace, who had a way of talking about holy books and one's own person that made a girl blush with pleasure. Briceño was living proof that not all women gave up their lives to a man, as Teresa's mother had done, sacrificing herself for husband and children in the name of honor. There were women who became such admirable people in their own right that they deserved and received the love of the Lord Himself. Teresa's dearest friend, Juana Suárez, had herself entered the Convent of the Incarnation, under the mitigated Carmelite rule, to follow that marvelous destiny alongside 180 other women—seculars, widows, undowried girls, as well as some genuine nuns who sounded rather jolly, by Juana's account.

Teresa was at a crossroads. Her young body was not appeased, but who could satisfy it? Her brother Rodrigo, her cousin Pedro, her best friend Juana? All possible and all forbidden. Everything ends, everyone leaves; the nothingness of all things, all things are nothing. Except Teresa wasn't as strong, yet, as María de Briceño or Juana Suárez; she wasn't ready to embrace the veil as a vocation. Not ready at all.

Her mother's devotion she found compelling, but her martyrdom was frightening. The dourness of her father's faith held her back: what a bind, that "point of honor" he kept on about, when Teresa only longed for excitement and adventures sweeping her up, up and away, into the Beyond! She cried out for love with every fiber of her being, she lacked for love. She would sponge herself carefully all over several times a day, dab her skin with perfume and scented oils, making herself pure and desirable—ready for anything, yet always in the anticipation of failure. And still that aching heart, still those floods of tears. Was she depressed or elated? She could not tell, and neither could the sisters at Our Lady of Grace. Teresa fell seriously ill. Best to send the Ahumada girl back to her father: too fragile . . .

* * *

Already disappointed and yet offered up, Teresa obtained her father's permission to convalesce at her sister's in Castellanos, where María had settled after her glittering marriage. On the way she stopped off at Hortigosa, to visit her uncle Pedro Sánchez de Cepeda, the third of her father's four brothers. Indisposition did not prevent her from wearing her red skirt with black braiding, black velvet bodice, and black lace shawl—an attire immortalized two centuries later by Bizet's sultry Carmen. On some level she was aware that don Pedro, though still in mourning for his wife, responded to her youthful beauty. For her part she enjoyed his company, like a more lenient version of her father.

"So you're not well, I hear?" inquires don Pedro, his eyes crinkling in a smile.

"Surrounded by dry rosemary bushes, and nobody to lean on," Teresa says nervously, alluding to her disappointments.

"Of fair Don Juan the king that ruled us, / Of those high heirs of Aragon, / What are the tidings? / Of him, whose courtly graces schooled us, / Whom song and wisdom smiled upon, / Where the abidings?"[11] Don Pedro is being kind or mocking, it's not clear which. He is said to be an Erasmist, something of an Illuminato. What could he mean? He's awfully well-read . . .

"Pardon, Uncle?" She feels on the verge of tears, again.

"Jorge Manrique." Don Pedro fetches the book from a library shelf; bibliophilic treasures outnumber worldly luxuries in this country manor. "Do you know him?"

Teresa likes to arouse desire, and yet the moment she senses the man's interest she retreats, introspectively, feeling guilty and soiled. Pedro de Cepeda notices this, and goes no further.

"Are you uncertain about marriage?" He realizes he must talk to this niece as an uncle, almost a father. It had not been a good idea to upset her with the verses of this old-school but very famous poet, who had enthused the whole of Spain.

"I'm not ready for the monastic life either, Uncle. My remorse at my mistakes is so great, the doors of Heaven are closed to me for ever."

"Mistakes, child?"

"My father suspects me, he can't be sure, of course, but it's true that I dissemble my desires . . . and I am incapable of understanding God, I am too hardhearted. I am not like a woman in that way."

"You dissemble, do you? You feel remorse . . . Is this a young lady speaking, or do I hear somebody speaking through you? You sound just like your father."

He feels caught out, and doesn't know how to pursue the conversation. Smart and pretty though she is, Teresa is clearly in a bad way. God alone could rescue a soul like that, a young woman like that. For this fresh-faced niece, scarcely more than a child, is undoubtedly a woman. Or is it precisely because of her febrile womanliness that . . . No, too confusing.

"Don't cry, my dear, we're all in need of consolation. I am myself, indeed I am, and without dissembling. I need . . . I need you to read . . . Here, read to me from Saint Jerome."

He puts Manrique back and pulls the *Epistles* from the opposite shelf, before stretching himself out to listen.

And what happens then for Teresa? She feels violently assaulted. "For without my desiring it, [God] forced me to overcome my repugnance," she wrote thirty years later.[12] She sits down by her uncle and fastens her dark gaze on the page.

* * *

Why Saint Jerome? Why was she reading, here in Hortigosa, the letters of the "learned ascetic" and first Christian translator of the Bible into Latin? Born in the sixth century on the border between Dalmatia and Pannonia, preoccupied with *hebraica veritas*, Jerome was the "author" of the Vulgate Bible, which replaced the Septuagint translation attributed in legend to the work of seventy-two rabbis. An accomplished rhetorician, he had studied in Rome, learned Greek in Constantinople and Antioch, and regarded himself as a disciple of Cicero. He had crossed polemical swords with Origen and disputed more amicably with Saint Augustine. What was his appeal for Teresa's uncle? Was it down to the Bible itself, which was only permitted to be read by the ecclesiastical elite (and whose mere presence in certain homes was evidence to the Inquisition of heresy or covert Judaism)?

It could also be because the future Saint Jerome had thrown himself into the solitary study of Hebrew in Chalcis, Syria, and spent years translating the Old and New Testaments in Bethlehem, where a Jew visited him at night "like Nicodemus," he said, had visited Christ. Pedro Sánchez de Cepeda, who was of converso stock, was very likely moved by the indefatigable Christian's return to the source. He would have known that a number of Marranos had been eager to join the Order of Saint Jerome, because this brotherhood's lenient rule allowed them to practice the Old Religion with impunity. Although their eventual condemnation on charges of "Judaization" had discredited the order, this would not have prevented Pedro from reading Jerome's *Epistles* or having them read to him. Far from it. Nor would it stop him, a few years later, from becoming a Hieronymite himself.

Then again, perhaps he wanted his tormented niece to read from this saint because Jerome had spent his youth enjoying the baths, circuses, and theaters of voluptuous Rome, and not a few reprehensible relationships, before he became an ascetic. Early on, at the wealthy home of the patrician Marcella, he became involved with a set of highborn ladies and gained the affections of a widow named Paula, along with those of her daughters, notably Eustochium—all recent converts to the Christian faith.

The great Hebrew scholar had also championed the superiority of virginity over marriage so rigidly as to be accused of Manichaeism; the most hostile antagonists found him guilty of "perversion and sin." His faithful Roman noblewomen came to join him in Bethlehem. All of them knew Greek and several applied themselves to Hebrew. Paula and Eustochium were later canonized. Why shouldn't Teresa follow a similar path?

* * *

Pedro's eyes are closed, but he is not asleep. He is trying to conjure up the monastery founded by Jerome in Bethlehem, with its great hall leading to the grotto where Jesus was born. Here Jerome translated, at a furious rate, the language of Teresa's paternal forebears into Latin. He was ultimately buried in another grotto nearby, opposite the tomb of his friend Paula, where Eustochium would soon join them.

"Here, read me the letter to Eustochium, if you please, Teresa."

"That epistle opens with Psalm 45, shall I begin, Uncle? 'Hear, O daughter, and consider, and incline your ear; forget also your own people and your father's house, and the king shall desire your beauty.'" Teresa's throat tightens, she stifles a sob, and pauses for a moment before resuming her reading. "I have left the home of my childhood; I have forgotten my father, I am born anew in Christ. What reward do I receive for this?"[13]

Don Pedro watches her intently, his body trembling all over at the sound of her young voice. He leads a secluded life; for some time now, books in Castilian and the joys of the mind are all he has had. Saint Jerome's letters would soon lead him, without transition, he thought, to become a friar.

He kept Teresa by his side for a few days more, soothed by her voice and by her hands as they turned the pages, talking to her about the vanity of the world.

* * *

The more Teresa read, the more she felt like throwing up. The more nausea she felt, the more interest she feigned: it was a point of honor. She had been torn in two. One part of her body dreamed of valiant knights and conquistadors like Rodrigo, and was mounted behind them, or being buffeted by wind and spray on the high seas. The other espoused the words of a father whose one concern was to save his soul and his children's; then Teresa scolded herself for her vanity, her frivolous temperament, and her womanly senses, which she hated to death, all on behalf of that judgmental father. There was only one way out, it seemed: "to leave the home of her childhood."

On the third day of her stay with her uncle, Teresa calmed down. She'd found that with him she could move between her conflicted states, casting off the divided self that sickened her and made her cry. It might even be possible to splice the two sides back together. Until she came to Hortigosa, Teresa had always seen the monastic option as a bastion against her low desires, while her intelligence discerned in this need for protection a sort of groveling, which put her to shame. But things were different with Uncle Pedro.

In the first place, he knew all about the vanity of the world, far more than other men she had encountered in the course of her young life. So much so that he had led her to forcibly overcome herself, as a protection against worldliness and against him, too—but in such a way as to introduce her to the pleasures of forcing herself. Uncle Pedro made her aware of passion and the inanity of passion at the same time; she discovered the allness and nothingness of the temptations that beset her at the nearness of Rodrigo, Cousin Pedro, Cousin Elvira, or her inseparable best friend Juana ... And he had done more than this. As she daily steeled herself to read, for his sake, from the edifying book which made her sick with the boredom of subjection to his whim, she found to her surprise that she was glad. Glad to please him, glad to encounter Saint Jerome and his psalms ...

Ah, that vigilant eye lodged deep in her young mind, which never ceased to observe, to judge, to comprehend what she was feeling in body and soul! She was beginning to get the measure of this night watchman inside, who never left her, who tormented and yet enhanced her! Was she really so glad to please Uncle Pedro? Or was she simply reveling in her own capacity to analyze what was happening on either side of this epistle by Saint Jerome: she, reading in the armchair; he, pretending to be half asleep on the couch? And between them this kingdom, *Audi filia* ...

Her nausea gone, Teresa felt ready in heart and body to push this willingness to please to extremes. There was no virtue in this dissection, though, she knew that too; nothing but an utter lack of discretion, boundless ambition, the sin of omnipotence.

The more she was intoxicated by her spiraling thoughts, the more the girl felt that her uncle was inducting her into a universe in which guilty passions and debating with those passions were not mutually exclusive, but simultaneous: a delectable surfeit, a world in itself, salvation perhaps. Teresa wasn't thinking about Jesus yet. She was simply afraid of her senses, while clinging to the sensuousness that Uncle Pedro allowed to the things of the mind. Blessed be voluptuous spirituality!

* * *

At this moment, he looked more like an Old Christian than a converso's son. Pedro Sánchez de Cepeda somehow but unmistakably reminded the convent girl of her late mother, the woman whose pious black garb concealed a love of prowess and exploit, the kind that would be dubbed "quixotic" less than a century later, and which drew mother and daughter toward the martyrdoms of the saints, or was it the other way around? Meanwhile the patriarch, don Alonso, remarked sententiously over their bent heads that only "good books" deserved such absorption, and in general, it was best to avoid anything in Spanish. Teresa acquiesced meekly to her father, as she was bound to do, but it made no difference: she secretly devoured the abominable romances at night. Did she intuit, however vaguely, that true devotion lay in her mother's impure purity, able to shed the same tears over the sweet pangs of courtly love and the agonies of decapitated martyrs? No man had ever seemed to live up to such completeness—not even Rodrigo, with his worthless vow of *para siempre*, still less the coveted cousin, and let's not mention the others. But Uncle Pedro? Maybe. He was so unlike Alonso that Teresa would have taken him for her mother's brother instead.

A strange alchemy took place in Teresa de Cepeda y Ahumada during those days of 1533, while she was staying with her uncle. Her senses recognized her host as a more modern, knowledgeable, audacious version of her mother; but in her memory, he was indissolubly linked to her father by virtue of their shared ordeal. Were senses and memory converging? To accelerate what impetuous decision?

We have mentioned that the court case brought by the municipality of Manjabalago against the Sánchez de Cepeda brothers for their refusal to pay a modest tax (100 maravedís apiece) had outraged the whole family. Joseph Pérez disagrees: his research suggests that the affair was actually a put-up job engineered by the brothers themselves, to obtain legal validation of a status they already enjoyed in practice. Either way, the case was heard, and it can't have been pleasant for the children. Castilian kids loved playing at Inquisitions in those days, even in the royal gardens. Avilan girls and boys piled up the logs for roasting heretics; one child once tried to strangle another who was playing the part of penitent, only with the noble aim of saving him from the stake! The town was abuzz with preposterous rumors, some branding the Sánchez brothers as criminals and apostates. The hearing was an alarming prospect in such an atmosphere. But what could it have meant to Teresa, aged between four and eight? Not a word was said at home, of course; the family *honra* was after all the highest value after God, if not on a par with Him. It was perfectly obvious that the Sánchez Cepedas were hidalgos, there could be no doubt about it, so the watchword must have been, walk tall and let tongues wag. Beatriz de Ahumada, a *cristiana vieja* by birth and proud of her lineage, would not have commented further, nor would the Sánchez de Cepeda brothers.

* * *

In fact Teresa was kept in the dark about the whole business, especially at the time. Her paternal grandfather, Juan de Toledo, was a converso merchant who dealt in silk and wool before moving into finance, where he handled taxes and tributes for a considerably juicier profit than before. In 1485 he fell foul of the Inquisition. In "reconciliation," and to avoid the stake, he had voluntarily presented himself on June 22 before the inquisitors of Toledo, confessing to "several instances of serious crimes and offences of heresy and apostasy against the Holy Catholic Faith." Juan was a Marrano, a "dirty pig" in popular parlance. The Marranos made a public show of Catholicism, and practiced the old Mosaic religion secretly at home. The monarchy decided that such people threatened a social cohesion founded on unity of faith and must be persecuted or eradicated. Between 1486 and 1500, the drive to flush out clandestine Jewry led to thousands of death sentences being passed down by the courts in Toledo.

Juan de Toledo escaped this fate. The merchant turned financier was treated with indulgence: he was nonetheless sentenced to do penance for seven consecutive Fridays through the city's churches, clad in the tunic of shame—the dreaded *sambenito* that denoted conversos and recidivists. Goya, still appalled at this persecution in the nineteenth century, sketched in his *Album* a group of convicts wearing the *sambenito* under a *coroza*, or conical hat. His caption reads: "*Por ser del linaje de judíos*," for being of Jewish descent.[14]

However "lenient" the punishment, it was symbolically devastating. Juan de Toledo's family had been stripped of its *honra*, and the disgrace was to weigh heavily on future generations. Juan had the good sense to leave Toledo and ignominy behind, settling in Avila around 1493. The sign above the shop now announced a new name, "Juan Sánchez." He prospered again, enough to buy a fake certificate of *hidalguía* that related him to a knight of Alfonso XI and exempted him from taxes, sequestrations, prison, debt, and torture. Had Teresa heard talk of this false certificate when she lamented her skill at "dissembling"? Juan Sánchez's sons took the name "de Cepeda" from their mother, who was of the petty nobility and a genuine *cristiana vieja*. They dropped the patronym Sánchez altogether when their father passed away in 1543. The statute of *limpieza de sangre* or "purity of blood," discriminating against both Jews and Muslims, was promulgated in 1547. Had they seen it coming? After the expulsion of the Jews in 1492, it was safer to be discreet.

★ ★ ★

At the hearing for nonpayment of taxes, held at the court of the first instance, the prosecution charged that the Cepeda brothers were not hidalgos but common taxpayers, or *pecheros*. The case was referred to the Ministry of Justice tribunal for disputes of *hidalguía* at Valladolid.

A procession of witnesses came to the stand. One of them brought up the disgrace of Juan's *sambenito* in Toledo: duly recorded, but irrelevant, for his conversion was sincere, and besides, he had married that unimpeachable Old Christian, Inés de Cepeda. All the rest testified that ever since they arrived in Avila, the Sánchez family had lived like hidalgos: it was common knowledge. They owned warhorses and weapons and were prepared to serve in the king's armies. Don Alonso had already proved himself . . . When at last the ruling came down it was favorable, and the Sánchez de Cepedas were publicly recognized as hidalgos, that is, members of the tax-exempted class. This status, duly inscribed at the close of proceedings, had the binding authority of res judicata. It could never be challenged, and the family *honra* was restored. But could a "trial" like that, a "secret" like that, ever be erased?

Ten years later, in 1559, the persecution turned brutal. In the wake of the discovery of pockets of Lutheranism, the Inquisition held two autos-da-fé, in

Valladolid and in Seville, where thirty and twenty-four heretics, respectively, were burned at the stake. Lutherans, *alumbrados*, *dejados*, disciples of Erasmus, and nonjuring clerics were all thrown into the same bag, along with some prominent aristocrats; the penitents were paraded in the green and yellow *sambenito* Teresa's grandfather had worn, plus miters decorated with devils and hellfire. The Carmelite nun, then embarking on her most prolific period of writings and foundations, would surely have been reminded of the court case endured by her family. If so, she never said a word.

* * *

Teresa the writer associates "these miserable little rules of etiquette [points of honor: *estos negros puntos de honra*]," "this miserable honor"[15] with the "merit" of a self given to overestimating itself, with the "calculation" of an ego which today we might call inflated, with upward social mobility ("it is a point of honor that [one] must ascend and not descend"),[16] with fear of public opinion or criticism from others, and with degrees of "rank" supposedly based on "laws." Against this she sets what real "honor consists in": attachment to God on the Cross unmarred by subjective or social criteria, nothing but an empty-handed alliance whereby *I* seek myself in *You*. "Help us understand, my God, that we do not know ourselves and that we come to you with empty hands; and pardon us through Your mercy."[17] Echoes of Saint John's Gospel: "and *another* shall gird thee" (21:18).

To me, this stringent quest for "what honor consists in" is the effect of an equally violent loss of the other, false *honra*, the "miserable" kind that was alleged to be lacking from the converso lineage named Sánchez, then Sánchez de Cepeda, and on down to the Cepeda y Ahumadas. In sixteenth-century Spain, the word *honra* meant something quite specific: families and individuals lived in fear of being stripped of that honor should it ever transpire that one of their ancestors belonged to the accursed race. The purity of blood statutes, though promulgated by religious and social bodies and not as strong as Crown legislation, still left your honor at the mercy of anyone who could produce evidence of your Jewish ancestry. Of course, you were free to preserve your honor by dishonorable means—such as bribing other witnesses who would swear to the contrary. Until 1524, the Inquisition was only interested in rooting out crypto-Jews; only afterward did it extend its remit to pursue all sorts of heretics, from Lutherans to Erasmists and Illuminati.

Your writings, Teresa, are silent on the subject of your ancestors' conversion and their stealthy Judaism or Erasmism; we find nothing about the court cases that stained the family honor. You never conceded that the dread of disrepute that haunted your family was less a feature of the old feudal aristocracy (indeed, Spanish nobles and royals thought nothing of frequenting Jews and converts) than an effect of the egalitarian sentiments of an Old Christian people eager to denounce the nonconformist ideas and conduct of those with "tainted blood." You operated under caution from the Inquisition, which by 1560 suspected your own foundational labors of Illuminism. Only the obsessive harping on the word *honor*—honor lost, but yet desired—shows up, like a scar, the pain that racked you for so long, Teresa, my love, the pain of being on both sides at once: being the wound as much as the knife. Judged and judging. Harder on yourself than all the suspicions of the purifiers, bloodier inside than the wound inflicted on your kin by the trial. "The fear of losing my honor was stronger in me," you say of the confused fourteen-year-old that you were.[18]

When I read the word *honra*, I decode as follows: here lies the accusation of *marranismo*. The cult of honor worked together with your upbringing to instill that fierce moral sense, that perpetual surveillance of oneself, of others, and of others in oneself. And you, Teresa, took advantage of this to transcend yourself. To escape from your origins but also from the society of those who would denigrate and persecute them. To the point of defying their world, the world, exiling yourself beyond "all things," which are but "nothingness." And finally— like a last flourish of honor that abolishes honor—by defying the Beyond itself, locating it inside you, where the Other resides. Is this a display of perfect humility, or of boundless audacity?

> The fear of losing my honor was stronger in me. This sense of honor gave me the strength not to completely lose my reputation. . . . Would that I had had the fortitude not to do anything against the honor of God just as my natural bent gave me fortitude not to lose anything of what I thought belonged to the honor of the world. . . .
>
> I was extreme in my vain desire for my reputation . . . I only had the fear of losing my reputation, and such fear brought me torment in everything I did. With the thought that my deeds would not be known, I dared to do many things truly against my honor and against God.[19]

★ ★ ★

Bizarrely then, but necessarily, the name of a great Hebrew expert, the scholar-saint Jerome, became associated with the quest for honor: as though to indicate that what was commonly judged dishonorable might become the very fount of honor, differently defined. The revision of tradition undertaken by the Erasmists (including Uncle Pedro, it seems), which led them to the rediscovery of Judaism, was a fillip for the supreme, unimpeachable honor constituted by the monastic life, or "taking the habit." "Reading the *Letters of Saint Jerome* so encouraged me that I decided to tell my father about my decision to take the habit, for I was so persistent in points of honor that I don't think I would have turned back for anything once I had told him."[20]

That confounded quest for honor! "Let any person who wants to advance and yet feels concerned about some point of honor believe me and strive to overcome this attachment";[21] "God deliver us from persons who are concerned about honor while trying to serve Him. Consider it an evil gain, and, as I said, *honor is itself lost by desiring it*, especially in matters of rank. For there is no toxin in the world that kills perfection as do these things."[22] That quest will now be replaced by self-exile in the Other, whom ultimately you will tuck deep inside your being. Does *greater honor* come with *greater bliss*? The interior castle in lieu and place of the hoarding of honor: a protected intimacy yet not a withdrawn one, an inwardness coiled in the Other, an impregnable space conquered and held in full view. Is this the revenge of those whose honor was impugned?

* * *

While staying with Pedro Sánchez de Cepeda at Hortigosa, Teresa was not sure of the path, but dimly felt her future taking shape. Did she have a notion that her father Alonso's fortunes would dwindle steadily over the years, as if to disavow his own father, the canny merchant Juan Sánchez—that father who always came out on top no matter what and shamed his son? Did she foresee that don Alonso would cling to the hidalgo lifestyle at all costs, neglecting his store, his trade, his taxes, all unworthy of the coveted status that had finally been legitimized—but lacking the land and property supposed to bring in income for men of that rank; and all this *para sustentar la honra*, for the sake of keeping his good name? Uncle Pedro would snub the old Marrano patriarch in his own way, by devoting himself to the Christian faith as a Hieronymite monk, no less, this being an order that welcomed converts, even if they were known to perform Jewish rituals. Among all the Old Christians of Teresa's acquaintance, she could not think of any more devout than this relative with his elegant synthesis of Saint Jerome and Jorge Manrique. Apart from her mother, of course; but she was a woman, an excellent custodian of honor in the admirable, terrible, female way: by the commitment of her womb and the illness that killed her. Teresa herself had the loathing of *honra* that we've seen, and the future nun would always make fun of those who spend their time "pretending" so as to hang on to it, instead of seeking another life, a loving life, a divine life, a life of divine love, a life divine with love, it's all one.

But is it possible? At this moment, reading Saint Jerome aloud to her learned uncle, Teresa's mind is made up. Here and now, beside don Pedro, with don Pedro, she has taken the habit already: she has entered the cloister, or *claustro*. In Spanish the womb is sometimes called *claustro materno*. Don Pedro has reconciled, for her, the monastic *claustro* with the maternal one.

Teresa was now ready to cloister herself in the maternal hollow, settle into the infantilism of faith, sink into the dream of dreams: the dream of love. Thanks to Uncle Pedro, or is it to Saint Jerome, reading would replace the weary alternation of pleasures and lonely regrets. "*Audi, Filia . . .*" (Ps. 45:10). She would not forget those words. As though the God-fearing scholar were authorizing her separation from the mother, that bond of love entwined with hate, and launching her search for sublimation—a paternal one, true, but as spiritual as it was sensual. *Audi* is *Shema* in Hebrew. Hearken to Israel and to Jesus, my daughter! They came together in Uncle Pedro. Did she know it? She could feel it. "Hearken, O my daughter, so shall the king greatly desire thy beauty; for he is thy Lord . . ." "All thy garments smell of myrrh, and aloes, and cassia, out of the ivory palaces, whereby they have made thee glad." She closed the *Poem for the Wedding of the King*, no longer crying, smiling broadly.

It wouldn't be easy. The tormented wanderer kept a strict eye on her wanderings: How was she to follow the path shown by don Pedro without betraying don Alonso? Because that's what it would mean: leaving home, leaving her younger siblings Agustín and Juana, to whom she had been like a mother, and renouncing "dangerous opportunities" and worldly "vices" from then on. Yes, vices: whether pious rhetoric or considered judgment, that's how Teresa defined her youthful longings in *The Book of Her Life*! Nor would she cave in any longer to her father's blandishments. She would "dissemble" once again, she'd try to bargain. Anything to secure the assent of a patriarch who didn't want to let his daughter go . . .

* * *

Until entering the Carmelite order, Teresa attracted quite some attention in Avila. Nobody would have predicted the nunnery for this fashionable young woman, gliding from one reception to the next, attending the festivities for the Empress Isabella in 1531, then those for Charles V when he stops over at the Dominican monastery in the spring of 1534. Both María de Briceño, her old schoolmistress, and Juana Suárez, happily ensconced in the Carmelite Convent of the Incarnation, urge her on at every opportunity. Is don Alonso holding her back, or is it her own weakness? It takes guts to announce the resolve to withdraw from the world to a father who used to impose godly reading lists upon the whole family (has he forgotten?), but has let himself go since the death of his wife, so that the business goes to rack and ruin and the family falls into penury, while still he refuses to give an inch.

Teresa knows she can't renege on her decision. "I was so persistent in points of honor that I don't think I would have turned back for anything once I had told him." But it's no good, his response is inflexible: "When I'm gone, you may do as you please. But not before."

She wonders whether her father has a genuine faith in God. Does he even believe that she does? A joust: point of honor against point of honor, daughter's honor against father's honor! Fortified by the loyalty of her Uncle Pedro, María de Briceño, and Juana Suárez, confident of the support of her father's confessor, Fr. Vicente Barrón, Teresa stands her ground throughout the mortal struggle with her beloved father. Two years later she persuades her brother Juan (he is thirteen, she is twenty) to join the Dominicans the same day as she became a Carmelite. They will run away together, *para siempre*, like she did with Rodrigo to the land of the Moors . . .

* * *

A fresh, clear morning in October 1535. Avila is still asleep. A few shopkeepers setting out their wares; a few maidservants selecting fruit and vegetables. The plazuela Santo Domingo is almost deserted. Nobody notices the two young people. The breeze that cooled the summer air now seems a cold herald of fall. Teresa's legs are numb; she strides through the hilly streets of the fortified town, under the Carmel Gate and north, toward the Convent of the Incarnation. . . .

When I left my father's house I felt that separation so keenly that the feeling will not be greater, I think, *when I die.* For it seemed that every bone in my body was being sundered. *Since there was no love of God to take away my love for my father*

and relatives, everything so constrained me [I was doing all this with such violence to myself: *era todo haciéndome una fuerza tan grande*].[23]

How could I not bring this moment of weakness to bear on my profane
reading of your way of perfection, my vagabond Teresa? Being at home with
Father pushed you toward worldly pleasures, despite or because of his efforts to
protect you from your own wayward impulses and infatuations, so as to keep
you immaculate, all to himself and for a better future. That much is clear. Uncle
Pedro came to the rescue, being at once a Marrano and a *cristiano viejo*, a sensual
father and a spiritual uplifter, a man of the flesh and a connoisseur of perfection,
representing the flawed, fallen world as well as the innocent world associated
with Mother and the Beyond. You would no longer be the prodigal child who
had suffered in "strange houses"—but did you feel like a stranger in your own
land, Teresa, my love? And what about this swine-feed you refuse to eat, as you
say forty years later in the "Second Dwelling Places"? Is this an allusion to Luke
15:16, where the prodigal son is denied even the "husks that the swine did eat"—
or an unexpected reminder of the dietary prohibitions secretly observed by the
Marranos? Perhaps "taking the habit," the vocation that was being decided, was
your intuitive, unconscious choice of a double allegiance, Jewish and Christian,
whose unlikely and inimitable alchemy would be primed by your own mystical
plunge into their depths.

You don't actually say so, but the book of your *Life* hints that at the moment
of decision, you were already at the bottom of yourself, outside yourself: you
thought of nothing but the Other-world as suggested to you by that fatherly,
motherly Pedro de Cepeda. Or more exactly, you suddenly saw the possibility
of reconciling that Other-world with your father's will: "For in this final decision I was determined to go where I thought I could serve God more or where
my father desired," as you put it so prettily three decades later. You elected to
break with the father in the name of the Father, to leave Alonso in order to
read Saint Jerome with Pedro, or ultimately to read by yourself. To overcome,
to transcend yourself so as to content the ideals of men and women over and
above their earthly needs. You hoist yourself up to Alonso's superego, whose
injunctions (to be a proper Catholic) he could not himself follow, then you
espouse the ambiguities and metamorphoses of a Pedro who hardly suspected
them (being an erudite, a humanist, attracted by Francisco de Osuna), and thus
you will merit the love of the Lord whom your mother (a *cristiana vieja*) has
gone to join. Your decision to be cloistered is at once a bid to unite the mother's uterus (*claustro materno*) with the father's ideals, and a total, hyperbolic,

consummation of your Jewish ancestor's conversion. By reuniting you with both parents, your adoption of the veil also reunites, in a paroxystic destiny, the Old and New Testaments.

Your kid brother Juan was stopped in time. He didn't become a Dominican; Alonso dissuaded him.

* * *

Witnesses say that at the end, feeling death's approach, you proclaimed firmly and proudly: "Lord, I am a daughter of the Church." These words, unremarkable from a nun, have more traction when coming from you. Were there doubters to convince, even now? You are not the product of your origins, neither the Marrano nor the Old Christian strand. You constructed yourself with and against the Church, while keeping faith with your idea of its perfection, and that idea could only come to fruition by reforming the Carmelite order in a way that accented the intimacy of contemplation and the visionary approach to theopathy, or "undergoing God." Because, in Hortigosa, at that crossroads of ascendancies and influences where the decisive days with Uncle Pedro had placed you, you realized that your terrible, your ravishing singularity could only blossom in that tradition, that institution: the Catholic, Roman, and Apostolic Church integrated by the New Christians. The fortuitousness of biography met the weight of history. Perhaps, too, it was an existential choice—one worthy of consideration, even today?

Neither tepid ecumenism, nor the domination of one group by another, your inner experience—at the heart of the Catholic Church—would enable you to translate your highly personal appropriation of both the secretive reserve of Marrano life and the feverish affects of the *alumbrados*. It enabled you to yoke a passionate monotheism, at odds with established institutions, to emergent rationalism and pragmatic humanism, by way of an unprecedented analysis of the amorous sentiment that lies at the root of our bonds with others and constitutes the secret of faith. Always faithful and yet unfaithful to the canon and to dogma, you were set to embark on a personal adventure that meant far more than a novation in the Catholic tradition. For while the sainthood bestowed on you did much to safeguard and lionize your oeuvre in the eyes of Catholics, the polyphony of your writing demands to be interpreted today as a universal legacy. You never pay the least tribute to your tacit Jewish background, but you don't deny it either, while you express stout opposition to the exclusions prescribed by the concern for *limpieza de sangre*. Likewise you don't espouse the dogmas of Catholic institutionality so much as humbly observe them, the better to get around them, with mischievous brio. Your inside-outside position, which proves to be one of irreducible vigilance, in other words, of a singular writing, is surely the best riposte to "the clash of religions." This is not to hail it as a route map for the inevitably contentious communities of the future. It's merely an invitation to experience, which is a boundless utopia.

* * *

Such considerations are far from your mind as you leave home, and yet your resolve appears to be unshakable. Nobody would suspect the battle being waged inside you and with your loved ones. Nobody but you, plus curious onlookers like myself, Sylvia Leclercq, who reads you almost five centuries later, intent on reconstructing your wanderings by way of your writings.

* * *

It took a year for don Alonso's wrath to subside. On October 31, 1536, he undertook before a notary public to endow his favorite daughter with a supply of best-quality habits—nothing less would do—and religious books. He also would furnish her with bedding, and gift the Incarnation convent with twenty-five fanegas of grain per year, half wheat and half barley, or failing that, 200 gold ducats. On her side, Teresa gave up all rights to an inheritance.

She took the habit on November 2, 1536: All Souls, the Day of the Dead. She was in floods of tears, but we know how easily she welled up, like Saint Ignatius Loyola, whom she hadn't yet encountered. The new novice was named Teresa de Ahumada, using her mother's patronym. "I suffered greatly at first, and later came to enjoy it."

The eternal issue of honor and pride kept her going to the point of pain, a pleasurable pain. Everything she did was "enveloped in a thousand miseries," but wasn't it all about being worthy of the Other? She liked to serve with trifling things, for the sake of it, like a "grain of sand" not yet lifted up by the waters of grace.

> I didn't know how to sing well. I was so worried when I hadn't studied what they had entrusted to me (not because I wanted to avoid committing a fault before the Lord, since being bothered about that would have been virtuous, but because of

the many that were listening to me), that just out of a sheer cult of honor I was so disturbed that I said much less than I knew. . . . I felt this very much in the beginning, but afterward I enjoyed it. [And so] I recited much better, and *in the effort to get rid of the accursed honor, I came to know how to do what I considered an honor*, which, incidentally, each one understands in his own way.[24]

Meanwhile, miracles were being performed by a fellow sister of the Incarnation: the candles this fortunate one lit to the Virgin were not consumed. Could it be a sign from God? Another, though wealthier than Teresa, slept in the paupers' dormitory. Ahumada felt very humble compared to them: but once she had left her cell, in 1543, she would not give up her two superposed rooms, an "oratory" and a chamber, where she received her numerous nieces and cousins while slapping her flesh with nettles!

One day, poor thing, you actually crawled on all fours into the refectory with a mule's packsaddle full of stones on your back and a halter around your neck, led by a sister, like a beast of burden. What wouldn't one do to humble oneself, to be worthy of Jesus's Passion! After professing full vows, it was not until 1562 that you took the name *Teresa de Jesús*. A heavy patronym indeed. Jesus's daughter, and also his spouse? At any rate, a fine promise of tortures and raptures, as we will see.

Your agonized, lacerated soul began to pass its malaise, again, to the body. Again you fell sick, more seriously than before: the time had come to mortify yourself to the point of bliss, of *jouissance* unto death.

Chapter 9

HER LOVESICKNESS

I hold that love . . . cannot possibly be content to remain always the same.

Teresa of Avila, *The Interior Castle*

I t began with a terror that literally broke you. You knew your health must suffer from this complete change of lifestyle, you remember losing your appetite. You were still a young woman who loved clothes and good food, but you went without. You threw yourself with gusto into all of the convent rituals. The practice of devotion brought contentment to replace the inner aridity of the unloved being you were, or thought you were. It opened you up to another life, the higher life of the true Christian, a full life much beyond what laypersons took to be plenitude—for as we know, their all, to you, was nothing. But with tenderness came fear; furtive rewards, dread of never being up to scratch. Courage and tears, tears and blood; your body became broken by pain.

You were brokenness itself, reduced to being nothing but the fault line that split you in two. Your heart pains (*mal de corazón*) grew worse, you kept passing out, and these fainting spells grew more frequent day by day.

By the fall of 1538, after three years of nunnery life with the Carmelites at the Convent of the Incarnation, you were in a pitiful state. The Mitigated Rule, which did not prescribe enclosure, left the door open to various sorts of "company" and, as a result, the life of the convent seculars blew hot and cold on impressionable souls. This could only aggravate your plight, torn as you were between the appetites of your thwarted body and the obedience demanded by a full life. The laxness of the calced order—preaching purity but inciting to the contrary, praying to God by day and smuggling the devil into the parlor by night—put you through months of excruciating pain.

The remedy? A stay with your half-sister María de Cepeda in the hamlet of Castellanos, the winter of 1538. You were carried there in a litter, and on the way you once more made a halt at Uncle Pedro's, in Hortigosa.

It was probably he, and not your less persuasive mother, who taught you that "if one proceeds with detachment for God alone, there is no reason to fear that the effort will turn out badly."[1] Artfully he centered you on the weakness that was rapture, the agony that was a choice. Having helped you to take the decision to join the Carmelites (though doubtless unaware of the part he played that day, when he made you read Saint Jerome), Pedro Sánchez de Cepeda was once more to be your guide. He gave you a book to keep: *The Third Spiritual Alphabet*, by the Franciscan friar Francisco de Osuna. This text taught you prayer and recollection, unleashing floods of tears, of course, and would remain a spiritual authority for you. For twenty years you practiced mental prayer in solitude, using the *Alphabet* and other "good books," as you were an insatiable reader. It was a long time before any confessor was able to understand you, leaving Osuna's work as your sole trustworthy compass: you read him against the Nothingness of the world.

Don Alonso was always there for you, too—but increasingly in the background, because you were trying to detach yourself, as you saw it: another cruel decision, but a firm one. Nobody would be allowed to question your will, you didn't need company, you didn't need a father or any man, you had made that crystal clear already. You weren't even interested in making friends within the convent. Some sisters were offended by this aloofness, and registered complaints. But all you needed was the *Spiritual Alphabet*, your prayer book, your one, irreplaceable, and constant companion. Whenever you were without it, your soul "was thrown into confusion and [your] thoughts ran wild."[2]

★ ★ ★

Naturally, I got hold of the famous *Alphabet*. It taught you the "art of love" as an exercise in yielding to the darkness of the sensible soul, which, unmoored from language and knowledge, and only on that extreme condition, may have a chance of fusing with the divine. Osuna's "mental prayer," as opposed to the vocal version prized by the Church, helped you to annihilate yourself, escape from yourself, cease at last to be an *I* or a *she*. You gave yourself up utterly to that new prayer in which personal pronouns and all forms of naming lose their outlines and surrender to the flux of affect: water of perceptions, oil of desires, tidal wave of feelings. Can this still be called prayer? Osuna writes: "This exercise is known as profundity with respect to the depth and darkness of the devotion, for it originates in the depths of man's heart, which are dark because human understanding has been deprived of light. Seeing the heart plunged into shadows, the spirit of God comes over the heart on the waters of desire to proclaim his divine light."[3]

To the understanding cherished by scholastics, Osuna opposes pure apprehension—not an all-engulfing affect, but an intelligence he calls immediate, a pure seeing "without looking," granted to the person in prayer who succeeds in identifying with the object of love, the object of faith. His injunction is not "to quiet the intelligence but the understanding. According to Richard [of Saint Victor], the comprehension of invisible things belongs to pure intelligence; the intelligence is said to be pure when the understanding is fixed on a supreme truth without the intervention of the imagination."

★ ★ ★

The shift from judgmental reason to the capture by immediate intelligence of every object as if it were an object of love was a thrilling game, at first, to our chess player: What could be more exciting for the mind? Very soon, however, these slippages began to chafe the inner wound: once more loneliness, weeping, nothingness of all things. Very soon Teresa let herself sink, abandoned herself. Did she pray with Osuna in the way that others sleep? She seems to have sought God as one seeks the comforts of sleep and was overcome with desire to nurse at the mother's breast, to suckle in the arms of the beloved—no: of the Beloved, the supreme Being who combines the attributes of both parents. Her copy of the *Spiritual Alphabet* can be seen at the Carmel of Saint Joseph. It bears the marks of numberless perusals, revealing a particular liking for this passage:

> Be especially careful of the time after matins, for that sleep is more for the soul than for the body, and never go to bed sleepy, but wide awake in desire for the Lord. *Emulating the bride, look for God by night in your bed. . . .*
>   Blessed are those who pray for a long time before sleeping and on waking up immediately begin to pray again, for they emulate Elias in eating a little, then sleeping, eating a little more, then sleeping again, and in this way *they pass their*

time reclining, as it were, on the Lord's breast after their meal, as children rest against their mother's breast where they sleep after having sucked, wake up, nurse again, and then fall back to sleep. In this manner they spend the time for sleeping in these glorious intervals so that the time is more for prayer than for sleep because their primary intention was to pray. And they use the majority of time others spend for sleep in prayer, and even during sleep they realize as soon as they awake that the soul slept in the arms of their beloved.[4]

Who invented dreams as the royal road to childhood memory, archaic, loving memory? Was it Teresa of Avila, Francisco de Osuna, or Sigmund Freud? Taking over from Pedro de Cepeda, the Franciscan friar introduced the Carmelite nun to a Godhead who could be tasted and suckled, whom she could look for by night in her bed, or after matins, when she wasn't sleepy. She ached all over with desire for love, hunger to be loved and to cuddle up like a child, like a bride, to dream . . .

* * *

Osuna leads Teresa to that white-hot spot where the "frivolous pleasures" that torment her intersect with the "thought of God" that reassures her: "For more than eighteen of the twenty-eight years since I began prayer, I suffered this battle and conflict between friendship with God and friendship with the world."[5] Indeed, when she was young, "as the sins increased I began to lose joy in virtuous things and my taste for them."[6] But her new spiritual master does not choose between the lusts of the body and the soarings of the soul, and neither does she. What his teaching achieves instead is to positively deepen the fault line the young novice had hoped to conceal in the convent. It immerses her in the unthinkable, and by instituting a prayer stripped of speech, it impells her to the prayer of abandonment (*dejamiento*) practiced by the *alumbrados* or Illuminati. What's more, this spirituality makes room for visions and supernatural revelations. After all, wasn't the *Alphabet* dedicated to the duke of Escalona, one of the foremost protectors of the *alumbrados* of Castile?

In contrast to the moralistic repression advocated by conventional religious instruction, the spiritual guidance of the illuminated *Alphabet* produces an effect of sustained, impassioned excitement that devastates the young nun, much like the first charged moments along the psychoanalytic journey. Lacking the interpretations of a therapist, not yet ready to trust in her own self-analytical lucidity, supervised by a string of confessors, Teresa settles into her crisis with Osuna's encouragement and blessing. She surrenders unreservedly to the amorous delights suggested by the Franciscan: "It seemed to me . . . that by having books and the opportunity for solitude there could have been no danger capable of drawing me away from so much good."[7]

But for the time being, after your stay in Castellanos and three months in Becedas with a healer who just made matters worse, these spiritual joys were helpless to check the advance of the mysterious illness that kept you bedridden for three years. The heart trouble you complained of since the start of your novitiate grew more acute: "Sometimes it seemed that sharp teeth were biting into me, so much so that it was feared I had rabies."[8]

★ ★ ★

No, not rabies but extreme disgust afflicted you. You couldn't swallow anything but liquids. Anorexic, burning with fever, this "inner fire," as you called it—condensing into a single interiority both organic spasms and anguished thoughts—was so violent that it inflamed your nerves, clenched your body, stabbed it with unendurable pain day and night, while a deep and unshakable sadness also chilled it through and through. Perhaps you were tubercular?

"Pain of the nerves is unbearable, as doctors affirm, and since my nerves were all shrunken, certainly it was a bitter torment. How many merits could I have gained, were it not for my own fault! [y como todos se encogían, cierto—si yo no lo hubiera por mi culpa perdido—era recio tormento.]"[9]—as you recall years later in *The Book of Her Life*, with that scientific-poetic knack for rhythmic concision.

Did Alonso, the loving father, on seeing Teresa brought back to him by the nuns, detect an element of play-acting in her plight? An exaggerated hankering to join the divine Spouse? Doctor Charcot would have called this "hysteria."[10] Be that as it may, the father wouldn't let her go to Confession, as she often liked to do. Too often.

"I will not let her have her way!" declares Alonso de Cepeda.

"Oh, the excessive love of flesh and blood!" responds the nun. (But to what love does she refer? Hers? Or His?) "How you have harmed me!"

That same night, Teresa "mounted" an almighty paroxysm that made her pass out.

* * *

Day of the Assumption, 1539. Your hands and feet are twisting in pain, there is no respite in Hell. Is it that you long too much for death? You lie in a coma for four days.

> At this time they gave me the sacrament of the anointing of the sick, and from hour to hour and moment to moment they thought I was going to die; they did nothing but recite the Creed to me, as if I were able to understand them. At times they were so certain I was dead that afterward I even found the wax on my eyes.[11]

* * *

Like most psychiatrists, not to say psychoanalysts, Charcot steered well clear of female saints, hastily dismissing them as "undeniable hysterics." He didn't leave any considered opinion with regard to your case.[12] However, we do have the diagnosis emitted by a Spaniard, Esteban García-Albea, who defines Teresa as an "illustrious epileptic."[13] More recently, in 2000, the French epileptologist Dr. Pierre Vercelletto contended that the saint's later raptures amounted to "ecstatic crises" typical of "temporal epilepsy."[14] My colleague Jérôme Tristan has nudged me in that direction already, as readers will remember.

The temporal lobe is a hugely complex node, I realize: it's the seat of sensorial, gustatory, and olfactory functions and is also involved in mnesic processes. Neuronal discharge can induce fleeting psychomotor phenomena in that area, experienced by subjects as "auras," almost invariably painful or unpleasant. Epileptic discharges can become generalized to trigger a convulsive crisis resulting in coma, like Teresa's four-day period of unconsciousness in August 1539.

The scientific term *aura*—applied to Teresa's raptures—simply means "breath," in an acceptation coined by Galen during the second century with regard to a patient who perceived "an impression of cold steam." We are forever obliged to Dr. Vercelletto for having pointed out, in his discussion of the precise value of the term *aura* in epileptology, that motor crises (characterized by clonic shaking, diverse paralyses of limbs or jaws, and speech difficulties—all of which Teresa reports) are linked to neuropsychological gains "specific to each person": in Teresa's case, her sensory, intellectual, even metaphysical peculiarities, and of course her tendency to hypergraphy! Few people are as peculiar as

Teresa, Vercelletto agrees. He cautions that while her saintliness can never be reduced to her temporal lobe, this factor should not be ignored. So, which is it, epilepsy or mystical marriage?

Other neurologists or psychiatrists would make short work of spotting in the young novice the specific symptoms of a hypersensitive predisposition, prone to regressions and exaltations, with a tendency to *alexithymia*. And what might that be? Don't act baffled, google it! The term denotes the incapacity of certain subjects to express emotion verbally, entailing consequences such as nausea, anorexia, and occasional instances of atypical epilepsy. All the same, while science knows more and more about this kind of brain dysfunction, as Dr. Vercelletto confirms, it is still uncertain of how a subject utilizes it in order to be free of it.

They can but think you are dead, Teresa, all except for your father, who refuses to bury you right away. He finally gives in. Your body has been laid out, the sisters have dripped funerary candle wax on your eyelids. The grave has been dug. Your younger brother Lorenzo watches over you during that last night, dozes off, the candle scorches the coverlet . . . you wake up.

⋆ ⋆ ⋆

Let's hear Teresa herself on the subject. In the light of her account I can confirm Dr. Vercelletto's diagnosis without hesitation: I am familiar with these symptoms, I've seen them before.

> Such were these four days I spent in this paroxysm . . . *my tongue, bitten to pieces*; my throat unable to let even water pass down—from not having swallowed anything and from the great weakness that oppressed me; *everything seeming to be disjointed*; the greatest confusion in my head; all shrivelled and drawn together in a ball. The result of the torments of those four days was that I *was unable to stir, not an arm or a foot, neither hand nor head, unable to move as though I were dead*; only one finger on my right hand it seems I was able to move. Since there was no way of touching me, because I was *so bruised that I couldn't endure it*, they moved me about in a sheet, one of the nuns at one end and another at the other. . . . *the lack of appetite was very great.* . . .
>
> I was very conformed to the will of God, and I would have remained so even had He left me in this condition forever. It seems to me that all my longing to be cured was that I might remain alone in prayer as was my custom, for in the

infirmary the suitable means for this was lacking. I went to confession very often.
. . . For if this patience had not come from the hand of His Majesty, it seemed it
would have been impossible to suffer so much with so great contentment.[15]

Don Alonso is forced to face the facts at last and to grant his daughter's stubborn wish to attend Confession. The ensuing Communion is accompanied by
copious tears. Though "the pains that remained were unsupportable," what a
relief! And it is so frightening to see "how apparently the Lord raised me from
the dead, that I am almost trembling within myself."[16]

* * *

Almost trembling, and almost amused, Teresa, as you describe this hysterical coma thirty years after the event. It would happen again. Maybe you were
secretly giggling about it under don Alonso's nose, he wasn't the kind to notice,
but then again . . . Distraught, contrite, he determined to follow his brother
Pedro's example by becoming a monk. This is what you were waiting for: the
relationship had come full circle! You hastened to foist upon your father the
famous "good books" he had been the first to recommend—the books to which
not he, however, but Uncle Pedro had introduced you with genuine passion,
and which you had already explored more deeply than either man. Naturally
you insisted on *The Third Spiritual Alphabet*: "Since I loved my father so much,
I desired for him the good I felt I got out of the practice of prayer."[17]

A great good indeed!. Father and daughter, praying as one, "in the manner of
Osuna." But . . . but you dissembled, you kept other pleasures from his knowledge: after returning to the convent in late August 1539 and spending three
years virtually bedridden, you rejoined convent life around Easter 1542, crawled
through the refectory on all fours, entertained plenty of visitors as a result, and
led a dissipated life, at least in your own view; you were not to tell him any of
this. And since he appeared to believe in your purity, whereas you were busy
"deceiving people,"[18] getting away with sensual worldliness and the cultivation
of "friendships and attachments that the devil arranges in monasteries,"[19] you
agonized even more deliciously over it all! In his *Vida del buscón Pablo*, Quevedo has great fun with the ruses people invented for the courtship of nuns, in
defiance of grilles and cloisters.[20] Ah, the *galán de monjas* or nuns' beau, what a
menace! Is he prowling nearby, perhaps? You do say that the freedoms of some
sisters led them to pass messages "through holes in the walls, or at night."[21]

A sharp sense of the indignity of such behavior made you desist from prayer altogether, and you told don Alonso of this, though omitting to explain in what way you had offended him and God at once. Your father did not condemn you, however. He believed your excuses of illness and infirmity, your symptoms worried him, and his candid acquiescence highlighted the affection between you: "My father because of his esteem and love for me believed everything I said; in fact he pitied me."[22] The piquant trials of father–daughter "negotiations" were reaching their pitch when, typically, the father suddenly caved in—I've seen it all before!

* * *

You entered him, he entered you. It was entirely for his benefit that you performed all that body-theater, my playful Teresa, confirming the hypothesis of a friend of mine who maintains that the hysteric's symptoms are directed at his or her spectator, whoever it may be. Another friend holds, on the contrary, that the hysteric prefers to bodily deliver himself or herself exclusively to the beloved. Don Alonso stood at the junction of both possibilities. He was more available to you than his brother Pedro, who merely fulfilled the ferryman's role (in my view; but what a ferryman!), and he was prepared to follow his daughter on the road to a perfection that would bring him nearer to—who? His wife, Beatriz? Or his brother, Pedro? Nearer to both, no doubt, thanks to the conquered nearness of his daughter.

You succeeded; you persuaded your father Alonso to pray as you did, in Osuna's style, as recommended by your Uncle Pedro. Full circle, I repeat. The daughter would teach the father to pray, in other words to love, as though she were her father's father. Such was your first triumph over . . . men.

* * *

And also, I might add, your first triumph over the Inquisition—the institution that humiliated your grandfather Juan Sánchez, came close to prosecuting Pedro and Alonso, and was soon to take an interest in your own case. For the moment, you rejoice at having got your father to pray: the Marrano's descendant is by way of becoming a mystic, a much more enviable destiny than that of *cristiano viejo*. A most remarkable success, in fact. He has at last been "integrated," in today's parlance, who knows whether on the edges or in depth, for both are possible once mysticism is accepted as an interiority external to, or exteriority internal to, true faith.

In fact, big brother Rodrigo, whom you coaxed into running away with you to court decapitation by the Moors (your first bid for sainthood!), was really just a twin, a double of yourself... and a provisional substitute for Alonso, perhaps? You father was, after all, now and forever, the first man conquered and in need of conquering, giving rise to evident "paternal" replicas in the form of that improbable string of confessors and other counselors whom you resorted to every step of the way. Early on in the book of your *Life*, you give the game away: "I was the most loved of my father."[23] In return you would draw your father with you, back to the prayers in which Uncle Pedro and Osuna the *alumbrado* taught you to search for love. To put it more precisely, thanks to Osuna, whom you discovered thanks to Pedro, you can share the pleasure with don Alonso. Your father and you, you and your father, separately and together, snuggle into that bed where it is right and possible, asleep against the Other's breast, to quench the eternal thirst to suckle that plagues human beings at night or after matins. Let time come to a halt: you are convinced your father belongs to you and you to him, the die is cast, and the man (Alonso Sánchez de Cepeda) is dead, transformed into a (religious) father.

⋆ ⋆ ⋆

Am I taking things too far? Not at all. It makes sense that at the very moment you relate your victory over him, you also mention the death of this man, the first man you ever wanted: "In losing him I was losing every good and joy, and he was everything to me."[24] Alonso Sánchez de Cepeda passed away in December 1543, a full eight years after you entered the Convent of the Incarnation. Eight years of upheaval and trouble to mark the start of your monastic career, eight years during which you were constantly feeling and fighting a passionate attraction to men, to that man. And yet, when remembering him in your memoir in 1560, you announce his death just after reporting his alignment with you on the religious plane. Why such haste to erase his presence? Why this anticipation of his decease? Why exclude *papá* from the passionate ordeals that shook your interior castle during those years, diagnosed by Dr. Vercelletto as a string of "temporal seizures" accompanied by the perception of "auras"?

You give us the answer yourself, with the breathtaking intellectual honesty that forbids you to equivocate: *porque le quería mucho*, because I loved him dearly. This admission escapes at the end of a passage on how you had to force yourself to keep your feelings, particularly those toward your father, in check. Your resolve to cut loose from worldly vanities entailed—among other sacrifices?—making the effort to appear insensible in his presence: "I had great determination not to show him my grief and until he would die to act as though I were well. When I saw him coming to the end of his life, it seemed my soul was being wrenched from me, for I loved him dearly."[25]

Can you see what I'm getting at? I suspect you, Teresa, of keeping quiet about the guilty attraction you felt for don Alonso despite—or because of—his Marrano fiscal lawsuit, his way of getting your mother pregnant ten times over until she expired at age thirty-three, his delusions of grandeur, his impossible integration, and the nonchalance with which he cultivated a hidalgo's lifestyle without the necessary assets, leading him to fritter away your grandfather's fortune until there wasn't even enough for a dowry. All the same, if the paternal cause of your hysterical conflicts remained in the shadows, you had plenty to say about some other sources of extreme emotion that seem to have pitched you repeatedly into a coma.

I want to pause on just two of them, which mesh so thoroughly with the father's sway over your early steps on the path to perfection that the spiritual battles against the devil you credit yourself for in those days appear in an indisputably erotic light.

First, the woman with the open abdomen, to whom you became so attached. The sight of her at the convent sends you outside yourself. Then—as if to escape her ill-being, or perhaps, again, to indirectly cause it—that unhappy sinner you found so appealing, the Becedas parish priest, succeeded with the same ambiguous purpose by a "person," an assiduous visitor to the nunnery, whose company you became "extremely fond of." What dangerous places they were, those Golden Age Spanish convents! You had excellent reasons for wanting to reform them, Teresa, my love!

* * *

She hasn't left her cell for three days. Each morning she is racked by vomiting fits, which make her unable to ingest anything until past midday. Her limbs contract, she cannot move, she is confined to her bed by absolute exhaustion.

"I am down to my bones," Teresa sighs to the nursing sister, who looks in on her several times a day.

She refrains from mentioning what gladness can be had from such affliction, how glad she actually feels ... In the evening, before darkness falls, Osuna's disciple makes herself throw up with the help of a goose feather, failing which she will feel considerably sicker the next day. At midnight her heart sets to thudding again, her arms and legs are twisted by waves of rheumatism, her fever soars.

What tortures her most, since the onset of this immobilizing condition, is not being able to keep watch by the bedside of the nun with the open belly. The poor woman's calvary is always on her mind, Teresa can see her, right here in her cell, though not of course with the eyes of the body. And yet she feels her bodily, she vomits her, loves her. The wretched sister's intestines are obstructed and have burst through the skin, a veritable sieve, and anything she eats now oozes through those holes. Like dribbling mouths all over the surface, stinking anuses puncturing her flesh. The other nuns, aghast, have retreated from the abject spectacle. Teresa alone is determined to sit by the deathbed. Too bad if her bones are wrenched by convulsions; she drags herself as best she can into the cancer-sufferer's cell, and there she stays.

"You're very brave, sister," gasps a Carmelite on a whirlwind visit, holding her nose and making for the door.

"I envy her patience in dying," Teresa replies dreamily, outside herself.

Instead of holding her nose, she begs God to grant her equal patience and send her all the afflictions He pleases. Sure enough the Lord fulfills her wish, and blesses her with the vomiting attacks she knows so well, the retching she provokes when the need arises. He sends her bone ache, exhaustion, new bouts of fainting, and an ever more infirm heart. Does He do it to torment or to ravish her?

Teresa thinks back to her mother, to all those mothers who die in childbirth: What else can a woman succumb to but her womb, the womb that's been impaired since adolescence, smelly and bleeding, a cancer in gestation for generations? If Teresa is a woman like her mother Beatriz, she will die like her, too, of her belly. Or like the cancerous nun, herself somehow a victim of that fertilized, fertilizable putrefaction, that sickening space every woman carries around inside. But how will you escape their fate except by being, precisely, sick; rejecting that matrix that inhabits you, that tumor, that pernicious motherhood, that mother, that mortality?

Teresa's condition worsens by the hour. The nuns have deserted the cancer patient to crowd around Teresa's pallet.

"She's gone!" wails the nursing sister.

A false alarm. Teresa sits up, but how tired she is!

* * *

Don Alonso, not yet initiated by his daughter into the art of prayer, decides to send her to Becedas, a village famed throughout Castile for its healer, whose attentions no ailment could withstand. The stay in Castellanos hasn't helped, and he can think of no other way to save his favorite child. Meekly obedient for once, the young novice sets off, accompanied by her half-sister María and the affectionate, loyal Juana, to endure three months of violent purges and other outlandish remedies at the hands of the *curandera*. Never mind, she's deep in Osuna's *Third Spiritual Alphabet*, the book her uncle gave her; searching for union with the Spouse, regardless.

Now, this prayer of quiet might last only the space of a Hail Mary, but from the lofty summit of her twenty-three years, when body and soul attain the state of grace, the young woman feels she has "the world at her feet." It seems to her that the yearning for perfect love is all that can lift her above the pestiliential stuff of human flesh; the stinking cloaca of the cancer-ridden nun, the puffy, flaccid, rotten female body.

Bones, bones alone have the dignity of hardness. Teresa enjoys the sensation of a hardening soul, it's just that the body doesn't follow suit. Or not yet. Her body is always going soft, and only stiffens as a preamble to collapsing senseless. The Lord has granted women one hardness, the hardness of bones. And even then, women can only appreciate them if they're thin, as a result of fasting, perhaps. One can't really feel *that* except through pain. Or by throwing up, which is simply a way of provoking pain in the deepest part of one. A way of emptying the belly, wringing it out, annulling it.

At Becedas church, a young priest catches Teresa's eye. Mental prayer is voiceless; it stokes the desire for love, but keeps it encysted inside. Teresa's body wants to be heard, it wants to empty its love-need into the ears of a man, a man of faith, of good faith: a man of God. Let voice break free of sickly flesh and climb to the heights of perfect love! How else to escape from her aching guts, as though tied by her own hand to those of the dying nun, which the healer was helpless to pacify? On the contrary, these viscera threaten to drag her into the female hell, into death. Teresa is overpowered by a sudden certainty: in order to escape the vicious circle of doomed womanhood, she must absolutely take this young priest as her confessor. It is a shining imperative.

"Of excellent intelligence and social status . . . learned, although not greatly so,"[26] the cleric in question is defenseless against the onslaught and soon falls for his penitent. Teresa, immersed in her quest for God as a bulwark against "noxious forms of recreation" (as she called them bitterly in 1560), against "mischiefs" and "frivolous pleasures" and her own palpitating body, talks to him of nothing but the Other. Her candid inebriation naturally fires him up still more, as she can't but notice, later explaining shrewdly: "I believe that all men must be more friendly toward women who they see are inclined toward virtue. And this is the means whereby women ought to gain more of what they are seeking from men . . ."[27]

The protagonists of their amorous skirmish swap roles along the way. When he begins to have feelings, he confesses them to the young woman, who finds his bashfulness increasingly seductive. Until the day this nameless man, this anonymous protagonist, makes a clean breast of his predicament: "I've maintained illicit relations with a woman for the last seven years, and yet I continue to say Mass."

Teresa pounces on the opportunity to get even closer to the unfortunate sinner. After all, remaining true to an errant friend is a virtue. Excitement mounts to fever pitch: the misdeed arouses as much desire as compassion, and the existence of a rival peps up the love potion with an acid tang of Mother, that first competitor for the father's love.

"What's he like, how does he live?" Thoroughly tantalized by the young priest, Teresa is becoming nosy; she grills the servants.

"Who'd have thought it, Sister!" Conchita the housekeeper, full of false prudery, does not hold out for long. "That woman has him in her clutches thanks to some charms she's put in a little copper amulet. The poor possessed creature wears the trinket around his neck, for love, and no one has been able to get it off him."

Teresa needs no more encouragement to turn herself into a Good Samaritan for her confessor, who is clearly under the devil's thumb:

> I used to speak with him very often about God. This must have profited him, although I rather believe that it prompted him *to love me greatly*. [Note that our therapist is not unaware of the deep springs of her spiritual magic: a matter of "love" and "pleasure."] For in order to *please* me, he finally gave me the little idol, which I then threw in a river. Once he got rid of this, he began—like someone awakening from a deep sleep—to recall everything he had done during those years. . . . Finally, he stopped seeing this woman entirely . . . Exactly one year from the first day I met him, he died.[28]

Here is one love affair whose terminal denouement would seem to affect only one of the partners, the hapless priest! We would be wrong to think so, because Teresa is not immune to these conflictive passions herself. Her seizures and ailments return with a vengeance, punctuated by further dangerous liaisons.

⋆ ⋆ ⋆

The Carmelite's body now turns into a veritable battlefield. Her impetuous desires clash constantly with her equally violent brakes on them. She wants to belong to a man . . . brother Rodrigo, cousin Pedro, don Alonso, don Pedro, a visitor here, a cleric there . . . she wants to yield to the tenderness of María de Briceño or Juana Suárez. Nothing doing, her defenses are unbreachable, everything—such as it is—will be resisted, honor will be preserved! That's don Alonso's first priority, isn't it, as well as the wish of doña Beatriz, still being beamed down from the Beyond . . . Carnal pleasure debases us, sex is dirty, like any other vital impulse: we must punish our lips, our skin, our loins, we must pull back ever deeper into the soul, cleansed to God's satisfaction by edifying texts. There, in that innermost self, reconciled with the Other, all is order and purity, luxury, calm, and chastity.* [*A variation on Baudelaire's lines in "L'Invitation au voyage": Là, tout n'est qu'ordre et beauté, / Luxe, calme et volupté.—Trans.] Teresa tries her best to lock herself into it, sobbing, sickened. But powerful as the prohibition may be, loudly as the voice of honor growls from above, and scrupulously as the vigilant conscience complies with the diktats of propriety, still the smothered drive sends its waves coursing through every fiber of her unhappy being. Hence another seizure, and another, in full view of both the sisters and the Lord.

The spasm grips her like the messenger of some secret, shameful pleasure, vibrating under the burning spear of a horseman, a double, an extraterrestrial, an angel, a Master. It starts with a helpless shuddering, the wringing of every muscle. It ends with a coma—a melancholy rerun of that osmosis with the lifeless mother's lifeless womb. Teresa doesn't want to get over her mother, she doesn't think about her at all, not any more, for mother inhabits her smarting skin, her rigid body, her frozen blood, even the quivering chassis of her bones. The only corpse is hers, Teresa's—the daughter who will never be a fertile woman, anything but that.

Given "the nothingness of all things," there's nobody to love and one is neutralized: there's no sense, no sensation. But the refusal of life still constitutes a vital protest, combating refusal itself with an explosion of destructiveness. Impeded desire mutates into an electric discharge—vomiting, stiffening, paralysis, disconnection, annihilation of the flesh and the spirit. Thus provoked, Nothingness is a resistance, the only possible resistance to the death of desire, itself desired. Or rather to the death of desire imposed, and consented to, in the name of the *point of honor*, which purports to lead you to the name of God.

★ ★ ★

You know your way around that point of honor so well, Teresa, my love, that you always push it a step further, eager to make it stricter and more demanding! Not content with blaming it for all your ills—epilepsies, comas, pathologies, desires and counterdesires, all umbilically linked to that merciless point of honor—you up the ante, you want more, and more! Combating the superego, that frenzied ideal, with an excess of perfection, at last you will enjoy those conflicts, always the same, which it will command for you throughout your life; they will grow milder with time and age, less a matter of *honor* and more simply *pleasant*. As the years go by you break in your Commander bit by bit, you put yourself in His place, you understand Him and He understands you better all the time. His tyranny begins to soften, to feel increasingly familiar and salutary. You will be reassured by an Other who is not stern and judgmental, but kind and fair; an Other who loves you, His cherished spouse, who prays and writes for Him alone . . . But we have not got there yet. Just now the point of honor is making you ill, my Teresa of anguish and pain.

> The Lord comes to the soul if we make the effort and *strive to give up our rights* in many matters.[29]
>
> God deliver us from persons who are concerned about honor while trying to serve Him. Consider it an evil gain, and, as I said, *honor is itself lost by desiring it*, especially in matters of rank. For there is no toxin in the world that kills perfection as do these things.[30]

In one of those portraits you like to sketch of "certain souls," you are highly critical of "one lady" whose great defect is the fuss she makes over points of honor behind a façade of humble piety. Knowing how censorious you are of your own frailties on that score, I wonder whether the lady with the neurosis about honor might not have something in common with the author of the below lines, who is perhaps taking a swipe at herself:

> I shall tell you about one lady in particular, for it is not long ago that I spoke with her in a special way. She was very fond of receiving Communion frequently . . . [and] experienced devotion in her prayer . . . She had never married, nor was she now at an age in which she could . . . it seemed to me that [all these virtues] were effects of a very advanced soul and of deep prayer. . . .
>
> After getting to know her I began to understand that all was peaceful as long as her self-interest was not affected. . . . I learned that although she would suffer all the things that were said against her, she would not tolerate anything said against her reputation even in *some tiny point concerning her honor* or the esteem she thought was her due. She was so overcome by this misery, so eager to know everything that was said against these and so fond of her comfort that I was amazed how such a person could spend even an hour alone.[31]

With matchless aplomb, aren't you caricaturing here your own "hysterical narcissism," to borrow dear old Jérôme Tristan's pet term? It's a failing you confess to throughout your writings: the "excessive pains about cleanliness" you took when young,[32] the hunger for gossip and society ("This [frivolous] relative was the one I liked to associate with"), the concern with "the honor of the world,"[33] and the "calculation" that leads some to seek out honor, not realizing that if it exists at all it is granted by others, and besides, "honor is itself lost by desiring it."

* * *

Another anonymous suitor, identified only as "a person" who visited the monastery, "distracted" her more than anybody before him, and offered a friendship of which she was, while it lasted, "extremely fond."[34] Might the mystery companion have been Francisco de Guzmán, the eligible eldest son of a wealthy, aristocratic Castilian family? Her enjoyment feeling incompatible, once again, with the exigencies of honor, Teresa derived as much pain from this friendship as fun, despite certain associates "with great importunity assuring me that it was not wrong to see such a person." That's all very well, but how was such a perfectionist to cope with compromise?

At this point, Teresa, you experienced—for the first time?—a kind of seeing that is not owed to bodily eyes but to those of the soul, as you recalled twenty-six

years later. Caught between fright and pleasure—halfway between your excitement in the person's presence and your shame at infringing the paternal and
religious interdict—the young woman that you were abruptly "saw." With scientific exactitude, the writer of 1562–1565 details the nature of this vision and
describes the two forms it took: the semblance of Christ and a toad.

> With great severity, Christ appeared before me, making me understand what He
> regretted about the friendship. I saw Him *with the eyes of my soul* more clearly
> than I could have with the eyes of my body. And this vision left such an impres-
> sion on me that, though more than twenty-six years have gone by, it seems to me
> it is still present. I was left very frightened and disturbed, and didn't want to see
> that person any more.[35]

But then you doubted what you had seen, Teresa, for you were a rational
woman, even if tempted by "noxious recreations." "It did me much harm not to
know that it was possible to see in other ways than with the bodily eyes." Had
it been an illusion, a chimera conjured up by the devil? "Although the feeling
always remained with me that it was from God and not a fancy," you hesitated:
"I did not dare speak about this with anyone."
   Truth to tell, your early "visions" were not exclusively of the Holy Countenance. A coarser brand of "character" also featured: the toad, for example.

> Once at another time, when with this same person, we saw coming toward us—
> and others who were there also saw it—something that looked like a large toad,
> moving much more quickly than toads usually do. In that part where it came
> from I cannot understand how there could have been a nasty little creature like
> that in the middle of the day, nor had there ever been one there before. The effect
> it had on me, it seems to me, was not without mystery; and neither did I ever
> forget this. Oh, the greatness of God! With how much care and pity You were
> warning me in every way, and how little it benefited me![36]

Note that the writer does not attribute the toad to a vision; she says merely
that "we saw" it, "we" being the couple she formed with her visitor and the
others who were there. But she has the integrity to point out that no specimen
of that size had ever been sighted before and that this abject apparition was
without doubt a warning from God. The toad as the obverse, the other face in
some sense, of Christ's forbidding countenance as He appeared to her earlier?

Heads or tails: divine wrath and foul toad, prohibition and sex. The first visions related to us by Teresa crystallize at the intersection of her desire for the masculine body and her shame at falling short of the inevitable "point of honor." She will have to banish guilt and secure her right to pleasure within a new construction, of which she will be the author if not altogether the inventor, since admittedly its inspiration lies in the Gospels.

* * *

Logically, necessarily, Teresa attempted to detach herself from these sinful attractions by becoming a devotee of the chaste adoptive father of her Beloved, Saint Joseph. The first discalced convent she founded, in Avila, was named for Saint Joseph and was followed by several more with the same patron.

> I took for my advocate and lord the glorious Saint Joseph and earnestly recom-
> mended myself to him. . . . For since bearing the title of father, being the Lord's
> tutor [subtext: this father is not a progenitor], Joseph could give the Child com-
> mand. . . . I don't know how one can think of the Queen of Angels and about all
> she went through with the Infant Jesus without giving thanks to Saint Joseph
> for the good assistance he then provided them both with. . . . He being who he is
> brought it about that I could rise and walk and not be crippled.[37]

"Being who he is"—an ideal father, removed from sexual commerce—allows Saint Joseph to be the missing link in the chain of don Alonso–don Pedro–Francisco de Osuna, leading to the creation of a sublimated vision of the loving father according to Teresa. He soothes the desire-ravaged body and quells its symptoms: Teresa finds she can walk again.

The cult of Saint Joseph pervades the first pages of the *Life*, which tell how the novice effects a rapprochement with her own father via religion, a development parallel to the process whereby her erotic temptations and reactive health crises gradually give way before the emergent vision of an optimal father figure, at once sublimated (in Saint Joseph) and sensuous (in prayer as prescribed by Osuna). At that stage of the journey, her spiritual road will be to accept that a Father exists who neither judges nor desires her but is pleased to "adopt" her as she is, in all her love-starved, dolorous interiority—so much so that He acqui-esces to her womanly passion for Him, thus releasing her from infatuation with attractive "persons" and from the concomitant dread of toads. This road will be a long one, and its stages will often need to be retraveled. Just now, however, battered by the physical and erotic storm, she hasn't yet found the path, and her "visions" will be the occasion of hellish ordeals for some time to come.

* * *

How long had death been making its slow way in you, Teresa? Since your father's lawsuit, with its diffuse threat of obliteration, the inevitable Marrano sacrifice? You met and desired death as a child, before trying to run away to be beheaded by the Moors; your encounter was more intimate when it came to the loss of your mother, Beatriz. After that you resolved to die to the world, by cloistering yourself in the Convent of the Incarnation. Your father's death in 1543, a passing prepared by his induction into prayer, sounded the final knell.

Other events modulated your withdrawal and your rejection of the family. María, the offspring of your father's first marriage, and her husband Martín Guzmán de Barrientos attempted to sue the executor of don Alonso's estate; you squabbled over rings and bracelets, even over the parental bed, in between vitriolic arguments about your parents' respective characters. The family hearth was left deserted: Lorenzo and Jerónimo departed for the antipodes in 1540, followed by Pedro and Antonio after Alonso's death. "I am a daughter of the Church," you would announce on your deathbed, in a statement that is, as I have suggested, only apparently banal. I do not only read it as the ultimate assertion of your monastic condition. Not even as a "refusal of origins," because the modern concept of "origins" was not in your habits of thought and you had no need to allay the meaninglessness of life by a wager on the "nature" or the "history" that preceded you: in your day those forces were in gestation, they had not yet supplanted "fate."

From that fateful day at Uncle Pedro's, which decided you to take the veil, and through the first years of your novitiate, you plowed a singular furrow of your own: both submissive and recalcitrant toward both origins and institutions. A reformer within. You needed His Majesty, the God-man proposed by Christianity. Your longing for an ideal Father found echoes in evangelical and biblical texts, and was informed by new dissident movements as much as by the teachings of the Church. You appropriated all these, just as His Majesty became yours: He was part of you, you took part in Him. The wandering continued, but in new forms, centered on the ideal Father: a Father who was ever more loving, protective, absorbed, resorbed . . .

Chapter 10

THE IDEAL FATHER AND THE HOST

There's no need to move the hand or raise it—I'm referring to reflection—
for anything, for the Lord gives from the apple tree (to which [the soul]
compares her Beloved) the fruit already cut, cooked, and even chewed.

Teresa of Avila, *Meditations on the Song of Songs*

Teresa was not averse to self-mortification; but she would not be like
those nuns of old, light-headed with fasting and pain, or like the teen-
agers of today who puncture their skin with nails and needles for the
scary thrill of the forbidden. Teresa was not the sort of hysteric who deprives
herself of feeling in order to avoid the agony of eternally unsatisfied desires. She
certainly knew phobic moments of frozen affect, withdrawal from the world,
nausea. But these alternated with hypersensitivity, and heightened perceptions
craving words, from which she managed to extract formulations as poised and
accurate as they were profuse.

She sought this rendering fiction, this verbal sap, in continual dialogue with
her confessors. They struggled to keep pace with her at times, they flagged,
they let her down; but they were the ones who urged her to write, the better
to explain herself. If the Dominican friar Pedro Ibáñez reckoned she should
commit her life to paper, that's what she would do. After a quarter century of
convent life, Teresa embarked on a first draft of *The Book of Her Life*.

Living in the bosom of the vast Cepeda y Ahumada tribe, she sensed early on
that desires, helplessly intense because reciprocated, are condemned to remain
unfulfilled in the game of supply and demand. Onto this incestuous trunk was

grafted the insecurity of her converso ancestry. But it was the fervor of Christ's message that activated the magnetism of the Word upon which that attraction in turn depended. In a sixteenth-century Spanish family mixing converts with Old Christians, utterance and writing were the ultimate bonds of a communication in which ineluctably lethal passions might take refuge, find clarification, and be relieved. Teresa's lovesickness did not stop her embracing the dogma shared by her parents: if the Word was made flesh in Christ, it continued to be made flesh, or truth, in the everyday stuff of conversations whose inescapable falsehood or contentiousness endowed them with relentless immediacy. Teresa deftly conveys early on the importance of the truthfulness that makes for intimate unions and underpins familial desire: "My father *believed* [me when I said: *me creyó*] that my illnesses were the reason for my not praying; for *he did not lie*, and by this time, in accord with the things I spoke of to him, *I shouldn't have lied either.*"[1]

* * *

It's springtime, a season for mellow dumbness and living life for its own sake; Jérôme Tristan is courting me, in his own peculiar way. My learned colleague tirelessly documents and enlightens me as to how he, at any rate, would tackle the subject of my saint. Last night, as we were coming out of a Psychology Society meeting, he lectured me as follows:

"As you are no doubt aware, dear girl, psychiatry has a word for hysterics who are emotionally unresponsive due to their inability to interpret their own feelings: we call them alexithymics. Their perceptions are conveyed by the senses and received by centers in the brain, as usual—there's no neurological deficiency associated with this disorder—but the perceiving subject refuses to 'read,' if you will, the neuronal signals, and to create the psychical representation of them which normally forms the grounding of self-awareness and is the precondition for language. Isn't that so, Sylvia?"

Oh well, I'll walk him to his car, parked miles away, just to stretch my legs. As we stroll along the railings of the Luxembourg Gardens I am entranced by the horse chestnut candles and the sound of bees reveling in the pleasure of a job well done. We kiss goodbye next to the Observatoire. Drunk on the notion of alexithymia I dash for home, deep in cogitation, blind to the parade of automobiles, traffic lights, and bright, bare shop windows.

* * *

By excluding the spoken word, Teresa's mental prayer may well have fostered the development of alexithymic states and even triggered the fits that plagued her during the first years of her novitiate; and yet her culture, education, temperament, and genius conspired to rebel against this verbal anesthesia. I am impatient to put Jérôme straight, and present him with the paradox that Teresa was actually *hyperlexithymic*. For not only was she a virtuoso at "reading" the least shiver of feeling and perception, she also registered in body and mind the cleavage (word vs. drive, language vs. affect, the verbal vs. the carnal) first displayed outrageously, inspiringly, by Christ—whose death and resurrection unfolded in and through the Word.

"And the Word was made flesh" (John 1:14). In her groundbreaking, personal way, Teresa recognizes herself in Christ's incarnation and resurrection and appropriates them, using them as a template and retracing their stations in her fiction. Following in Christ's wake, from the starting point of her family history and within the critical limits of her physiology, she rediscovers willy-nilly how intrinsic to the human condition is the capacity for representation-sublimation-idealization, and how perpetually under threat. Then she takes on board, illustrating it in her own impassioned way, the biblical and evangelical intuition to the effect that humanization—understood as the ability, always in jeopardy, to make meaning—depends on the celebration of an ideal Father.

I don't suppose Jérôme will be following me down that road.

And yet he knows that Freud traced the "construction" of that ideal Father, Father of the Law or loving Father (the model was constantly being refined by the Viennese thinker) to the "prehistoric fable" of the murder of the father by his sons, the brothers of the primal horde. Only because they have killed him can they found a society in the name of his law. The ideal Father is the recto of the verso that is the dead Father. This fable expresses an anthropological truth that is confirmed by what we hear from our patients, right, Jérôme? Broadly speaking, Freud invites us to accept that the Bible and the Gospels reveal the truth of the psychic workings of countless generations of *Homo sapiens* for the last hundred thousand years. To acknowledge this truth might help us, Freud thought, not perhaps to believe in the ideal Father or to delegate ourselves in Him, but to make a go of reuniting words and drives with a view to moderating the latter and speaking more truth, indefinitely speaking.

Now, could this human-specific capacity for making sense "in the name of the Father" be on the wane, not to say on the way out? My learned colleague would certainly concur with me on that. If Dr. Tristan has a fault it would be to overdo the Lacan, working back from the *Seminars* to that "seminal essay," as he calls it, "'Family Complexes in Pathology,' from 1938, Sylvia dear, do you know it? Bang in the middle of the rise of Nazism comes a text that emphasizes the determinism of psychosis as found in the failure of fathers, and hence mothers, to stick to their roles. Do you follow my gist?" (He's asking *me*?)

Either way, many contemporary scholars—philosophers, anthropologists, and psychoanalysts, not forgetting the feminists whom he finds so annoying, including Aude, his therapist wife—are currently trying to work out the constructions-deconstructions of the paternal function by following the path of "eternal recurrence" toward myths, beliefs, and mystical experiences. They are interested in the maternal function, too, but that's a different and rather trickier story.

Teresa of Avila contributes to this research with her own experiments in faithful infidelity to the dogma of the ideal Father; her testimony enables us to measure its necessity and probe its impasses, while opening up dizzy vistas of its overcoming, of freedom. So, what is an ideal Father?

I have been following his emergence in Teresa's autobiography, observing the way family and personal vagaries combined with the dogmas of faith. The ideal Father is one who refrains from enjoying his children (in the sexual sense of *jouissance*), just as he refrains from sacrificing them, in order for frustrated desire (his and theirs) to metamorphose into a capacity for imagining and thinking. This myth goes back to Isaac's aborted sacrifice at the hands of Abraham, and culminates in Christ's Calvary on Golgotha, abandoned by his Father, before rising from the dead to sit at His right hand in Heaven; it rests on a complex perlaboration of Father–Son desire. First, this desire must be conceived as susceptible of deferral: it must be frustrated, suspended, forbidden, and yet sustained, indeed fueled. A late flutter of the amorous imaginary attributes this original suspension of desire to the Father Himself: unlike animal progenitors, this Father is already a Subject who cares about his offspring's future and the quality of relationships among them. Freud tracks the formation of this figure through the mutations of the "father of the primal horde," the sexual tyrant and omnipotent killer who, once dispatched by that band of brothers, his sons, is gradually transformed into a symbolic authority that no longer threatens but protects bonds that become, by the same token, cultural bonds.

★ ★ ★

At this point of my private novel, Dr. Marianne Baruch objects that this fanciful construction, invented by the celebrated founder of my discipline and updated by me with the help of Jérôme Tristan (not that she knows the last bit, she's jealous enough already), which I'm running past her as a distraction from the rather tiresome routine of the MPH, simply adds to the myths she's out to demystify.

"Look, Freud tells a story that repeats the story that certain anthropologists and psychologists got out of this or that myth. These days, they don't even agree among themselves about the dead Father. It's what you call the 'unconscious.' Whatever! Except nothing like that ever comes up on my MRIs. Scientifically speaking, I'm afraid all your precious Freud discovered was the power of fiction. People tell each other fictions and it makes them feel better, period." Marianne shoots me a commiserating glance; she doesn't want to lose me.

She's had to postpone her Spanish trip by a month. Hardly surprising. Director Toutbon was never going to let her waltz off just like that, on a whim, with no notice. "Where's your sense of responsibility? What about your patients?" Poor Marianne, the one time she had something other than the office on her mind! Disgraceful! But let that go, we'll deal with it later.

So, our house psychiatrist reckons I've been snared by a fantasy, Freud's and mine. She's not wrong.

"A fantasy? And why not? Because fantasies *think*, like dreams think; and their thinking—which is not the same as reasoning—uncovers emotional truths that are opaque to reason." I'd ask her to lie on the couch and try it out, but I'd be wasting my time.

Marianne makes a face. But, pill-pusher though she is, she can't entirely fend off what she calls "your goddam psyche-schmyche stuff," and lets me carry on. Why, the august Doctor may even be lending an ear.

"I'd go further," I tell her. "What if the fantasy of the ideal Father wasn't just a story, a fiction, a fantasy as you say, but the prototype of *every* fantasy?"

Or maybe she isn't listening after all, just pretending. That business about her father, now there's a story . . . Will she be able to understand, being so tied into her love-hate for dear Daddy, who'd wanted a boy? Too bad, on we go. The ideal Father *is* the fantasy, I say, being a gendered representation that rises above sexuality: he is a "father," and so a progenitor, but "ideal" because defined by his symbolic function. A crossroads figure that stands between desire and meaning, passion and thought. By "fantasizing" over the "ideal Father" I've reached the same crux, the origin of imagination and thought.

Marianne stops teasing. She's paying attention, for once. This ideal Father who spurs us to imagine and think, is he a sublimating father, then, after having been—or while still being—a procreative one? (I wonder if my crazy notions are initiating her into psychoanalysis. Unlikely. But she's storing them up for her trip with Haïm, for sure!) He's a "dead" father in the fathering sense, because having "lived" by begetting, he is now forced to find himself a new purpose, to be reborn, this time in a symbolic role: that of laying down the Law, forbidding what lies outside it, making us think in our turn. So, if we need the father who defers his desires in order to speak-imagine-think, it follows that for us—speaking-imagining-thinking beings—there can be no other father but the dead Father? I pause, to give Marianne a breathing space: her convoluted backstory with Aimé-Haïm, added to my talk of ideal Fathers who are, for good measure, dead, have shaken her. She is about to say something. But her pager goes off: a resident is having a fit.

I carry on with my novel in my head—accompanied by my roommate, naturally. The paperwork can wait: Paul is on an outing, and Élise is staying with her dismal father. I've got time.

* * *

The price of this fantasy of the ideal Father as dead Father can only be anguish. If, before and after becoming the *I* of cogitation, *I* is a *fantasizing* subject, and if *I* fantasize the ideal and/or dead Father, this means that I am owed at once to a desire and its frustration, a begetting and a sublimation together. How am I to keep my equilibrium over this foundational imbalance, this trial, this Cross?

Christianity leads the subject into this anguish as its own special truth, it fans and embeds it. Woven into the very structure of the desire for meaning, Christianity is the paradise of neurosis, lined with hopes for its appeasement. *It* will be sorted out in the fullness of time, for ever and ever, amen! With neurosis aplenty for eternity and beyond, Christianity is in no hurry. Especially as it is not satisfied with perpetuating anguish: it illuminates it. A procession of apostles, saints, martyrs, and mystics have mapped the highways and byways of love unto death. In these explorations of the heavens and hells of desire, anthropologists and psychoanalysts were quick to pick up that anguish is the compulsory tribute exacted by the very activity of fantasizing, in other words the imaginary buttressed by desire. You can dispense with the fantasy of the ideal Father and/ or the dead Father, you can stop fantasizing, but you will thereby be deprived of the imaginary itself: such is the gist of the message sent down by these observers of the soul's journey toward the Other. You are left to tick over in the realm of calculating, operational thinking. You become superhuman, you start somatizing, or you sign up as a suicide bomber.

Religion as an institution coalesced around the foundational fantasy of the ideal Father, embodied in a wide variety of complex hierarchical "father figures": shamans, wizards, high priests, gurus, monks . . . The Catholics were especially proficient here, leading to a highly centralized papacy with aspirations to universality. By decanting the fantasy of the ideal Father into a class of men (the clergy), Catholicism conducted the paternal function through a doubling or splitting of male sexuality, with consequences that ranged from the glorious to the appalling. On the one hand, the erotic, channeled into human procreation; on the other, an ideal, sublimated fatherhood, steeped in death to self and haloed with eternity.

In so doing the Church authorities entrusted to the "Holy Fathers," the men of God, the task of relieving ordinary men of that impossible and yet essential "paternal function" that presided over our humanization in some remote prehistory, and whose civilizing works are the milestones of history. It did not follow, however, that this exemplary figuration of the ideal Father exempted the mass of the profane from the effort required by civilization to shoulder, willingly or otherwise, this impossible, symbolic "paternal function" at the same time as carrying out the everyday chore of biological paternity.

With regard to the female religious state, where it exists (as in Christianity), it is predicated on the same sublimated renunciations as the male, with an added prohibition against acceding to higher office, the latter reserved for the paternal function. However, although treated as secondary, "spiritual maternity" does not appear, any more than the "maternal function," to differ in specific ways from the "spiritual paternity" of the ideal Father. In fact, nuns are expected to turn themselves into homologues of this ideal paternity. Thus Teresa can be "the most virile of monks" without forfeiting her genius for springing very feminine, very personal surprises. But she strains toward the ideal Father, and it is with Him she seeks to be conjoined.

And what has this to do with us? A lot!

* * *

The current crisis of religion, and by extension of the priesthood, affects more than just the various churches and their congregations. Over and above the differences between the faiths espoused by the world's populations early in the third millennium, regardless of bellicosities here or internecine quarrels there, it's the very function of the ideal Father that is in jeopardy, and this can be observed even in the "neutral religions" constituted by the legal, pedagogical, and moral codes of the advanced democracies. The crisis is most patent at the everyday level: we need look no further than the oft-lamented "absent father," now that men neglect their ideal role of head of the family in favor of professional success or the frantic pursuit of women—when they're not risking their lives by having gay sex, or courting jail with an online pedophilia habit.

Such perversions have always existed, but today they impair the fantasy of the ideal Father while undermining the foundations of our societies, magnified by the joint effects of biotechnological progress and social permissiveness. There are reports from every quarter of this multiple collapse of the ideal Father along with his unconscious double, the dead Father. My own position at the MPH forces me to note how, in every single case study, we invariably come up against the same fateful "collapse of the paternal function." Not even my Teresa, I suspect, was altogether untouched by this phenomenon: the "Fathers" often strike her as inadequate to their task! Her solution was to look to her Spouse. And I presently feel great admiration to see how my wanderer relied on the One who did preserve the function of the ideal Father, by restricting Himself to the sublimated version of paternal desire.

* * *

When Jesus was born, miraculously, from a virgin womb, when He performed miracles by the sole power of His Word, when He died only to be resurrected by the intercession of the Spirit in order to sit at His Father's right hand, what was He saying? *There is but one desire that counts, the desire for the name, for the representation of meaning.* The intensity of this desire can and must be such that it merges with itself by renaming and representing itself: *to desire* will be *to name, to represent.* That is enough to revive us body and soul, or I should say for us to be reborn or resurrected, since our carnal appetites are not sacrificed so much as relayed by their representations. Are they thus mastered, or empowered? *Mysterium fidei*, from which the Church draws its strength. Writers know this: they experience it every time a new poem or novel endows them with a new body. I can't convey this insight to Marianne, too great a leap for her.

Reading Teresa, I perceive Christianity—particularly in its apotheosis of Catholic monastic life—as the stimulation and simultaneous thwarting of infantile desires for the father, which must be compensated by being displaced, but to where? Marianne is definitely listening now. Teresa herself would back me up here, since throughout her writings she practices her faith as a source of anguish, ordained, continually fueled, and indefinitely allayed.

The neurotic can only bear this chiasmus between desire and sublimated creativity by escaping into the symptom: the chasuble of faith hides a host of psychosomatic disorders. Is there any way out? There may be, for the mystic of either sex who strives to identify with the supposed *jouissance* of the ideal Father, rather than with his function; a *jouissance* that fantasy locates at the junction of flesh and word. Mystics intuit that the same *jouissance* is universally accessible if—and only if—we experience it as the desire for representation-verbalization-sublimation. They are ready to mortify their bodies with artful refinements of masochism in hopes of deadening the sexual drive and attaining the purity of the ideal Father, while unconsciously (and with experience, increasingly consciously) aware that the more they try to deaden it the more the drive flares up, and the greater is the resulting *jouissance*. For their torture places them at the crux where the ideal Father stands, between here and the Beyond, body and spirit, desire and meaning.

It's true, Marianne, I promise, Teresa soon realized that mortification doesn't still the flesh: the excess of penitence is demonic. She wound it down, though without stopping completely, and warned her sisters away from it, as well as John of the Cross; I'll tell you about that later.

* * *

The experience reconstructed by Teresa's works amounts to a laboratory of masochism and sadism, of which the nun herself became rapidly aware. Might the devil not have a hand in these thrilling blends of arousal and pain? The answer is found as early as *The Book of Her Life*. Provided one maintains the humility of the link with God, demonic delights (by which are meant sexual or worldly ones) devolve back to Him:

> If the quiet is from the devil, I think an experienced soul will recognize this because it results in disturbance . . . And if it is *a humble soul and not inquisitive or concerned about delights, even though they be spiritual,* but a friend of the Cross, it will pay little attention to the consolation given by the devil. . . . Anything the devil gives is like himself; a total lie. When the devil sees that in this consolation the soul *humbles* itself (for in this experience it must have much humility, as in all matters of prayer), *he will not return often,* because he sees his loss.[2]

If we don't give them weapons against us, do devils truly exist? Demonic desires lurk within: "How frightened these devils make us because we want to be frightened through other attachments to honors, property, and delights! . . . For we make them fight against us with our very own weapons, handing over to them what we need for our own defense. This is a great pity";[3] for it is considerably harder to project the light of the Spouse into the interior castle. Pain must be "delightful" when sent by God, hateful and "melancholy" when it's the devil's work. But how do we distinguish? God's "favor" brings a sense of joy and repose, emanating from a "region other" than the "outside" of our being, the devil's domain. It is furthermore girded with "determination" and impressed with certainty, poles apart from any illusory "fancies."

> You may wonder why greater security is present in this favor [the gift of "delightful pain"] than in other things. In my opinion, these are the reasons: First, *the devil never gives delightful pain like this.* He can give the savor and delight that seem to be spiritual, but *he doesn't have the power to join pain—and so much of it—to the spiritual quiet and delight of the soul* [*mas juntar pena, y tanta, con quietud y gusto del alma, no es de su facultad*]. For all of his powers are on the *outside,* and the pains he causes are never, in my opinion, delightful or peaceful, but disturbing and contentious. Second, *this delightful tempest comes from a region other than those regions of which he can be lord.* Third, the favor brings *wonderful benefits* to the soul . . .
>
> That *this favor is no fancy* is very clear. Although at other times the soul may strive to experience this favor, it will not be able to counterfeit one. . . . *There's no basis for thinking it is caused by melancholy,* because melancholy does not produce or fabricate its fancies save in the imagination. This favor proceeds from the interior part of the soul.[4]

However, it is not always easy to tell the gifts of God from the tricks of the devil. Albeit divine grace appears greater, "it can be more dangerous, and therefore I shall pause a little to consider it." For God's word is multiform: "There are many kinds of locutions given to the soul. Some seem to come from outside oneself; others, from deep within the interior part of the soul; others, from the superior part; and some are so exterior that they come through the sense of hearing, for it seems there is a spoken word."[5]

How patiently you dissect yourself, Teresa, my love, along the road undertaken in the name of the Father!

* * *

Marianne has administered an injection to the patient in crisis; he's asleep now, and she's back in my office. She settles quietly into the easy chair, lighting a cigarette, a habit she knows I hate. She just wants my company, and lets me read in peace. I look up, leave her in her anxiety, pick up my own train of thought.

"The thing is, Marianne, Teresa gets as far as saying that only God is able to link the greatest suffering with the greatest joy and restfulness of the soul! She says that *that* can only come from God, not from the devil, because—and I'll try to keep this short, but it's major, just you wait—it is restful and does one good, in other words, it's true to the teaching of the ideal Father. I mean, you wouldn't expect such beneficial results from the devil, would you? This splendid reasoning, along with the experience you and I have had with our residents and other patients, authorizes me, in turn, to affirm that Christian mysticism feeds on perversion.* [*Spelled in the original as *père-version*, father-version.— Trans.] Calm down, bear with me, I know I'm repeating myself but I want to be clear. What I mean is that Christian mysticism is hard-wired for perversion, it depends on it, colluding with the father's arousal as well as with his frustration of the child. Hardly exclusive to mysticism, did you say? Absolutely not, that's why I find it so interesting. So we're on the same wavelength after all! Now, mysticism pretty well exhausts the perversion or father-version by elevating it into an entirely imaginatory-meditatory-elucidatory pleasure. The 'way of perfection'—a perfect image in itself, isn't it?—when it leaves the fantasy of the ideal Father behind, can lead to the borders of atheism. Meister Eckhart asked God to make him 'free of God,' and Teresa says 'My Sisters, you have the power to checkmate God.' On the way to perfection, the mystic is the custodian both of the ideal Father and of the possibility of representing the father-version. Conversely, any thought that has broken with its fantastic foundations and their prototype, the fantasy of the ideal Father as a dead Father, is devoid of imagination, right? It's been severed from its roots in the pleasure of words and the turmoil of desire. You know what? Such a de-imaginarized thinking may be fine for managing basic needs, but useless for desire. Mysticism testifies to the strenuous efforts of our civilization to keep hold of the ability to think, even if that way lies madness. Just look at Teresa's amazing journey from Alonso to Pedro to Osuna, right up to that fabulous 'checkmate'! She wrote that, you know, but she cut it from the authorized version in the end."

Marianne is dumbfounded by this avalanche of assertion, which has surprised me not a little myself. She doesn't say anything, so I go on.

"I know what you're thinking." She loathes that expression but I can't help it, I'm getting carried away. "You're wondering, and you're right, about the equivalent mother-version that must shadow this journey toward the Father. You think I'm keeping mum about the mother-version perversion, because there's a problem with it? Hold your horses. The furrows of that backcountry are even more hidden, more pungent, more dangerously authoritative and also, as it happens, more cheerful."

Marianne crushes her cigarette in the saucer of my teacup (that *really* annoys me), lightly kisses the top of my head, and walks out. She's done for the day; I, on the other hand, am staying all night on call at the home. Alone at last, with Teresa!

⋆ ⋆ ⋆

The Host is the one thing that can soothe the Carmelite's commotions. The thin flake of unleavened bread is bland and tasteless, without nourishment, like a film placed between tongue and appetite. It tantalizes as if to trigger famished dreams of invisible presences, stealthy caresses, a feathery touch deep inside. Teresa likes her wafers large, the better to bait her hunger, to tease and subdue it. She parts her lips with glee to feel the brittle disc dissolve on her tongue without sticking to the dome of the palate. There's nothing plump or maternal about it, nothing that smacks of nipple. Nothing feminine or pampered, no resemblance to meat or cake or cherries. A presence of nothing. The host is a sliver on the way to being a spirit, a substance that fades away to regale you with the taste of absence . . . no, to make you swallow the presence of an immaterial reality made of words, images, dreams. It produces the gustatory certainty (that most intimate and singular of certainties) of the way this world of voracious bodies and coarse gobbling creatures is in contact with a different place: an invisible, frustrating world and the more exciting for it, abuzz with daydreams, thoughts, silences, nothings. A far-off world where you are free to roam, not dependent like an infant on its mother, not oppressed by the species' need to eat. This spiritual, eternal world is also the body of a man who was crucified and came back to life. You enter it by way of a wafer, a membrane, a substance that loses all consistency in contact with your tongue.

Teresa swallows this intangible world, gulps it down and takes possession of it. The stranger is inside her now, filling her. Swallowing gives her a clearer sense of what she often confusedly feels, and the wafer now underlines this at the back of her mouth and throat and then in the pit of her stomach. A glorious antibody is housed inside her body. Could it be that one's heart of hearts is nothing but an elusive, fugitive presence? Whether grief or overflowing joy, image or thought, unquiet company. Could this be the Word that refuses to be uttered? A tasty Word at all events, pleasure incurved, incarnate. Is she savoring the source, the unnameable wellspring of every word and fear and wish?

★ ★ ★

"Corpus Christi," murmurs the priest as he places the wafer on her tongue. All of a sudden the cloudy intuition that *I* is an *other*, that burning frontier Teresa has always sensed without being able to put a name to it, the summit where her flesh is elevated into meaning and where meaning rejoins the flesh, acquires the flavor of a cannibalistic feast: so it's the heavenly Father, the Savior whom she is cradling in her mouth! "Whatever you do, don't chew." Teresa is filled by a man's body while holding her appetite in check. If gluttony is a vice, restraint only intensifies the pleasure in her mouth. So long, mother's breast, adieu the cookery of women! The Host links me to the substance of the ideal Man. I absorb a splinter of his hardness, his bones, his suffering, his impregnable Calvary. Do not say "of his sex": I reject such devilish fancies. I consume the anatomy of Absence. I eat my fill of desire for the Impossible. No more absence, no more impossibility, we are together.

As soon as the Eucharist spread through medieval Christendom, the churches began teeming with women. Were they reveling in being fed at last, those women whose life was spent in feeding others? Did the nurturers find their own nurturing mother in the Church? A replacement for the mother they had lost forever, for whom every woman pined with a lifelong nostalgia when she married, or was forced to marry, in order to reproduce; the mother nobody wanted to know about?

The Church is a good mother, Teresa subscribes to that. The Virgin, always in tandem with Saint Joseph, remained a constant patron of the convents she founded. The Lord's male breasts spurt "streams of milk," a fat dry white drop lands on Teresa's tongue: at that moment the thought of doña Beatriz flashes through her mind, and her soul empties out with a curious loneliness.

But already it is not the mother who lies upon the tongue that tastes the spirit of God. What this cannibal appropriates is the gaunt, drained, translucid body of Jesus; He is the one she ingests, the one she digests, who runs through her veins and pierces every cranny of her body like a white-hot spear.[6] That's it: the Host frees Teresa from her mother at last. She doesn't depend on Mama any more, she has no need of maternal sustenance; she only pines for Him. "The Lord almost always showed Himself to me as risen, also when He appeared in the Host."[7] A man's body for sure, a fountain of sperm-milk, an androgynous being equipped with the bountiful breast of the Virgin Mother when the praying woman reaches the holy of holies: "for from those divine breasts . . . flow streams of milk bringing comfort to all the people of the castle."[8]

* * *

In her *Meditations on the Song of Songs*, La Madre addresses the sisters in her recently founded institutions. She imparts to these women the oral side of the love Catholics harbor for the Lord, evoking the succulent imagery of the Song with epicurean relish. Like an anti-Eve blithely biting into the apple and every other fruit, Teresa feels licensed to enjoy them: "All the soul does is taste, without any work on the part of the faculties [aquí todo es gustar sin ningún trabajo de las potencias]."[9] Fully cognizant of the essential orality of the union with this maternally endowed Spouse, the writer celebrates it, and moves with disarming breeziness from the pleasures of suckling to the pleasures of utterance. "Previously, the soul says, it enjoyed sustenance from His divine breasts."[10] Teresa cites the famous first verse, "Let him kiss me with the kisses of his mouth," and goes on: "I confess that the passage has many meanings [interpretations: *entendimientos*]. But the soul . . . desires nothing else than to say these words [desires none of them, but only: *el alma no quiere ninguno, sino decir estas palabras*]."[11] Pleasure of sucking, pleasure of saying: where's the difference? Isn't it one and the same *jouissance*? Teresa is on the path to perfection. Unless it leads rather to . . . psychoanalysis?

She's not there yet; the symbolic assumption of the praying woman implies a strong identification with virility and a denial of the genital phase that replaces the joy of rebirth through the mouth. A veritable parthenogenesis occurs in this oral and verbal self-engendering—through the Eucharist and through the word, never one without the other.

What overflowing *jouissance* it is for the soul to receive this communion! It makes Teresa both a breast-feeding infant and a woman penetrated by the male iron, and what's more it makes her a man, the same as all men! La Madre dislikes any whiff of femaleness, though it might be inescapable in a convent; she would rather see her charges transcend womanhood, doing away with those bleeding or infected wombs that haunted her own life as a novice. "Nor would I want you to be like women but like strong men.[12] For if [women do what lies within: *que si ellas hacen lo que es en sí*], the Lord will make [them] so strong that [they] will astonish men."[13] By the grace of Communion, what lies within is the presence of the Lord, who espouses our entrails. Further, if we in turn are faithful to Him to the point of espousing His Calvary, He will render us so manly that men will be amazed. And why not? If the Lord created us from nothing and bore us into the world of the Spirit like a mother, why should eating His body not turn us into men like Him?

The breast of Beatriz de Ahumada is forgotten, as swiftly glimpsed as it was dispelled by the grace of the Host into the sweet taste of Christ's masculine body. Masculine, yes, but not as other men's bodies are, for the Son of God's is cavernous, like a woman's: passionately wounded, punctured, tortured, and yet resilient, eternal, immortal. Male and female both? Superhuman, resurrected.

★ ★ ★

If she could gobble every one of those wafers, destined for the eager mouths of the nuns queuing behind her, she would. But she doesn't go that far, she aspires only to receive the very largest crumb of divine Body and admits as much to her confessor. The amiable priest always saves the largest, roundest one for her. It's their little secret, it brings them together, although in reality Teresa only communes with the Other. What harm can there be in wanting the biggest part, insatiable as she is for Jesus? It's merely a sign of how greatly her devotion surpasses that of the other nuns. The man of God indulges her.

Only John of the Cross, much later, manifests any objection to the arrangement. In September 1572, Teresa invites her "little Seneca" to become resident confessor at the Convent of the Incarnation. Obsessed with asceticism and self-punishment, when this perfect Father tires of punishing himself he takes it out on Teresa. He shares her zeal for the reform of the order, and yet one day, when at the communion rail he sees those sensuous lips approach, radiant with expectation, instead of rooting out the largest Host—as is customary for this insatiable female—he proffers the first he finds. Then pauses, draws back his hand, breaks the wafer in two, and places a meager half on Teresa's tongue, keeping the other half for the nun behind.

What's come over him? There's no shortage of wafers, is there? John is obviously bent on reprimanding her hedonism, but the rebuke backfires: since Jesus is wholly present in each particle of what exists, how much more must He inhabit the smallest scrap of Host! This is logic enough for Teresa, in whom reason will always be greedier than taste buds. She won't give John the satisfaction of seeing her chastised, let alone allow him to deprive her of pleasure in the tiniest flake of wafer as though it were the largest. So long as she is replenishing herself with the body of the fatherly, motherly Jesus, nothing—within the bounds of discipline and obedience—can spoil her enjoyment.

And in the privacy of her soul the Lord appears, holding out His right hand pierced by a nail: "Don't fear, daughter, for no one will be a party to separating you from Me." How could it be otherwise, since she has just swallowed Him! And what's the puny nail John has tried to drive into her soul, by denying her the best Host, compared to the nail in Jesus's palm? Nothing. No deprivation can ever hurt the Carmelite, for every hurt brings her closer to the One who endured agonies beyond imagination! Every time she takes Communion—and Teresa loves that sacrament, as her father don Alonso had noticed—the Host reconciles her with the ideal Father while allaying her disgust at the maternal-feminine taint.

The teat and its milky streams are henceforth fused with the steely tip of the nail and with the thorn of absence, disgust has mutated into ceaseless hunger, and frustrated voracity into hunger for imagination. Teresa accepts her half of the wafer as yet another token of her osmosis with His double Majesty, father and mother in one. Actually, John of the Cross has given her the opportunity to celebrate her nuptials with Jesus in fine style. The union of the lover with the Beloved is the more unbreakable for being marked by a gash, a thwarting, a lack. John knows this, of course! He cannot fail to read his friend's feelings. With humility, more than ever filled with the Other, La Madre moves imperturbably away, leaving the great spiritual poet to reflect upon sensual Teresa's response to the lash of his rigor. It's not the first time their paths have crossed and diverged, nor will it be the last.

Meanwhile His Majesty soon confirms His approval of the beloved daughter, in these words: "Behold this nail: it is a sign that you will be My bride from today on."[14]

Part 4

Extreme Letters, Extremes of Being

The devil cannot give this experience, because there is so much interior joy in the very intimate part of the soul and so much peace; and all the happiness stirs the soul to the praises of God. . . . St. Francis must have felt this impulse . . . those who at one time listened to [Friar Pedro de Alcántara] thought he was crazy. Oh, what blessed madness, Sisters!

Teresa of Avila, *The Interior Castle*

After all, the patron saint of hysterics, St. Theresa, was a woman of genius with great practical capacity.

Joseph Breuer and Sigmund Freud, *Studies on Hysteria*

Chapter 11

BOMBS AND RAMPARTS

It is foolish [*es desatino*] to think that we will enter heaven
without entering into ourselves, coming to know ourselves . . .

Teresa of Avila, *The Interior Castle*

July 7, 2005. Castile is baking hot. Cracked earth, stony gullies, parched
shimmer of yellow air; a lunar landscape under a sun of fire. Here water
is a saint's dream, a figure of speech. Madrid lies behind us; we're heading
to Avila in a bright-red rental KA from Hertz. I twiddle the dial for the midday news, they're talking about bombs in London: explosions in subway tun-
nels near Aldgate, King's Cross, Edgware Road, and on a double-decker bus
in Tavistock Square. Aldgate is also one of the stations for the area where the
2012 Olympic Village will be built. Is that significant? We speculate about the
number of devices, of casualties, of missing people . . . The Madrid bombings
were just over a year ago. Thirteen bombs, ten of which exploded in three minutes in four suburban trains coming from Alcalá de Henares toward Atocha
station. There were ninety-one fatalities at a scene of twisted, gutted carriages
littered with the dead and injured; Aznar's party lost the elections and the
Spanish troops were pulled from Iraq. Like every tragedy that feeds the global
media machine, there is little sign of it today; only in the sorrowing hearts of
the victims' loved ones. One almost expects Al Qaida cells in Madrid. But in
London! What was Scotland Yard doing? Where was James Bond? Where was
Tony Blair?

"We were braced for it. It wasn't a question of if but of when." My Mexican pal Juan preempts the BBC and other globish media platitudes. Juan lives in London, and knows all there is to know about Spain's Golden Age. Here, his voluble campiness irks the local studs: gas station attendants, waiters, and vendors look daggers at him, and we always get served last. I pretend not to notice.

"The Piccadilly line must be hell. The tunnel's really narrow, you know, it nearly touches the sides of the train. Like hurtling at high speed through the eye of a needle, and in rush hour! To think I was on it the day before yesterday." Andrew's blood drains from his skin whenever something happens. He looks like a snowman in a heat wave.

* * *

I've lost all sense of time with him. How long is it since we met? "Young writer from New York," that's how he introduced himself at the Kristeva class we both attended at Columbia. Cocktails, dinners at the Top of the Sixes, the Nirvana, the Soho—all of them gone now. Memories, memories. . . . But the sexual attraction persists. Andrew is the only American I know without a jot of religious sensibility. His Methodist parents hammered him so hard with the Bible that his Oedipus obliged him to make a "clean break," as he says wryly. His ruthless retaliation is becoming more ironical with age. He's raw and sensitive the way I like them, while being outwardly cool, sexy, and witty. Just the ticket for an occasional flutter; each of us is irrevocably alone, but every time we meet it's like we'd never been apart.

* * *

"Our pilgrimage to your Teresa," as dear Andrew teasingly calls it, becomes shadowed by current events. The radio keeps updating the material damage and the number of fatalities, it's unimaginable . . . Other countries are shaking off their torpor. Spain's wounds are still fresh. France gloats: of course, Paris is smarting from the failure to bag the 2012 Games. And then there are the various "European opinions" conveyed by the referendums rejecting the Lisbon Treaty. We tried to forget that "they" were still around, but "they" reminded us, and how. Who are "they," anyway?

"A bunch of fanatics, what else? The world's full of 'em. One was even spotted in Avila!" Andrew's jocularity falls flat. Juan and I don't respond, and Andrew segues sideways: "I've always preferred *Lazarillo de Tormes* to weddings with God, and at this rate history's bearing me out."

On the road and around the table, alone and with friends, the erotic thrust and parry between him and me takes the form of scholastic disputes. The sex of angels, Bush and Chirac, Nietzsche and Heidegger, French politicians Villepin and Sarko, *Le Monde* versus *Le Nouvel Observateur*, the tele-evangelism phenomenon, the refurbishment of MoMA, the Hispanization of the Big Apple, the relative merits of Philip Roth and Philippe Sollers—nothing escapes us, and everything makes us laugh. Before we end up in bed, we never know how the sparring will pan out. We're even in terms of weapons, but poles apart in style. I'm notoriously dogged and consistent. Whereas Andrew, who changes his mind as often as his shirt, will suddenly start defending an idea he trashed five minutes ago, just for the novelistic fun of trying a different character. I don't sulk or cry foul, it could wreck the game. I catch the ball in the air, run to the net, *smash*! Or sometimes it's the other way around, I'm not saying that never happens. On this occasion, I let the whole thing go.

Juan is hunched over his cell phone: none of his posh friends who work in the City around Aldgate can be reached. The radio says the phone signals have been jammed to prevent the terrorists from detonating a new wave of attacks. We're scared.

"What of? Come on, there's no use being scared!" Andrew's blood has flowed back, now he's red in the face with temper. At least the London bombings will have had the effect of concentrating my on-off partner's mind on the faith wars. So far, the Teresian landscapes we've seen have only impressed him with their storks! "You wait and see, soon all will be revealed: Islamic suicide bombers," he continues in a mocking drawl. "James Bond don't know it yet, but when he finds out, he'll be awful scared of scaring the populace. Dear me, bombers in our bosom! All those chaps flooding in from North Africa, Pakistan, the Philippines! Or even better, homegrown, from some run-down inner city, smart enough to become engineers or teachers, Her Majesty's socially mobile subjects. . . . Remember 2001, how surprised we were at the high educational levels of the pilots, mostly Saudi, who crashed into the Twin Towers? And how that didn't stop them identifying with the losers of globalization and turning themselves into human bombs? I say! Even the most phlegmatic Brit might ask himself a few questions. One point to me! And what about the G8, keeping awfully quiet back there; just as mad for God, and unlikely to change the opponent's way of thinking, if you see what I mean. Because there's a hair in the soup of the rich, and that's religion. The rich are pretty keen on religion, the fuse of the human bomb! Can you see them deconstructing it?" (Besides the Kristeva course, Andrew has attended rather too many Derrida seminars for my taste.) "Another point to me! Nope, few takers for that job."

Even an occasional lover is loath to admit that his partner has had the same insights as him, not to say before him! The jagged peaks of the Guadarrama are bristling with wind turbines in the distance, like a hi-tech version of the windmills Don Quixote mistook for giants. I kick the ball into touch.

"The suicide bombers are the windmills, you mean, and the politicians are our Quixotes? So we're waging war on an unfindable enemy, attacking effects instead of causes, and hitting back with futile militaristic campaigns, like the Man of the Mancha charging forth on his Rocinante, instead of undertaking the necessary social reforms? We'd do better to change the wind than sit in judgment on the windmills. If the wind keeps blowing from that direction, it'll drive all the world's windmills insane, it really will."

Juan and Andrew have stopped listening. Good old Sylvia, talking through her hat again. They turn up the radio. In fact I'm getting closer to Teresa, I never left her. Her wind, her sun, her peerless energy of Love with a capital L, which draws her irresistibly to the divine Spouse—did she construct or deconstruct them? In La Madre as in the Islamists, it's their faith, the "hair in the soup," the fuse that interests me, *pace* Andrew. That exaltation that makes a person ill with love, ill unto death.

"Forty-nine dead, 700 wounded, 350 still in hospital, of whom 22 are in a critical condition . . ." It's enough to have the radio on: the same figures ride the airwaves in every language.

"And that's just the beginning! Over to you, G8!" Andrew's sarcasm is not funny anymore.

* * *

Ocher and gray, streaked with red, the ramparts of Avila rise before us like a brusque eruption of the arid land we are traveling, piously nestled in the heart of the Sierra de Gredos, ice-cold in winter and windblown in summer. Many peoples once settled this hilltop, but now all that remains of them are the stones and bricks packed into the two and a half kilometers of the majestic perimeter wall, twelve meters high and three meters thick, with nine gates, four disused posterns, and eighty-eight massive semicircular towers. The fortification raised between 1090 and 1093 by Count Raymond of Burgundy, don Raimundo, at the express command of Alfonso VI, recycled the rubble of earlier Roman walls that had been demolished and rebuilt by Muslims and Christians in a string of legendary clashes that foreshadowed the Crusades.

Our little red KA is unfazed. It speeds from gate to gate, whips through the steep and winding streets like a lizard, and is soon parked in front of the Parador. Strange how that dragon of a wall has taken over our bodies, pushing us in and out without our hardly being aware of it, like a constant swinging: Teresa's birthplace is a vertigo. Getting as close as possible—my saint's manuscripts themselves can't be touched, sequestered under glass in the worthy museums of the *Guía Teresiana*—I come across pre-Roman altar stones, carved with geometric designs and the shapes of plants and fish; dressed stones; Latin inscriptions; funerary stelae adorned with primitive reliefs of human heads. Although the piling of histories one on top of the other added up to a citadel dreamily reflected in the Adaja River as if in a tale of knights and ladies, this Romanesque edifice looks brand-new to my eyes, like a flimsy set built to accommodate one of those "duties of memory" our contemporaries go in for. The Avilans are so proud of their fortress that they fix every damaged stone at once and repair the least crack as soon as it appears. The blinding Castilian sun makes the ramparts look as artificial as a pasteboard backdrop for son et lumière shows on summer nights. We remember the London bombings; we'll observe a minute of silence later on.

As soon as you step inside the walls, you realize that the fortified space of the saint's home city is the model for her *moradas* or Dwelling Places, misleadingly named *The Interior Castle*, as she described them late in life, in 1577, at the request of her friend and confessor Jerome Gratian. The *moradas* could not have been conceived without the *Hekhalot* and Avila: a haphazard agglomeration of little houses, plazas, and barrios, partitioned off from one another and yet open and permeable. By the monumental grace of those eighty-eight towers that bulge and snake rhythmically around the holy of holies, the *moradas* or "abodes" of Avila communicate with one another just as they do with the mountains, fields, and sky.[1] Avila "expands in its smallness" as an effect of those walls, wrote Miguel de Unamuno.[2] No, Avila is in no sense "small," because all of its boundaries are membranes. Instead of enclosing and compacting it, that great concertina of a wall inflates and transcends it. Here, every indoors is halfway to being outdoors; Avila streams with greatness.

Of the family home and little garden, the place where Teresa is said to have been born, nothing remains to feed the nostalgia of her fans. Located on the plaza de La Santa, between the home of the Avilan notable Blasco Núñez Vela and that of her uncle Francisco Álvarez de Cepeda, whose sons were her first heartthrobs, it was once a stolid block of granite adorned with the Ahumada crest. In 1630 the Discalced Carmelites purchased the abandoned property, whose direct heirs had emigrated to the New World, and six years later an ostentatious church in the worst baroque taste was erected on the site.

I think about the inventory drawn up by don Alonso on the death of his first wife, Catalina del Peso y Henao, a victim of the plague in 1507. This document shows Teresa's Papá in a different light than do her own sketches. We find a conscientious hidalgo who in 1512 rode off to fight in Navarre under the king of Aragon, ruler of Castile on behalf of his daughter, Juana. But did Alonso's breastplate hide the soul of a collector? The list of tackle for mules and horses includes harnesses, saddles, girth-straps, stirrups, curb chains, halters, and bells. Mule blankets were "red, with dark green diamonds" or "white and red," and there were "several Rouen coats in red and yellow" for the horses. Alonso rejoices in the enumeration of luxuries and seems to have had a fetishistic love of swanky textiles. He mentions a "crinkled doublet made of fustian from Milan, with aiguillettes," another of "purple damask," and another of "crimson silk." He is no less precise about the wardrobe of his late wife: a "scarlet gown trimmed in black velvet," a "skirt of *zeïtouni*—moiré satin from China—slashed with yellow taffeta, lined in red." These treasures were set off by splendid jewelry: a pair of gold chains that encircled the neck four times, six chiseled gold bracelets, earrings of pink and yellow gold, and a crucifix inlaid with precious gems.

By the time Teresa came along, this sumptuous lifestyle was already, or nearly, over; she recalled her mother only ever wearing black. The modern setting for the cult of Teresa contains no hint of her father's pampered tastes, any more than it suggests the raptures and tortures consigned in her writings. Inside the church, a plaster Teresa swoons for all eternity against a blinding gold background. Awed pilgrims shuffle past a display of relics, the sight of which makes me feel quite ill. There's a finger from her right hand, a staff she used on her travels, her rosary, and—more endearing—the soles of her sandals. A medley that is supposed to authenticate the handful of letters kept in a jar, which have no need of such a reliquary.

"You wanted to see it, and here it is!" crows Andrew. This time I'm inclined to agree: the tacky mummification of La Madre marks the high point of Catholicism and the beginning of its decline. Scenting my tacit accord, Andrew launches into a rant. "Examples abound everywhere, obviously, but your Teresa takes the cake, and I think you know it! This religion is a model for all the personality-cult peddlers who dreamed of absolute Truth incarnate on earth: whether fighting it or inspired by it, it's all the same, they dream of it. Royalists, Bonapartists, communists, Maoists, fascists, Nazis, fundamentalists, bin-Ladenists, evangelists, creationists, the lot. Every despot sees a pope in the mirror, I can assure you! The Sun King, the Führer, the Little Father, the Duce—and, right here on this dry plateau, General Franco, the grand sponsor of national tourism with specialism in holy sites, who never went anywhere without the left hand of your roommate packed snugly in his pocket, you told me so yourself. And further allow me to point out that it was your precious Counter-Reformation that sowed the seed of the interactive spectacle, thought by cretins to be a modern invention. Look around, this is where Disneyland got started—for the entertainment of the humanoids aka 'children of all ages' who've overrun the planet! Just look at the kitsch: here's where the Spectacle finally vanquished the Spirit. And from then on, the way was open to mass hypnosis in front of the TV. That's what you, Sylvia, have got to wake up to here, if you can open your eyes at all. How could Catholicism ever offer the antidote to the poison it pioneered so brilliantly itself? Because that's what you want us to believe, isn't it! But how could it?" His blue eyes stare at me with lover-like fixity; I'd rather interpret it that way than suspect he's making fun.

"Take it easy, will you? You should follow my example and read more about it," I tell him with mock severity.

"Later." He pulls me close and we kiss in a less than saintly manner. I've got over Bruno, though my American writer is quite mean enough to bring up the subject sooner or later. Teresa herself was a saint in a very special sense.

Juan brings us back down to earth.

"The bombers were from the suburbs of Leeds. Seemingly well-integrated Brits, who had had some further education in madrassas in Pakistan. Blair must be *so* proud of his multicultural model!" As a former Maoist Juan has no time for Blairism, and is glued to the radio whenever the political juncture looks insoluble. What times we live in!

"Thank goodness for the storks." I'm unreservedly on Andrew's side in this; he films them obsessively. Another artsy video is all we'll get out of this trip, no use whatever for my research, I should have known!

I prefer to go alone to visit the convent and church of Our Lady of Grace, outside the city walls to the southwest, where don Alonso sent his daughter to school after her mother died. It's my favorite Teresian site, and it doesn't even show up in the guidebook; a handful of Avilans come to Mass here as if seeking the safety of a swallow's nest hooked to the eaves of the hillside. The sisters' gliding forms can barely be distinguished through the grilles. Those elderly bodies, cloistered and unseen, emit a musical twittering like eternal adolescents, head over heels about everything and nothing.

★ ★ ★

Beyond the ramparts to the north, near the Ajates district where stonecutters, weavers, and market gardeners once lived, the Monastery of the Incarnation has become a special station for Saint Teresa's pilgrims. A clutch of dignified storks nests above the ancient door, and the clatter of their beaks, like wooden sticks knocking together, imparts an inhuman tension to the triumph of the bells. Did these migrants ever come in Teresa's day? She only seemed to notice the doves, she even called her convents "dovecotes." Was this to compare them to cages, crowded confinements, prisons? Not necessarily; Teresa says that she felt "very happy and at ease" in her parents' house. Oddly enough, all that remains of the family hacienda on the wide Morana plain, near Avila, is the dovecote.

There's not a dove or pigeon to be seen at the Incarnation, any more than inside the fortified town; only solemn storks. They look like black-and-white Carmelites mounted on red stilts, clacking gutturally about their raptures. The rosebushes in the neat courtyard never knew Teresa. Nettles used to grow there, and she would make bunches of them into stinging whips, believing that only the soul must enjoy bliss. Gazing out at the ramparts, she dreamed of water in this courtyard—cool water to refresh her mortified inner garden.

★ ★ ★

The building where Teresa spent thirty years of her life is spare and simple in a rustic way that induces meditation, and must have attracted many souls that were, like hers, disappointed by the world's stupidity. The cloister was built, it was said, on ground that once contained a Jewish ossuary. This was not the only fateful sign: the monastery chapel was inaugurated on the same day as Teresa was baptized, April 4, 1515.

In a reconstructed cell we are shown an austere cot, with a wooden pillow. Unlike many other religious houses, the Incarnation lacked wealthy patrons, and so the garden was surrounded by plain clay walls, and the rooms and tiny cells were whitewashed. A flimsy roof of abutting tiles covered the choir. Repairs, extensions, or modest improvements would drag on for years, and the nuns sometimes had to be housed elsewhere for works to continue. In winter, snowflakes would fall on their breviaries; in summer, they hid from the heat behind closed shutters, in a dark, damp purgatory where you could hardly see to read your holy book. Faith was invigorated by these trials. The call to matins came two hours before sunrise; lauds and prime were sung before first Mass, vespers in midafternoon, and compline at evening, before retiring. Terce, sext, and none were also chanted at their due hour, so that each occupation was part and parcel of worship. Holiness, cleanliness, decency: these humble premises sought to be worthy of Carmelite purity and to reflect it. Teresa, supremely mindful of cleanliness in both the literal and the figurative sense, made sure of it by setting exacting standards, before and after her appointment as prioress in October 1571.

A rough cherrywood bench, seemingly the work of a country carpenter, serves as the Communion table in the lower choir. Two grilles rise above it, like those in the parlor, from behind which the nuns can follow Mass. That narrow doorway to the left, generally used by cleaners and suppliers, is the one Teresa was forced to pass through when she returned to her former convent to take up her duties as prioress. Since the community's susceptibilities forbade the reformer to use the main entrance, she had no choice but to take this lowly, humiliating alternative. Yet I want to think that she didn't particularly resent it; on the contrary, she took every slight as a sign of being "chosen."

A fifteenth-century painting hangs at the entrance to the choir in the lower cloister, a naïf work from an early Beguine establishment. I decide I like it. The Virgin is shown sheltering Carmelite monks and nuns under her cloak—a subject that was very powerfully treated, too, by Piero della Francesca.[3] This Madre, protecting and dominating her sisters and confessors on the wall of the Incarnation in Avila, bearing the Infant Jesus in her heart and recalling a winged angel in her regal cloak, its tips outspread by two cherubs—is she only Mary? Or is she already Teresa, following her way of perfection from prayer to prayer toward a serenity fit for a queen?

* * *

Silence was the rule in the chapel, the choir, the refectory, and the dormitory. Compared to the majestic, frugal austerity that enveloped this tension-ridden little world during the Golden Age, the kitchens look cheerful and cozy, with ceilings that graze the tops of our heads. Copper pans hang next to musical instruments: the community of 190 women must have had great giggles and gossips behind the double bars of the parlors or between prayers.

Juan smacks his lips at the sight of the pots and pans.

"Oh, look! Everything they needed to rustle up a wicked *salpicón*!" Andrew chuckles, and I join in with slurping noises. Juan riffs on, inspired by the kitchen.

Since giving himself the title of Doctor of Low Food, our Golden Age specialist has got the bit between his teeth.[4] Historians, it seems, recently discovered that before you can have any notion of what people thought, you've got to know what they ate. Sancho Panza, for instance, was partial to *salpicón de vaca*—cow's meat salad—garnished with onions and seasoned with pepper, pimentos, or crushed peppercorns, and sometimes vinaigrette, with boiled calves' feet on the side. Juan pauses, beaming, intent on making our mouths water. I demur: "That might be all very well for Sancho, and maybe the Don, but Teresa . . ."

This gets him going again, as if trying to block out the shock of Al Qaida with tantalizing evocations of food.

"Well, the ingredients varied according to class. Mutton cost more than beef, and a lot more than cow. Basically it's easy, you chop it, salt it, and boil to a bit of a mush. Like what they call a 'melting pot.' So picture a conventful of nuns, what do they get up to after feeding their souls? They prepare a delicious *salpicón*, that's what. A chunk of hock bacon and some chopped onion goes in with the boiled cow, then you add pepper, salt, vinegar, and some raw onion rings on top: delicious! With extra spices sprinkled on, it was a popular baroque delicacy very like the French *saupiquet*. Same root, yes. *Saumure, saucisson*, German *sauerbraten*, English sausage, sauce . . . From *sau* or *sal-*, salami, salmagundi, salmi, and so on. It's all in the *salpicado*, isn't it, the sprinkling. Which being a function of the weather and the mood of the cook, these ones here must have piled it on, in their low-ceilinged hole, either freezing or baking to death!"

What does he know? Between the fruits of the earth sustaining Teresa and the unappetizing stew described in the *Quixote*, I'm not hungry. I wander away. To each his drug, to each his taste wars . . . Juan isn't done with it, though. He combs all the restaurants in Avila in search of *salpicón*. The waiters shrug pityingly: local cuisine means cured ham and sangría, you can whistle for the low food of the Golden Age. Even in Avila, globish rules!

But Juan does score one hit. Avilan bakers have not forgotten the delectable sweets the sisters used to make, and you can still buy *yemas de Santa Teresa*, a rich confection involving twelve egg yolks, 175 grams of sugar, fourteen spoonfuls of water, a stick of cinnamon, and the zest of a lemon.

* * *

The cloister Rule had been relaxed, as everyone knows, and one result was that it became easier to get permission from the mother superior for extramural leave. Since money was tight, an absent nun allowed significant savings to be made; at any rate, this was the argument used to justify the laxity the future foundress would condemn before reinstating the rigors of the Primitive Rule. Meanwhile Teresa herself took several, sometimes lengthy, breaks outside the convent (six months in Toledo staying with Luisa de la Cerda, three years in the home of Guiomar de Ulloa). Inside, it's no exaggeration to say that the nuns were cloistered or locked away behind those finely wrought bars. Their dovecote was indeed a cage, allowing little squares of light and air to filter through the ingenious grilles behind which a Carmelite could see without being seen, leaving the visitor clinging to the sound of her voice. For extra security there was always a third, a chaperone nun who presided over parlor conversations. But, like every rule on earth, the Rule only existed to be circumvented, and the sisters at the Incarnation were good at circumventing it: the young Teresa couldn't help but notice, as we've seen.

The Incarnation was not known to be particularly forbidding, then, and word soon got around town that a most agreeable Carmelite could be encountered there. The parlor became the site of maximum temptation, and also, now and then, of the most decisive liberation.

It was here that Teresa held her long confabulations with John of the Cross, whose "miraculous" chair, miraculously preserved, is a big draw for tourists: they picture it hovering in the air as it is said to have done one day when the two friends and reformers talked themselves into a state of ecstasy over the mystery of the Trinity. It was here, too, that the noble and influential lady Guiomar de Ulloa announced the arrival in Avila of the great Franciscan contemplative, Pedro de Alcántara. Doña Guiomar obtained leave for Teresa to spend a week at her house so that the saintly friar (one of whose self-imposed mortifications was never to lay eyes on a woman) might vouchsafe, by his righteous authority, that Teresa's visions really did come from God. Many other visitors came here to meet her, some of them well-known, like Francisco de Borja[5]—who urged her to persevere in silent prayer despite the doubts of her current confessor—or certain princesses well placed at Court. And let us not forget the attentions of the "person" in whose company she saw the toad . . .

* * *

We continue our exploration of the old convent. This tidy museum and its piously exhibited relics mean little unless they send a modern visitor back to the writings. Well, do they? Not if Juan and Andrew are anything to go by, but it doesn't bother me; let them be instructed, entertained, or bored by what they call my "fetish saints." Everyone sees what they can or want to understand. Perhaps it was necessary to institute this baroque cult in order to protect La Madre's works from creeping oblivion, and gold-sprayed mummification is, I'm sure, effective for enriching the faith of many weary pilgrims from Portugal or Valencia who follow in the footsteps of the saint inside their buses, on the trail of values that elude them. And yet it's the living Teresa, alive though my reading of her books, that I am trying to conjure back—into this space between its stark walls, amid the murmurous bustle of mothers trying to keep their kids from stampeding, and even into the flight of those impertinent storks, not content with flapping slowly over these haunted halls but seemingly settled in the saint's very lap.

"Those two-tone clickety guys were the only Carmelites around, in the end," says Andrew, true to type. "No, I take that back: they were the only living creatures of any kind! Because those pilgrims of yours, frankly . . . Sacred space is fast turning into a desert, isn't it?"

I don't say anything. What space? Jokers, admirers, visitors, pilgrims, storks—Teresa tears us all away from our spaces, from space itself, to deposit us in time.

Teresa's greatest "torment" as a novice was not undergone in that aseptic cell reconstructed around a few of her belongings. I can't help smiling at her travails, but not callously. Let's see. The young woman was mystified by the "special love" she felt for anyone who preached "well and with spirit," but "without striving for the love myself, so I didn't know where it came from." At all events the pretty young recruit "eagerly" listened to every sermon, even when "the preaching was not good." "When it was good, the sermon was for me a very special recreation." A guilty one, she means. Why so? Perhaps because this pleasure was prompted by a human, an all too human, factor—the personal charms of God's representative rather than the quality of his message. My poor, supplicant Teresa, ever torn between duty and pleasure, you won't miss out on a single one of the "torments" so familiar to neurotics! "On the one hand I found great comfort in sermons, while on the other I was tormented . . . I begged the Lord to help me."[6]

Teresa felt restless, inadequate, unsure of her vocation.

> I didn't understand that all is of little benefit if we do not take away completely the trust we have in ourselves and place it in God.
>
> I wanted to live (for I well understood that I was not living but was struggling with a shadow of death), but I had no one to give me life, and I was unable to catch hold of it.[7]

Can this weary soul, impatient to be re-converted, ever find the extremity which will be her road? The great event takes place at last, after eighteen years spent "in this battle and conflict between friendship with God and friendship with the world,"[8] one Lenten day in 1554.

Chapter 12

"CRISTO COMO HOMBRE"

Let Him kiss me with the kiss of His mouth. . . . I confess that the passage has many meanings. But the soul that is enkindled with a love that makes it mad [*que la desatina*] desires nothing else than to say those words. . . . God help me! Why are we surprised? [*¿Qué nos espanta?*] Isn't the deed more admirable?

Teresa of Avila, *Meditations on the Song of Songs*

One day entering the oratory I saw a statue [*una imagen*] they had borrowed for a certain feast to be celebrated in the house. It represented *the much wounded Christ and was very devotional*, so that beholding it I was utterly distressed in seeing Him that way, for it well represented what He suffered for us. I felt so keenly aware of how poorly I thanked Him for those wounds that, it seems to me, my heart broke. Beseeching Him to strengthen me once and for all that I might not offend Him, I threw myself down before Him with the greatest outpouring of tears.[1]

This was not yet a vision; it was a carved image, a work representing the Beloved—"In this very place, Juan! You see, Andrew?"—which the approaching feast day caused to be placed in the oratory of the Incarnation, where it caught the nun's eye. The sight of Jesus moves her, distresses her utterly [*toda me turbó de verle tal*]. What perturbs her so? His "wounds" and His weals, of course, His sweat and His grief. Teresa interiorizes this bleeding, hurting, body of a man: "Since I could not reflect discursively with the intellect,

I strove to represent Christ within me [*procuraba representar a Cristo dentro de mí*] . . . it seemed to me that being alone and afflicted, as a person in need, He had to accept me."[2]

It was not enough for Teresa to identify with a man in pain, underwriting her own feminine anguish. "I could only think about Christ as He was as man (Yo sólo podía pensar en Cristo como hombre)."[3] She must bring him literally inside, and the man of the statue—far less tortured, incidentally, than a Christ by Matthias Grünewald—now dwells in the Carmelite's entrails.[4] But the God-man is also all around her, and His presence contains her "so that I could in no way doubt He was within me or I totally immersed in Him" [yo toda engolfada en Él][5].

★ ★ ★

The extravagance of this embrace is not only justified by the experiences of illustrious predecessors. Teresa is thinking about Mary Magdalene's conversion, of course, as she weeps before the statue, but she laments the way "the tears I shed were womanish and without strength since I did not obtain by them what I desired."[6] She would retreat from female role models, and it was not until discovering Saint Augustine's account of his conversion that she felt she recognized herself: "I saw myself in [the *Confessions*]."[7] By the start of 1554 the *Confessions* were finally available—in Catalan—to the former boarder at the Augustinian Convent of Our Lady of Grace, who responded to their content as to a clarion call from God.

> As I began to read the *Confessions* . . . I began to commend myself very much to this glorious saint. When I came to the passage where he speaks about his conversion and read how he heard that voice in the garden, it only seemed to me, according to what I felt in my heart, that it was I the Lord called.[8]

Thanks to her identifications, first with Mary Magdalene and then, even more strongly, with Saint Augustine, Teresa's transference onto Jesus was doubly validated and reinforced. Meanwhile the naive freshness of her effusions, as bookish as they were spiritual, did not preclude an analysis of her relationship with what can only be called a fantasy incarnate, apprehended through images, mental constructs, and imaginary representations. And, on top of all this, through something more: a genuine revelry of the senses, a feast for the flesh. The paroxysm of Communion.

Not as "immersed" (*engolfada*) as all that, the writer lays out, with peerless probity, the many facets of her experience.

She shares her love of images with us first, firing a sly shot at the reformed Church in passing: "Unfortunate are those who through their own fault lose this great good. It indeed appears that they do not love the Lord."[9] This leads to the admission that for her (and, perhaps, for most of us) the visual thrill of a likeness, be it of the Lord or of any cherished person, lies at the bottom of the feeling of love itself. The cells in hermitages, those secluded outdoor cabins or the retreat rooms in Carmelite monasteries, ought to be decorated with holy pictures, according to the foundress. Further, "try to carry about an image or painting of this Lord that is to your liking, not so as to carry it about on your hearts and never look at it but so as to speak often with Him; for He will inspire you with what to say."[10] *To love seeing* and *to love* were synonymous for Teresa in her process of re-conversion. Thus did a Carmelite of the Incarnation rediscover Plato's *Banquet!*[11] Only to reconfigure it in her own, Catholic way, charging the images with love, before passing, with love, to the other side of the images, like Alice through the looking glass.

The vision of the suffering Man is thus an "amorous" one, leaving her "distressed" to a degree that corresponds to what is far more than a visual gratification. It is a sensation that, though linked to sight, at once kindles Teresa's every sense and triggers an avalanche of ideas. More than merely seeing, the "vision" of the Beloved Other becomes a "tenderness" felt as a gift, but "neither entirely of the senses nor entirely spiritual" (un regalo que ni bien es todo sensual, ni bien es espiritual).[12]

Ideal and desire, both the one and the other, as that which is experienced by way of sight gathers the flesh back into the spirit. The amorous gaze transports the lover into her Beloved and vice versa, body-and-soul, inside-and-outside, presence-and-immersion. On this day in Lent, 1554, more than ever before, after the reproving Holy Countenance and on the heels of the outsized toad, the vision of the suffering Man would initiate a period of auras, levitations, and other transverberations.

Far from the macabre expressionism of Grünewald, the future Counter-Reformation saint only contemplated the Calvary so as to turn it inside out like a glove. If at first, admittedly, she tended to wallow in masochism, she cast this off bit by bit and her experience rapidly ascended its radiant beam of pure pleasure, climaxing in the exultation of the elect.

In Teresa's work, Christ's wounds appear free of the carnal abjection that attracted Grünewald. At one point they actually metamorphose into jewels. The Carmelite "sees" Christ take the crucifix from her hand, and when He gives it back, the presence of the Beloved so often sensed by her side ("It seemed to me that Jesus Christ was always present at my side; but since this wasn't an imaginative vision, I didn't see any form"[13]) has transformed the wounds into gems:

> It was made of four large stones incomparably more precious than diamonds— there is no appropriate comparison with supernatural things. A diamond seems to be something counterfeit and imperfect when compared with the precious stones that are seen there. The representation of *the five wounds* was of very delicate workmanship. He told me that from then on I would see the cross in that way; and so it happened, for I didn't see the wood of which it was made but these stones. *No one, however, saw this except me.*[14]

We know that the epileptic aura is prone to such extreme states of perception and imagination, and to their inversion, but even so Teresa seems to transform them into an unprecedented sensual intelligence. She links them to the glorious tradition of Mary Magdalene and Augustine, the better to appropriate them for her personal gallery of images, within the religious culture of her time, in a soft yet punctilious idiom, while subjecting them to the most honest introspection her levels of knowledge at the time would permit.

Carefully, tenderly, the writer probed her emotional state, dissociating this love from any hackneyed daydream or vision in the common acceptation of the word, and labeling her experience—for the first time—one of "mystical theology."[15]

> This did not occur after the manner of a *vision*. I believe they call the experience "*mystical theology.*" The soul is suspended in such a way that it seems to be completely outside itself. *The will loves*; the memory, it seems to me, is almost lost. For, as I say, *the intellect does not work*, though in my opinion *it is not lost*; it is as though *amazed* by all it understands because God desires that it understand, with regard to the things His Majesty represents to it, that it understands nothing.[16]

Chapter 13

IMAGE, VISION, AND RAPTURE

Although I say "image" let it be understood that, in the opinion of the one who sees it, it is not a painting but truly alive . . . Almost every time God grants this favor the soul is in rapture [*arrobamiento*], for in its lowliness it cannot suffer so frightening [*espantosa*] a sight.

Teresa of Avila, *The Interior Castle*

L oving recollection cuts loose from the gaze that prompted it, to excite all of the senses: from now on the Carmelite will be engulfed by an all-inclusive sensibility, in the fusion of touch and sight. "I tried as hard as I could to keep Jesus Christ, our God and our Lord, present within me."[1] The efforts she had made from the beginning of her monastic life were finally crowned with success. Now she beholds Him, but not as an image; she alone sees Him thus, and her solitude curves ever more inward, toward that interiority where He dwells for her, immovable, inoperable, inseparable from her inner being; she is as though pregnant with Him, hollowed out inside where He unfolds: "The spirit may be shown how to work interiorly. One should strive earnestly to avoid exterior feelings."[2] Teresa only formulated that assimilation of the Other, that led her to feel that she *was* the sacramental body, when she came to write *The Interior Castle* (1577); but the experience was already in progress, especially since her re-conversion in 1555.

In *The Book of Her Life*, the degrees of prayer (the prayer of quiet; ecstatic contemplation; spiritual marriage) would be catalogued with a care for self-analytical precision, but also with a view to instructing her "daughters," like the ambitious reformer she was. In its untended garden, irrigated by the four waters, the soul first labors like a gardener toward mystical union. Humbly suspending the intellect the better to surrender to the Spouse, it nonetheless still strives to live out its fantasy while submerged in prayer. Next come the prayer of quiet and the prayer of union, until finally, with no more need of a gardener or the least "labor," it reaches the fourth prayer, which is rapture. The union is henceforth sealed, as lover and Beloved merge into each other like water poured into the sea.

For thirty years, within the sheltering walls of the Incarnation, Teresa exhibited states of paroxysm at which some marveled, while others feared the devil's doing; she was scrupulous enough to suspect them herself, veering between the possibilities and applying to both the scalpel of introspection and retrospection.

Thus she extols the perfection of prayer that is "union" with the Beloved while observing that here the soul, melting into Him, is still "upon our earth";[3] union, as opposed to rapture, remains always the liaison between two distinct identities, Him and me.

In the *Way*, warning against the separation of mental from vocal prayer, Teresa continues to advocate a "union" of differences: it is right "to consider whom we are going to speak with, and who we are."[4] Only in "rapture" can prayer reach the heights, and the dispossession of self be consummated in wholesale transformation: at that eleventh hour the osmosis with the Other causes one to be torn from oneself in excruciating pain, which blissfully abates into relief. Unendurable desire is thus transmuted into the ineffable *jouissance* of the transfixion[5] immortalized by Bernini's sculpture. The joy of mutual penetration spawns metaphor upon metaphor, she is a sponge soaked in the sacred liquid of the Trinity, which is impossible to contain, for it is He who captures and incorporates her into His sovereign presence:

> There came the thought of how a sponge absorbs and is saturated with water; so, I thought, was my soul which was overflowing with that divinity and in a certain way *rejoicing within itself and possessing the three Persons* [*gozaba en sí y tenía las tres Personas*]. I also heard the words: "Don't try to hold Me within yourself, but try to hold yourself within Me [*no trabajes tú de tenerme a Mí encerrado en ti, sino de encerrarte tú en Mí*]."[6]

The description and interpretation of such visions vary somewhat in the course of Teresa's oeuvre, but there is no radical departure from the accounts given in the *Life*. The Dwelling Places make more of the "intellectual" character of these "images," which are no longer either "sensible" or "imaginary." Nevertheless, while that distinction is a feature of the raptures evoked in the *Life*, the moment the writer tries to express it in words the difference she finds between her "spiritual" visions and those that imbue the senses imposes a style that is helplessly sensible, metaphorical, metamorphic. Not even the purest contact with the Other can be written other than in image-laden fiction.

* * *

I prowl beneath the low ceilings of the mythic Carmel of the Incarnation, thinking about a woman happily in thrall to her visions. *The Interior Castle* was not written until 1577, far from here, in Toledo, and then revised in Segovia in 1580. The very last accounts of the future saint's mystical trances testify to the maturity of her experience, inseparable from that of her artistry with the language of vehemence and lucidity alike. In the meantime Teresa has read much, learned much, and founded a great deal. Her theological knowledge has outgrown the *Spiritual Alphabet* of her early mentor, Osuna. And yet the original "tempest" of love is still there, whether in the practice of quiet, of union, or of rapture.

I like to think about her final virtuosity, here in the corridors of the Incarnation that saw her first steps. Time condenses for me, too, as through Teresa's work I inhabit the dilated instant of thought. Before, now, and afterward no longer flow by but soar upward in a vertical eternity, suddenly lifting the vaulted ceilings, enlarging them, spinning them into the *moradas* of a fabulous interior castle. Hers and ours, in words, in text.

Here, with a biblical, scriptural sense of the unrepresentable vision, Teresa painstakingly expounds the way "imaginative visions" differ from "intellectual visions":[7] how the first "remain so impressed on the memory that they are never forgotten," "inscribed in the very interior part of the soul," whereas the second are "so sublime that it's not fitting for those who live on this earth to have the further understanding necessary to explain them" (que no las convienen entender los que viven en la tierra para poderlas decir). These "intellectual visions" can only be spoken of "when the soul is again in possession of its senses." Jacob's ladder (Gen. 28:12–16) and Moses' burning bush (Exod. 3:2–6) serve as examples, for even "if there is no image and the faculties do not understand," it is possible to remember by the power of faith:

> I do understand that some truths about the grandeur of God remain so *fixed* in this soul, that even if faith were not to tell it who God is and of its obligation to believe that He is God, from that very moment it would adore Him as God, as did Jacob when he saw the ladder.[8]

And further:

> Nor did Moses know how to describe all that he saw in the bush, but only what God wished him to describe. But if God had not shown secrets to his soul along with a certitude that made him recognize and believe that they were from God, Moses could not have entered into so many severe trials. But he must have understood such deep things among the thorns of that bush that the vision gave him the courage to do what he did for the people of Israel. So, sisters, we don't have to look for reasons to understand the hidden things of God.[9]

Now, no sooner has Teresa reserved for her ultimate union with the Beloved all these "hidden things," which cannot be named and baffle reason, than she returns to her passion for explication and tries afresh to explain by means of some comparison. (Deseando estoy acertar a poner una comparación para si pudiese dar a entender algo de esto que estoy diciendo.) She begins by pointing out that, when the soul is in ecstasy, it "cannot describe any of [the grandeurs it saw]."[10] But in order to make this experience intelligible (Is it "imaginative"? Is it "intellectual"?), the writer takes refuge, modestly, in her lack of "learning" and her "dullness" in order to avoid making the choice.[11] Unnameable as it may be, the vision is still *fixed*, *impressed*, or *inscribed* on the memory—like writing? Like a graven image? La Madre has already mentioned elsewhere the true, the living book His Majesty had so vividly impressed upon her: "His Majesty had become the true book in which I saw the truths. Blessed be such a book that leaves what must be read and done so impressed that you cannot forget!" (Su Majestad ha sido el libro verdadero adonde he visto las verdades. ¡Bendito sea tal libro, que deja imprimido lo que se ha de leer y hacer, de manera que no se puede olvidar!")[12] Suddenly, in a startling flash of insight, the writer associates the unforgettable inscription with a proliferation of riches. The word *camarín* or "treasure chamber" around which her comparison revolves can also mean boudoir, or a closet for a holy statue's accoutrements.

> You enter into the room of a king or great lord, or I believe they call it the treasure chamber, where there are countless kinds of glass and earthen vessels and other things so arranged that almost all these objects are seen on entering. Once I was brought to a room like this . . . and I saw that one could praise the Lord at seeing so many different kinds of objects . . . I soon forgot it all. . . . Clearly, *the soul has some of these dwelling places* since God abides within it. . . . *The Lord must not want the soul to see these secrets* every time it is in this ecstasy. . . . After it returns to itself, the soul is left with that representation of the grandeurs it saw; but *it cannot describe any of them*, nor do its natural powers attain to any more than what God wished that it see supernaturally.[13]

Do you hold deep inside, Teresa, my love, a dwelling place of such a kind, a *camarín* crammed with treasures and other curiosities? *Camarín*: an alcove, an actor's dressing room, a washroom, a study? A swarm of objects, elements, bodies in evolution, preparation, defenseless gestation? A chaotic emotional boudoir you will be compelled to inhabit, sort out, and move on from.

✴ ✴ ✴

Quite explicitly, Teresa introduces the sensible into the intellectual in order to weave a *third space*, that of those "intellectual visions" whose task it is to rename and rewrite the felt experience of an invisible overcoming and dispossession: "[The soul] will feel Jesus Christ, our Lord, beside it. Yet, it does not see Him, either with the eyes of the body or with those of the soul. . . . Since she didn't see anything she couldn't understand the nature of this vision."[14] Moreover it is the very force of the sensation, "impressed" rather than figured, but distilled by the delicacy of the formulation itself, that constantly attests to the divine rather than demonic origin of such "sightless," "suprasensible" visions. And the flesh becomes Word.

She *felt* He was walking at her right side, but she didn't experience this with those senses by which we can know that a person is beside us. This vision comes in another *unexplainable, more delicate* way. But it is so certain and leaves much certitude; even much more than the other visions do, because in the visions that come through the senses one can be *deceived* [one might fancy it so: *ya se podría antojar*], but not in the intellectual vision. For this latter brings great interior benefits and effects that couldn't be present if the experience were caused by melancholy; nor would the devil produce so much good; nor would the soul go about with such peace and desires to please God, and with so much contempt for everything that does not bring it to Him. Afterward she understood clearly that the vision was not caused by the devil, which became more and more clear as time went on.[15]

With a semiological finesse that is equally startling, Teresa distinguishes these images, which are her way of thinking metaphorically, from paintings and other ornamental objects. Her images when enraptured are "truly alive," the fruit of an interior seeing: there is no pictorial effect but a fleeting dazzle, like a veiled sun, only communicable to those who have been granted the same favor.[16]

Finally, a discovery we might call pre-analytical: it is possible to translate the unnameable pangs of impassioned sight into a named image, an identifiable representation, if—and only if—the love object calms the sensory and potentially demonic violence of the praying lover by occupying it, fixing it, engaging it. The "loving words" of the Other ("Do not be afraid, it is I") steady the soul and ratify the amorous meaning of its visions:

> For if the will is not occupied and love has nothing present with which to be engaged, the soul is left as though without support or exercise, and the solitude and dryness is very troublesome, and the battle with one's thoughts extraordinary [*si falta la ocupación de la voluntad, y el haber en qué se ocupe en cosa presente el amor, queda el alma como sin arrimo ni ejercicio*]."[17]

Only the love of the Other, that fixed and eternal object, can endow one with the "talent for discursive thought or for a profitable use of the imagination"[18] whose absence Teresa bewailed when recalling her first stumbling steps in faith. Imagination, thus understood as existing in and by the love of the Lord, is now free to be the intelligence that transforms the sensory imprint into an "intellectual vision": it can now be lived as the wonderfully "delicate" presence of the Other at the very core of subject Teresa. I understand that there were for her none of the "contradictions" with which some commentators have seen fit, by the lights of their own logic, to tax her. But the "fancying it so" (in which Teresa admits there can be a whimsical desire, an *antojo*) and the cancellation of delusion or subjective impulse are in action together. They touch like the front and back of the growing "certitude" of the praying woman, physically and mentally dispossessed of herself in the union with the Beloved.

* * *

Adjoining the "boudoir" of the soul, these visions—which must remain secret—lead to still more "interior" intimations: the spiritual betrothal that occurs in the "Seventh Dwelling Places." Finally, dispensing with imaginary visions, there is nothing but an intellectual vision uniting the lover with the Beloved—the sheer light and unbridled joy of the *pax vobis* (John 20:21).

The soul, or "I mean the spirit," becomes "one with God" in that "center." Now, over a few concise lines, the rhetoric of comparison turns from the feeling body to evoke metamorphosis in the form of two candles close together. The image is developed, apophatic thought *oblige*, into a mingle of waters, and then into streams of light:

> Let us say that the union is like the joining of two wax candles to such an extent that the *flame* coming from them is but one, or that the wick, the wax, and the flame are all one. But afterward one candle can be easily separated from the other and there are two candles; the same holds for the wick. In the spiritual marriage the union is like what we have when *rain* falls from the sky into a river or fount; all is water, for the rain that fell from heaven cannot be divided and separated from the water of the river. Or it is like what we have when a little *stream* enters the sea, there is no means of separating the two. Or, like a bright light entering the room from two different windows: although the streams of light are separate when entering the room, they become one.[19]

In the private deeps of her experience, Teresa thinks by employing sensorial images that are largely free of anthropomorphic or erotic connotations. By virtue of this ultimate, climactic surge toward sublimation of the state of love, this repertoire is like "thought in motion." A highly wrought passage in the "Fourth Dwelling Places"[20] recalls how some four years earlier (we are in 1577, so this was in 1573, after undergoing "anguish" and "interior tumult of thoughts") La Madre came to the realization that "the mind (or imagination, to put it more clearly) is not the intellect." Against the numbing abstractions of the intellect she makes room for *a certain imagination*—or *imaginative* faculty—able to convey the truth of thought without completely severing its links to the body. Neither abstraction nor "imaginative vision": what Teresa is after is an imaginary that is thought, a thought that is felt, and the sheer pleasure of metamorphoses.

How often, my philosophical Teresa, will you force me back to the dilemma that haunts scholastic masters past and present: intellect or imagination? Not to put too fine a point on it, is this thinking or delirium? Neither one nor the other, but always swaying between the two: that would be your answer, I reckon. Or rather you wouldn't answer, you would continue weaving the a-thought of your letter addressed to the extremes of being: oscillation, flux, body and soul, flesh and word, the inception of the imaginative faculty and the ardent desire to share it.

* * *

Mercedes Allende salazar correctly notes that Teresa's confessors were not all of one mind with regard to the area of thought she sought to explore.[21] Where La Madre wrote "thought is not intellect," adding "thought or the imaginative faculty" in the margin, Jerome Gratian attempted to clarify the gist of the argument by inserting between the lines: "thought or imagination, for this is how women commonly refer to it." In contrast, the Jesuit Jerónimo Ribera grasped something of the distinction she felt inside and strove to verbalize as clearly as possible. He struck Gratian's insert and wrote firmly at the top of the text: "Nothing to be expunged."

I'm delighted by this disagreement, for it shows that there is indeed a "third way," perceived (by Gratian) as feminine but accepted (by Ribera) as universal, which is no more nor less than *thought*. Distinct from both the alleged truth of abstract understanding and from imaginary fancies, a thought exists that only thinks inasmuch as it is an "imaginative faculty"; an infinite elucidation of fantasies, setting out from their amorous source, in the betrothal of understanding and imagination.

Thank you, Fr. Ribera, for not erasing a word!

Chapter 14

"THE SOUL ISN'T IN POSSESSION OF ITS SENSES, BUT IT REJOICES"

> And even though the vision happens so quickly that we could compare it to a streak of lightning, this most glorious image [of His sacred Humanity] remains so engraved on the imagination that I think it would be impossible to erase it until it is seen by the soul in that place where it will be enjoyed without end.
>
> Teresa of Avila, *The Interior Castle*

It is in the fourth degree of prayer, then, that what Teresa calls "this exile" of the soul [*este destierro*]¹ is accomplished. Banishment extirpates the person at prayer from the understanding, will, and memory that set so many traps for her, the very same as our desires set for the neurotic subjects we are—Andrew, Juan, Bruno, myself, to name a few.

Teresa deals with it differently from us. Or rather she doesn't deal with it, she throws herself in, she plummets to the bottom, but she is then reborn by writing about it: writing the adventure of abandonment and exile for us. Inverting the fear of divine judgment into a mystical marriage, her "banishment" places her inside an oblatory Other, loving/loved; henceforth she becomes this Other. This bears no resemblance to the relationship between the lover and the Beloved in preceding prayers, for there they would simply and easily decant into each other, to the point of merging like twin fountains into a single stream. Here, in the fourth degree, there is no longer any "work" involved, only "rejoicing." "In this fourth water the soul isn't in possession of its senses, but it rejoices without understanding what it is rejoicing in [Acá no hay sentir, sino gozar sin entender lo que se goza]."²

There is a good that fills her with joy, but she does not know what it consists of. All of the senses are involved but without a precise object, interior or exterior. Intensity and self-perdition: no border, no identity can withstand this transport. And now the metaphor-metamorphosis of fire comes to join that of water to signify the blissful annihilation of the person at prayer: "the soul sometimes goes forth from itself . . . comparable to what happens when a fire is burning and flaming,"[3] "for at the time one is receiving [these favors] there's no power to do anything."[4] Deprived of "sensory consciousness," the faculties "remaining for several hours as though bewildered," the "bothersome little moth, which is the memory," getting its wings burnt—the soul is lost to itself.[5] Yet this annihilation is the source of "heroic promises, of resolutions and of ardent desires; it is the beginning of contempt for the world because of a clear perception of the world's vanity."[6]

The writer does not address the origin of this reversal conducting the soul from desiccation to water and fire. Modern neurologists are inclined to think that the trigger is an electric or hormonal dysfunction of the brain. Psychologists talk of hypomaniacal feedback from the fantasy of marriage to the ideal Father, turning depression into feelings of paranoid omnipotence. But one cannot reduce to scientific buzzwords the rhetorical power of the biblical and evangelical tradition from which Teresa drew the necessary authority to legitimize and reinforce her "states." And were such medical concepts genuinely to designate the neuronal and psychological conditions of her experience—and as a psychologist myself, I wouldn't argue with that—they still fail to explain the verbal re-creation achieved by the saint: What have they to say about the exactness and intensity of these metaphor-metamorphoses in perpetual reversal?

Teresa didn't wait for Andrew and me to come along before indicating, with her usual clear-sightedness, the incommensurable hiatus separating the state of prayer ("very edgy, very borderline," quips Jérôme Tristan) from the writing of it. Another state must arise to mediate between the two: "inspiration." Not the same thing as prayer, then. You are not very prolix on this point, my secretive Teresa; you are content to say that you have God's pattern before you and are following it, like an embroiderer does with needle and yarn.

I know you're always delving into the books that are your faithful companions in solitude—the Bible, the Gospels, the writings of saints and churchmen. You never forget that your identification with Jesus relies on your remaining immersed in the intertextuality of canonical sources. Since these have become your vital environment, your prime reality, you are able to recast their rhetoric as though *I* were *He*. Your "inspiration" is thus an inhaling of the Other, a loving rewrite of His body—through the rewriting of His word in your imaginary, receiving it as something that sprang from an exterior seed. *It* is written in you, by you, foreign and penetrating without, private and bereft within. It was also essential to possess the genius of your language in order to pin *it* down, for failing this, prayer would remain a foreign language, like Arabic, say:

> I write without the time and calm for it, and bit by bit. I should like to have time, because when the Lord *gives the spirit* [*da el espíritu*], things are put down with ease and in a much better way. Putting them down then is like *copying a model* [sewing: *sacando aquella labor*, a pattern, sampler: *dechado*] you have before your eyes. But if the spirit is lacking, *it is more difficult to speak about these things than to speak Arabic*, as the saying goes, even though many years have been spent in prayer. As a result, it seems to me most advantageous to have this experience while I am writing, because I see clearly *that it is not I who say what I write*; for neither do I plan it with the intellect nor do I know afterward how I managed to say it. This often happens to me.[7]

$$\star \ \star \ \star$$

You leave it at that, Teresa, my love, but it's precious enough, and I bet our modern Illuminati, who think themselves so smart, don't know half as much as you do about writing. Do they, Andrew?

"Whatever. It's her grand mal that interests me." Andrew is very keen on the work of Dr. Vercelletto, that's as far as he'll go.

But still, from all the psychosomatic conditions propitious to prayer, Teresa did take a "magic recipe" unrelated to the temporal lobe, which looks simple, once the writer has formulated its application: *He* is an all-powerful lover, and their union introduces His omnipotent presence into her. We're a long way from encephalograms, aren't we, and much closer to the Song of Songs as rewritten by Teresa, right? "Serve Me and don't bother about such things," He tells her soothingly.[8] Andrew's not listening, he's had enough of the Incarnation, of me, and of everything; he goes out for a smoke. I carry on with my monologue in silence, much better.

Was Teresa's ecstasy a narcissistic triumph over depression, probably over postcomatose exhaustion as well? Was it achieved by means of manic exaltation, itself induced in her by the intromission of her ideal Father endowed with the strength of absolute love?

Certainly it was, but not only that. The Carmelite herself retraces this movement of the psyche with a psychological precision rich in sexual allusions. The rare libertines who venture into Teresa country are soon clamoring for more; the pilgrims, if ever they read her, discern only allegories. But Teresa holds out for both at once, honesty *oblige*!

You mustn't think (this is for Andrew, outside in his smoky fug) that I've been dazzled by the sheer sensual perspicacity of a sick woman with a genius for self-analysis. My grand Teresa offers something more: the artistry with which she stages the fantasy penetration of her inwardness by the Other, and conveys it in a narrative as capacious as it is concise—in a word, convincing. Proof of this, do you agree, is her notorious *jouissance* at being run through by an angel disguised as a debauched aristo or Little Lord Fauntleroy, at least in Santa Maria della Vittoria. Those fabulous passages, the only texts of hers familiar to the educated public at large, make her into much more than a precursor of baroque art. My contention is that she invented it—before Bernini, before virginal Assumptions, before the whimsical undulations of Tiepolo![9]

* * *

At the heart of the sixteenth century, from behind the iron grilles of the Convent of the Incarnation, this woman knew that the repression of desire can gnaw your flesh and snap your nerves, to the point of falling into coma. She came up with a stunning, because postmodern, analysis of the lethal nature of desire, and of *jouissance* as a firewall against lust. The frigidity of repressed women, the compulsive discharges paraded by their uninhibited sisters— together they spin the wheel of female hysteria into madness. Did Teresa know that from experience? Or did her restless vigilance spy the danger from afar? Did she find the solution?

The Carmelite naturally didn't reveal the sexual sources of her distress, but nor did she content herself with a rational, reasonable censorship of such illbeing. At once true and untrue to monotheism, Teresa devised a "third way." By the blending of the mind and senses into nothing but touch, the touch of the Other, she sought to "divert" desire, nothing more! She would put it down to that ideal of the self constituted by the ideal Father, the loving, loved magnetism* [*The author makes a play on the proximity in French of "lover," *amant,* and "magnet," *aimant*: "*A(i)mant*."—Trans.] that penetrates her. The resulting *jouissance* is termed "elevation."

Andrew advises me to save it for my publisher, Zonabend, who doubtless adores this kind of waffle. He's off for a breath of air on the ramparts. If he knew how little I care for Bruno these days! Men spend more time thinking about other men than do the women allegedly concerned. I don't say a word. Everything in my life conspires to leave me alone with my roommate, in our very own mystical marriage. That's fine by me for now.

★ ★ ★

"And I said, Oh that I had wings like a dove! For then would I fly away, and be at rest" (Ps. 55:6). Teresa goes back to her Bible, taming it into a wondrous tale: "The flight is given to the spirit so that it may be elevated above every creature—and above itself first of all. The flight is an easy flight [*vuelo suave*], a delightful one [*vuelo deleitoso*], a flight without noise [*vuelo sin ruido*]."[10]

Unlike the psalmist, who *implores* the Other to give him wings, I note that Teresa *already possesses them*: secure in her status as the Bride, she is already aloft. The writer juxtaposes the New Testament to the Old in the image of the dove of the Holy Spirit, and she herself embodies the resulting amalgam. The experience Teresa describes is lived as a "spirit," for the nun-dove seems to overlook the flying "body": Is this the prudish evasion of a woman conscious of her religious vows? Or is it rather the sign of the intellectual probity with which she wants to be clear that this elevation is only a mental act, a "spirit's-eye view," a sublimation? Then again, perhaps spirit and body are all one to her? This last hypothesis is the strongest. Teresa's experience differs as much from metaphysical dualism, which segregates spirit from flesh, as it does from the *Spaltung* of psychosis, which impedes the contact of the symbolic act with the instinctual energies and leads to delirium. Constantly revolving around dualism and desymbolization, steeped in metaphysics and a connoisseur of "borderline states," Teresa (like other mystics) invents a different, incarnate psyche and a different body entirely devoted to the love object.

In the work of art that is the speaking subject thus recast, the "exiled soul" cannot suffer from isolation, hindrance, abandonment, division, or delirium, for is it not governed by the conviction of possessing the Other's love? Were any of these misfortunes to befall her, she would only attribute them to her Guest, and thus set in motion the dialectical spiral of repentance and salvation: eternal promise of an eternal recurrence of the same elevation, the same inextinguishable *jouissance*.

* * *

An amphibious creation, an almighty alloy, ecstatic rapture is a sense of soaring above every creature, and "above itself first of all." Ecstasy is like a doublet spiraling up: one (spirit-and-body) becomes detached from a part of oneself (also spirit-and-body), which remains earthbound, in order to "rise upward" (*para levantarse*). La Madre has a clear understanding (*entiéndese claro*) of the motion of this liftoff, in which the body-spirit helix coils around itself, manifests itself to the faculty of reason, is understood and is thought: "*Entiéndese claro es vuelo que da el espíritu para levantarse de todo lo criado.*" The soul, Teresa goes on to say, from up there both "beholds everything without being ensnared," and at the same time is given "dominion," being "brought here by the Lord." Endowed with memory, the spirit-flesh doublet also surveys its own past, and as it contemplates from above its erstwhile distress, it/she marvels at its "blindness" at the time "when it was ensnared."[11]

No sign now of convulsions or vomiting. From now on *it* glides in the pure pleasure of touch and hearing: ecstasy is soft (*es vuelo suave, es vuelo deleitoso*) and noiseless, rapt in the silence of the spheres. Away from the world of the senses, the soul is more sensual still.[12]

Could Teresa's rapture be a way to *lift* depression? Not in the sense of throwing off the weight of melancholy, but acting as a corkscrew auscultation-palpation, a highly charged annihilation? Against depression Teresa invents not an antidepressant but a "sur-pressant" that annuls her—not because she lacks the love object to the point of madness, as is the case with melancholics, but because He overwhelms her with His superabundant presence; body-and-soul together, over and above the absence of all the hes and shes who can possibly be imagined.

* * *

The saint's celebrated beatitude may cause the hasty reader or the superficial lover of baroque art to forget that there are two aspects to this magical rapture. It is an excruciating bliss that transports the soul, for "it is the soul alone that both suffers and rejoices on account of the joy and satisfaction the suffering gives,"[13] while the body is left racked and dislocated by pain: "Sometimes my pulse almost stops, according to what a number of the Sisters say who at times are near me and know more, and my arms are straight and my hands so stiff that occasionally I cannot join them. Even the next day I feel pain in the pulse and in the body, as if the bones were disjoined."[14]

Seized by "anxious longings for death," fearful "that it will not die,"[15] the soul yet comes to take pleasure in the process. The love of the Lord means eternity, after all. More prosaically, Teresa has survived other epileptic fits and awakened from comas at death's door. She has since arrived at the certainty that enjoyment is possible: the soul experiences itself as a construct dependent on this Love, just as much as on the comas that herald it. Teresa does not say it in so many words, but with that intellectual integrity that spares us nothing of her mental and physical states, she clearly implies it. The suggestion is indeed that pleasure is felt *against* the sick body, for at this stage the soul communicates only its torment to the body, keeping all the pleasure for itself: "The body shares only in the pain, and it is the soul alone that both suffers and *rejoices on account of the joy* and satisfaction the suffering gives." It is the soul, in short, that makes the body sick by shifting anguish onto it, communicating torment to it, and loading it with ill-being. And if it, too, suffers in its way and for good, the soul is just as capable, in the same movement, of enjoying its suffering unburdened from fear of death. Is it always so lonely in bliss, detached from the tortured body, radiant and victorious without it? The transfixion causes us to doubt it, as do the metaphors-metamorphoses describing the exile of the soul in the Beloved by means of a cascade of sensations. As always it is your writing that speaks truth, Teresa. Your self-analysis told you that the soul alone, provided it be magnetized by the love Object, can reverse suffering into joy (in the name of the Other)—even if it means that this blessed reversal takes it out on the body, whether plunging it into a coma, as neurologists have observed, or exalting it to the point of orgasm, as shown by the baroque sculptor.

* * *

When you wrote, you did not say everything at once. Sometimes, too, you were writing under the eye of your fathers and counselors. Bernini himself must have grasped this double scene, for he displayed the Transfixion that dispossessed you of body and soul right in front of the cardinals of the Cornaro family, the patrons of the chapel where you recline. Their eyes are on you, and it must have been from the gazes of such fathers, rather than from ours, that you sought to remove yourself, to banish yourself. Who knows, perhaps the paternal and paternalistic surveillance you were under pushed you, even more powerfully than your own personal history would have done, toward that inversion of pain into pleasure that ravished you and took you out of yourself?

There were times when Teresa felt the union with the divine as an annihilation, a brush with death. I picture her pacing under these low ceilings, beside herself, down the corridors and narrow stairways of this modest Convent of the Incarnation with its burden of temptations and hostilities; body and soul on a knife-edge, shaking with epilepsy, hopelessly sad. Writing after the event, she feels able to say that it was the prayer of union with the Spouse that led to such a loss of all her "faculties." Or maybe it was the other way around: maybe it was the seizures, the neurological dysfunction, that first put her vigilance into abeyance and melted the borders between herself and the Other? No understanding, no will, no memory; no communication, no words. This abandonment, which to her is beatitude, cannot possibly be conveyed. A senseless beatitude?

> Here ... the soul rejoices incomparably more; but it can show much less since no power remains in the body, nor does the soul have any power to communicate its joy. At such a time, everything would be a great obstacle and a torment and hindrance to its repose. And I say that if this prayer is the union of all the faculties, the soul is unable to communicate its joy even though it may desire to do so—I mean while being in the prayer. And if it were able, then this wouldn't be union.[16]

This may be the description of a swoon induced by a comitial crisis; we are reminded of time standing still for Mohammed's pitcher, in the epileptic euphoria evoked by Dostoyevsky in *The Devils*. Although "this suspension of all the faculties is very short" (half an hour "would be a very long time"), and it is difficult to know what is happening, since "there is no sensory consciousness," even so, "these faculties don't return to themselves so completely that they are incapable of remaining for several hours as though bewildered."[17]

This is where the strength of the love union comes in. Thanks to this construct (an embodied fantasy, as I see it four centuries later), it is not I who speaks, but Him; I is Another, *[*"*Je est un autre*": in a letter by Arthur Rimbaud.—Trans.] I is God, a Voice that makes me hear things, reassuring explanations—for God is a protective rationality in Teresa's Catholicism. Unable to speak or to read, the soul (when united with the Other to the point of fusion) is nevertheless flooded with "the most marvelous and gentlest delight" in the most sensitive part of itself.[18]

* * *

Other elevations, more painful still, are like veritable trysts with death:

> In these raptures it seems that the soul is not animating the body. . . . one under-stands and sees oneself carried away and does not know where. Although this experience is delightful, our natural weakness causes fear in the beginning. It is necessary that the soul be resolute and courageous—much more so than in the prayer already described—in order to risk all, come what may, and abandon itself into the hands of God and go willingly wherever it is brought since, like it or not, one is taken away. . . . At times I was able to accomplish something, but with a great loss of energy, as when someone fights with a giant and is worn out. At other times it was impossible for me to resist, it carried off my soul and usually, too, my head along with it, without my being able to hold back—and sometimes the whole body until it was raised from the ground.[19]

These brutal forces that "carry her away" suggest the violence of the elec-tric discharges neurologists speak of, and only the divine "cloud" that conveys the lover to her ideal Father bestows mystic value upon the trauma. The sacred comes to the rescue of ill-being.

Embarrassed by these prodigies, Teresa forbade the other nuns to talk about the "carrying-off" effect when it happened to take place in public. Some-times, feeling it coming on, she stretched out flat and asked the nuns to hold her down; "nonetheless, this was seen."[20] At such times she is "greatly fright-ened," then comes a "rare detachment."[21] Although playing no "active role" in the pain, Teresa feels stranded in a "desert so distant from all things" that she "doesn't find a creature on earth that might accompany [her]."[22] Union or no union, God then seems achingly distant from the soul; the dereliction is total. Mental pain coupled with physical pain provokes a catatonia compounded by an insuperable melancholy: "Usually when unoccupied [my soul] is placed in the midst of these anxious longings for death; and when it sees [the pains] are beginning, it fears that it will not die."[23]

Throughout these "clinical" descriptions, we can clearly make out a sequence: the detonator is anguish, accompanied by fits, followed by a neuronal disconnection, and ending in the physical relief that succeeds to fatigue. I shall not fail to deliver my novel interpretation of Teresa's raptures to my colleague Jérôme Tristan. I am out to impress him, of course, by encroaching upon his professional terrain as a neuropsychiatrist, but I also plan to mention that my way goes further than science. I'm trying. So is he, but the poor fool holds back, with his cramped little life as a specialist in who knows what. With Teresa, the prodigious amorous construct of the lover penetrated by the Beloved is what downshifts the postcomitial distension. A micro-fiction of eroticism in fits and states that would have interested Andrew, if he weren't acting the sniffy Voltairean, purely to annoy me.

Chapter 15

A CLINICAL LUCIDITY

> Despite all these struggles . . . there remains a spark of assurance so alive . . .
> though all other hopes are dead, that even should the soul desire otherwise,
> that spark will stay alive.
>
> Teresa of Avila, *The Interior Castle*

Voice message from Bruno on my cell: "Hiya! Not too hot down your way? How's it going? Found a title yet?" (Long pause. Clink of ice cubes swilled in JB. It's probably not my book that's on his mind.) "Everyone well, I hope . . . Listen, so what does a woman like your Teresa think about jealousy? I mean, no big deal, it just occurred to me. I imagine God comes in very handy for shielding her from that kind of human emotion, a bit *too* human, right?" (He can hardly expect an answer to this kind of provocation.) "Nobody's jealous of God, are they? Or are they? Call me. Byeee."

Bruno jealous, that's all I needed. I have no intention of calling back. He'll just have to wait till I give him the book.

Musing on the ways to take a woman, Marguerite Duras's vice-consul says: "I should play on her sadness."[1] He says. Marguerite says. She used love to help her die to life. Her pain was her cry, Hiroshima. Outlawed, out of reach. Anne-Marie Stretter confirms it with her absence, imprisoned in a sorrow too old to weep for. The ravishing of Lol V. Stein is not a pleasure either, passion suffocates her; unhappiness crushes Tatiana Karl, a woman never gets over it. "Destroy, she said," cried Élisa, afraid of hunger, poverty, and truth.[2]

In the book that first brought Bruno and me together, I wrote—and it's been held against me—that Duras is a witch. A witch who passes on to her female readers a boundless misery of which these victims endlessly complain in sing-song voices, so badly infected that their only escape is often the psychiatric hospital of Sainte-Anne; I'm one, I know what I'm talking about. People resented my insight, but it was true. Bruno confirmed it to me: "You know what, Bruno darling, I recognize myself in Sylvia's portrait of me." That's what she told him over a drink, Duras the survivor, who between a corpse and her own body saw only "similarities . . . screaming at me."[3]

Nothing to do with my Teresa, all this, or very little . . . Bruno doesn't understand much; Juan, my London pal, is happily grazing the sunny slopes of the Golden Age; as for Andrew, I've no idea, he's too well barricaded behind his sarcasm to give a hint of what he really thinks. Pain is certainly the hidden face of philosophy, its mute sister, and Proust, who used to kill himself laughing while paying tribute to perpetual adoration, came close to making Albertine into a social suicide. Gomorrah is depressive and Sodom is criminal, as everybody knows, but writing in search of lost time replaces the amorous impasse with the narrative of jealousy. "Little Marcel" becomes a storyteller, after all, when he realizes that what was torture to imagine about Albertine (or Albert) was actually his own unrelenting desire to please new people (whether male or female is another matter), and even more powerful, his desire to sketch out new novels. "Only from one's own pleasure can one derive both knowledge and pain."[4] Enough to perform the miracle of transubstantiation all over again, and contend that language, by the power of fiction, becomes flesh once and for all. At last this "fresh and pink" material, the work, can replace pale "substitutes for sorrows," and compete with cathedrals.[5] "I thought he was Jewish," whispered Maurice Barrès, as he followed the Catholic funeral of a writer who had been among the earliest supporters of Dreyfus, while at the same time opposing the closure of cathedrals.[6]

Teresa, too, believed in transubstantiation, and my guess would be that she subscribed to it even more resolutely by the grace of her writing than by any submission to the dogmas of faith. What's more, she managed to climb out of the frightening sloughs of despond that accompanied her epileptic episodes without lingering in the thickets of autofiction.[7] Her own brand of fiction (*hacer esta ficción para darlo a comprender*[8]) aimed directly at exile in the Beloved, sidestepping—unlike Colette—the purity of plants and animals. The Burgundian writer wept as painfully as a man and savored her "idle" misery with something akin to greed. "What I lack I can do without,"[9] proclaimed the high priestess of buds and blooms, despising the surface froth of some "good fat love."[10] Down she would go, pen in hand, into those "feeling depths" to which "love can't always accede," disguising herself as a female Dionysus, a dream-cat. "I swear to you it's not really a mental thing," the miscreant would say.[11] She never thought that Teresa was by her side in this crossing, this extreme pass where we "are burned," because "we possess in abstention, and only in abstention"— hence the "purity of those who lavish themselves unstintingly."[12]

But Dostoyevsky is the one who resembles my Carmelite the most, when he has Kirilov describe the sensations that precede a seizure, or indeed suicide:

> "There are seconds—they come five or six at a time—when you suddenly feel the presence of eternal harmony in all its fullness. It is nothing earthly. I don't mean that it is heavenly, but a man in his earthly semblance can't endure it. He has to undergo a physical change or die. This feeling is clear and unmistakable. . . . It is not rapture, but just gladness . . . Nor do you really love anything—oh, it is so much higher than love! What is so terrifying about it is that it is so terribly clear and such a great gladness. If it went on for more than five seconds, the soul could not endure it and must perish. . . . To be able to endure it for ten seconds, you would have to undergo a physical change . . ."
>
> "You're not an epileptic?"
>
> "No."
>
> "You will be one . . ."[13]

And yet Fyodor Mikhaylovich has no pleasure in transfixion; for him, the main thing is "despondency," and this is the whole difference between Orthodoxy and Catholicism.[14]

* * *

Dare I admit it to my friend Marianne? Since spending time with Teresa, I prefer her way of crossing the Acheron: the fairy Mélusine's cries drowning out the moaning of the saint.*[*An allusion to Gérard de Nerval's 1853 poem "*El desdichado*."—Trans.][15] I even dare say I understand her, which doesn't mean that I recommend her solution to an age of surrogate mothers and homoparental families. It's simply that Teresa knocks me out with the power of her self-destructiveness, as much as with the vigorous efficacy of her rebirths.

Let's see, who invented the bitter joys of the inner life? I wager it was the melancholics, sucked in by their injured narcissism ("Negative narcissism, Sylvia dear," Jérôme Tristan reminds me), so injured that it melts into Nothingness and thrives on denigration. The black sun of introspection is something Teresa knew well. She liked to distill this knowledge, as did medieval monks before her with their acedia. But the self-destructive energy of my roommate goes much further than that of her predecessors or imitators, for at the same time as sweeping body and soul away in the comitial crisis, it sublimates itself, with renewed and no less impetuous violence, into exile in the Other, a magnified ex-portation. And I never get tired of tracking her in the microanalysis of her desires.

$$\star \quad \star \quad \star$$

Although she speaks of the "impossibility" of conveying the force of her transports, the Carmelite convinced herself, with the corroboration of visions, that the very brutality of the epileptic fit was proof of its divine source: who but a loving Spouse would inflict such violence upon you? And so the malady of love undergoes a metamorphosis: without really departing from the letter of the Gospel ("God is Love"), the writer inscribes her personal story into it so as to transmute—through the Passion of Christ—the most unbearable suffering into indelible grace.

Strongly felt, but fleeting, is another aspect of rapture: the certainty of oneness with God surrounds the writer with the aura of a glorious identification that "lasts only a short time,"[16] for "rapture is experienced at intervals,"[17] but the soul, lifted up "to the highest tower," unfurls the "banner for God . . . as someone who in a certain manner receives assurance there of victory."[18]

Teresa is conscious of the twofold nature of this regenerative alchemy. The combination of "pain" with "glory"[19] is a source of rapture as much as of peril. The influx of ambivalent, excitable affects ultimately blows up the castle of intimacy, that haven where the nun, deep in recollection, succeeded in more or less conquering her centrifugal desires. The passing safety of purity cannot resist the magnet, it shatters to smithereens and sweeps away, along with conscious understanding, the confines of the very self: "The soul is suspended in such a way that it seems to be completely outside itself";[20] "nothing satisfied me, nor could I put up with myself; it truly seemed as if my soul were being wrested from me."[21]

The capacity for introspection that Teresa seems to have displayed since childhood was blunted by the practice of prayer in Osuna's mode; perhaps she sought to elude the vigilance of that merciless night watchman, the judging conscience, always discoursing, dissecting, condemning, making her miserable. The drawbacks of such a retreat did not escape her, however. For eighteen years, she remarked lucidly, silent prayer was the occasion of undergoing "this trial, and in that great dryness": the ordeal of "being unable as I say to reflect discursively" (*por no poder, como digo, discurrir*)[22] But any trials were gladly accepted, since they came from the Lord, and Teresa readily recognized the advantages of such regressive pleasures; the benefits of narcissistic *jouissance* (as Jérôme and I refer to it) in the masculine-feminine bosom of the combined parents whom she projected by exiling herself, powerless and speechless, in the Other. And yet in the same stroke of writing, the nun also indicated the advantages she expected from Confession. Shared speaking and listening offered far more than a "shield" against importunate thoughts; they put her through a veritable initiation process, which paved the way for writing. That need to "reflect discursively," satisfied by Confession, throws light on the inexhaustible eagerness with which the future saint was always seeking guides (who were for their part conquered by her paroxysms and verve), confessors whom she hassled, subjugated, and cast aside. Reading, confession, and writing fell gradually into place to mobilize rapture, to provoke it and push it to the limits of endurance. And to provide her with the optimum framework for surviving and sharing.

* * *

Family tradition, Augustinian schooling, personal culture and flair, all helped her to find in books the concrete reality of the grace she awaited from the Beloved: armed with a book,

> which was like a partner or a *shield by which to sustain the blows of my many thoughts*, I went about consoled. For the dryness was not [invariably] felt, but it always was felt when I was without a book. Then my soul was thrown into confusion and my thoughts ran wild. *With a book* I began to collect them, and *my soul was drawn to recollection*. And many times just opening the book was enough; at other times I read a little, and at others a great deal, according to the favor the Lord granted me.[23]

When this love of books came to feed the writing of Teresa's own works, her pitiless self-analysis reached a peak of rigor, grace, and wit. The solitary reader, the frustrated talker, would begin to hone sharp insights—often connected with utterance itself, the secret object of her desire—that anticipated Madame de Sévigné by a hundred years: "So often do we say we have this virtue that we end up believing we have it."[24] I cannot decide, my voluble Teresa, what I envy more: your aptitude for transfixion, or your skill at converting your *discurrir* into chiseled maxims.

However much the writer stigmatized the "faculties" of intellect, imagination, and will that were not propitious for "mystical theology," she made use of them for getting to her own personal truth. It was a truth that only emerged, for her as for us, gradually, through the process of committing herself to paper.

For the first time, a person—a woman, what's more—describes with clinical lucidity the states of depersonalization caused or aggravated by epilepsy, along with their transcendence through faith in, and love for, the Other. It is generally agreed that Moses (maybe), Saint Paul, Mohammed, and Dostoyevsky (certainly), had similar experiences. But with how much more discretion and abstraction they reported them! Going well beyond the restitution of symptoms, basing herself on Judeo-Christian passions, Teresa exacerbates the melancholic moods attendant on the seizures and traces the successive stages whereby she has managed to turn them into exaltations of subjective omnipotence. The fact that the latter never hardens into delusions of grandeur, a paranoid structure, or harmful enactments in the real world is not the least mark of Teresa's genius. She took care to soften that triumphant self-affirmation into a concern for better relations with others, through the moral, sensorial, and intellectual perfecting of herself—without being blind to her own tendencies toward *père-version*.

This alchemy took shape here, at the Incarnation, in a very intense fashion from 1554 to 1562, until an inspired confessor (the Dominican Pedro Ibáñez) asked the nun to write down this folly, this heresy, this novelty. Predecessors like Francisco de Osuna, Luis de Granada (with his *Treatise on Prayer*), Bernabé de Palma (*Via spiritus*), Juan de Ávila, and Pedro de Alcántara had already challenged the split between the "natural" and the "supernatural," the created and the uncreated, on grounds that in faith, dualism merges back into one: only through faith could visions and prophecies operate, only through faith could divine illumination be received.

What Teresa added to the service of faith thus understood by this earlier current of mystical theology was her neuropsychic pathology and her feminine sensuality, her melancholy and her hysterical passions, her literary artistry and psychological acuity coiled around bodily agony. Thus she affirmed in a wholly new way—humanly forceful, as well as politically necessary by the end of the sixteenth century—that to take the love of the Other to its logical extremes constitutes the bedrock of Christianity and, even more intensely, of Tridentine Catholicism. And it casts light well beyond that moment of the Church, onto the various monotheisms fighting today over our globalized planet.

Chapter 16

THE MINX AND THE SAGE

May it please the Lord that I be not one of these but that His Majesty
favor me . . . and a fig for all the devils, because they shall fear me.
Teresa of Avila, *The Book of Her Life*

"**I**ntellect, Sister, what have you done with the intellect?" (Her confessor,
Fr. Vicente Barrón, treading carefully.)

* * *

Bruno is not altogether in error, I'm making progress. This trip to Spain with
Andrew and Juan has helped me gather up the threads of Teresa's story, which
continues to haunt my reading and my dreaming. Her encounters are fleshed
out before my eyes, I can feel her living her life.

Teresa has need of the spiritual direction of Fr. Barrón, on condition of dilut-
ing it with the more amicable advice of Francisco de Salcedo, who picked up the
relay of her young soul from Uncle Pedro. Salcedo also assures a constant supply
of *aloja*, a magic potion made from honey and spices, that soothes the fevers to
which Teresa is so often prey. This "blessed and holy man, with his diligence, it
seems to me, was the principal means by which my soul was saved";[1] not only
does he practice prayer, like Uncle Pedro, but prior to his ordination in 1570,
he was romantically involved with the same Pedro's wife's cousin. No, Salcedo
is not one to drone on about intellect. The mercurial Teresa nonetheless proves
a handful, far exceeding his capacities. Maybe he should pass her on to Maestro

Gaspar Daza, a close friend he had already told her about? Maybe not. She's more up the street of Diego de Cetina. Sure enough, this twenty-five-year-old Jesuit makes her very happy: here at last is someone who understands! She determines to follow Cetina "in all things." He finally persuades her to concentrate on Christ's Passion, and to set her face against unsuitably personal mystic graces . . . This judicious young man is destined to go far, all the way to the chair of theology in Toledo.

★ ★ ★

"Poor intellect, it has gone strangely astray in me!" (Teresa loves to *discurrir* in the confession booth. Her respect for the young padre does not inhibit her from blurting out all the truths that pop into her mind. "I want to tell, tell, tell, tell all I know, all I think, all I guess, all that enchants me, and hurts, and surprises me," sings the nightingale in Colette's memoir.[2]) "This intellect is so wild that it doesn't seem to be anything but a frantic madman no one can tie down. Nor am I master of it long enough to keep it calm for the space of a Creed. Sometimes I laugh at myself and know my misery, and I look at this madman and leave him alone to see what he does; and—glory to God—surprisingly enough he never turns to evil but to indifferent things: to whether there is anything to do here or there or over yonder. I then know the tremendous favor the Lord grants me when He holds this madman bound in perfect contemplation."[3]

"You must be sorely tried . . ." The confessor is doing his best to slip in a word edgewise, to show this woman the right path, to fulfill a most difficult duty.

"Sometimes I am sunken in a foolishness of soul."

"Hmm!"

"Yes, I think my soul then is like a little donkey eating grass, almost without perceiving that it does so."

"No movement or effects by which you might perceive this?"

"It seems not, Father. On the contrary, in the other states I have told you of, my desires are restless and impossible to satisfy. And then great impulses of love make the soul like those little springs I've seen, which never cease to move the sand upward. 'This is a good example of, or comparison to, souls that reach this state; love is always stirring and thinking about what it will do. It cannot contain itself, just as that water doesn't seem to fit in the earth; but the earth casts it out of itself. So is the soul very habitually, for by reason of the love it has it doesn't rest in or contain itself.'"[4]

She makes his head spin, this loquacious nun, in ceaseless motion! She shows distinct promise, but still . . . After racking his brains, Diego de Cetina advises her to meet Francisco de Borja next time he comes through Avila.

$$\star \; \star \; \star$$

You are a minx, Teresa, for the more you act the sage, the more you aim your seductress's beam at the objects of your love, the more your confessors—and your readers—want. Some take fright, naturally, and there was even a move to have you exorcised.[5] But your spells deceive others, not yourself, and while keeping a low profile as befits those inquisitorial times, you dose your feverish outbursts with bitter bouts of soul-searching. How well I understand you!

"The soul must strive above all to represent to itself that there is nothing else on earth but God and itself." Diego de Cetina is slightly taken aback, but does not argue. After all, you are no more "united" with your Master than the Sulamitess was with her Spouse, in the Song of Solomon! So what's the problem?

The good fathers wish earnestly to believe you. But you move too fast for them. Diego de Cetina and Gaspar Daza have time only to wonder whether it is really seemly for a charitable soul to shrink from the world as much as you do. Beware the sin of pride, the fault of disrespect . . . Is this behavior licensed by the canon? You've gone beyond that already, you're in a rush.

You are well aware, for that matter, that the presence of the Lord both inside and around you is pure grist to your ego. Your raptures often take place, as if accidentally, in public,[6] and you worry far too much about what people think. Some disapprove in whispers, others praise the Lord for granting you the favors that you claim. Either way "would be advantageous to me" (*que entrambas cosas eran ganancia para mí*).[7] There's no avoiding narcissism if you're set to be the Other's great love, and you know it, my perceptive Teresa. Your harshest critic will always be yourself, isn't that so, my implacable one? For much as you profess humility and devoutness, temptations assail you and, shamefaced, you feel "I was deceiving everyone."[8] Fair enough! "Such a subtle self-dissection is not without benefits on the side," smirks Dr. Tristan. "Your roommate got more than her share of *ganancias*, did she not!"

Next, by a fresh and by no means final twist of watchful lucidity, you realize that the "appearance of humility came from serious imperfection and from not being mortified." Because if you had truly surrendered to your Spouse, you wouldn't care what people said about you, good or bad. You would have been ready for any amount of persecution. Talking of persecution, you expected it! You foresaw it, and it did not spare you, right to the end. Isn't that always the best gift for a . . . persecutee? You don't need telling, Teresa, all's fair in this cohabitation with the Almighty that you created for yourself with so much pain and rapture!

And all is for the best in this best of all possible out-of-the-worlds. There is no outlet for zealousness, vanity, or simulated seduction. You knew, long before we did—we of the Parisian Psychoanalytical Society—that there's no outlet for narcissism. Negative or positive, narcissism is understood, foreseen, and justi-fied by the love between the two of you, the Beloved and the woman who prays, the Lord and His Bride. "Everything seems to be a heavy burden, and rightly so, because it involves *a war against ourselves*. But once we begin to work, God does so much in the soul and grants it so many favors that all that one can do in this life seems little."[9]

* * *

I like your quip about the world down here being like a "bad inn." Your trium-phant narcissism thus spares you from both the utter disconsolation of earthly life and from the suicidal urge that can tempt the depressed to think that there is only safety in the Beyond. Nothing of the sort afflicts you, Teresa, my love: a temporary visitor to our squalid hostel, you couldn't care less for the condi-tions, since He is waiting for you.

"Let us not desire delights, daughters; we are well-off here; the bad inn lasts for only a night [Bien estamos aquí; todo es una noche la mala posada]."[10]

Fond though he is of you, Diego de Cetina frowns at this. You notice.

"Never think, Father, that I am not pained by the sins of our fellow men. Of course I am! And yet I ask myself: what if it was another temptation?" (Intel-ligence tells you that it would be a good thing to step back from the exclusivity, so prized by you, of the bonds between you and the Lord, and take an interest in other people. So many sinners, after all!) "But then again—might it not be another kind of vacuous hankering for honor, when one tries to do too much for others?" (You switch directions in a flash, like a will-o'-the-wisp; the young Jesuit is getting dizzy, he's not sure whether to breathe deeply or try once more to bring you back to earth. He sighs.)

"Are you quite well, Father? Now, doesn't this bid to save our neighbors, like every other effort of the kind, betray an excess of zeal? It's a sin of pride, perhaps? A want of humility? I would have done better to open my eyes to myself, I should have been more circumspect." You have an answer for everything, vigilant Teresa. Fortunate confessors!

"Very good, carry on with your prayers and penances."

Did Cetina get you to study the *Spiritual Exercises* of Ignatius Loyola? Nobody knows.

Chapter 17

BETTER TO HIDE . . . ?

For they have healed the hurt of the daughter of my people slightly, saying
Peace, peace; when there is no peace.

Jeremiah 8:11

Teresa is agitated, sure, she's into splitting hairs, that's clear; at the moment, however, the excesses of body and soul are far from being the chief cause of her unhappiness. In 1547, the chapter of the Cathedral of Toledo, soon followed by other powerful authorities, had decreed the *estatuto de limpieza de sangre*, the Statutes of Purity of Blood, which banned the descendants of converted Jews from holding ecclesiastical office.[1] Anybody might suddenly be required to prove the *limpieza* of their ancestry and their soul! But who is truly pure, *sin mancha*, "without stain"? An Old Christian? Don Quixote, the creation of a man with converso roots, described himself mischievously as a Christian from the land of the stain: "*En un lugar de la Mancha, de cuyo nombre no quero acordarme . . .*"[2] "In a village of La Mancha, whose name I have no desire to call to mind . . ." One can guess why.

Among the Illuminati or *alumbrados* were many converts from Judaism, and many women. Shunned by official institutions, they were positively welcomed by more unorthodox congregations in search of spiritual renewal. For some ten years, from 1550 to 1560, Teresa too had been influenced by new spiritual masters, in addition to Osuna. She had engaged in an intense dialogue with herself so as to adjust her experience to their teachings; but for all her commitment to honesty and truth, she could not confide in anybody about this development.

The first of these masters was Juan de Ávila, the "Apostle of Andalusia," born, like Teresa, to a converso father and an Old Christian mother, and the author of a book about and for women, *Avisos y reglas cristianas sobre aquel verso de David: "Audi, Filia."*[3] Teresa had of course devoured the first edition, in 1556. *Audi, filia!* For her, this title would always be associated with the *Epistles* of Saint Jerome and his commentary on Psalm 45: "Hearken, O daughter, and consider, and incline thine ear: forget also thine own people, and thy father's house; so shall the king greatly desire thy beauty." These were the words she read out loud to Uncle Pedro, the words that were so important in her decision to take the veil. But the preacher Juan de Ávila was suspected of Illuminism, something the inquisitors tended to confuse with interior spirituality and the whiff of Protestantism; Teresa had to tread carefully. *Audi, Filia* was placed on the Index of Prohibited Books in 1559.

The Inquisition also prosecuted the Franciscan friar Pedro de Alcántara, because that holy man took it for granted that God could reveal himself to the weaker sex. He had gone as far as teaching that Heaven was for the poor and the rich could never be saved; he called the victims of the Inquisition "martyrs" and disapproved of the term "dogs" to describe converts from Judaism or Islam. Dangerous, again. *The Book of Prayer and Meditation*—signed by Luis de Granada[4] but a vehicle for Alcántara's ideas—was also placed on the Index in 1559. Pedro de Alcántara himself was acquitted, with a warning to moderate his tone.

Bernardino de Laredo was also a Franciscan, and a personal physician to João III of Portugal. Although he had no scholastic training he went further than his master Osuna in the *Ascent of Mount Zion*, a work that fascinated Teresa—but she balked at Laredo's rejection of any human representation of Christ. After all, she could never dispense with the humanity of the Crucified One. So, let's thrash it out! What a splendid time to be *discurriendo*!

* * *

On second thoughts, better not. The chief inquisitor, Fernando de Valdés,[5] and his right-hand man, the Dominican Melchor Cano,[6] were on the warpath. In 1551 they drew up an Index of Prohibited Books, revising it in 1554, ahead of the *Index vaticanus* promulgated by the pope in 1559. It had become imperative to eradicate crypto-Jewish and Muslim practices, to repel the advance of Lutheran propaganda on the wings of the new technology of printing (already in 1517, the

Ninety-five Theses pinned up in Wittenberg by Martin Luther were printed),[7] and to censor both the production and the possession—the reading—of heterodox works. "They" banned all spiritual treatises in the vernacular and any complete editions of the Bible that were not buffered with duly authorized commentaries.

Teresa's new friends the Jesuits were also targeted, due to their links with Rheno-Flemish mysticism. It was whispered that "they" had attempted to arrest the archbishop of Toledo himself, Bartolomé de Carranza, an ally of the Jesuits and a friend to the champion of inspired faith, Juan de Valdés, who had died in 1541.[8] These controversies were a great topic of conversation among the best of the Carmelites, and Teresa drank in knowledge, steeped herself in it, constructed herself with it. A new Bible had been circulating since 1522, published by the recently founded University of Alcalá, which had retranslated the Old Testament from the Hebrew and the New Testament from the Greek, after Chief Inquisitor Cisneros had embraced the humanist point of view.[9] As a matter of fact, Friar Luis de León—your posthumous editor, my audacious Teresa—went further still. He stood up for Arias Montano, the scholar protected by Philip II who directed the literal translation of the Hebrew Old Testament into Latin, and an interlinear Latin translation of the New Testament from the Greek.[10] One thousand two hundred copies (far more than those issued by Alcalá) of the eight-volume Bible rolled off the Antwerp presses of the king's typographer, Christophe Plantin, in 1573.[11] Luis de León had the gall to maintain that the Vulgate and the Septuagint texts were not always faithful to the original Hebrew; he translated the Song of Songs into Castilian and was jailed for four years. "They" were well aware, besides, that the future philosopher-poet was of Jewish ancestry: his great-great-great grandmother on his father's side, Elvira, was a conversa. Undaunted, on his release, he wrote *The Names of Christ*, a work that delved into the literal meanings of the Hebrew texts and attacked the statutes on purity of blood.

You, too, would be in "their" sights. An early charge of Illuminism was refuted by your confessor, the Dominican Pedro Ibáñez, in 1560. Posthumously, the scourge of the *alumbrados* in Extremadura and inquisitor in Llerena, the Dominican Alonso de la Fuente, denounced you as a "mistress of Illuminism" before the Council of the Inquisition in 1589. Thanks to God, there are no passages of yours that genuinely challenge religious discipline or dogma, and the affair petered out. Later, another Dominican, Juan de Lorenzana, denounced you to the Holy Office, as did the Augustinian Antonio de Sosa and, in 1598,

Canon Francisco de Pisa, the historian of Toledo. None of these accusations were followed up.

How were you supposed to handle all this, as the ignorant woman you pretended to be—which of course you were, but one endowed with high intelligence and a sense of history? Fierce arguments opposed grammarians and humanists to some (but not all) theologians: the Jesuit Mariana advocated a return to the literal meaning of the Bible, directly based on the Hebrew, while a number of Thomist Dominicans appointed themselves the guardians of dogma.

You would hardly have been eager to draw down on your head the lightning bolts of any sort of "trial," in view of your family history. Undoubtedly passionate, you were also shrewd. You cited the innovators with diffident humility; when the innovation was yours, you presented it bravely or diplomatically, depending on the circumstances. The Council of Trent, launched in 1545, was still in full swing, and its lengthy debates would give rise to new ways of confronting heresy, Protestant or any other kind. Since the Church was a *corpus mysticum*, a notion the unfolding Counter-Reformation took very seriously, it would have to provide the populace with saints: these were to fortify the sacrament of Communion, facilitating a suprasensible union with Christ while inspiring a communal solidarity able to compete with that of the Protestants or the humanists, strong enough indeed to outdo them. Meanwhile, all things considered, people in Avila were not cut off from such issues. Your services will be needed, Teresa. Just not yet. . . .

* * *

Meanwhile, there's good reason to fear lest the spiritual favors you report be seen as demonic temptations, or heresy, or insanity . . . How reassuring to have a trustworthy confidant in Diego de Cetina, a man who understands you, and knows his Juan de Ávila as thoroughly as his Francisco de Osuna!

"Father, I have been released from my captivity on earth." Teresa wants to shout it out, but warnings have been "raining down on her" in these troubled times; she'd rather be reasonable.

"That is not the humblest of sentiments, Sister, as they must have told you already."

"I only wish to explain myself to those I love! Truly, the transport lifts me up, as the clouds or the sun draw up the vapors of a stone."

Diego de Cetina is doubtful, he doesn't trust your double spirals. Evidently this Carmelite is no hoaxer, though Lord knows there are enough of those in these dark times, especially in women's convents. Is she like the *beatas* with whom rustics and aristocrats alike, rightly or wrongly, are so besotted? She says what she feels, with beautiful precision. But there are limits.

"I would advise you to concentrate on the Passion of Christ, preferably on a single aspect, without haste. Follow *The Imitation of Christ* by Thomas à Kempis, it will teach you discipline. I sometimes feel that you undertake too much at a time."

"I am willing to do everything you say, Father. But it's stronger than I am. 'The more I strove to distract myself, the more the Lord enveloped me in that sweetness and glory, which seemed to surround me so completely that there was no place to escape.'"[12]

"Resist, Sister, resist. Willpower too comes from God, and He has given you a great deal of it. Stand fast against these mystical graces, humility must be preserved."

Even this young, modern priest, a member of Loyola's Society of Jesus, even he tries to hold her back. He's not wrong, certainly, and Teresa vows to do her best.

She abandons prayer for a year, with the sole result of "putting myself right in hell."[13] "In sum, she is a woman; and not a good but a wretched one" (En fin, mujer y no buena, sino ruin).[14]

⋆ ⋆ ⋆

She tells him so, because she thinks it's true, and because she thinks he thinks so, too. Teresa thinks that more women than men are blessed by grace. She has noticed this independently, and Pedro de Alcántara will confirm it to her:[15] women do progress more rapidly along the spiritual path. A holy man who mortifies his body to the point of death, Alcántara is so knowledgeable about the female soul that he reckons it preferable for a woman to marry again, below her social rank if necessary, than for her to take the veil without a genuine vocation to serve God. There are excellent reasons for this, according to Alcántara, and also according to Teresa, who is not as erudite as the Franciscan but feels it in her heart.[16] Let it go for now; all will be addressed in good time.

Five years have gone by since that memorable, and incontestably genital, communion with Jesus, when standing in front of a carved effigy of the

Suffering Man and sobbing harder than the Magdalene, Teresa knew that "the Lord was certainly present there within me" (como sabía estaba allí cierto el Señor dentro de mí).[17]

On June 29, 1559, a quite different vision comes to her: more disturbing, more incisive, more decisive in fact, given the absence of any form of pictorial, sculptural, or textual support. She *hears* the One she seems to see:

> I saw that *it was He, in my opinion, who was speaking to me.* Since I was completely unaware that there could be a vision like this one, it greatly frightened me in the beginning; I did nothing but weep. However, by speaking one *word* alone to reassure me, the Lord left me feeling as I usually did: quiet, favored, and without any fear. *It seemed to me that Jesus Christ was always present at my side; but since this wasn't an imaginative vision, I didn't see any form.* Yet I felt very clearly that He was always present at my right side and that He was the witness of everything I did. At no time in which I was a little recollected, or not greatly distracted, was I able to ignore that He was present at my side.[18]

Later, Pedro de Alcántara assures her that this kind of vision is "among the most sublime."

> For if I say that I see it *with the eyes neither of the body nor of the soul*, because it is *not an imaginative vision*, how do I *know* and affirm that He is more certainly at my side than if I saw Him? . . . The vision is represented through knowledge given to the soul *that is clearer than sunlight*. I don't mean that you see the sun or brightness, but that a light, without your seeing light, illumines *the intellect* so that the soul may *enjoy* such a great good.[19]

"Without being seen, [this vision] is impressed with such clear knowledge that I don't think it can be doubted." It is not so much "visible" as "impressed," that is, already inscribed, carved, sculpted, and she also compares the Holy Presence to effortless sustenance: "as though the food were already placed in the stomach without our eating it or knowing how it got there."

What's more, it is as though she was pregnant with a child that is her own internal composition, that has no need to enter from outside, and that is "there," regardless of her awareness of or desire for it. An unconscious creation? "It is clearly known to be there, although we don't know what food it is or who put it there. But in this case I do know, *yet not how it got there*; nothing is seen or understood, nor was the soul ever moved to desire it—nor had I been informed that this was possible [entiende bien que está, aunque aquí no se entiende el manjar que es, ni quién le puso. Acá sí; mas cómo se puso no lo sé, que ni se vio, ni se entiende, ni jamás se había movido a desearlo, ni había venido a mi noticia podía ser]."[20]

Whenever she tears herself away from her inner being in order to envisage an external agent of love, it is aurally—as for the Mary of the Visitation—that the nourishing inscription enters in.

> God makes the intellect become aware—even though it may not wish to do so—and understand *what is said*; in that experience the soul seemingly *has other ears* with which it hears, and God makes it listen, and it is not distracted. . . . It finds *everything prepared and eaten.* There is nothing more to do than to *enjoy*, as in the example of someone who without having learned or done any work to know how to read, and without having studied anything, would find that all knowledge was possessed inwardly, without knowing how or where it was gotten since no studying had been done. . . . The soul sees that in an instant it is wise. . . . It is left full of amazement. . . . Even without signs, just by a glance, it seems, [God and the soul] *understand each other.*[21]

Like a book, engraved and heard by the soul—that other inside her—thanks to Him? The book has still to be written.

⋆ ⋆ ⋆

There ensues a series of repetitions of that experience, with precise physical and spiritual variations that merely assure the Carmelite of her visual, tactile, aural, and gustatory interpenetration with the Beloved's presence. The hands of the Lord appear to her, then His "divine face,"[22] then the lovely whiteness of the whole person. Will she be ravished by this, or fall to fear and trembling? On June 29, the feast of Saint Paul, "this most sacred humanity in its risen form was represented to me completely, as it is in paintings, with such wonderful beauty and majesty."[23] Teresa is exultant:

> If I should have spent many years trying to imagine how to depict something so beautiful, I couldn't have, nor would I have known how to; *it surpasses everything imaginable here on earth, even in just its whiteness and splendor.* . . . God gives it so

suddenly that there wouldn't even be time to open your eyes, if it were necessary to open them. For when the Lord desires to give the vision, it makes no more difference if they are opened than if they are closed; even if we do not desire to see the vision, it is seen.[24]

A resplendent whiteness, a vision without form, Jesus has impressed himself indelibly on her; the Spouse has become her embodied phantasm, on the way to becoming . . . her double.

Conscious of this absolute identification with the object of her worship, the praying woman at the peak of her mystical experience described herself as "transformed into God"; the censors—whose job it was to protect her from her own heretical leanings and so assure the publication of her testimony with the imprimatur of the Church—struck out this phrase and replaced it with "united in God." The attentive reader will gather, however, that, more than a "union" between two distinct beings, Teresa's raptures enact a veritable assimilation of the divine into the praying woman.[25] Needless to say, she never enters the castle without being impelled to do so by the Other: "I understand this union to be the wine cellar where the Lord wishes to place us when He desires and as He desires. But however great the effort we make to do so, we cannot enter. His Majesty must place us there and enter Himself into the center of our soul."[26] And yet, since "there is no closed door"[27] between the Fifth and Sixth Dwelling Places, the soul at last reaches its "center" where "the main dwelling place" is found,[28] and becomes "one with God" (*una cosa con Dios*).[29] Dispossession of the self, transport into the Other, absorption of the Other into the self, in the infinite round between dwelling places.

Teresa sometimes implied, misleadingly, that she had cut down on paroxystic prayer; on the contrary, it remained essential for the molding of La Madre's position with respect to her faith. What did change over time and with the benefit of maturity was that her undeniable Illuminism, continually revisited, questioned, and imparted by her writing, ceased to be a source of confusion and distress and evolved into the fantastical support of a matchless entrepreneurial realism, the impulse that led her to found a string of reformed Carmelite religious houses. *The Book of Her Life* and the *Foundations* retrace the meticulous elaboration of this cleavage and this equilibrium.

The most extreme consequence of the identification underway—of the beloved turning into her Beloved—will be that "in the enjoyment of that divine presence *the vision of it is lost*. Is it true that it is forgotten afterward? That majesty and beauty remain *so impressed that they are unforgettable*."[30]

"Our effort can neither do nor undo anything when it comes to seeing more or seeing less. . . . The Lord desires us to be very clearly aware that this is not our work but His Majesty's work."[31] Teresa takes leave of herself in the living image of the Other whom she carries inside. After having *seen*, the time comes for *hearing*. At the junction of these two perceptions, truth is *written*.

* * *

Although her raptures made Teresa one of the elect, La Madre was anxious to disclaim any of the "pride" that lesser souls might feel to possess such a gift. She only felt the indignity of it, especially when her confessors hinted at that aspect. As time went by, penitence changed into a delightful restoration of triumphant pride; manic emotionality was calmed by the omnipotence of the Resurrected Lord, if not by the authority of a spiritual Father; in the last instance she bowed, serenely, to therapeutic necessity. And so she received that plenitude as a "truth," her truth, and advanced two reasons for the "certainty" she felt.

First, the Jesus who surrounds her and delights her is no longer a "comparison" but a "living image," because He radiates the majesty of the risen Lord, which faith dictates to the believer and which dissolves her being:

> I don't say this example is a *comparison*—for comparisons are never so exact—but the *truth*. The difference lies in that which there is between living persons and paintings of them, no more nor less. *For if what is seen is an image, it is a living image*—not a dead man, but the living Christ. And He makes it known that He is both man and God, not as He was in the tomb but as He was when He came out of the tomb after His resurrection. . . . Especially after receiving Communion . . . He reveals Himself as so much the lord of this dwelling that it seems the soul is completely *dissolved*, and it sees itself *consumed* in Christ.[32]

And then, since it is to Him that she owes her *spark of certainty*, hers cannot possibly be a subjective truth but only *the* Truth:

> Within this majesty I was given knowledge of a truth that is the fulfillment of all truths. I don't know how to explain this because *I didn't see anything*. I was told without seeing anyone, but I clearly understood that it was *Truth itself telling me* . . . "*Do you know what it is to love Me truthfully? It is to understand that everything that is displeasing to me is a lie. By the beneficial effects this understanding will cause in your soul you shall see clearly what you now do not understand.*"[33]

Strangely but logically, Teresa perceives this truth as an inscription etched into her physical and psychic being, like an "indescribable" trace that remains to be translated, uttered, retranscribed ad infinitum. Far from "dissolving" her, indeed, the Truth that invades her by virtue of Love for the Other invites her to make It known, by setting down *her* truth. Confessors did not suffice: the writer needed to ask a spiritual master who was himself suspect in those dark times—the author of the reflections on *Audi, filia*—to approve her decision to translate the "inscribed" or "impressed" into "fiction." She sent the manuscript of her autobiography to Juan de Ávila, whose letter of April 14, 1560, was already highly encouraging: hearken to Christ's words, the master told her in a nutshell, for He did not offer His counsel to men sooner than to women.

Is there any point in hiding, then? Not really.

Chapter 18

"... OR 'TO DO WHAT LIES WITHIN MY POWER'"?

> It is no good inflating our conceptions beyond imaginable space; we only
> bring forth atoms compared to the reality of things. Nature is an infinite
> sphere whose centre is everywhere and circumference nowhere. In short it
> is the greatest perceptible mark of God's omnipotence that our imagination
> should lose itself in that thought.
>
> Blaise Pascal, *Pensées*

When Teresa's Dominican confessor, García de Toledo, asked her
in 1565 to complete the second draft of the *Book of Her Life*, the
author replied that since she had had no time to re-read it, he
must feel free to proceed "by tearing up what appears to you to be bad"; meanwhile she would "do what lies within my power" (*hacer lo que es en mí*).

> I ask you to correct it and have it transcribed if it is to be brought to Padre Mae-
> stro Ávila, for it could happen that someone might recognize my handwriting.
> I urgently desire that he be asked for his opinion about it, since this was my
> intention in beginning to write. If it seems to him I am walking on a good path,
> I shall be very consoled; *then nothing else would remain for me than to do what lies
> within my power*. Nevertheless, do what you think best, and remember you are
> obliged to one who has so entrusted her soul to you.[1]

Later, she wrote: "For if they [women] do what lies in their power [*si ellas hacen lo que es en sí*], the Lord will make them so strong [manly: *varoniles*] that they will astonish men."[2]

* * *

This concern to be faithful to "what is in her power" or, more literally, to "what is within," evolved with maturity into the "center of our soul," an immutable "certainty," a "peace" that persists through "war, trial, and fatigue."[3] At that moment, though, her fidelity was strained by fear of betrayal: "As for what I say from here on, I do not give this permission [to Toledo and other confessors]; nor do I desire, if they should show it to someone, that they tell who it is *who has experienced* these things, or who has written this. As a result, *I will not mention my name or the name of anyone else*, but I will write everything as best I can to remain *unknown*."[4]

And yet, the feeling she had of having begun a new life did nothing but grow. It dated from her re-conversion, of course, and was reinforced by the act of writing itself, which "freed" her from herself and made her a subject of the Other—in times to come, and in the time of others.

> I now want to return to where I left off about my life, for I think I delayed more than I should have so that *what follows* would be better understood. This is *another, new book from here on*—I mean *another, new life*. The life dealt with up to this point was mine; the one I lived *from the point where I began to explain those things about prayer is the one God lived in me*—according to the way it appears to me—because I think it would be impossible in so short a time to get rid of so many bad habits and deeds. May the Lord be praised *who freed me from myself* [*que me liberó de mí*].[5]

* * *

The first draft of the *Life* being lost, all we have is the one written between 1563 and 1565 for the Dominicans García de Toledo and Pedro Ibáñez, and with the blessing of Francisco de Soto Salazar, her Inquisitor friend (believe it or not); Salazar also urged her to send a copy to Juan de Ávila. The Inquisition was naturally packed with skillful diplomats and subtle theologians . . . Three years later, in April 1568, despite the misgivings of Fr. Domingo Báñez, who was reluctant to let the book stray beyond a restricted circle, Teresa finally sent her autobiography to Juan de Ávila by the intermediary of her good friend Luisa de la Cerda.

Much later, in 1574, the Grand Inquisitor Cardinal Gaspar de Quiroga opened a copy of the same book with great interest. He had received it from the princess of Eboli, who had borne a grudge against La Madre ever since her spoilt ways had gotten her expelled from the Pastrana convent. This act of revenge misfired: the "Great Angel," as Teresa dubbed him, told Luisa de la Cerda of his admiration for the writer. Six years later, in 1580, when Teresa's reforms were beginning to prevail and she called on Quiroga for permission to found a Carmelite community in Madrid, he confirmed his appreciation of the book. However, the manuscript was not to leave the precincts of the Holy Office until 1588, when her executors Ana de Jesús and Luis de León retrieved it for publication purposes.

However subjective, the Truth the nun sought to transmit by articulating her own small truth turned out to be highly shareable, and shared it was. Teresa was thrilled to discover that García de Toledo had actually had his own religious experience of the states she described. Pedro Ibáñez, too, the alert, faithful companion of her mystical experience as much as of her projects for reform, was to retire to a contemplative Dominican monastery. Domingo Báñez, Teresa's confessor and director of conscience during the years of writing the memoir (1562–1568), lecturer in theology at Saint Thomas of Avila, professor at Salamanca, and consultant to the Inquisition in Valladolid, tried to impress on her that she should not confuse God's action in her with her own action in His name, for each was "complete in its way." Speaking as a witness for Teresa during her beatification proceedings in 1592, Báñez declared that mysticism and theology, the desire for God and the knowledge of God, albeit two distinct things, came together in her. Was the truth according to Teresa on the way to becoming *the* truth, validated as such by the highest echelons of the Church?

* * *

The unstinting support of the Dominicans did not prevent La Madre from expressing her gratitude to the Jesuits.

Since His Majesty desired now to enlighten me so that I might no longer offend Him and might know my great debt to Him, this fear increased in such a way that it made me diligently seek out spiritual persons to consult. I had already heard about some, because they had come to this town and were members of the Society of Jesus, of which—without knowing any of the members—I was extremely fond, only from hearing about the mode of life and prayer they followed. But I didn't feel worthy to speak to them or strong enough to obey them, and this made me more fearful; it would have been a difficult thing for me to converse with them and yet be what I was.[6]

And again: "I have been *reared in, and given being*, as they say, by the Society."[7]

In the highly competitive wasps' nest that was religious life under the eye of the Inquisition, every support was precious; the inner book had great need of it, and so did the books to come. Teresa, with unbeatable pragmatism, made sure of surrounding herself with every "network" in sight to fend off the suspicions, calumnies, and persecutions that were a perennial feature of her life. But if these powerful shields kept her safe from the Inquisition, a more important factor was the intimate persuasion that acted like the magical spring of her pragmatism: she was convinced of having attained and incorporated the Absolute, the "*centella de seguridad*," even if only intermittently.

* * *

The sun is blazing hot this afternoon, my traveling companions are sated with sightseeing and running out of speculations about the terrorist attacks in London. Andrew has been reduced to leafing through Teresa's letters (volume 2 of my French edition of her *Complete Works*), while lending half an ear to my expoundings. As usual he only wants to be contrary, and now he pounces, with an evil grin.

"So Teresa only made it into odor of sanctity because she turned her neurosis around by barricading herself behind a demented exultation?" He doesn't pull his punches.

My friend is too impatient to discern the nuances of the multihued biography I am trying to refashion, in my fashion, of my roommate, or to explore her kaleidoscopic frames of mind. Otherwise he would have seen how in the icy furnace of Teresa's psychic life, the traps of paranoid delusions of grandeur were dismantled one by one, step by step, finding compensation elsewhere. This came about thanks, firstly, to the woman's humility, real or feigned, revealed by her many depressive doubts and by that quickness to berate herself in which masochism vied with irony. But it was no less due to the more or less friendly harshness, the more or less harsh friendship, of her spiritual guides. Lastly and above all, it was due to writing, her indefatigable lookout by night and by day; the writing she did not neglect from the 1560s onward, with or without the input of ecstasy. Thus contained behind a triple security barrier, her raptures restored her to health and the pleasures of hard work. The Carmelite mystic was reborn as a businesswoman.

"Andrew, listen to me." I'm groping for clincher arguments to awaken my wayward American to the benefits of heeding a long-dead Catholic saint; no easy task, in all the rawness of that fundamentalist outrage in London. "Look, Teresa knows that this 'living water' she's submerged in, to drowning point, and I'm talking about depression inverted into stimulation by way of comatose states and epileptic auras—so, this living water is called *desire*. She knows that ecstasy is a disconnect that interrupts that unbearable arousal and transforms it into *jouissance*, a rejoicing in self-abandon, relaxation, a therapy-*jouissance*. That's her weapon against the deadly violence of desire. How do I know? Listen to this," and I pick up volume 1 of the *Complete Works*. "Here, *Way of Perfection*, chapter 19, section eight. 'The love of God and the desire for Him can increase so much that the natural subject is unable to endure it, and so there have been persons who have died from love.' That's what she says! The fact that the desire is for God doesn't alter the fact that it's *desire*. Real desire, whose object is nowhere, the objectless kind—you know the sort, as well as I do. The divine aspect only makes it greater. She goes on: 'I know of one'—she often uses that formula to talk about herself—'who would have died if God hadn't succored her immediately with such an abundance of this living water, for she was almost carried out of herself with raptures. I say that she was almost carried out of herself because in this water the soul finds rest.'[8] So, are you listening, Teresa is the vessel and God is the glassmaker who blows it into the shape he wants, but also the man who fills the vase as he pleases. This coupling, whose sexual symbolism surely hasn't escaped you, is analyzed by Teresa in all its ambiguity. Pain and sweetness, nourishment and penitence, dissembling and longing—divine perfection meets human imperfection, in short. Teresa analyzes herself in the language of the Gospels, but once she inserts this into a semi-novelized introspection, it becomes a prefiguration of psychoanalysis. Well, yes, I take that as a compliment, it's an occupational hazard! Here's more, a bit farther on.

"'However great the abundance of this water He gives, there cannot be too much in anything of His. If He gives a great deal, He gives the soul, as I said, the capacity to drink much; like a *glassmaker* who makes a *vessel* a size he sees is necessary in order to hold what he intends to pour into it.

"'In *desiring* this water there is always some fault, since the desire comes from ourselves; if some good comes, it comes from *the Lord who helps*. But we are so indiscreet that since the pain is sweet and delightful, we never think we can have enough of this pain. We eat without measure, *we foster this desire as much as we can, and so sometimes it kills*. . . . I say that anyone who reaches the experience of this thirst that is so impelling should be very careful, because I believe he will have this temptation. And although he may not die of thirst, his *health will be lost* and he will give *external manifestations* of this thirst, even though he may not want to; these manifestations should be *avoided at all costs*.'"

* * *

While "mortal life" makes her breathless with desire and this asphyxia horrifies our nun, the desire to possess the ideal Father comes to her rescue once again, giving her another enjoyment to savor. This one, unlike desire, is not deadly, for sensual plenitude is here relieved by being ideally transferred onto the amorous ideality of Man. Some (in Lacan's line, as we've seen) think today that this "other *jouissance*" is accessible only to women. Others contest this. There are writers, for example, male to all intents and purposes, who are not so far from opening up to it, from expressing it, and more.

Andrew looks skeptical—just to annoy me, I guess. I give up, and resume the discussion with Teresa: It's easy, she exists but doesn't answer. Like God. "Like my father," said Paul, my favorite patient.

By contrast with the average suicide bomber, you believe, Teresa, that the celestial glassmaker formed you as a vessel whose size is commensurate with what He wishes to pour into it. Loving as He is, and albeit flattered by your penances and mortifications, He will not summon you to die, let alone to blow yourself up. Your mating is thus so divinely tuned that the water He provides will never be too much, even though you sometimes drink an awful lot of it, don't you, Teresa! The female "vessel," mouth agape, hollow-bodied, is begging to be filled, for your desires are still childishly, archaically oral, I've told you before. Your arousal calls for food, nourishment without end. Alternating bitter grief with sweetness, you are "so indiscreet" as to castigate yourself relentlessly, my black-browed Teresa, you can never have enough, your voracity (or frigidity?) is unassailable, you were made for dying of desire. And would that be a blessed death, or a stratagem of the devil? Good question, and one that your various mortifications, succumbing to the same demonic impetus as your pleasures of the mouth, are not about to answer!

You are no longer fighting anorexia but its flip side, the secret, untold cause of many anorexic or bulimic behaviors: the "desire that kills," unquenchable thirst, the avidity you feel as an empty female vessel. In this battle you are your own best doctor, a complicated one you'll admit, downright dangerous at times, but as effective as most other medics. When you were writing that chapter 19 of the *Way*, you thought that "losing your health" was to be "avoided at all costs." You'd learned the futility of trying to conceal the symptoms, "for we will be unable to hide everything we would like to hide." Not only because it's God's love that wills all this, but also because "our nature at times can be as much at work as the love." Something of an Illuminata, certainly, but no less a woman of the Renaissance, you are aware, my searching Teresa, unschooled as you claim to be, of the role of human nature as an adjunct to God's: "There are persons who will vehemently desire anything, even if it is bad."[9] To whom do you refer? Do you know these persons from the inside, as you know yourself? Suppose you do. What then? Should these persons be penalized? Should their vehemence be brought within limits?

Not at all. You have come to a different answer, which I imagine you trying out on Francisco de Borja in an effort, no doubt successful, to convince him. He sums it up.

"In short, you are seized, like Paul, by a strong desire to live a bodily life while at the same time longing to be delivered of the prison of the body in order to be united with God." This former grandee of Spain, duke of Gandía and marquis of Lombay, titles he has renounced by joining the Jesuits, could never be called unschooled. He quotes from the letter of Saint Paul to the Philippians, which he knows by heart: "For I am in a strait betwixt two, having a desire to depart, and to be with Christ; which is far better: nevertheless to abide in the flesh is more needful . . ."[10] Borja is a man of the world. He does not preach, so much as rely on the easy charms of conversation.

"And the pain of it can be so dreadful that it almost takes away one's reason, Father." You enter into the game at once, introducing a little story, novelistic Teresa. "Not long ago, I saw a person in this affliction. She was in such great pain, and made such an effort to conceal it, that she was deranged for a while. Yes, quite delirious." Your diagnosis is correct, Teresa; you fear for your own reason.

The Jesuit grandee smiles in silence, glad to note that the authorization he gave you to continue in the practice of prayer was not taken lightly: you keep a scrupulous eye on your own progress. But he never expected you to outwit him at the game of casuistry.

"For my part I don't believe it is a matter of cutting off desire, only of moderating it." What a finely poised performance as a moralist, prefiguring those of the eighteenth century, my mutant Teresa! "That's right, it's good to create diversions, and I do mean diversions: to divert desire. To transmute it, if you like, by the power of thought (*que mude el deseo pensando*).[11] Don't you agree, Father?" You desire in thinking, Teresa, you are a thinker of desire. Could Borja have been one of the first to notice?

* * *

For three years, from 1555 to 1558, you borrowed your friend Guiomar de Ulloa's confessor, Fr. Juan de Prádanos. Your soul, you wrote later, was not strong but very fragile, "especially with regard to giving up some friendships I had. Although I was not offending God by them, I was very attached." To Prádanos, as to the friends he was warning you from, you were "very attached, and it seemed to me it would be ingratitude to abandon them." How well I understand you! Prádanos was not so distant from your substantial states and words, he did not forbid anything, he simply abandoned you to . . . God. Were you expecting it? Between these two father figures, human and divine, came "the first time the Lord granted me this favor of rapture." The long-awaited moment of "mystical nuptials" has arrived, it is Pentecost 1556, you are forty-one years of age. "I heard these words: 'No longer do I want you to converse with men but with angels.'"[12] Here is a grace that will reliably protect you from that manly Fr. Prádanos, not yet thirty . . . but never from his angelic side! Still, that is nothing to guard against, since the Lord Himself enjoins you to converse with his like. Honest as a person and sincere as a writer, you say so fair and square: "These words have been fulfilled, for I have never again been able to tie myself to any friendship or to find consolation in or bear particular love for any other persons than those I understand love Him and strive to serve Him; nor is it in my power to do so."[13] Fortunate Prádanos!

Young Fr. Baltasar Álvarez, also a Jesuit, stepped in to help you draw up the constitution and rules for discalced nuns. From 1562 to 1565, he was your confidant in Avila before being appointed rector at Medina del Campo. "I had a confessor who mortified me very much and was sometimes an affliction and great trial to me because he disturbed me exceedingly, and he was the one who profited me the most as far as I can tell";[14] "I knew that they told him to be careful of me, and that he shouldn't let the devil deceive him by anything I told him."[15] But shouldn't so solemn a *letrado* follow you with ecstatic transports of his own? You write: "I saw some of the wonderful favors the Lord bestowed on the rector of the Society of Jesus whom I have mentioned . . . Once a severe trial came upon him in which he was very persecuted and found himself in deep affliction."[16] Is this a reference to Fr. Álvarez, as Fr. Gratian notes in the margin, and as Fr. Larrañaga believes? Or is it to Gaspar de Salazar?[17] Later on, a few months before the death of Baltasar Álvarez, you sound a more personal note, writing to Isabel Osorio: "You should know that he is one of my best friends. He was my confessor for some years. . . . He is a saint."[18] Finally, a year before your own death, you write sadly from Palencia: "Nonetheless, regarding matters of the soul, I feel alone, for there is no one here that I know from the Society. Truly, I feel alone everywhere, because before, even when our saint was far away, it seems he was a companion to me, because he still communicated with me through letters. Well, we are in exile, and it is good that we feel this life to be one."[19] He must have been pretty special.

* * *

What you invented, Teresa, my love, was neither censure nor sublimation, but a transfiguration of desire and its mutation into *jouissance*. The future saint Francisco de Borja must have been somewhat startled, but I think that he listened and heard you. His benevolent presence was enough for you to pursue your train of thought. The pair of you met at least twice, and this "great contemplative" helped you to tie Martha and Mary, the monastic and the active life, together.[20] Later he became general of the Society of Jesus and you wrote to each other for eighteen years, a fact that was taken into account during the process of your beatification. Those letters have unfortunately not survived; what a testimony they must have contained! The former nobleman's encouragement, you let it be known, reinforced your conviction that it was possible to modulate desire between action and contemplation in the way you did, since "he answered . . . that it had happened to him."[21] Good gracious!

* * *

Today, listening to your nun stories, Borja holds his peace. Silence is as much part of the father's role as of the analyst's.

"Do you remember the hermit that Cassian speaks of?" (You like to impress the good fathers, my strategical Teresa, and that includes Borja. I can see why: they love it!) "The one who threw himself into a well, in order to see God sooner." Like a suicide bomber in Baghdad, Tel Aviv, or London? Or like one of the "consumed" whom Colette dwelt upon, those men and women who are even more numerous today, junkies of desire unto death by way of hard sex? "Well, if that hermit's desire had been faithful to God, he would not have put himself forward like that. For everything that comes from God is discreet and measured, I mean, luminous. Therefore we must be on our guard, always on the lookout! And we must curtail the time of prayer, no matter how enjoyable we find it. For otherwise our bodily strength will falter and our head will start to throb, trust me. I'm sure that moderation is necessary in all things, Father. And I dare to hope Your Honor will pardon me for thus advancing my humble opinion."

A father, still more a father of the Church, cannot but approve of such sensible opinions, Teresa. Which neither add nor detract, of course, from your intimate conviction of harboring the Lord at the center of your castle—like a precious jewel, you say later.[22] Your written ecstasy is a syncope that soothes you so as to link you to everybody, for "the Lord invites all [*convida el Señor a todos*]."[23] Your precious, blissful solitude is kept intact by weaving a net in the external world, like the "circumference" around your "center." Is this what you are telling your learned, blue-blooded Jesuit? He hardly needs to be told, surely, that any excess is always a fault! But "*perinde ac cadaver*" and "*AMDG—Ad majorem Dei gloriam*"!

Borja knows that you reprise Matthew ("Come unto me, all ye that labor and are heavy laden" [11:28]) in your own way. The divine feast you enjoy is obviously not intended for you alone: "If the invitation were not a general one, the Lord wouldn't have called us all."[24] Indeed, the more inclusive the invitation, the greater your *jouissance*. How so? Because the spiral of narcissism is so constructed that it sweeps the beloved toward grandiosity the moment he or she sets foot on it: we have touched on this already. It is in order to spread out this feast for everybody that you make yourself a writer in your castle-laboratory, at the same time as you set forth on the highways and byways of Spain, bringing reform to the Carmelite order.

$$* \; * \; *$$

"You of all people should understand, Andrew, as someone who's only interested in politics in order to get out of it! Teresa's grandiose perversion, her *père-version*, demands far more of her than the conventional charity that's enough for the average neurotic nun, trying to do good left and right so as to merit the sufferings of Christ. Politics as a form of connection has always been a magnet to paranoiacs, as you've often said yourself, and when it does not breed tyrants, it offers vast building sites to reformers and benefactors of humanity. Today's tyrants have dwindled into virtual clowns of the generalized spectacle. So what? They're still running after power and glory, aren't they? Going back to Teresa, her transports of ecstasy are just one side of a coin whose other side commands her to act politically. Ravished by the heights of her elevation in the Spouse, dazzled by union with Him at the heart of her castle, her only concern now is to grasp hold of the religious link that subtends the power of Church institutions, in this case the Carmelite order, and adapt it to her very own style of *jouissance*. After all, she is the Truth of the Other! Luckily this wild certainty only possesses her on and off. Not letting it hold her up, she manages to domesticate the incommensurable desire for the Other—paranoia, if you like—and exhibits her appeasement in institutionalized form, as an example to the whole world. She's saying: have a go, and then we'll talk! By founding a new monastic order, the Discalced Carmelites, Teresa proclaims to all and sundry that it's possible to infinitely transmute the meaning of the bond with others, and that this is what life, properly lived, is about! In all humility, needless to say. That's her ambition, don't you think? Stop harping on her pathology, this is a patient who has intuited your clinics already. She says in the "Sixth Dwelling Places": 'Through experience we have seen that it'—the jewel, or vision of Our Lord—'has cured us of some illnesses for which it is suited.'[25] Her faith is her therapy, and she spells it out. . . . Come on now, quit grumbling and let's read some more."

Chapter 19

FROM HELL TO FOUNDATION

But it seems to me that love is like an arrow sent forth by the will.

Teresa of Avila, *Meditations on the Song of Songs*

W e are in 1560, and Teresa, despite being taken out of herself in raptures and overwhelmed by the love of the Lord, is not at peace:
she frets about whether she is truly fulfilling her vocation. The
Convent of the Incarnation seems awfully big, despite its cramped conditions,
and far too agreeable: the Mitigated Rule, that governs the Carmelite order following the papal bull of 1247, is downright lax. And yet some find the regime
too frugal: meat no more than three times a week, a single meal on other days,
fasting during Lent and Advent—to hear them complain, you'd think it was
draconian. But why? Can this really be called a life of abstinence, abstention,
and poverty? What about the day trips, and the callers, and the semi-authorized
socializing? Only the ordeal of Calvary is worthy of God, and by that standard,
there's certainly nothing Christly about the Incarnation! Why was the Primitive Rule ever relaxed? Are they so wrong, the men and women who practice a
more austere and demanding spiritual code, abroad and in Spain too, and call
for an end to the laxity of this modern, rather too modern, Catholicism? Laxity, who said laxity? The sisters are all for it. Here's one now, returning from the
parlor, her mouth full of cake—yes, didn't you know, there are splendid refreshments to be enjoyed at the Carmelites' place, along with good talk!

"Beware the vice of gluttony, Sister!" Teresa rebukes her with a smile, not
sure of being immune to that temptation herself.

"Small fry compared with your outings, Sister," comes the swift retort. (These nuns can be nasty. Ill feeling reigns until nightfall, when there is singing and dancing after dinner between prayers. Even then, some persist in resentment against the Ahumada woman, who thinks she's a saint.) "Everyone knows that certain high-ranking persons, whose requests and alms no mother superior can refuse, apply to have you stay with them? Tee-hee . . ."

"I only go when I am ordered to do so."

"Oh, of course, but go you do. You go all steeped in God, they say, unless the devil's hand is in it!"

Teresa swallows back her anger. The girl is cheeky, but not completely wrong. Ahumada has an intimate circle of her own: her cousins Ana and Inés de Tapia, for example, and, at the moment, the young widow, daughter of a first cousin, who has become a lay sister and faithful companion, María de Ocampo. All these women admire her, and love to hear her tell the lives of the saints; sometimes she confides her own torments and the parts played in them by God and the devil.

Last night, for instance, Teresa had a vision she plans to share with her friends. They will surely understand, for the Lord often sends such terrifying images to women in particular, so as to deflect them from the temptations that are legion even here, in this mitigated convent where outings are allowed.

"I saw before my eyes, before falling asleep—and so it was not a dream, but truly a vision, of those that God grants not to our eyes but to the visceral depths of the soul—I saw, Sisters, the frightful punishment of some vices (*de algunos vicios el castigo*).[1] Yes, vices. Oh, no, I can't name them, they are so iniquitous that the words would burn my lips. I saw, I tell you, with the eyes of the soul, the terrible spectacle of those sinful creatures chastised. God did me the favor of sending me that vision with the sole intention of frightening me."

"A vision of Hell!" exclaims María de Ocampo.

"No, María, for the Hell to which one may be conveyed by means of prayer, as I have been, is impossible to describe: nothing but excruciating agony and nothing to see. But in this vision of the vices, the images seemed even more frightening than the tortures of Hell. I saw the pincers the demons use upon the damned, and other Dantesque horrors. There are plenty of descriptions in our good books, I have often read them to you, and altarpieces have been painted on the subject. Is it not strange, Sisters, that I experienced neither fear nor pain at the sight of such torments? Is it because those vices and their punishments did not concern me? But I felt a great revulsion, as I used to when I was a novice. Ah, Satan is a wondrous painter, my dears, he plays his tricks and sets his traps in the imagination, and we know that he does so the more with women.[2] Everything can be harmful to those as weak as we women are."[3]

"But Teresa, you have no cause to undergo the pain of such punishments. There are many here who would deserve them more! God forgive me for presuming to give Him ideas! After all, the Mitigated Rule itself ushers us into the path of temptation." Like many young widows, María de Ocampo struggles against depravity with an almost excessively high moral sense.

"We can't be angels down here, María. On the contrary, we have a body."[4] Does Teresa want to appear less intransigent toward human vices than her cousin?

"I'm very scared of the devil!" says Ana de Tapia, who is apt to be hard on herself. And yet she goes out less than many other young nuns, and her daydreams can hardly be very salacious.

"Are you, indeed! I fear a discontented nun more than many devils."[5] She hasn't the heart to chide her companions; she would always rather make them laugh.

But today, she is not in the mood for pleasantries. The jibes from the greedy sister, plus this conversation about vice and temptation, have plunged her back into the unspeakable Hell that God was good enough to let her glimpse, in order to set her free. She was not there for long, just long enough to understand that the Spouse wanted to show her the inconceivable place the devils had prepared for her, the fate she had earned by her sins.

* * *

Hell has no images because it is without space. That's what Hell is, first and foremost: no space, no location, no extension. You yourself hardly exist, either. You are present, fully inhabiting time, but deprived of space. Can one conceive of a place without space?

That impossibility is called Hell. A kind of unthinkable, nameless hollow, scooped out of a filthy wall. Only Christ has known this, as the psalmist foretold long before, and Theresa can't but follow her Spouse: "He made a pit, and digged it, and is fallen into the ditch which he made" (Ps. 7:15). Not for the first time, however, the Bride outdoes the Groom. In her vision, there is no measure at all; Teresa's Hell is pure constriction.

If seeing were possible in this nonexistent space, Teresa would have seen nothing but ghastly walls crushing her under their weight. In the absence of all light, she senses or feels what would have appalled her sight. A long, narrow alleyway enclosing her on every side, its floor muddy and foul smelling, swarming with putrid vermin; this pipe is a sewer. At the end of the stinking bowel, a cupboard in which the Carmelite finds herself confined. No reality can give the least notion of what she endures, her soul consumed in a furnace, while a thousand miseries harrow her cramped body.

Hell. It cannot be compared to the agonies Teresa has already been through, racked by nervous crises whose ferocity every doctor had recognized, nor to the torments visited on her by her demons.

Devoid of space and representation, is this journey to the underworld, this Sheol, a tearing apart? On one side anguish, oppression, the flesh stabbed through and through; on the other boundless desolation and despair, a terrible grief, impossible to convey. That your soul is being torn out of you would be an understatement; it splits of its own accord, while somebody else takes your life away. Thus cut in two, the writhing spirit converges with the body's frightful pain. Suffocated, cramped, damned, she is on fire, dislocated into pieces. Long alleys, pitch darkness, an entrance like the smoking mouth of an oven, a foul and slimy cul-de-sac, a crawling heap of maggots. Oh, my distraught Teresa, at the far side of night.

* * *

Did you dream your own birth? Does this body and this soul, squeezed almost to death, reenact the irrevocable expulsion from the womb, that one-time haven turned foul cloaca? "I found it impossible either to sit down or to lie down, nor was there any room," "unable to hope for any consolation."

Or is this perhaps a disgusted perception of your own body, a fetid prison from which you are "unable to hope for any pleasure," from which the only thing to do is escape, fleeing away from yourself into the Paradise of the ideal Father?

Or again, perhaps this infernal vision dramatizes the painful coming-to after a comitial cataclysm, recalled only as experiences of asphyxiation, discharge of stinking matter, glutinous sphincters, feverish larval teemings? It could well be the aftermath of exhaustion, prostration, the memory of desperate gagging that is no longer a torrent of woeful tears, but rather the epileptic strangulation of "a fire in the soul that I don't know how to describe . . . I don't know how to give a sufficiently powerful description of that interior fire and that despair."[6]

This truth branded on your whole being, my martyred Teresa, cannot be laid at Satan's door. Paul Claudel trembles with you when you are reduced to being a worm in this Hell; for all his precious rhetoric, he is one of your secret admirers.[7] Between tapeworm and turd, neither male nor female, neither beast nor monster, a paltry, stubborn abjection, you are ground down to the degree zero of life in this spaceless Gehenna: merely a lump of horribly compacted flesh. So terrible a trial could only have been imposed on you by God, in order to make you see with the eyes of your whole body the hideous abode from which His mercy will, without a doubt, deliver you. Isn't this a sovereign gift, the ultimate sign of His concern for you?

But perhaps you *are* guilty, as much as the sinners who were atrociously punished for their vices in that vision you shared with your friends. Let's see. Temptations, like the ones in that nightmare, are not unknown to you: you mention them often enough. But the toad thoughts you beat out of your body with the help of bunches of nettles, preferably lashing the sores inflicted by a hair shirt— can they really be called vices? Possibilities, perils, certainly. But vices? As basely vulgar as that?

Not you. You deserve more, you deserve better: you are worthy of a far worse punishment than any God reserves for ordinary reprobates. You merit nothing less than the Truth of Hell, in its total, crushing, absolute version. Because God loves you more, He cares more about your fate than about that of common sinners, and so He strikes fear into you with a condensed season in His worst Hell. Conclusion: He loves you the best!

By one of those blessed reversals you are so deft with, you, the unworthiest of all, deem yourself to be the favorite; you are the most tested and rejected, because the most cherished. It's a maneuver of genius, my unsinkable Teresa, informed by the impregnable logic of the Catholicism that precedes and sustains you, anchored in the extravagant belief that the Other exists, whose name is Love. Whatever else may happen. But a love that is inseparable from the twin that fuels it: suffering. Or perhaps this twin is hate?

$$\star \;\; \star \;\; \star$$

The little group around Teresa continues their discussion. At some point the sisters notice that Ahumada is abstracted: engaged in prayer or meditation, who can tell? That's how she is—a holy woman, whatever her detractors say. They respect and love her. She'll come back to earth when she's ready.

"And what if we became discalced?" says María de Ocampo suddenly. "Like Saint Francis, or the Poor Clares? They had no truck with the worldly pleasures we Carmelites indulge in." She seems agitated by the very idea, unless it is the thought of the infernal compressor that's upsetting her.

The others are surprised and a little disconcerted. What does Teresa think? A silence falls. A silence from Hell. Does it cause her to waft up from the abyss or to descend from glorious summits? Immortalized by Velázquez, or perhaps by a pupil of his, her holy gaze is lifted upward, the better to plumb her own depths. A double interiority. The small company holds its breath.

"What do you mean, María?" Ahumada does not immediately grasp the scope of the proposal, but it does not surprise her: in it she hears an echo of her own wish.

"We could set up a new convent! With stricter rules!" María bursts out.

Dreamy Teresa can be briskly efficient when required. No more thoughts of Hell! No time to waste.

"The first thing to do is find a source of income for the future convent!"

Is this project unfeasible? Ahumada is too pragmatic not to think so at first. Then, one day after Communion, our Lord chips in, ordering her to pour all her energies into getting the initiative off the ground.

A foundress is born.

* * *

Andrew has quit teasing me. Oh, I know he's a long way from coming around to Teresa's virtues, and his sardonic asides will always be the best way of proving he exists while loving me. But he's now prepared to continue the trip—a change of plan on his part.

"So we just follow the trail of your saint's foundations, okay? We start with Saint Joseph of Avila. What's next, remind me, Medina del Campo? Malagón? Valladolid? Toledo? Pastrana? Salamanca? And then Granada? I'll drive, Juan can twiddle the radio. What's the latest on the human bombs?"

I never know whether he's kidding or writing a novel. Will it be my novel this time? Will it be Teresa's? Anything can happen. Personally, I always travel best in the company of books.

We're off!

Part 5

From Ecstasy to Action

What is necessary is a different approach,
the approach of a lord when in time of war
his land is overrun with enemies.

Teresa of Avila, *The Way of Perfection*

Chapter 20

THE GREAT TIDE

The purpose of this spiritual marriage: the birth always of good works,
good works [*de que nazcan siempre obras, obras*].
Teresa of Avila, *The Interior Castle*

Now the tide's breath gusts over the island, there's a confetti of rose
and wisteria petals whirling toward the waters of the Fier, the birds
have vanished, and I am looking out from my veranda, which defies
the winds as stoutly as the Baleines lighthouse. Here on the Île de Ré, the late
August storms tear through the nonchalance of summer, and none too soon.
I'm used to them. Is it because my roommate never leaves me for a second? I
tend increasingly to the view that repose is not a thing of this world, and everything else is a lie.

I buy magazines to read on the beach, I listen to the radio, I watch TV. All
sorts of dramatic events are happening. Nothing is happening. The culture
pages pretend to get worked up about the imminent literary season. The new
pope reassures the synagogue (somewhat), and tries to rationalize (elementary)
faith, or vice versa, while the president of all the French jets off to foist our
national compassion on someplace in the Hexagon or in the world: one deed of
republican charity is worth two pledges on paper. Tide for tide, the surge pow-
ered by the media is lapping these days around the feet of the sacred—or of its
absence. That's my opinion, anyway. I won't mention it to Andrew (who sends
me cryptic, i.e., besotted, daily e-mails), or to Marianne—who since her return
from Cuenca has been studying Hebrew and Freud, and is planning to go into

analysis in September. Happy news! I can guess what they're both thinking, differently and spontaneously: Oh, just another of Sylvia's obsessions, an optical illusion created by the saint's works, in league with the bad weather that's keeping her on her island. No two ways about it. Unless . . .

This fall's literary season, with apologies to my publisher Mr. Zonabend, I mean Bruno, is pure marketing, considerably more so than usual, in fact. I'm not one of those who bemoan the extinction of Literature with a capital L, plaintive aesthetes left high and dry by the tsunami of the spectacle. I've sweated long enough in the august precincts of Jussieu and Columbia, and then over my Duras book, to know that literature has got to roll with the breakers. The smart wave to which I made my own modest contribution has ebbed. Adieu well-wrought language, high-flown style, writerliness, textuality! Too hard and too slow. Now that form is dead, courtesy of TV, long live the platform! A few fastidious mourners for the world of belles-lettres bleat on about the philistinism of the "society of the spectacle," but they don't mind raking in the profits. Nobody has yet read the novel already labeled the best seller of the *rentrée*, but every arts-and-leisure reader knows that it cost millions, as befits a fine sci-fi synopsis written in French for Hollywood; they know the author is ready to trot his pooch up the red carpet at the Cannes Film Festival or the Élysée Palace, and that lawyers for Muslims, Jews, women, and God are lining up to sue him.

As a matter of fact, everyone will get hauled over the coals around this probable Prix Goncourt and the scandal it's bound to create. Destroy, he said, she said, with a jaundiced laugh; some laughter is just a dressing over the inability to have a good time. And a way of stirring up the sex wars that in turn drive many a righteous female memoir of rape and abuse—poor little girls who loved it, really.

In the past, the masses wanted fascism. No longer. Today, in our leaderless civilization, the masses only aspire to a dismal smirking. What masses, anyway? The survivors of the class struggle have adopted the mores of the petty bourgeoisie. The petty bourgeois have traded their cultural pretensions for the artificial paradises of instant gratification. The spectacle numbs and revolts us, and yet the exploits of technology have captivated our dreams, and some of the brightest brains are researching the regeneration of this tawdry species to the point, perhaps, of immortality. So it doesn't take much for the most apocalyptic of despairing scribblers to push us over the edge, doped by a chain of promoters with scores to settle and profits to make—we laugh fit to bust, we buy the product. Jaded, depressed, without a future, sulky as spoiled kids full of rancid grudges and aimless lusts, we wallow smugly in the consumption of bitter disenchantments and mirth without catharsis. I understand you, clones of toxic nihilism that you are: you relish the ultimate pleasure of lording it over manipulated spectators of whom you're one, as am I, with only the forlorn hope of getting the hell out, clutching your loot, sooner than put an end to it all.

And yet your Hell is just a cry to Heaven, which must exist someplace not far away, otherwise the earth would not be round. Sure enough, while I glance through the splutterings of the so-called literary press, the pageantry of World Youth Day in Cologne is being broadcast on TV. A dazzling multilingual show of flawless intellectual mastery over the need to believe! Baby Jesus at the wheel and holy wafers on arrival, in a choreography of chaste young bodies, beatific smiles, and the jazzy lilt of postmodern hymns. The Vatican could not have achieved a more universal triumph.

On another channel, Jewish settlers wearing yellow stars brandish babes in arms, as if that would stop the Israeli army evicting them from their moshavs in the Gaza Strip. Muslim guerrilla groups, meanwhile, divided into pro- and antisuicide tactics, are at each other's throats, and it ends up in slaughter either way. Next there will be footage of car bombs in Baghdad, Hamas shooting up Fatah and vice versa, Hezbollah wreaking havoc in Lebanon . . . one humanitarian disaster after another.

Who said there were no more masters at the helm, no great mentors anymore?

There is one: Jesus Christ Our Lord, relayed by his deputy on earth. Humanity needs a Lord who loves it, and needs still more a Child-Lord, a Loving Child-Lord. This crying need had to be discovered, had to come forth, and now it has. It doesn't have to be satisfied. It is enough to manifest it, to make it apparent, to voice it. Be content to receive the message: fulfillment will follow in and through the mere hope of fulfillment. Waiting for God may be like waiting for Godot, yet this festive imagery of tambourines and trumpets is a world away from parsimonious Protestant patience, Beckett style. The need for love is a need for unbridled communication, and communication is a rich promise of love: Catholicism has never revealed the secret of its message better than in these popular fêtes punctuating our planetary age. These adolescents in quest of love—which is to say, every single one of us in the four corners of the world—have yielded to the one true religion, the faith that has come to dominate all others (which are green with envy!) and outlived the ideologies (which succumbed to terminal totalitarianism, and good riddance): the religion of Love.

I gaze at the trusting, well-behaved, well-policed crowds. The mystery of love subjugates all these young people, and smoothes its balm through the screen onto the hurts and desires of the world's viewers, who were all Catholics for a day—remember?—when John Paul II was buried. The essence of communication, especially when it adopts the guise of a spectacle, is Catholic: childish, affectionate, clinging to the Father and prepared to suffer unto death, to destroy itself, the better to resume the search magnetized by the promise of a possible Good, for later or for never. Irrespective of the decline in vocations and the emptying churches, this promise of and patience for love is all that survives in these dark times, transmitted by the evidently "catholic" magic of Christianity, to the whole of a humanity that has lost its way and needs to believe.

I'm not denying that the citizens of the consumer society are slower to sacrifice themselves for their fellow man—whether out of love for the latter or for the Lord—than the saints and martyrs of old. Or that the pleasure–pain tandem that once underpinned both self-mortification and the spirit of charitable giving has noisily decamped into SM clubs and backrooms. Is the love imperative that communicants and spectators seek here compatible with the work upon oneself, and for the democracy of proximate community, which Christian morality demands, or demanded? We may well wonder. The Holy Father, himself an exacting theologian, is sufficiently preoccupied by the question to impress on his splendid, young, festive listeners that the time has come to "give yourselves." It was the right moment. Is it still?

The chortling nihilist and the incestuously abused seductress of the new literary season are not beyond rescue; they could still be fished out by that universal net. A believer in Evil is simply an orphan of Good. This hardly prevents such a one from devoting himself or herself, body and soul, to personal advancement. Fine. But when they are the first to say so, while delivering themselves into the jaws of the spectacle, are they not aching for a word from the loving Father? As graceless depressives, or tireless officiators at the altar of one-night stands, such artists could well be Catholics in waiting. They receive indulgence even before they get the Prix Goncourt.

The most pathetic need of all, the most impossible to satisfy, the need to believe is unlike other needs in that it links biological survival to the pleasure of making meaning. It became entwined, two thousand years ago, with the love of an ideal Father inseparable from a Virgin Mother; this is a dogma that contains plenty of involuntary wisdom, nuggets of which come across in the stories my patients tell me. I would go so far as to contend that human beings owe many achievements to this need to believe, and particularly to the Christian and post-Christian versions of that amorous, fretful logic: infinitesimal calculus, Picasso, Joyce, Cantor, the hydrogen bomb, and the space shuttle, to pick a few at random. Provided we tear ourselves away from it with infinite subtlety, because if it is done too abruptly, blunders ensue, and then Terror— we have seen it often enough.

* * *

I don't think I ever underestimated the presumptuousness of my loving desire to understand Teresa of Avila. Faced with the spectacle of devotion this late-August storm has forced me to watch, cloistered indoors before the TV, the enormity of my absurd ambition comes home to me more forcefully than ever. In the world that's hardening into shape today—on one side, this youthful embrace of faith, whose most peaceful, most triumphal, most irritating (after reconsideration of its long history) manifestation is doubtless the Catholic faith; on the other, the shrill misery of a would-be iconoclastic culture of success—there seems little room for my "third way."

Here are the options. One, you are an eternal adolescent mooning after love, in which case, knowingly or not, you are a believer: you need that ideal Father in whom you shall recognize another eternal adolescent, not to say the Infant Jesus himself, who a good father who knows his business will not fail to advise you to cultivate in your innermost being. That's how it goes, faith is a dialectical spiral, and the logic of the same name lost no time in giving it an extra twist. At this point you take refuge in the bosom of the Virgin Mary, whose orthodox icon you may parade along the banks of the Rhine in order to scare Protestants, for example. You trust in the pope, a Holy Father who utters truths you had not been aware of, truths your dreams had been awaiting, all impatient, in the dark. You are saved.

Two, you know a bit more about sex. In which case Love—as preached by the churches, and, in a different key of virtual salvation, by the media—does not strike you as being the basis of everything, the cornerstone of morality, society, and progress. Your experience tells you that this pesky Love tends to break down into numberless splinters of lust and hatred. You succumb to the vertigo of being the last person standing in a vile, debased world. One hope left: to snigger all the way to the bank when your novel proves a hit. Alternatively you might heed the president's summons, and join the club of power. Anything is possible, but whatever it is it will be televised.

No room for a third way, then? I fear not, especially when I look around me, rather than skulk in a tower immersed in the writings of a Counter-Reformation saint, a junk-shop curiosity of no interest to anyone except a handful of oddballs like me.

All the same, I've been following that third way myself for a while. Forty years of a woman's life is not nothing, even if it's not very much, counting back from Bethlehem! I've got no choice. Love, that is, faith, is not something I "stepped in," as the sniggering author said, being a depressed rationalist and egregiously scatological, just to warn everybody off. But I don't ritually bend the knee before Eros or Agape, either. With Freud I listen to them, lie them on the couch, question them. With Kafka I sidestep, estrange myself from the ranks, analyze. Does the essential remain? What remains is the movement, and the eyes open to the road, which is also open.

Since I count myself a Freudian, I've obviously taken seriously the question of whether we are a sect, a sort of die-hard branch of post-Judeo-Christianity. And if we are (it's not inconceivable), are we living through one of those metamorphoses of love's call and response that aspire to the renewal of infinite truths? Our tenets do not posit the "death of God" in the sense dear to the zealous disciples of "pleasure with no strings attached," of self-loathing, of terror painted as revolutionary and Nothingness painted as philosophical—and I'd rather forget the stalag-cum-gulag exterminators who appointed themselves to decide which human beings were surplus to requirements. Are we carrying out, on the contrary, with our psychoanalytical way of comprehending and doing, one of those endless queryings of the divine? Or should I say, queryings of the very lucidity of love—of its elucidation?

Putting Teresa back on the agenda, Lacan thought that Catholics couldn't be analyzed. I, Sylvia Leclercq, have the gall to contradict that wild-eyed post-Catholic post-Freudian. Backed up by my cherished research, much of which has been conducted at the MPH (for my sins!), I hereby declare that it is possible to put the mystery of the Lord Himself through the scanner, and analyze the need to believe in love.

In this cavalier adventure you are, investigative Teresa, my unwitting accomplice in lunacy.

* * *

The tempest over the Fier is abating, and through the window the bell tower of Ars stands placidly outlined against the horizon. Me and the old salt-marsh worker down there, perfecting his pyramid of crystals, we live in a Christian land. I'm not sure he either knows or cares. It doesn't matter. Next to him, with my geraniums on the wall, I lose the sense of time. But when time catches up with me again, like an inescapable occupational hazard, I get back to the magazines and the TV, to history swinging by. That's when there's nothing to beat you, Teresa, my love, for keeping me connected—and completely unplugged.

Chapter 21

SAINT JOSEPH, THE VIRGIN MARY, AND HIS MAJESTY

> Between me and You, an "it is I" disquiets me. Ah, let Your "it is I" remove my
> "it is I" from in between us!
>
> Mansur al-Hallaj[1]

To found her house of God: Teresa's desire, irrepressible and majestic, had altered course. But what house, hers or His? The difference is a matter of voice: henceforth Teresa hears His Voice becoming hers. No longer is there a loving Spouse, the vision of whom carries her toward exile in Him body and soul, and whose presence envelops her here and now—both things simultaneously and alternately. Instead a third person intervenes, more overwhelmingly than ever: His Majesty or the Lord speaks to the foundress at crucial moments of the enterprise and buoys her up; indeed, He often dictates the plans of battle. The sight and touch of the Spouse is increasingly superseded by hearing, the most intellectual of the senses, tailored for decisiveness and action. In Teresa's case, that is; I could name a few (in my workplace, as it happens) whose experience of hearing voices does nothing to bring them back to reality, quite the opposite—but that's another story.

Teresa did not lack for logistics advisers. There was her confessor, the Jesuit priest Baltasar Álvarez, and the Dominican Fr. Pedro Ibáñez, and her Carmelite superiors, including Fr. Gregorio Hernández and the ecclesiastical provincial Angel de Salazar, as well as the rectors of the Society of Jesus: Dionisio Vázquez, followed by Gaspar de Salazar. There was that affectionate Franciscan and loyal accomplice, Friar Pedro de Alcántara. But over and above these it was the word of His Majesty that carried most weight with the nun, imposed itself upon her confessors and counselors, and, having become indistinguishable from the word of La Madre, held them all under His sway. This imperious Third Person—the Voice of the ideal Father converted into Teresa's ideal superego—was a resolutely *interior* Other, with whom Teresa would not lose a contact that was ever more vocal as she continued to analyze herself through writing and through making foundations.

Mind you, to be agreeable to His Majesty did not simply mean *jouissance*, it also involved hearkening to the ideal Father's words as constructed by Teresa in her readings and prayers. More precisely, to please Him was to respond to His teachings: to embody them in *acts*, in works. She would have to adjust her thoughts, her body, and her transactions in the world *with* that ideal Other who spoke *within* her.

* * *

And thus you set forth on a new stage of the journey, my attentive, my realistic Teresa.

* * *

To hear that Voice transcends listening, it is rather a new kind of enjoying: a matter of com-prehending the Voice in Itself without self. Of being agreeable (*agradable*) to it outside oneself, at the same time as pleasing the Other in oneself as though pleasing another self. An altered self that begins to stir, to strain toward the Other without cease, to almost merge with It at times; nothing would stand between them were it not for the tympanum, her hymen as it were, like a fine Dutch linen or a translucent diamond partition filtering the Master's light through the psyche and body of the nun turned foundress. The *Dwelling Places* tirelessly accumulate metaphors that might convey this mysterious alteration-cohabitation with His Voice. For it is only by co-responding to the Voice of the Third Person incorporated inside her that Teresa de Ahumada can consider herself worthy to become *Teresa of Jesus*. Thus and only thus persuaded of the truth of her task, the future Madre feels unassailable, irrefutable, armed against all obstacles or conflicts—for that correspondence demotes them to the rank of lies.

The Voice of His Majesty speaking through her mouth is certainly categorical: "Do you know what it is to love Me truthfully? It is to understand that everything that is displeasing to me is a lie [*entender que todo es mentira lo que no es agradable a mí*]."[2] In this comprehensive hearing and understanding, "truth," "love," and whatever is "pleasing" are synonymous, provided it is the ideal Father, identified with Teresa, who is speaking. Or, to put it another way, provided Teresa is projected into Him by way of that vocal Third Person, His Voice. From now on she is more than protected, she is untouchable. "Paranoid visions": my colleague Jérôme Tristan pounces straightaway, it's his job, the symptom is patent, "too patent, Sylvia dear." Of course it is, who does he think I am? Ah, the amiable paternalism of men . . . La Madre "sees" in visions "all kinds of people" who are "preparing to attack her," to "persecute" and "harm" her. I could hardly fail to spot it, my anxious Teresa. All you can rely on is God, the God you hear while He speaks through your mouth!

Not content with savoring His penetration and habitation of her, from around 1560 Teresa heard Him and made His Voice heard *urbi et orbi*. Persecuted as she perhaps or certainly was, the praying woman was far from being left all alone with her visions, as she had recently written. In aid of her ambition to be agreeable to His Majesty, two supportive figures stepped forward: Saint Joseph and the Virgin. With them by her side, her metamorphosis took the form of a re-foundation, a reformation of the Carmelite order.

> One day after Communion, His Majesty earnestly commanded me to strive for this new monastery with all my powers, and He made great promises that it would be founded and that He would be highly served in it. He said it should be called *St. Joseph* and that this saint would keep watch over us at one door, and *Our Lady* at the other, *that Christ would remain with us*, and that it would be a star shining with great splendor. He said that even though religious orders were mitigated one shouldn't think He was little served in them; He asked what would become of the world if it were not for religious people, *and said that I should tell my confessor what He commanded, that He was asking him not to go against this or hinder me from doing it.*[3]

But how to get this vocal injunction, this new understanding of the nun with the divine, publicly acknowledged? After all, she could hardly inform Fr. Baltasar that what she heard was not the fancy of a poor deluded woman, but the utterance of His Majesty Himself! Teresa's quandary was not induced by her awareness of being a woman in a man's world, nor by her dependence upon validation by a higher authority, as feminist commentators have suggested. The Voice that dwelt within her was rooted in psychic depths way more radical than the perception of such restrictive imbalances of social power. Teresa wavered, dreading as was natural the reaction of her confessor; yet, with still greater lucidity, she also feared the "lights of reason" that the good man strove to share with her and that she was conscious of betraying by her "understanding" with the Voice. On the borderland of reason, like a chess player she assessed the risks she incurred with this business of voices, and gambled on controlling the game. A Jesuit, therefore a Tridentine, Fr. Baltasar did not contest the existence of Voices from the Beyond, but he was not about to offer a blind endorsement on the mere strength of Teresa's word; let her discuss it with the superior of her own order! Where foundations were concerned, he advised Teresa to ask doña Guiomar to write to Rome in support of the project.

Teresa sought in vain for a confidant to whom she might expound her new way of being with His Majesty. She knew from experience that even old friends are not always trustworthy, particularly female friends. María de Ocampo was only a lay sister as yet, and even though the foundation idea was originally hers, she was merely contributing a "legitime"; it would be a further ten years before she took full Carmelite vows under the name María Bautista. And when this same cousin was appointed prioress of the Valladolid monastery, she was noticeably sympathetic to the calced persecutors of Teresa's discalced tribe, enough said! All in all, few people can be counted on in this world.

* * *

Thanks to God, doña Guiomar de Ulloa undertook to help out in launching the longed-for overhaul of the Carmelite regime. She submitted the foundational project to the Carmelite provincial, who, man of faith though he was, would be more amenable to a petition from a wealthy noblewoman than from a humble nun. The idea of a monastery housing thirteen Carmelites in accordance with the Primitive Rule of poverty and enclosure appealed to him; he pledged his full support. Guiomar sent the official request in his name and started the paperwork with the Vatican to obtain the permissions; they even dared hope for the endorsement of Francisco de Borja, whom Pius IV had summoned to Rome not long before. But the story leaked out in Avila. The Convent of the Incarnation took umbrage and advanced jealous objections: How was any foundation possible in the absence of a secure source of income? Other orders grumbled that alms intakes were skimpy enough already, so imagine an extra convent without a cent to its name! All this was enough to unnerve the provincial, who changed his mind.

Teresa was not especially disappointed: such was her confidence in His Majesty within, she never doubted she would prevail. On the other hand, she was not at all sure whether the others believed in her claim that He spoke through her! Judiciously she examined her predicament from every angle, and opted for prudence:

> Sometimes I gave them explanations. Yet since I couldn't mention the main factor, which was that the Lord had commanded me to do this, I didn't know how to act; so I remained silent about the other things. God granted me the very great favor that none of all this disturbed me; rather, I gave up the plan with as much ease and contentment as I would have if it hadn't cost me anything. . . . and I remained in the house, for I was very satisfied and pleased there. Although I could never stop believing that the foundation would come about, I no longer saw the means, nor did I know how or when; but I was very certain that it would.[4]

The problem lay, she thought, in her *being* as it had been gradually forged by prayer, for "there is a great difference in the ways one may be"—*habéis de entender que va mucho de estar a estar.*[5] Henceforth her *being* would be defined by this experience of alteration-cohabitation with Him: Jesus is His Majesty within, speaking though her in order to act through her. "Seek yourself in Me," the Master would command in years to come. For the moment, it was imperative to convince everyone who was anyone in the Church that she had been chosen by the Third Person, chosen to be and to found as though she were He.

★ ★ ★

Teresa of Jesus, or Teresa as in Moses? God speaks through her, the Voice inhabits the burning bush that she is. I can picture from here the frowns of the Carmelite fathers, the contortions of the Jesuits, and the hairsplitting of the Dominicans who now endorsed her, now deplored her, depending on moment and individual temperament. And I'm fascinated by the "theological" seduction La Madre worked on them. She managed to get them onside without neglecting to cover her back by creating personal networks of useful friends of both sexes, establishing practical bulwarks, and organizing a solid intendancy to tide her over everyday setbacks.

Teresa was well aware that the subtle variations of her being, which were the strong points of her praying and its modulations, were weaknesses in the eyes of the world; the challenge was thus to continue to cultivate them, but secretly, silently, shrouded in caution, while she conducted a diplomacy of prudence and influence, even—or especially—with prelates. Like the psychologist she was, she began by probing the difference between the Voice of His Majesty as heard inside and her own reason: the ideal Father turned into the ideal enamored Self was not the same as the self.

> Many of the things I write about here do not come from my own head, but my heavenly Master tells them to me. The things I designate with the words "this I understood" or "the Lord said this to me" cause me great scrupulosity if I leave out even as much as a syllable. Hence if I don't recall everything exactly, I put it down as coming from myself; or also, some things are from me. I don't call mine what is good, for I already know that nothing is good in me but what the Lord has given me without my meriting it. But when I say "coming from myself," I mean not being made known to me through a revelation.[6]

In the current state of her being, this myself without a self, governed by the Other, is shorn of personal will and consciousness, and yet by virtue of this very alteration feels more certain than ever of its sovereign governance:

> There come days in which I recall an infinite number of times what St. Paul says—although assuredly not present in me to the degree it was in him—for it seems to me *I neither live, nor speak, nor have any desire but that He who strengthens and governs me might live in me.*[7]

And then sometimes this assurance collapses into stupor. Teresa goes through periods in which the bright transference, the revelation, have gone: "It happened just now that for eight days it seemed there wasn't any knowledge in me—nor could I acquire any—of what I owed God, or any remembrance of His favors; my soul was *in a terrible stupor* and in I don't know what kind of condition."[8]

But there are also moments in which the fusion with the ideal Father reaches its apogee, so that His truth becomes "hers" in perfect exaltation:

And what power this Majesty appears to have, since in so short a time He leaves such an abundant increase and things so marvelous impressed upon the soul! O *my* Grandeur and Majesty! What are You doing, *my* all-powerful Lord? Look upon whom You bestow such sovereign favors! Don't You recall that this soul has been an abyss of lies and a sea of vanities, and all through my own fault?[9]

Even so, in a final twist of self-observation, the analysand Teresa is skeptical enough to wonder whether the entire experience might not be a dream, after all. A wonderful dream that will only become reality once she has confronted the humdrum chores and travails of foundation, the "business affairs" she mentions in Letter 24.[10]

★ ★ ★

The first of these travails would be the foundation of the Convent of Saint Joseph. Teresa was just beginning to invent that blend of vocation and pragmatism, the supernatural and the efficient, whose permutations would underpin the sixteen further foundations accomplished over the twenty years she had left to live. Some people applauded the reformer, others attacked her. On balance, however (and she was a compulsive balancer of accounts, whether in direct relationships or by means of letters), our chess player felt so bolstered by her exchanges with His Majesty that she could only laugh at her adversaries and persecutors of every stripe:

> Likewise the devil began striving here through one person and another to make known that I had received some revelation about this work. Some persons came to me with great fear to tell me we were in trouble and that it could happen that others might *accuse me of something and report me to the Inquisitors.* This amused me and made me laugh, for I never had any fear of such a possibility. If anyone were to see that I went against the slightest ceremony of the Church in a matter of faith, I myself knew well that I would die a thousand deaths for the faith or for any truth of Sacred Scripture. And I said they shouldn't be afraid about these possible accusations; that it would be pretty bad for my soul if there were something in it of the sort that I should have to fear the Inquisition; that I thought that if I did have something to fear I'd go myself to seek out the Inquisitors: and that if I were accused, the Lord would free me, and I would be the one to gain.[11]

Thanks to God, the practice of silent prayer had penetrated into every milieu; even the Dominican priest Pedro Ibáñez was a keen practitioner. The great theologian retired for two years into a monastery of his order so as to freely immerse himself in that mental prayer of union with God that was so important for Teresa, thanks to Osuna and in part also, let's not forget, to Uncle Pedro. Could the experience be contagious? There is a great difference in the ways one may be. . . .

As a further sign from Providence, the Society of Jesus appointed a new rector. Father Dionisio Vázquez, who had reservations about Teresa's project, was replaced by Fr. Gaspar de Salazar, "another very spiritual one who had great courage and understanding and a good background in studies." Her confessor urged her to confide in this man, especially as her conflicts with the authorities who resisted reform meant her soul "couldn't even breathe"; was it out of anguish?[12]

The first meeting between Teresa of Avila and Gaspar de Salazar was a rarefied moment of pure love that she, naturally, distilled in writing:

> I felt in my spirit I don't know what that I never recall having felt with anyone, neither before nor afterward; nor would I be able to describe what this experience was, or draw any comparisons. For it was a spiritual joy and understanding within my soul that *his soul would understand mine and that mine would be in harmony with his*; although, as I say, I don't know how such an experience was possible. For if I had spoken with him or had heard enthusiastic reports about him, it wouldn't have been a great thing to experience joy in knowing he would understand me. But *he hadn't spoken one word to me*, nor I any to him, nor was he anyone of whom I had any previous knowledge. Afterward I saw that *my spirit was not deceived*, for in every way it did me and my soul great good to speak with him. His attitude is very suited to persons whom it seems the Lord has already brought very far along, for *he makes them run* rather than walk with measured step. His method is to detach them from everything and to mortify them, for the Lord has given him the most remarkable talent for doing this, as well as for many other things.[13]

* * *

The beneficial effects of this "incomparable" rapport with Fr. Salazar were not long in coming. The conversation with the ideal Father promptly resumed, and

His Majesty (obviously residing "in heaven," far above the effusions of the two soul mates, but speaking through Teresa's mouth) "urged" the nun to return to matters of foundation:

> A little while after I had got to know [Salazar], the *Lord began again to urge* me to take up once more the matter of the monastery and to give my confessor and this rector many reasons and arguments why they shouldn't impede me from the work. Some of these reasons made them fear, because this Father Rector never doubted the project was from the spirit of God, for through much study and care he considered all the consequences. After much reflection they didn't dare venture to hinder me from carrying out this work.[14]

Although she was deeply attached to this Jesuit (who would later, under suspicion of Illuminism, suffer persecution and imprisonment), from a business point of view my political Teresa was always grateful to the Society as a whole for the support it gave to her reformist designs. Despite the tensions and severe exigencies to which the Jesuits had often subjected her—trials she had the sense to appreciate as formative—she gave them a flattering role in some of her prayerful visions:

> I saw great things concerning members of the order (of the whole order together) that this Father belonged to, that is, of the Society of Jesus. I saw them *in heaven*, sometimes *with white banners in their hands*, and, as I say, other very admirable things about them. Thus I hold this order in great veneration, for I've had many dealings with them and I see that their lives are in conformity with what the Lord has made known to me about them.[15]

The Dominicans were equally petted, for Teresa was always at pains to preserve the balance between the two orders. Humbly and without favoritism, she acknowledged the help and support her reforms had had from priests like Pedro Ibáñez, Domingo Báñez, and García de Toledo. His Majesty was kind enough moreover to send her premonitory visions that reassured her about the brilliant future of their order at a time when it was "somewhat fallen":

> Once while I was praying near the Blessed Sacrament, a saint [Saint Dominic] appeared to me whose order was somewhat fallen. He held in his hands a great book. He opened it and told me to read some very large and legible letters.

This is what they said. "In the time to come this order will flourish; it will have many martyrs."

At another time when I was at Matins in the choir, there were shown or represented to me six or seven members—it seems there were that many—of the same order, *holding swords in their hands. I think this meant that they will defend the faith.* For at another time when I was at prayer, my spirit was carried off to where it seemed to be in a large field in which many were in combat, and *those belonging to this order were fighting with great fervor.* Their faces were beautiful and very much aglow. They conquered many, throwing them to the ground; others, they killed. It seemed to me this battle was *against the heretics.*[16]

Clearly, a battle plan was taking shape: with His interior Majesty on one flank and sympathetic priests on the other, Teresa's strategic weapons were primed. Every element was in place for the next step, although money was still short. Her reason "governed" and "fortified" by His Voice, Teresa was soon to discover that the Carmelite Primitive Rule actually prescribed making foundations without an income—thus neutralizing her adversaries' major argument at a stroke. But she did not know this yet. She was alone with His Majesty, attentive to that Other who was renovating her soul; estranged from herself, reassured and at peace in this new, sonorous love, less psychic, more active, enterprising, and detached. True, she lacked resources. To be realistic, though, she had the support of some highly influential clerics. In the solitude and grandeur of enthusiasm, the ecstasy of transfixion here mutates via a new alchemy. In it are mingled the exaltation of knowing she must act and the fear of being unable to do so: ambition and persecution. Despite the obstacles, the dread, the dead weight of so many difficulties, a female self triumphantly convinced of being the Other's mouthpiece gains self-awareness over the course of these pages. And aspires to become . . . freer still!

"All the rest of the trouble was mine [*y todo el más trabajo era mío*], trials of so many kinds that now I'm amazed I was able to suffer them. Sometimes in distress I said: 'My Lord, how is it You command things that seem impossible? For *if I were at least free*, even though I am a woman!'"[17]

* * *

And, as if the better to embody Teresa's vow to operate through His Majesty's Voice, a triangular construction comes to her aid, composed of Teresa, the symbolic Father (Saint Joseph), and the Virgin Mother:

Once when in need, for I didn't know what to do or how to pay some workmen, St. Joseph, my true father and lord, appeared and revealed to me that I would not be lacking, that I should hire them. And so I did, without so much as a penny, and the Lord in ways that amazed those that heard about it provided for me. The house struck me as being very small, so small that it didn't seem adequate for a monastery . . . And one day after Communion, the Lord said to me: "*I've already told you to enter as best you can.*" And by way of exclamation He added: "*Oh, covetousness of the human race, that you think you will be lacking even ground! How many times did I sleep in the open because I had no place else!*" I was astonished and saw that He was right. I went to the little house and drew up plans and found that although small it was perfect for a monastery.[18]

On one of those same days, the Feast of the Assumption of our Lady while at a monastery of the order of the glorious St. Dominic, I was reflecting upon the many sins I had in the past confessed in that house and many things about my wretched life. *A rapture came upon me so great that it almost took me out of myself.* I sat down; it still seems to me that I couldn't see the elevation or hear Mass, and afterward I had a scruple about this. It seemed to me while in this state that *I saw myself vested in a white robe of shining brightness,* but at first I didn't see who was clothing me in it. Afterward *I saw our Lady at my right side and my father Saint Joseph at the left,* for they were putting that robe on me. I was given to understand that I was now cleansed of my sins. . . .

The beauty I saw in our Lady was extraordinary, although I didn't make out any particular details except the form of her face in general and that *her garment was of the most brilliant white,* not dazzling but soft. *I didn't see the glorious St. Joseph so clearly,* although I saw indeed that he was there, as in the visions I mentioned that are not seen. Our Lady seemed to me to be *a very young girl.*[19]

★ ★ ★

In order for you to hear the Voice of His Majesty within, Teresa, my love, you had to transcend the paternal seduction that was so disturbing and malign as to send you into coma. You had to persuade yourself that your "real father" was a symbolic one: Saint Joseph, the non-procreator, the paradigm of all symbolic fathers, who dispels the fantasy of seduction, oedipal rivalry, and incest. And your mother had to be a virginal young girl. But was this an idealization of your mother in her youth, before she was worn out by her many pregnancies, or was it rather a vision of yourself, projected in the place of this ideal because untouchable woman, this immaculate body? Either way, you truly live out the *being* in which I discover you at this point of your adventure (and of mine). You write it as the deliverance from your limited condition as a begotten creature. Because of the way they transmute father and mother into ideal figures, Mary and Joseph will always accompany you in your upward flight toward eternal othernesses, eternal and yet possible, for when you are outside yourself these ideal constructs burn on, inside: "I remained for some time . . . almost outside myself. I was left with a great impulse to be dissolved for God [*un ímpetu grande de deshacerme por Dios*]."[20]

Chapter 22

THE MATERNAL VOCATION

> I heard the words: "While one is alive, progress doesn't come from trying to
> enjoy Me more but by trying to do My will."
>
> Teresa of Avila, *Spiritual Testimonies*

N ow everything can be speeded up, it's time to leave the footdraggers, the ill-wishers, the antagonists behind: let's get moving!

On August 15, 1561, Teresa settled her sister Juana and brother-in-law Juan de Ovalle into a small house she had bought in their name, located west of Avila outside the walls. The couple would live on the ground floor—the future chapel—while thirteen monastic cells were planned for the upper story, as well as service areas. The first Convent for Discalced Carmelites, to be called after Saint Joseph, was about to see the light. Money had been found: Aldonza de Guzmán, Giomar's mother, had given 30 ducats and Jerónima Guiomar de Ulloa had given whatever she could spare, on top of the dowries of two of Teresa's nieces (200 ducats from Isabel de la Peña, and maybe from Leonor de Cepeda) and the 200 ducats sent by brother Lorenzo from Peru.

It was a modest building, unworthy perhaps of being a monastery, and Teresa was frustrated by the cramped spaces that cruelly belied the magnificence of her project. Still, we must take things as they come, we'll improvise, just get it done, we'll do better next time. Surprise attacks and shows of strength became the "trademark" of La Madre's campaigns. Where foundations were at stake, she was not above taking possession at dead of night of premises disputed by her enemies!

This, the first of the works to be dictated by His Majesty's Voice, was coddled by Teresa like a newborn babe. She drew up the plans, whitewashed the walls, designed the close-grilled jalousies that would enable the nuns to see without being seen, directed the workmen. Her sister Juana's family seconded her efforts, as did old friends like Francisco de Salcedo and Fr. Gaspar Daza. Did she notice them at all? Was she aware of the lives around her? Or was she simply hovering over the taut thread of the Other's Voice?

★ ★ ★

One morning Teresa stumbles over the body of her little nephew Gonzalo lying unconscious on the floor beside the door. From the heights of her mirage with His Majesty she descends precipitously to earth, sweeps the insensible body into her arms, rubs her face against his, warms him under the rough cloth of her veil. Gonzalo rapidly revives in her arms.

"You resurrected him!" cries the boy's mother, sobbing with joy at the miracle, while doña Guiomar and Salcedo clasp their hands together, awed to witness such a sign from God.

"Stuff and nonsense," retorts Teresa briskly, batting away the sin of pride. Or is she just more reasonable than the others, always lucid in the midst of her dream?

Juana's firstborn, so early snatched from the jaws of death, will soon be presented with a little brother. Does Teresa, the perceptive midwife, recognize his frailty straight away? While others celebrate the birth, the aunt's worried diagnosis cuts through the theological platitudes required by the occasion: "If you are not destined to be a man of God, I pray God to take you, little angel, before you come to offend Him . . ."

The child does not live long. Far from being moved, let alone upset, by this death, Teresa goes into raptures: "Praise God for the sight of one of those little souls ascending into Heaven, and the throng of angels gathered to welcome it!"[1]

Since life in the Beyond trumps life down here, Teresa, my love, you must have thought that the child was well "saved," spared the journey through this vale of tears. Fair enough. And yet I feel, along with your biographer Marcelle Auclair who picks up on the story, that you behaved heartlessly toward that baby and toward Juana, who might have preferred to see her sickly son alive at her side rather than buried beneath the earth, angel or not. But you don't really like mothers, do you, and deplore still more the motherhood of your younger sister—almost as much as you disliked your own mother when she was surrounded by a gang of pestering brats.

Furthermore, La Madre has a horror of imperfection. Years later you explain in a letter to one of the great benefactors of your foundations, María de Mendoza, sister of the bishop of Avila, that you will not accept a certain postulant into your Valladolid establishment, on grounds that she has only one eye. You proffer a somewhat glib excuse: "In a house where there are many nuns, one can overlook whatever defect there may be; but where there are so few, it makes sense to be selective."[2] Teresa envisions her discalced nuns as akin to an elite corps, in the image of La Madre herself, who suffers, to be sure, but also causes suffering. She expects vocations to be ironclad, constitutions to be robust, and minds to be keen. Lord preserve us from birdbrains, melancholics, and females possessed by the devil! Pitiless she undoubtedly was, at times. "I am not at all like a woman in such matters, for I have a robust spirit [a tough heart: *tengo recio corazón*]."[3] I shall always remember that remark, for it does not express regret. Yours was undoubtedly a merciless pride—the logical outcome of your fusion with His Majesty and an indispensable condition for your work. A superhuman, inhuman, mesmerizing hardness: such was the price of the diamond of your soul.

* * *

Life treads water and the longing gets fiercer, as the brief from Rome authorizing the foundation of Saint Joseph's has still not arrived. Anguish, cramps, and vomiting ensue. Intense exchanges with the confessor Pedro Ibáñez: he proposes to Teresa that she write about her life. She enjoys frequent stays at the house of doña Guiomar, who continues to activate her high-society network: "For more than four years we have been . . . closer than if we were sisters"—but the true family is that of the works, the Work. Teresa naturally mobilizes all of her most successful relatives to help with the Carmelite reforms, first among them the conquistador of the family, her younger brother Lorenzo, who has married a wealthy woman in Quito, Ecuador. As befits the gravity of the circumstances, she addresses him as *señor*—later on, she will exert a steely spiritual direction over him. But just now the date is December 23, 1561, the *señor* has generously offered 40 pesos, and she is overcome:

Señor. . . . Certainly all those to whom you sent money received it at such an opportune moment that I was greatly consoled. . . .

I have already written you a long letter about a matter that for many reasons I could not escape doing, since God's inspirations are the source. Because these things are hard to speak of in a letter, I mention only the fact that certain saintly and learned persons think that I am obliged not to be cowardly but do all I can for this project—a monastery of nuns. There will be no more than fifteen nuns in it, who will practice very strict enclosure, never going out or allowing themselves to be seen without veils covering their faces. Their life will be one of prayer and mortification . . .

That lady, doña Guiomar, who is also writing to you, is a help to me. She is the wife of Francisco Dávila, of Salobralejo, if you recall. Her husband died nine years ago. He had an annual income of 1,000,000 maravedís. She, for her part, has an entailed estate in addition to what she has from her husband. . . . *For more than four years we have been devoted friends, closer than if we were sisters.* . . . At present she is without funds, so it is up to me to buy and prepare the house. . . . But then His Majesty comes along and moves you to provide for it. And what amazes me is that the forty pesos you added was just what I needed. I believe that St. Joseph—after whom the house will be named—wanted us to have the money, and I know that he will repay you. In sum, although the house is small and poor, the property has a field and some beautiful views. And that's sufficient.[4]

With regard to papal briefs, the one received in August will not suit, because it has to derive from the ordinary authority, that is, the authority of the bishop of Avila, and not that of the Carmelite provincial, who has declared himself incompetent. On Christmas Eve of 1561, the same provincial commands Teresa to go to Toledo: the daughter of the duke of Medinaceli, doña Luisa de la Cerda, is in a bad way. In fact she is delirious, and only Teresa can help her. While awaiting permission to found, the future saint will act as a "psychological cell," and failure is not an option.

Despite her six children, doña Luisa remains inconsolable for the death of her husband Antonio Arias Pardo de Saavedra, marshal of Castile, nephew of the archbishop of Toledo (and General Inquisitor) Juan Pardo de Tavera, and one of the richest men in Spain. The grieving widow has lost her mind, ceaselessly repeating "I believe in the resurrection of the flesh." Teresa, a woman of faith if ever there was one, recognizes the emergency of the situation. For it is the Carmelite provincial, Ángel de Salazar himself, who has "sent an order, under precept of obedience, to go immediately" and minister to the unhappy soul! Besides, there is great "consolation" and "security" in the fact that by the grace of God, she can also count on a house of the Society of Jesus established in Toledo, near the home of the bereaved noblewoman! Teresa is not the sort to hesitate in such circumstances.[5]

Toledo was far away, however. You need only look up a map of Spain, and recall that in 1561 there were neither trains nor planes nor cars. It was winter, snow was falling, the roads were slippery and impassable. Accompanied by her brother-in-law Juan de Ovalle and her good friend Juana Suárez, Teresa reached the town of her ancestors by early January. She could not have failed to think of her disgraced grandfather in his *sambenito*, the rich merchant Juan de Toledo, alias Juan Sánchez, who fled the town to save his *honra*. Who mentioned honor? We will see what we will see!

Teresa stayed for six months. Six months of luxury living, of exquisite female friendships, of rubbing shoulders with grandees and making useful contacts with eminent churchmen and highborn ladies. Luisa de la Cerda turned out to be a conscientious person of great piety and kindness. Deeply attached to Teresa, she followed her like a shadow, lavishing elaborate attentions upon her and even a set of diamonds, to the amused indifference of the recipient.

> Once, when I was with that lady I mentioned, I was ill with *heart sickness*; as I said my heart trouble was severe, although it isn't now. Since she was very charitable, she gave orders that I be shown some of her *jewels of gold and precious stone* that were very valuable, especially one of the *diamonds* that was appraised highly. She thought they would make me happy. Recalling what the Lord has kept for us, *I was laughing to myself* and feeling pity at the sight of what people esteem. . . . In this way the soul has *great dominance*, so great that I don't know whether anyone who doesn't possess this dominion will understand it. It is the *detachment* proper and natural to us."[6]

* * *

At Luisa de la Cerda's you meet the cream of Toledan society, Teresa, my love, and these people impress you, but not at the expense of your critical sense or knack for making use of them at the right time: the duchess of Escalona, the duchess of Maqueda, the duchess of Medinaceli, the duchess of Alba. You also make the acquaintance of doña Luisa's niece, Ana de la Cerda de Mendoza, princess of Eboli, who will denounce you to the Inquisition; but that's another story, in which animosity between women plays its part, a far trickier business to handle than the skirmishes with your confessors, whose fingers you slip through, by now, like a fish. We will return to that later.

For the present, in Toledo, you proceed to analyze these Spanish grandees with the inexorable delicacy hitherto reserved for your musings on yourself. Immersed in His Majesty, you're used to mortifying yourself or stepping "outside yourself"; but also, as I know, to conducting a meticulous dissection of your experiences, in terms commonly regarded as "mystical." Now we see this strenuous introspection turning its hand to reportage! The glittering circle around sweet, sad Luisa de la Cerda inspires passages of high dramatic realism. Your feats of social psychology, my novelistic Teresa, are doubtless less amusing that those of Cervantes, and never plebeian in the manner of *Lazarillo de Tormes*. Refusing to be either duped or dazzled by these celebs *avant la lettre*, you portray them with lofty feminine exactitude:

> I realized that [Luisa de la Cerda] was a woman and as subject to passions and weaknesses as I, and how little should be our esteem for the status of nobility, and that the greater the nobility the more the cares and trials. I observed the solicitude they had for preserving their composure in conformity with this status, which doesn't allow them to live, obliging them to eat without rhyme or reason because everything must be done in accordance with their status and not with their bodily constitution. (They have often to eat food that is more in harmony with their position than with their liking.) As a result I totally abhorred any desire to become a lady of the nobility . . . This is a kind of subservience that makes calling such persons "lords" one of the world's lies, for it doesn't seem to me that they are anything but slaves to a thousand things.[7]

$$\star \;\; \star \;\; \star$$

Could it be the very luxury you enjoy in this milieu that awakens in the hardness of your heart an unprecedented "compassion for the poor"? Unless I am very much mistaken, it is here, in the Cerda palace stuffed with gold, wrought furniture, fine porcelain, and precious stones, that for the first time in your life you notice the existence of paupers and register the hellish existence of outcasts whose misery doesn't need the spur of penitence:

> It seems to me I have much more compassion for the poor than I used to. I feel such great pity and desire to find relief for them that if it were up to me I would

give them the clothes off my back. I feel no repugnance whatsoever toward them, toward speaking to or touching them. This I now see is a gift given by God. For even though I used to give alms for love of Him, I didn't have the natural compassion. I feel a very noticeable improvement in this matter.[8]

During these six months in Toledo you also find the necessary seclusion to write, something that will prove crucial both for you and for history. But you have not forgotten the little discalced Convent of Saint Joseph, back in Avila. And since your mystical life takes the form of a series of coups de théâtre, like a picaresque novel of the soul's pilgrimage toward the Other, recast as His Voice in you—so, before building your inner mansions, you continue to have extraordinary encounters that move the action forward.

* * *

A pauper, excuse me, a *beata*, knocks on the door of the palace: her name is María de Jesús Yepes. Born in Granada, widowed when still young, this bizarre, freewheeling character had become a Franciscan beguine (or *beata*) after giving away all her worldly goods. She had then trekked to Rome on foot and obtained an audience with Pope Pius IV himself. To what end? To implore him on her knees to let her found a Carmelite house under the Primitive Rule. (The same idea you had, and on the same day: isn't that funny?) Flabbergasted, the Holy Father called her "a mannish woman"—he had his reasons—and ordered his entourage to comply with her request, referring her to Cardinal Rainucio, who gave the authorization. Once she returned to Granada, however, the local Carmelites and the population at large were all for flogging her in public! Princess Juana, the kingdom's regent, advised her to speak to a Jesuit whom you, Teresa, know very well—Fr. Gaspar de Salazar—and he in turn dispatched her to see you in Toledo. María laid before you her project for a Carmel governed by absolute poverty; eventually she would found the reformed Carmelite Convent of Alcalá de Henares.

Illiterate but gifted with a prodigious memory, María knows the Primitive Rule by heart, rather better than you do, admit it. Historians today even suggest that you were thoroughly ignorant of this first Rule, composed at the beginning of the thirteenth century by Saint Albert of Jerusalem. I can inform you that it went through two subsequent versions: the Rule was amended and approved by Pope Innocent IV in 1247, and then softened by the mitigations Pope Eugene IV granted in 1432.

María de Jesús Yepes's most important revelation is that, according to the Primitive Rule, the nuns must live without patronage, subsisting on their labor alone, and not give way to any power, whether of bishops or secular rulers. This lesson does not fall on deaf ears! Between ourselves, the *beata* also imparts a few lessons in Vatican diplomacy that will not come amiss for the task in hand.

For two weeks you observe each other, admiring, agreeing, and disagreeing. The beginning of the Discalced Carmelite Constitution gradually takes shape. Your supporters are impressed, and at the same time concerned: can one rely on Providence alone for such an ambitious work?

★ ★ ★

Father Pedro Ibáñez himself has some misgivings and writes you two pages of theological objections. You understand that further supporters are called for, more powerful than Ibáñez and possessors of a bold, ascetic, saintly spirituality. An idea comes: you could consult Brother Pedro de Alcántara. You are well acquainted already with the authority of this ideal arbiter, the only man capable of cutting the Gordian knot in which you are presently caught between the plaudits and critiques elicited by your reforms. He is already a great partisan of the project, given his fervent endorsement of the desire for poverty—an evangelical principle he will have you commit to—and to the dignity of women, whom he declares equal to men in the love of Christ. Admit it: Pedro de Alcántara was extremely helpful to you when he wondered why you were consulting *letrados*, those jurists or theologians who might be excellently qualified for legal disputes and cases of conscience but knew nothing of the life of the spirit! Thus comforted, you are able to parry the theological arguments deployed by Fr. Ibáñez against your notion of foundations without funds.

Backed up by some, contested by others, you assert your own authority more and more, my resistant Teresa. No woman before has been seen to stand up to her superiors the way you do in the text you will shortly deliver to Fr. Ibáñez, in which you address all your confessors—whose greater knowledge and competence you acknowledge in all humility, for it stands to reason that you need them, every one.

On the one hand, you like to draw them toward prayer:

I told [Fr. Gaspar de Salazar] about [my trials of soul] under the seal of confession. He seemed to me wiser than ever, although I always thought he had a great mind. . . . *As soon as I see a person who greatly pleases me, with longings I sometimes cannot bear, I want to see him give himself totally to God.* And although I desire that all serve God, *the longings come with very great impulses* in the case of these persons I like; so I beg the Lord very much on their behalf. With the religious I'm speaking of, it so happened to me.[9]

On the other, you sleep with one eye open:

Since I believe that my confessors stand so truly in the place of God, I think they are the ones for whom I feel the most benevolence. Since I am always very fond of those who guide my soul and since I felt secure, *I showed them that I liked them.* They, as God-fearing servants of the Lord, were afraid lest in any way I would become *attached and bound with this love,* even though in a holy way, and *they showed me their displeasure.* This happened after I became so subject to obeying them, for before that I didn't experience this love. *I laughed to myself* to see how mistaken they were.[10]

It is a source of satisfaction to you that Luisa de la Cerda likewise visits, and often the dignitaries of the Carmelite order, including the provincial father, Ángel de Salazar, come to call. The latter informs you around this time that a new prioress is to be elected at the Convent of the Incarnation; you are free to return there or not, as you please. In such a conundrum, of course, it falls to His Majesty to have the last word, and as usual His Voice promptly comes through. Your ideal superego commands you to leave! By the grace of God, the papal brief so long awaited by doña Guiomar arrives on February 7, 1562: a coincidence, no doubt.

* * *

The moment has come to act with even greater celerity than usual, especially in the wake of that long sojourn with Luisa de la Cerda. Not that the interlude was one of pure repose, as we have seen: rather, a flexing of soul sinews before the great leap. It was at her house that you completed the first draft—since lost—of the book of your *Life.* Enough writing for now! You hasten back to Avila, where trouble awaits, as one might expect after the absence of the foundress.

Juan de Ovalle has fallen prey to double tertian fever, which strengthens the case for his return to the convent house he and his wife Juana moved out of after Teresa's departure. But consent is required from the bishop of Avila, don Álvaro de Mendoza. Nothing doing! Such a man cannot conceive of a monastery without money!

"I don't want penniless nuns," complains this noble lord to Pedro de Alcántara, summoned to the rescue by Teresa yet again. After writing to Mendoza, the friar has journeyed on mule-back all the way to El Temblío to meet the intransigent bishop face to face.

Alcántara (who was to die on October 18, 1562) must have moved don Álvaro all the same, for the bishop turned up, it seems, at the parlor of the Incarnation. It was up to the foundress to play the charisma card, and Teresa of Jesus dispelled any last doubts he may have had. From that day on, the bishop of Avila, grandee of Spain and of the Church, acted as a staunch and efficient champion of the discalced reform.

* * *

As for Pedro de Alcántara, did you intuit the nearness of his death, Teresa? Before seeing the indomitable Franciscan on his way, you, the intermittent anorexic, made a point of rustling up the most delicious dishes for him, recipes inherited from that excellent housewife, doña Beatriz de Ahumada. The Rule strictly forbids the consumption of meat, except for unavoidable reasons of "necessity." What greater necessity than the entertainment of so dear a friend? An Old Christian saying held that after the Friday fast, the next best certification of Catholic orthodoxy was to tuck into eggs and bacon on the Saturday. The erudite Juan assures me that you would have made him some *olla podrida*, my lip-licking Teresa: a hearty potpourri of mutton, beef, and bacon with plenty of white cabbage, turnips, onions, and garlic, smothered in spicy coriander, and cumin. One could even throw in the heads and feet of birds! (A bottomless well of knowledge, that Juan.)

I don't buy it, too over the top, and what about her Marrano background . . .

"Meat was banned? If you say so." My Hispanist is trying his best to oblige me. "Well then, La Madre would dish up some caviar. Absolutely! Sturgeon eggs imported from the Black Sea! I swear! Okay, that particular delicacy might not have reached Avila, but Don Quixote . . ." (Oh, him, I might have known: Juan thinks of nothing else all day long.) He's off again: "Don Quixote and his sidekick thought nothing of quaffing down at least six skins of wine to lubricate the local caviar made of gray mullet, sea-bass, and chub roe all mashed together.[11] Honestly, Sylvia, in those days people all along the north Mediterranean coast were total fans of this confection. It made a change from boring old ham and cheese, pieces of which, and I quote, 'if they were past gnawing were not past sucking. They also put down a black dainty called, they say, caviar'—*cabial* in the Spanish—'and made of the eggs of fish, a great thirst-wakener.' You see? Verbatim, I assure you!"

Juan preens, he's got me, bravo, I give in. In fact he's on my side: "A woman like that, who gets off so jubilantly on her writing, she can't have been anorexic for long, eh, Doc?"

I say that Teresa may well have enjoyed that black dainty, I like the idea, it suits her. As it suits her friend Alcántara, like black lights in interior castles.

And so it was that Pedro de Alcántara's last memory of you, my tongue-smacking Teresa, was a "seraphs' banquet."

* * *

By this point, your staff was eager and ready for the consecration of the first discalced convent. Julián de Ávila would be the chaplain, Gaspar Daza would say the first Mass. Four novices were preparing to receive their habits from Teresa's own hand: Antonia de Henao, one of Alcántara's spiritual daughters, who took the religious name of Antonieta of the Holy Spirit; Úrsula de Revilla de Álvarez, of Daza's circle, who became Ursula of the Holy Angel; a lady-in-waiting of doña Guiomar, María de la Paz, renamed María of the Cross; and the sister of chaplain Julián, María de Ávila, now María of Saint Joseph.

On Saint Bartholomew's day, August 24, 1562, the bells of Saint Joseph pealed out to all of Avila the creation of a "monastery" in obedience to the so-called Primitive Rule. Among those attending the ceremony were Teresa, Daza, Juana Suárez, Inés and Ana de Tapia, Juana and her husband Juan de Ovalle, plus Francisco de Salcedo, the "saintly gentleman" who had "helped in every way."[12] Also present were don Gonzalo de Aranda and, of course, Teresa's faithful, indispensable, inevitable, noble "sister" and benefactress, Jerónima Guiomar de Ulloa—dressed like a poor person, in accordance with the Primitive Rule.

* * *

Yesterday you were so emotional that you vomited before the inaugural Mass. The day before, you were stitching habits, veils, and bonnets. Today, your cup spills over . . . And yet, on reading your account four centuries later, I find that you're not easy in your mind, for there are threats looming over the foundation. In the very lap of success you're still a persecutee, Teresa:

> Well, for me it was like being in glory to see the Blessed Sacrament reserved . . . and to see a work accomplished that I knew was for the service of the Lord and to the honor of the habit of His glorious Mother—for these were my concerns. . . .
>
> After all was over and about three or four hours had passed, *the devil stirred up within me a spiritual battle* . . . He brought doubts to my mind about whether what I had done was *wrong*; whether I had gone against obedience in having made the foundation without my provincial's orders. . . . And all the virtues, and my faith, were then suspended within me *without my having the strength to activate any of them or defend myself against so many blows.*[13]

The happiness of August 24, 1562, did not last long. The Incarnation felt betrayed, and anger mounted against Teresa. Her insolence had to be punished. It was a serious error, surely, to seek to undo the Mitigated Rule and go back to total enclosure, penitence, silence, fasting, and bare feet? Positively medieval! That Ahumada woman is not keeping up with the times. Who does she think she is? She has committed a serious fault, clearly, but is it merely "serious," "more serious," or "extremely serious"? Does she deserve two strokes of the scourge, or life imprisonment, sorrow, and abstinence forever?

Avila was abuzz with rumors.

Despite fear, distress, and melancholy, those "devils" that embattled you, you held firm, Teresa, His Majesty being duly at His post inside you.

The prioress of the Incarnation, Mother María Cimbrón, orders you to come back "at once" to her monastery. Julián de Ávila, that faithful squire and chaplain, escorts you to the meeting. A veritable tribunal: your sisters don't mince words. On top of that, the Carmelite provincial, Ángel de Salazar, deals out a "serious reprimand." Allegedly you "gave scandal to the people" and were "promoting novelties." What have you to say for yourself? Fortified, once more, by His Majesty's Voice, you stick to your guns. And like the Machiavellian diplomat you are, you confound your adversaries by feigning to bow to their wishes, my crafty Teresa: "None of what they said caused me any disturbance or grief, although I let on that it did so as not to give the impression that I didn't take to heart what they said."[14]

Father Salazar, as smooth an operator as yourself, is playing a double game: on the esoteric side, he reassures you; on the exoteric side, he pretends to espouse the mood of the institution and the city. "Afterward I spoke to him more freely, and he was very satisfied and promised—if all went well—to give me permission to go there once the city quieted down, for the clamor throughout the whole city was vehement."[15]

Formidable measures are taken. The consistory meets with the *corregidor* (the mayor or highest city authority, representative of the royal power), and leading members of the chapter. It is a Grand Tribunal, practically the Last Judgment! All the participants call for the destruction of your monastery.

> Only one member, a *presentado* of the order of St. Dominic [Fr. Domingo Báñez], although he was opposed (not to the monastery, but to its being poor), said that it wasn't something that had to be suppressed, that the matter should be considered carefully, that there was time for this, that such a decision pertained to the bishop [Álvaro de Mendoza, bishop of Avila since 1560] and other things of this nature. What he said was very helpful, for they were so furious that it was a wonder they didn't carry out their decision straight away.[16]

The story didn't end there. Royal constables were sent to Saint Joseph's to evict the novices *manu militari*. The girls refused to let them in; not without an order from the one who had brought them here, period! The *alguaciles* did not dare break down the door.

★ ★ ★

On August 30 all of Avila's political authorities gathered together to deliberate, notables side by side with Church delegates, and the hostility was unanimous; some were for appealing to the Council of State, as though the convent threatened the security of the realm.

I can see you from here, Teresa, swaying between your devils and the unfailing Voice of His Majesty, which fortunately proved the stronger: "'Don't you know that I am mighty? What do you fear?'"[17] Confident in that unswerving Third Person who expresses Himself in your style, as we know, you went on to deal as one must with earthly men, my subtle Teresa. Given that several of these powerful individuals were theologians, it was important to approach them:

> Afterward, when the negotiations were on their way toward a settlement, another person, a very zealous servant of God, came to me saying the matter should be put into the hands of *learned men*. As a result I had *many worries*. Some of those

who were helping me agreed with this proposal; this snarl in the affairs, which was caused by the devil, turned out to be the most complicated tangle of all. *The Lord helped me in everything*; for in a summary like this you can't explain all that took place in the two years from the time this house was founded to the time the litigation ended. This last phase and the first were the most laborious.[18]

As for the provincial who had promised to support you, he was now back-pedaling, cowed by the animosities and rancors you aroused. You, somewhat fed up by now, have the nerve to remind him that it's not Teresa talking, but His Majesty. How can he not realize?

"Consider, Father, that we are resisting against the Holy Spirit!"

Who can resist a majesty like yours? It was the big bazooka. Your biographers are keen to highlight this, and I'm happy to go along.

* * *

After the rain, here comes the sun. Spring 1563. With official permission to leave the Incarnation, you move to Saint Joseph's in the company of four more discalced postulants eager to follow you: Ana de los Ángeles, María Isabel, your cousin Isabel de San Pablo, and Ana de San Juan, daughter of the marchioness of Velada.

You have prevailed, Teresa, but this is only the beginning. Sixteen more battles of this kind remain to be fought and won, all different and yet similar, an extravagant amalgam of foundations and persecutions.

* * *

The representation of Saint Joseph will stay with you for good. His image will preside over all your creations, like a prototype of the ideal Father you always strive to see in your spiritual fathers on earth (an effort of faith leading to much fervor and disappointment)—those confessors and other ecclesiastics whose approval and support you seek.

Inseparable from Joseph, the portrait of the Virgin your mother left you is another permanent companion. On the day of the Assumption 1561, in the church of a Dominican monastery, you prayed to a "very young" Mother of God for her help, whereas you "didn't see the glorious St. Joseph so clearly."[19]

Now that you have founded Saint Joseph's, in August 1562, Jesus Himself crowns you as a reward for what you did for His Mother:

> Christ . . . seemed to be receiving me with great love and placing a crown on my head and thanking me for what I did for His Mother.
>
> Another time while all were at prayer in choir after compline, *I saw Our Lady in the greatest glory clothed in a white mantle; it seemed she was sheltering us all under it.* I understood how high a degree of glory the Lord would give to those living in this house.[20]

In this homage of yours to the Mother of God I discern the supreme elevation of your own maternity: the promotion of your personal fervor hoisting you up to the rank of Mother. Don't you experience the glory of Mary's virginal, royal Assumption as though it could be yours, provided you suffer enough?

> One day, the feast of the Assumption of our Lady, Queen of Angels, the Lord desired to grant me the following favor: in a rapture He showed me her ascent to heaven, *the happiness and solemnity with which she was received,* and the place where she is. I wouldn't be able to describe how this happened. *The glory my spirit experienced* in seeing so much glory was magnificent. The effects of this favor were great. I was helped in having a deeper *desire to undergo difficult trials,* and I was left with a longing to serve our Lady since she deserved this so much.[21]

When in the next paragraph you evoke the vision of "a very richly made pallium" hanging over the heads of the Jesuit Brothers at the College of Saint Giles in Avila, is this not a vision of the pallium formed by Mary's robe, as it is often represented in painting, like a protective canopy over the servants of the Church? The "longing to serve our Lady" makes you feel her "glory" and "trials" in lieu and place of the Mother of God herself.

Henceforth you are in no doubt: you, the Lord's spouse, His beloved lover, are also the Mother of the Man of Dolors, as much as of the divine Child. That infant appears to you in the penumbra of the convent, and your idolaters were quick to immortalize the vision in stucco—in order to "plaster" maternal piety into place for ever and ever?

The circle has closed: you are a daughter, wife, and mother. The Other within you is a son, husband, and father. But He can just as easily take on the attributes of His Virgin Mother, since He showers you, you don't know how, not with His sperm (you have a horror of toads, but you don't mind lizards; in time, you will let them dart under your habit!), but with the mother's milk overflowing His bountiful breast:

> And notice carefully this comparison; it seems to me very appropriate: the soul is like *an infant* that still nurses when *at its mother's breast*, and the mother without her babe's effort to suckle puts the milk in its mouth in order to give it delight. So it is here; for without effort of the intellect the will is loving, and *the Lord desires* that the will, without thinking about the matter, *understand that it is with Him* and that *it does no more than swallow the milk His Majesty puts in its mouth*, and enjoy that sweetness. For the will knows that it is the Lord who is granting that favor. And the will rejoices in its enjoyment. It doesn't desire to understand how it enjoys the favor or what it enjoys; but it forgets itself during that time, for the One who is near it will not forget to observe what is fitting for it. If the will goes out to fight with the intellect so as to give a share of the experience, by drawing the intellect after itself, it cannot do so at all; it will be forced to let the milk fall from its mouth and lose that divine nourishment.
>
> This is the way this prayer of quiet is different from that prayer in which the entire soul is united with God, for then the soul doesn't even go through the process of swallowing this divine food. *Without its understanding how, the Lord places the milk within it.*[22]

Nevertheless, in this blissful kaleidoscope of the soul's permutations of attributes, your chief role will be *the maternal role*. You will perfect it over the course of the twenty years you still have to live before meeting the Other face to face: death, so dreaded by unbelievers, is for you the absolute event.

It's not easy, it's impossible to step into the role of symbolic Mother. Modern women are just beginning to realize this fact. Perhaps they are getting wise to how after more than a century of assorted feminisms, the mystery of maternal passion remains more obscure than that of gestation—pretty well mastered by science—or that of in vitro fertilization, or cloning, or artificial wombs. Nothing in contemporary culture prepares them for the mystery of motherhood— no more than anything prepared you for it, Teresa, back in the heyday of the Church Fathers during the Spanish Renaissance. The books you wrote after the *Life* are continually tackling the question: How to be a mother? How to conduct another person, man or woman, toward self-transcendence in affective bonds that are both strict and open, and all the while affirming your own transcendence, because that is what confers the most credible authority: the authority of the ability to start again?

You know from experience that *suffering* is an inescapable part of our bond with others, even more, and otherwise, than in the transcendence of the bond with the self-as-other. But you deny the exaggerations of that suffering, to which your friends are more prone than you—not that this prevents you from overdoing your mortifications (pardon me for bringing that up again) while attempting to invert them into joys, and succeeding! There is no miracle recipe for being a good mother, as you will discover over the course of your foundations. However, from the moment you shoulder the new role of Mother on top of the role of the Spouse's beloved lover, you grasp that the essence of the maternal vocation lies in the balance to be found between *jouissance* and *will*. You will *enjoy* the ideal more than ever, but without abandoning yourself to it, for it falls to you now to *accomplish* the ideal with a well-tempered *will*, deferred away from self into the "third person"—into His will. Could this be a path to self-forgetfulness, a way of "depsychologizing" oneself, as my colleague Jérôme Tristan puts it, of effectively thinking from another person's point of view?

Thus the exile of *jouissance* outside oneself is compounded by the exile of the will as exerted on behalf of self and of others, upon self and upon others. The first exile transports you into the Other, the second gathers His Majesty into the fluidity of an acting soul. Forever in an altered state, reassured or preoccupied, transparent and decisive, the mother lives off the other and acts for him or her. To the prayer of abandonment, to the fetus or baby bathed in the waters of ecstasy, the fabulous dynamism of the businesswoman is now added, my disappropriated Teresa. Motherhood appropriates nothing, it delegates itself through the Other to engender new life. The will to abandon oneself to the Other's will in order to found a new creation just as if it were one's own, while knowing it is not: that is maternal.

A few days after the experiences mentioned above, while thinking about whether they who thought it was wrong for me to go out to found monasteries might be right, and thinking that I would do better to be always occupied in prayer, I heard the words: "*While one is alive, progress doesn't come from trying to enjoy Me more but by trying to do My will.*"[23]

Autoeroticism is no longer enough for you, any more than the words that force women into the background. The Mother is one who is "considerate of others": she thereby becomes the equal of the Lord, and nobody can "tie her hands."

"The Lord said to me: '*Tell them they shouldn't follow just one part of Scripture*' [1 Cor. 14:34: 'Let your women keep silence in the churches: for it is not permitted unto them to speak; but they are commanded to be under obedience, as also saith the law'] *but that they should look at other parts, and ask them if they can by chance tie my hands.*"[24]

This point in your thinking helps me to divine the meaning of your reform: you, Mother, *Madre*, are not content to be a woman in ecstasy. You become a *gangway* between that singular *jouissance* acquired in the love for and of the Other and the possible transmission of that *jouissance* to others. It begins with an amorous dialogue with the Spouse who creates for you an imaginary incarnate, relieved of your will: *I* (man or woman) am nothing but the spouse of the loving Beloved who wants me. It goes on with the sensorial identification with the Other, of an intensity such that I want to and can assume His will—the will that by being no longer outside of me, or judging me, but invested and thus agreeable, speaks through me. Our ideal Father who art in Heaven, Thou art henceforth in Me divest of myself who am transfused into Thee in the love of Thee.

* * *

"Another I," "God naturalized," the nun proclaims, here enjoys an extraordinary "sharing" or participative freedom. Integrated with the Other because penetrated by Him (*cuando te entrañares con este sumo bien*), this "other I" protects itself from the risks inherent in "free will" with its threat of sin and hence of "enslavement," preferring to be "fastened" [nailed: *enclavado*] to the exploration of love and fear toward the Other: a *jouissance* that for Teresa seems to be the only truth worth knowing.

> May this "I" die, and may another live in me greater than I and better for me than I, so that I may serve Him [Muera ya este yo, y viva en mí otro que es más que yo, y para mí mejor que yo, para que yo le pueda servir]. May He live and give me life. May He reign, and may I be captive, for my soul doesn't want any other liberty. . . .

O free will, so much the slave of your freedom if you don't live fastened with fear and love of your Creator [O libre albedrío tan esclavo de tu libertad, si no vives enclavado con el temor y amor de quien te crió]! Oh, when will that happy day arrive when you will see yourself drowned in the infinite sea of supreme truth, where you will no longer be free to sin! Nor will you want to sin, for you will be safe from every misery, *naturalized* [*naturalizado*] by the life of your God!

He is blessed, because He knows, loves, and rejoices in Himself without any other thing being possible. He neither has nor can have—nor would He be a perfect God if He did have—the freedom to forget Himself or cease loving Himself. Then, my soul, you will enter into your rest *when you become intimate with this supreme Good* [*entrarás en tu descanso cuando te entrañares con este sumo bien*],[25] understand what He understands, and rejoice in what gives Him joy. Now, you will find you've lost your changeable will; now, there shall be no more change! For God's grace will have done so much that by it you will be . . . a *sharer* in His divine nature [*particionera de su divina naturaleza*].[26]

Have you become a . . . creator, on a par with God himself?

* * *

Who am I, then? Not merely a lover, not really the ideal Father Himself, I am the Mother. Obviously, I surround myself with scholarly fathers whose counsels I follow and to whose authority I submit, and yet it is I, Teresa of Jesus, alone with His Majesty, who take the initiative of realizing His Truth in and by an "I" empty of me. The rebirth, the re-foundation of His new houses in me will unfold in the dwelling place that I am—that is, in Him—but I can build the place and dwell there, indeed I "will not have finished doing all that [I] can" when "to the little [I] do [*mi trabajillo*], which is nothing, God will unite Himself, with His greatness."[27] The world will understand that truth is newness, and that newness is a rehabilitation of tradition at the auspicious moment I have just now seized. And that this reorganization of Time is simply my way of hearing the Other's Voice: I, the foundress, the Mother. To be a mother is to found; or rather, to re-found. Indefinitely.

Has your depression flipped into erotomania? Has the paranoid fear of other people drained away in love suffering, in loving suffering, in warlike dominance? Of course. And yet, all the facets of your new way of being—"there is a great difference in the ways one may be"—are defused in the detachment from others and from self, in relinquishment and dispossession: the more I abandon myself before the inanity of power, money, honors, the sharper grows my will to shatter or circumvent all obstacles by means of cunning, stubbornness, or sweetness, and reach my goal. Which is not my goal, you understand, but the Other's . . . of Him who resides in me empty of me!

We are at the heart of the alchemy that constitutes the speaking subject: the alchemy of amorous alteration. The contrary of alienation, or its other side. The entrepreneurial singularity of the individual shaped by monotheism—especially the Catholic version—highlights and hardens its universal logic. But it is Teresa who unabashedly explores it in the paroxysm of her extravagant passion for the Other.

⋆ ⋆ ⋆

Teresa, my love, I cannot leave you in that year of 1563 without mentioning two events that, by revealing the seriousness of the first foundation, vouchsafed it a fabulous destiny.

First, as I have already pointed out to anyone who has come with us this far, the striking coincidence between the completion of your first book, the *Life*, and the achievement of your first foundation. You founded because you wrote, and you wrote because you founded. We find a staggering overlap between, on the one hand, the dangerous and delightful dispossession of yourself in Him, the wretchedness and rapture of writing, and, on the other, your lucid pragmatism, astute charm, and skillful toughness. This high-wire balancing act did not make you the first modern female writer, if we understand by modernity the valorization of a text or a written oeuvre becoming a value in itself. Nor do I consider that the test you set yourself, to restore the Carmelite order to its Primitive Rule, was the mark of an archaic age, the symptom of a masochistic renunciation of modernity in favor of a purity derived from the higher spiritual authority with which you identified.

But what if you were the precursor of a way of being, already obscurely sought in those days and still being sought—through writing among other means—between self and non-self, self and other, self with others? Neither art nor politics, neither religion nor social activism, but something through, with, and against *all of that*? The *everything* which is *nothing*, as you so well put it; sought for with the (feigned or genuine) unconcern you expressed to your mentor and "editor" (if you'll forgive the anachronism), Fr. García de Toledo, shortly before completing your text:

> I believe your Reverence will be annoyed by the long *account* I've given of this monastery, but it is very short in comparison with the many trials we suffered and the wonders the Lord has worked for it. There are many witnesses who are able to swear to these marvels, and so I beg your Reverence for the love of God that if you think you should *tear up what else is written here* [*romper lo demás que aquí va escrito*] you *preserve whatever pertains to this monastery*. And when I'm dead, give it to the Sisters who live here that when those who are to come see the many things *His Majesty arranged for its establishment* by means of so wretched and dreadful a thing as myself, they might be greatly encouraged to serve God and strive that what has been begun may not collapse but always flourish.[28]

Myself is wretched, but His Majesty—whose will is henceforth mine, His Majesty that *I* am here below by virtue of my works of writing *and* foundation—is only attached in a special way to this piece of writing; feel free to destroy what you like of it, except the trace of the "account" I have provided of all that "His Majesty arranged" to establish "this monastery," that *I founded*. Speaking, writing, working through me and in me, His Majesty broke new ground. For after my death, for those who will come after us, preserve if you please the trace of that innovation.

All that interests me is to reverse Time. By writing and/or by founding, I place myself in the infinity of Time, as the Other's Bride, in order for His presence to begin afresh. Since under the Primitive Rule the Other's presence is more desirable than it is, by now, under the Mitigated Rule, more stimulating than it is among those who let it wither, then my innovation, infinitesimal as it may be, suffices to spark the Other all over again. So will my reformation be, minuscule and magnificent—in response to the Erasmists whose humanism brings me to appreciate Christ's humanity all the more, and in response to the Lutherans whose harshness fills me with holy rigor against the laxity of my side. By restoring to the present the infinity of the past I am doing far more, for that matter, than to combat or crush my enemies: I am inviting them to welcome into themselves the infinity of the Passion in the infinity of time. Such is my reformation: a counter-reformation. The Counter-Reformation will eventually recognize the intentions that drive me, although as I write these lines to Fr. García, I cannot be certain of it. We shall see.

All I know is that what I've written has no importance in itself. Change the letters, the handwriting, whatever you like, but preserve that relationship to time which I have founded for myself and for those who may wish to follow me. The point is to open up the course of time to a return of that Time in which we lose any care for our needs, in which we lose ourselves, merging with the infinite Time of His Majesty, or again with the outside-time of my desire, when I coincide with His Majesty the ideal Father, with the ideal tradition.

During the two years it took to found Saint Joseph's, I lived at the intersection of ordinary time and the outside time in which my will merges with the Ideal. I succeeded in implanting His Majesty, a Third Person, my outside-time chimera, my ideal, in the worldly time of human relationships. The world's time already registers this graft: my scandalous innovation is being combated, denounced, or approved. As for me, I fearfully observe my own folly, but I also triumph over it. I can see that I have embedded a new Time in time, bent the flight of time into multiple spaces that lodge in people's souls, to enhance them and make them live. In these tragic times of religious war—but isn't every worldly time rent by religious wars?—what is there to do but to let His Majesty live, that ideal Other who dwells in our soul, who *is* our soul? Please keep, Father, the meaning of this *fiction*, the account of this adventure; I care little about the text itself, you may tear up the rest (*romper lo demás que aquí va escrito*).

What "rest," Teresa? Do you mean whatever does not concern the small Carmelite house of Saint Joseph? There is no surplus to your excesses. Everything forms part of the adventure, writing included, and García de Toledo (like your later publishers) understood this very well. They jealously preserved the "account," word for word, even if they made certain deletions or alterations here and there where your more audacious formulations made you an emulator of the Lord, not to say an advocate of gender parity; after all, somebody had to save you from the claws of the more zealous witnesses at the court of the Inquisition!

★ ★ ★

The second event of this new beginning in your life was the visit you paid to the Basilica of San Vicente, after leaving the Incarnation on your way to perpetual seclusion in Saint Joseph's.

Halfway between the two, outside the city walls, Saint Vincent's is a commemorative shrine on the spot where in the year 306, three Christian siblings, Vicente, Christeta, and Sabina, were martyred. Perhaps you knew the legend,

Teresa: they say that a snake came to guard the bleeding, tortured bodies from wild beasts. Such devotion on the part of so repulsive a reptile was clearly implausible. But there's more: a wealthy Jew who hiked up there, intending to desecrate the corpses, was himself stopped by the snake coiling itself around him. Deeply shaken, he converted to Christianity there and then, causing the frightful snake, or phallic monster, to release him. This converted Jew built the first temple on the crime scene dedicated to the three martyrs. In the seventeenth century, when Raymond of Burgundy was beginning the reconstruction of the dragon wall that encircles Avila, the Basilica of San Vicente was erected on the site of the old temple, following a design inspired by the architect Giral Fruchel, who had built Avila's cathedral.

At this pivotal moment of your life, it wasn't the majestic and highly official cathedral that drew you; you headed instead for the basilica. You went down into the crypt, took off your shoes, and prostrated yourself before the Virgin of Soterraña. This statue is supposed to have been brought to Spain by Saint Peter as an offering for San Segundo, then bishop of Avila. It is a Romanesque sculpture carved in walnut, housed in the central baroque chapel of the crypt. A side chapel exhibits the stone on which the three early saints were put to death.

The Book of Her Life often evokes the white veil worn by the Virgin Mary, something many commentators associate with this "subterranean" Virgin, Virgen de la Soterraña. But they seldom mention the converted Jew, the first founder. I picture you kneeling before Mary, your holy patroness inseparable from Saint Joseph, and I can't imagine you not sparing a thought for the builder of the first temple, the Jew of the snake.

⋆ ⋆ ⋆

Today, you're the founder. Not you alone, mind you, His Majesty is still within, but you have just said farewell to Teresa de Ahumada along with her Toledan ancestors, her father, and her mother. You are outside yourself, Teresa, in the conjugation of ecstasy and will: no longer Teresa de Ahumada, you are Teresa de Jesús.

Nonetheless, rarely and discreetly, the past seeps through:

> One night, being so ill that I wanted to excuse myself from mental prayer, I took my rosary in order to occupy myself in vocal prayer. I tried not to recollect my intellect, even though externally I was recollected in the oratory. When the Lord

desires, these devices are of little avail. I was doing this for only a short while when a spiritual rapture came upon me so forcefully that I had no power to resist it. It seemed to me that I was brought into heaven, and the first persons I saw there were *my father and my mother*. I saw things so marvelous—in as short a time as it takes to recite a *Hail Mary*—that I indeed remained *outside myself*; the experience seemed to me too great a favor.[29]

You went to San Vicente because here, in this Romanesque basilica, the memory of a virgin awaited, a *cristiana vieja*. And the echo of a converted Jew of whom you never spoke. You could not have done otherwise than to visit this crypt. Without a word. Pure rapture.

Chapter 23

CONSTITUTING TIME

This twofold immersion in the fathomless depths of the divinity.

Angela of Foligno, *The Book of Visions and Instructions*

To make foundations, to constitute, to write a constitution: but how? In the event, your reform of the Carmelite order would rest on two pillars: constitution and fictions. On one side, the strict regulation and jurisdiction whose great purpose was to guarantee the right conditions for the *outside-time* of contemplation in worldly time. On the other, the "account" or narrative of inner experience, linking the journey toward the infinity of the Other with the humdrum trials of dealing with the passions of women and the history of men.

On completing the *Constitutions* by writing (yes, that again!),[1] *The Way of Perfection*,[2] then the *Foundations*,[3] you imbued your sequestered sisters—whom your tongue often did not spare—with a psychic and indeed political life that was utterly without precedent, not only in the religious world but in any community of women, and perhaps of men, at that time. The story of your interior experience, resonating with the experience of your sisters and the other protagonists of the foundations, helped to literally unlock these cloistered souls. The narrative tenor of your writing (labeled "account" or "fiction"), which falls outside "genre" by mixing them all, appeals to the freedom of the spirit with an audacity, humanity, and distinct mastery of the moderns that contrast with the searingly rigorous texts of Ignatius Loyola, your senior by twenty years,[4] as much as with the skepticism of the *Essays* of Michel de Montaigne, your junior.[5]

And it's precisely this theological and philosophical "ignorance," this "unlettered" freshness that would turn *The Way of Perfection* and the *Foundations* into a breviary and a chronicle at once, mingling sensual delicacy and pragmatic intrepidity in a thought whose universal historic range and scope have still not been fully fathomed.

Just now, however, in 1566, you are contemplating the idea of *constituting* with María de Jesús Yepes, drawing on her knowledge and borrowing from her experience. It is to all appearances a bid to bring the Carmelites back to stricter standards. Is this to combat the laxity and drift of the Mitigated Rule and the whole epoch itself? To stand up more effectively to Lutheran rigor? Your implacable severity signals a far grander ambition, Teresa, my love, than any feebly moralistic design: you are intent upon inscribing into the accelerating time of history the outside-time of your understanding with the Other. Enclosure, poverty, and austerity are but three ways to convey the love of war and to acknowledge the war on love.

So now, along with María de Jesús Yepes, do you seek to return to the Primitive, ascetic Rule, the way she observed it at the Carmelite convent in Mantua where the nuns are, it is said, "walled up"? In a way; but it is rather more a matter of returning to that point in order to rethink, to recommence anew. "Constitution," for you, will contribute to inaugurating that other time that inhabits you already, the one I have read and seen taking shape in you.

The cornerstone will be enclosure, a shield against the levities and licenses you observed at the Incarnation, which it is high time were abolished, now that France has fallen prey to calamity, thanks to the "havoc" wrought by that sect of "miserable" Lutherans, as you put it.[6] María de Jesús wants to add on another cornerstone that is just as necessary for embarking on the way of perfection: absolute poverty.

"Until I had spoken to her, it hadn't been brought to my attention that our rule—before it was mitigated—ordered that we own nothing." This was something that "I, after having read over our constitutions so often, didn't know."[7] A descendant of wealthy merchants like you, Teresa, can't do less than begin to "constitute" by renouncing, firmly and finally, the chattels of this world! Before, "my intention had been that we have no worries about our needs; I hadn't considered the many cares ownership of property brings with it." So far so natural, and so Christlike. To cap it all, María nudges you toward the third principle of your reform: the discalced nuns are to live from their labor alone, and forgo all private income and allowances. Nothing but alms and personal effort!

Saying Mass, preaching, teaching, even tending the sick—these are tasks for men; your "daughters" will be encouraged to spin at the wheel, weave, sew, embroider. As a purist, you ban the more elaborate forms of needlework. Spinning and weaving are fine, but beware of lacy fripperies, guipures, and tapestries, for too much sophistication (*labor curiosa*) leads minds to stray from God! And no working with gold or silver, that's forbidden above all.

* * *

Between the Carmelite provincial, Ángel de Salazar, who disapproved of such austere, impoverished convents; Bishop Álvaro de Mendoza, who took you under his wing; the Dominican Domingo Báñez, who supported you; and the Franciscan Pedro de Alcántara, who inspired you, slowly but surely you drew up the future constitution. In 1567, with the approval of the Carmelite general, the Italian-born Juan Bautista Rubeo, the new rules were written out with the assistance of María de Jesús, before she went off to found the Imagen convent at Alcalá de Henares. The text was then passed on to John of the Cross for him to use as a template for the discalced male regime. As the original has been lost, the only version we have has been reconstituted from the Alcalá copy and the rules for the Carmelite friars. To my mind, this short text (twelve sixteen-page chapters, of which you authored only the first six), regulating solitude within group life by dint of a wise balance of asceticism and tenderness, is the very condensation of your art of founding time.

* * *

After all, can anything be regulated without regulating time? How to make best use of time has always been a concern for monastic orders. Hence chapter 1, rule 1:

> Matins are to be said after nine, not before, but not so long after nine that the nuns would be unable, when finished, to remain for a quarter of an hour examining their consciences as to how they have spent the day. The bell should be rung for this examen, and the one designated by the Mother prioress should read a

short passage from some book in the vernacular on the mystery that will serve as a subject for reflection the following day. The time spent in these exercises should be so arranged that at eleven o'clock the bell may be rung to signal the hour for retirement and sleep. The nuns should spend this time of examen and prayer together in the choir. Once the Office has begun, no Sister should leave the choir without permission.[8]

Matins at nine, "examen" for fifteen minutes with meditation in Spanish upon a particular mystery, all "together in the choir." Alone and together, meditation and work; the hours of the day are planned in such a way that time does not elapse but stands up straight, vertical, the frozen present of the contemplation of the Other. There are no distractions: your authorization of the vernacular tongue is not a license, it merely helps familiarize each nun with her Spouse and assimilate Him to whatever is most "her own," both infantile and maternal. Likewise with chanting: to forestall possible backsliding, you prohibit the seductive runs of Gregorian notation, stipulating "a monotone and with uniform voices." As for the rest of the rite, even Mass will be "recited," to save time, "so that the Sisters may earn their livelihood."[9]

Thus set up, the absolute present of contemplation will be paced according to the rhythms of the seasons and the movement of the sun. The bell rings out the calls to prayer, morning, noon, and night, and organizes the space of solitude with others: indoors or out, chapel or cell, garden or kitchen. The hours of the divine office (matins, prime, terce, sext, none, vespers, compline, lauds) and the milestones of the Catholic calendar (Christmas, Lent, Easter, saints' days) divert the quantitative flow of "passing time" into the outside-time of contemplative suspension.

The reform of time imposed by your *Constitutions*, Teresa, does not create a new calendar. Obviously not, since you are consciously aware of not founding a new religion. To take refuge in Catholic time as it exists (your Spouse's calendar, the holy feasts and liturgies) enables you to better *hollow out* this time in which you recognize yourself, and of which you demand that it recognize you—the better to shoot it like an arrow deep inside toward the amorous intensity, carried to extremes, that will help you to detach from the world in order to cleave to the Other until "participating" in Him. Recognition and exile: never one without the other. Your genius lies in this paradox, which conformists (traditionalist and modernist alike) refused to accept, and could only be admitted by bolder dialectical minds in the wake of the Council of Trent.

* * *

This headlong rush into the worlds of business, diplomacy, funding, this accumulation of ruses, affinities, seductions, and humiliations—what were they for? To hollow out places beyond place, enclosures harboring an outside-time, protecting the Infinite. The discalced universe founded by your *Constitutions* is your last oedipal assault, a cold disavowal of the world of families, wealth, secular honor. Could it be in veiled resonance with the secrets of the Marranos disclaimed by your father and uncle, though they "participated" in them? Silent prayer welded a secret world inside you, which the Carmelite reform will institutionalize. In that world, the parents' world, you make a kingdom that is not of this world. At the gate of the discalced houses you leave the Cepeda y Ahumadas and everything to do with them behind. Because from now on, you're plain Teresa of Jesus.

Taking your vows thirty-five years ago at the Incarnation, with the secret complicity of Uncle Pedro and the support of your readings of Osuna, had not been, after all, enough of a break with the order of families, of family, the law of management-gestation-generation. From now on, there's no ambiguity: at the cost of the sadomasochism that your joyous lucidity ceaselessly modulates into willpower or serenity, you are free. But at what a cost! It's another paradox, my baroque Teresa, and it won't be the last.

* * *

Before throwing yourself into the race that will keep you busy for the next fifteen years, the time of Infinity thus negotiated with ephemeral, worldly time nudges you to etch a thousand meticulous details into your regulations. The most essential are as follows.

Enclosure, you say That means solitude, silence, and detachment from the world.

No nun should be seen with her face unveiled unless she is with her father, mother, brothers, or sisters, or has some reason that would make it seem as appropriate as in the cases mentioned. And her dealings should be with persons who are an edification and help for the life of prayer and who provide spiritual consolation rather than recreation. Another nun should always be present unless one is dealing with conscience matters. The prioress must keep the key to both the parlor and the main entrance. When the doctor, barber-surgeon, confessor, or other necessary persons enter the enclosure, they should always be accompanied by two nuns. When some sick nun goes to confession, another nun must always be standing there at a distance so that she sees the confessor. She should not speak to him, unless a word or two, only the sick nun may do so.[10]

Outside-time in time demands total dispossession from the outset: nothing for oneself. The sisters cannot own anything, not even a book:

> In no way should the Sisters have any particular possessions, nor should such permission be granted; nothing in the line of food or clothing; nor should they have any coffer or small chest, or box, or cupboard, unless someone have an office in the community. But everything must be held in common. . . . the prioress should be very careful. If she sees that a Sister is attached to anything, be it a book, or a cell, or anything else, she should take it from her.[11]

You who were once such a stylish young thing, you now bear down on every sign of caring about appearance or comfort. Attire will be austere, with rope-soled sandals made of hemp, habits of coarse cloth or rough brown wool, hair chopped short under the wimple; no colors, no mirrors, Spartan cells, and straw pallets.

A fast is observed from the feast of the Exaltation of the Cross, which is in September, until Easter, with the exception of Sundays. Meat must never be eaten unless out of necessity, as the rule prescribes.

> The habit should be made of coarse cloth or black, rough wool, and only as much wool is necessary should be used. . . . Straw-filled sacks will be used for mattresses, for it has been shown that these can be tolerated even by persons with weak health. . . . Colored clothing or bedding must never be used, not even something as small as a ribbon. Sheepskins should never be worn. If someone is sick, she may wear an extra garment made of the same rough wool as the habit.
>
> The Sisters must keep their hair cut so as not to have to waste time in combing it. Never should a mirror be used or any adornments; there should be complete self-forgetfulness.[12]

For those who haven't grasped that this detachment is the imperative condition for belonging to the Other, *The Way of Perfection* sets out, in greater psychological detail, the implications of your juridical-constitutional rigor:

I am astonished by the harm that is caused from dealing with relatives. I don't think anyone will believe it except the one who has *experienced it for himself*. And how this practice of perfection seems to be forgotten nowadays in religious orders! I don't know what it is in the world that we renounce when we say that we give up everything for God, *if we do not give up the main thing, namely, our relatives*.[13]

Once nature, that is, "the relatives," has been dealt with, there naturally follows the need to guard against any special affection between sisters. Teresa is careful to put bounds on female passions, veritable poisons that she compares to the tumultuous feelings between siblings and to a "pestilence":

All must be friends, all must be loved, all must be held dear, all must be helped. *Watch out for these friendships*, for love of the Lord, however holy they may be; even among brothers they can be poisonous. I see no benefit in them. And if the friends are relatives, the situation is much worse—it's a *pestilence*![14]

Let no Sister *embrace another or touch her on the face or hands*. The Sisters *should not have particular friendships* but should include all in their love for one another, as Christ often commanded His disciples. Since they are so few, this will be easy to do. They should strive to imitate their Spouse who gave His life for us. *This love for one another that includes all and singles out no one in particular is very important*.[15]

The inevitable pleasures between sisters (female homosexuality is endogenous!) must be closely watched out for, then. Beware elective affinities! Transform them into "general" bonds, into the cement holding the group together! Is that your message? Sooner said than done!

With rather more finesse, your Motherhood—sensual and prudent—softens these rigors by drawing attention to another, more delightful Cross that afflicts those who care for others, and know them down to "the tiniest speck [*las motitas*]": "On the one hand [these lovers] go about forgetful of the whole world, taking no account of whether others serve God or not, but only keeping account of themselves; on the other hand, with their friends, they have no power to do this, nor is anything covered over; they see *the tiniest speck*. I say that they bear a truly heavy cross."[16]

When, in situations of mystical ascesis and the acquisition of this insight into human relationships, penances seem called for, you are careful to qualify them: "Should the Lord give a Sister the desire to perform a *mortification*, she *should ask permission*. This good, devotional practice should not be lost, for some benefits are drawn from it. Let it be done *quickly so as not to interfere with the reading*. Outside the time of dinner and supper, no Sister should eat or drink without permission."[17]

Moments of relaxation—an innovation of yours—will be allowed:

> When they are through with the meal, the Mother prioress may dispense from the silence so that all may converse together on whatever topic pleases them most, as long as it is not one that is inappropriate for a good religious. And they should all have their distaffs with them there.
>
> Games should in no way be permitted, for the Lord will give to one the grace to entertain the others. In this way, the time will be well spent. They should strive not to be offensive to one another, but their words and jests must be discreet. When this hour of being together is over, they may in summer sleep for an hour; and whoever might not wish to sleep should observe silence.[18]

It goes without saying that delicacies are forbidden: the menu is meager, and fasting lasts for six months. The Constitution for Saint Joseph's bans meat, save in cases of absolute necessity, as we have seen, but it does allow for fish and eggs, as well as unlimited bread and vegetables. Positively mouthwatering! Lest we forget, there's nothing like frugality to condition the detachment from self that solitude is expected to foster.

Good spiritual nourishment, equally under surveillance, will feed the souls whose stomachs have thus been purified:

> The prioress should see to it that good books are available, especially the *Life of Christ* by the Carthusian [Ludolf of Saxony], the *Flos Sanctorum* [a collection of lives of the saints, including the *Golden Legend* by Jacobus de Voragine], the *Imitation of Christ* [Thomas à Kempis], the *Oratory of Religious* [Antonio Guevara], and those books written by Fray Luis de Granada [the *Book of Prayer and Meditation*, the *Sinners' Guide*] and by Father Fray Pedro de Alcántara. This sustenance for the soul is in some way as necessary as is food for the body. All of that time not taken up with community life and duties should be spent by each Sister in the cell or hermitage designated by the prioress; in sum, in a place where she can be recollected and, on those days that are not feast days, occupied in doing some work. By *withdrawing into solitude* in this way, we fulfill what the

rule commands: that each one should be alone. No Sister, under pain of a grave fault, may enter the cell of another without the prioress's permission. Let there *never be a common workroom.*[19]

I see that the list of books authorized by the prioress is short but edifying, and the cleverest of the discalced nuns would be able to commit their salient passages to memory, so as to form part of a duly indoctrinated, elite corps.

I also note that this austerity wisely applies to one and all, fomenting a kind of equality between the sisters that even includes the mother superior:

The Mother prioress should be first on the list for sweeping so that she might give a good example to all. She should pay careful attention to whether those in charge of the clothes and the food *provide charitably* for the Sisters in what is needed for subsistence and in everything else. Those having these offices should *do no more for the prioress* and the older nuns than they do for all the rest, as the rule prescribes, but be attentive to *needs and age*, and more so to needs, for sometimes those who are older have fewer needs. Since this is a general rule, it merits careful consideration, for it applies in many things.[20]

Over the years, the various foundations would show that it was better to establish the prioress's authority from the start and enshrine total respect for the hierarchy; for the moment, however, Teresa refers to herself as an "older sister." Such were the optimistic beginnings of an institution that dreamed of equality. When at length she realized that the human animal, even behind the bars of a cloister, requires steering by an unambiguously firm hand, La Madre would duly take this into account.

But this is still only the start of an unimaginable adventure. The goal was no more or less than to found, in this world, the interiority of an absolute love beyond the reach or ken of this world; to noise abroad the work of this love by isolating it, rendering it invisible and indeed untouchable, and by the same token infinitely desirable. Nothing could have gone more against the grain at this time, the apogee of the Renaissance, as colonization was spreading and industry beginning to develop. But the repercussions of the Council of Trent subsumed this Teresian casuistry into the cultural revolution that was the Counter-Reformation, without anyone knowing where exactly this would lead: to the impasse of an archaism in whose swamp of supernatural manifestations Renaissance or Protestant progress would find itself mired? Or to the awakening of unsuspected energies and fruitful singularities, as enigmatic and confounding today as they ever were?

* * *

In *The Way of Perfection*, the three points that summarize the *Constitutions* allude to a Paradise located at the intersection of the "inward" and the "outward":

> I shall enlarge on only three things, which are from our own constitutions, for it is very important that we understand how much the practice of these three things helps us to possess *inwardly and outwardly* the peace our Lord recommended so highly to us. The first of these is *love for one another*; the second is *detachment* from all created things; the third is true *humility*, which, even though I speak of it last, is the main practice and embraces all the others.[21]

The fundament is love according to prayer: in these days of religious war, you must pray (inwardly) and make it known by taking up as much space as possible (outwardly). Recollect yourself at the very heart of your interior castle, but swarm through the mountains and valleys. In a Carmel harking back to the old ways, contemplation amounts to a warrior kind of love. Are some "unfortunate heretics" attacking the Catholic fortress in which La Madre desires to house her reform? To arms, to war! But one cannot gallop into battle without first outlining the Paradise of love; without exploring in every direction love's exaltations, which only thus, accepted at last, open up into Nothingness.

> Let us return now to the love that it is good for us to have, that which I say is *purely spiritual. I don't know if I know what I am saying. . . .* For I don't think I know which love is spiritual, or when sensual love is mixed with spiritual love, nor do I know why I want to speak of this spiritual love. . . . The persons the Lord brings to this state are generous souls, majestic souls. They are not content with loving something as wretched as these bodies, however beautiful they may be, however attractive. . . . And, in fact, I think at times that if love does not come from those persons who can help us gain the blessings of the perfect, there would be great blindness in this desire to be loved. Now, note well that when we desire love from some person, there is always a kind of seeking our own benefit or satisfaction . . .
>
> It will seem to you that such persons do not love or know anyone but God. I say, yes they do love, with a much greater and more genuine love, and with

passion, and with a more beneficial love: *in short, it is love.* And these souls are more inclined to give than to receive. Even with respect to the Creator Himself they want to give more than to receive. I say that this attitude is what merits the name "love," for these other base attachments have usurped the name "love."[22]

Who said enclosure? Inwardly and outwardly, you constitute whatever is necessary to harbor love, to set it ablaze with ecstasy, indifference, endurance. You are ready, Teresa, to confront the world from the vantage point of that nonworld. Comfort does not sit well with prayer, ecstasy is not a pampered but a painful act, incompatible with easy living: *"regalo y oración no se compadece."*[23]

Are you, like Angela of Foligno, perpetually engaged in a "twofold immersion in the fathomless depths of the divinity"? Not really. What you do instead is to walk it, explore it, elucidate it. The idea is to create the optimum conditions for attaining, through recollection, the intimate secrecy, the "closet" (Matt. 6:6) of prayer, the prayer "all night" (Luke 6:12) engaged in by Jesus himself, for "it has already been mentioned that one cannot speak simultaneously to God and to the world."[24] Time to withdraw from the world, then, to step back from its "frenzy"; but also from "bad humors" or melancholia, on "days of great tempests in His servants."[25] To stand never so far from the Master "that He has to shout," close enough for the person at prayer to "center the mind on the one to whom the words are addressed."[26] This pact with the Other should neither be a fusion, nor an obstacle to comprehension: "It will be an act of love to understand who this Father of ours is and who the Master is who taught us this prayer."[27]

And yet, with no striving on the part of the spirit, a transfer of intimacies is what occurs, an outpouring of pleasure between communicating vessels. The "divine food" of happiness, then,[28] the understanding of the "nothingness of all things," which together transmute the "pain" into "joy." Let "reason" itself "raise the banner"![29] The "interior" of every person will thus find itself appeased: "If the soul suffers dryness, agitation and worry, these are taken away."[30] In a word, the soul is returned to bliss. "The delight is in the *interior* of the will, for the other consolations of life, it seems to me, are enjoyed in the exterior of the will, as in the outer bark, we might say."[31]

Severed from this "exterior life," the cloistered soul—which Teresa reveals and instructs in the *Way*—will not allow itself to be held back by any obstacle. Of course, La Madre laments those "scattered" souls who behave like "wild horses . . . always restless,"[32] and this remonstration could just as well apply to herself. However, the enclosure of Heaven, irrigated by the Other's water or milk, is not impervious to the "active," "powerful" fire, "not subject to the elements," whose inability to extinguish its opposite, water, "makes the fire increase!" Far from being passive, the soul Teresa summons up in her writing is a blaze of love, tantamount for La Madre to the fire of "liberty": "No wonder the saints, with the help of God, were able to do with the elements *whatever they wanted*."[33] The "poor nun of St. Joseph's" licenses herself to wage war in order to "attain dominion over all the earth and the elements."[34] War against herself, by practicing "interior mortification";[35] war to "conquer the enemy," meaning the body first of all. Once souls have become "lords of our bodies,"[36] they wage war against the last enemies, among whom must be counted those "learned men," who "all lived a good life—incomparably better than I,"[37] but who have not been blessed with true "consolations [pleasures, refreshment: *gustos*] from God."[38] Or against what she calls the "night owls" or "cicadas," those Carmelites of the observance who haven't gone along with Teresa's reforms.[39]

* * *

Thus inflamed, the soul on its path to perfection never encounters a "closed door," for its state of "suspension"[40] makes an invincible combatant of it. Cloistered but not tied down, its deep refreshment in itself, at once water and fire, compels it to brave the antagonism of those who are content with the "exterior life," the "outer bark":

> I had no one with whom to speak. They were all against me; some, it seemed, made fun of me when I spoke of the matter, as though I were inventing it; others advised my confessor to be careful of me; others said that my experience was clearly from the devil. My confessor alone (even though he agreed with them in order to test me, as I came to know afterward) always consoled me.[41]

* * *

Not even devils can scare you anymore, Teresa. Fortified by your union with the Beloved, you ignore them, like so many pesky flies! "For although I sometimes saw them, as I shall relate afterward, I no longer had hardly any fear of them; rather it seemed they were afraid of me. I was left with a *mastery* over them truly given by the Lord of all; *I pay no more attention to them than to flies*."[42]

Contemplative and secluded as you are, you harbor a military vision of the world, my dear Teresa; the Parisian Psychoanalytical Society crowd would call it paranoid, and they wouldn't be completely wrong. Witness this vision:

> I saw myself standing alone in prayer in a large field; surrounding me were many different types of people. *All of them I think held weapons in their hands so as to harm me*: some held spears; others, swords; others daggers; and others, very long rapiers. In sum, I couldn't escape on any side without putting myself in danger of death; I was alone without finding a person to take my part. While my spirit was in this affliction, not knowing what to do, I lifted my eyes to heaven and saw Christ, not in heaven but quite far above me in the sky. He was holding out His hand toward me, and from there He protected me . . .
>
> This vision seems fruitless, but *it greatly benefited me* because I was given an understanding of its meaning. A little afterward I found myself almost in the midst of that battery, and I knew that *the vision was a picture of the world* . . . But I'm referring to friends, relatives, and, what frightens me most, very good persons. I afterward found myself so oppressed by them all, while they thought they were doing good, that I didn't know how to defend myself or what to do.[43]

How lucky you are: your ideal Father still protects you! What's more, his protection has modulated. The ecstatic union has already become a matter of listening and hearing. From now on, and more and more, His Voice does not simply comfort and reassure you: it reasons, judges, ponders, counsels. You would never have succeeded as a foundress without pulling back from the Beloved a little. Where previously you were enclosed in a garden irrigated by pleasure, cut off from a world you perceived as rejecting you, His Voice has opened up an evaluating distance; the love-rapture has been amplified by understanding and a kind of mastery. In professional jargon, I'd say that the ideal of the ego has become endowed with a reasonable, domesticated, sympathetic superego. To build the little Convent of Saint Joseph's, you followed David's example: "I will hear what God the Lord will speak: for he will speak peace unto his people, and to his saints" (Ps. 85:8).

And with time, indeed, you will outdo David. Is that an overstatement, brought on by a fit of feminism? In 1577, the Voice you hearken to in prayer is that of Jesus himself as he tells you to "Seek yourself in Me" (Búscate en mí).[44] *Listening* to the Other is not the same as *seeking* oneself in Him. Your inner experience is renewed; you are searching, you are a seeker; not content with hearing voices—divisions-hallucinations—*you recompose, modulate, compose them.* You write. David played on his harp while waging war, and he was a king. You are a warrior with no sovereignty beyond that of fiction in the Castilian vernacular. I can't help thinking that your writing has more than one string to its harp.

* * *

Four years, the quietest and most restful of your life, had gone by in the company of the select group you gathered together at Saint Joseph's,[45] when a missionary friar fresh from the Indies told you of the horrors being perpetrated on the natives by the glorious *peruleros* whose adventurous freedom you had once envied.

Then the father general of your order, Juan Bautista Rubeo (Giambattista Rossi) arrived from Rome on his first visit to Spain. You were in dread of his opinion—but he only encouraged you to undertake further foundations, further afield. You acted surprised, but you were as ready as can be. It's all you were waiting for. You got a little band of three of four nuns together and hopped into a wagon, under canvases stretched over a frame of rushes so nobody would see you, enclosure *oblige*—and off you went!

Did someone say "enclosure"?

* * *

And they're off! At a trot, at a gallop, never at a walk, with detours, ruses, and ambushes galore, you're a racehorse, Teresa, valiant and highly strung. A nun, with such a passion for the road? For the next fifteen years you will crisscross Spain, trudging on foot, mounted on a mule, rattled boneless in a coach. Escorted by a few devoted sisters and obliging men—secular priests who double as technical advisers, the occasional infatuated confessor—all undaunted by the hardships of nature and the iniquity of humans. Your energy as an epileptic prone to migraines astonishes your contemporaries, as well as posterity; from here, four centuries further on, it's your tempo that fascinates me: you are a true composer of time.

Your impetus in this dash is loving and warlike. "Grant me trials, Lord, give me persecution!" Let's go! Trotting, cantering, on horseback, on mule-back,

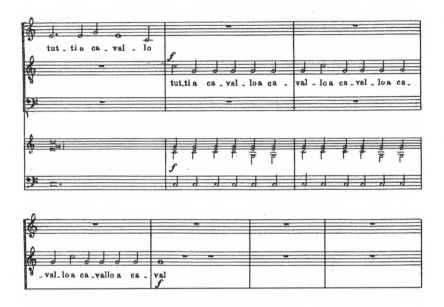

in a coach, on foot! Bring your quills, your contacts, your wallets, your kind hearts! You, devout noblewomen, and you, knights and merchants, bishops and courtiers, kings and queens, let us mount and sally forth together in a glittering cavalcade, for the insidious enemy is on the prowl. But how to tell friend from foe? It's war, the war of love.

If your blows fall short of the frail rampart, let's sally forth again, to arms! I watch, I think, I burn, I complain, O love that fortifies my heart. Quick, each man to his post! The journey is in me, the battle too, brutal and furious: they alone can bring me peace. Peace, what peace? There is no peace. One hand alone cures and wounds me. And because my suffering never reaches its limits, a thousand times daily I die, and a thousand times am born, so far am I from my salvation. Here we go again, to horse, to horse, to horse, every soul a horse, there is no soul if not loving and warlike, warlike and in love.

All of a sudden the Babel of times and languages carries me away, too, me, Sylvia Leclercq, a therapist in my spare time, and suddenly Teresa's tempo comes back to me in Italian: it's the loving warlike gallop of Monteverdi,[46] born fifty years after you, Teresa, my love; it's his beat I hear drumming through your writings, rising, resonating, and harmonizing with you. Suddenly he supplies the sound I felt was missing as I read your texts. To lend meaning to his runaway music, the conductor at Saint Mark's Basilica in Venice borrowed lyrics from Petrarch[47] and from Giulio Strozzi,[48] the first translator into Italian of *Lazarillo de Tormes.*

I hear you clearly now, Teresa, speaking to me in the voices of Petrarch, Strozzi, Monteverdi, all three Catholic Latins, and you excel in the race of love unto death:

E E E E G E C
Tut-ti tutti a ca-val-lo . . .
E E E E G E C
Tut-ti tutti a ca-val-lo . . .
C G G G G G C G G G G G
Tut-ti a ca-val-lo a ca-val-lo a ca-val-lo a ca-val

Quick, love is near, as near as the enemy, every man to his post, not a moment to lose, to your souls, to your souls, to your souls, there is no soul but one that's warlike and in love:

E E E E G E C
Tut-ti tutti a ca-val-lo . . .

When I was young I dreamed of writing like that, galloping off on a text by Strozzi or Petrarch to the rhythms of Monteverdi. Quite recently—had he sensed this hidden attraction?—a president (but which?) blurted out to me: "Sylvia Leclercq is a racehorse!" This strange compliment, which I received with a proud gratification that baffled the friends who were present, brought me back to you, Teresa, via my Italians:

E E E E G E C
Tut-ti tutti a ca-val-lo . . .

But it's no good, I will never, ever, neither in body nor on paper, possess anything like your fever; your velocity, suppleness, abrasiveness, and cunning; your jubilation, humility, and perfidy; your sharp claws and soft lethargy; your dexterity with a deathblow; your violent triumphs and grievous defeats, simplicity and glory, suffering and sadism, annihilation and perseverance, carelessness and obstinacy, serenity and anguish, toughness and tenderness;

your spiteful kindness, amorous indifference, and desperate tenacity. Nor will I ever have that furious, caressing lucidity and unflagging watchfulness, always on behalf of that infinite Love of the Other, infinitely unfindable, infinitely imbued in you. Never, Teresa, my love! You were, they said, a true "spiritual conquistador."

It's raining, snowing, blowing up a storm. You're feverish, you throw up, you scourge yourself, you mount a bad-tempered mule that bucks you off, the axle of your coach snaps on a rutted road, you fall over, you hurt yourself, you break a leg, you feel cold, you feel too hot, there's nothing left to drink, you haven't had a scrap to eat since goodness knows when, you were promised great things but it's all fallen through, never mind! You'll find another way in, a different path; you'll prevail on one of your accomplices, quick, no time to lose; your purse is empty but you always find money somewhere; it matters and it doesn't, the re-foundation has no need of a steady income, as you explain to all and sundry, and also they—sisters, brothers, creditors, friends, or foes—don't matter either. What matters are deeds, what's needed are works and more works.

Your love leads the dance, that sole, single, inexhaustible love, on the trot, at a gallop, no love but in the loving warlike soul, and for that soul, your soul, galloping along the highways and byways of Spain, of the world, of perfection, of the interior castle, of everything, of nothing:

E E E E G E C, E E E E G E C.
Tu-tti, tutti a ca-val-lo, tut-ti, tutti a ca-val-lo

Religious houses founded by Teresa of Jesus.

1562	Saint Joseph's in Avila	1575	Beas de Segura
1567	Medina del Campo	1575	Seville
1568	Malagón	1576	Caravaca
1568	Valladolid	1580	Villanueva de la Jara
1569	Toledo	1580	Palencia
1569	Pastrana	1581	Soria
1570	Salamanca	1582	Burgos
1571	Alba de Tormes	1582	Granada
1574	Segovia		

Chapter 24

TUTTI A CAVALLO

"That is too high-minded," I replied, "and consequently cruel."
Fyodor Dostoyevsky, *Humiliated and Insulted*

I'm daydreaming, eyes wide open beneath their lids: I can see and hear her now, Teresa's on her way, twenty years stretch ahead, counting from the first lines of the *Life*, and the only thing that will stop her is death. She's got clean away from the family, from yesterday's sisters, from the fathers of here or there, in order to be exiled in the Other and to carve Him a new place—invisible, impregnable, segregated from the world—in the world. She writes of transforming herself into God, uniting with God. At any rate, His Majesty cannot be winkled out of her. Neither "I" nor "we," this dual entity sets off, arrives, struggles, founds, sets off again, battles with itself, starts over. Nothing but new beginnings. Let's try to follow.

★ ★ ★

1567. Medina del Campo: a large market town with an international fair. Unexpectedly, wealthy converso merchants such as Simón Ruiz are prepared to back these nuns determined to live on nothing but alms and their humble crafts of embroidery and needlepoint . . . Did such fledgling entrepreneurs seek a place in the sun of the Church? Was it easier, more exciting, more promising to obtain this via innovators like Teresa, instead of hoary notables "who have the fat of an old Christian four fingers deep on their souls," as Sancho puts it in *Don Quixote*?[1]

La Madre could not fail to interest them, for she did not comply with the *estatutos de limpieza de sangre* that excluded converted Jews from the more prestigious convents, as well as from university colleges and town councils.

Since she began making foundations, La Madre has been blessed with more than visions: voices, too, are heard, whose messages she eagerly transcribes. The difference is that visions induce states of rapture, whereas voices spur to action. The voices—obviously the Lord's—speak disparagingly of human prescriptions and laws: they convey the Word of the Beloved differently from how the world's kingpins understand it. To speed things up—and Teresa is moving faster every day—it seems that thanks to these voices she, too, stands against the law, against the world, against the grain. "You will grow very foolish, daughter, if you look at the world's laws. Fix your eyes on me, poor and despised by the world. Will the great ones of the world, perhaps, be great before me? Or, are you to be esteemed for lineage or for virtue?"[2]

At Medina, then, a new house opens on August 15, 1567: cousin Inés Tapia, now Inés de Jesús, will be the prioress. There are malcontents in town who grumble that this foundation is a fraud. Let them say what they like, God has given Teresa some true friends here: Pedro Fernández, the Dominican principal; the Jesuit Baltasar Álvarez, who accompanies La Madre in her spiritual life; and the Dominican García de Toledo, of course, dependably busy and protective, almost affectionate. No sooner has this inauguration been celebrated, than permission arrives to found two male monasteries under the Primitive Rule! Where should they be located?

Antonio de Heredia (Antonio de Jesús), a Carmelite of the Observation from Medina, takes an interest. But he's too old, too difficult, Teresa balks, no. Let's speed up:

> *tutti, tutti a cavallo*
> *tutti, tutti a cavallo*
> *tutti a cavallo a cavallo a cavallo a cavallo a cavallo a caval*
> *tutti, tutti a cavallo*
> *tutti a cavallo*

Father Antonio introduces to the discalced nuns a bright young man fresh out of theology school at Salamanca, twenty-five-year-old Juan de Yepes, ordained as Juan de San Matías. Short and skinny, round-skulled and sharp-faced, he is the son of a rich weaver from Toledo (Toledan forebears and of

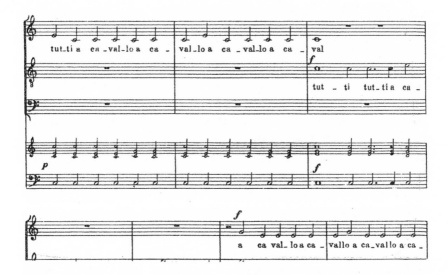

Jewish stock, it seems—just like Teresa!), the hidalgo Gonzalo de Yepes, who was reputedly ruined by marrying Juan's mother, a woman of Moorish and hence Muslim blood. This Juan de San Matías is an ascetic, disillusioned by the calced life; he yearns to withdraw from the world in the mountains of Segovia. He has shining eyes, an elliptical wit, and the fieriness of the Carthusians he wanted to join. He's the one! Onward!

No, hold your horses, wait!

Luisa de la Cerda, Teresa's generous patron and friend, slows things down again. This noble lady, who aspires to Heaven above all else, insists, absolutely *insists* that Teresa found a branch at Malagón, a little hamlet in the sticks. Teresa can't see the point of dispatching her nuns to the middle of a field, when all they know is weaving and sewing. But Báñez is keen as well, and it's hard to say no to him. Aha! Malagón, as she recalls, is not a million miles from Montilla, the home of Juan de Ávila. Doña Luisa, who often visits Andalusia, could deliver to him the manuscript of the *Life*, which Báñez has just returned to the author. Shush, not a word to Báñez, who doesn't want the text to circulate and might feel sore if the other priest were roped in; best to take responsibility oneself and entrust the precious pages to Luisa. The foundress has embarked on a new chase. How to make sure her manuscript will reach its destination? It would seem writing a book is no less complicated than founding a new religious order!

To begin with—she's always beginning—she must get in touch right away with Juan de Ávila, tell him of her forthcoming visit to the area, and send him the book in advance through Luisa. Although she dared to hope as much, Teresa is thrilled when the learned sage replies without delay and even looks kindly upon her journey: "You can better serve the Lord with this pilgrimage than by staying in your cell."[3] No hesitation, she'll go to Malagón.

Meanwhile there's no end of checking, finding out, keeping up to date: they stop in Alcalá de Henares on the way, at the discalced convent founded by María de Jesús. Poor woman, she hasn't got a clue: too tough, too many penances. María is an innovator whose notions came in useful for the *Constitutions*, to be sure, but only on condition of being revised through and through, adapted to inner virtue, stripped of external rigors. That's also what it means to be a foundress: the readiness to start over, over and over again, relying on one's powers alone—besides the Voice of His Majesty, of course!

The problems pile up at Malagón. Where to find a spiritual director for a new monastery in this godforsaken spot? How about getting Tomás de Carleval from Baeza, Bernardino's brother, a disciple of Juan de Ávila . . . But Bernardino was arrested by the Inquisition back in 1551. It might be reckless, a way of courting trouble.

On the other hand, attentive to the guidance of the master of Avila, Teresa doesn't think twice before accepting converts at Malagón, that is, sisters in white veils, and starting a school for local girls. The young recruits have got to learn to read, otherwise they haven't a hope of donning the black veil one day and reading the holy office!

And then, since troubles never come singly, how on earth is one to eat fish, as stipulated by the *Constitutions*, when there's no fish to be had in Malagón? Never mind, let them eat meat, we're in Spain after all, a carnivorous country if ever there was one, and too bad for the Constitution, decrees Teresa. Off they go again.

```
E   E   E   E   G   E   C
Tut - ti tutti a ca - val -  lo . . .
E   E   E   E G   E   C
Tut - ti tutti a ca - val -  lo . . .
C  G   G   G   G   G   G  C  G   G   G   G   G
Tut - ti  a  ca - val - lo  a ca - val - lo a ca  -val-lo  a  ca  -val-
C   G    G   G  G   G
lo   a ca- val -lo  a  ca  -val
```

But it's not that simple. La Madre does not for a moment forget about her manuscript: the Business she must attend to amongst her business.

May 18, 1568. Letter to Luisa de la Cerda: Why has she not yet sent the book of Teresa's *Life* to maestro Ávila?

May 27. Another letter to Luisa. "Since you are so near him, I beg you . . ." Not to mention that Fray Báñez is also waiting on it, and since there is no way to photocopy the original, and Báñez must not find out about the author's contacts with Juan de Ávila, "I'm distressed—I don't know what to do."[4]

June 9. Fresh bid to jog her ladyship's memory. "In regard to what I entrusted to you, I beg you once more . . ."[5]

June 23. "Remember, since I entrusted my soul to you . . ."[6]

November 2. At last! "You have worked everything out so well . . . So I'm forgetting all the anger this caused me." Juan de Ávila has emitted a positive verdict, the future saint "is satisfied with everything. He says only that some things should be explained further and that some terms should be changed."[7]

Good grief! It took all of five letters to Luisa de la Cerda during that summer of 1568 to set the ball of the *Life*'s acceptance rolling: not that Teresa was really "attached" to the text, at least she claimed not to be; but it's not that simple. Was it not essential for her to write down (or to "communicate," as we say today) the "treasure" she concealed in her "center," so as to found an interior Time within time as it flies by?

✳ ✳ ✳

Summer 1568. To Valladolid. A great Mendoza, Bernardino of that name, wishes to settle the Discalced Carmelites into a house there, with a garden and vineyards. She cannot refuse, when the gallant gentleman is brother to the bishop of Avila, Álvaro de Mendoza, who blessed the foundation of the Convent of Saint Joseph's in Avila!

Teresa stops off at Duruelo to visit the little house additionally offered by Bernardino, with a view to setting up the first convent for discalced monks. She makes a detour to Medina to bring back Juan de San Matías, promoting him to the rank of associate founder in the Valladolid venture.

Let's see, how are we getting along in these noble lands so handsomely lavished upon us? There are so many mosquitoes in this lovely countryside that the sisters get malaria and die like flies. Teresa won't be bullied, enough is enough, we'll move into town. Álvaro's sister María de Mendoza donates another house, it's just what we need, we'll put up all the fittings ourselves: cells, chapels, grilles,

Teresa won't settle for less than perfection; María Bautista will be the prioress. La Madre wants everyone to know that a convent must be to La Madre's taste, she won't bow to pressure from any quarter, whether the Mendozas or some estimable Jesuit such as Fr. Ripalda.

Four years later, on March 7, 1572, Teresa writes to inform María de Mendoza that she will not accept two postulants recommended by that lady. Is it because by her high standards, the young ladies showed an insufficient vocation? She's a perfectionist, as we've seen: she doesn't want one-eyed or sickly girls in her convent.

You're hard-hearted, Teresa, and you know it, you're proud of it, you're not as Christlike as your voices make you out to be. A masochist overall, you are not above being a sadist at times, I will remind you of that. It helps, certainly: the times are as tough as you are, the Carmels hard to control, one has to fight, to keep tense as a bow in order to keep making foundations. But still!

* * *

The previous year, an auto-da-fe was held in Valladolid. Men and women accused of Lutheranism were burned at the stake. Most were conversos with connections to the Cazalla family; Agustín Cazalla, preacher to the king and his mother, was among them. There had been some contact between these circles and doña Guiomar, involving Teresa herself: although they were no longer in touch, prayer continued to link them. The world was coming down hard on the new paths she was trying to clear, it was out to silence His Voices, that much was clear. Oh well. Just distrust everyone and everything, follow your way of perfection more and more perfectly, and we'll be off again,

E   E   E   E   G   E   C
E   E   E   E   G   E   C

Blessed be His Majesty, this hostile world is not only composed of enemies: some pure souls do exist, like that young Juan de San Matías. Might His Majesty have created him expressly for Teresa's project? His is a life devoted to intelligent thought and great penance; "I believe our Lord has called him for this task."[8] In November 1568, Juan and Teresa, now a close-knit team, founded the masculine Convent of Duruelo. A shabbier, more frugal holy house can scarcely be imagined. Teresa stitched with her own hand the habit of the young monk who now took the name of Juan de la Cruz, John of the Cross.

* * *

And yet you are going to abandon him in the dark night of this utterly impoverished place, Teresa, my love, a pang of sorrow and pride in your heart, admiring him, but already a little distant. For he is passionately in thrall to the realm of the invisible, whereas you are committed to scattering the glints of the diamond of your soul, which encases the Third Person. John of the Cross will lose himself ever more in the purity of agonized contemplation, whereas you pursue your furious cavalcade for God.

F F F F A♭ F D♭
F F F F A♭ F D♭
D♭ A♭ A♭ A♭ A♭ A♭ A♭ D♭ A♭ A♭ A♭
A♭ A♭ D♭ A♭ A♭ A♭ A♭ A♭
F F F F A♭ F D♭
F F F F A♭ F D♭

Yes, I hear you clearly: after every conversation with John of the Cross, your gallop is slightly faster and yet slacker, dampened by melancholy. No, John's nothingness will never crush the jewel of your inner dwelling places, it can only unleash a shiver in that heart of yours, which wants to be hard, which has to stay that way.

* * *

Now then, time to pull yourself together, to check your first foundation and tighten the bonds with the sisters at Saint Joseph's in Avila. Indeed, but it's impossible! A fresh proposal has arrived, supported by your new Jesuit friend, Pablo Hernández: to found a house in Toledo.

Toledo, is it? The city where grandfather Juan was traduced, where the *sambenito* embroidered with the Sánchez family name was hung up in the church of Santa Leocadia. A metropolis that presently numbers no fewer than twenty-four monasteries! A foundation in such a place is a crazy gamble! Maybe so, but that's what La Madre likes about it.

A rich trader named Martín Ramírez has engaged to bequeath his worldly goods to the discalced institution at Toledo; in exchange, he wants to be buried in the chapel. Is this acceptable? A commoner giving himself the right to be buried in a convent, as though he were a nobleman? It goes without saying, however, that they will welcome the daughters of converso Jews. But Toledans are sharply divided over the fate of Archbishop Bartolomé de Carranza, arrested in 1559 and slammed into a Roman jail due to his friendship with Luis de Granada and other "spiritual" adepts of mental prayer; he has numerous enemies here. Some pious women nevertheless club together to have him freed, defying the Inquisitor General Fernando de Valdés. As though this were not enough to torpedo the Toledo venture, it soon transpires that the Ramírez bequest is no longer available; the permission to found keeps being delayed, and conservatives rail against the cheek of this little woman who proposes to found a religious house by cutting deals with tradespeople! Can anything else go wrong?

No need to panic. Teresa, who can be sweet and gracious when she chooses, pushes on with the works. Finally the ecclesiastical governor of the diocese, don Gómez Tello Girón, agrees to guarantee the project, on one condition: in order to avoid infection by the taint of trade, the convent must have no revenues and refuse any donation or patronage (thus shutting the vulgar Ramírez out of the picture; was he the problem all along?) The foundress feigns surprise. But Father, who suggested anything else? Our Constitutions impose a strict rule of poverty, I thought you knew.

Mother Teresa has three or four ducats to her name, enough to buy two straw pallets and a blanket. A mischievous *pícaro* who goes by the name of Alonso de Andrada offers help, in the form of the keys to a building he's wangled who knows how. Teresa prefers not to inquire about such details, especially when they give off a whiff of irregularity. She is physically attacked by a neighbor, who hates the discalced movement. None of this prevents her from persevering with the work in hand—sweeping, repairing, and decorating the premises. At this point the owner of the place changes her mind, decides she doesn't want the newfangled style of convent either. But at last Tello Girón returns from a trip, and the council grants permission. The happy ending is courtesy of the Voice of the Lord, who has demanded superhuman obstinacy from Teresa, mixed in with a degree of machination and shady dealings, it must be said.

On May 14, 1569, the first Mass is said in the new foundation at Toledo. More than a foundation, it has been a brilliantly forced passage, a seduction strategy, a feat of errancy and endurance. Nothing can resist you, Teresa. Perhaps your poverty is a form of high ambition? Your humility, a piece of brazen chutzpah?

E E E E G E C
E E E E G E C

This gallop might have been smoother had it not clashed with other equally bold and no less brash schemes, usually from women. At this precise juncture, your soaring energy came up against that most formidable of Spanish grandees: Ana de Mendoza de la Cerda, princess of Eboli, wife of Prince Ruy Gómez— the most powerful personality after King Philip II—and great-granddaughter of don Pedro González de Mendoza, cardinal and archbishop of Toledo, dubbed "the third king of Spain." Quite a package! She was a haughty, peremptory woman, minus an eye (could that be another reason why you didn't want that sort of defect in your convent, Teresa?), capable of setting fire to everything around with "just one sun," as the saying went, a spoiled and spendthrift princess. You were about to find this out, unfortunately, for here she was, nagging you to drop everything and go to Pastrana to found another convent, there's no end to it. Off you went, willingly enough, since in the intoxication of your status as the go-to foundress, giddied by your ascent, you were still blind to the traps the Eboli woman would set for you, my naive Teresa.

No question of a wagon this time, it's an unworthy vehicle for a Madre like yourself. The princess sends a stately coach, a fairy carriage! Along the way, your gallop—a golden gallop now—draws breath at Court, in Madrid! We know that His Majesty's Voice is essential to your foundations, but that of King Philip II is not to be sneezed at either, is it?

The great ones of this world are solicitous, they promise to help. The great ladies are not to be outdone: Leonor de Mascarenhas, for instance, introduces you to a pair of hermits who will become your disciples, or almost. One can never be sure of seeing eye to eye with such original characters, but you're an original yourself, aren't you? The characters in question are Mariano de Azzaro and his friend the painter Giovanni Narducci, of whom more later.

At Pastrana you are given a suite in the Eboli palace and showered with treats, fueling the gossip of evil tongues: what behavior from a woman who always purports to be holier than thou! And yet sparks have flown between you and your hostess Ana de Mendoza from the beginning of your stay. You of course have no time for the courtiers and their "artificial displays" of lordship (*autoridades postizas*),[9] and you say so bluntly. For her part the princess insists on an Augustinian sister to keep you company, although it is common knowledge that you only care to frequent nuns affiliated to your own discalced Rule. And so on. Eventually you settle on a prioress: Isabel de Santo Domingo, the spiritual daughter of the great reformed Franciscan Pedro de Alcántara who was such an inspiration to you, as we've seen. And a second monastery for men takes shape not far away, this time under the auspices of the prince of Eboli.

A change of decor is noticeable here: luxury congeals into morbidity and the atmosphere is sepulchral. As at Duruelo, the monks' cells are adorned by crosses and death's-heads. The hermits you recently met, Azzaro and Narducci, have renamed themselves fray Ambrosio Mariano de San Benito and fray Juan de la Miseria—that's right, the painter whose portrait of you you weren't too pleased with. These two introduce the practice of perpetual worship to Pastrana: night and day, the Holy Sacrament must be attended by two praying brothers! This overwrought asceticism is as distasteful to you as that of young John of the Cross. The mournful rituals at Pastrana and Duruelo are beyond you; impressed but already somewhat detached, you think only of continuing the journey.

> *E   E   E   G   E   C*
> Tut - ti tutti a ca - val - lo
> *E   E   E   EG   E   C*
> Tut - ti tutti a ca - va - lo

Her Highness of Eboli can stay put, she's got what she wanted, her very own Carmel, like her relatives María de Mendoza and Luisa de la Cerda; in fact she's got two of them. Let her stay in Pastrana, you won't be climbing into her golden coach again, that's a solemn vow; there have been too many compromises already.

* * *

The galloping is far from over, and you are more and more attentive to His Majesty's Voices so that they might speak through your lips. Voices that dictate the proper balance between the gruesome penances favored by the recently discalced, and the worldly temptations entailed by princely palaces, but also by convents with questionable standards: between macabre skulls and the licentiousness of paradisiac illusions. The followers of Juan de Ávila and the Jesuits are alone in hearkening to those voices in your mouth; they alone hear you at this time, one of the most testing of your whole itinerary. Isn't that enough encouragement to press on?

Meanwhile, family ties must be reorganized. You relegate the family of your sister Juana de Ovalle to its rightful place: too much familiarity is damaging. On the other hand you empower the role of your brother Lorenzo, who has returned from the "Indies" with a splendid fortune and a burning faith. It's a good time to regulate your relationship with money: not too much but more than none, just enough for peace of mind and galloping on, but even so . . . Whatever the precautions, money comes at a price, and one that's always too expensive. "Miserable is the rest achieved that costs so dearly. Frequently one obtains hell with money and buys everlasting fire and pain without end." ("Negro descanso se procura, que tan caro cuesta. Muchas veces se procura con ellos el infierno y se compra fuego perdurable y pena sin fin.")[10]

* * *

Fall 1570. Departure for Salamanca, this time. Another Jesuit, Martín Gutiérrez, has asked Teresa to start a house in this city of students and high-flown culture. Where can premises be found to rent in such a densely populated place? The Dominican Bartolomé de Medina is displeased: from the heights of his university chair, he advises the "little woman" to "stay at home." Teresa trusts in her powers of persuasion. All she needs to do is pay a call to this snooty academic, and he'll drop into the bag of her rhetoric like so many others.

Done: the inauguration is scheduled for November 1. The locale has not yet been decided, everything is provisional, but the main thing, the foundational gesture, has been achieved. The rest will follow. Ana de Tapia, now Ana de la Encarnación, has been chosen as the prioress.

Tut-ti tuttia ca-val-lo tut-ti tuttia ca-val-lo
tuttia caval-loa caval-loa caval-loa caval-loa caval
E E E E G E C, E E E E G E C

No chance of going to sleep on one's laurels. At Medina, a new prioress must be appointed. The Carmelite provincial, Ángel de Salazar, uneasy about the reforms from the start, is opposed to the re-election of Inés de Jesús. He would prefer to have an unreformed nun from the Convent of the Incarnation; he is, moreover, backing the claims of the family of Isabel de los Ángeles, Simón Ruiz's niece, fearful lest her fortune—money misery again!—be handed to the convent at their expense. Salazar angrily orders Teresa off the premises: what an excruciating humiliation! There will be no more galloping for a while, as she slinks crestfallen out of Medina on the bony back of a water-carrier's donkey. She goes for succor to John of the Cross, and together they set off to make a foundation at Alba de Tormes.

* * *

January 1571. An accountant at the court of the dukes of Alba, prompted by his wife Teresa de Layz, had already called on Teresa to establish a convent in the rural surrounds of Alba de Tormes. By now, the foundress has learned the hard way that some minimum income is necessary, simply for the convent to exist and the sisters to live: in those days, many succumbed from their penances but also from starvation. She strikes a bargain: you will provide for food, clothing, and the needs of the sick, and accept all vocations without inquiring into "purity of blood."

As always, La Madre travels to the sound of His Voice. Tested to the limit, but more than ever sure of the Other, Teresa is definitively a Third Person, you can't miss it. A writer who outlines her own character, combined with a pragmatic woman—that's what you call a foundress. Martin Gutiérrez, a few years younger, the rector of the Society of Jesus college in Salamanca,[11] understands and supports her; but doesn't their intimacy jeopardize her liberty? Since, she tells his Reverence, "I don't think I'm attached to any person on earth, I felt some scruple and feared lest I begin to lose this freedom." The Lord's Voice responds promptly to this attachment anxiety, and reassures the troubled woman beneath the Carmelite habit: "Just as human beings desire companionship in order to communicate about *the joys of their sensual nature*, so the *soul* desires when there is someone who understands it to communicate about its joys and pains; and it becomes sad when there is no one."[12] Communication between souls, on a par with the sensual joys, is therefore not altogether banned between the Jesuit and the nun. That is certainly good news. Otherwise, how could she possibly proceed with making her foundations?

The Dominicans prove more resistant, this time, to Teresa's charms. Pedro Fernández, the illustrious theologian who defended Teresa in the early days of her project, has gone over to the side of the provincial, Ángel de Salazar, who remains suspicious of it, as we've seen, and has begun to express his own reservations. Fortunately the Voice of His Majesty is once more on hand to confront the Dominican father who has become such a *père-sévère*: every time Fr. Fernández reproaches her for some failing, the Voice brings Teresa back to life. It's perfectly true that I am incompetent and a sinner, Father, is the gist of her retort; but your objections help me to improve. I am profoundly grateful to you, for if I surpass myself it's thanks to you, please don't stop, it's going rather well, don't you agree? It's going well, and better, and faster. Dash on!

tut-ti tut-ti a cavallo
tut-ti tut-ti a cavallo
tut-ti a cavallo a cavallo a cavallo a cavallo a cavallo a caval
tut-ti tut-ti a cavallo
tut-ti tut-ti a cavallo

October 1571. As the apostolic visitor to the Carmelites, the same Dominican father, Pedro Fernández, appoints Teresa as prioress to the Incarnation in July 1571. Such a strange idea must be the brainchild of Provincial Salazar—that would make sense. Being so deeply opposed to her foundations, it would suit him to nail her down inside a convent of 150 nuns, while appearing to honor her with a promotion! It's nothing but a punishment, and Teresa sees right through it, as she writes to Luisa de la Cerda: "Oh, my lady, as one who has known the calm of our houses and now finds herself in the midst of this pandemonium, I don't know how one can go on living."[13]

The investiture ceremony goes horribly wrong. Afraid to lose their freedoms as calced nuns, the conservative Carmelites won't let Teresa in. Protests, booing, and jeering greet the provincial when he utters the name of the Incarnation's new prioress. "No!" shriek the incensed sisters. The only contrary opinion comes from Catalina de Castro, who pipes, almost inaudibly: "We want her, we love her!"

This staunchness is all it takes to rally a small, timid group of supporters. The antis grow heated; the timid camp grows larger. Scuffles break out. The constables are called in. At last the controversial prioress manages to slip inside the choir by the side door. Clutching an image of her father, Saint Joseph, Teresa sits down in the same stall she had occupied for twenty-seven years, when she was just a little nun. A blunder, in the daze of emotion? Or, on the contrary, a clever diplomatic ruse, a conscious diffidence that is sure to pay off? No, rather a divine inspiration. And that's just the beginning.

You are a mistress in the art of mise-en-scène, Teresa, my love. Oh yes, don't misunderstand me, the right judgment of mise-en-scène is an art, like music, a kind of sanctity. Then you disappear for a moment, and return with a statue of our Lady, dressed in embroidered silk. Slowly and solemnly you place her in the prioress's stall. You give her your official keys, you kneel at her feet and say in a soft voice (yours or His Majesty's?):

"Behold our Lady of Mercy, dear daughters. She will be your prioress."

Your words fell the rebels like a bolt of grace—a *coup de foudre*, indeed. From that moment on, the Incarnation was yours. No more insistent visitors, sensual dissipations, flirting in the parlor. During Lent, even fathers and mothers are excluded.

All the same, this new and unaccustomed rigor is not accepted by your subordinates without a struggle. It's only human. A party of enterprising young blades decides to have it out with you: Does this prioress think she's God? You receive their spokesman and continue spinning, without looking at him, through a torrent of cavalier eloquence. Finally you cut in:

"Henceforth Your Grace will kindly leave this monastery in peace. If Your Grace persists, I shall appeal to the king."

* * *

Notwithstanding such smart raps on the knuckles, you are still a good mother who knows how to feed her daughters, I grant you that, my fixer Teresa. Francisco de Salcedo is in charge of provisions: sixty head of poultry, plenty of pulses, lettuces, and quinces. Your sister Juana is going to send some turkeys. All of the ingredients for some *ollas podridas*, as well as *salpicón*, perhaps, and endless supplies of *yemas*, my chum Juan would be delighted! The fine ladies of your acquaintance—the duchess of Alba, doña María de Mendoza, doña Magdalena de Ulloa—will contribute as much and more.... You are not anorexic, Teresa, or not any more, it's a false rumor extrapolated from your early days. But you forbid jewelry and profane dances, it's the least you can do. His Majesty knows only the music of angels and the spirit, and you do likewise.

The one thing lacking in this refashioned Carmel is a good confessor, and you know just the man. Summoned from the college in Alcalá where he was teaching the prince of Eboli's novices, John of the Cross takes the post. The ideal circumstance for conversing with this holy man: among mutual ecstasies and levitating chairs (phenomena certified by the nuns who keep an awed eye upon the sayings and doings of the two protagonists), the pair of you advance together and yet on different tracks toward your respective sainthoods, divergent but forever convergent.... The sort of love you share, lucid and remote, is only possible this way.

★ ★ ★

The moment of spiritual marriage has arrived at last. We are in November 1572. The holy humanity of Jesus inflicts wounds on you that match His own, and lavishes immeasurable joy upon you, since you've succeeded in pleasing Him by your prayers as by your deeds, in *ficción* as in *obras*:

> While at the Incarnation in the second year I was prioress, on the octave of the feast of St. Martin.... His Majesty ... appeared to me in an imaginative vision, as at other times, very interiorly, and He gave me His right hand and said: *"Behold this nail; it is a sign you will be My bride from today on. Until now you have not merited this; from now on not only will you look after My honor as being the honor of your Creator, King, and God, but you will look after it as My true bride. My honor is yours, and yours Mine."* This favor produced such an effect in me I couldn't contain myself, and I remained as though *entranced*. I asked the Lord either to *raise me from my lowliness* or not grant me such a favor; for it didn't seem my nature could bear it. Throughout the whole day I remained thus very *absorbed*.[14]

Throughout all this you make an excellent prioress, ergo your mission has been accomplished. But Avila does not suit you, the climate is icy, you're surprised you could ever have been born here. It's time to go on the road again.

New foundations await you.

Fussier than a Lutheran, more illuminated than an *alumbrada*, you are a magnet for condemnation but also for hope, hopes of all kinds. You are a pioneer of the Counter-Reformation and a saint; they don't know that yet, but they will after your death. But there are some who suspect it and go out of their way to smooth yours. People like the duchess of Alba, who obtains permission in February 1573 for you to leave the Incarnation for a few days and go stay with her. Shortly afterward you receive authorization from Pedro Fernández, the apostolic commissary, to establish a house in Segovia.

* * *

1573. One of Teresa's confessors, Fr. Jerónimo Ripalda, comes to Salamanca as La Madre is passing through, in the course of her three years at the Incarnation; he instructs her to write down the story of her foundations. Following on your autobiography, now tell us about your work. How impatiently you had waited for this! The text had been flowing ever since the final chapters of the *Life*. The Voice had suggested you write the book in 1570, and nothing had come of it. Now, you feel founded enough to be able to pass on the art of founding.

Ten years ago, after all, the act of writing had spurred you to make foundations. Conversely, now, the creation of your godly houses redirects you to writing, a different writing in which psychological subtlety, a hardheaded sense of reality, and the lucidity of rapture are intermingled. You begin work on August 24 and compose the first nine chapters of the *Foundations*. One certainty bolsters you: having managed to flesh out your visions in the real world, you are confident they don't come from the devil. "So after the foundations were begun, the fears I previously had in thinking I was deceived left me. I grew certain the work was God's."[15]

* * *

From 1573 to 1582, the *Foundations* relate the loving and warlike adventures of Teresa the politician. They are the visible face of another adventure, the one that invented the depths of intimacy, as related in *The Interior Castle*. In 1577, at the request of Fr. Gratian and the order of Fr. Velázquez, her current confessor, the Carmelite penned the latter text, which would "found," effectively, dwelling places that appear, with hindsight and against the background of the *Foundations*, to be the antithesis of the worldly business of the militant traveler. Or were they instead the ultimate condition for the success of those pragmatic endeavors? Perhaps it is a case of a foundation of the foundations, since at this point— halfway through the time it will take to reform the Carmel and at the very heart of Teresa's personal experience—the demons confronted and trounced on the outside had not disappeared altogether. In her private and most intimate depths they teemed, in the form of numberless mental and emotional resistances to be overcome, walls of the soul to be broken through, an inner mobility to be made suppler. The exterior war was sustained by interior analysis. She had no shield, it was simply the elucidation of the inner self, made fluid and habitable, that enabled Teresa to live in the present, past, and future time and world. "To live" henceforth meant to overcome the fear of *hatefatuations* that cannot be other than diabolical, and the agony of obstinately morbid symptoms, in order to be continually reborn inside, while tirelessly forging ahead outside. At the sunset of the Golden Age, the foundress's constant peregrinations across the arid lands of Spain, her conflicts with Church institutions, all of which were pretty well obsolete and derelict, and her wrangles with their convoluted administrations drew strength from that interior journey, which achieved the construction of a space of wholesale serenity: "a jewel," she calls it in a letter to Fr. Salazar.[16] And *The Interior Castle* closes upon Jesus alone, among enamels more delicate than ever, gold and precious stones—mystical graces unseen, hidden in anonymity, and yet flashing forth. Tensions and charms of the . . . baroque: *barroco*, an irregularly shaped pearl.

Once again it was in writing that Teresa erected her ultimate habitat, entered into so it might be publicly revealed. Here is an irregular space if ever there was one, made of antitheses, strong images targeting the senses and aiming to dazzle, to unbalance, to set in motion, to celebrate the inconstancy of feeling in a perpetual mobility that can only be appeased by profusion and the eternity of the ephemeral. The recesses in the cut of these precious stones, these luminous diamonds studding the fabric of Teresa's text, render them surely more decorous, less boldly ostentatious than the institutional work of reform? More private, allegorical, and polyphonic than the very real epic of the foundational race?

That's not how Teresa saw it. From early on in the *Life*, by dint of prayer, she was always struggling to extricate herself from "the teeth of the terrifying dragon,"[17] the devil, so as to sing the praises of God's goodness and mercy; "that I may sing them without end"![18] By the time of the *Interior Castle*, secure in the knowledge of being the loving and loved spouse, she builds an interior space of impregnable riches that, opening up room by room in parallel to her race, is capable of withstanding real setbacks in as much as it challenges Hell itself— that placeless place, that gash in the soul, that unrepresentable trauma that makes you die of fear and diffuse excitement, whose horrors La Madre once described at length to her sisters at the Incarnation.

Today, as her race through the world crosses with her surge toward the Beloved within, at the intersection of *Foundations* and *Dwelling Places*, Teresa has just made a "baroque" discovery—as we will understand later—which enchants her: bliss beats torment if, and only if, the soul manages to inhabit itself in such a way as to perceive itself as a generous polytope, a kaleidoscopic mobility sustained by the Other's love. Thus at ease in her spacious interior, she can defy the cramped Gehenna as well as the demonic alleyways of worry in which the couples and groups of creatures confront one another. With its dwelling places thus equipped and made good for enjoyment, the soul can endow itself with a new imagination, fertile in strong and serene ramifications within and without. The antics of the devils, by comparison, appear as what they are: deadly substitutes spawned by another imagination, the kind Teresa calls "weak," illusory because constrained, intimidated, frozen by the fear of external or internal aggression, wearisome and worn out, defeatist—in a word, melancholic. The soul in love with the Other and loved by Him at the core of itself well knows that the Enemy, that is, the devil, has no reality beyond this wretched counterfeit imagination. But rather than exhaust itself in sterile wrestling, the fortified soul in its dwelling places transmutes that cringing imagination into a triumphal one, deft at assimilating the infinite facets of the logics of love.

"For even though it may seem that good desires are given [by the devil], they are not strong ones."[19]

It is *in the imagination that the devil produces his wiles and deceits*. And with women or unlearned people he can produce a great number, for we don't know how the faculties differ from one another and from the imagination, nor do we know about a thousand other things there are in regard to interior matters. Oh, Sisters, how clearly one sees the degree to which love of neighbor is present in some of you, and how clearly one sees the deficiency in those who lack such perfection![20]

How can we identify the souls with a high degree of "love of neighbor"? The judgment of the inside-outside traveler is instant: those incapable of true love are those she observes as "earnest" and "sullen," who "don't dare let their minds move or stir." "No, Sisters, absolutely not; works are what the Lord wants!"[21]

Bestir yourselves, then, get moving, body and soul, send your thoughts on a journey: *tutti a cavallo*, inside and out! Be swift, don't ever stop, don't fasten on anything, neither on yourselves nor on the one you love, for the Other is always elsewhere, a bit further on, a step ahead, go on, keep going! Do something not for the love of this or that person, but because that's how it is, a given, given by the good Being himself, it's the will of our Master, if you like, for the Good runs through us. "It" is beyond our ken because it loves us. That is why, if we are truly to participate in the will of the good Being, it is important to seek, always and above all, that delicious and peaceful gladness that disconcerts our exterior being and thwarts all those chicanes, which can only be external, minor, and thus deceptive. *There is a great difference in the ways one may be*, the infinitely good Being desires its own bounteousness and appropriates itself indefinitely, penetrates and travels its own being, like the time of the characters in Proust; the time of its racing extends into space, reversible dwelling places hatch and stack up ad infinitum, evidently.

It's clear from inside the plural and delectably amorous intimacy of my *moradas* that "the devil never gives delightful pain like this." Oh, I know Satan is capable of affording us tidbits and pleasures that can seem spiritual, but it is beyond his power to join great suffering with quiet and gladness of the soul; the devil does not unite, his work is always a scattering. Likewise "the pains he causes are never . . . delightful or peaceful but disturbing and contentious," whereas the "delightful tempest comes from a region other than those regions of which he can be lord."[22] Thus Teresian interiority effects a masterly transformation of Saint Augustine's *regio dissimilitudinis*, created by original sin, for which the Protestants were developing such an appetite. No doubt about it, the *muy muy interior* is nothing less than Heaven down here on earth.

* * *

But then, if the questing soul is certain of its reciprocated love for the Other, what pains it? What greater good does it want? Another discovery, as baroque as the last, comes to resolve this dilemma in your writing, my blissful Teresa. As with the inconstancy of the Divine Archer who, like the Spouse of the Sulamitess, comes and goes in His nevertheless absolute goodness, and whose wounding "reaches to the soul's very depths" before He "draws out the arrow," the pain, like the soul, "is never permanent." It's as though a spark leaping out from "the brazier that is my God" so struck the soul that "the flaming fire was felt by it," but "not enough to set the soul on fire," so leaving it with elusive pain; the "spark merely by touching the soul produces that effect [*al tocar hace aquella operación*]." An arousal the more exciting for being unsatisfied, a pleasure forever unconsummated, the "delightful pain" remains nameless, fluid, without identity. It is "pain" and "not pain," and this uncertainty—baroque in itself—means that it is fluctuating, "not continuous," mutable and tantalizing to the end. "Sometimes it lasts a long while, at other times it goes away quickly"; the soul in search of loving interiority is not master of itself, it always depends on the Other . . . although the Other is within it, like a blinding flare. The insatiable seeker, never quite ablaze, begs for more, for as soon as the spark makes contact it goes out, and the desire for pain—or is it pleasure? No term seems right for this erratic, multiple state (porque este dolor sabroso—y no es dolor—no está en un ser)—once more stokes up "that loving pain [He] causes."[23]

* * *

Frigidity? Masochism? Voluntary servitude compensated by a runaway imagination? Good old Jérôme Tristan, beating us over the head with his diagnostics, my mercurial Teresa. He's right, no doubt, but it's more than that. If that were all, it'd be the devil's work. On the contrary, in your penetration-appropriation of the good Being by itself, this operation "is something so manifest that it can in no way be fancied. I mean, one cannot think it is imagined, when it is not."[24]

The test of the imagination by the senses emerges as the ultimate proof of the truth of the experience, unmistakably stamped with the Other's trademark, not that of the devil. Kinetic, sensitive, bittersweet, the endlessly relaunched imagination ("again!") with its exorbitant intensity and rosary of metaphors, creates the geometry of an authorized serenity, authorized because shared with the ideal of the Self, the ideal Father. Touching, sparks, braziers, extinctions, pains ... and again ... and again ... and again! "Lack," "frigidity," "masochism," you say? All that is nothing but trials sent by the devil, fit to be reversed into an infinite winging toward the space packed with obstacles overcome, toward the capacity for love proper to the Beloved incorporated in me. Toward the Other who is Love, inaccessible and yet so present that He can be possessed to the infinity that He is, an infinity I too am becoming.

If the devil is no more than a puny, death-dealing imagination—a "melancholic" one, Sisters, I should have warned you—the only way to defeat him is via the baroque kaleidoscope of a psychic space erected against the nonplace of Hell, but also against the headlong rush to the uninhabited outside, from which the soul should remain apart. Only when the plastic mobility of this interiority is in place (or rather, in motion) and unhealthy impotence is transmuted into fresh ramifications, an eternal nativity, will the world itself be available for conquests without end and interminable re-foundations. *Tutti a cavallo*, yes, on condition of retaining the malleable castle of the soul, laminated into degrees of love.

* * *

As Teresa travels Spain on donkey-back and in carriages, and the writer's pen establishes her home base in a polyvalent space, the vagabond desires instigated by the devil and stirring in the soul "some passion, as happens when we suffer over worldly things [things of the age: *cosas del siglo*]"[25] give way to another, more dominant movement. Instead of taking one's worldly hankerings for "something great," resulting in "serious harm" to health,[26] and instead of condemning them, what matters is to put them to work. Should they become excessive, these impulses must be "fooled." What else can we do, faced by the wiles of the malevolent genie inside us intent on preventing us from entering the interior space where the soul moves in the certainty of meeting its Other? Watch out, illusion and error are recognizable because they do harm; logically, harm cannot be anything but illusion and error in the good Being and the castle I am building to its scale!

Tears themselves are only beneficial for watering the desiccated soul when they come from God; then they will be "a great help in producing fruit. The less attention we pay to them the more there are";[27] but in tears, too, "there can be deception."[28]

Fragmented and restless, forever tempted by the devil, the soul (again this third party, probingly observed as it endlessly unfurls within her) is not hopelessly in thrall to demonic falsehoods all the same. However infinite the way of perfection, union lies at the end of it—that is, at the "center," right here, in the labyrinth of dwelling places. The writer already senses a premonitory excitement, "feelings of jubilation and a strange prayer," an "impulse of happiness" comparable to those experienced by Saint Francis and Pedro de Alcántara, carried away by "blessed madness."[29] What could this be?

By a further twist of alert lucidity, Teresa analyzes the phenomenon as a "deep union of the faculties"; an osmosis of the intellect, memory, and will into the good Being of the Lover/Beloved. A flexible osmosis, though, since the Lord "leaves [the faculties] free that they might enjoy this joy—and the same goes for the senses—without understanding what it is."[30]

And so you arrive, Teresa, with full freedom to enjoy, at the faceted jewel of your writing, which condenses your union with the Beloved and your freedom vis-à-vis Him into a cascade of metaphors-metamorphoses. Clinging proximity mixed with flighty expansiveness, brief touches, darting escapes. Centripetal and centrifugal, your *jouissance* is a nameless exile, a fascinating and yet appalling estrangement. What? How? Our souls cannot know. But it's a disturbing ignorance all the same, reviving the memory of another escapade, equally both real and symbolic, which was supposed to take you and brother Rodrigo to the land of the Moors with a view to getting beheaded, thus winning martyrdom and sainthood.

In a burst of writing that soars high over the "somersaults" of the devils, you depict a soul, your soul, rushing toward the dangerous, bewitching strangeness that is so hard to express (it might sound "like gibberish" or Arabic, *algarabía*). It recollects itself, but without losing the élan of its euphoric activity (*que aquí va todo su movimiento*). At the very heart of this compacted, stony intimacy—diamond or castle—the soul is driven to making expansive proclamations.

"What I'm saying seems like gibberish, but certainly the experience takes place in this way, for the joy is so excessive the soul wouldn't want to enjoy it alone but wants to *tell everyone about it* so that they might help this soul praise our Lord. All its activity is directed to this praise."[31]

The journey, interior or through the outside world, is here a synonym of serenity, as prodigal sons and daughters reconcile to a world made safe at last. Revolts have been shelved, self-denials forgotten, frustrations transcended. To want to "put to work" and even pacify one's irksome desires by the grace of loving oneself in the Other is perhaps madness, as Teresa is aware; but a blessed madness. And surely preferable to grim truth, belligerent folly, or deceptive, gloomy nihilism.

Today, as I am reading you and speaking to you, your "activity" is being widely publicized, everyone is being "told about it." You are being rediscovered. Everybody has his or her Teresa. *Tutti a cavallo.* You seem to be intriguing the world all over again, beginning with me, Sylvia Leclercq, to speak only of my own headlong race.

$$\star\ \star\ \star$$

1574. En route to Segovia, you are escorted by just four stalwarts: John of the Cross, Julián de Ávila, Isabel de Jesús (whose fine voice you discovered in Salamanca), and a layman, Antonio Gaytán: a widower whose enthusiasm for your work led him to entrust his home and daughters to a governess while he goes on the road with you. You assign to him the daunting task of spiriting fourteen nuns out of the Pastrana convent, where your fearsome friend Ana de Mendoza de la Cerda, princess of Eboli, is holding sway. Donning the habit after her husband's death, this pretentious woman seems obsessed with aping you. The noble lady climbed into a "cloistered" carriage and took herself off to Pastrana, where she lives secluded under the name Ana de la Madre de Dios. Eaten up by envy, she has lost all proportion: everybody is to obey her, never mind the constitutions, and especially yours. The Rule is what she says it is!

Out of kindness to the unfortunate nuns left at the mercies of this capricious aristocrat—or maybe out of a desire to get even with one of your bugbears, the epitome of "artificial displays" of lordship and authority—you arrange for the fourteen sisters to be kidnapped by Julián de Ávila and Antonio Gaytán. You ought to be ashamed, Teresa, you female *pícaro*, you *pícara* of faith! After that you go ahead and make a foundation without an order from the bishop, merely with his verbal approval.

The princess turned Ana de la Madre de Dios lets you get away with it, busy preparing an exquisite revenge of her own. Have you forgotten how in 1569, when you were founding Pastrana, you gave in to her pleas and lent her the copy of the book of your *Life* that had just been authorized by some saintly men? Eboli left the manuscript lying around, and the servants took a peep at it. People began jeering at your visions, comparing your ecstasies to the impostures of Magdalena de la Cruz, who'd pretended to be a holy woman as well—some heretic *she* was! They burned her at the stake for faking, and serve her right! One-eyed Eboli has got you now. You snatched her girls, she'll denounce you to the Inquisition!

Without the slightest inkling of these schemes, you buy a house in Segovia and move in the fourteen nuns you acquired in a less than Catholic way, perhaps, but too bad, here goes another foundation:

```
E   E   E   G   E   C
E   E   E   E   G   E   C
C   G   G   G   G   G   G   C   G   G   G   G   G
C   G   G   G   G   G
E   E   E   E   G   E   C
E   E   E   E   G   E   C
```

John, your "little Seneca," is lost in rapture in front of a Cross he perceives floating against the lime-washed wall of the cloister. You are writing your *Meditations on the Song of Songs*. The sisters all worship you, without the least discretion. It's too good to last. Squalls and storms are about to catch up with you again.

Your confessor, Fr. Yanguas, quotes Saint Paul's words commanding women to keep quiet in church, as a way of telling you that women should know their place; he is no fan of the *alumbrados* toward whom he feels you incline. The Inquisition begins to rummage through your past and scrutinize everything you ever wrote. Father Domingo Báñez is the only one with the finesse and the forcefulness to defend you—but not before making alterations here and there, and prefacing your works with a beautifully wrought screed of scholarly approval.

On the way to Avila, you can't help stopping off at the grotto where Saint Dominic used to pray. Prostrating yourself for a long time before the saint's apparition, you will not depart until he promises to stay by your side in your work of foundation. You are in sore need of him—but of Saint Dominic, or of Domingo Báñez?

You write: "I saw a great tempest of trials and that just as the children of Israel were persecuted by the Egyptians, so we would be persecuted; but that God would bring us through dry-shod, and our enemies would be swallowed up by the waves."[32]

The Egyptians are not through with you yet, Teresa. And you, the "child of Israel," will help whip up the tempest.

★ ★ ★

1575. Springtime at Beas de Segura, at the border of Castile and Andalusia. In the warm climate of the slopes of the Sierra Morena, almond and orange and pomegranate trees are covered in blossom. Two highborn ladies, the Godínez sisters, have donated a house worth six thousand ducats and invited La Madre to make a foundation there. The eldest, Catalina, handsome and wealthy, always refused to get married; to spite her parents, who wouldn't hear of her going into religion, she ruined her complexion in the sun, a proper Donkey Skin. Miserable and ill, finally released by the death of her parents, she summons Teresa: the only salvation for the two orphans is a discalced convent. Saint Joseph of the Saviour at Beas thus saw the light of day on February 24, 1575. But it's not because Beas will be a breeding-ground for saints that it stands out in Teresa's story; it's because this is where she meets "the man of her life."

Such a corny cliché is not unwarranted at this point in the holy gallop. In her own words:

In 1575, during the month of April, while I was at the foundation in Beas, it happened that the Master Friar Jerome Gratian of the Mother of God came there. I had gone to confession to him at times, but I hadn't held him in the place I had other confessors, by letting myself be completely guided by him. One day while I was eating, without any interior recollection, my soul began to be suspended and recollected in such a way that I thought some rapture was trying to come upon me; and a vision appeared with the usual quickness, like a flash of lightning.

It seemed to me our Lord Jesus Christ was next to me in the form in which He usually appears, and at His right side stood Master Gratian himself, and I at His left. The Lord took our right hands and joined them and told me He desired that I take this master to represent Him as long as I live, and that we both agree to everything because it was thus fitting.[33]

Teresa hesitates only for a second. Recalling her affection for other confessors, she feels guilty, attempts to rein back her desires—putting up a momentary "strong resistance," she tells us. But twice more the Voice of the Other encourages her: there can be no mistake, her orders are "for the rest of my life, to follow Father Gratian's opinion in everything."[34]

Thunderbolt of love, *amour fou*, spirit made flesh. A young man of thirty, the son of a secretary of Charles V, the apostolic visitor for Andalusia, finally slakes the desire of this sixty-year-old woman. He is a son to her, obviously, but this Mother who could have been his mother is also his daughter, since he is her father confessor. Flesh and spirit at one, Teresa revels in a different ecstasy, of a kind she had never known at prayer. It resembles the paradox of the Virgin Mother as seen by Dante: "Thou Virgin Mother, daughter of thy Son, . . . The limit fixed of the eternal counsel" in the *Paradise!*[35] Is this Paradise on earth, perhaps? Here is the last missing link in the chain that resorbs the immemorial incest prohibition in Teresa's experience: the daughter of her father, who became the heavenly Father's Bride, has now become a mother in love with her son who is at the same time her father. The fantasy of incest, purified by the theological canon, has now become embodied in earthly affects, bonds that are as real as can be.

The new water in which the ecstatic Carmelite will bathe flows precisely from this transport, in which the little girl merges with the mother. Joys of symbolic motherhood, folded into a child's imagination; joys of infant innocence, conjugated with the omnipotence of masterly maturity. More than hysterical excitability, it is female paranoia that Mary satisfies and appeases when, from being a mother, she moves to being the daughter of her son/father, and only thus a fiancée and a wife, in the suspended time of the eternal design. Teresa does the same. She has never been so sure of herself, so triumphal in the passion of her faith: nor has she ever been as fragile, more exposed to the trials of reality, more attentive to the violent thirst of desire,[36] than to the Voices of His Majesty. But the latter is bound to smile upon these new transports with a young father-brother-son-husband; there are no worries on that score.

Loving and being loved by Gratian reassures, stabilizes, and makes her feel secure, far more than did the protection of the sound and prudent Domingo Báñez. But this new connection also makes her more vulnerable than ever as she hunts for new, efficacious "fatherhoods," both spiritual (angling for the support of the great Dominican writer Luis de Granada, she writes him a markedly humble letter on the advice of their mutual friend Teutonio de Braganza) and institutional (she doesn't shrink from appealing to Philip II for help when her darling Eliseus—one of Gratian's many code names—gets into trouble).

Your passion for Jerome Gratian, infantile and pragmatic at once, cannot be compared—although some have done so—to the vaporous swoons of Madame Guyon's "pure love" for Fénelon. The more in love you are with your cherished son-father—at last, an *hombre* of flesh and blood by your side, a physical replica of the Lord, would you have settled for less?—the more realistic, militant, astute, and active you become, a businesswoman all over. Besides, for all that you may be the "daughter" of your son-father-partner, you are the boss in this couple, my headstrong Teresa, from the start, and increasingly as you pursue those business affairs at your usual furious pace:

tut-ti tut-ti a cavallo
tut-ti tut-ti a cavallo
tut-ti a cavallo a cavallo a cavallo a cavallo a cavallo a caval
tut-ti tut-ti a cavallo
tut-ti tut-ti a cavallo

I try to keep up with that pace, I pant and struggle, unlike you. I count with you the foundations you continue to make until your last breath, always against the backdrop of your love for Gratian, naturally, as he "replaces" the Lord: "*Y díjome que éste quería tomase* en su lugar *mientras viviese*"! Isn't that something? Have you thought about what such a *replacement* could possibly mean? No? Is it that you don't do much thinking anymore, carried away by your passion for that man? Of course not, that's not it at all. Actually the intoxication doesn't last long, you soon perceive the limits of the man and of the thing, but you cling to the game, believing without completely believing in it; we'll take a closer look at this later, you and me. For the moment let me ride with you, come on, everyone to horse:

E E E E G E C
E E E E G E C
C G G G G G G C G G G G G
C G G G G G

E   E   E   E   G   E   C
E   E   E   E   G   E   C

So your Eliseus wants you to found a house in Seville? Seville it is! In fact, by this move the apostolic visitor Jerome Gratian of the Mother of God was disobeying—again!—the general prior of the Carmelite order, Juan Bautista Rubeo. A tricky predicament that soon proved untenable when Gratian found himself trapped between the pincers of Philip II's wish to accelerate the Teresian reform and the obduracy of the order, reluctant to be reformed. You use your Pablo-Eliseus-Paul and he uses you, bestowing little pet names like Laurencia or Angela... All in the cause of reform, as we have said, but one can't dig in the spurs without incensing the laggards and drawing persecution down. The next five years will be a perfect tempest of trials and thunderbolts.

Seville is a long way from Avila, and Andalusia is a sly country; it scares you. The local churchmen don't even respect the authority of the general, Fr. Rubeo: they actually condemned a disciple of Juan de Ávila to burn at the stake! No matter, you are at the height of your fusion with Gratian, you pledge him your "total obedience" for "as long as you live," and you hurtle on, keener than ever.

Father Ambrosio Mariano lends a hand, but he gets ahead of himself: he persuades you that Archbishop Cristóbal de Rojas has given his permission, when he has done no such thing. Worse, Mariano thinks nothing of leaving you all by yourself in Seville in a frightful situation: comprehensive hostility to discalcement and not a cent in donations! Those giddy Sevilleans only care about having fun. It's a port city, where whores count more than nuns, but this trite pleasantry doesn't make you laugh. The things you learn, on the road! The calced community are outraged, your program is seen as meddling, as "interference"! But you get your way: on May 29, 1575, a convent for discalced nuns is founded in Seville, once more under the patronage of Saint Joseph.

How happy it makes you! New novices, charming Andalusian girls, join up. They intrigue you, too: the confirmed *Madre fundadora* starts to explore a new country, the landscape of the female soul. The text of the *Foundations* begins to sound as though the chronicle of your works were also, or chiefly, the novel of these sorely tested and often castigated lives. Take the chapter on Beatriz de Chávez, aka Beatriz de la Madre de Dios, the spiritual daughter of your dear Eliseus. What a handful, that girl! You try to understand her, in writing. We'll come back to it at the end of our ride.

One thing has never been plainer than it is here, in Seville: the world threatens to gag you, Teresa, my love, it may end up by burning you alive. What do you expect when you move from pure ecstasy to the work of founding, when you aspire to found pure ecstasy in the world, against the world, but with the world? Tensions between the women are rising, too; nothing new about that, but it's getting more dangerous. Your own niece, María Bautista, feels licensed to disobey you and speak ill of you, she even finds fault with Gratian. She receives a wrathful letter from you, dated August 28, 1575;[37] but will this tongue-lashing suffice to bring her to heel?

It gets worse. Copies of the *Life* are circulating, the princess of Eboli has filed a complaint against you, and the book is submitted to the court of the Inquisition; even Fr. Báñez is growing peevish. And María Bautista makes a point of seeing the influential Dominican every day—emphatically not for your or Gratian's benefit.

But Domingo Báñez is an honest man in the end, thanks be to God. He rescues your book in exchange for a modicum of censorship, emendations which of course you accept. It's better than being burned. You've won, but be prudent!

* * *

Another piece of good news: your brother Lorenzo is back from Peru with a fortune, money that will help reflate the beggarly convent in Seville. He will be "consigned" for his pains, since your enemies are alert, they will do anything to sabotage you; it's lucky they didn't put La Madre's brother behind bars! This pitiful imbroglio does not stop you giving him a good telling-off. It is ridiculous, nay, unacceptable, to call oneself "don" on grounds of one's fiefdoms in Indian country! Now that you are sure of yourself and of him, there's no need to be flattering him with titles. You can dress him down as he deserves, beginning with the matter of *honra*, the good old family vice. Well, you had bones to pick with the new and fervently discalced brother, and you like being the only captain on board; family take note: you'll make foundations as you see fit!

This claim to autonomy doesn't stop you requisitioning Lorenzo's nine-year-old daughter, Teresita, for the convent. Gratian is against it; but she won't take vows just yet, of course, you only want her for "her education." And also to spread a little merriment in halls that often lack it, truth to tell. You established asceticism for it to be sublimated in joy, Teresa, you established joy to be elucidated by asceticism; Teresita will be your great weapon in this debate, because the little one is an "imp" and highly "entertaining." People should know that Teresa de Jesús's holy houses are not disdained by merry little imps, quite the contrary.

Meanwhile the persecutions continue, and it's your job to face up to them, to think of everything, to tie down everything that can be, and when the storms blow too hard, simply to hang on. Gratian helps out, but not always, and not really. You already know how impulsive he is, always too harsh or too lenient, clumsy with some people and ingratiating with others: "Difficulties rain down on him like hail."

Now for the latest dirty trick: Gratian is packed off to a monastery of the Observation. How appalling, he must be rescued, I'll write letters, pull every string I can . . . Right, it's over, he's back. But in early 1575, the general chapter of the order at Plasencia resolves to dismantle the convents Gratian founded in Andalusia without permission from Fr. Rubeo. And again it falls to Teresa to intervene. She writes to the general of the order, Rubeo, pleading for his continued support.

★ ★ ★

December 1575. An anonymous Carmelite nun denounces Teresa to the Inquisition. "And nonsense also was what she said of us, that we tied the hands and feet of the nuns and flogged them—would to God all the accusations had been of that sort."[38]

But it's the last straw for Provincial Ángel de Salazar. Finally out of patience, he commands Teresa to repair to a convent in Castile: "[He] said that I was an apostate and excommunicated." It seems the bell is tolling for Teresa's enterprise.

Searches, interrogations; are you about to be arrested, Madre? A vehicle belonging to the Inquisition is stationed before the door of your convent in Seville. But only a deposition is required, which you will send to the Jesuit Rodrigo Álvarez, the acknowledged expert in matters of delusion and error.

But you, skillful Teresa, not only bewitch your world with the grace of a writing that thrills us today, four centuries after the tempest; you also carry out a veritable plan of military encirclement! First, you present a long list of ecclesiastics prepared to testify to your good faith: Fr. Araoz, the Jesuit commissary; Fr. Francisco de Borja, the former duke of Gandía; and numerous others. Then comes the epistolary race, the gallop of letters:

tut-ti tut-ti a cavallo
tut-ti tut-ti a cavallo
tut-ti a cavallo a cavallo a cavallo a cavallo a cavallo a caval
tut-ti tut-ti a cavallo
tut-ti tut-ti a cavallo

Humbly you confess your penchant for mental prayer in the wake of Pedro de Alcántara and Juan de Ávila, well aware that that's your major transgression in the eyes of the authorities. You swiftly move on to reference the many illustrious scholars who helped you protect yourself from this unconscionable error, Dominicans this time, necessarily; chief among them the councilor of the Holy Office at Valladolid, the ubiquitous Domingo Báñez.

But don't expect to get out of trouble so easily. The investigation has only just begun. You are summoned again—to justify your ecstasies! Kindly provide a new deposition!

You're enjoying this gallop of writing, after the race of the roads. Here's how you sum up that phase of the adventure in a missive to María Bautista, on February 19, 1576: "Jesus be with you, daughter. I wanted to be in a more restful state when writing to you. For all that I have just read and written amazes me in that I was able to do it, and so I've decided to be brief. Please God I can be."[39]

Of course, it pleases Him to fulfill your every wish. His Majesty is hand in glove with you, His Voice speaks through your lips, as you don't fail to remind us. And you're capable of convincing anyone who takes the time to listen. Indeed, the wind is momentarily turning to your advantage. How could even the wind resist your galloping?

A new house is purchased, the recalcitrant Franciscans eventually come around, they didn't want you in the neighborhood, poor things, and now they do.

Teresa is triumphant. She leaves Seville, where María de San José takes over as prioress. Before departing she sits for Fr. Mariano's painter friend, Giovanni Narducci, now Juan de la Miseria. Writing to Mariano on May 9, 1576, she sounds elated, hopping gaily from one topic to the next, as if the Sevillean ordeal had been nothing but fun and games, a period of ebullient agitation:

> The house is such that the sisters never cease thanking God. May He be blessed for everything.... This is not the time to be making visitations, for [the friars] are very agitated.... Oh, the lies they circulate down here! It's enough to make you faint.... Nonetheless I fear these things from Rome, for I remember the past, even though I do not think they will be to our harm but to our advantage.... We are receiving many compliments and the neighbors are jubilant. I would like to see our discalced affairs brought to a conclusion, for after all the Lord won't put up with those other friars much longer; so many misfortunes will have to have an ending.[40]

Prior to departure, after kneeling before the archbishop to be blessed, Teresa cannot believe her eyes and ears when the same archbishop, don Cristóbal de Rojas, the source of so many vexations, kneels in turn before her and asks for her blessing. It is June 3, 1576.

★ ★ ★

1576–1577. Enjoying the mild climate of Toledo, housed in a pleasant cell, you receive from Lorenzo the manuscript of the *Foundations* you had left at Saint Joseph's and continue composing your text. The updates concern Gratian, the calced and the discalced, your idea of creating a special province of the Carmelite order with Gratian as the provincial, a project you already mooted in your letter to Philip II. Separately you draw out the political lessons of past experience, from the Incarnation to Seville. Firstly, it is important to consolidate the temporal sphere by a "government" that is temperate and yet clearly hierarchical, in order to advance the spiritual good: "It seems an inappropriate thing to begin with temporal matters. Yet *I think that these are most important* for the promotion of the spiritual good."[41]

Respect for hierarchy is essential from your point of view as foundress, especially among women who are duty-bound to acknowledge their chief, that is, yourself:

> I don't believe there is anything in the world that harms a visitator as much as does being *unfeared* and allowing subjects to deal with him as an equal. This is true *especially in the case of women.* Once they know the visitator is so soft that he

will pass over their faults and change his mind so as not to sadden them, he will have great difficulty in governing them.[42]

Is that because obedience is harder for a woman? For a woman like you?

"I confess, first of all, my *imperfect obedience* at the outset of this writing. Even though I desire the virtue of obedience more than anything else, beginning this work has been the greatest *mortification* for me, and I have felt a *strong repugnance* toward doing so."[43]

Be this as it may, the works are multiplying. You maintain a prolific correspondence (200 letters up to 1580), dispense advice of all sorts, circulate *The Way of Perfection* and keep an eye on its reception. In 1577 you begin *The Interior Castle*—a metapsychology *avant la lettre*, the quintessence of your journey toward the Spouse and ultimate nuptials with Him. Nothing is left to chance, and all these works are created while managing in hands-on fashion the establishment and staff of twelve nunneries, without neglecting the affairs of the male counterparts founded in accordance with your new-old Rule.

You have the gift of asserting your authority without dispelling good cheer, your own or that of others. Witness that sparkling *vejamen*, also from 1577—a response known as the *Satirical Critique*, mixing faux pedantry with schoolboy humor, to a solemn colloquium held in your absence in the parlor at Saint Joseph's in Avila. You had requested Julián de Ávila, Francisco de Salcedo, John of the Cross, and your brother Lorenzo de Cepeda to reflect on those words the Lord once spoke to you, "Seek yourself in Me." Once the bishop who was also present had arranged for the various speeches to be sent to you in Toledo, you replied with the jovial irony of one who had just escaped the clutches of the Holy Office: "I ask God to give me the grace not to say anything that might merit being denounced to the Inquisition."[44] And you then proceeded to mercilessly tease each of your friends for their contributions; we shall reread these remarks once you have passed away.

I have a notion that the months from July 1576 to December 1577 constitute the most luminous period of your later life. You are given over to writing, elucidating, and transmitting. You don't have much longer to live, but for the present, time has ripened: you experience it fully, soberly, and laughingly.

The papal nuncio who championed your reforms, Nicolás Ormaneto, has died. You leave for Saint Joseph in Avila; could it turn out to be a definitive "prison"? Your fevered race repudiates such a thought. Let's wait and see.

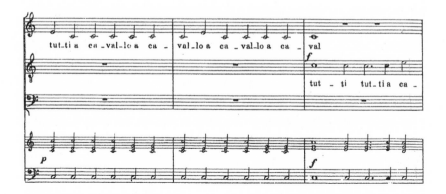

The new nuncio, Felipe Sega, bishop of Piacenza, loathes the discalced movement and brands you a "vagabond and a rebel." Accusations rain down once more on Gratian, relating to his licentious ways with women. That's the situation, and nothing's going to change: Gratian needs your protection more than you need his presence or his affection. Another letter to His Royal Majesty is called for. You write and sign it on December 13, 1577.

All is not well at the Incarnation, either. On the order of Gerónimo Tostado, vicar-general of the Carmelites in Spain, the calced provincial Juan Gutiérrez de la Magdalena arrives to preside over the election for prioress. He threatens to excommunicate anyone who votes for you.

Such is the frayed atmosphere in which you continue exploring the Dwelling Places of *The Interior Castle*, that masterpiece of introspective analysis. Yet the work is completed on November 29, 1577, in less than six months. However did you do it, Teresa?

"Hosts of demons have joined against the discalced friars and nuns," you complain to your friend Gaspar de Salazar on December 7.[45] Matters reach such a pass that John of the Cross and a close associate, Germán de San Matías, are taken captive by Gutiérrez. Where to turn, when the general of the order and the nuncio are both ranged against you? To your pen, Madre!

For the fourth time you write to Philip II, outlining the conflict between the two rules and pleading on behalf of John of the Cross, for "this one friar who is so great a servant of God is so weak from all he has suffered that I fear for his life. I beg Your Majesty for the love of our Lord to issue orders for them to set him free at once and that these poor discalced friars not be subjected to so much suffering by the friars of the cloth."[46]

Absorbed in founding, in writing, in Gratian, have you not rather neglected your "little Seneca"? Is he too ascetic for you, too saintly in his inhuman self-mortification, too inaccessible in his elliptical purity? Are you feeling guilty, Teresa? It's time to make amends! Between you and me, John deserves salvation more than Gratian. But you'll save both of them, my future Saint Teresa.

Christmas Eve, 1577. Teresa falls down the stairs and breaks her arm. The traveler is getting old. Her morale is as solid as ever, but her bones are getting brittle.

Don Teutonio de Braganza, appointed to the archbishopric of Evora in Portugal, who was a Jesuit from 1549 to 1554 and knew Loyola in Rome, asks you to make a foundation in his city. Alas, it's impossible. Your reforms are under threat in Spain, and there's still many a road to be galloped down in your native country; it's no time to be going abroad. But can his lordship do something for Gratian, perhaps, and for John of the Cross? The latter "is considered a *saint* by everyone . . . In my opinion, he is a *gem*."[47]

Her arm in a sling, the aging Teresa can still write. A deluge of diplomacy, of piety, of courage and craftiness will come to drench everyone who has the honor of knowing her, closely or from afar.

But where is John being kept? Rumor has it that Germán, his companion in misfortune, is coughing up blood, and that John has been sent away, but where, where? Doña Guiomar, a saintly lady and unswervingly loyal, can't stop crying. Is Gratian really doing everything in his power to have John released? You feel that the apostolic visitor, the much-cherished Eliseus-Paul-Pablo, has hardly noticed John's absence: Might people be put off by that odd brand of sanctity that aspires above all to self-annulment? "I am shocked by the imprisonment of Fray John of the Cross and the slow pace of all our negotiations."[48]

That's the problem, Gratian is too slow. Whereas sanctity is speed, and John is the swiftest of us all, the most condensed; and in consequence the most unfindable, the one who escapes us, is always already beyond us.

I tell you I am certain that if some influential person were to ask the nuncio to have Fray John set free, he would at once give orders that he be returned to his house. It would be enough to tell the nuncio about this father and how he is kept in prison unjustly. I don't know what is happening that no one ever remembers this saint. If Mariano were to speak to the Princess of Eboli, she would intercede with the nuncio.[49]

Precisely because he is like lightning, gentle John didn't need help from anybody in the end. He's escaped on his own from the prison of the order, in Toledo, where he had languished for nine months in a dungeon so cramped that even he could not stand up in it, body and soul compacted in that Nothingness that stands him in lieu of sanctity. He's taken refuge with the Discalced Carmelites. Will he be safe from persecution there? Teresa is vigilant, leaves on a trip, keeps watch again, goes off on a tangent, follows her own path....

Even the Society of Jesus becomes infected by the climate of suspicion, and the friars are divided; repression smites Teresa's Jesuit allies. Baltasar Álvarez, who defended Teresa at the time of her first raptures, is charged with "wasting his time among women and chiefly Carmelites," instead of following Ignatius Loyola's *Spiritual Exercises* to the letter. He will be sanctioned.[50] Gaspar de Salazar, another Jesuit who wants to join the discalced friars, becomes the target of malign insinuations relating to Teresa. In a curt letter to Fr. Juan Suárez, the Jesuit principal, in February 1578, La Madre goes bravely out on a limb to defend her right to "friendship," however misunderstood:

> I will never deny *the great friendship that exists between Padre Salazar and me or the favor he shows me*. Yet I am certain that in what he has done for me he has been moved more by the service it renders our Lord and our Blessed Mother than by any friendship. Truly, I think it has even happened that as much as *two years went by without a letter passing between us*. If *the friendship is an old one*, it is because in the past I was in greater need of help, for this order only had two discalced Fathers. At that time I would have had a greater motive for wanting him to transfer than I do now. Thanks be to God we have more than two hundred, I think, and among them not a few who are especially suited for our poor manner of life. I have never thought that the hand of God would be more sparing toward his Mother's order than to the other orders.[51]

* * *

March 15, 1578. The Inquisition arrests Juan Calvo de Padilla, who had often lent a hand in the management of Teresa's convents and whom she had recommended to King Philip in 1573.

Events continue to accelerate, in contradictory ways.

The nuncio issues a brief to strip Gratian of all his powers.

On August 14, Roque de la Huerta, one of Philip's right-hand men, announces that on the ninth the king promulgated a counter-brief: Gratian retains his functions as a visitator.

It is vital not to take sides between pope and king, you know that better than anyone, my careful Teresa; it's all about wriggling through . . . with rectitude; above all one should not bristle, act "foolishly," or indulge in gloomy "prophesying," like dear Gratian is prone to do. In love, but not blindly, La Madre is frank with her Eliseus in a letter written at the end of August 1578.[52] To any purpose, one wonders?

The worries don't let up. The discalced convent at Almodóvar holds its second general chapter: La Madre is furious, what a moment to choose, it's crazy! In Gratian's absence, old Antonio de Jesús is elected. John of the Cross is sent, or should we say banished, to El Calvario, near Beas. The discalced communities are placed under the baton of communities of the cloth; Gratian's punishment requires him to retire to Alcalá. There's a rumor that he plans to defect to another order, in disgust. Will he abandon Teresa? To cap it all, the calced friars march into Saint Joseph's accompanied by policemen and lawyers to oversee the handover.

The situation in Seville is even worse. The provincial appointed by the nuncio Felipe Sega starts defamatory proceedings against Gratian, while the prioress María de San José is replaced by Beatriz de Chávez, who spreads all sorts of slander against the discalced nuns and is completely under the thumb of Diego de Cárdenas, the provincial of the cloth in Andalusia.

Has the galloping switched sides? The adversaries are the ones charging forward now: Teresa's clan is badly weakened, and it's all it can do to resist. But she does not give up, just adapts her ammunition. Ever carriers of His Majesty's Voice, her letters increasingly do the work, in place of mules and stagecoaches.

⋆ ⋆ ⋆

January 31, 1579. A trustworthy friend, the octogenarian Hernando de Pantoja, asks Teresa to vouch for the moral propriety of her nuns and to deny all those stories of extravagant mortifications at Seville. Can it be true that they hang sisters from the ceiling to flog them? Outraged, the *fundadora* hastens to reject all such lies and accompanies her indignant response with an open letter to the

"Discalced Carmelite nuns, Seville" designed to share this defense of her order's holy, wholesome lifestyle with the community concerned.[53]

Either Teresa's epistolary battle was beginning to bear fruit, or the king's reformist zeal was exerting its irresistible effect on the course of events. Personally I feel sure that what weighed heaviest in the balance of history was your graphic pressure, my single-minded Teresa. Philip II appointed the Dominican Pedro Fernández, a veteran of the discalced cause, as a counselor to the papal nuncio. Gratian and María de San José were rehabilitated. And yet Teresa never regained her trust in this eccentric woman, María; was it a question of female rivalries, stirred up by the slippery Gratian? We shall keep an eye on that. Teresa sent a new friend of hers, the Genoese banker Nicolo Doria, to call on the prioress in Seville and get her to acknowledge her mistakes. An educator and a politician underlay the businesswoman and the mystic. Could it all be one and the same person?

* * *

1580–1581. High time to be back on the road, after two years' immobility. Her traveling companion is Ana de San Bartolomé, acting as both nurse and secretary. First they visit Valladolid, then Malagón, where the convent projected since 1568 can at last be made reality in a new, harmonious, simple space. After that, a new foundation at Villanueva de la Jara. On the way back, they stop, with Gratian, in that fateful Toledo where the cardinal archbishop, don Gaspar de Quiroga (painted by El Greco as the grand inquisitor general), grants Teresa permission to take back *The Book of Her Life*, something forbidden until now. The "Great Angel," as he is dubbed, addresses the Mother in these terms:

> I am glad to make your acquaintance. I have long desired to do so. You have in me a friend who is ready to help you in your undertakings. Some years ago, one of your books was submitted to the Inquisition; the material was most rigorously examined. I myself read it from beginning to end. You expound very solid arguments there, of great profit to readers. You may have it collected whenever you wish; you may do as you like with it; I hereby grant permission. Pray for me.[54]

Eight years later he will make no objection to returning the manuscript to Ana de Jesús and Luis de León when they decide to have it printed. What a victory! Is the Inquisition to be forgotten at last?

Teresa makes more foundations, at Palencia in 1580 and Soria in 1581. And then excellent news arrives: the nuncio Felipe Sega himself is calling for the separation of calced and discalced orders, something La Madre had demanded in vain. They're off again:

```
E   E   E   E   G   E   C
E   E   E   E   G   E   C
C   G   G   G   G   G   G   C   G   G   G   G   G
C   G   G   G   G   G
E   E   E   E   G   E   C
E   E   E   E   G   E   C
```

Letters, interventions, contacts, tactful mediations, amours, and adversities . . . La Madre, the daughter of her Eliseus, prepares her friend Gratian to be elected principal of the discalced order. And that's what happens on March 3, 1581.

* * *

Teresa of Jesus is weary, but glad to be back home as the prioress of Saint Joseph's. The road is mostly behind her, and many deceased loved ones are waiting for her on high: her sister María passed away in 1562, her brother Lorenzo and her friend Francisco de Salcedo both died in 1580. Gratian is usually away, that's how it is, although she can't get used to it. As for the rest of her family, Juana and the children, unfortunate brother Pedro, the nephews, they're all the same as ever—always needy, like every family, always the victims of money and *honra*.

There are issues in Valladolid with young Casilda de Padilla: Is she being manipulated by the local Jesuits, hostile to the discalced nuns? That's what Teresa thinks, but it can't be helped. We are not about to change our attitude to the Society, when "most of the nuns who come here do so through them."[55]

And John of the Cross is pestering for a foundation in Granada! No, Madrid and Burgos. Is she worn out at last? Her legs may be faltering, but not her love of new acquaintances. Gratian being somewhere else as usual, Teresa falls back on Pedro Castro de Nero, a friend of Gratian's from Alcalá days, whose "intelligence, charm, and manner of speech please me very much." She makes a point of informing Gratian of this appreciation on October 26, 1581;[56] she wants her fickle Pablo to know that his Laurencia is still alive, more than he imagines, even without him.

Teresa is sixty-six years old. Regarding this pleasure in Pedro, "I don't know whether that may be due to the fact that he is so close to you," you say coyly; "If I didn't have a confessor and it seemed all right to you, I would go to him." Later the young understudy for Eliseus is privileged to read your book, after the duchess of Alba sends over a copy, and "he never stops talking about the benefit he derived from [it]."[57]

In December she goes to Burgos. The midwinter jaunt will drag on for twenty-four days, complete with accidents, snowstorms, the wagon capsizing in the river with eight Carmelites inside, and La Madre in the grip of fever. Sometimes she feels paralyzed, sometimes racked by shivering, her tongue seized up in her mouth, spitting blood, unable to swallow anything but fluids... Teresa is plainly exhausted, the body can't keep up with the exalted soul, and yet somehow it does.

tut-ti tut-ti a cavallo
tut-ti tut-ti a cavallo
tut-ti a cavallo a cavallo a cavallo a cavallo a cavallo a caval
tut-ti tut-ti a cavallo
tut-ti tut-ti a cavallo

Catalina de Toloso, with two daughters already in the Carmel, proposes a new convent at her home. The archbishop of Burgos, don Cristóbal Vela, agrees to the idea. But humiliation lies in store again, Teresa girl, you didn't expect that, did you, at the end of your life?

You were intensely excited by the honor of meeting this great man: he reminded you of childhood, and you hoped he would recognize, respect, and esteem you. After all, he was the nephew of Francisco Vela de Núñez, that revered neighbor of your father who was godfather to little Teresa de Ahumada, how long ago now... sixty-seven years already? But it was not to be. The great don Cristóbal only wants to "negotiate" with you, what did you think? He never suggested that you should go ahead and found, or not yet, and maybe never. We're simply "negotiating." Do you grasp the distinction?

Twenty-four days' arduous trek, only to be snubbed! Such rudeness and disdain! Toward a lady your age! You dig your heels in, true to type. The wrangling stretches on for three months. Gratian does nothing but complicate things: he's either euphoric or depressed, never the cool-headed realist you need for such discussions.

It's now or never for unsheathing your invincible weapon, your blade of eloquence alloyed with humility. As the sadism of the quasi-kin archbishop hits home, you counter with the diplomacy of mortification:

"My poor daughters are so desirous of obtaining the authorization of your Lordship, they are flagellating their bodies as we speak," you murmur, heartrendingly.

Don Cristóbal Vela remains unmoved.

"At this very instant, they're offering up to God their use of the scourge." Your voice grows soft, Teresa, you abandon yourself, your calm gaze rises to the Beyond: as a masochist, you know the drill!

"Let them, it won't change my mind." Don Cristóbal knows from experience that there's no limit to masochism, it leaves him cold ...

His retort stings worse than a slap in the face. It's the baptized goddaughter in you that is humiliated, it's your converted lineage he scorns, it's your inspired foundations that are being trampled underfoot ... You know it, and you take it. In the name of His Majesty within. It's not over yet.

The Burgos Jesuits are being uncooperative, too: they take every opportunity to disavow you. For example, said gentlemen will only accept a convent set up in a duly purchased house. Fine, but where? You'll have to work it out. The race is on again.

tut-ti tut-ti a cavallo
tut-ti tut-ti a cavallo
tut-ti a cavallo a cavallo a cavallo a cavallo a cavallo a caval
tut-ti tut-ti a cavallo
tut-ti tut-ti a cavallo

You manage to remove Gratian from the scene. You won't give up on your goal. So His Lordship wants nothing to do with you? So there are no premises in which to lodge your religious house? You get hold of two small rooms in the hospital, and you go to work there. Here's a new experience even for a practised woman like you, how amusing! Caring for the sick and crippled, you who had so little time for people with one eye or otherwise infirm! It's never too late to learn, when one is in dialogue with the Voice of His Majesty.

At last you find the perfect house. On April 18, 1582, the inaugural Mass is said in the presence of the archbishop. The whole of the royal town of Burgos is delighted, it could not be otherwise. Don Cristóbal de Vela is more delighted than anyone, naturally. And even the Jesuits are amicably on board.

* * *

A new stage begins at Valladolid. The convent is getting harder and harder to run, what with all those complicated women, sadly submissive when not experts at intrigue and scandal. Casilda leaves to become a Franciscan; Beatriz de Ovalle, Juana's daughter, is lambasted for her relationship with a married man of means; and the prioress herself, María Bautista, is definitely lacking in charity. There are headaches at Salamanca, too, involving the prioress Ana de la Encarnación. And at Alba de Tormes with Teresa de Layz, that estimable donor who seems unable, since she became prioress, to stop bothering the nuns. The exception proving the rule, you are getting along well with Soria's prioress, Catalina de Cristo. She may be illiterate, which alienates Gratian, but what a nice person she is!

Women are hard to govern, but never boring. And letter-writing is such a splendid invention: swift as a horse, more to the point than an arrow! Teresa loves it, there are always letters to write, as much when business is ticking over as when it isn't; the founding sequence follows the same beat in any case.

```
E   E   E   E   G   E   C
E   E   E   E   G   E   C
C   G   G   G   G   G   G   C   G   G   G   G   G
C   G   G   G   G   G
E   E   E   E   G   E   C
E   E   E   E   G   E   C.
```

Leaning on her stick, Teresa goes to Mass and never fails to deal with the problems: reasoning with the overly authoritarian Teresa de Layz, arguing with the rector of Salamanca who has come to complain about Ana de la Encarnación. . . .

And all the grandees who want to see her! Today it's the young duchess of Alba, who is soon to give birth; the house of Alba needs Teresa as it did long ago, that memorable Christmas night of 1561. Father Antonio de Jesús, who has taken over from Gratian as the provincial of Castile, tells her to go there at once.

The month is September 1582. Chilly goodbyes at Valladolid. The weary old lady sets off with Antonio de Jesús and Ana de San Bartolomé. Her last letter to Gratian is dated September 1: disappointed, embittered, resigned, she tells the absent one that "your servant and subject" will be in Avila at the end of the month, "with God's favor." "Oh, *mi padre*, how oppressed I have felt these days."[58] An appeal to her darling Eliseus? The anguish of never seeing him again? The premonition of the end?

Jolting along the rutted roads, Teresa grows hungry and enfeebled, her pulse abruptly slows. A faint: they fear she is gone, but she straightens up. At the town gates, a messenger delivers good tidings: the duchess has been delivered of a healthy child. "No more need for the saint, then, thanks be to God!" mutters the dying woman. Dying or not, she can still crack a joke.

tut-ti tut-ti a cavallo
tut-ti tut-ti a cavallo
tut-ti a cavallo a cavallo a cavallo a cavallo a cavallo a caval
tut-ti tut-ti a cavallo
tut-ti tut-ti a cavallo

She receives a glacial welcome at the Convent of Alba de Tormes. The new prioress, María Bautista, doesn't even come out to say hello, and La Madre is left alone in her room like a nobody who's just passing through. She is in a desperate condition. While Gratian dallies in Andalusia, Teresa wastes away in her cell, stiff-tongued, vomiting blood. Catalina de la Concepción, Catarina Bautista, and Ana de San Bartolomé take care of her in her last days. Teresita is there, too.

At dawn on October 4, 1582 (October 15 by Pope Gregory's calendar), the feast of Saint Francis, Teresa departs to join her Beloved.

Finis the melody of war and love.

It is said that when Antonio de Jesús asked her whether she wanted to be buried in Alba or in Avila, Teresa replied: "Do I possess anything that is mine? Will they not give me a patch of land here?"

The new prioress of Alba and the *conversa* Teresa de Layz, with the help of Antonio de Jesús, make haste to bury the precious body of the future saint beneath a pile of earth, quicklime, and stones. What a treasure for the convent! "In the final accounting, Lord, I am a daughter of the Church," she repeated while receiving the Last Sacrament. To convince herself? Or to persuade her friends and foes?

Part 6

Foundation — Persecution

The Lord said to me: "Don't be sad, for I shall give you a living book." . . . His Majesty had become the true book in which I saw the truths. . . . Who is it that sees the Lord covered with wounds and afflicted with persecutions who will not embrace them, love them, and desire them?

Teresa of Avila, *The Book of Her Life*

Chapter 25

THE MYSTIC AND THE JESTER

Our body stands between the spirit it is bound to serve and the desires of
the flesh, those dark powers that make war on the soul, like a cow stands
between the farmer and the thief.

Bernard de Clairvaux, *Sermons*

From: juan.ramirez@free.ac.uk
To: sylvia.leclercq@FMP.fr
Subject: Miguel and Teresa

Monday, November 1

Dear Sylvia,

No news from you for ages, what's up? Indian summer, lazing about on the warm
sands of the Île de Ré? It's All Saints, who'd have thought it, no computer and no
Internet! Unless that "civil war" in your Parisian *banlieues* has pitched you back into
politics! Are you giving up on the microcosm of dreamy introspection? I wouldn't
believe that even if I saw it; I expect you're still galloping along with your flatmate,
with no time to think about old Juan. So, to remind you who I am, I'm attaching a few
articles by yours truly and other top folks as you asked for when you were pretending
to consult me about your peregrinations in the land of my forefathers and through
the Golden Age. You may not have time to read the whole of this lengthy epistle I've
been pondering for a while now and which I'm just putting down as it comes, for
your own good and mine—a kind of rough draft for a future article, if that's okay.

Contradicting what I said under the ramparts of Avila, I don't actually think Cervantes is as remote from the passions of your saint as I figured, as the unrepentant aesthete you take me for. You've sown a doubt—but I'm not convinced, so don't crow too soon. Your Teresa may well pave the way for baroque art, but she's very far from the comedy that lies at the heart of humanism as I imagine it, when I'm playing at thinking the future is before us, provided we look behind us properly. Fasten your seatbelt!

Don Quixote's tilting at windmills—I'll stick to the windmills for now, not to bore you with other images from that fabulous novel I've been living in for years as you know—that crazy battle waged by the old hidalgo is more, I think, than a satire on the literature of chivalry, whose obsolete rituals and pretensions to glory seemed comical to Renaissance types in 1605, the year Cervantes's book was published. Teresa was about thirty years older than the great novelist (he was nearer the age of Jerome Gratian, alias Eliseus, alias Pablo, alias Paul, and so on—the darling father-cum-son your Madre was so madly in love with and you find so amusing!). Well, Cervantes was around for her beatification in 1614, two years before he died; one day I plan to comb through the work of this unbelieving writer for any traces of Teresa's presence I might have missed. It's a future piece of research, no hurry. For the moment, here goes with what I think brings your mystic weirdly into contact with my jester.

Knightly romances are not the only, or even the real, target here. The sailor-novelist was attacking delusion itself. I mean, look: he fights in Lepanto, Corfu, Naples, and Tunis; then, thrown into jail by Barbary corsairs, he makes four escape attempts before being ransomed from Hassan Pasha by the Trinitarians, and after that he goes as Philip II's envoy to Oran. He's even more of a vagabond than Teresa, isn't he, but then he's a man and he's young, that counts for a lot, plus he's closer to us in time. Between bouts of piracy and diplomacy he pens a kind of novella in the courtly tradition with a decently perverse twist, La Galatea. And a handful of comedies. He also commits a few minor swindles that get him excommunicated by the vicar-general of Seville; fathers a child out of wedlock, Isabel; and is claimed as a husband by Catalina de Salazar, in a transfer of assets she made out in favor of her brother. The author of Don Quijote ends up taking vows as a tertiary friar in the order of Saint Francis. You have to admit, my elusive Miguel led a rather more eventful life than your Teresa, for all that she made a picaresque foundress and a downright offbeat lover!

What compelled her was the Other. What intrigued him was delusion. In Spanish, maravilla means both marvel and miracle, the fantastic and the divine—putting us right into the postmedieval transition, when the Church set out to replace the obscurantism of pagan myths and fairy tales with the bright light of faith. Faith versus superstition. Teresa explores the love of the Other in a way that makes her immortal for every lover on earth, and especially for those who profess the Tridentine Catholic religion, as you point out. Miguel, on the other hand, puts delusion center stage and laughs at it, which doesn't mean he abolishes delusion, just that he makes it endearing.

Delusion is the one thing that makes him act, write, and laugh throughout his life as a writer and adventurer. Inside and outside delusion, inside and outside the deluded, the one inseparable from the other, no fixed position, no "message," always on the alert. See what I'm getting at? Next.

Over and above the values and positions of chivalry, and at the armored heart of the Man of the Mancha's inflated nuttiness, which provokes sarcasm and pity, Cervantes the writer simultaneously, in a single movement, admires and pillories the ardor of human beings in search of an ideal. He's tickled by believers: the earnest knight with his faith in Dulcinea and his own sacred destiny, sure, but also the whole of Christian, knightly Europe with its faith in the values of the Christ-centered Middle Ages, values that still persist today. Yes, I'm afraid that when you look for "values," those are all you'll find, which may be a shame, but there we are.

Query: Do the windmills only represent the summits of the courtly literature which, after *Lancelot* and *Amadis of Gaul*, fired the amorous imaginary of the Christian world in the days of Teresa of Avila and Miguel de Cervantes?

For starters, Don Quixote, what a name! *Quijote—Quijada—Quesada.** [*Some of the names Cervantes advances for his hero at the opening of the book.—Trans.] You know that *quijada* means "jawbone"? Maybe the don is a derisory replica of the great Charles V, whose legendarily prognathous mandible prevented his upper and lower teeth from meeting, so that his speech was rather garbled. How do you like Don Quixote as a jawbone that pokes fun at royal greed, the devouring greed that's as ludicrous as he is, in both appearance and essence?

Quesada, which sounds a bit like *quijada*, means cheese tart. Don't tell me, you think I've gone too far this time with my culinary obsessions! Well you're wrong. Contrary to what some of my colleagues think, Dulcinea's suitor was not a "knight of the sad table." Not a bit, and I can prove it! "Una olla de algo más vaca que carnero, salpicón las más noches, duelos y quebrantos los sábados, lentejas los viernes, algún palomino de añadidura los domingos . . ."[1] In English it goes, "An olla of rather more beef than mutton, a salad on most nights, scraps on Saturdays, lentils on Fridays, and a pigeon or so extra on Sundays, made away with three-quarters of his income." You see? The King of France's *saupiquet* was stuffed with gammon, truffles, and calves' sweetbreads, indeed, but not everyone lived in Versailles. To return to my cheese tart.

This *quesada* smells quaintly of the country. It sends my lovelorn knight, together with anyone else who claims parentage with the *quijote* (here a derivative of the French *cuissot*, meaning thigh-piece, part of the protective armor worn by God's intrepid pilgrims) back to the more primary pleasures of the palate, to prosaic reality.

I recap by riffing on the name: What is Don Quixote, an emblem of holy war or a cheese tart—a custard pie, if you like? A hybrid, invented composite, does he exist to any greater degree than the windmills he tilts at? Or are those windmills imaginary enemies fueling the paranoia, sorry, the enthusiasm of the potential warrior who slumbers in all of us since time immemorial, the soldier of unavoidably holy wars during the sixteenth, seventeenth, or twenty-first centuries?—Not forgetting Toumaï!* [*Name given to specimen of a new possible human ancestor whose skull was found in Chad in 2002.—Trans.]

Beyond his satire on the madness surrounding rank and status, Cervantes has it in for the act of faith in itself, and that includes being madly in love. Don Quixote exposes the absurd underside of human passion, the jester side of the saints, if you will. Teresa isn't unaware of this facet: it comes out now and then in her laughter and the farcical scrapes she gets into as a traveling founder. But she needed it to remain a secret, stowed away by His Majesty in the very cellars of the interior castle.

Less than half a century after the death of your Discalced Carmelite, along comes Don Quixote, who has mystical Spain splitting its sides over the pathetic amours of crazed knights-errant, the very love that fired the simple hearts and fathomless transports of John of the Cross or Teresa of Avila. Mystical Spain is tangled up body and soul in the sails of the windmills—or to take another great scene from the novel, it rolls on the ground with laughter, still flapping its powerful wings: wings of windmills, wings of angels and conquests, resilient, ridiculous engines.

On our last journey in the footsteps of the saint, we were both very struck by the wind turbines on the hills around Avila, their slow rotation churning the memory of Castile as much as anything. I agree with you about the paradoxical complicity between the mystic and the jester. As explorers of love, the one proceeding in deadly earnest, the other mockingly, they're poles apart, for sure. But both of them construct and dismantle our machines for producing fantasies, passions, and beliefs. Adventures and high winds.

That laughable hidalgo, "of a hardy habit, spare, gaunt-featured, a very early riser and a great sportsman," whose "brains got so dry that he lost his wits"—isn't he unmistakably a man in search of absolute love? He is sold to us as a saint, but in pathetic mode, having turned up fifty years too late for waxing earnest about the Beyond and about oneself. He has a go, all the same. And we're still having a go today, aren't we?

When Teresa felt the need of someone or something, she would turn to the Master. Don Quixote, on the other hand, "came to the conclusion that nothing more was needed now but to look out for a lady to be in love with." His lady would be a version of himself, the febrile male, for in resolving to christen this imaginary damsel "Dulcinea del Toboso," our literary knight was selecting "a name, to his mind, musical, uncommon, and significant, like all those he had already bestowed upon himself and the things belonging to him." This game of mirrors isn't completely alien to Teresa's erotic logic, is it, when she's communing with His Voice? With or without the capital letter, it's the same. And the deconsecrated love affairs of the moderns, as you're in a position to know, partake of the same beliefs and credences that magnetized Teresa toward her Father and those spiritual fathers . . .

By that point, who cares if the Quixotic visor is made of pasteboard! Our visionary was able to turn a swineherd driving his pigs through the stubble into a dwarf sounding a horn to herald his arrival at the next castle. And who cares if Jesus is not really walking by the Carmelite's side? She enjoys him deep in her guts, skewered by the dart of the heavenly lad who appears in her dream. The force of desire is enough to transform an inn and its host into a great fortress commanded by a splendid lord, girls of easy virtue into noble maidens, and a laborer on an ass equipped with a saddlebag and a bota of wine (one can't imagine Don Quixote without Sancho Panza!) into a faithful squire.

The novelist and the nun seem to be saying the same thing: that the love-fevered imagination must never, God forbid, be asked for evidence! You have to understand that in these misty regions of human truth, things are neither demonstrated nor disproved, they are imagined.

"If I were to show her to you," says Don Quixote to those who doubt the beauty, not to say the existence, of his Dulcinea as others doubted the existence of His Majesty, "what merit would you have in confessing a truth so manifest? The essential point is that *without seeing her you must believe, confess, affirm, swear, and defend it*; else ye have to do with me in battle, ill-conditioned, arrogant rabble that ye are."

A few years ago, in a paper I e-mailed to you, I wrote that Cervantes the humanist was a committed debunker of religious faith, practically opening the door to unbelief. But now, after rereading him with Teresa in mind, I think it's more complex. The normally sardonic Miguel smiles with compassion at the ineluctable, indefectible passion of faith. This passion makes him laugh, because he shares it. He manages to detach himself long enough to write, but he doesn't rid himself of it. This way of being inside and outside at once makes him, and us, laugh louder. What else is one to do, when belief—like unbelief—is impossible, and sometimes deadly? Let's write, let's laugh.

Teresa, as you see it, had already taken that road. We'll keep this from the worshippers who sanctify her and will go on doing so for ever and ever, why spoil their fun? But it's good to know it between ourselves and to pass the word to a few other people who would never read her unless we pushed them. Conversely, they might see Cervantes in a new light if they read him along with Teresa's works.

Decades before Cervantes and the don, Teresa knew that her visions were not perceived by the eyes but by the whole body before crystallizing them into "intellectual visions." I took in what you told me in the hired car. Basically, while immersed in her carnal fantasies, she never stops wondering whether it's a state of grace or a state of sin to believe that her body has merged with the Trinity, that our Lord has entered the garden of her soul, that the Other dwells within her, that she is penetrated by Him, and infinite, like Him. And the more she gives voice to these doubts that enrapture and terrify her and sometimes make her laugh, the more of a novelist she becomes. The more of a novelist she is, the better she founds. The better she founds, the more questions of this kind she asks herself.

What's different with Cervantes? In his case, he exits the interior castle and observes it from outside, not abandoning the grounds altogether. "I chuckle at that poor believer of a Quixote, who is what I am when I'm not writing," the diplomat-pirate seems to say. Standing at the intersection between the gullible hidalgo and the unbelieving boors who fancy themselves as modern, Cervantes mocks the whole lot of them: Don Quixote, Sancho Panza, and himself.

Teresa enjoys and suffers in the incarnation of her fantasies, in her *raptus*, whether illnesses or foundations, and pushes on in writing, further and further. If she's readier to laugh than most other saints, with her it's the laughter of a naughty girl, who giggles at La Madre swooning over her Husband like the little brat she remains to the end. Teresa is also a great writer, of course, and she senses it, but that matters less to her than her pleasure-pain in the Other and their common works on earth, pleasure-pain in the foundations of His Majesty, of the Third Person incorporated within her. La Madre likes to think that she's a vehicle for the reason of the Other, and only wakes up intermittently to the fact that she is an unreasoning confabulator. And whenever she allows herself that grotesque insight, she turns into a precursor of—Cervantes! Do you follow me?

Descartes was born in 1596, when Teresa had been in the grave for fourteen years. It would be Cervantes's irony that carried out, and with what elegance, the instruction the Carmelite liked to give her sisters, though she never included it in the authorized copy of *The Way of Perfection*, because its brutality probably made her laugh with fear, the instruction that's one of your favorite quotes: "Play chess, Sisters, you could checkmate God!"

You see, I'm feeling provocative, I'm being blasphemous, just hope I'm not muti-lating the complexity of your saint, as if she hadn't been pruned enough already by a finger here, an arm there, courtesy of the relic hounds, the "faithful" who really take love to catastrophic extremes . . . I'll stop, with apologies for such a long message. In London it's freezing cold, these luminous chrysanthemums won't warm me up, I do miss our Mexican Day of the Dead, a much more Cervantesque occasion.

I miss you. Hugs to Andrew.

Later,
Juan

From: sylvia.leclercq@FMP.fr
To: juan.ramirez@free.ac.uk
Subject: Re: Miguel and Teresa

Dear master-expert in the Golden Age,

I miss you too, and you were right. Neither the Indian summer nor the civil war are enough (so far) to unseat me from my gallop with Teresa. And what you wrote really hit home with me, as ever. After a quick jog through the Luxembourg Gardens, to wash my saint *and* the arsonist youngsters out of me for a moment, I wanted to pick up without breaking stride but can't quite manage it, you see, so my reply will be leisurely and won't resist the pleasure of contradicting you; you know how I am.

Cervantes describes delusionism, or the illusory part of faith, in other words, Love. I'm with you there, he is one of the greats who opened the shutters of the European and universal soul, letting fresh air into the dank cellars of their neuroses.

But—there's always a but—do you really think idealism is the same thing as faith? I'm asking that question of myself, as well as you. A colleague of mine, Dr. Barbier, claims that there are three kinds of idealism: dynamic, delusionistic, and fundamentalist.

Teresa is undoubtedly a species of fundamentalist when she imposes her vicious mortifications on herself and the rest of the reformed Carmel. It's too high-minded and hence cruel, a familiar pattern. It's hard to figure out, but I'm going to try. She's certainly a sadomasochist, although with a big dose of humor! She becomes a "fun-damentalist" as a matter of "historical necessity," as you put it with your knowledge of the Inquisition period, and with a view to bringing me down to earth! Let's assume that's the case. She is obliged to harden her stance against slackness (that of the rul-ing classes battening on the spoils of conquest, that of the decadent religious orders, that of the warmongers stirring up hostility to the Marranos, and more—thanks for the relevant attachments), but she also seeks to exalt the supernatural in opposition to the overexclusive asceticism of other groups (Lutheran rigor, for example). Basically, she wants to modernize the Church without severing it from its traditional sources and popular audiences.

La Madre is just as plainly a delusionist. She would be incapable of Cervantes's sardonic distance when mocking Don Quixote's fancies.[2] She dreams of becoming one with her fantasies, turning body and soul into the Other she lacks, incarnating their fusion—and standing back at times with the intromission of a little water here, a scrap of Dutch linen there. Now for the thousand-dollar question: Can this embodied fantasy really be termed a "delusion," when it is experienced as a potentially lethal reality (as when Teresa imagines that God condemns her desires, or when she somatizes her guilt until falling into a coma)? And the term seems even more far-fetched when "delusion" is experienced as a life-giving reality (as when her nuptials with the Lord hoist her into physical and spiritual bliss). Here, words become things and ideas grow into genuine forces: we are closer to Judge Schreber than to Madame Bovary. And yet the pragmatic advantages of this real delusionism—note the paradox—could appear negligible or absent if they merely shut Teresa into a dungeon of narcissistic megalomania, or, worse, into masochistic mortification. Although, even then, the experience would be worthwhile for the sake of the summits Teresa reaches and reports on. Many others have sought such thrills to enliven the dull world, after all, in a different way but following a similar logic of extremes: from Sade to Mishima, with God or without Him, as a Christian, a Samurai, or an atheist.

It is the dynamism of Teresa the delusionist that astounds me as a modern, if that's what I am. Not losing sight of Cervantes, let me play (just provisionally, stepping into the inviting dance of your message) the advocate of delusion, Teresa-style, against the jesting of the novelist. What's more, I think the energy of her prayer actually challenges the novelist's laughter, not to say refers him back to his own infantile facility.

It's because I am a delusionist, in the sense of assuming my delusions, that I don't tilt against windmills but instead make foundations: What do you say to that, Miguel? Don't you think Teresa might have said that to Cervantes, had she lived until 1605? And if I'd been present at their encounter, I'd have asked another question: Is it possible to act without being a Quixote? Including one who is self-aware when combining windmills with the spirit of enterprise? It isn't? Then what's the difference between the sterile delusionism of a knight-errant lost in the Renaissance, and the genuine, dynamic delusionism of a founding Mother? Who draws the line between them, the Church? The commission that decides on the canonization of saints? The judgment of history? The Nobel Prize committee? The League of Human Rights? Or does the power of decision over where "madness" stops and "genius" begins come down to that elucidation of the longing to believe known as "writing," "analysis," or whatever you want to call it? It's a process that leads to works, and sometimes to action.

My dear Juan, let me sum up my answer in brutally concise fashion, hoping that one day I'll be able to develop it further, given the courage and the time. Teresa turned the embodied fantasy of the ideal Father, that brought her both joy and pain, into self-knowledge; into a journey, argued in writing, through her "interior dwelling places." She managed to extract what is real about the fantasy that "the Ideal exists"— i.e., its foundational component, indispensable to the constitution of the human psyche. Yes, that's it, I'm talking about the inner life of our contemporaries, about you and me, about humankind as it emerged from the last Ice Age and progressed through a civilizing process that climaxed with the cult of the dead, the dead Father, his authority and his love, in short, the fantasy of the Beyond. Now, this psyche and this humanity, ours, are in crisis, increasingly sapped and enervated, clones or no clones, take a look at *American Idol* if you don't believe me; or else they are exploding in the night courtesy of the arsonists in our suburbs and elsewhere. As for so-called atheists like me, we are just as susceptible to other, mostly violent, delusions, if you care to examine our intellectual pretensions or the latest trendy cop series more closely . . . Before different psychical lives or different humans arrive to populate this globalized earth, let's try, at least, to understand the metamorphoses undergone over the centuries by a believing humanity and the experience of faith.

Teresa in particular did not succeed in flipping the fantasy that "the Ideal exists" into a caustic guffaw at the very notion of idealization, as Cervantes did, and relatively few others, for instance Voltaire and Nietszche, in their way. But she did convert her belief into a relentless investigation of the recesses of the soul capable of idealizing, or of loving, if you prefer. That *was* (past tense) capable of idealizing and loving?

Cervantes blew faith and love to smithereens of derision, not abolishing them, you're right, but regaling humans with the gift of disabused pleasure. Whereas Teresa uses faith and love in order to recondition the belief- and love-producing machine. She ventures as far as possible along the route that beckons the person who doesn't give up on believing, the person who talks as a way of sharing, and who loves in order to act. With all the benefits and all the follies involved in this expectant belief, and while describing it with disturbing, seductive subtlety.

- But Cervantes's attitude won out in the end, didn't it? Look around! What's left of that universe of faith and love, what's left of the windmills? Chimeras, TV soap operas for avid women and their partners. Or God's madmen, the suicide bombers who pretend not to realize that He (the Almighty, the Master, the One and Only, the True, the Beyond) has mutated into pure spectacle, and twist their alleged faith into murderous nihilism. Dogmatic, moralistic, terrifying and terrified, or just as often insubstantial, drunk on images, there they are, with no knowledge of Teresa, Cervantes, or any of a few others, bent on deleting our memories, too.

Still, dare I suggest those dangerous maniacs of the virtual Absolute might not really be so scary? Cervantes's laughter will get the better of them. Their fundamentalist rage would be defused if they just read him instead of burning flags, embassies, and Danish cartoons. And he could detoxify the rest. I know, there's a long way to go—fanatics are no good at reading, or laughing, and the inner halls of my nuanced Teresa would be way above their heads. What would it take? Nobody knows, not even me. Missionaries? Believers? Educators? Committed people opening up spaces for reading and writing? People daring to analyze the "fundament," to renew it? Maybe some of that will happen eventually.

Don't get me wrong, I'm not asking for Teresa to be dusted off as a model for the third millennium. I'm only saying that she encourages us to think again about the place of ideal Love in the soul—or if you prefer the psyche—of the talking beasts we are. She invites us to open up the interior castle of our need to believe, death-dealing and lifesaving at once. Can we manage without such a place? And who's "we"? Stammering humanoids with embryonic psyches, currently unable to be contained by any family, tribal, or ideological refuge whatsoever. We're all suffering from a disease of the ideal, all nihilists. It's because this species of humanoid surrounds us with waves of globalized fanaticism, or is lying in wait for us inside, that I'm so beguiled by Teresa's story. And that's why I persist in my efforts to decipher her embrace of the Other.

So there's my profession of faith signed and sealed, you asked for it!

Otherwise, everything's fine. The MPH keeps me busy, the sun is shining, and Andrew sends his love. He's in Paris, sitting right here, listening to news bulletins about cars ablaze in the suburbs and bunches of men hollering about the cartoons of the Prophet. He says to tell you that Paris, far more than New York, is the place to write about whatever's wrong. Will you come over and see us some weekend soon?

Looking forward to it, with lots of love,
Sylvia

Chapter 26

A FATHER IS BEATEN TO DEATH

The "Christian"—he who for two thousand years has passed as a Christian—
is simply a psychological self-delusion. Closely examined, it appears that,
despite all his "faith," he has been ruled only by his instincts—and what instincts!
Friedrich Nietszche, *The Antichrist*

"I love because I am loved, therefore I am": that seems to be your credo, Teresa, my love, but this solar face of your rapture is dependent on a bizarre figure: the man who loves you and whom you love is both suffering son and suffering father, scourged and put to death before resuscitating. As you will have guessed, my dialogue with you is also a dialogue with Freud: the founder of psychoanalysis believed that the "beaten child" we are in fantasy can (sometimes) resort to the paradoxical solution (as in your case) of another fantasy: *a son-father is put to death*.[1] Is this not the basis of Christianity? Or one of its bases, at the very least, in my atheistic eyes! I will here insert a parenthesis in the story of my cohabitation with Teresa, addressed to my psychology colleagues, as well as to believers who might be interested to see how their experience can be approached from the outside. I shall inquire into the fantasy of the "father beaten to death," arguing that it is a cornerstone of Christian faith, and I shall do so via Freud's text upon that other fantasy: "A Child Is Being Beaten."

A Coptic manuscript, translated from the Greek in the third or fourth century and exhumed during the 1970s, appeared in *National Geographic* in April 2006. Its gist was that Judas did not "betray" Jesus so much as "fulfill" the latter's design, which was to be put to death. Thus the image of the bad disciple, which had fueled Christian anti-Semitism for two thousand years, was shattered. The analyst, for her part, has no need of this kind of "evidence" to know that the execution of Christ was not an unfortunate accident (due to some betrayal or some internecine quarrel in Judaism, etc.), let alone a Gnostic revival of the Platonic soul (which must discard the body in order to ascend to the idea of Goodness and Beauty). At the intersection of "A Child Is Being Beaten" with *Totem and Taboo*, and in light of what Freud called "the desire of the father," of sadomasochism and its sublimation, it seems to me that the scenario of the "father beaten to death" expresses a logical necessity in the Christian construction of the subject of desire.[2] Indeed, the Passion displaces upon the son-father the guilt and pain inflicted on us by the prohibition of incest and by abandonment (it is not me but him who is punished, who undergoes the passion of pain); it cannot be otherwise, if love of and for the father is finally to be authorized in a "reconciliation" wrought by "infinite intellectual love," by sublimation.

Postulating the unconscious existence of *primal fantasies* (*Urfantasien*) derived either from the witnessing of certain events or from a "pre-historic truth" going back to the "earliest times of the human family," Freud evokes the "primal scene," "castration," and "seduction." Introduced in the same breath, the fantasy of the beaten child seems to occupy a specially privileged place among these primal fantasies, which are set to structure the psychoanalytic reading of desire and the range of sexual scenarios in which each person's specific eroticism may be deployed. Halfway between the primal and the individual, between myth and poetry, "a child is beaten" constitutes the dawn of individuation— the decisive moment when the subject begins to sketch out his or her sexual choice and speaking identity in the ternary structure of kinship. Whether male or female, excluded from the primal scene, "I" seek my place between father and mother, both to mark my difference from them and to enter into bonds that are the inseparable ties of love and speech, erotic and signifying.[3]

It was Christianity's genius to appropriate this fantasy (unwittingly, needless to say) in order to recast it and proclaim it *urbi et orbi* in the shocking, unbearable, and ultimately liberating—despite its ambiguities—form of Christ's Passion. Only thus can the Man of Suffering, beaten to death, abandoned by his Father, reach the Father, and resurrect.

Jesus is human, like me, says the believer (and a fortiori Teresa). He is a brother beaten to death before coming back to life. But this human is also a god, the only God. After the Last Supper and before the Passion, the man who calls himself the Son of God tells Thomas: "If ye had known me, ye should have

known my Father also; and from henceforth ye know him, and have seen him."
He tells Philip: "He that hath seen me hath seen the Father . . . Believest thou
not that I am in the Father, and the Father in me?"[4] Since Jesus is consubstantial
with the Father in the knot of the Trinity—Teresa leans heavily on this point—
Jesus is also a beaten father.

✶ ✶ ✶

The outrageous idea of the violent killing of a Father, a martyred God, is repulsive to many rebels against Christianity, the most inspired being Friedrich
Nietzsche. To abase God the Father to the level of a Man of Suffering could
only, for him, produce a slave religion, fit for weaklings and infrahumans.[5] How
wrong he was! Teresa does not separate the Father from the Son; the praying
woman likes to feel that she receives into her soul, by means of Communion,
both Christ *and* his Father, thanks to Jesus's sacrifice: "How pleasing to the
Father this offering of his Son is, because He delights and rejoices with Him
here—let us say—on earth."[6] "How did the Son take on human flesh and not
the Father or the Holy Spirit?" she wonders, struggling with the idea that the
three Persons are really "separate." She goes on, archly: "This I haven't understood. The theologians know."[7] I don't mean to shock you, Teresa, my love, but
Freud's audacity is what encouraged me, Sylvia Leclercq, to detect in this divi-
nized suffering a gigantic defensive scaffolding against the surfeit of desire and
a hefty dose of sadism. It seems to me that the paschal scenario satiates desire
and violence, but by turning these in every direction to play with them, defuse
them, . . . and appease them.

✶ ✶ ✶

The better to convince you, I must go back to childhood, it's an occupational
deformation of mine! The narrative of "A Child Is Being Beaten" opens with a
scene in which I see someone being beaten. I don't know who it is, but it's not
me, it's him—someone else. The narrative progresses through three phases:

"Daddy loves only me," says the little girl or little boy. "He cannot love anybody else, because whoever he is beating, it is somebody else." I, the author of
this fantasy, am not being beaten. I am only a budding sadistic voyeur. Why?
Because my desire for Daddy is so great, I have to repress it into guilt. And so
"this early blossoming is nipped by the frost," as the Viennese doctor put it, in

such a way that precocious genital arousal undergoes a regressive debasement to the lower level of orality, anality, or onanism, and becomes crystallized in the pleasure of whipping-punishment . . . displaced onto the anal zone of another. Thus the sadistic pleasure in the spanking meted out by Daddy to another in fact curbs my own genital excitement and guilt toward the all-powerful father I desire.

Note that at this stage of the script, the fantasizing child is not itself being abused, and the beaten "object" remains as yet indeterminate. The fantasizing subject is dominated by the excitement of its voyeurism alone, which arose as a bulwark against its genital organization. This voyeurism is "not clearly sexual, not in itself sadistic," Freud hazards cautiously, "but yet the stuff from which both will later come." That is to say, voyeurism contains genital excitement and sadism in embryo. We will remember this when we encounter a believer prostrate in unnameable veneration of his ill-treated God, his speechless contemplation less a matter of decorous discretion than of shameful relish.

The scenario changes in the second phase of the fantasy. "Daddy does not love me: he is beating me," says the little boy or little girl; but this masochistic inversion does not mean the same to both sexes.

To the boy, "Daddy is beating me" signifies that he is guarding against his passive desire to be loved by his father, as well as against latent homosexuality, before attempting to invert this passivity and feminization and turn them into weapons against the father, waging an oedipal war that launches him on the high road to male emancipation. Unless the boy enjoys masochism, in which case he changes the sex of the punisher: "Daddy loves me, and so the person beating me can only be a woman, it's Mom! She's the one I have to separate from, and yet it's her place I want to take beside Daddy. Hateful Mom, that evil, desirable witch, she'll never stop taking it out on me!" That's how the script reads for a man who feels the thrill Sacher-Masoch described under the lash of a Venus in furs.[8]

But in girls like you, Teresa, matters are more warped still. The defensive inversion of potentially sadistic voyeurism ("A child is being beaten, I don't know who, but it's not me") into masochism ("I am being beaten") remains unconscious. Because you don't experience this inversion as a punishment alone; it also implies the "secondary erotization" of the pregenital zones, as the same Viennese doctor explained; a regressive substitute for genital satisfaction. Sure enough, in the fantasy "A Child Is Being Beaten," that satisfaction is discharged in masturbation. And since this intense, victimized, and self-focused eroticism is as much a source of guilt as a yearning to be loved, it too will be repressed into the unconscious. That's how the permanence of unconscious female masochism becomes instilled, on top of the passivity expected of women and drummed into them by traditional cultures.

Finally the second phase of the fantasy is inverted in its turn, still as an effect of repression, and safeguarding the little girl's masochism even more effectively, the better to impress it into the unconscious. "It's not me who Father is beating, it's a boy," runs the formula for the third and last defensive step. It's not me, and not a woman at all, it's a man who undergoes the physical action of the Great Other! This has the effect of excluding the little girl from the erotic scene and, moreover, from any "scene" at all: social, political, cultural, and the rest.

⋆ ⋆ ⋆

Let us attempt to understand the stages of this progression. The little girl (and the woman) shields herself from her incestuous love for the father (phase 1: "He loves me") and from her own masochism (phase 2: "He is beating me") by projecting them in inverted form onto another, preferably of the same sex as the coveted paternal object (phase 3: "He is beating a boy"). How does this delegation of female desire onto another object of the same sex or the other sex take place, to safeguard her from being a subject of desire? How does this inverted delegation of desire come about, when it is not a repression properly speaking, but what I call an introjection of paternal attachment, of perversion (*père-version*)?

Unlike the boy, who concentrates the desires of the entire lineage and posits himself as a fairly happy Narcissus from the moment of the primal scream (why has it been forgotten that Narcissus, in the eponymous myth, is a young man? Why is the "second sex" generally regarded as more narcissistic?), the girl, from earliest childhood, always compares herself to someone else. A woman exists only as a function of this other, who is, in the first instance, the mother. As I have noticed with my female analysands, little girls have their first "oedipal complex" toward their mother: they turn the mother into this premature otherness, this sensible, preverbal presence, this pole of simultaneous attraction *and* adversity they can never stop comparing themselves to, measuring up to, separating from.[9] You or me? That's the little girl's initial question, for she is incapable of setting herself up as a self-complacent Narcissus, replete with his own image. She tries to put herself "out of bounds," to safeguard herself from the unsettling excitement running through her. She defends herself from her passion—first incestuous, then masochistic—by focusing it on another: "He doesn't love *you*," she says, "because he is beating you." Who is that "you," that abused second person who shields my little-girl desire, guilty as I am of loving and being loved?

Every little girl, says Freud, has an irrevocable childhood memory of the way little boys are the ones who are given the rod. In his interpretation, the repression that succeeds desire inverts the father's love into the punishment of another person who is the object of the girl's jealous hatred. The prototype of this other beaten person can only be the mother, enabling a due humiliation of the little girl's rival, even in the best patriarchal families. In Teresa's family, the dignified, handsome Beatriz de Ahumada—prematurely ravaged by continual pregnancies and rapidly succumbing to sickness—could easily have been regarded as a "beaten woman."

And yet the little girl's ambivalent love for her mother persists in protecting the envied matron and seeks out other targets to deflect the beating from the loved/hated maternal object. In the girl's fantasy, other children take the place of the abused rival, drawing on the parents' libidinal transference to her siblings. Why this displacement, this masquerade?

Freud points to everyday scenes children witness at home or at school. When a child is punished, he is viewed by the others (inevitably in competition with him) as having forfeited the father's love, leaving the father available for the not-beaten, unscathed onlookers or voyeurs; or more precisely, for the unscathed *voyeuse*!

But Freud goes further. He suggests that it is the guilt inherent in the repression of the voyeur's desire that creates the necessity of punishment, irrespective of whether scenes of punishment have been observed. His inquiry now goes deeper, asking what is the source of that guilt-inducing repression of love felt for and returned by the father, which peaks in fantasies of punishment, of whippings?

There can only be one answer: this repression, whose violence depends partly on personal factors (such as the premature development of genitality in some children between the ages of two and six, or the excessive sensitivity and vigor of the sexual drive in others), partly on the nature of incestuous currents within the family, is simply the reiteration of the incest repression that underlies human history and is prescribed by it. As the founding element of the culture that distinguishes our species, the repression of incest necessarily and

universally engenders guilt and its corollary, masochism. In specific circumstances, however—such as a highly strung family background and the exceptional sensibilities of someone out of the ordinary (like you, Teresa)—this
prehistoric guilt entails a marked regression to earlier stages of psychical development, before the development of genitality: to the oral/anal level (spanking),
to onanistic relief, or to the variations on punishment-whipping that treat the
whole body as an erogenous zone.

All this resonates with us, doesn't it? But I follow you, Teresa, my love, when
I say there may be "something" wanting in Freud's neat explanation; something
that would account for your manner of *jouissance*, side by side with your "guilt"
and your worship of the "Tortured Man." We saw this in the course of your
foundations/persecutions/jubilations: you are extraordinary. The physical suffering that inflames you carnally is gradually deployed just as much, and then
more, in your mind. It invests language, writing, the multiplicity of attachments, and remains sublime. Better still, it becomes ever more sublime, ever
more verbal and active. Bodily and spiritual, your suffering is always reversible, and that's how it gives itself the chance to be distilled into an intense
symbolization-elucidation-creation.

* * *

I suggest, then, that to the Freudian view of endogenous masochism ensuing
from the repression of incest be added the fact that incest provokes a final displacement of arousal, not this time onto a different "object" (a boy), but onto
the means of expression and communication itself. The repression of incest
leads to an investment . . . in language and thought! Do you follow?

So, in parallel with the fantasy that "someone else is being beaten," which
protects me from forbidden genital pleasure and/or from the incestuous desire
to love and be loved (by Daddy, but also by Mommy; Freud has less to say about
her, since her love strikes him as more natural, less prohibited; I wonder!), in
parallel with that fantasy, then, I the little girl will transfer the intensity of my
desire onto words and thoughts, onto representation and psychic creativity.

This displacement is more than a barricade against culpable genital desires,
creating a new object of desire that proves to be a new source of satisfaction,
complementary to the pleasure of the erogenous zones; it consists of an infinite
capacity for representing and naming, to the point of endowing genital arousal
with words and meanings or nonmeanings, besides the exaltation of masochism

itself. All this in hopes not only of finding partial substitutes for the forbidden love that is incest, in the shape of my own symbolic activities or works, but also of meriting that forbidden love, rendered guilty and reversed into masochism. Meriting it through the wild capacity for sublimation all humans possess, a skill that I, smart little girl that I am, noisier than the others and Daddy's favorite to boot, employ to outdo everyone else.

To perversion in its masochistic ("I enjoy the fantasy of being beaten") or sadistic ("I enjoy seeing a boy being beaten") forms is added the sublimatory *jouissance* of my own power to speak and think *for and with* the beloved/lover. You see, at the beginning, sublimation accompanies the perverse (*père-vers*) defense, and perversion (*père-version*) is the other face of *sublimation*. It is easy to imagine the possible variations of their joint destinies: sublimation and perversion can splice together, or part, or cross paths; they can be mutually oblivious, or reunite, or jointly stimulate each other . . .

To formulate it in terms akin to yours, in the dynamic of that third phase of the female fantasy resulting from the incest prohibition ("It's not me, it's him who's being beaten"), guilt comes accompanied by a longing for redemption. There is no other way of meriting recognition and grace from the Other, that is, of rising above the unmistakably anal score-settling with those around me, than by overinvesting the psychic representations that are language and thought. My thought and my word are redemption; my writing and my creations likewise.

Unlike boys, who are bound to engage in interminable bouts of physical and erotic contests with the father and his doubles, merciless duels that will dominate and absorb all their most elaborate intellectual activities, girls exhibit (over and above their individual genetic dispositions and favorable or unfavorable developmental contexts), through their academic and intellectual prowess, commonly greater than boys', a precocious overinvestment in the activity of thinking. Thinking may thus take on a "redemptive" value for little girls, in the sense of endowing them with a symbolic, phallic power that is the fantasy equivalent of the Other's power. Some boys also take this more delicate, spiritual, intellectual road; they include artists and intellectuals, of course, and men of God, it goes without saying. This is how they sublimate their "psychic bisexuality" (according to Freud, again). In the end, at the top of this road to sublimation, to which sex do we belong? An inept question, since, properly speaking, once we reach the heights where Flesh and Word merge into one, each person belongs to the unique sex that she or he constitutes at her or his own peril. There's a certain happiness in it.

* * *

Let us recapitulate. The terminal fantasy of "A child is being beaten" erases, from the girl's conscious mind, the representation of the masochistic scene ("He is beating me") and replaces it with a twofold movement: On the one hand, the sadistic version of the fantasy "He is beating him"; on the other, its accompaniment by a heightened level of imaginative and cognitive activity, alongside a critical moral conscience identified with the parental superego. The female superego roots itself in this movement, as does a critical vigilance liable to go to delirious extremes of self-scrutiny. It's understandable, then, that the conflicts between this strongly invested symbolic construction and an equally consistent sensibility may cause the symptoms manifested by such conflictive, divided personalities labeled "hysterical." They are particularly common among women, although they are also found among men who have followed a similar path. In the right family and historical circumstances, the same tensions may stimulate and develop women's symbolic creativity. This occurs against the background of a domesticated masochism that can only in that way be tempered.

* * *

Let us pause for a moment on this strong identification, defensive and creative at once, that girls have with the paternal superego merged with the phallic function, at the expense of female identifications. It leads to a repression of the mother seen as castrated or infirm, prompts imitations of virile attributes, and propels the subject into a glorification of spirituality alone—so as to reunite the little girl, and the woman she will become, with the symbolic Father.

In line with this logic, masochism is preserved and cultivated while undergoing a final inversion, this time under the pressure of the superego, into hyperactive talking and thinking and other busy activities (in accordance with individual capability), an exhausting program that requires a . . . sadistic dominion over others. We are back with the sadistic voyeurism that characterized phase 1 of the little girl's fantasy, and she makes the most of it: "I excel in my representational and symbolization activities, they also comfort me, and by thus drawing near to the agent of the Law, I seal a pact with the symbolic Father. I also take my revenge on the boy who has the penis, when he is beaten in place of me: I am the Phallus."

However, as far as the girl's unconscious is concerned, the beaten boy is just the mask of herself, which causes her sadistic *jouissance*, underpinned by a virile identification with the Father, the agent of the Law who dispenses punishment, to rely on a masochistic *jouissance* that is even more deeply buried in the unconscious ("I know it's my own incestuous desires—for Daddy and Mommy both—that are being punished. But what advantages come with it!"). Ah, the impressive contortions and interminable polyphonies of the hysteric's progress! Few can come up with an answer to the question, "What do women want?"

Boys for their part are not impervious to this sadomasochistic economy (John of the Cross and the monks at Pastrana attained heights of masochistic euphoria that made even Teresa feel queasy). Except that the boy's whipping fantasy is always experienced as passive: "I am loved by the father" (subtext: like a passive woman). Thus male masochism, culminating in the scenario of his flagellation by a whip-wielding woman, in reality protects the subject from the father's sadistic desire, something that must at all costs be kept at bay, for this paternal desire persists at once as unconscious homosexual attraction and as the ultimate danger. So, although the masochistic fantasy of being beaten by a woman by no means prevents a man from occupying a feminine position in the sense of a passive role, this fantasy nonetheless affords him a double boon. In the first place "it" isn't happening between two men, for I'm getting pleasure from a woman; I might be playing a passive, female role, but my choice of object is heterosexual; furthermore, the child-beaten-by-his-mother who I have become is not even a passive female, since the man suffering from his mother, that is, I myself, mirrors the suffering I always divined in my own father—a humiliated man, always weighed down by the power of maternal hysteria. By being punished myself, I become one with my debased father: we are united at last in a kind of wedding beneath the whip. However you look at it, my masochism as a man beaten by a woman is the one thing that makes a man of me, an abused man, no doubt, but one who exists, by reason of his injury and his castration, just as I exist exclusively through my experience of pain. This man is my mother's man, of course, the one I always desired with a cowed and fearful longing, but whose sadism I need no longer dread, since I have taken his place and erased him from the scene with Venus and her whip.

Such are, on the female side and on the male, the agonies and ecstasies of sexual identity. Does each sex suffer and die apart?

* * *

And what of the Passion, in this strange perspective? What if Jesus were not only a Son, but also a consubstantial representative of God the Father? A Father who is tortured to death?

We know that for the Freud of *Totem and Taboo*, the murder of the father was a foundational act, a historically real event in the course of human civilization. In the same way Jesus Christ is, for Christians, a historical character, and the faithful commemorate a murder that really happened. I'd rather keep a distance from these issues: leaving aside the question of whether the events actually took place, I shall confine myself to assessing the psychic reality they generate among subjects who literally believe in their fantasies and representations. In addition, while the Christ of the Gospels is a Son, I am interested in the logic that would have God the Father likewise put to death in the Passion (Saint Paul touched on this long before Hegel and Nietzsche). Given the inextricable knot of the Trinity, it would be hard to delink the suffering unto death of the Son from that of the Father, which is consubstantial with it.

To recap, what would happen if Jesus were not only a beaten child or brother, but a beaten father—beaten to death?

For the little girl, this situation implies that the one she loves—the object of her mother's desire and the phallic function upholding her access to representation, language, and thought—is equally as victimized as the boy of her sadistic fantasy: "It's not me being beaten, it's a boy. Now here's a father being beaten. This father must then be a sort of boy, or brother-figure."

Mixing the son with the father, this scenario has the advantage of simultaneously alleviating the incestuous guilt that imbues the desire for the sovereign Father, the Other, and encouraging the girl's virile identification with the abused man. A glorious and gratifying identification, to be sure, but under cover of the masochism this twofold movement promotes, not to say incites: "This beaten father and/or brother is my double, my likeness, my alter ego— me, equipped with a male organ."

The way is thus cleared, in the unconscious, for the Father as agent of the Law and the Forbidden to merge with the subject of the guilty passion, that is, myself, the cherished daughter of that same father. The superman Father becomes humanized and, more importantly, feminized by the suffering he undergoes; as a result he is at once my ideal and my double. A cozy "us" is constituted by and in the passion of the Father, whose love, guilt, and punishment we both share. As far as my unconscious is concerned, not only is the Father the agent of prohibition and punishment, he is also, manifestly, the object of the interdiction itself and suffers from that prohibition and punishment just as . . . I do! Hence my idealization of him, in which the ideal of the ego and the superego are mingled, and which, by superseding my experience of myself as junior, ignored, and excluded from the primal scene, staunches that exclusion. This returns me to the first stage of my oedipal fantasy: "I love him and he loves me." But in the light of our osmosis in the father's passion, this love is formulated differently: "We are both of us in love and guilty; we deserve to be beaten to death together, to be reunited in death."

For the unconscious, this father–daughter reunion suspends the incest prohibition in and through the suffering of the two protagonists, jointly in love and punished. Their pain will necessarily be felt as a wedding. A suffering sexualized under the "whip of faith," in the ordeal of the father beaten to death, is seen and felt as a "merciless love" (to paraphrase Baudelaire).[10] The only way out of this masochistic paradise lies in sublimation.

By placing the fantasy of the father beaten to death at the summit of the evangelical narrative, so that it calls out for our identification, Christianity does more than reinforce the interdictions: paradoxically, it displaces them and paves the way for them to be worked through or sublimated.

On the one hand, neurotics of either sex continue to be inhibited and/or stimulated by the threats of judgment, condemnation, and expiation that mutilate desire. Nevertheless, by being beaten, like the son-father, the subject can liberate his or her unconscious desires from culpable suffering, moving on to a suffering that could be qualified as sovereign or divine. Once past the guilt linked to transgression, the issue will be one of passion as the sole highway to union with the ideal Father. This new type of suffering, Christlike or Christian, is not the reverse of the Law so much as a suspension of Law and guilt in favor of the *jouissance* in a suffering that is idealized, precisely—the *jouissance* of calling, pining, crucially failing to satisfy the desire for the Son-Father; the pangs of pain-delight in the ambivalence of perversion, *père-version*. God's Calvary unto death does not normalize suffering, nor does it authorize incest. However, by virtue of its glory and thanks to our desire for and with the father, this shared agony, this com-passion hover on the verge of admitting, and justifying, both the sin of incest and the pain that punishes it.

This goes beyond pleasure. We speak here of *jouissance*, in as much as plea-sure taken with the Son-Father is a pleasure unto death. John of the Cross expressed this better than anyone: "Where have You hidden, / Beloved, and left me moaning? / You fled like the stag / And after wounding me; / I went out calling You, and You were gone" ("The Spiritual Canticle"). "And spread his shining arms, . . . / And hung by them, and died, / His heart an open wound with love" ("Song of Christ and the Soul").[11]

* * *

The worship of the beaten Father entails a fundamental consequence: along with, and beyond, my surreptitiously avowed incestuous link with the Father, it is symbolic activity itself that the Father's passion invites me to eroticize, to develop, to magnify, to love. How does this occur?

Reinforced by the incest taboo and the punishments the father metes out in order to maintain it, repression creates the neurotic and his or her repre-sentational capacity. We have just seen how the fantasy of the beaten Father establishes another structure inside me, the underside of the neurotic appara-tus: his Passion, as physical suffering infused with value, incites me to resexual-ize and load with affectivity my own movement of idealization of the father. But this masochistic variant of *père-version* affords me little more than partial, largely unsatisfying pleasures, and the resulting frustration unleashes a cascade of somatic or functional disorders.

As it is by means of thought and language that I connect with the Other, the activity of representing my (however frustrated) desires is clearly favored by the Father-as-Passion, the figure poised to replace the Father-as-Law. The resexualization of the ideal Father into the man of the Passion fosters an unprecedented resexualization of representation itself—of all fantasy- and language-producing activity. First, in a way that induces compassion, the abused Father's Passion invites me to realize my sadomasochistic drives in physical reality, by way of extravagant rituals; this is what is usually encour-aged in self-mortification and atonement. In parallel, the religious and espe-cially the mystical experience tend to deflect my sadomasochistic impulses, beyond the reality of pain unto death, into the realm of representation where language alone is fit to appropriate it. This is because it is through thought, imagination, and language—far more than through the fantasized communion—that I create around the subject of the "Father beaten to death" and become his chosen one, the Other's elect.

Acts of representation-speech-thought, activities attributed to the father in patrilineal societies and that link me to him, become—in the Christic system— the foremost domain of a *jouissance* that embraces and transcends sadomasochism; this activity ultimately emerges as the "kingdom" where suffering, thus metabolized, can be expressed and appeased.

Following Freud, this displacement of pleasure from the body and sexual organs into representation has been termed *sublimation*. Perversion and sublimation impose themselves as the two faces, underside and upper side, of this relaxation or indeed fabulous suspension of the incest taboo, brought about by the Son-Father being beaten instead of me.

No other religion, including Greek polytheism, has proved as effectively auspicious for the experience of sublimation as the religion of the Son-Father beaten to death. By way of this fantasy, Christianity maintains, on the one hand, the inaccessible ideal (Jesus is a God, which makes Him a forbidden Father who forbids me to approach or to touch Him). On the other hand, and without avoiding the contradiction, Jesus is a son, a brother, a man who redeems our guilty desires by submitting to the lash as though he were a party to our transgressions and sins. On the one side, legalistic coldness and apathy; on the other, fervent *jouissance* filtered through the passion of pain. The alternation of the two can play out within an individual (feeding into autoerotic sadomasochism) or between a subject and his or her erotic object (boosting the sadist–masochist oscillation enjoyed by partners in perversion).

Not a father who begets, in the manner of the biblical patriarchs, Jesus as the Man of pain and the abused Son-and-Father sets in motion a spiraling cycle of repetitions that displace carnal passions into mental rewards. Coming after the figure of Baby Jesus and the sacralization of birth as an eternal starting over, the figure of Jesus as the beaten Father shows that the repetition of pain is the supreme act of atonement. By beaming back to me from the heights of his Fatherhood the mirror image of my own nonshareable pain, Jesus reinstates the symbolic or spiritual element of human suffering, and ennobles it by so doing. He reveals and reinforces the psychic participation that is intrinsic to the pain of beings with the power of speech. That is his lesson for those who would tend to overlook it, and that's why Christianity acted for two thousand years as a laboratory for modern psychology and even psychoanalysis. But at the same time, as we know too well, it is susceptible to the idealism of indiscriminate pyschologization. Isn't there an ersatz kind of Christianity lurking in the "heart of hearts" of globalized TV spectators, for whom nothing is "universal," bar the universality of amorous or spiritual pain?

* * *

Whatever the truth of past excesses and their contemporary exemplars, my aim is to salvage the kernel of intrapsychic truth they contain, which with Teresa's help can be summed up as follows: the myth of the murdered Son-Father tells us that the prohibition of incest is not simply about the deprivation of pleasure; it invites sexual excitement to perform a *jump on the spot* in order that, while remaining contained in me, it travels through my sensorial and genital apparatus to become fixed in *psychic representations* and acts—ideality, symbolism, thought.

Shockingly, but not without veracity or profit, Jesus as the beaten Father is the figure of language experienced as a representation that encompasses bodily pleasure and pain, travels through them, and wrenches itself away to reach the ideal. This language in its Christian version—though who has ever lived that version in all its transubstantial complexity, apart from Teresa and the great artists?—is not a pure abstraction, but rather an exaltation that heals suffering by means of a *jouissance* that is forever open and forever wanting. The speaking being's life is a continual starting over, over and over again, in a series of communions with the Man put to death: "Sown in destructibility, indestructible we rise."

Catholicism was more propitious than other religions in this respect, because it simultaneously maintained and transgressed sexual or carnal prohibitions and inscribed this happy culpability into signs. It ostentatiously highlighted that *bis repetita*, the desire of the speaking being, as a desire that infringes the Law insofar as the Law is prohibition (resulting in the feeling of suffering) and also as a desire to be recognized by the Law insofar as the latter is a symbolic code (resulting in the blooming of the self in *jouissance* outside the self). Pierre Klossowski invokes that very point when he writes that the reiteration of the carnal act in language not only provides an account of transgression, it is itself "a transgression of language by language."[12]

* * *

I hear your question: In this theater of sadomasochism, does not Jesus as the beaten Father set free the death drive at the very moment he seems to "reconcile" it, to distill it into a Beyond? Absolutely, and we are all too familiar with the way Christianity has presented itself at certain points in its history as a justification of vengeance and a summons to the Crusades, to the Inquisition, or to sanguinary pogroms.

However, whereas some religions positively aggravate the same fundamentalist deviations, the Christic knot (particularly in Catholicism) of desire, *suffering*, and sublimation also gave rise to the perlaboration and analysis of these fatal excesses, thanks to the tremendous development of theology, writing, and art. Great artists like Mozart or Picasso responded to the intensities of this dialectic in a sustained fever of creation. Thus "set free," the death drive was also set on a path toward its own deliverance, relieved of a certain . . . becalmedness.

* * *

Another crucial moment in the fantasy of "a father being beaten to death" does not stop at releasing the death drive as sadomasochistic aggression, properly speaking, but hoists it to a paroxysm of *jouissance*. The death drive in its radical, Freudian sense is pushed to the point of dissolution of bonds and uncoupling from the plane of the living. This is exactly what transpires in the story of the Passion.

For when Eros and Thanatos are released to "freewheel" down the Way of the Cross, the identity between body and soul comes apart in the transition from suffering to Nothingness. Here we confront the supreme difficulty always implicitly hanging over the figure of Christ, but coming tragically to the fore at Easter: Christ is not only a Son abandoned by his Father ("My God, my God, why hast thou forsaken me?")[13] but also, yes, a Father (remember what he told Thomas and Philip) beaten to death (Saint Paul's "Christ died") before rising again.[14]

Let us pause over this death of the Father, a concept only very cautiously explored by Catholic scholars; it seems to appeal more to Protestant and Orthodox Christians.

The Father's "descent into the bowels of the earth" is denoted in Greek by the noun *kenosis*, meaning "nonbeing," "nothingness," "emptying," "nullity," but also "senseless," "deceptive" (the adjective *kenos* can mean "void," "of no account," "futile," and the verb *kenoun* "to purge," "to sever," "to obliterate"). Calvary confronts us with the complete suspension of the paternal function and the elimination of the representational and symbolization capacities that this function, in psychoanalytic theory, assures. In theological terms, it is purely and simply the death of God. In philosophical terms, with reference to the death drive as the "carrier wave" of all other drives, we can declare with Gilles Deleuze that only "Thanatos *is*," in the sense that only Nothingness is.[15]

God himself is "pending" or *en souffrance* in Christ's suffering, and this outrage, which theological scholarship has trouble facing up to, prefigures a later, modern time when the "death of God" seemed to be a fact. "God has died, God Himself is dead," writes Hegel: a prodigious, "frightful" representation, confronting representation with the deepest of cleavages or ruptures.[16]

But no sooner mooted, the death of the Father and/or the symbolic realm is negated: Christ resurrects! What astonishing therapeutic power resides in this bracketing of recognized, longed-for death with the negation of death! What a prodigious restoration of the capacity for thinking and desiring is effected in this dread exploration of suffering to the point of loss of the mind, to the point of death! It is because the Father and the Holy Spirit are themselves mortal, abolished by the intervention of the Man of pain, whose thought endures all through his suffering unto death, that they can be reborn. Thought can begin again—a different thought! Thought as resurrection? Might that be the ultimate form of the freedom proclaimed by Christian suffering? Nietzsche was not blind to the fact that this letting go into kenosis lent to the human and divine death on the Cross "the freedom from and superiority to every feeling of resentment."[17]

One can understand the potent effects of this fantasy on the unconscious. This breaking, even for an instant, of the link that couples Christ to his Father and to life, this caesura, this hiatus does not offer an *image* so much as a *narrative* to the psychic cataclysms that endanger the putative equilibrium of the individual, and in so doing it thinks and heals them.* [*The author makes a play on the homophony of *penser*, "to think," and *panser*, "to bandage or heal": "et, de ce fait, les panse."—Trans.]

* * *

We are each the result of a prolonged "work of the negative": birth, weaning, separations, frustrations, bereavements. By staging this rupture at the heart of the absolute subject that is Christ, by presenting it in the guise of a Passion, the inseparable reverse of the Resurrection, Christianity brings back into consciousness the dramas inherent in our becoming, thus endowing itself with an immense, *unconscious* cathartic power. Only the gradual progress of science, the human sciences in particular, plus the psychoanalytical leap, would help us move toward the psychosexual interpretation of these variants of suffering. At the time that concerns us, we had hardly embarked upon that long road.

What if it were only through kenosis that the divine was able to recuperate the most beautiful consciousness of its new beginning? I say "the most beautiful" because, next to the suffering of com-passion, the sovereign suffering of kenosis is paradoxically a process of "dis-passion": I contend that it de-eroticizes the agony that voyeurs feel along with the God-man when they contemplate the Calvary. More than this, the absolute necessity hardwired into the human spirit to aspire to the Other, to desire the divine, to hunger for meaning, is abruptly revealed—in kenosis—to be empty, futile, of no account, and senseless.

Extreme passion, extremes of delinking. Due to the conjoined presence of the Absolute-and-Nothingness of desire, Christianity touches the limits of the religious. With kenosis we move from religion into the terrain of the sacred, understood as the trespass of thought into the unthinkable: the space of Nothingness, futility, vanity, and meaninglessness.[18] Medieval mysticism ventured into that space with Meister Eckhart: "I pray God to make me free of God."[19] But it may be John of the Cross who best encapsulated that presence of the impossible in the tension of desire and thought—the Nothingness that gives voice to the hopeless chase ("I went out calling You, and You were gone") characteristic of the need to believe.

Teresa, more attuned to resurrection, finds bliss in the reconciliation in which the Son-Father's death is resolved. Spinoza's formulation may help modern man to interpret this ultimate mystery: "God loves himself with an infinite intellectual love," he writes in the *Ethics*, in terms that recast what is, for the believer, absorption of suffering into the "new body" of the risen Christ, seated at the right hand of the Father, and into the resurrection.[20] Because "infinite intellectual love" (God the Father) coexists with the existential pain (God the Son and the believer) which it elucidates, it is called God and is a joy.

Having emphasized, in a completely novel way, values of compassion and an implicit kenosis without ever divorcing them from "loving intelligence," the genius of Christianity fashioned a formidable counterweight to pain, namely the sublimation or perlaboration of pain in mental and verbal activity. I, a being that suffers because I desire/think, because I am loving/loved, am capable of conceiving my passion as a representation that will be my resurrection.

My spirit, in love with the Passion, recreates it in works of loving intelligence, such as thoughts and stories and pictures and music.

* * *

Christianity both admitted and denied the Father's ritual killing. Such was the solution it managed to impose on the universal "murder of the Father" that is the bedrock of human civilization. From then on, Christianity—more especially Catholicism, after the revolution of the Counter-Reformation—appropriated the Greco-Roman body to itself. It took the body of antiquity rediscovered by the humanists and pushed it to the limit in the Passion of Man. Painting, music, and literature were to nurture the passions of men and women, announced by mysticism prior to baroque art, and to radically overturn the subject of monotheism.[21]

The tension between desire and meaning—the definitive trait of speaking beings and the motor of the sadomasochistic logic of human experience—is doubly resolved, then. I renounce incest in order to gain access to the desiring and desirable father as a symbolic father, and to be associated with him if, and only if, I succeed in appropriating his symbolic and imaginative powers. And yet this new beginning ("In the beginning was the Word") is painful. The child who speaks must renounce its desires and repair its guilt; the verbal child is a beaten child. If it can conjure it up in thought, the way of perfection stretches ahead.

Soothing that infantile, incestuous, speaking humanity—for speaking humanity is suffering humanity—with his suffering as a Father who became incarnate in the Son in order to be beaten to death, Jesus does not merely act as therapist. He overturns capital components of the human condition.

The eroticization of his ordeal makes manifest the torments of the desiring body within the family triangle: incest with both parents, and more specifically with the Father, is not just an unconscious desire, for it turns into a preconscious one. With girls, the father–daughter encounter, unconsciously courted and sublimated in passionate nuptials with Christ's "sacred humanity," goes to stimulate the cultural and social energy of the Christian woman. With boys, the fantasy of a homosexual encounter with the father, equally unconsciously courted, ends up favoring social attachments based on warrior and political fraternities, with the risk of drifting into multiple forms of deviance and permissiveness.

* * *

In this situation the heroics of antiquity, and in another way the phallic omnipotence of monotheistic man, are clearly untenable. There are no supermen, proclaims the martyred Son-Father of Christianity. The only sovereignty is symbolic, propped up on the quasi-avowed sadomasochism of our desires and only thus qualifying for limitless transcendence. The libertines of the Enlightenment or the Sadean explosion went on expanding this unprecedented breakthrough, whose insights fostered a new European renaissance via the baroque. The repercussions continued with the rise of the bourgeoisie, whose moral code based on the law and its transgressions continues to hold sway today.

Given the fact of repression, there is no solution to *père-version* other than to re-verse it through sublimation. Given that no subject is not perverted (*père-vers*, toward the father) the subject can become a "glorious body" if, and only if, it confines itself to the remit of the ideal—but a resexualized ideal. Art, whether thinking as art or art as thinking, in many modulations still to come, will demonstrate the truth of this. But I don't mean to suggest that Christianity will end up as aesthetics, on the contrary. Over and above works of religious art, it is *sublimation*—at the core of the body-mind, murder-idealization transference—that reenacts the drama of the Father-Son, the metamorphosis of the Word into flesh, the transfiguration of thought-through passion. Sublimation ensures the planetary impact of all this, its human universality.

Was Teresa's the first attempt to articulate the strange status of a thought that is neither abstract understanding nor unbridled fancy? An imaginary a-thinking? That way of being is barely comprehensible to us now, and for that reason seems more enviable, trapped as we are by technologies that have turned us into alienated, profiteering robots. Meanwhile the "hard-core" perversions are being decriminalized and normalized across the secular world.

As for the death of the Father (the kenosis) that interrupts the sadomasochistic flow with the promise of resurrection, it does more than to de-eroticize incestuous passion. It throws wide open the daunting possibility of another psychic upheaval: the abolition of symbolic or paternal power itself, with all the attendant risks of mental, social, not to say biological disorders, some of which are already to be glimpsed amid the globalized desolation of the world. And yet the death of the Father is also pregnant with the great libertarian potential that comes with the end of religious constraints, but will be delivered only if we can invent fresh versions of the "loving intelligence" that was once called God, that Teresa so faithfully depicted, and to which the love known as transference is presently making its own modest and markedly unsettling contribution—invented by the still youthful discipline of psychoanalysis.

Chapter 27

A RUNAWAY GIRL

> We women have no learning . . . within us lies something incomparably
> more precious than what we see outside ourselves. Let's not imagine that
> we are hollow inside.
>
> Teresa of Avila, *The Way of Perfection*

"That saint of yours is going to kill you, give it a rest! When you're
not scouring her writings like a Benedictine, or a damn lunatic I
should say, you're on her trail! On foot, by plane, on wheels and
online, from castle to castle, from convent to monastery . . . So where are you
now? Salamanca? Toledo? Burgos? Pastrana? Slow down, for Pete's sake, do
you hear? Don't patronize me, either. You've turned into a complete workaholic!*" [*"Workaholic," like "runaway girl" in the title and passim, appear in
English in the original.—Trans.] I'm not kidding. Just my luck, me the pleasure
artist, laid-back Taoist sage, lover of eternal peace and quiet . . ."

Andrew is irate, under cover of chivalrous airs as though I were a real woman
who needed protecting by a real man. Can he think for one moment that I'd
fall for his promises to help me with anything and everything? Poor darling,
flying to the rescue of his workaholic (well, at least not alcoholic) damsel. He
couldn't even make me a cup of tea! And who is he to talk, when he's always
rushing between New York, Paris, and London? He's been acting extra virile of
late, when not affecting a touch of the aristos—that's a new one! Lord Andrew
detests the plebs, and there's nothing plebbier than working one's socks off like
poor, benighted Sylvia. The fact is, he's jealous. All my attention is on Teresa,

I don't make enough time for my American writer; he can tell my mind's else-where and I'm not really listening. I haven't got time to go to art shows with him, or to the opera to see the latest gimmicky production of *Don Giovanni*, no thanks, not even to see the first night of Halévy's *La Juive* (now there's an author awaiting his Proust).

"Are you crazy, it's four hours long!"

"It never bothered you before," Andrew says grumpily.

Before Teresa, he means. All we share now is the bed, that's something, the most essential, surely. Or is it? I think he may be wondering about that, even though he's an American writer. Oh well.

"'Workaholic' suits me," I say, pretending to take his dig as a compliment.

"It's what Louise Bourgeois used to call herself, like that, in English. She was a hard worker, addicted to it, you know." I know: the more he contrasts me with other women, the more he loves me.

* * *

My New World aesthete has been in London, making a DVD on Louise Bour-geois, who is showing at Tate Modern.[1] His admiration for this sculptor is recent; when first we met he couldn't stand the Spiders, and the Teats didn't turn him on at all. Now he's putty in her hands! It seems incongruous to find Andrew Garnett, the brooding novelist who rocks like Philip Roth (minus the wealth and the glory, but what can you do?), producing a hi-tech survey of Bourgeois' works in the Turbine Hall, but there's no mistake. Having always claimed to despise gadgetry, he's become an electronics wiz and knows all there is to know about Bourgeois.

"Getting on a bit, isn't she?" An experimental sword thrust from me.

"But still just a runaway girl," parries Andrew, with heated self-assurance.

He's right. The young Louise dropped everything: the family workshop steeped in the odor of wool dyes, the Aubusson tapestries they repaired, the suburb of Choisy-le-Roi; the libertarian mother, a reader of Zola, Louise Michel, and Rosa Luxemburg. But most crucially she dropped the libertine father, living under the family roof with his mistress Sadie, who was supposed to be the children's English governess. Adieu sweet France, gray skies, banks of the Seine: Louise ran away to marry an American history of art teacher—an Anglophone, obviously, like Sadie. She settled in New York under what she called its cutting, humorless sky (*ciel coupant qui ne plaisante pas*), and began frequenting artists with a knack for creating outlandish spaces. "Settled" is not the word, though, since the emigrant was constantly switching her aesthetic, borrowing and appropriating different styles right and left. So mutable was she that the clerics of modern art often wondered, and still do, whether this Frenchwoman possessed a style at all, whether she was "anybody" in her own right.

"Ah, they don't understand a thing, they seldom do," says Andrew, making a face. "Her style, it's . . . well, it's a *runaway* style, do you see? It's not about breaking up space, but accumulating spaces."

He's repeating himself, but it's interesting. After all, this approach to adventure is not altogether foreign to me.

"So leave Teresa alone, and come see Louise."

★ ★ ★

Andrew slots the DVD into my computer without asking. He clicks away enthusiastically. I watch the film, but I'm thinking about Teresa. Not that I say so, why bother. He's on a roll.

"Space doesn't exist, you see!" My writer's eyes are full of what he saw in London.

That austere and lively city intoxicates me, projects me inside of myself, erases me, all the opposite of New York's crystal clearness, which gets me going. In London I feel available, like an empty page, I visit, listen, read; I am receptive. My friend Juan, the Golden Age man, introduces me to his youthful fans, who learn about the new maladies of the soul with expressions of mild disgust. I let them talk, I daydream, I can't help it, it's out of my control; Christopher Marlowe put it nicely, echoing Shakespeare, or was it the other way around? "It lies not in our power to love or hate, / For will in us is overruled by fate."[2] In New York I'm like myself, I get excited, fired up, purposeful; I make efforts. I should have gone to London with Andrew and saturated myself with the Egyptians at the British Museum and Louise B at the Tate, why didn't I . . . Andrew's voice breaks in:

"Space is just a metaphor for the structure of our existence, she says." Andrew speaks solemnly, and I repress a giggle to respond in the same tone:

"So perhaps our castles, interior or exterior, are projections of our psychic lives?"

Am I here with him and Louise B, or am I still, as ever, with my Teresa?

Andrew zooms in on details, lingers on them, talks me through them, draws me into Louise's motionless travels. Like everyone in her milieu, Louise rejected religion as such, considering that 140 religions on this earth are way too many. But since she believed herself to have a religious temperament, she signed up for the 141st, which is art.

In the beginning was fear. "Fear makes the world go round." "It's the story of someone so frightened by his love that he withdraws." Fear turns into depression, together with an inexorable lowering of self-esteem. "A man and a woman lived together. On one evening he did not come back from work and she waited. She kept on waiting and she grew littler and littler. Later a neighbor stopped by out of friendship, and there he found her in the armchair the size of a pea." But it's a fortunate pea. It, or she, realizes "that you can stand anything if you write it down." She starts snatching at all the ideas buzzing around her head, buzzing through the air like flies, and converts them into pen-thoughts, pink or blue, like butterflies. Once written down, these thoughts will become drawings, then paintings, then sculptures. For the little pea discovers that sculpture alone is liberating: it's a tangible reality that encases emptiness, desertion, separation. Death. You must never think that the pea is interested in anxiety. Like her mother, it—meaning she, this woman—is conceptual, and assesses the situation objectively, scientifically, and not emotionally. "I was interested not in anxiety but in perspective, in seeing things from different points of view." And: "I am not interested in the appearance of the body; I'm interested in how things work." Obviously, since the body is a mechanism, and mechanisms are stronger than women and men and fear and death.

In the beginning was loss of innocence. "You cannot understand erotic forms if you are completely innocent, and a symbol is a symbol only if what it stands for is known." Do sexual forms provide a way out of depression or emptiness, then? She clarifies by saying that to sculpt is "to record confidence or pleasure," which take the place of depression and emptiness and modify them. Then it can be called "a formal problem," that of reorganizing the world.

And that's how the little pea became the architect of the world. The Aubusson tapestries played their part in this loss of innocence; French tradition is totally to be run away from—provided one revisits it often, it's so terribly chic! The "tapestry" is henceforth named Restif de la Bretonne, Colette and Willy, Guillaume Apollinaire, André Breton, Céline, Antonin Artaud . . . all of them French. But, for the pea/woman who "travels herself," it is also named Norman Mailer and the constellation of Americans whose courses she attends and whose

shows she sees. They initiate her into the brazenness that culminates in this tribute to Francis Bacon: his inebriation doesn't depict "things" but an "indisputably violent desire" of "terrific brutality"; "his suffering communicates." "I want
to share it." "To look at his pictures makes me alive."

* * *

From one beginning to the next, Louise Bourgeois confirms the vagabond destiny of creators from time immemorial, but especially during the twentieth
century. Among the frontiers to be crossed were those of language, political
regime, the family, the father. An absolute necessity for girls in particular, especially those who were born, like Athena, from the head of Zeus after he had
swallowed their mother Metis, goddess of crafty thought. Equally important,
never omit to jump every fence: Athena was the first, and already an accomplice of Ulysses the traveler, of course. It's essential "to free oneself" from self
and from home, and more so as a woman. "I married an American. I left France
because I freed myself, or escaped from home. . . . I was a runaway girl. I was
running away from a family situation that was very disturbing."

* * *

Hannah Arendt felt great affinity with this line from Schiller: "*Eine Mädchen
aus der Fremde*," "A maiden from afar"—seeking the father, fleeing the father.
Or rather, taking the place of the progenitor and faithful-unfaithful to the intellectual mentor; situating herself in the indefinite, cut loose from foundation.
In perpetual re-foundation, perhaps, budding forth moment by moment? "*Une
éclosion de tous les instants*": that's how Colette phrases her floral adventure in the
company of her mother, the sublime Sido, recreated by the writing of a daughter
endlessly nourished by the maternal tongue; cleaving to her rooted matrix. But
cleaving away from the father, the captain with a wooden leg, the impotent writer
with a "membered" need to write, and equally rejecting the trio of husbands—
Willy, Jouvenel, Goudeket. Melanie Klein did something similar by reinventing
psychoanalysis in order to understand mutism in children and making the cure
for desire a thought cure. Klein had to leave, first her mother, and then Mr. Klein,
who had given her three children; she had to tear herself away from German and
struggle for English; finally she had to get away from Freud himself in order to
found her own school—from depression, via matricide, to sublimation.[3]

Louise Bourgeois didn't have to resort to such brain-clutching upheavals. More recent, more modern, and a lot luckier, an American in the cosmopolitan sense, she "only" had to reinvent the terrain of her "structures of existence," and make far-fetched spaces in three dimensions. She "travels herself" (*elle se voyage*), to borrow the neologism of the journalist Stéphanie Delacour in Julia Kristeva's metaphysical detective novel, *Murder in Byzantium*.[4] Kristeva is Bulgarian by birth, French by nationality, a European citizen—and an adoptive American? She's a journalist, a psychoanalyst, a semiotician, a novelist, and how many other things? She too is made up of mobiles and kaleidoscopes . . .

The father's daughters rediscover the mother's depths when they appropriate the father's ambition, while taking tactful care of the male urge to power: "The phallus is a subject of my tenderness. . . . I lived with four men, I was the protector," explains Louise B. Had she lived today my Teresa might have endorsed that sentiment, thinking of her own family, of father-uncle-brothers, and then confessors . . . These "runaway daughters of the father" thus manage to transmute their fear, and maybe they end up not being afraid, whether of the phallus, or of betrayal, or of fear itself, the fear that petrifies most "liberated" women into hardened militants.

"A bit psycho-babbly, don't you think? These days, even in New York . . . it comes over as rather intellectual, for an artist. Not sure I'll keep that bit." Andrew moves the DVD on, unhappy with his art-star's line on phalluses. I don't blame him. I hide a smile. Men, really, ever since they turned into the second sex . . . On with our viewing!

⋆ ⋆ ⋆

It's surely a prime achievement for a sculptor to rid himself or herself of rigidity. "I dream of being a reasonable woman," is how Louise describes her latest metamorphosis. Out with stiffness and brittleness—and yet: "I was supposed to apologize for being only a girl. My brother was born later, of course." "Ever since I was born, I was pushed into constant rivalry with other people." Is that any reason to bend? To throw in the towel? Of course not! Though it's never definitive, let's try to attain serenity without dependency. "I feel good. I feel independent."

Teresa "feels" as well, there's no doubt about that, she burns with longing to feel herself being this or that. They were all at it, during the late sixteenth century: "little Seneca," the towering John of the Cross, "Doctor in *Nada*," cares only for "substantial words," the kind that resonate viscerally, in the flesh, that are one with substance. If the soul were to be told, "'Be thou good,' it would then substantially be good."[5] Loyola's *Spiritual Exercises* had the Jesuits wrap up their meditations with the "application of the five senses": after cogitating they were to find repose in looking, listening, tasting, touching, smelling. Teresa, however, has no need to "apply" herself, for simplemindedness or *bobería* comes naturally to her, she boasts of it, it's a state that does not cancel the intellect but subordinates it to simplicity: "Here there is no demand for reasoning, but for knowing what as a matter of fact [*con llaneza*] we are and for placing ourselves with simplicity [*con simpleza*] in God's presence, for He desires the soul to become ignorant [*boba*] in His presence, as indeed it is."[6] And the more this ignoramus feels, the more she feels herself, and the more she senses her friends and enemies, until she feels, and becomes, independent. Independent *with* His Majesty or *of* His Majesty? It makes no difference, since He was inside her by the time she began to write and to make foundations. She feels both things at once. The writing, fighting Madre is also a "runaway girl," indeed the epitome of one—she who is always escaping from what precedes her toward what exceeds her and always re-founding herself by founding institutions. *Tutti a cavallo* . . . "Everything depends on your ability to sublimate," says Louise's voice on the DVD.

Is there a deconstruction of the father going on? Some of Bourgeois' works, like *The Destruction of the Father*, would make us think so. Andrew's film has wicked fun with this one, shadowing the artist through her labyrinth of paternal forms with an unabashed pleasure in their vacillations between tumescence and detumescence, deformation and formation. Suddenly my favorite filmmaker starts horsing around, I like him best like this, playing the fool without his deep-and-serious-writer mask on. He whirls away from the computer and bounces around me like a chimpanzee, shrieking at the top of his voice:

"Hey, Nobodaddy, Nobodaddy, Nobodaddy! Why art thou silent and invisible, father of jealousy? Why dost thou hide thyself in clouds from every searching eye?"[7]

* * *

Has La Bourgeois bewitched him? Jigging and giggling, oblivious of the deconstructive Seventies, Andrew is a carnival king. With a few lines of rhyming verse, he flies off into unbearable father love, it's hysterically funny; is libertarian

Christianity alone in legitimating and cultivating such a thing? Jesus the imagination is a silky tiger made of wrath and pity, and the revolution will be libidinal or it will not be. I dare you, go cross swords with the Commander, go taunt Daddy, see how you make out at squishing him into Nobodaddy! A burlesque dig here, an obscene jibe there, poor old fellow left to rot, coughing and cowering, who "jumps up off his seat and turns thrice three times around," some passion! Nowhere else has Daddy love, confessed to death, pushed artists and others not belonging to that weird species into such a rebellious, savage tenderness, the banality of evil revised and corrected, male anality rehashed to the nth degree. They call it freedom and Andrew is acting it out to me this minute, jabbing a faux-sardonic finger at the ceiling.

"'That ole Nobodaddy got stuck up there, burping and farting without a care! He read out a big sermon that made heaven shake, and then got to yelling for William Blake!' That's pretty good, getting Blake in there. In subtitles, or as voice-over? 'Why darkness and obscurity in all thy words and laws, that none dare eat the fruit but from the wily serpent's jaws? Or is it because secrecy gains females' wild applause?'" My friend is getting quite carried away, capering and cackling; then he stops dead, and strikes a Gallic pose. "'Upon seeing this, the moon blushed scarlet.' Curtain."

He stares at me with dark, crazed eyes. He's not laughing now.

Silence.

If he only knew how his clowning vindicated my own very personal theology . . . But let's not go there.

"Shall I paste that into Bourgie's film? What d'you reckon? Too strong for her, maybe? Oh, she blasphemes with her dad's organ all right, bingo! But it's like she envies him . . . or like she's holding back even so, do you feel that or not? Couldn't be further from my poet-engraver, anyway. Uncommercial maniac."

I think of Teresa, it's far from her too: she's into chess, not chisels.

"Mind you, Louise ain't so bad for a woman. We'll see at the editing stage. Ready for the rest?"

He presses Play, more calmly.

* * *

I understand his disquiet. Louise's hand-to-hand combat with her father is also an indefatigable reweaving of the maternal web: it's the restoration of Joséphine, the mother who was her companion in depression as much as in good sense. Before the artist found out how "ridiculous" life is. Becoming a mother herself—an experience Louise B accompanies and reflects, like a refracting mirror—led her inevitably to this detachment; but most mothers don't know it. Andrew's heroine, who is not an ordinary mother (But what woman is? Certainly not Madre Teresa!) turns space into a kind of fecund receptacle, a topography of udders and breasts. Cows, sows, women, all are "interesting, moving, live and flexible landscapes." We're a long way from your subtle dwelling places, Teresa, my love! Apart from the flexibility, the liveliness, the mobility, a certain simplemindedness, *alma boba* . . .

Warlike violence nonetheless persists beneath the decorous indecency that is always being petted and cajoled. It simmers like the tantrum of a child who is loved and yet quick to flare up, flounce off, blow her top. Who can stand anything if she writes it down and then makes of it a sculpture, which is her preferred script.

But then is this nomad nothing but an eternal adolescent, a phallus worshipper cloaking the dreamer of breasts? What is a woman, in the end? A woman must dare to be "arrogant and ambitious," declares my writer's latest muse. Great! Anything else? I won't tell Andrew that Louise sounds like a feminist from Milwaukee, because I do know by now that if a woman isn't minimally arrogant or ambitious she simply is not, period. But then . . . Oh, it would take too long, you'd have to write a novel!

Every beginning is a new life "organized around hollowness." That's quite a discovery. Does it apply to the female body? Maybe, or it's an overstatement, we'll see. For the time being the pea-woman is a "house-woman," necessarily an empty one like the empty homes it/she left behind, clearly "a metaphor for existence," for abandoned, abandoning, abandonistic space. Excellent start if you want to become a sculptor, or sculp*tress*. Nice and particular, without precluding an element of the general. And so it was, claims Andrew's film, that the arrogant and ambitious little pea took on the great Bernini himself, Gian Lorenzo Bernini, seventeenth-century virtuoso, Italian sculptor, architect, decorator, painter, playwright, and poet. Good gracious, that's someone I didn't expect to meet at Tate Modern! He adored La Madre and was the first, in my humble opinion the only, artist to see her with the eyes of a marveling connoisseur, in a way that still shocks the faithful. I have knelt before his sculpture in Santa Maria della Vittoria (not before Teresa, who only exists in her writings). Andrew doesn't need to know this; it's my secret garden. I've said too much already and can't take any more of his sarcasm; today we are at the altar of the contemporary.

In the video still unfolding on my plasma screen, Louise pays due homage to the master of the baroque. But she objects to his love of drapery: "There was no emptiness [in this work], not an inch that was not filled with folds, as if emptiness was Bernini's enemy."[8] It takes guts to stand before the Praxiteles of modern times and dedicate to him a great galumphing ball with a hole inside! Come off it, Louise!

I stop myself there.

"Hang on, hang on . . . from one beginning to the next . . ." Andrew's squeezing it for all it's worth. We are treated to *Eye to Eye*, *Blind Mind's Bluff*, *Harmless Woman*, *In and Out*, and *Passage dangereux*, in sequence.

"Hey, did Louise ever go into analysis?" I'm reading a statement that's splashed on the screen in an achingly avant-garde font: "Unconscious is something which is volcanic in tone, and yet you cannot do anything about it, you better be its friend, you better accept it and even love it if you can, because it might get the better of you, you never know."

No answer. Andrew looks smug to have caught me out on my home ground. I continue, in a careless voice:

"Well, she's read her stuff, as artists go! She talks the talk . . ."

"Yes," murmurs Andrew, "but it's embodied in the space of the works. That's where words get canceled out, you see, in bronze, iron, glass, wood . . ."

He sounds husky and thoughtful, he really admires her.

* * *

B kept a diary, noting down the fleeting ideas or "butterfly-thoughts" that helped her to keep depression at bay. Those thoughts fed and illuminated the gestures of making. Finally the made objects in turn evolved into a mishmash of borrowings from here and there, a multifarious bric-a-brac compacted into private, provisional spaces, the thresholds of new departures. Plural landscapes of rebirth, labyrinthine buddings with multiple facets, kaleidoscopes of absent identities, polymorphous ambiguities, polytopical vitality.

"It's a female thing, isn't it, this perpetual starting over, you'd think it was a whole different person," muses Andrew. Is he wondering aloud, or stating a fact? "Nietzsche was the great pioneer . . . but he went mad."

"Syphilis, I believe."

After all, I don't really know. I think of Teresa's re-foundings, her perpetual variations upon those same but always different states of prayer, loss, exile, loss of self, selflessness in Majesty, elucidation . . .

The repeated new starts that characterize the trajectory of Louise B are not just psychological stages in a therapy of survival. In her borrowings from analysis, self-analysis, and, inevitably, the "intertextuality" of contemporary art, most art critics have merely seen the "subjective cures" of an idiosyncratic artist rather too involved with her own moods. But observed close up in Andrew's video, these artistic departures don't strike me as illustrative. Instead they seem to be generated by their own products, in an oeuvre of sudden leaps and eternal returns. In the later, more mature achievements, they manage to condense the ruptures and reprises into polymorphous geometries. Neither a cubist nor a surrealist, although bearing the marks of both "schools," Louise B juxtaposes without breaking and links without isolating.

"I like *Cells* the best." I'm only saying that because it's a good idea to have a favorite work when approaching an artist. I've picked one: *Cells*.

These cells—whether the units that comprise a sculpture or an installation, or the actual series entitled *Cells*—are not impenetrable castles. They are merely embryos or shards of life, calling out to one another. Sometimes the link between them is conducted via mirrors, which like the membrane partitions that demarcate the rooms inside Teresa's interior castle, protect the impregnable singularity of the alveoli. But there are paradoxical gangways between the enclosures: oneiric narrative threads, unthinkable and yet now peaceful anecdotes, open to the gaze.

Take *Cell (You Better Grow Up)*, from 1993. Andrew's lens slides as lovingly as his prose over the materials, hugs the surfaces, brushes the contours. Steel, glass, marble, ceramic, wood. Here the polyphony of textures materializes in the diversity of forms and voids. A ring of phallic cylinders, old favorites with Louise, variously erect or flabby, twist in this particular *Cell* like granulated substances heaped into towers, liable to blow away or to collapse. The erectile, sperm-fat Babels of earlier periods are starker here, in these twists of broken glass. Crystals pile up, spinning skyward—threatening at every moment to dwindle, thin, deflate, lured earthward, tempted to come crashing down. On another plane in the same cohabited space, three hands poke up, straight out of another era, Greek, Renaissance, or baroque. It might be a child's two hands in an adult one, or else a man's two hands folded in prayer, clasped by a woman's hand, or vice versa. A glass-paned pagoda stands like a transparent hourglass counting the seconds, which this sculpture will not allow to become petrified; our participative contemplation flows through it. Light spirals over the curves of the building. Three circular, pivoting mirrors encompass these objects, mingle and dissolve them, fracture and recompose them. Not forgetting the spectators and visitors roped into the pirouette of art by these membrane-mirrors, their inner children rediscovering long-lost fantasy caves: the title reminds them that they'd better grow up. Maybe moving into one of these cells is a fine way to do it . . .

Andrew pours himself a drink. I remain before the screen, watching the documentary.

★ ★ ★

"Or maybe I'll go for *Topiary IV*, takes up less room than the so-called *Cells*. Just right for my apartment on place d'Italie?" I can't stop teasing him.

After birds, my favorite beings on earth are trees and shrubs. Like outsize flowers, not content to defy beauty but challenging the tempests of time, they seem to embody the best of human yearning. *Topiary IV*, from 1999, is a kind of tree-woman, the anti-mermaid par excellence. Instead of swapping her lower body for a fishtail that dreams of water, the tree-woman knows that one day her legs will give way and she'll be on crutches before she dies. But she keeps her lower woman's body, sporting a flimsy adolescent frock below the profusely ramifying crown. Her sap has risen, and despite her scanty foliage the tree-woman continues to beguile us with jeweled clusters along her branches. A hybrid made of steel, fabric, beads, and wood, for me this shrub is the heavenly resurrection of Beckett's *Not I*. Sometimes a male or female artist, female in the present case, manages to attain the psychic plasticity that transforms a failing body into a blossoming tree.

But Teresa does that too, Andrew, wait! I haven't got there yet! Let's see more of your Louise meanwhile.

Oh, this sculpted shrub is nothing like the flowering cherry of the teenager's body, and yet its bunches of emerald, raspberry, or purple beads caught in the looking glass of time have a vitality that reminds me irresistibly of the freshness of the cherry trees under the Great Wall of China, where I stood in admiration, dreaming I was pregnant. As Andrew and I gaze at it now, the *Topiary* body seems to be clad in an elegant white satin shift or a teenager's nightgown, but the body's missing a leg, she can't stand up, she needs a crutch, the artist makes no bones about it. And yet for all its dry branches and trunk, the organism grows tall, sprouting and budding—if not into juicy flavors, then into emerald gems. The seduction of crystallization. And what wonderful details: the arms of the artist-arbor, snaking out like the limbs of a Hindu divinity, are full of surprises! Two garnet-colored raspberries, when we expected pink! Plus, I ask you, what's that sort of orange wineskin doing in a female head that's a leafless tree tipped with blossoms? Is it a nest for butterflies or caterpillars? Or, given that black hole it's got, is it a watchful eye, mocking so much assurance on the part of a woman artist, even a runaway one?

At the end of *In Search of Lost Time*, Proust saw his characters mounted on stilts. They had grown because their bodies incorporated the time of years and turned it into space. Only one of them didn't age, Odette, the cocotte, associated in the writer's mordant imagination with his own mother, how blasphemous is that! Odette (and/or the mother) stops time inside her: men can age or grow, she'll remain in bloom until the end, in spite of everything.[9] The femininity of Louise B, outside time in its own way, is not afraid to stand tall like a tree of life in defiance of death, laughing at death. Teresa's the same, which is odd for a Carmelite, isn't it? You'll see . . .

* * *

Andrew has finished his whiskey and gets back into gear, clicking on this and that, coming up with more surprises.

"Look at that! I'll take *Seven in Bed*, how's that for a Tantric dream?"

What does he see in these lewdly entwined rag dolls? A three-way orgy mixed with a four-way swinger's party, at least three of the figures have two heads . . . Bisexuality, incest, and betrayal. The hurts inflicted on Louise B, in childhood or early youth, are apparent here in rose-tinted version. Are the nestling bodies deceased, aligned in a sarcophagus and already petrified by the lava of memory, that bestows innocence but does not purify? Or are they floating in a state of weightlessness, in some ultra-ecstasy beyond sexual pleasure, in postwrestling reconciliation? Human puppets either way, makeshift stuffed bolsters, tacky and ugly, touching and touched. Evil has not disappeared into some banality or other, but suffering has been staunched by the urge to hug; touch, that most essential of the senses, can be seen and felt in this "sculpture." Does it posit the victory of the breast over every other kind of eroticism, exhibited, assumed, and dealt with at last? Not really. It represents the same search for the origins of space (the metaphor of our desires, according to Louise B) that her work tirelessly inquires into—in ricochets, with no end in sight.

* * *

Teresa veiled her body, she had no choice, modesty and faith required it. But the fiction enacted in her foundations stripped her bare, embraced the Spouse, and diffused their caresses as felt by her—a majestic solitary orgy, a polytopical, kaleidoscopic vitality—through centuries to come. And in all innocence. If Andrew doesn't want to know, that's his problem. From the heights of the Tate Modern he looks pityingly down on me, stuck God knows where with my saint. He only has eyes for Louise B, who's old enough to be his mother or grandmother, as if I cared. We all have our fictions.

It is fate. "It lies not in our power to love or hate . . ." He hands me a glass of claret, closes the computer, kisses my cleavage, and pulls me toward the bed.

Chapter 28

"GIVE ME TRIALS, LORD; GIVE ME PERSECUTIONS"

Comfort me with apples . . .

Song of Solomon

A total transformation into God, as what Teresa went through—albeit momentary and climaxing with a translucent castle—is still a living sculpture carved out with blows of programmed death. Andrew admires the edifice and the haste; my pleasure lies in detecting the survival that germinates in the work of death. Ah, the space-time of women! As a child I never cared for snowmen, I used to dig with frozen fingers into the thick, crisp crust in order to free the snowdrops. There had to be some.

$$\star \ \star \ \star$$

To merge with the murdered Lord until the husband-Father becomes a brother-husband, a double, an alter ego, is more than a passion for Teresa, it's her way to be. To suffer through and for Jesus is hard, but given her complete confidence in His existence, His approval, and her future recompense in the form of His eternal grace, this hardship is clearly preferable to unsatisfied desire and the want of love that damages health as a symptom of hysteria. Teresa knows it and spells it out: "I am my usual self, for trials are health and medicine for me."[1] The tribulations prompted by the fantasy of reciprocal love relieve her somatic conversions, migraines, and convulsions; the heartaches of love are always "trials," but far from being experienced as maladies, they are like vehicles of healing to her. In the spiritual life, "everything seems to be a heavy burden, and *rightly so*, because it involves a war against ourselves."[2]

All trials and all persecutions remind her of those Jesus endured, so they can only be glorious. This narcissistic reward, as well as a phallic assumption into identification with the Lord in His troubles, is felt in the short and long term as intense pleasure: "Give me trials, Lord; give me persecutions."[3] Teresa longs for these with complete sincerity, before she gets to reap the still more gratifying rewards of the art of victory. But since the duty of humility most often forbids her to articulate her satisfaction, not to say her personal glorification, all her pleasure will be in "somehow imitating the laborious life that Christ lived."[4] Being without self, her *jouissance* derives from the Other: entirely projected into the Other, she is the Other's protecting, saving, nonperson.

At that point a further step is possible: the praying woman gives herself leave to consider the pact with the ideal Father as a matrimonial contract, or rather a patrimonial and indeed notarial one, under the rules of a kind of universal community of assets ("what is Yours is mine"). This alliance between proprietors confers on Teresa a far higher dignity than the unlikely "honor" she had struggled for hitherto. *La honra* is only vanquished by virtue of this most seigneurial (*con señorío*) marital agreement, and the "friendship" of the divine Father, by whose side she walks for the duration of the Passion, can be received as comfort and more, as a rightful property:

> And the Lord said: "You already know of the *espousal* between you and Me [*ya sabes el desposorio que hay entre ti y Mí*]. Because of this espousal, *whatever I have is yours*. So I give you all the trials and sufferings I underwent, and by these means, *as with something belonging to you*, you can make requests of My Father [*con esto puedes pedir a mi Padre como cosa propia*]. Although I had heard we *share* these [*somos participantes de esto*], now I had heard it in such a different way that it seemed I felt great dominion [*pareció había quedado con gran señorío*]. The *friendship* in which this favor was granted me cannot be described here. . . . since then I look very differently upon what the Lord suffered, as something belonging to me—and it gives me great *comfort* [*como cosa propia, y dame gran alivio*]."[5]

Extolling the rights, duties, and benefits of suffering, your most radical passages employ the pronoun "she," my exiled Teresa. Who is this *she*? The human soul? The female soul? The Bride in the Song of Songs? It's your own soul you observe, Teresa, but from so close that its/your contours are blurred, there is no more I, I is overlaid by her, absorbed in her. But you are not erased by this osmosis into the nonperson, you grow bigger by it, and create another, impersonal I; "I" becomes a nonperson in the Christian faith you hoist to its zenith by ceaselessly transcending yourself in your ideal Him, until you become Him. Although you call her "she," it's a selfless, sexless "I" that rejoices in being the Other in you, in all senses and meanings, burned away in a wholesale cleansing that is itself re-sexualized. By "putting a cross" over your person, you are not interring yourself, as the ingenuous might think; you are exiling yourself "in majesty." Among apples, as in the Song of Solomon: "Comfort me with apples." "Asking to be sustained doesn't seem to me to involve a request for death but for life and the desire to serve in some way the One to whom she owes so much."[6]

The transference that transmutes suffering into fruitful jubilation comes at a cost: carnal fulfillment must be renounced, and persecution endured, although you exaggerate the latter at times, as though every moment of your life were a battle. Exhausting, no doubt—but a great deal more bracing than the repose of ennui between bouts of somatization. The benefits of outwitting your harassers far outweigh the drawbacks of being harassed: you obtain the reunion with the Great Other, which not only satisfies an incestuous desire to possess the Father, but also promises the grace of your metamorphosis through the Word that He is, into Eternity. By your work as a founder and re-founder, you taunt the passage of time with spaces of rebirth that are secluded and yet noticeable, incisive. You broaden the course of the world; your way of being, your deeds and your writing drive it outside of itself; with the Other and like the Other, you are outside time.

This surplus *jouissance* (*plus de jouir*) in your total transference, which nonbelievers regard as fanciful and affords scant consolation even to regular believers, becomes a physical reality for you, Teresa: the joy of the union with the Beloved is so powerful that it obliterates the perception of ill-being and transforms it into continual jubilation, perpetual acquiescence.

Having reached this fork in the road of psychic experience, you choose neither of the two paths available; but you definitely tilt toward the second.

* * *

The first is mortification. Your guilt at transgressing the prohibition (of incest, of carnality), magnified by and through your identification with the sacrificed Father-Son, turns you into a dab hand with scourges and hair shirts. You flagellate yourself diligently, nothing special, until you add an extra twist: your niece Teresita swears she's seen you rubbing nettles on the welts. There, how's that for pain! Malicious tongues, out of envy or cynicism, wax ironic on the disinfectant properties of nettles. Even if you knew of this, I doubt there have been many volunteers for such a biting balm. Fasting days are prescribed by the liturgical calendar, but one is welcome to fast more, and you often do. In addition, as an intermittent but proud anorexic, you make yourself throw up by tickling the back of your throat with a goose feather—a quill too far! But that's the kind of refinement a nun thinks up when competing with the sisters. You want to be the first, the best, the only one to merit the Other's grace.

For twenty years, and more intensely from 1591 to 1597, more than 1,500 people testified before the Sacred Congregation of Rites for the Counter-Reformation Church to beatify, and then canonize, Teresa of Avila. After death her sanctity rested upon the basis of this collective memory, detailed in the numerous depositions whose accuracy was no doubt tinged with subjectivity. But the reports concurred on one point: Teresa inflicted appalling injuries on herself. "There was nothing she liked more than to martyr her body for the sake of our Lord" (Ana de la Trinidad); "Her haircloth is made of sharp-edged patches to cut the flesh into bleeding wounds" (María de San Ángel); "Her body is covered in sores caused by the scourge and the hair shirt" (Ana de San Bartolomé, her nurse, who testified that even when she was old and sick, Teresa went in for savage penances); "This was a woman who disciplined herself so often that her confessors grew concerned; owing to her constant use of the cilice, her skin was permanently raw, despite her frequent illnesses and convulsive fits" (Beatriz de Jesús); "This torture was so excessive that the confessors often had to intervene" (Alonso de los Ángeles). But Teresa persisted, even when her sores became infected: "The wounds on her body grew empoisoned and turned into pus-filled sacs" (Ana de la Madre de Dios). The precision of these accounts suggests they were genuine observations, not the histrionic hyperbole of zealous companions trying to boost her chances.[7]

Nevertheless, you frowned on the reckless mortifications of friends such as Mariano de San Benito, and even on John of the Cross's elaborate taste for pain. Nor had you any sympathy for women who are always miserable, plaintive, and ailing; you hated any such weakness in yourself. It's one thing to take care of nuns who are poorly: the *Constitutions* prescribe it; but too much melancholy is unacceptable. Sisters, beware! Even love, supposed to be the universal remedy, often induces a lamentable mushiness.

"But I thought Love was our God, Madre?" simpers María Bautista. She is a crooked soul who cannot help being disingenuous and will ultimately prove treacherous.

"Certainly it is, but mind: it must be virile love." Teresa stares at her with eagle eye. "I would not want you, my daughters, to be womanish in anything, nor would I want you to be like women but like strong men."[8]

"Like men?!" Cheeky scrap, either pretending to be dim or else asking to be punished.

"The soul understands that so as to reign more sublimely, the only true way is that of suffering. You know that much, María Bautista, don't you?"[9]

The unfortunate girl didn't expect such a put-down. Had she forgotten that the truly virile way was to be put to death? That the worst humiliations, when endured in place of the Man, are glorious? Her initiation has only just begun.

Teresa doesn't let go yet. With regal poise she seizes a rotten cucumber from the table and proffers it to her insolent cousin, transfixing her with the same predatory stare.

"I order you to go plant this in the ground."

The sarky girl musters up a last show of sham obsequiousness, which does her case no good at all:

"Shall it go upright, or sideways?"

"Sideways!" And with that the superior turns on her heel in disgust. Teresa de Jesús has better things to do than to linger where it stinks of women.[10]

* * *

You are implacable, Madre, when it comes to the frailties of young nuns. Such as those who seek permission to leave one Carmel for another, right after taking their vows of enclosure: the very idea! General Juan Bautista Rubeo himself authorized one sister to move to a different convent, because she didn't like the climate! Whatever next? "The devil doesn't want anything else except to foster the opinion that something like a transfer is possible."[11] You warn Fr. Gratian against such lax indulgence, for you understand "women's nature" better than he. Is it that self-knowledge you have, of yourself as a woman, that drives you to be so callous? You add, "It is better that some die than that all be harmed."[12]

You surprise yourself by thinking such thoughts aloud, but the sisters don't appear alarmed. You've drummed it into them, after all, that there's no better life than to die for the sake of the Lord.

Sadism? Masochism? An urge to raise yourself to the level of the humiliated Phallus, suffering/rejoicing in that humiliation? Words are inadequate to describe the ever-praised sacrifice that enables you to dream of being at one with the Other's Passion, and yet to find yourself forever wanting, forever falling short of Him.

* * *

You have a horror of the weak, the crippled, and the mad ("melancholics," manic-depressives). You don't let them in, there's no place in your convents for them. But what if a woman succumbs to ill-being when she's already inside? What would happen if an elite nun, the kind you welcome, lost her reason? *There's* a grievous trial for you! Why? You're not upset for that person's sake, my prideful Teresa. That sort of modern, humanistic, bourgeois notion is still a long way off, even if your blissful osmosis with the Other is preparing the ground, along tortuous and unsuspected paths, for its emergence. No, you are sorry because mental illness in a nun is liable to unsettle all the others, as you write to Mother María de San José in Seville. The order takes precedence over all else: your compassion is simply a form of perfectionism. For that matter, compassion is not the right word: "Perhaps a thrashing will get her to stop screaming. This wouldn't do her any harm."[13] You've said it. With melancholics, "use punishment; if light punishment is not enough, try heavy; if one month in the prison cell is not enough, try four months."[14]

Your severity becomes legendary, and while your followers are all for it, your enemies brand you a criminal. Rumor has it you're an ogre, a bully who enjoys abusing her flock, more a witch than a mother! Well, people are notoriously quick to speak ill of nuns, but watch out, the Inquisition pricks up its ears at this sort of talk.

"The reformed Carmelites tie each other up by the wrists and ankles and flog each other! That's what people are saying, Mother. The woman who left the Seville convent, María del Corro, is accusing Isabel de San Jerónimo and you, too, Mother, of such practices." Your daughters wonder, whispering, whether the gossip could be true. Little Teresita is dismayed: What if it were? Tell us it's not so, Auntie, unless . . .

"Please God they're saying nothing worse!" You kick it into the long grass, rather than deny it outright. The compulsion to domination over yourself ("lord of all the elements and of the world")[15] and others must inevitably lead to some gratuitous nastiness toward your "daughters," and they don't spare you either, as we've seen. The cruelty of female passion!

* * *

In fact, your line on religious suffering is not fixed. In this as in other dwelling places, you are never buoyed by certainty, you waver, groping toward the right path, slipping between the walls of the translucent diamond of your soul. Suffering is the way, agreed. But not absolutely, not always, not to the end. The *Constitutions* enshrine certain rules, of course, while allowing some leeway for initiative and indulgence:

> Work with a time limit should never be given to the Sisters. Each one should strive to work so that the others might have food to eat. They should take into careful account what the rule ordains (that *whoever wants to eat must work*) and what St. Paul did. If someone should volunteer to take on a fixed daily amount of work, she may do so but ought not to be given a penance if she fails to finish it.[16]

The rules limit some penances:

"Should the Lord give a Sister the desire to perform mortification, she should ask permission. This good, devotional practice should not be lost, for some benefits are drawn from it. *Let it be done quickly so as not to interfere with the reading.*"[17]

If punishments are designed to conduct the body toward the Christly ideal, reading could perform the same job, if wisely directed. Would you instate reading in place of penitence?

In response to other infringements, however, you gave yourself free rein— with considerable and undisguised glee:

> She should likewise be punished who says something falsely about another. And she should also be obliged to restore, in so far as possible, the good name of the one whose reputation was harmed. And the one who is accused should not respond unless ordered to do so, and then should do so humbly, saying "*Benedicite.*" And if she answers impatiently, she should receive a heavier penalty, according to the discretion of the presider.[18]

You are even wise enough to acknowledge the existence of desires that "offer something good," as distinct from the egregiousness of "violent thirst." What's the difference? Unacceptable desires are those whose pain is so "sweet and delightful" that we, being "indiscreet," "never think we can have enough of this pain."[19] You suspect this melancholy masochism of being fomented by the devil, who "tempts one to perform indiscreet penances" purely to wreck one's health, "take away one's reason," and render one finally "deranged."[20] You are certainly the last person who would ever encourage such deviations! We are guilty enough at birth, aren't we? No need for the devil's "stratagems"! Your successors, when they completed the regulations, classified potential "faults" in five chapters appended to your section entitled "On the Chapter of Grave Faults." They were numbered in ascending order, from light faults (49), medium faults (50), and grave faults (51), to "graver faults" (52), culminating in the "gravest faults" (53). You personally counsel prudence in the management of passions, showing your consummate proficiency at settling human scores: "the punishment should be given after the anger has subsided."[21] It's always sensible to postpone the reckoning, my subtle Teresa; what is to be done with passionate love and hate, joy and suffering, except give them time to percolate into the senses, to attach to words, and with any luck, to be illuminated in thoughts? Always postpone: *Sea el castigo después de la pasión aplacada.* No vindictiveness, no sanctions in the heat of the moment.

All in all, you are for punishment with a cool head, never in anger. Because raw emotion, whether painful or pleasurable, is a *jouissance* that summons another; it leaves little room for judicious decisions. You, on the contrary, are lucid in passion, my moderate Teresa. You don't trust your moments of incontinence, your penchant for punishing yourself and others is quite objective. Is this to appease the expert torture-mistress in you, Teresa? Good luck with that!

You go as far as calling yourself "not very penitential," and I guess you're right in comparison to other paragons, like Antonio de Jesús or Catalina de Cardona, to name a couple. In 1576, the more moderate flagellant you had lately become wrote to Fr. Mariano:

> I have to laugh that Fray Padre Juan de Jesús [Roca] says I want you all to go barefoot, for I am the one who always *opposed* this to Padre Fray Antonio. He would have found out that *he was mistaken* had he asked me. My intention was to attract people of talent, for they would be *frightened away by a lot of*

austerity. What was set down was only so as to distinguish ourselves from the other Carmelites. . . . What I have insisted on with him is that the friars be given *good meals*. . . . The other thing I urged that he impose is manual work . . . Understand, padre, that *I am fond of strictness in the practice of virtue but not of austerity*, as you see in our houses of nuns. This is perhaps so because *I am not very penitential*.[22]

In your view, then, suffering is not the one and only "true way," but a means among others—a secondary means?—for attaining the spiritual ideal. In any case it is subordinate to joy, which takes precedence in your experience of faith understood as a wholly fulfilled love. But pain is not entirely discarded, either; how could it be, when your ideal Father is a "beaten Father," like Jesus, or like don Alonso Sánchez? But you still prefer its sublimation in reading, and even more in writing, which became your "true way" after 1560.

$$* \ * \ *$$

Language is not the only ruse you deploy against rampant masochism. I like to imagine, Teresa, my love, that your dolorism lessened in the same proportion as you became more aware of the eroticized (and preconscious?—no, highly conscious) link with your confessors.

A lot of water has flowed under the bridge since your very first visions and trances, since the sighting of Jesus's severe countenance or of that horrid swollen toad. You don't suppress your desire for the Other or for others any more than anyone else, indeed rather less, as we have seen over and over. Aged sixty-one, on June 15, 1576, you embark on a perilous idyll with your confessor Jerome Gratian; it must surely have had an erotic side, no matter how platonic in practice. It's you I choose to believe on this point, rather than the slanders passed on to the Inquisition. Cloistered, clad in shapeless rough wool, full of repentance as you are, this romantic friendship authorized and reciprocated by Gratian himself channels desire and redirects its turbulence away from the ever-lurking temptations of self-harm. How restful!

"Although . . . I reflected that this suffering would be very beneficial to my soul, all these actions helped me little. For the fear didn't go away, and what I felt was a vexing war. I chanced upon a letter in which my good Father [Gratian] refers to what St. Paul says, that God does not permit us to be tempted beyond what we can suffer."[23]

After meeting Gratian, the flesh would no longer be an obstacle. Present or absent, the close friend's body was more than a dream: it became another incarnate, guilt-free fantasy.

"One night I was very distressed because it had been a long time since I had heard from my Father [Gratian]. . . . He suddenly appeared to me . . . coming along the road, happy and with a white countenance. . . . And I wondered if all the light and brilliance that comes from our Lord makes [people in Heaven] white. I heard: 'Tell him to begin at once, without fear . . .' It couldn't have been my imagination."[24]

This was reassurance. If Gratian shared in the "holy humanity" of Jesus—and your love was so strong that you amalgamated the priestly father with the ideal Father—then there was no reason to feel guilty or to literally beat yourself up!

And you went further, Teresa. You invited the gaze of your correspondent Jerome Gratian to creep under your habit, to crawl over your bare skin, and not by itself: a toad—no, a lizard this time, anyway a critter, was there too:

Oh, *mi padre*, what a terrible thing happened to me! While we were sitting on a haystack considering ourselves lucky to have found it, next to an inn that we were unable to enter, *a large salamander or lizard got in between my tunic and my bare arm*, and it was the mercy of God that *it didn't get in somewhere else*, for I think I would have died, judging from what I felt.[25]

You are a wicked flirt, Teresa, a perverse little girl, an irresistible seductress armed with a diamantine pen. You submerge the sorrow of lovelessness into the four waters of prayer, you wash it clean and dissolve it in the trust you have in the infinite sublimation within you, that jewel of your carnal being. In short, you drown "all things" and their "nothingness" in that magical charm of yours, which priests and nuns alike have fallen for, hooked by your compelling, seductive motherliness.

By allowing yourself these "friendships"—though you're not deceived about them, thank God—suffering and passivity in the mind are experienced better than ever with detachment, *dejamiento*. You are "altered" in the Other (as I call your "exile" toward the Beloved), but since this "alteration" slips between your tunic and your bare skin, but gets no farther, you turn into placidity what some would have felt as alienation. You are altered, not alienated. The symptoms and other penances are converted into a kind of effortless cooperation with His Majesty's Voice, and this sustains you through the other cooperations you might be involved in, including with "distracted" or "corrupt" people:

"I understood well that these effects didn't come from me, nor did I gain them through my diligence, for there wasn't even time for that. . . . I do hardly anything on my part . . . it is the Lord who does everything. . . . souls upon whom the Lord bestows these favors . . . could be placed in the company of *any kind of people*. Even if these people are *distracted and corrupt*."[26]

This kind of detachment, without efforts or judgments, does not require any physical punishment. Preached by Osuna, explored from the very beginning of your monastic life, *dejamiento* becomes—together with writing, and the bonds formed by dint of making foundations—a cheerful serenity tinged with moral masochism, accepted as a chastening deserved, and meekly consented to: "It calls for great humility to be silent at seeing oneself condemned without fault."[27]

* * *

In the ardor of her ascesis, Teresa exhibits an ambiguity that gives rise to the second path her dolorism would follow before being quieted at last. She often writes to criticize too much intemperance in pain, warning her brother Lorenzo, for instance: "Don't take the discipline any more than is mentioned [in my letter], in no way should it be taken more than twice a week."[28] Already in the *Life*, Teresa had argued that to "long to be martyrs"[29] often indicates a demonically inspired failure of humility. With insistent ambiguity, though, she delivers her body to the very martyrdom she has just advised against:

Since I am so sickly, I was always tied down without being worth anything until I determined to pay *no attention to the body or to my health*. Now what I do doesn't amount to much; but since God desired that I understand this trick of the devil, who put the thought in my head that I would lose my health, I said: What difference does it make if I die; or at the thought of rest, I answered: I no longer need rest but the cross.[30]

But she is still seeking some precious balance. "It seems to me now that this kind of procedure is a desire to *reconcile body and soul* so as to *preserve one's rest here below and enjoy God up above*. And if we walk in justice and *cling to virtue*, this will come about."[31] Extreme austerity being the devil's gain, the temptation to look "more penitential than anyone" must be resisted and the supreme challenge faced: to obey her confessors or the mother superior, "since the greatest perfection lies in obedience."[32]

Teresa couldn't fail to be impressed by the spectacular mortifications performed by Catalina de Cardona at Pastrana. This highborn lady had left the court to spend eight years living in a cave, with only beasts for company, eating roots, and inflicting ghastly tortures on herself.[33] Then she came to the reformed Carmel, in somewhat mannish garb, and continued with her extreme program of penitence. Half wanting to outdo the amazing Catalina, Teresa was goaded to rivalry until the day His Voice—His Majesty's—rescued her from the command of the *Père sévère* to harm herself without restraint. It was a good Voice: it saved La Madre from her deadly *père-version* and reconciled her with an ideal Father who is content with mere filial docility.

"The Lord told me: 'You are walking on a good and safe path. Do you see all the penance [Catalina de Cardona] does? *I value your obedience more.*'"[34]

Whence came this bifurcation, this appeasement? How could you, my fervent Teresa, renounce pain unto death in exchange for "obedience," choosing that active passivity you constructed in view of the recommencement of time? How were you able to replace "jouissance unto death" with that hyperactive passivity, your symbolic maternity? In opposition to Catalina de Cardona and her vehement masochism, you chose life.

"The desires and impulses for death, which were so strong, have left me, especially since the feast day of St. Mary Magdalene; for *I resolved to live very willingly* in order to render much service to God. There is the exception sometimes when no matter how much I try to reject the desire to see Him, I cannot."[35]

Instead of being penetrated to death by the Other, you make yourself receptive. You replace oral-anal-muscular violence, the kind that swallows-excretes, bites-vomits, that is spasmodic and paralyzing, with an overflowing pragmatism backed up by a real or feigned detachment—"obedience" treated as a mental genitality under the sign of acquiescence and receptiveness, interleaved at times (rarely, but still) with lucid interrogation. "Humility?" you say; your infectious complicity with the Beloved, your tender reliance on Him, emboldens you. In the final analysis, obedience is inflected into a continual mutual nesting of the transcended into the transcendent, the nun into His

Voice, the feminine into the masculine . . . I challenge anybody to separate container from contents!

In the meanders of this movement, with regard to the senses the *raptus* itself, the forcible usurpation, the abduction of your own body by the Other, who debars you from any other creaturely love object, become transformed into replete orality. You feed on the Voice and Word of the Other that satiates you to the extent of imparting "manly strength" (*fuerza de varón*). No more anorexia, no more vomiting as you greedily ingest the God who, you do not doubt it, "even in this life . . . gives the hundredfold."[36]

> I was also thinking about this comparison. Since what is given to those who are further advanced is totally the same as that given to them in the beginning, we can compare it to *a food that many persons eat.* Those who eat just a little are left only with a *good taste* in their mouth for a short while; those who *eat more,* receive nourishment; *those who eat a great deal receive life and strength. So frequently can these latter eat and so filled are they from this food of life* that they no longer eat anything that satisfies them other than this food. They see how beneficial it is to them, and their taste has so adapted to this sweetness that *it would prefer not living to having to eat other things* that serve for no more than to take away the pleasing taste the good food leaves behind.[37]

Now that the guilt of incest has been lifted, now that He has convinced you, you have the right to love Him and be loved in return. His Voice neither forbids nor judges: it is simply a lovely taste that penetrates with the Voice into all the body's cavities. Deeper down than the mouth, the guts themselves are touched by it. And this feeling spirals up toward the Other who authorizes the pleasure and gives it a meaning, the meaning of reciprocal love. Orality and genitality, mingled and disinhibited, are no longer felt as "rape" or abduction (in French: *un rapt*; in Spanish: *arrobar*, "to tear," "to mutilate," "to damage") but as *rapture* (French: *ravissement*). To "ravish" in the sense of entrancement is another cognate; "one" is torn out of oneself, but in a situation of trust. You entrust your bewilderment (*desconcierto*) and your folly (*desatino*) to Him so that He might contain them and contain you, as one cradles a baby, and so that you might contain Him as the perforated female body contains a lover. "We are not angels but we have a body."[38]

* * *

Catalina, who wanted to be a man, couldn't unite with Him except by sadistically hurting-killing herself. You, just as much of a tomboy and more virile than many of the monks around you, accede by means of fantasy (and who knows, in reality too, perhaps?—the texts are discreet, but undoubtedly suggestive) to female genitality as well as to symbolic motherhood. How was this possible?

Let me hazard an enormity that psychologists and writers might understand. Your appropriation of language by writing revealed another Teresa to you—a new Teresa who transformed the fear of divine judgment into attentiveness to the Other's Voice. By speaking and writing about your culpable (hence frustrated and painful) desires, you take onto yourself both divine judgment and its redemption. Because you are in the place of the Other, the Other takes Its place in you. Fear is compounded, or rather superseded, by receptiveness: openness, welcome, abandonment to the gift.

* * *

This is how from being feared, then heard, the Other rewritten becomes an Other touched, felt via all the senses. Writing does not enact the respect for otherness (for evil, for impossibility, for crime, for "characters" . . .) as morality would wish, although this can happen too. Through writing, the Other and all forms of alterity cease to be forbidden, cease even to be separate from me. By writing I think them, perceive and possess them, touch and am touched by them. Writing is the supreme, innocent move from word to deed, the consummation-assumption of all prohibitions, including the primal one of incest. Henceforth, by authorizing herself to write, Teresa is "another," capable of *feeling* in the fundamental sense of *touching*. All those "others" who frightened or at least impressed her are inside her, and she is inside them—a reciprocal interpenetration. The Scriptures and Gospels, the family superego, the demands of *honra*, or the aspiration to the Ideal and to eternity no longer assail you as external imperatives, Teresa, my love, since you have the audacity to assimilate them into your own sensory experience and to impregnate your style, your *fiction* with them. Others, the Other, are your fiction, which is not even "yours," since you exist outside yourself, in the third person.

Your writing was born, as we have seen, in the wake of amorous transferences with your confessors (akin to psychoanalytical transference) and with variably loyal fellow nuns and female friends (akin to every heightened attachment between women), all of which unlocked your desires. A sensual body, alive to the passions of men and women, was thus made available to your pen. Through guilt and repression, and despite renunciation and punishment, you built yourself a new corporeal and psychic space; sensual, ravished, in a continual state of elucidation, and, by all these tokens—I say this confidently—a glorious body.

If masochism and its twin, sadism, are not entirely avoided here, they are nonetheless crowned by ravishment, or rapture, and surpassed in "marriage." Meekness vanishes in a surge of loving elation, and the imaginary flows back into the body and its erogenous zones to relieve them of the tensions that so harrowed the young novice. La Madre's potency and impotencies together diminish, her dominion and humiliation of self and others abates, her comitial or flagellant mortifications become few and far between. Relieved of desire itself, body and soul find peace in the fusion of everything with nothing, of nothing with everything, of self with Other, of flesh with Word, and vice versa.

You achieved this entrance into the writing of *fiction* around the age of fifty, with the book of your *Life*, and you consolidated it through the trials of founding houses, themselves objects of love and writing. I interpret this, also and simultaneously, as a reiteration of the immemorial founding metamorphosis of the speaking being: when the *infans*, touching and feeling, undergoing and rejecting, begins to move through the language of its home environment and to appropriate it, at which point its sensations become refined into meanings. How many years did it take Toumaï, our prehistoric ancestor, to learn to speak? Did language come about at a stroke or after some protracted evolution? The children who come to my consulting room, my patients' and my own dives into the forgotten, teach me that I accede to language when the words of other people do not seem a menace or a violation; when other people do not inflict on me either their incomprehensible opacity or their judgments, let alone their blows, frustrations, or neglects. I welcome their voices as they welcome me, I co-take or *com-prehend* a voice, it does the same to me, in a flowering of sensible intelligence and intelligent sensibility. This leaning on the other voice and its leaning on me place me in a different connection to others: the persecutory other invaginates into the receiving-received other. I cease to be an *infans* and become a speaking-desiring subject, a thinking child; I build sexual theories; I am a potential seeker.

As its final surprise and greatest benefit, this reciprocal receptiveness is not, or not feared as, a victimized passivity, aggravated throughout one's life until it is time to merit—maybe—a posthumous reward in heaven. If at the start of my graduation to speaking subject I acquired the use of language through *jouissance*, then language will never be just a utilitarian communication code for me. I will understand and practice it as a co-penetration: not rape but rapture. Is this a delusion? No, it's a constant therapy, which takes over from original fear and unpicks the cascading chains of infantile hatefatuations and primal abjections into the trials and pleasures of speaking.

Chapter 29

"WITH THE EARS OF THE SOUL"

If reality were indeed a sort of waste product of experience . . .
Marcel Proust, *Time Regained*

En lo muy muy interior . . .
Teresa of Avila, *The Interior Castle*

Your visions, Teresa, are not perceived with the eyes of the body, you often insist on this point; rather they are built by a listening that avails itself of touch. Does this relate to the infrastructure of language, the gradual intelligibility of sensation, the primary molding of meaning which Julia Kristeva calls "the semiotic"?[1]

> She never saw anything with her bodily eyes, as has been said. But what she saw was so delicate and intellectual that sometimes at the beginning she thought she had imagined it; at other times she couldn't think such a thing. Nor did she ever hear with her bodily ears—except twice; and these times she didn't hear what was being said, nor did she know who was speaking.[2]

* * *

I read and reread your words; might not that "intellectual delicacy" that pertains to your visions be the very element of your interior castle, body and soul included? With the scalpel of your self-analysis, you probe into the deepest, most *intimate* region, where metaphysical categories overlap and combine—body and/or soul, matter and/or spirit, space and/or time, subject and/or object . . . From another perspective, an evolutionary one, you might be auscultating the emergence of thought: as a writer, you stand at the borderline where thought is not yet a thought. It is no more than the delicacy of a wholly intelligent flesh, whose understanding is a function of its smelling-listening-seeing-tasting: each sense a threshold you approach and step across in order to come into contact with the Other, and with others, without being raped, frightened, or hurt. Ravished, yes. "In spite of the halo of light surrounding his form, the youthful Persian god remains obscure to us," writes Freud, dumbfounded by the incestuous bliss of Mithras-Zarathustra.[3]

During your ecstatic visions that is the face you wear, Teresa, over the body of an infant prior to its separation from the mother, prior to the prohibition of incest.

Here the psychologist in me discerns the glee of the fabulous infantile satisfaction you preserve intact beneath and throughout the separation that prompts humans to speak and which you acquired, like all law-governed humans, by force of grief and melancholy—only to conquer the independence of existing. You are always reconquering that realm, that paradise, while facing up to the ache of prohibition and abandonment.

And yet your sensual reconquest is not confined to a regression, far from it. It is not before, but *after* separation and prohibitions that you give yourself leave, accompanied by the Voice, to reconquer those delectable depths (the "interior of the soul," as opposed to "whimsical imagination"), and it is this belated reconquest, on the other side of frustrations and sufferings, that you so scrupulously observe and name. Reconciled with your tempests and attendant comas, you distinguish these from the "external part of our being" that, being prone to sorrows, agitations and disturbances, remains the domain of the devil. Thus you're able to separate suffering, the kind we call masochistic and which seems connected to an unacceptable "melancholia," from that "delightful tempest [that] comes from a region other than those regions of which [the devil of disturbing, contentious desires] is lord."[4]

The Voice of His Majesty, issuing from a different region, is no longer received as an imaginary favor, a "fancy [caprice: *antojo*]," a flattering, trying, or agonizing injunction from the superego. Instead you hear it as unmistakably as a "loud voice is heard" by the ears of the body. No doubt about it: "There's no basis for thinking it is caused by melancholy, because melancholy does not produce or fabricate its fancies save in the *imagination*. This favor proceeds from the *interior part of the soul*."[5]

$$\star \ \star \ \star$$

Your enamored state, identified with incest with an Other endowed with the attributes of both parents, profoundly alters your relationship with meaning. Meaning becomes sensible for you, which helps attenuate the cruelty of the prohibitions and the judgment inherent in them. Your relationship to the body is also changed; you take possession of a new body that flourishes in the delicacy of that sensual intelligence made possible, no matter how intermittently, by its incorporation of thought. "A person with the ears of the soul seems to hear those words . . . so clearly and so in secret."[6] The intelligence of your interpenetration with the Other alleviates the spasms, labors, and agitations of illbeing, and allows you to "enter" into the "tempest" of contacts with the Other, a turbulence that carries you away without obliterating you in psychosis. Your union with the Other does not destroy you; there's no threat of identity catastrophe. On the contrary, you succeed in meticulously depicting the yearning for nonseparation.

"Sometimes my pulse almost stops. . . . All my longing then is to die . . . if anything could give the soul consolation, it would be to speak to someone who had suffered this torment. . . . So it seems to me that this desire for companionship comes from our own weakness . . . *the desire the body and soul have of not being separated* is what makes one beg for help."[7]

True enough, that separation can only be consummated in the eye of the storm; I am reminded of the "depressive position" Melanie Klein considered a psychic precondition for the acquisition of language.[8] But in your case, Teresa, after that long meditation upon your states of prayer, with which I'm familiar thanks to your accounts, the unbearable separation is redressed by reunion. Confident in the knowledge—or is it faith?—that reconciliation makes up for suffering, the soul feels neither abandoned nor guilty, neither helplessly depressed nor inexorably excited, neither melancholic nor hysterical, even though it has known all of those states. "The soul is purified," you say, "purged like gold in the crucible." You're an alchemist, Teresa, since you can't be a psychologist. You borrow from the masters of the occult to explicate how, by going through depressiveness with its ascetic temptations, you became worthy of "the enameled gifts" from the Lord. A new "purification" occurs, fulfilled and gratified, a "golden" purgation that preempts the one awaiting sinners in purgatory, with its expected mortifications: "Que en esta pena se purificaba el alma, y se labra o purifica como el oro en el crisol, para poder mejor poner los esmaltes de sus dones, y que se purgaba allí lo que había de estar en purgatorio."[9]

* * *

The prayer of union finally leads your soul to a "complete transformation . . . in God,"[10] which although it "lasts only a short time" makes you feel "healed." A therapeutic prayer, then (unlike the one that used to send you into a coma as a novice!) replaces the judgmental, fearsome *Voice* with a *new Voice* that offers itself, touching and penetrating while letting the other senses penetrate it.

This new topology of intimacy imbuing your lover's rapport with the Beloved completely changes the experience of suffering: were you to feel pain, you couldn't assign to it the negative value of ill-being. This rather undermines the sadomasochistic nosography that I'm pinning on you from the outside! Here, "separation" and "the incest prohibition" are not scotomized; you don't pitch into psychosis or even perversion, Teresa, my love—I'll sign you a doctor's note on that—you only teeter on the edge. Instead, like all the suffering in your realm, separation and prohibition allow themselves to be veiled by a "transparent covering,"[11] as you describe in your Dwelling Places—in other words, by your fantasy incarnate, carnal and permissive, as though by a caressing, flimsy veil. As you write it, the pleasure of love in the form of incest with the Son-Father turned Spouse is wiped of guilt by the fable of a "union" you desire so much that you experience it as a physiological reality. Is it a veil, or a penetrable hymen? Nothing licenses me to jump to the conclusion that one or another of your confessors, some intrepid explorer of female desire like your adored Eliseus-Gratian, might have given you the opportunity for congress itself. But we know for a fact that spiteful contemporaries, and you had your share of enemies, did not refrain from hints to that effect.

* * *

Given and received, the Voice uttering the words of the Beloved—and therefore also the words of the Bride "transformed" into the Beloved—are freighted with a "supreme authority," far more powerful than any abstract verbal message. In the new economy of amorous writing, of Teresa's new body that is constituted by the acts of writing and foundation, there cannot possibly be a barrier between words and things, writing and making, reading and doing work in the world. There are only transitions to and fro through the "veil" (in place of the *repression* that governs *consciousness*): "locutions from God effect what they say [speaking and acting: *hablando y obrando*]."[12] It is not surprising that if He speaks-and-acts, as one would expect from a Creator, Teresa "transformed into Him" also writes and acts (i.e., makes foundations), both things together.

Make no mistake, Teresa is not calling upon human beings to do as they say and say as they do. Her experience is not a morality. Indwelt by a speech reconciled with her desires, she pushes incarnation as far as erasing the last borders between *speaking* and *being*, meaning that she only speaks by being and only is by speaking; there is no barrier, just a "veil." Manic agitation and its symmetrical other face, the melancholic-masochistic guilt generated by forbidden desire, which racked her before, are no longer a threat. Voices and words alongside acts of foundation become, in this great alchemical flask, of "great repose" and "engraved on our memory."[13]

A great repose engraved in memory?

* * *

This experience of incorporation, authorizing the embodied fantasy of incest over and above the incest taboo, will require a new "imaginary vision" if you are to convey it to your sisters and confessors—and to us, your readers in the third millennium. It will be the story of a hidden treasure, the casket enclosing a secret jewel.

The alchemical metaphors and the metamorphoses of this radical experience travel from invisibility to light, from imprint to brilliance, from the casket of empty space to the density of the diamond, from blinding sunlight to the veil of fine linen or the transparency of the gem, from impenetrable stone to infused light. None of these extremes immobilize or alarm her, for they have eased into thresholds, landings, membranes, in the journey of the *I* toward the Other, of the body toward the soul, in an indefatigable to-and-fro.

* * *

The recasting of identities and the suspension of categories was already intrinsic to the Christian dogma of the Incarnation, in which God became a man. But you pushed this logic further, Teresa, to extremes that must have shocked many a theologian. What a heretical notion, this access to an inaccessible "jewel" in a "reliquary" whose keys are in the Beloved's keeping, but which you, a simple nun, are capable of appropriating! As if you could house the very sun inside yourself, making your conjoined body and soul into a "case" so thoroughly penetrated by the scorching star that nothing separates them any more from Him, beyond a transparent veil. And this diamond, the Other within, is the most precious thing you have—or better said, the most precious thing you are. To have or to be: to have is not enough for you, you must *be* the gem. Therein resides the effrontery, the heresy, the paranoia (as Jérôme Tristan insists, and I let him, I share, I murmur: To each his alchemy).

So I think you write a madness you have faced up to and yet worked through, in the *jouissance* of devotion, in a masochism precisely sublimated by writing, and in the realities of foundation, the cherry on the cake.

And since for you the jewel is the "sacred humanity of Christ," His desiring and desirable body, tortured and glorified, it's understandable that the contact with Him in visions—as you journey through the permeable dwelling places of your interior castle—no longer kindles fear in you, but only an unbridled ecstasy.

* * *

When the Other forbids you from acceding to Him, He is telling you: "Suffer!" and you instantly become melancholic and driven to penitence. When you permit yourself to love Him as a Bride loves her Spouse, you are threatened by delirium: "I am the Other" is an exalting temptation . . . sent by the devil, perhaps? You step back from the manic extremes of both anguish and excitement, Teresa, shielded from them by that refraction of hallucination—the a-thought of writing—that operates as a self-analysis. Bedazzlement curves back into inscription, ecstasy meets reflection, and the exile outside oneself returns to the reasonable self so that the latter may chart its path.

* * *

Only thus can the sublimation of the Passion for the Beloved into sensible, appeased intelligence take over from sex and fear. The quailing of the child before the father's seductive authority and its terror before the idealized Father, the indomitable proprietor of the enviable, painful maternal destiny, arouse fear and trembling in the eternal infants we are—that Christian believers acknowledge themselves to be. And yet all it takes is to stop living as a beaten child, or even as a beaten father, and recast one's familial role into that of the receptive wife—so receptive, indeed, that she manages to "transform herself" into Him through their "union." All it takes is for a delicate intelligence to accompany the desire thus authorized, so that in place of wrath there descends the peace of the elect, the sovereignty of the kingdom. All this occurs within and beyond the strictness of the Primitive Rule that you have no intention of relaxing; in fact you would like to reform it into something stricter still, wouldn't you, Teresa? And you don't forget that one must still fear the Father, in view of the Last Judgment; for when He comes "with so much friendliness" to speak with His Bride, it fills her with "such fear": a fear tamed by writing it.

> I say "*frightening*" because although the Lord's presence is the most beautiful and delightful a person could imagine even were he to live and labor a thousand years thinking about it (for it far surpasses the limitations of our imagination or intellect), this presence bears such extraordinary majesty that *it causes the soul extreme fright.* . . .
>
> O Lord, how we Christians fail to know you! What will that day be when You come to judge, for even when *You come here with so much friendliness to speak with your bride, she experiences such fear when she looks at You?* Oh daughters, what will it be like when He says in so severe a voice, *depart ye who are cursed by My Father?* (Matt. 25:41: "Depart from me, ye cursed.")[14]

Fear is not relinquished altogether, but increasingly overlaid with the self-assurance brought by contact with the Other to the point of dissolving into Him, becoming impregnated by Him; and thus you have become, Teresa, someone else. I is another. A Mother.

* * *

Is Teresa, body and soul, like a small jewelry box in which the humanity of the Spouse, that desired and desiring body, is secretly lodged? Does she emit sunbeams, the visceral heat of His Majesty within, only separated from her by a scrap of gauze? Or is she perhaps the texture itself, a homemade hymen softly linked to Him? And finally, the diamond: Is it the Other's precious humanity?

Or the indestructible glint of that ecstatic and most intimate inner core, as Teresa is transformed by Communion into Him?

"Once after receiving Communion I was given understanding of how *the Father receives within our soul the most holy Body of Christ* . . . There are deep *inner secrets* revealed when one takes communion. It is a pity that these bodies of ours do not let us enjoy them."[15]

* * *

You are evading the issue, Teresa. Allow me to remind you that, contrary to what you claim above, "this body of yours" was right there with you when you communed so blissfully with the Other. Everybody knows that now, thanks to Bernini. I'm willing to admit that "deep inside your soul," which precedes and entails the metamorphosis of your body—or possibly the other way around—you equated yourself with the nuptials joining Father to Son (since you had "transformed" into Him!). Might you be the Father who contains within Him the Child Jesus, His Majesty pregnant with the God-man, or are you only (if that's the word) the receptacle of their reconciliation? Here is a curious but ravishing fitting together of forms, a nesting that leaves many of us pensive. Might you embody all by yourself the mystery of the Trinity, Father, Son, and Holy Spirit, whose ins and outs you once discussed in such rarefied fashion with John of the Cross that the pair of you were seen to levitate in your seats, according to the nuns of the Incarnation, all agog at this communion between future saints! And, more miraculously still, the mystery that lifts you above the ground is played out in your woman's soul-body, no more, no less! The way "that body of yours" never kept you from *jouissance* is proof enough; your prayerful revelry in Him simply endowed you with a new body, capable of incorporating fantasy and molding itself as it pleased.

The old body has not disappeared, though. All your life you'd have done anything to get rid of it, enduring everything from the slightest mortification to the agony of abrasive hair shirts. The inventive range of punishments you relentlessly inflicted on yourself would be the dark underside of rapture: "A fault this body has is that the more comfort we try to give it the more needs it discovers. . . . The poor soul is deceived [by these demands] and doesn't grow."[16] You are reminded of "many women who are married," and imagine one who—like your own mother?—"suffers much adversity without being able to receive comfort from anyone lest her husband know that she speaks and complains about it."

"Indeed, we have not come here to receive more comfort than they!"[17] Being married to Jesus, do you atone for the sins of all married women?

To suffer is a woman's fate, that's well known, and to die is human, naturally. You seem to bow to this, Teresa, but you don't really: for you, subjecting the body to "heavy trials" can only serve to prevail over it when the goal is to purify suffering and even to abolish it in order to "enjoy repose." Repose after Calvary, masochistic joy, is that it?

Or is it rather a question of reaching that "other region" of jubilation disconnected from suffering, pure *père-version*, exquisite *mère-version*? You reach it, it seems. Because you write it. I am prepared to believe you. Well, almost. We obviously won't breathe a word of this to Andrew or Jérôme or Marianne, will we?

★ ★ ★

You are torn with indecision again, Teresa; sometimes it's one, sometimes the other, or presumably both at once. Indecision? Or should I say sinuousness, playfulness? Because the ambiguity that plagued you all your life between suffering and sublimation finds an exact designation, an uncanny synthesis, in the verb "to mock." This word falls abruptly from your nib, to suggest not so much a cruel denial of ill-being as a kind of jaded detachment or mild irony: "So what if we die? If our body has *mocked* us so often, shouldn't we *mock* it at least once?" ("De cuantas veces nos ha burlado el cuerpo, ¿no burlaríamos alguna de él?").[18]

Your body, that cumbersome object, was a burden; now it is a toy. Instead of putting it to death, you dedicate it to the saints, to Jesus, to God—to "our God the Logos," as old Freud used to say. And here you are, not only rid of your fleshly envelope but delighted to play tricks on it the more it taunts you, what am I saying, the more it tries to knock you out for the count! For example, you think you've earned the Other's love and your sisters' admiration by performing so many penances. You make yourself vomit in order to have something to offer God ("the Lord is served by something"),[19] for you reckon that He expects treasures from you: "In this life there could be no greater good than the practice of prayer." Prayer will constitute the exercise that helps you skirt anorexia, and with it the body, but by raising frustration to the rank of a pleasure shared . . . with the Father-Son. And with your own father, don Alonso Sánchez himself, as we have seen.[20]

My reading is as follows: so as to resist the impulse to offer your life (your body) to your father, you begin by offering your death (your vomiting body) to the Lord, but you marry your father indirectly, coming together in the Lord: a pretty tortuous defense, admit it! You keep fanning the faith of your father Alonso, so as to lead him to the supreme Good, of course, and to have done with *la honra* . . .

After all, none other than Jesus is showing you the way in this. Since he is a *man*, the Son of Mary gives you "understanding through experience,"[21] in other words the union with the Beloved is *corporeal*: Is this your way of disavowing the "spiritual books" your father valued, he who placed God's immaterial divinity far above the bodily presence that doña Beatriz, like most women, hankered for in novels of courtly love? But you, praying over the Passion and the Resurrection, don't dissociate God from the flesh. It is clear that the "most sacred humanity of Christ" does not count among the "corporeal things" from which we must "turn aside." "It is clear that the Creator must be sought through his creatures." ("Está claro, se ha de buscar al Criador por las criaturas.")[22] How could you possibly dispense with your body, since His is always present for you—contacted, contagious, penetrating, or enveloping?

A daughter of the Renaissance, a woman of zestful vitality, you never forget for a moment that your Lover is "human." And it is that understanding through experience (*por experiencia me lo daba a entender*) of the mystery of the Incarnation you are so sure of sharing with Jesus—"incarnate fantasies," in psychoanalytical terms—that led you to revolutionize the Catholic faith at the end of the sixteenth century.

You interpret Christ's Passion, with its descent into Hell and ascension into Heaven, as an invitation to acknowledge the violence of human desire, with the ultimate goal of tempering it so as to have a firmer dominion over the world. If the majority of human beings are "scattered" souls, skittish as "wild horses no one can stop," you consider that the saints, by contrast, could do "whatever they wanted" with God's help, merely to gain "dominion over all worldly things."[23] This course is surely the way of perfection you aim to follow.

* * *

By uniting with the Other until it becomes Him, the soul goes beyond humility; in its very abandonment, it transcends suffering and acquires "power and authority" ("*poderío y señorío*")[24] as well as a "great quiet," a "devout and peaceful recollection."[25] We gather that ideal Fatherhood is no longer punitive for you, but instantly pleasurable and nourishing; it satisfies the person, affirms the advantages of being alive, brings joy. In consequence the task now is to make your word live up to that, to become agreeable so as to be like Him—to be Him? "Think, daughter, of how after it is finished you will not be able to serve Me in ways you can now. Eat for Me and sleep for Me, and *let everything you do be for Me*, as though you no longer lived but I."[26]

To be agreeable to the Third Person, to the nonperson in you; maybe that's the definition of happiness.

You prefigure the seventeenth-century moralists, Teresa, my love, with that obligation of happiness that you think comes from the Other. "There is . . . only one duty, to be happy," Diderot wrote. I wonder whether the inspired encyclopedist ever suspected that one of those nuns whose fanaticism so infuriated him had preceded him along that path?[27]

* * *

With no strain, the soul becomes a babe in arms that "nurses" and comprehends "without effort of the intellect."[28] No more "frenzy";[29] Teresa is through with suffering and punishing, she is all consent and contentment, she says *yes*. "During the time of this prayer, everything is 'yes.' The 'no' comes afterward upon seeing that the delight is ended and that one cannot recover it."[30]

Negativity, ill-being, angst, discontentment, and criticism only arise "afterward," as a temporary eclipse of the *yes*. More than a subjective choice, Teresa's *yes*, emanating from the Other, presents itself as an ontological *yes* she appropriates by appropriating "the sacred humanity of Christ"; perhaps, too, as an unconscious spur to gratitude? The *no*, on the other hand, along with every species of negativity, mortification, penance, or active realization of sadomasochistic impulses, is only apprehended as a cessation of the essential *yes*.

Jérôme Tristan keeps looking over my shoulder; I can feel him breathing down my neck as I write. Certainly, my friend, one can interpret this masterly reversal of depression and sophrology into manic exaltation as the paranoid temptation to ensure absolute dominion and control. But you can't overlook the fact that while this temptation exists, it is both checked by the framework of the Catholic institution with its many rituals and hierarchies and continually deconstructed by the self-analytical discipline of a writing undertaken for the long haul.

* * *

I spend my sleepless nights dissecting, with the aid of the magnifying glass and scalpel of my daytime clinical duties, the psychic metamorphoses that make the Teresian castle into a work of art that's more unusual and differently admirable than the great cathedrals of the Christian West. Has time wiped out these pneumatic dwelling places? Or do they survive beneath various disguises and renovations, like the walls of Avila loom before the handful of tourists who still appreciate their splendor—or rather, their pasteboard-scenery quality?

Teresa the writer who turns to making foundations is no longer the punished child or the beaten Father-Son. The thought-sensation of her tremendous introjection of the loving-loved Other is turned into action, into works. Although the "faculties" (understanding, will, and imagination) may persist in fretful agitation, and there may be no end to struggles, trials, and sufferings, nothing will prevent the soul from joining, not the "sound of the Voice," but the "work" of the Spirit—the soul's spirit, or mind:

"This greeting of the Lord must have amounted to much more than is apparent from its sound. . . . *His words are effected in us as deeds.* . . . For it is very certain that in emptying ourselves of all that is creature and detaching ourselves from it for the love of God, the same Lord will fill us with Himself."[31] For "the Lord puts the soul in this *dwelling* of His, which is the *center of the soul* itself":

> This *center of our soul, or this spirit*, is something *so difficult to explain*, and even believe in, that I think, Sisters, I'll not give you the temptation to disbelieve what I say. . . . To speak of pain and *suffering* and say at the same time that the soul is at *peace* is a difficult thing to explain. I want to make one or more comparisons for you. Please God, I may be saying something through them; but if not, I know that I'm speaking the truth.[32]

Does this mean He *is* the soul? The soul *is* Him? Pain is peace? Peace is pain? What is the meaning of the verb *to be*, here?

"*Mas habéis de entender que va mucho de estar a estar*": there is a great difference in the ways one may be.[33] Teresian "ontology," succeeding to her *raptus* sublimated into gratitude, does not, however, fall back on quietism. The movement that appropriates *be-ing* conjugates the verb in the plural: *I* is an amassment of others. Identity must be porous, presence must be penetrated, and the feeling-thinking subject engaged in a cascading chain of reciprocities with other feeling-thinking subjects. The consent to incest with the ideal Father-Son restores the world as a place of grace and joy: *Yes* to requited desires and reconciled alterities. *Yes* to the affirmation of co-presence, to the acceptance of otherness that founds the subject of desire, *yes to the infinity of being.*

* * *

Could this message I have gleaned from Teresa's words be a universal truth? It is certainly not a call to solidarity with the host of wronged humanity, "the humiliated and insulted," even if this humanist commitment is embedded in many modern branches of Christianity. Via Teresa's experiences, a prodigious subjective space is being built before our eyes, one that makes an impression upon the European mentality, even where it does not impose upon it. Unless it be just a grandiose illusion, the crowning glory of the aesthetic religion now fading into globalized virtuality?

The existential joy of Teresa of Avila was (ontologically, unconsciously) founded on the delegation of the Self into the Other—a delegation that had to negotiate any amount of frustrations, separations, travails, punishments, and penances before adhering to the alterities in the self that are manifest in the insatiable activity of representation, that is, the narrative I am capable of producing for, and with, another. This entails a constant translation of the estranged inside oneself, the assumption, body and soul, of I into Him; and this elation reshapes depressive angst into energetic pragmatism. Words thus become not things, but affirmative deeds: *yeses*, works. The Creator is succeeded, not perhaps by a Creatress, but certainly by a re-foundress.

* * *

"Yes," says Teresa, while writing and founding. And even while dying—especially then. Her "amen" to the Other-Being defies time: that *yes* falls outside time.

Today, in Alba de Tormes, she is leaving this world to meet her Beloved face to face.

Part 7

Dialogues from Beyond the Grave

And even as he, who, with distressful breath,
Forth issued from the sea upon the shore,
Turns to the water perilous and gazes;
So did my soul, that still was fleeing onward,
Turn itself back to re-behold the pass
Which never yet a living person left.

Dante, *Inferno*

Chapter 30

ACT I

Her Women

Nor did You, Lord, when You walked in the world, despise women.

Teresa of Avila, *The Way of Perfection*

They are very womanish . . . [be] like strong men.

Teresa of Avila, *The Way of Perfection*

LA MADRE, on her deathbed, watched over by:
ANA DE SAN BARTOLOMÉ and TERESITA, La Madre's niece, Lorenzo's
   daughter, TERESA DE JESÚS in religion; with them are
CATALINA DE LA CONCEPCIÓN
CATARINA BAUTISTA

Followed by entrance of:
BEATRIZ DÁVILA Y AHUMADA, Teresa of Avila's mother
CATALINA DEL PESO Y HENAO, the first wife of Teresa of Avila's father,
   Alonso Sánchez de Cepeda

Characters passing through, in alphabetical order:
ANA DE LA CERDA DE MENDOZA, Princess of Eboli
ANA DE LOBRERA, ANA DE JESÚS in religion
ANA GUTIÉRREZ
ANA DE LA FUERTÍSIMA TRINIDAD
PADRE ANTONIO DE JESÚS

The image of the Virgin that Teresa always kept with her. Private collection.

BEATRIZ DE JESÚS, a niece of La Madre

BEATRIZ CHÁVEZ, BEATRIZ DE LA MADRE DE DIOS in religion

BEATRIZ DE OÑEZ, BEATRIZ DE LA ENCARNACIÓN in religion

CASILDA DE PADILLA, CASILDA DE LA CONCEPCIÓN in religion

CATALINA DE CARDONA

ISABEL DE JESÚS

PRINCESS JUANA, sister of Philip II

JUANA DEL ESPÍRITU SANTO, prioress at Alba de Tormes

JERÓNIMA GUIOMAR DE ULLOA

LUISA DE LA CERDA

MARÍA DE OCAMPO, MARÍA BAUTISTA in religion

MARÍA DE JESÚS

MARÍA ENRÍQUEZ DE TOLEDO, Duchess of Alba

MARÍA SALAZAR DE SAN JOSÉ, prioress at Seville

EMPRESS MARIA THERESA of Austria

TERESA DE LAYZ

AN ANONYMOUS NUN

With the portrait of the Virgin Mary bequeathed to Teresa by her mother, whose blue veil casts its iridescence over the deathbed scene.

⋆ ⋆ ⋆

ACT 1, SCENE 1

LA MADRE

TERESITA

ANA DE SAN BARTOLOMÉ

JERÓNIMA GUIOMAR DE ULLOA

LUISA DE LA CERDA

ANA DE JESÚS

and CATALINA DE LA CONCEPCIÓN, CATARINA BAUTISTA

Although La Madre had wished to go up to Heaven in a flash, her niece Teresita will testify that her death was neither easy nor quick. And yet Teresa is not distressed at entering into her final agony. The twilight of her awareness fills her with blue-tinted voluptuousness, blue as the wintry dawn over Avila, blue as the Virgin's cloak in the picture her mother bequeathed to her before she died.

She knows she's not alone. Ana de San Bartolomé, the young conversa nun who is nursing her, and Teresita—now in the bloom of her sixteen years—keep watch with tender solicitude by her bedside, accompanied by Catalina de la Concepción and Catarina Bautista. Sounds of padding footsteps, rustling habits, murmuring voices; scents of skin, clean towels, cool or warm water. The dying woman cannot see the faithful companions by her side, but they inhabit her visions.

* * *

Is it possible to die, when she is already dead to the world so as to live more completely in God? Teresa thinks death is delightful, an "uprooting of the soul from all the operations it can have while being in the body"; because the soul was already, while the body lived, "separated from the body" in order to "dwell more perfectly in God." Often, as during those terrible epileptic comas, the separation of body and soul was such that she didn't "even know if [the body] had life enough to breathe." Soon, now, it will not. The rest is unknown, something even more fearsome and delightful, since she loves. "If it does love, it doesn't understand how or what it is it loves or what it would want."[1] The unknown is love. Teresa never stopped wondering about love, and writing about it. There's no reason to stop now.

* * *

The blue Virgin has her hands crossed over her breast, and the face of Beatriz Dávila y Ahumada. With the folds of her azure robe she protects the fortress of Avila, but the Mother of God does not say a word to the dying woman. How long ago did this "mother without flaw" abandon her daughter? Some fifty years?

Teresa sees one of her own texts materialize on the pale silk. To write about the inner life means spewing out "many superfluous and even foolish things in order to say something that's right." It required a lot of patience for her to write about what she didn't know. Yes, sometimes she'd pick up her pen like a simpleton who couldn't think of what to say or where to start.[2]

It required patience to get people to read her, and then to reread herself. Torrents of engraved words, funerary columns, whole pages stamped into the translucent walls of the interior castle, which Teresa can retrieve with no help from the "faculties"—whether understanding, memory, or will—it's just there, just like that. "Hacer esta ficción para darlo a entender":[3] literally, to "make this fiction to get my point across." "Hagamos cuenta, para entenderlo mejor, que vemos dos fuentes":[4] "Let's consider, for a better understanding, that we see two founts." Let's pretend, pretend to see. Let's tell stories. Let's write them down.

⋆ ⋆ ⋆

TERESA. Converse with God. What else could I do, being a woman and a conversa? (*Lengthy pause.*) My Lord and Spouse! The longed-for hour has come! It is high time we saw each other, my Beloved, my Lord! (*Listening.*) *Conversar con Dios.* Such things can't be explained except by using comparisons. To grasp them, one must have experienced them.[5] (*In a rush.*) A conversa who wants the world to be saved . . . with my daughters . . . After the return of Fr. Alonso de Maldonado from the Indies . . . Who'd have thought it? . . . I have been out of my mind . . . I'm still delirious . . . the Lord says that I must look after what is His, and not worry about anything that can happen . . .[6] (*Quick smile.*) The long-awaited time has come! (*Long pause.*)

⋆ ⋆ ⋆

A new page imprints itself upon the Virgin's blue cloak outstretched over the ramparts of Avila, a page La Madre wrote regarding another Beatriz, a relative of Casilda de Padilla. She'd never met Beatriz de Óñez, or Beatriz de la Encarnación, but had heard much about her God-given virtues from the awed sisters at Valladolid. This was one daughter that Teresa was going to take with her when she flew away from the Seventh Dwelling Places toward the Lord.

TERESA, *in a tone of fervid reminiscence.* Beatriz, daughter, woman without flaw . . . Mother . . . pray God to send me many trials, with this I'll be content . . .

As she mutters to herself in this vein, pious Ana de San Bartolomé recognizes the words La Madre had written in a section of the *Foundations*, glorifying the nun whose "life was one of high perfection, and her death was of a kind that makes it fitting for us to remember her."[7]

> TERESA, *feverishly*. Have you asked the monastery nuns? Did they ever see anything but evidence of the highest perfection? High perfection is an interior space free of all created things, a disencumbered emptiness, a purified soul and God divested of all character, dispossessed of Himself, turned in on Himself.
>
> TERESITA, *in tears*. She's dreaming . . . as if reciting something . . .
>
> TERESA. "She was next afflicted with an intestinal abscess causing the severest suffering. The patience the Lord had placed in her soul was indeed necessary in order for her to endure it." Just like my mother. It was wonderful to behold the perfect order that prevailed internally and externally, in every way . . .

But wasn't her muddled mind confusing Beatriz de Óñez with the nun who had cancer, the one she had cared for when a novice at the Incarnation? Or perhaps with Beatriz Dávila, the mother Teresa pitied as well as honored, but assuredly praised to the skies? She wanted to follow in her footsteps to the Beyond, but by choosing another way of perfection: the monastic way.

> ANA DE SAN BARTOLOMÉ, *to* TERESITA, *interrupting her prayers for a moment*. She's calling on her mother for help before going to join the Lord.
>
> TERESITA. Do you think so? I think she's seeing her mother *in* the Lord. She wants to find peace in her lap, to know herself to be perfect, in her and like her.

Teresita surrenders to emotion: for the foundress, her little Teresica, as she called her, was always the impish nine-year-old she welcomed into the Discalced Carmel at Valladolid. Even so, the little one is often more insightful than other sisters about the extremes of mind and body, as she has just demonstrated.

* * *

La Madre can barely hear them. Immersed in visions, she continues to murmur the text unfurling across the blue robes of the Virgin above the walls of Avila. Nothing but her text, chiseled into what is left of her body and soul, the second nature etched into her by writing. It takes up all the space of her dwelling places, the whole castle.

LA MADRE, *reading.* "In matters concerning mortification she was persistent. She avoided what afforded her recreation, but unless one were watching closely, this would not be known. It didn't seem she lived or conversed with creatures, so little did she care about anything. She was always composed, so much so that once a Sister said to her that she seemed like one of those persons of nobility so proud that they would rather die from hunger than let anyone outside know about it."[8] (*Pause.*)

    Who is speaking? Who speaks through my lips? I know you're near, daughters, even if I can't see you with my bodily eyes. I am not yet dead, so there's no need to weep or to rejoice, it comes to the same thing. I'm thinking, that's all, dying people do that, didn't you know? (*Pause.*) In fact, the approach of death is the best time for the strange activity of thinking by writing. I think, therefore I am mortal; I question myself, I wonder what right I have to see the Beloved face to face. (*With fervent reminiscence.*) That sister who was talking through my lips, who is she? Or was it me thinking aloud, a witness to my mother's distress? Me, wrapped in the suffering of Beatriz de la Encarnación?

Although Teresa's brain is growing feebler, she keeps qualifying everything she says, as she always used to. The coming end merely adds leisure to her lucidity. One can't approach God with trepidation, one can't serve Him in despondence.

LA MADRE, *reading.* "The highest perfection obviously does not consist in interior delights or in great raptures or in visions or in the spirit of prophecy, but in having our will so matched with God's that there is nothing we know He wills that we don't want with all our desire; and in accepting the bitter as happily as the sweet, when we know that His Majesty desires it."[9]

ANA DE SAN BARTOLOMÉ, *repeating in simplified form the lessons Teresa has imparted, as she follows the murmuring voice.* Now she's talking about honor, she's against it, she can't bear all those people scrambling after it.

TERESITA. At home, she used to accuse my father Lorenzo of doing that. But the honor of Grandma Beatriz, I mean, her flawlessness . . . I'm confused . . .

Teresita isn't sure whether she is supposed to revere the perfection of her grandmother or seek other, happier models. But still, Beatriz Dávila couldn't have been all gloom, however miserable her life, since La Madre's mother used to read novels of chivalry, apparently. Fancy that! I've also heard that when she was young, Auntie Teresa would get the giggles playing chess!

* * *

The dying woman has turned the page. For fifty-five years now, the magic of Beatriz Dávila y Ahumada has been diffracted into a long procession of women who are now filing past one by one, under the closed eyelids of the traveler on her last journey toward the Spouse. They move through Avila's narrow streets, climb the towers, pop in and out through the gates. The philosopher Dominique de Courcelles, who was no more present than I was at the final days of the future saint, has had the same insight as myself, Sylvia Leclercq, regarding the lifelong hold of the maternal magnet upon Teresa and the powerful way it was projected on her daughters. When La Madre was busy with her foundations she was also exploring the secrets of this relationship, repeatedly testing the proximity she cultivated to her progenitor, as well as the distance she kept from her.

Her "sisters" and "daughters" were not all natives of Avila, except perhaps for María Briceño, teacher of the young lay students at Our Lady of Grace, and Juana Suárez, the dear childhood friend who led the way to the Carmelites; but the nearness of death makes her gather them all together, loved or hated, all of them without exception, in Avila. Time regained unfolds in maternal space.

* * *

Doña Jerónima Guiomar de Ulloa opens the procession, dressed alternately in a gold-spun gown and in rags, the way she was on the day she took the veil.

TERESA. Was I mistaken to write that women are more gifted than men at taking the path of perfection?[10] On the whole they are . . . with some exceptions. I like exceptions. Doña Jerónima, you turned your palace into a convent, and you were the first to donate your fortune to sustain the Work. I can never thank you enough, O Lord God, for allowing me to meet this highborn widow, wedded to prayer, who was closely in touch with so many Jesuit fathers . . . (*Gazes at her for a while. Pause.*)

We really became good friends when you directed me to your confessor, Fr. Prádanos.[11] (*Doña Jerónima blushes at the memory.*)
(*Teresa's lips, mumbling inaudibly.*)

You knew my needs, you witnessed my sorrows, and comforted me. Blessed with a strong faith, you couldn't help recognizing the doings of God where most people only saw the devil. (*Moving lips.*)

DOÑA JERÓNIMA, *as a loyal disciple*. And where even men of learning were baffled, let me remind you.

TERESA. At your home, and in the churches you know, I had the chance to converse with Pedro de Alcántara . . . (*Lips.*)

(*Smiling.*) I must confess, I had something to do with the favors the Lord was pleased to grant you. And I received by that means some counsel of great profit for my soul.[12]

Doña Jerónima Guiomar de Ulloa goes on her way, all absorbed in her own soul.

* * *

Doña Luisa de la Cerda is next in line. Long ago she lavished on Teresa her endearing madness and her jewels; she shared, after all, some of La Madre's passions and frailties. She too was on excellent terms with some influential prelates, such as Alonso Velázquez who was instrumental for the foundation of the Carmel at Soria. The dying nun is content to smile at this ghost. Her strongest linked memory is the sense of triumph that buoyed the granddaughter of the converso Juan Sánchez in the great city of Toledo: while she was staying, that time, in the opulent palace of Luisa de la Cerda, a violent transport lifted Teresa toward the dove flying over her head. It was quite different from earthly birds—the dove of the Holy Spirit, soaring aloft for the space of an Ave Maria. That *jouissance* was followed by a deep sense of rest, like the grace accorded to Saint Joseph of Avila himself in the hermitage at Nazareth.

DOÑA LUISA, *anxious, dreamy*. Will I ever see it again?

TERESA. As I saw it in the city of my ancestors?

Yes, there is the dove again, flying away after Luisa de la Cerda.

* * *

Ana de San Bartolomé can only make out murmurs, stray words here and there, she can only follow in prayer: so she invents La Madre's reverie.[13] She imagines it, just like I, Sylvia Leclercq, am doing.

TERESA. And you, dearest Ana, my faithful little conversa . . . my sweet and unas-
suming secretary, companion, nurse . . . You were illiterate when you arrived, and
you learned to read and write by copying my hand. Oh yes, I know how strong
you are: didn't you fend off your first suitor by covering your head with a dish-
cloth? (*Leaning back.*) I can see it from here, you will be sent to found the Carmel
at Pontoise in France, where you will be prioress, yes, absolutely, I can see it all, no
use shaking your head. Go and rest awhile, go on, Teresita can look after me very
well. You can see that I'm better, God doesn't want me yet . . . Run along! Who's
this I see coming now?

ANA DE SAN BARTOLOMÉ, *hopelessly shy, walks on tiptoes, talks in a whisper.* It
looks like one of your nieces, Madre . . .

TERESA. Come forward, then, niece—no, not you, Teresita. It's Beatriz de Jesús,
visiting just in time . . . You will be appointed under-prioress at Salamanca, my
dear. Don't goggle your eyes at me, I know it, that's all . . . You have a lot of nerve,
and more importantly the pluck to retort to the pamphlet that Quevedo will
circulate against me . . . My being canonized by Gregory XV, he'll not begrudge
me that, but to be anointed "patroness of all the kingdoms of Spain," that's going
too far! The great satirical poet prefers the Moor-Slayer . . . of course, a warrior
saint like the apostle James, our Santiago Matamoros, whose help was so invalu-
able during the *Reconquista*, cuts a finer swagger than a mousy nun who wasn't
even a *letrada*! As for the Marranos . . . no, let's drop it. Well then, you, Beatriz,
will stand up for me, yes you will . . . Though we saints obviously don't need
that kind of accolade. His Majesty is enough for us, as I have often said . . . it's a
futile quarrel . . . You won't call it a stupid one, but that's what you'll be thinking. What a lamentable affair. In the end, Quevedo or no Quevedo, the pope
approves the court's decision . . . the all-powerful minister, Olivares, was rather
fond of me . . . So were you, dear child . . . *Be like strong men, my daughters*!
(*Smiles.*) You understand me.

* * *

The silence is suddenly torn by the sound of a woman singing and clapping her
hands, Andalusia-style.

TERESA. What a surprise! Who can this be, singing and dancing like myself in
younger days?

The voice approaches, to reveal the face of Ana de Jesús.

TERESA. So it's Ana de Lobera! (*Falling into excited reminiscence.*) Of course! Come closer, my child! You've always been different, Ana de Jesús. A queen among women, go on, don't look so innocent, you knew you were, in spite of your genuine and heartfelt humility, which I don't deny! You were the most attractive of all. Yes, plenty of people thought so—my little Seneca, for instance, not to use his real name. (*In a jaunty tone.*) There are great beauties among the nuns, you know. I have my own views on this. I've urged you often enough: be of good cheer, sisters![14] You will all be beautiful and queenly, worthy of the Lord, or almost . . . For you have to learn how to be cheerful while coming to me "to die for Christ, not to live comfortably for Christ."[15]

So it is you, Ana de Jesús! Come nearer, come on, I can see you with the eyes of my dear Seneca! (*Lips.*) The best of prioresses, who directs Beas like a seraphim—it was John of the Cross who said that. Approach, child. After I am dead, you will gather all the manuscripts left by the Holy Mother you'll remember me as, and hand them to fray Luis de León for publication. It's not that I'm particularly concerned with my writings, as you know I hardly ever reread my work. But *The Way of Perfection* must, please, remain in the form that I have given it. The rest I leave up to you, do the best you can . . . You and Fr. Gratian will take care of printing the *Foundations* that our Lord commanded me to set down in writing . . . in Malagón, but when was it, exactly? The command Fr. Ripaldo finally asked me to carry out, much later, in . . . I'm not sure . . . Salamanca . . . (*Staring fixedly at Ana.*)

ANA DE JESÚS. I'll be reproached for supporting Fr. Gratian, Mother. It's already earned me the hostility of Nicolo Doria.

TERESA. His fury, to be accurate. You'll get three years' reclusion, that's all, a trifle for an inspirational muse like you. And eternity into the bargain! Not just in the heart of John of the Cross! And fray Luis de León will compose his *Exposition of the Book of Job* especially for you.

ANA DE JESÚS. You flatter me, Holy Mother.

TERESA. Not a bit of it. And since you find me so holy, hear this prediction: You will introduce the Discalced Carmelite order into France, with the help of little Ana de San Bartolomé who's kneeling right there. She will be of great service. But we'll leave that to Madame Acarie, at Bérulle . . . And you'll go to Paris, and to Dijon, and maybe even to Brussels and the Netherlands . . . (*Pause.*)

Ana de Jésus. Sixteenth century. Carmel of Seville.   Private collection.

TERESITA, *bending low over the pallid face.* What was that you said about John of the Cross, Mother?

Teresita and Ana de San Bartolomé are avidly drinking in the murmured words; the old lady's life-breath seems in no hurry to desert her. She smiles at her visions, tongue in a knot and throat coughing up blood, making it hard to articulate. Her words must be guessed at, they guess, they love her. She turns toward the two nuns.

TERESA. John met her in 1570, you see, when she was just a novice. When he came out of the dungeons in Toledo in 1578 he dedicated his *Spiritual Canticle* to her, the poem she'd asked him to write as well as the commentary on it. I haven't been able to read it, unlike the other texts. . . . I tell you again, Ana de Jesús has the works, I only have the noise . . . (*Pause.*)

La Madre's lapidary way with words stays with her to the end, whether for laughter or tears. The two nurses stroke her forehead and wipe her lips with a cold cloth. They are not sure what would be most restful for Teresa of Jesus; should they talk or keep quiet? She was never like other people. Why would she conform now?

* * *

As she prepares to depart, she finds it sweet to remember the kind, the gentle, the maternal ones. There was Ana Gutiérrez, remember, who cut her hair one day when Teresa became overheated in an ecstasy. The girl thought the hair wonderfully soft and honey-scented.

LA MADRE, *curtly.* Stop that at once! Throw the hair on the nettle patch!

Exeunt the sainted strands, Teresa remembers it well. Alas, it was just the beginning.

TERESA. To think they're going to chop me into relics, dear Ana, and you'll all stand back and let them! I suppose it could be a fashion, one of those inevitable human foibles . . . No, if the Lord tolerates these macabre orgies, even among my friends, it can only be because I've sinned.

She shakes with laughter on her narrow cot. The sisters glance sidelong at each other: Is she losing her mind? "No, never, not a saint like Teresa of Jesus!"

> TERESA. María de Jesús Yepes, she was something else, awfully manly! (*Wrinkling nose.*) The pope said that about her. Not quite my type, that lady, but don't forget she helped me draft the *Constitutions.*
> (*She lifts her head, tired eyes sparkling with mischief.*)
>   Do you know what would give me pleasure, girls? (*Speaking fast.*) Bring me Isabel de Jesús, she could sing me a *villancico* in her crystalline voice. Or better not, leave it, it's too late at night—not even Princess Juana, the king's sister, could get her to come around at this time. Why did Her Royal Highness come to mind just now? She wanted to imitate me, that's right, I seemed awfully simple for a saint! It was too great an honor for me. And not simple enough for her, as it turned out. One must turn things inside out in order to grasp what's really going on in someone's head, especially a woman's . . . She was a great help, the lovely Isabel, I mean. So was Princess Juana.

Teresa straightens up suddenly. Those two girls mustn't think the found-ress is in any hurry to meet her Spouse! And the faithful pair rejoices at the improvement.

> TERESITA. A sip of water, Mother?
> TERESA. Why not? God keep you, darlings. I'm not thinking of water just now. I've drunk too much, said too much . . . "Just being a woman is enough to have my wings fall off—how much more being both a woman and wretched as well"![16] No matter, a person's soul, male or female, is nothing but an abject pile of dung, and only the Divine Gardener can change it into a fragrant bank of flowers. And even then He needs a great deal of help! You look frightened, you two. What are you afraid of? That I might die? Or of what I say? (*Knowing smile.*)
> TERESITA and ANA lower their eyes and kiss her hands.
> TERESA. "We women are not so easy to get to know!" Women themselves lack the self-knowledge to express their faults clearly. "And the confessors judge by what they are told," by what *we* tell them![17] (*Broad grin.*)

Racked once more by a dry cough, Teresa can't laugh, the spasms block her throat. Another sip? No. She thinks some confessors incline to frivolity, and in such cases it's advisable to "be suspicious," "make your confession briefly and bring it to a conclusion."[18] Then she falls back onto her pillows and closes her eyes again. (*Pause.*)

TERESA. Not too much affection, if you please, and refrain from too much feminine intimacy. Beware, it smells a bit too much of women around here, don't you think? (*Wrinkles nose.*) How often have I told you, daughters, not to be womanish in anything, but like strong men? And if you do what is in you to do, the Lord will make you so strong that you will amaze men themselves. . . . He can do this, having made us from nothing.[19] Do you understand, Ana, Teresita? Do you, Catalina de la Concepción, Catarina Bautista? Be like strong men!

(*Her lips sticky with dried blood can barely part to let the hoarse voice out. La Madre is almost shouting, to the alarm of the nurses she has so sternly told to change sex.*)

ANA DE SAN BARTOLOMÉ. This is most unwise, Madre! Calm down. A nineteenth-century writer called Joris-Karl Huysmans will credit you with the virile soul of a monk.

TERESA. I thank him! But he clearly doesn't know me very well. (*Reading.*) Ah, daughters, I have seen more deeply into women's souls than any future pathologist! No, I am not referring to my admirer and enemy, the one-eyed Ana de la Cerda de Mendoza, princess of Eboli, in religion Ana de la Madre de Dios; after all, she and her estimable husband Prince Ruy Gómez provided for the foundation of two discalced monasteries.[20] You'll remember nonetheless that as soon as her husband died, the lady ditched her six children and became a Carmelite, to be more like me, and then caused me no end of trouble with the padres of the Inquisition! God have mercy on her soul! A formidable battle-ax, that Eboli. Good King Philip was right to summon her back to her maternal duties . . . (*Pause.*) Is that true, or am I dreaming, in revenge? Calling herself Anne of the Mother of God, as if she were Mary's child, that was bad enough. Girl child or boy child, who's to say? (*Wrinkling nose.*) Did I tell you how she arrived at the convent? In a hermetically sealed cart, again to be like me, but with a full team of maidservants and luxury furniture for her cell. . . . You see the kind of person she was? I could weep![21]

(*La Madre starts choking again, and Teresita hastens to fetch a jug of cold water.*)

ANA DE SAN BARTOLOMÉ, *fussing is her way of showing love.* Are you sure she wouldn't prefer it hot?

TERESA, *revived by anger.* Finally earthly justice dealt with that pretentious woman as she deserved. Did you know, girls, that Eboli was convicted of plotting with the secretary of our dear King Philip to assassinate Escobedo, the secretary of don John of Austria? She was locked up in the Pinto tower. I can see it now, she will die in prison at Pastrana, and then it'll be up to the court of the Last Judgment. In all humility, grave sinner though I am, I am glad not to be in her shoes.... (*Falls backward.*)

⋆ ⋆ ⋆

ACT 1, SCENE 2

LA MADRE, with her carers

ANA DE LA FUERTÍSIMA TRINIDAD

BEATRIZ DE LA MADRE DE DIOS

CASILDA DE PADILLA, CASILDA DE LA CONCEPCIÓN in religion

CATALINA DE CARDONA

AN ANONYMOUS NUN

MARÍA DE OCAMPO, MARIA BAUTISTA in religion

MARÍA DE SAN JOSÉ

EMPRESS MARIA THERESA of Austria

TERESA DE LAYZ

With, passing through:

ISABEL DE SANTO DOMINGO

ISABEL DE SAN PABLO

ISABEL DE LOS ÁNGELES

ANA DE LOS ÁNGELES

After swallowing some water from the glass proffered by Ana de San Bartolomé, Teresa sinks back onto the white sheets. There will be no rest. The specter of the princess of Eboli hovering around the bed charges her with fresh energy. The dying woman finds great entertainment in the parade of complicated female souls.

But she lacks the strength to name her thoughts; they are only visions floating before her open eyes, blurred by tears, a down of memories; hazy shadows, opalescent or brightly hued, filling the frigid cell, flowing out of Alba de Tormes and rising heavenward with Teresa.

Here is María de San José, the prioress at Seville, the cleverest and craftiest, the one to watch. She is wearing a fox pelt over her habit.

LA MADRE. I noticed you at the palace of Luisa de la Cerda, do you remember, daughter? (*Stares at her for a long time.*) Trained by the greatest lady in Spain, you were a scholar, a rare jewel, speaking and reading Latin, an enchantress in prose and verse and all the rest.
(*Teresa is thinking these memories, but not formulating them in words.*)
MARÍA DE SAN JOSÉ. Your sanctity entranced my soul at once. "She would have moved a stone to tears," I kept saying to anyone who'd listen. (*Remembering, silent.*)
LA MADRE. How many letters did I write you after by the grace of Jesus you became prioress at Saint Joseph's in Seville? Dozens? And I'm sure you knew why at the time. (*Pause.*) Out of respect for your wisdom, undoubtedly. But also, or more so, because our mutually cherished Fr. Gratian wouldn't budge from Seville. (*Falls back. Palpitations.*) You knew, didn't you? What I mean is, he wouldn't budge from your side. (*Her throat tightens further, no air gets through.*)

María de San José has not forgotten the tensions, the recriminations, the quarrels. A blend of affection and jealousy linked and opposed her to La Madre. Today she lowers her eyes, she won't say a word. Teresa for her part is mentally rerunning the many equivocal pleas she addressed to the prioress.

TERESA, *reading, vehemently.* "Give us even more news about our *padre* if he has arrived. I am writing him with much insistence that he not allow anyone to eat in the monastery parlor ... except for himself since he is in such need, and if this can be done without it becoming known. And even if it becomes known, there is a difference between a superior and a subject, and his health is so important to us that whatever we can do amounts to little."[22] Serve him some fish roe, an *olla podrida* if you can, and why not some *salpicón*. ... (*Smothered laugh.*)
MARÍA DE SAN JOSÉ, *unable to resist self-justification.* You're saying, Mother, that we should make an exception for him?
LA MADRE. If only you love me as much as I love you, I forgive you for the past and the future. (*Teresa is not listening. While she lived, didn't she do everything in her power to look into the soul of this fascinating woman? Tonight, let the visitor listen to her.*) "My only complaint now is about how little you wanted to be with me."[23] (*She looks steadily at her. Over and above their mutual fondness, the pivot between them was Gratian. Who could fail to realize it? Not they, at any rate.*)

TERESA, *thoughtfully.* "For goodness' sake, take care to send me news of our *padre*."[24] (*Pause.*) "Oh, how I envy your hearing those sermons of Father Gratian."[25] "I am worried about those monasteries our *padre* has charge of. I am now offering him the help of the discalced nuns and would willingly offer myself. I tell him that the whole thing is a great pity; and he immediately tells me how you are pampering him."[26] (*Wrinkles nose.*)

"Please ask our Father Gratian not to address his letters to me, but let you address them and mark them with the same three crosses. Doing this will conceal them better."[27] (*Lips moving.*)

"Never fail to tell me something just because you think his paternity is telling me about it, for in fact he doesn't."[28] All this commotion about Fr. Garciálvarez, the meddling of Pedro Fernández and Nicolo Doria. . . . Write to me without delay, for charity's sake, and tell me in detail what is going on. (*Smile fades.*)

The sentences roll through her mind. In 1576 she was obsessed with Fr. Gratian, while he was loath to leave Seville—he obviously preferred the sparkling company of María de San José. Or did he?

LA MADRE, *an incisive dialogue breaking into her dreamy monologue.* Do you remember when the superiors of the order wanted to send me to the Indies to separate me from you? That is, to separate us, me and Fr. Gratian.[29] (*Teresa sinks back feebly. María looks unruffled: she knows all about this kind of female play-acting.*) Was Gratian so naive? He timed his moves too cleverly between the two of us for that. . . . Yes, he was a chess player too, not as good as me perhaps, but not bad. . . . (*Pause. Long silence from both Mothers.*) "Our *padre* sent me your letter written to him on the 10th."[30] Above all, and this is an order, "do not oppose or regret Father Prior's leaving." Don't be like me. "It is not right for us to be looking out for our own benefit."[31] (*Pause.*)

"You must have enjoyed a happy Christmas since you have *mi padre* there, for I would too, and happy New Year."[32] . . . (*Another choking fit, her lungs are full. That confounded prioress from Seville!*) I don't see why I shouldn't tell you that I saw more clearly into Gratian than you thought. "I was most displeased that our *padre* refuted the things said against us, especially the very indecent things, for they are foolish. The best thing to do is to laugh at them, and let the matter pass. As for me, in a certain way, these things please me."[33] (*Leaning back again.*) But let's get back to you, if we may. "I would consider it a very fortunate thing if I could go by way of Seville so as to see you and satisfy my desire to argue with you."[34] Now we are in 1580 and I am very old, aren't I? Tell me how you feel, and how happy you must be to have our *padre* Gratian nearby. "For my part, I am happy at the thought of the relief for you on every level to have him in Seville." (*Lips. Wrinkled nose. Retching.*)

Have they made up, these true-false friends, now that the end is near? That would have been too easy. A gob of blood. The dying woman gasps for air. And spits out the anger pent-up in her old body, anger that had filtered through her pen at times but will now burst unrestrainedly from the compression of her thoughts: judgment before forgiveness.

LA MADRE, *beginning quietly.* What can I say, you are a great prioress, by all accounts. And a famously learned woman, a *letrada*, no one else comes up to your ankle, let alone me, my lovely, you're a *letrada* all over. . . . (*She gets the giggles, chokes, marks time.*) But take it from me: I was upset by your foolishness, and you lost much credit in my eyes. (*Stares at her for a long time.*) You are a vixen, and I don't use words lightly. If death is an almighty carnival, and hardly an amusing one, our masks still get truer as we pass over toward the truth that only exists in the Beyond, and I know you follow me on that point at least. . . . Where was I? . . . No surprise to see you wearing the skin of that crafty beast I compared you to, over your habit! Because you introduced, into our saintly community in Seville, a greed I could not bear. (*Flared nostrils.*) You're certainly shrewd, beyond what your position required. Very Andalusian, really. You were never openly on my side. I can tell you, I suffered a lot on your account. Whatever possessed you to put it into the poor nuns' heads that the house was unhealthy? It was enough to make them fall ill. When you couldn't sort out the interest payments on the convent, you had to infect them with this strange extra fear. (*Bends head, reading.*) Do you suppose such matters are part of the prioress's vocation? Well, I finally complained to Fr. Gratian about you, absolutely, I got it all off my chest. And why shouldn't I?[35]

(*María de San José remains silent, looking down.*)

LA MADRE. Stop avoiding my eyes, it's over, I'm done here on earth. . . . It's no use, she doesn't dare look at me. (*Shakes head from side to side.*) You are tough and pigheaded, my dear, you resist me like you did when I wrote you those furious letters. It was like trying to make a dent in iron. Get away with you, then, adieu! What's keeping you? Of course I forgive you, away, be off![36] (*Waves hand, turning face to the wall.*)

* * *

La Madre has hardly regained her breath when another of those complicated females appears before her tired but vigilant gaze: María de Ocampo, the cousin whose idea it was to revive the Discalced Carmel, and who would be prioress at Valladolid. Another snooty soul, and sly-faced with it—passing judgment on all and sundry from her lofty perch. She rushes, cooing, to embrace the patient. La Madre withdraws to her innermost refuge, closes her eyes, holds her breath, plays dead. Her thoughts are more eloquent.

> TERESA, *reading, in an angry voice.* "I don't know how from such a spirit you draw out so much vanity."[37] No, I won't let her brag of having seen me on my deathbed. Let her reread my letters. I told her and wrote her a thousand times: it is selfish of you to care only about your own house! I dislike the way you think there's no one capable of seeing things as you do. You think you know everything, yet you say you are humble. How dare you presume to reprimand Fr. Gratian! (*Wrinkled nose, nausea.*)
>
> (*The defendant remains silent.*)
>
> TERESA, *staring intently at María de Ocampo.* Yes indeed, this woman, my own relative, who I myself propelled into the coveted post of prioress, had the impertinence to meddle in what was none of her business! How could she have the slightest idea of what it means to talk to Gratian? Speaking with him is like speaking with . . . an angel, which he is and always has been. My friendship with this father troubled her soul, did it? Well, I did what I could, and I'm not sorry. (*Straightens up in bed, lodges a pillow at her back, harangues the insolent phantom with closed eyes and disdainfully moving lips.*) I call it a friendship, if you want to know. Friendship sets one free. It's completely different from submission, and that's what you never understood, my poor child. To think you wanted to "save" me from Gratian! (*Forcefully.*) Save me and send me back to Fr. Báñez, whom I was neglecting, in your opinion! So off you went almost every day with your nasty gossip to the illustrious Dominican, trying to turn him against me and Gratian! You proved inflexible, a stance no one has ever taken with me. Yes, inflexible, to put it mildly.[38] (*Pause.*) No, I won't open my eyes, you will have to leave unseen. You will be pardoned without the light of a look, without brightness. That's all. It's too much already. But forgiveness is my religion, as it is yours, in principle. "A wise man does not bar the room of pardon, for pardon is fair victory in war."[39]

Who wrote that? (*Teasing smile.*) A "wise man," perhaps, does not. Much harder for a woman. So what am I? Nothing. Go away now, you have my forgiveness, of course. But for pity's sake spare me your presence.... Farewell, daughter!

$$\star \; \star \; \star$$

Teresa represses a desire to vomit. She mustn't, it only suits young bodies, young women; the dying must make do with the rising gorge of revulsion. She clings to her friendship with Gratian, just to show María Bautista what it is to be a woman: a woman of God, obviously, both here and in the afterlife. But a woman nevertheless, always in want of something or other—in want of love, what else.

TERESA. That prioress of Valladolid was smarter than me, perhaps. For one, she never wrote Gratian until he'd replied to her previous . . . at least, that's what she said.[40] It's different with me, I've always been the servant of our *padre*, his true daughter, and it's no concern of María Bautista's what went on between him and me, Him and me.... Who is He? May our Lord be with us.... My head is so tired.... (*Voice cracks.*)

Muffled footsteps, rustling habits, wet towels, cold water. Catalina de la Concepción and Catarina Bautista have come to take over from Ana and Teresita. La Madre meets their tender, vacuous gazes, her eyes try to smile, her lips quiver almost imperceptibly.

TERESA. We are not lovely to look at when we die, but some of us are luminous. I don't mean that a confession trickles at last from our naughty-baby mouths— for babies is what we become at the end—but . . . (*pause*). What comes out are ranting commonplaces, ready to be staged years hence by a certain Beckett. Rarely something original or striking. But one doesn't fear Nothingness, and when not cursing this vile world while waiting for Godot, one may find one's tortured, waxen countenance becoming lit by a futile glow.[41] (*Fast.*) All things are nothing, and that's fine. (*To the two carers.*) Don't you worry, my dears. There is a great difference in the ways one may be....

Having tasted of spiritual wedding in life, Teresa now expects nothing from her Spouse but total dispossession. She will be emptied of Gratian, also. The ultimate mystery: Could Nothingness actually be Being? "Mas habéis de entender que va mucho de estar a estar."[42] The two nurses are bewildered: Is La Madre delirious, or is she seeing the Spouse? Already? Probably the latter, since she's smiling. . . . A hideous smile all the same, stretching the lips that babble sounds in which the carers can only make out two, wearisome, obsessive words: *all* and *nothing, nothing* and *all . . . todo* and *nada. . . .* Silence.

* * *

In a flash, look, a few vice-ridden little hussies skipping past. One is the anonymous novice, who will remain anonymous: it was she who spread the rumor about discalced nuns scourging each other while suspended from the ceiling.

And this better-looking one, Ana de la Fuertísima Trinidad, a nosey parker who was always ferreting through my business, as if she wanted to impose an illegitimate proximity on me, or maybe she was a spy, but whose? The princess of Eboli? Officials of the Inquisition?

As vices go, I prefer ambition and scope, thinks Teresa. In the style of Catalina de Cardona, say. Here she is: I project the black shadow of this melancholic soul over the Alcázar gate that pierces Avila's girdle of walls.

> TERESA, *calm and composed.* You exerted quite a pull on me, as the daughter of the duke of Cardona, I can tell you that now, in the endgame of the end. (*Pause. Cheeks reddening, elbows sunk into the mattress, makes huge effort to straighten up, fails, tries again.*) You were governess to the ill-fated prince don Carlos, son of Philip II, weren't you? And also to don John of Austria, the illegitimate child of Charles V? (*Wrinkles nose.*) Because I'm always attracted by rank and honor, nobody escapes the family sin, I know it. Your noble self, as a doña, had considerable appeal for me, I must admit. (*Hands fingering veil, adjusting it on head.*) Then, suddenly, aged forty, you marched into the desert of La Roda, laden with penitentiary chains and blood-soaked hair shirts, in the sole company of your demons—gray serpents and fierce mountain cats. Not to mention fasting, dear me, every day but Tuesday, Thursday, and Sunday! (*Gabbling, out of breath.*) You chose to wear a monk's cowl, and I'll be frank, to me you're just a kind of transvestite. At the Escorial palace, did Princess Juana and King Philip invite you in that guise? I had to put up with you; my penances were small fry, compared to

yours. I wanted to equal you, which was confusing. That's it, I was overcome with confusion when I thought about you—especially when the Toledo community, a convent you once briefly visited, described being enchanted by the odor of sanctity emanating from your clothes, although it strikes me that your grimy habit could not but stink to high heaven. I can't help it, you see, I hate bad smells, I dread them, I run from them, there we are. (*Getting redder and more voluble.*) I trust my corpse will not be smelly, I'm sure it won't be. Here, have a vision, I'll share it for free: long after my death some good sisters will discover my fragrant body—so unlike yours, do you get me?—under a heap of limestone rocks (of course), and the news will astound the world. Jealous?

(*Catalina de Cardona's shadow remains mute. No sign, no sound, petrified in its transvestite pose.*)

TERESA, *in a hammy, pseudo-humble voice.* I felt all mixed up before you, oh yes I did, and I confess it. His Majesty understood, and reassured me: "I value your obedience more," His voice told me; you can imagine my relief. I didn't ever get to be as mortified as you, or as dirty, and certainly not a man, needless to say—ha ha ha! (*Open-mouthed, is she expiring, gagging, or laughing?*) I know all about obedience. Most of the time I obeyed as sincerely as I could. Quite often I did so playfully, I can say that now. The Lord knew it, for nothing eludes His infinite wisdom, and He let me, because if I was pretending it was only to please Him. (*Pause.*) I know how to obey, then. Despite the hardness of my heart, which is certainly male. Harshness, too, I cultivated just to please my Spouse! But not in your way, oh no! A female I was and a female I find myself to be, for the purposes of suffering, of course. And for those of enjoyment, obviously! Especially! Not like you, no. But sure of His love, in sovereignty, like Him, whatever else might happen. With or without Gratian. With everything and with nothing. . . . You'd never understand. You see, we belong to two different species. There is a great difference in the ways one may be . . . (*Smiling.*) To bud forth, to be drenched in water like a garden, streaming with joy, to say *yes* to everything, to nothing. . . . (*Smiling again.*) What else is there to do? To write, to make foundations, to hurry, because time is getting short, to lie . . . Truly I say this unto you. . . . (*Lips.*)

At these words the black shade of Catalina de Cardona disappears from the place where Teresa was amused to see it—the Alcázar gate in the ramparts of Avila—and takes refuge, offended, in Carmelite memory.

ACT 1, SCENE 3

LA MADRE, with
ANA DE SAN BARTOLOMÉ and TERESITA
CASILDA DE PADILLA
BEATRIZ DE LA MADRE DE DIOS
TERESA DE LAYZ
MARÍA ENRÍQUEZ DE TOLEDO, Duchess of Alba
The voice and ghost of the EMPRESS MARIA THERESA

The opalescent light of the death scene grows paler as the hours tick by. Even though La Madre knows her Spouse is waiting, her old, shrunken body cries out for motherly caresses. Does she really exist, this "mother without flaw"? Teresa no longer utters a word. Only her mind, the thoughts that leave her behind as they flee toward the Lord, clothe the visions—those wings, those ships—carrying her to Him.

$\star\ \star\ \star$

That young noblewoman advancing toward her bed, isn't that Casilda de Padilla, the daughter of the Castilian *adelantado*, Juan de Padilla Manrique? Her father died when she was very young, leaving her to be raised by her mother, María de Acuña Manrique, and guided by her confessor Fr. Ripalda—the inspired Jesuit priest who ordered the writing of the *Foundations*.

> TERESA. I miss you, daughter. (*Now her words run through the dying woman's mind, through neurons that obstruct or let them pass, but no word is uttered.*) Why did you leave me? Barely a year ago, it was. For the Franciscans of Santa Gadea, near Burgos, I seem to recall. (*Long stare.*) I recognized myself in you, or rather not— you ranked so far above me. And again, I hated that stubborn taste of mine for the finer things that drew me to you, that ambushed me in my unwitting state as a semi-Marrana determined not to know, that made me laugh at myself when I caught myself being so frivolous! First, from tender youth, like me you despised the world. (*Fast.*) They found a way to betroth you to a brother of your father's, so as to keep the fortune and the family name; your brother and one sister had already taken vows, that was enough, they thought. Your parents obtained a papal dispensation to license the match with your uncle. You were only twelve at the

time. You fled to a convent, they dragged you out, you went back, your uncle-husband got you out, you fled again, but this time you came to me, to the house at Valladolid.

(*The film rewinds inside her head, the brain sees, speaks without uttering, scrambles, speeds up, bumps into itself.*)

Let's begin at the beginning, shall we. Your story reminds me of my own paternal uncle, the pious, unforgettable Pedro Sánchez. (*Jumpy encephalogram.*) No connection? You're right, there isn't. Except, and this is the point, that Uncle Pedro was the one who made me decide to take the veil. I can admit it now. Nobody knows, only you. Do you see? My story was the exact opposite of yours: I didn't marry my uncle, he made me marry Jesus. Strange, isn't it? By the grace of God, I escaped sooner than you did from the fate reserved for women, mothers, families. You took your time. You tried to do it through me. At last you obtained what I offered, didn't you? (*Pause.*) In matters of love only the Other's love endures, don't you agree? The rest, including the attractions we feel as women, or especially those, is insoluble: the shadow of the mother gets in the way, do you follow me?

Teresa contemplates her reflection in Casilda de Padilla's specter, plunges into the other's life before retreating, lucidly; doubles briefly back onto the self to loop the loops of the writing and the girls' portraits sketched out in the *Foundations*. That's not me, is it? It's not me so who is it, who is she, what is a Me? Exile or castle? Dwelling places, maybe, but no me, there is no Me . . . unnameable Me that tells lies, basely splashing in the unnameable fount divine, of the Word rejuvenated. . . .

TERESA, *like an excited little girl.* Is that still you, Casilda, or have I got you mixed up? Do you know you're dressed like doña Catalina, my father's first wife? In the clothes that were packed away in wardrobes and precious chests. How can that be. . . .

CASILDA. You dressed me yourself, Mother, just now, with your own hands. (*She's trying to explain that it's all happening in the older woman's foggy mind. Or is it La Madre speaking, taking Casilda's role? She stares at the visitor for a long time. Superimposed images, chromatic deluge.*) You picked out this shantung skirt, made from the watered silk of old China, with a bias binding in slashed yellow taffeta and a red lining. And this violet damask bodice, ribbed with black velvet. You used to say your mother Beatriz used to put them on when she wasn't feeling sad, until, near the end of her life, she wore nothing but black . . .

TERESA. That's right, I did, I remember now! (*Carried away by reminiscence.*) And you used to speak so sweetly about your own mother, and the joy and fun she gave you every day, that I felt quite at home. And yet that same wonderful mother provoked violent inner struggles in you, with her sainted praying. (*Raising hands and holding them up, open, before eyes.*) To be faithful to such a perfect mother, as I tried to be to mine, you couldn't do better than leave the world that had caused her such grief, reject your marriage, and keep all your love for the holiness she herself aspired to, though she lacked the courage to pursue it wholeheartedly. Are you with me?

CASILDA. I thought I cared for my betrothed, Madre, much more than his age might warrant. Rather as you loved your Uncle Pedro, if I understand correctly . . . (*Reading from the* Foundations.)[43] "At the close of a day I had spent most happily with my fiancé . . . I became extremely sad at seeing how the day came to an end and that likewise all days would come to an end."

TERESA. All is nothing, I realized that at the same age you did. Or earlier. (*Pause.*)

CASILDA. I began to hate the world in the midst of its pleasures. (*Pause.*)

TERESA. We are much alike, daughter, and I love you because you persevered. Your mother couldn't bear to lose you to a nunnery. God bless mothers who pray on the one hand, and cherish worldly vanities on the other; such mothers sow war in the souls and bodies of their daughters. And war is the only thing worth living, my daughter; I mean it. Peace? (*Pause.*) Ah, peace! You too, you mouth it like everyone else, "Peace! Peace!" You, of all people! Peace doesn't exist, my heart. There is no peace, remember Jeremiah! (*Voice cracks.*)

Casilda de Padilla will never know the thoughts of a mind now beyond the power of speech. She is full of her own story, as we all are.

CASILDA. Father Báñez believed in the sincerity of my vocation. Twice I entered the convent at Valladolid, and twice I was expelled, even though I'd already put on the habit. I got no support from my mother; did she think I was being childish, or that I was possessed? (*Pause.*)

TERESA. Maybe she wanted to test you? That's what she told me, and your mother was a holy woman, my girl, believe you me. (*Momentary smile.*) So you worked out a compromise between you as follows. You signed away all your goods and assets, dear Casilda; that's what it comes down to, choosing the religious life.

Which is to say, choosing me—clear as day. Then your mother arranged with Rome to whisk you away from my lowly Carmelite house to become abbess at Santa Gadea, a convent founded by your own parents. Thus the family honor remained safe; but as for ours.... Let's drop the subject, shall we? (*Breathes out.*) (*Teresa is smiling, yet there's no detectable expression on her placid face. Ana de San Bartolomé thinks she must be with her Creator. But she's not there yet. Her mind wanders back to her part in Casilda's story, for this was one of her favorite daughters.*)

TERESA. I can still see the way you lost your pursuers! (*This movie doesn't bother her, on the contrary, it's entertaining.*) Once you got safely into our house, your habit went straight back on. It suited you, it still does, I must say. But I hope you don't mind if I like you better this way I dressed you just now? In that festooned skirt and purple bodice, Sister, you bring my mother's youth back to me! Between ourselves, our rough habits never make us forget that we're women. (*Pause.*) There's always something underneath.... Do you find that funny? (*Pause.*) And those unspoken wars the mothers waged, they passed them down to us, via invisible and downright twisted paths. But I can't stop thinking that those paths, those secret conduits, are precisely what make us so quick to turn toward the Lord, and so amenable to that divine Spouse. (*Forcefully.*) Come now, don't look so embarrassed! Keep them, keep the skirt I put on you and the top as well, I'd have given you all of Catalina's clothes if I could. I like you. You please me because you please the Lord, it's that simple, there's no sin in it. It's a game, let's be merry, daughter, it's only a game.... And playing is not forbidden, take it from me. Only today, for instance.... (*Pause. Asleep. Dreaming.*)

(*The mind journeys, but the stiffened body does not move. Has she become paralyzed?*)

Ana, Teresita, I don't sense you anymore, are you there? (*Wakes up, full face.*) I know you can't hear me, my voice won't come out. I'm cold. This blue air chills me to the bone, I wish there were some warm arms around my neck. I long for nurturing breasts, soft lap. Hot water, the four waters of the divine garden. Can't you see that I'm a newborn babe? Bathe me, fill my mouth with warm milk! (*Convulsions. Thin trickle of blood from corner of mouth.*)

I'm shivering, but only because I'm too lightly dressed. This fresh breeze, so airy and sharp-edged, tells me I'm in Avila, is that right? (*Fervid reminiscence. The serial goes into historical-epic mode.*) Father let me wear the white silk gown with pearl trimmings and lilac-pink stitching over muslin sleeves, the one Mother wore when Charles V came to town. And those leather ankle-boots I loved to see on her. Today's a holiday, I'm sixteen, and the Empress Isabella is coming with little Prince Philip, who is only four and who will become His Catholic Majesty King Philip II. (*Fast.*) To swap one's infant garb for a sovereign's finery, what a tiresome ceremony: flamboyant celebrations, head-spinning fuss. Then that feeling of emptiness and discomfort, me trembling and shivering like I am now, look, in this lovely dress of white and old-rose silk you've decked me out in, I know you meant well, but it's the middle of winter, be sensible, children.

(*No answer. La Madre can no longer hear the nurses whispering, her mind spins upon itself inside the crystal castle of her soul. No, it's a castle of snow and ice that's either melting or hardening, it depends. A delicate confusion merges dwelling places, years, silks, contours, beings.*)

Is it me arrayed in queenly splendor, or is it you, my daughter? Father Gratian's favorite, little Beatriz Chávez? (*Stares at her for a long time.*) Another one with my mother's name; the Beatrices are definitely keeping me company on this last voyage. And you even took the religious name of Beatriz of the Mother of God! Like our dear *padre*, that noble squire of the Virgin, who chose the same name to become Jerónimo Gracián de la Madre de Dios. I presume you noticed the coincidence? (*Pause.*)

Ah, that Mother of God, how desperately we reach for her when our own fails us! It would be an understatement to say you lacked a mother, Beatriz dear. (*Attempts sweeping movement with arm. Falls back.*) She was unkind and a bully, quite unlike other mothers that have been coming to my mind ever since I've lain dying in this freezing cold, for how many days now?... Anyhow, not really a mother at all, not like mine, nor like the way I attempted to be a mother myself, although, God forgive me.... (*Pause.*) He knows how flawed I am. (*Pause.*)

(*Beatriz de la Madre de Dios makes the most of this sentimental moment by acting the little girl, and a pretentious one at that: she'll never change.*)

BEATRIZ DE LA MADRE DE DIOS. In centuries to come, people will say that I was an abused child, won't they, Madre? You went into detail about my ill-treatment in the *Foundations*, in the chapter about the painful process of foundation in Seville.

TERESA. Appalling, to leave a seven-year-old mite with her aunt! They may have been rustic mountain folk, but your parents were Christians, like everyone else! (*Falls back.*)

(*Beatriz doesn't reply at once, intent on her own history as though drunk on bitterness.*)

BEATRIZ DE LA MADRE DE DIOS. And then those three servants, who were after my aunt's inheritance, accused me of trying to poison her with arsenic!

TERESA. To be honest the idea doesn't seem to me so far-fetched (*full face again*), in an abandoned child who would do anything to get home to her mother. We can admit these sorts of things now, can't we? This Hell on earth is well behind us, I mean behind me, and the cold air is already carrying my body, if not yet my soul, up to Heaven.

BEATRIZ DE LA MADRE DE DIOS. You are more *au fait* with all that than I, Mother. How can I remember what happened when I was so little? I do know that when Mother got me back, she gave me a scolding and a whipping and made me sleep on the floor every night for more than a year.

TERESA. And yet your mother was virtuous and devoutly Christian, like mine! (*Long pause. A joyful expression gradually forms.*) Aren't human beings strange! You'd think the Creator had not made us all of a piece, but out of mismatched scraps. As a result we all have several faces. You in particular, my child, it's a veritable curse. . . . Unless it's a stroke of luck, a kind of grace or freedom, do you follow? One of the most enviable of God's gifts, the ability to travel through our innermost spaces in a kind of pilgrimage. . . .

(*Beatriz goes back to poring over the twisted threads of her misfortune, not listening to La Madre. Teresa, carried away by storytelling, is not listening either. She has already written this drama, she contents herself with gleaning a word here and an image there. Hopeless, toxic female contiguity. . . .*)

TERESA. Ah, so your father passed away? (*The movie allows itself some melancholic frames.*) You never told me about that . . . and your brothers died as well? The Holy Virgin had to take you under her wing to ensure that when you were around twelve, you stumbled on a book about Saint Anne and developed a great devotion to the saintly hermits of Mount Carmel. (*Joyful expression returns, more intensely.*) Like me, you chose virginity. Clearly the best choice of a bad bunch. Fatherless and miserable, harried by your poor mother, who couldn't help taking it out on you, you barricaded yourself behind your hymen. (*Thin smile, fading.*)

BEATRIZ DE LA MADRE DE DIOS. I wanted to die a martyr, like Saint Agnes. Father and Mother beat me almost to death, then they tried to choke me. . . . I was confined to bed for three months, unable to move. . . . I wanted desperately to lose myself.

TERESA. Lose yourself, child? (*Leans back to inspect her.*) Thanks to the love of Christ, you were saved! To suffer like Him is pure glory. Once you felt affinity with the martyrs and the Passion, your family's harassment was transmuted into a token of love, wasn't it? (*Long pause.*)

BEATRIZ DE LA MADRE DE DIOS. There was only one way out for me: to become a nun.

(*Teresa seems to be suffocating again, she gasps for air to the alarm of Teresita and Ana. She thinks of the other Beatriz: Beatriz de Óñez.*)

TERESA. Beaten children, abandoned children, it's all the same: that's what you are, my darlings. (*The sequence of images is overtaken by darkness.*) Primed to take shelter in the bosom of the tortured Father whom I call our Lord. (*Turns to face us.*) My sisters, you are, and I along with you, we are the paler twins of the Lord on Calvary. The Lord who allowed Himself to be tortured, abused to death if you like, in order that we might merge with Him, fuse our flesh with His, and thus and only thus be saved along with Him. (*Sudden vehemence.*) You see, little one, you can escape from a degraded or violent mother, flee a falsely respectable and profoundly distressed family, but you can never, ever, get away from Him. We poor mistreated creatures—and what creature is not?—could only be saved by a Father as cruelly flogged as we were, who loves us and saves Himself, and thereby saves us too. (*Voice cracks.*)

(*The Chávez girl will never hear the catechism lesson La Madre recites to herself in order to make sense of her life and death. Beatriz is still hung up on her own adolescent yearnings.*)

BEATRIZ DE LA MADRE DE DIOS, *in a perverse whine.* I couldn't find a good father confessor anywhere, Mother.

TERESA. That's the way it goes, perfectly natural, my child. (*Smiles.*) But you are a shocking little flirt, let me tell you plainly. . . . As plainly as I allow that your mother was a wicked bully, in her way. (*Knowing smile.*) No need to blush! I can tell your cheeks are on fire, even with my eyes closed. (*Turns her back, settles on side with face to wall.*) I've known you long enough. . . . (*Breathes out.*)

I know you like the back of my hand, in fact, and you hardly need me to tell you why: because of Gratian. Yes, him again. (*Pause.*) Not knowing how to become a nun, you became depressed, and started haunting churches, looking haggard. An old white-bearded Carmelite did his best to convince you that God had already made you strong, since you'd survived your decomposing family, but that wasn't enough, you were on the lookout for something else. What could it be? (*Smile fades. Lips.*) The arrival of young Fr. Gratian on the scene lifted you to seventh heaven. You went to him for confession at least twelve times—oh, I know every detail!—you stalked and harassed him, in fact. (*Vehemently.*) He was wary of pretty airheads like you, I made sure of that, I wrote to him endlessly on that topic, as on many others. . . . Finally a lady interceded for you, and the painful richness of your soul was comforted: you clung to him like a limpet, determined not to let go!

(*It would take a lot more to dislodge that little pest of a Beatriz.*)

BEATRIZ DE LA MADRE DE DIOS. It was the feast day of the Holy Trinity, 1575, when you came to Seville, Madre, that I ran away from my parents' house to take refuge in the convent. I was your first novice, remember? You made me eat properly, I put on weight, I made peace with my mother. A few days after my profession of faith, my father resigned himself to die, and Mother came to join me at the convent.

TERESA. Nothing ever made me so happy as to see mother and daughter devoted to the service (*effortfully turning over, stares at her for a long time*) . . . the service of One who proved so generous toward them.

BEATRIZ DE LA MADRE DE DIOS. Mother and I? Or do you mean you and I, Madre?

TERESA. Mothers and daughters, you know, can never be reunited in this world. (*Rubs finger over lips.*) So much passion, so much rivalry, with love thrown in; and love is at its murkiest between a mother and a daughter. But there is a way to solder them, the only way! Remember what I am about to tell you, *hic et nunc.* Were female cohabitation possible at all, it is only possible in the name of His Majesty, a Third Person: that's what the true, Catholic, Roman, and Apostolic religion teaches. Will you remember that? I hope so, for your sake! As for the rest, between ourselves. . . . (*Nose, lips.*) Some of the father confessors God sends us are deplorably frivolous, in my experience. (*Reading from* Way.) "If this confessor wants to allow room for vanity, because he himself is vain, he makes little of it even in others."[44] Be forewarned! (*Pause.*) You aren't obliged to agree with me. In reality, Sister, you are quite incapable of having any opinion on this subject. Besides, these gentlemen are inclined to render us mistrustful of one another, it's well known. . . . (*Gravely.*) Why do you suppose I wrote a whole chapter about you, the twenty-sixth of my *Foundations*? It was because I knew the story would gratify him, who adored you. Of course I mean Fr. Gratian, who else? A foundation, you see, rests upon a host of stories like that, what did you think? (*Tries mechanically to adjust veil, forgetting that she is bare-headed.*) And it has a great deal to do with raptures, something else I daresay you know nothing about. Ah, they are impossible to resist, and cannot be disguised. On those days I am like a drunken man, I entreat God not to let it come over me in public! As for the lascivious feelings that come afterward, and that other people have mentioned to me, I pay no attention to them and I advise you to do the same. (*Knowing smile.*) Actually, I have never experienced this.[45] The truth is that I am so cheerful at departing at last toward His Majesty that I can confess all these trivialities to you, trivial creature that you are. But how I always distrusted you! (*Rueful smile, followed by nausea.*)

(*Three knocks at the door. Who is it? Who wakes La Madre from her coma?*)

TERESA. Let me go in peace! Dear God, You will not despise a repentant heart? (*Lifts beseeching eyes heavenward.*)

Father Antonio de Jesús, the old companion of John of the Cross, now a vicar-provincial, has come to witness the agony of the foundress. With him is the new prioress at Alba de Tormes, Juana del Espíritu Santo, a sweet and gentle girl but excessively fond of fasting, in Teresa's opinion. On grounds that Teresa was junior to the prioress, Juana offered her white linen bedclothes in place of the usual straw mattress, but then left her alone . . . so as not to be importunate! Father Antonio seemed not to notice this underhand score-settling between women. And now, at the end of the end, sensing the approach of the final hour, the two of them decide to show up—the Carmelite may well become a saint, you never know! But Teresa can't be relied on to collaborate. She is already floating on another level, waiting to be seized by the "royal eagle of God's majesty," "esta águila caudalosa de la majestad de Dios."[46]

TERESA. Ah, you must be here to talk business. (*Condescends to open eyes a crack.*) The battle for the Salamanca Carmel will be my last, and I have some concerns about this latest institution, having formally prohibited that the house be bought. But the prioress Ana de la Encarnación had set her heart on it. (*Turns page.*) So, it's you, Teresa, my daughter, Teresa de Layz, I regret that we must meet in these circumstances, but never mind, since it's God's will. Come closer, don't hang back. (*A new lease on life, briefly: foundational affairs stimulate her to the last.*) I took you, too, for another myself. It was you who founded this discalced convent at Alba de Tormes where I now lie, by God's grace, on this final leg of my journey. (*Reads.*) I devoted a nice little "short story" to you, as it will be called, in my *Foundations*. Don't thank me, thank the Lord for making you as you are. You had everything to be the beloved daughter: a well-heeled family, noble, pure-blooded parents so as not to feel "sold into a foreign land"[47] the way I sometimes did . . . I won't dwell on it, but I'm telling you, know it and don't forget. But no, that's wrong, it wasn't like that at all. . . . (*Rubs her eyes, nose, lips.*) God wished you to be abandoned also; soon after you were born, your parents left you unattended for a whole day from morning to night, as though your life mattered little to them. So many abandoned girls it pleased God for me to gather up—a sign from Providence, was it not? Providence, no doubt about it, decreed our paths should cross. . . . What was I saying. . . . (*Hacking cough.*) You were their fifth daughter, and people have no use for girls in this ignorant world.[48] Now listen, and retain what I say to you: "How many fathers and mothers will be seen going to hell because they had sons and also how many will be seen in heaven because they had daughters!"[49] (*Stares at her for a long time, then bows head to read from the pages that continue to unfold on the blue cloak of the Virgin, caressing the body on the brink of death.*) The times will have to change, that's all, and I have a premonition that it will be soon . . .

TERESA DE LAYZ, *in a faint voice.* The village woman who found me thought I was dead, apparently she said to me: "How is it, child, are you not a Christian?" And I piped up, "Yes, I am," despite being only three days old, because I knew I'd been baptized; and said no more until I reached the age when all children start to talk.

TERESA. That's quite a story, my dear; these women tell so many of them! Be that as it may, tell yourself that God willed it so, and don't attempt to fathom the mystery, we all of us bear its stamp (*Stares at her again, with incredulity.*) Forgotten by both parents, you knew you were a Christian. An excellent Christian! I myself recognized this about you, or else I should never have let myself be awoken by your visit at this stage. When your parents heard what their baby had said, they were amazed. They would have been amazed by far less. (*Coughs again, clears throat.*) Full of remorse, they began to lavish love and care upon you. . . . They were also troubled by your subsequent lack of speech that went on for a long time, I believe! (*Widens eyes. Pause.*)

TERESA DE LAYZ, *reciting her homily.* I didn't want to get married. But then, on hearing the name of a man who turned out to be both virtuous and rich, Francisco Velázquez, I consented at once. He loved me and did everything to make me happy, while on my side, God had equipped me with all the qualities he could wish for in a wife.

No, women never stop telling stories. . . . And this is another, stranded on its sandbank, jumbling times and places, high on love, children, and disappointment. Teresa isn't listening, she knows it all in advance, always did. What she had to do was swim on by, let the rest sink, wash herself down, escape.

>TERESA. A happy marriage, then. Like my marriage to my Spouse? (*Broad grin.*)
>
>TERESA DE LAYZ. Not all that happy, Madre, in that it was barren.
>
>(*At these words the foundress falls back into her blue chill of agony. The visitor continues prattling about the desire for children,* hijos, posteridad, generación, *and the many devotions and prayers she offered up, all in vain. Teresa thinks nothing. Nothing but the cold that sends icy fingers through the entrails that once were enflamed by the spear of transfixion.*)
>
>TERESA DE LAYZ. "Do not desire children, for you will be condemned," I was told by Saint Andrew, a powerful patron of these causes. And then I seemed to see a patio, Mother, and beyond it green meadows as far as the horizon, dotted with white flowers. Like your gardens, Mother, irrigated by the four waters, fragrant and in bloom. Saint Andrew appeared to me again, saying: "These are children other than those you desire." At that I understood that our Lord willed me to found a monastery. (*In a metallic, conquering voice.*) I no longer wanted to have children. (*Teresa remains silent for a long time. Why must this other Teresa rekindle such hoary griefs, incommunicable, forgotten, overcome and buried long ago?*)
>
>TERESA. I never wrote about what is now burning the tip of my tongue, and will remain as pure, unformulated thought.... (*Fervid reminiscence.*) Your story finds an echo in me. Two Teresas, de Cepeda and de Layz, two barren wives who begat religious houses instead of offspring.... (*Pause.*) You and your faithful husband eventually created Our Lady of the Annunciation at Alba de Tormes, a fine convent, and I'm proud of it. (*Pause.*) Sincerely proud. (*Weeps. Another long, heavy silence.*) And now, they tell me that the good donor that you were torments those great souls? (*With sudden violence.*) "I fear an unsatisfied nun more than many devils!" There!

Teresa de Layz feels the fear of sterility come over her again. If a mother upbraids her daughter, if she deserts her, is it not because the mother is herself unhappy, numbly inadequate, afflicted by some inexpiable infirmity? A dried-up fig, in short.

(*The dying woman pushes herself up on her elbows in the white bed with its freshly changed sheets.*)

TERESA. Ah, dear lady, one cannot serve God in disquiet. All this is infantile, mere attachment to self. How different it is wherever the Spirit truly reigns! (*Turns the page.*)

Teresa of Avila can be cruel, all right—just enough to restore order. Up to her last breath, and, if God wills it, piercing her foremost alter egos to the quick. Father Antonio de Jesús shows Teresa de Layz the door.

⋆ ⋆ ⋆

TERESA, *to Ana de San Bartolomé.* Tell me, child, are we still in Alba de Tormes, on the duchess of Alba's estates? (*In a childish tone of regressive nostalgia.*) Ah, the duchess! She delivered me for a time, like the exit from Egypt, she nurtured me. . . . It was her, doña María Enríquez de Toledo, wasn't it? Or am I out of my mind? I see her now. . . . (*Tries to rise onto elbows, falls back.*)
(*Doña María Enríquez de Toledo, the duchess of Alba, walks past holding a trout.*)
TERESA, *in a changed, respectful, courtier's voice.* The grace of the Holy Spirit be always with Your Excellency. Have you received my letter imploring your kindness regarding the house founded in Pamplona by the Society of Jesus? I know, the duke your husband is leading an army into Portugal, and the constable is your brother-in-law the viceroy. . . . (*Whispered aside to Ana de San Bartolomé.*) We must absolutely protect the Society as it protects us, don't forget that, my child . . . a testament, if you will. . . . (*Respectful voice.*) I am very sick, You Excellency, I am bleeding, I am on my way . . . it is important to me that the favor you show me in everything be known.[50] (*Quick sigh, soft voice for herself.*) The duchess is definitely worth keeping on side. After all, it was she who helped to have my little nephew Gonzalo exempted from serving in the duke's Italian campaign, dear Gonzalo, who caused me so many headaches after that. . . . Oh well, I did my best and so did she, and at least he didn't get killed.[51] (*Pause, broad smile.*) I'll always remember the nice fat trout you sent me, Excellency, when I was here in Alba, a good ten years ago it must be; a gift from God. . . . (*Tired voice, sigh. Suddenly sits up, reads in emotive voice.*) "If you favor us in this regard it would be like liberating us from the captivity of Egypt."[52] (*Silence.*)
(*Broad smile, repeating.*) Like liberating us from the captivity of Egypt . . . liberating us from the captivity of Egypt . . . from the captivity of Egypt . . . the captivity of Egypt. . . . "Let my people go, that they may hold a feast unto me in

the wilderness. . . . And I will bring you in unto the land, concerning the which I did swear to give it to Abraham, to Isaac and to Jacob . . . I am the Lord."[53] Let my people go . . . my people . . . from the bondage of Egypt . . . deliver me . . . deliver. . . . (*Coughing fit, long silence. Rest.*)

(*Teresa wastes not a second of this respite, the clarity that precedes death. She addresses Ana de San Bartolomé.*)

My dear child, as soon as you see that I am a little better, please order a cart. . . . (*Barely audible.*) Settle me in it as best you can and we will go, you, me, and Teresita, home to Avila (*voice breaking*). . . . Do you promise?

ANA DE SAN BARTOLOMÉ. Planning to travel, even with her last breath!

TERESITA, *plaintively, in tears*. She wants to be close to her parents. . . .

ANA DE SAN BARTOLOMÉ. I don't think so. She wants to leave Egypt.

TERESITA. But that's been done, way back in the Bible!

ANA DE SAN BARTOLOMÉ. Not like that. I think she's still caught in her own personal Egypt. . . .

⋆ ⋆ ⋆

Suddenly, after a few slow bars of introduction, a slender, diffident but cultivated soprano voice is heard. Delicately it sings an unaccustomed *Kyrie* for a funeral service—from the *Missa Sanctae Theresiae*, the Mass for Saint Teresa by Michael Haydn. The work was commissioned by the Empress Maria Theresa, and the voice we hear is hers.[54]

TERESA, *surprised, intrigued, attentive*. Don't be afraid, my daughter, nervousness inhibits the voice . . . as well you know, since at home in Austria you regularly sing the soprano solos of sacred music compositions. (*Motherly smile, timidity.*) Relax, let yourself go . . . you are after all the wife of Emperor Francis I of Austria! Come closer, let me hear your tuneful little voice. . . . Everybody will agree one day that Your Majesty's musical sensibility was the finest of all the Habsburg line. . . . You can believe me, it's your own patron saint telling you. . . . (*Vertigo, slackening, peace invades the spasm-shaken body.*)

EMPRESS MARIA THERESA, *singing the first movement of the Mass composed for her by Michael Haydn. The choir remains in the background throughout.* "Kyrie eleison. . . ."

LA MADRE. "Bravo!" "Superb!" "Majestic Haydn!" Are those your words or mine? I am not very musical, Majesty, as is well known, and you honor me by associating

me to that sort of faith which music is . . . being the most spiritual . . . or rather
the most physical . . . that is, both at the same time . . . or not? (*Dreamy voice.*)
Majestic, yes, that's what you called the little brother of the greater Haydn, for
you could see he wasn't so little . . . a Kapellmeister of Salzburg Cathedral, no less.
. . . The young Mozart will learn a lot about sacred music from Michael, no secret
there. . . . He mentions him in letters to his father Leopold. . . . They will remain
friends, even after Wolfgang's turbulent break with Prince-Archbishop Colloredo. . . . Music specialists will have a great deal to say about him, as time goes by
. . . yes, I assure you. . . . Some will point out that Mozart's celebrated *Requiem*
has much in common with the *Requiem* composed by Michael on the death of
Prince-Archbishop Sigismund von Scrattenbach, another friend of Amadeus.
But we're not at the requiem stage yet, are we, Majesty? . . . In my case, at least. . . .
Sing on, my daughter, and may God bless your lovely voice. . . . (*Peaceful smile,
falls asleep.*)

EMPRESS MARIA THERESA, *solo voice for the* Benedictus, *once again an unusual choice for Haydn in his homage to the empress and the saint.* "Benedictus qui venit in nomine Domini. . . ."

TERESITA, *crouching at the foot of the bed.* It seems the empress is giving her voice to La Madre. . . . What am I saying, La Madre gave her voice to her. . . .

ANA DE SAN BARTOLOMÉ. Is this really a Mass? It sounds more like a prayer, the sound of peace. . . .

(*Empress Maria Theresa is oblivious. She exits, carried on the* Benedictus *by Michael Haydn.*)

⋆ ⋆ ⋆

La Madre's spirit floats over the eighty-eight towers of fortified Avila, protected under the hem of the Virgin's blue cloak. At the same time she addresses the cortege of dark female silhouettes filing past her bed:

TERESA, *in a chanting voice.* Farewell, ladies, I am on my way to different skies. (*Pause.*) With no regrets. That is, I don't think so. (*Subtle smile.*) You did a good job of filling my life, as I filled yours. Enough is enough. . . .

The procession of nuns and prioresses includes Isabel de Santo Domingo, Isabel de San Pablo, Isabel de los Ángeles, Ana de los Ángeles....

TERESA. If the soul is a woman, she grieves to see that her nature, or rather her sex, hinders and ties her down. (*Reading.*) "Si es mujer, se aflige del atamiento que le hace su natural.... (*Short silence, then rapidly.*) She can't enter into the midst of the world to praise God. ... And she envies those who have the freedom to cry out and spread the news about this great God of hosts.... (*Short silence.*) Those who are free to proclaim to all the world the greatness of the God of cavalries."[55] (*Turned toward them, gazes after the procession of women leaving the scene.*) (*La Madre's head rolls back onto the fluorescent white pillow, an exceptional concession to the dying in this Spartan place.*) (*Long silence. A voice is heard in the distance.*)

> When the breeze blew from the turret
> Parting his hair,
> He wounded my neck
> With his gentle hand,
> Suspending all my senses."[56]

TERESA. What song is that? I never wrote that. ... (*Voice breaking.*) Could it be dear John of the Cross speaking through my lips? Is that you, Father, by my side? (*The voice stills. The eighty-eight towers, a glimmering girdle of Avila blue, encircle the dying body of La Madre.*)

Chapter 31

ACT 2

Her Eliseus

> I knelt down and promised that for the rest of my life I would do everything
> Master Gratian might tell me. . . .
>
> Teresa of Avila, *Spiritual Testimonies*

> It will seem inappropriate that he should have informed me of so many
> personal matters about his soul. . . . he told me about these things and
> additional ones that cannot be suitably put in writing. . . .
>
> Teresa of Avila, *The Foundations*

ANGELA, a code name for Teresa in correspondence with Jerome Gratian

LAURENCIA, ditto

LA MADRE, out of breath

ISABEL DE SANTO DOMINGO, prioress at Segovia, passing through

FATHER JEROME GRATIAN OF THE MOTHER OF GOD, permanent presence
    Aliases:

ELISEUS, PAUL, JOANES

TERESITA and ANA DE SAN BARTOLOMÉ, at prayer

SYLVIA LECLERCQ, psychologist

VOICE OF HIS MAJESTY THE LORD

VOICE OF A FUTURE EDITOR OF TERESA'S WORKS

ACT 2, SCENE 1

Cast as above, minus the VOICE OF HIS MAJESTY THE LORD

The soul in agony here enters a terrain that rather resembles that of my MPH, were it not for the way the Holy Mother's faith has changed it into a well-watered, flower-filled garden. Here, at the extreme of being, extreme beings trail their sufferings and raptures, their obsessions and exaltations, deliriums and OCDs, hysterical passions, manic self-punishments, dull melancholies, and searing moments of lucidity. Filtered through the body and the word, these states at the limit—hers, theirs—appear as alluring as passion, as beautiful as Paradise, as necessary as ideals.

La Madre has rallied a little: it's the upturn before the end. She can speak again, although with difficulty. The words that garland her memories and premonitions elude her throat and mouth. Almost silent, voluble inside, she relies upon the body more than ever, and marks the passage of time in beats of sound, touch, taste, smell. The failing Madre's flesh is no more than a love letter by now, a letter endlessly edited, corrected, and rewritten.

The skin thirsts for cooling waterfalls. The tongue cries out for pungent tastes. The shattered bones dream of strolling among fragrant lilies. When loneliness is so immense, to whom can these entreaties be addressed? Absence makes one mad. So does the longing for presence.

ANGELA, *in a normal voice.* One day in 1575 . . . was it in February or May? At the Convent of Beas . . . the Lord told me that He could grant my wishes. (*Pause.*) And as a token of that promise He put a handsome ring onto my finger, an amethyst. What divine bounty toward my sorry life, worthy of the fires of Hell! I know it was delirious nonsense to have felt this wedding to be real, in broad daylight. Christ as a marriage broker, *un casamentero*, that's insane! Foolishness . . . I can laugh at it now.

VOICE OF A FUTURE EDITOR OF TERESA'S WORKS, *attempting to moderate the harshness of a judgment that shows her, even on the brink of death, being as tough on herself as ever.* Madre, you noted in that context "I am writing this foolishness,"[1] but the fragment is apocryphal, of dubious authenticity, and the Church does not recognize it.

TERESA: You, too, love me too well, Father. (*Looks at him for a long time.*) Let me confide what comes to my mind about all this now. Was it not foolishness on my part to have seen—around the time I received the amethyst ring—the Lord join my right hand to Fr. Gratian's? And to have heard Him say that I should take that master as His representative, all the days of my life? (*Raises chin, looks straight ahead.*) Now, then, Father, don't back down, I pray you. I take it upon myself to admit that I committed that *desatino* and many more, fair enough. Neither right nor wrong, but inevitable. Logical. Well, yes, I'm a logical woman! If you think about it, all that kind of thing derives straight from the sacred humanity of Christ. And there aren't many of us prepared to take on the full implications of *Cristo como hombre*. (*Knowing smile.*) Please don't make that face, Father, I know the repugnance I inspire in you. I have felt my abjection and soiling intimately, I assure you. (*Stops smiling.*) But after so much pain and contrition, the disgust turned even so to pleasure, to desire, and—but I'm not telling you anything you don't know—into a clandestine relationship with my Eliseus, my Paul, my Joanes. He needed me. He needed that secret friend, code-name Laurencia, or sometimes Angela. . . . That's what I called myself in letters to him that he most certainly has kept, you'll see. (*Hand stroking the veil she imagines is still covering her disheveled head: incorrigible coquetry.*) His letters, no, I haven't kept them. He didn't write often, anyway, we'll never know what he really thought, or how different it was to what I suggested he think. . . . (*Tender voice.*) I elevated dear Gratian to the place of God, outwardly and inwardly, I confess it. I needed those *antojos*, cravings, whims, and on reflection, they weren't incompatible with the Incarnation. (*Pause.*) That's all. Mad! (*Broad smile.*)

The enigmatic grin brightens La Madre's face for so long that her two nurses suppose she must be getting an early glimpse of her Spouse.

She is not contemplating Gratian as he looked the day of their first meeting, but as he is in the seventeenth-century portrait of him that hangs in the Carmel at Seville. Because Sylvia Leclercq has no other way of picturing him.

LAURENCIA. You're a charmer, *Padre*. Had I had no other reasons for serving God, your angelic grace would have sufficed to convince me. And "in a certain manner it is a delight for me when you tell me about your trials."[2] I can think of someone— me—who will know how to defend "her son Eliseus better than anyone else in the world."[3] (*Reading.*) "I was pleased that Paul wrote me as 'your dear son.'"[4] "Oh Jesus, what a wonderful thing it is for two souls to understand each other, for they neither lack something to say, nor grow tired."[5] "*Mi padre*—and my superior, as you say, which delighted me and gave me a good laugh. . . . (*Chuckles.*) What little need there was for you to swear—neither as a saint nor much less

Fr. Jerome Gratian of the Mother of God. Sixteenth century. Carmel of Seville.
Private collection.

as a teamster—for I am fully persuaded. . . . I only want to remind you that you
gave me permission to judge you and think whatever I want about you."[6] (*Still
reading.*) Oh, my soul grows lonelier every day, so far from you. . . . (*Normal
voice.*) I feel as though I'm "always near Padre José,"* [*A code name for Christ.—
Trans.] but who is he? Jesus Christ or you? "In this way one passes through life
well, without earthly consolations, yet continually consoled. It seems you are no
longer of this earth, since the Lord has withdrawn the occasions of becoming
attached to it and filled your hands with what keeps you in heaven."[7] (*Big smile.*)

⋆ ⋆ ⋆

Here, Sylvia Leclercq grows irritated. Despite her years of graphomania, our poor Madre remains a slave to her passions! (The therapist will not speak of her irritation, but allows herself a moment's intrusion into the deathbed scene of this most unusual patient.)

SYLVIA LECLERCQ. After so many years of, um . . . (*hesitates, clears throat*) . . . of flattering, supporting, and shielding your precious genius of an Eliseus, mightn't it be a good idea to give it a rest? And for you to find rest in the peace of the Lord Himself, rather than in some stand-in or other?

Teresa is not best pleased by this interpellation. Under the guise of protectiveness, could the stranger be seeking to discredit her?

LA MADRE, *trying to get a clear view.* How very sensible of you, my dear! Kindly refrain from treating me as an invalid who has lost her marbles. (*Tries to point a finger at the intruder, hand falls back onto sheet.*) Think what you like, but pray keep this in mind: "The important thing is not to think much but to love much."[8] Consider if you will, clever lady, that by 1575 I had already started seven convents and was having some trouble with the friars of my Order. There weren't many discalced men in those days, and not one, frankly, who could hold a candle to Fr. Gratian. (*In a wheedling voice.*) And so, you understand, a fellow like that who as a young man in Madrid used to beseech an image of our Lady, whom he called his "Beloved"—all right, it's a bit pretentious, but with such disarming humility! He fell in love with our order in Pastrana, where he charmed the socks off the prioress, Isabel de Santo Domingo. . . . (*Snort.*) Who succumbed like all the others, male or female, to the magic of his conversation. . . . Finally he decided to take his vows with us, after trying out the Jesuits. . . . (*Widens eyes.*) An *hombre* with that kind of mettle is something to treasure, don't you think? (*Knowing smile.*)

Defeated by the evidence, Sylvia Leclercq keeps quiet.

ANGELA. When he came to see me at Beas, a few years later, in that unforgettable year 1575, he was already widely esteemed as a discalced white friar. Considering that, three months before his profession of faith, he had had to vanquish some very powerful temptations; he told me a little about it. . . . (*Absorbed in Gratian's travails, the voice grows dreamy, quivers, melts. Is Teresa taking the path of ecstasy already?*) Anyhow, he had been called upon to be a captain of the Virgin's sons, and he was fighting with great valiance.

SYLVIA LECLERCQ, *trying to get through to her via realism.* So you needed him, just as he needed you? Gratian would be the organizer you had been hunting for in vain, the man to coordinate the renovation of the Primitive Rule. And yet he didn't include your name in the Alcalá *Constitutions* published in 1581; there's no mention of you at all!

LAURENCIA. That was our agreed strategy. You are being petty. (*Normal voice.*) True, Fr. Gratian drafted the *Constitutions* for the discalced friars.[9] (*Silly voice.*) He was plainly helped by our Divine Majesty, and our Lady had clearly chosen him for the task of restoring Her Order. Of course, wretched sinner that I am, I strove to hide my imperfections from my daughters—although my flaws are so many that they must have noticed some. For instance, my affection for Paul, not the same today as it was, perhaps, but it persists. . . . (*Tragic voice, reading.*) And the concern I have for him. "I often point out to them how necessary he is for the order and that I am under an obligation—as if I could act otherwise if I didn't have this reason."[10]

SYLVIA LECLERCQ. I see. Not only was he useful to you, you loved him. (*She advances a simplistic, coarse interpretation, as one does with smart-ass patients who try to hide their cards. Take it from me, such patients are conscious of all sorts of things that are assumed to be unconscious!*)

Teresa has stopped listening, doesn't reply, plays dead. The psychologist, somewhat embarrassed, circles the bed. Not a flicker. Sylvia withdraws, resigned. La Madre remains with her Pablo-Paul-Joanes-Eliseus.

* * *

Isabel de Santo Domingo walks across the stage.

LA MADRE. You've come to say goodbye, dear child, God be blessed, I was expecting you. You met Fr. Gratian when he was a student, and I know it was you who steered him toward the Carmelites. In short, I met him thanks to God . . . and to you! (*Quick smile.*) "I had never seen perfection combined with so much gentleness."[11] You feel the same way, I know. (*Lingering smile. Lips.*) Go in peace! (*She turns to the wall. Not dreaming, but rereading her life.*)

ANGELA, *reading, with a little smile.* "I am now very old and tired, but not in my desires."[12]

LAURENCIA. For pity's sake, write to me! She has a point, that psychologist: why don't you write? (*Tragic voice.*) I stand up to the censors, I do battle with Nuncio Sega here and with Nicolo Doria there, all for the sake of our joint work, and also to please you, but you leave me to pine. . . . If at least you'd give up the fight, and give me up, cleanly. But instead you maneuver, you're equivocal; another sign of your genius, no doubt. I beg of you, write me, *Padre,* instructing plainly what I must and must not do. (*Imploringly.*) It's not fair of you to touch on these matters so confusedly. And also you must pray for me, a lot. . . . I am surprised you don't tire of me; I suppose God permits it so that I can bear a life in which I enjoy so little health or satisfaction, apart from what pertains to you. (*Pause.*) Lord, I well remember having written that to my Eliseus. And this: if, by wounding me, they wound my Paul no matter how slightly, I cannot bear it. I was not upset in anything that concerned me. . . . There, that's how I lived my life. (*Raises hands and holds them before eyes.*) Love will never be a sickness. . . . I hope that little psychologist who was trying to guilt-trip me has left. It's obvious the silly woman has never read the First Epistle of John (3:14): "He that loveth not his brother abideth in death." I've read it. Pablo and I, we knew that. . . . For charity, write to me, *mi padre*! (*Broad smile.*)

(*Silence from Jerome Gratian. He will not respond to the woman on the brink of death.*)

LAURENCIA. Is he still in Seville? Traveling through Andalusia? (*Silly voice.*) With María de San José? Or Beatriz de la Madre de Dios? What do women want, cloistered or not? A father to reign over, of course. But a man? Jesus, in his sacred humanity? What does a man want? To be loved by women, so as to escape from his brothers and be elected by the father? My mind is wandering. . . . The Dominican Juan de la Cueva, an eminently sensible man, observed that Gratian had a tendency to act alone, without consulting others. (*Suddenly vehement.*) Did my Paul think he was some kind of spoiled Infant King? He didn't even come back for the solemn vows of Lorenzo's daughter at Avila, although I begged him to, and poor little Teresita was so looking forward to it. Where are you, Eliseus dear? (*Silence from Paul.*)

ANGELA. I'm talking to you, pleading with you. Laurencia does not often enjoy her confessor, Paul, whom the Lord gave to her, because in the midst of so many troubles he is always far away. . . .

(*Silence from Paul.*)

ANGELA, *reading.* "But what learning and eloquence Paul has!"[13] And he has an honorable and agreeable family for whom I came to care, especially his mother, doña Juana Dantesco. . . . I hope that beastly psychologist isn't listening, God knows what she'd make of that! (*Pause.*) Ah, my darling Paul, I did all I could to protect you from Methuselah, our pet name for the nuncio Ormaneto, do you remember? (*Normal voice.*) Now that it's behind us, I'm wondering whether the most egregious aspect of the affair might not be my passion for your mother, doña Juana. (*Long silence, smile; collapses heavily back onto mattress, fondly shaking head from side to side.*) I was as crazy about her as I was about you. (*Warm smile.*) Who wouldn't be? Because I've seldom, or probably never, met her equal for talent and character. (*Reads.*) "She has a simplicity and openness that put me in seventh heaven," I can't repeat it too often; and "in these she greatly surpasses her son."[14] That was naughty! You'll forgive me, Father, won't you?

$$\star \ \star \ \star$$

At this point Sylvia Leclercq feels compelled to tiptoe once more into the scene: Will Teresa's free-associating cast any light on the (pretty indiscreet) pathology of that godly woman?

ANGELA, *silly voice.* It was very amusing, Eliseus my sweetheart, when you told me to open the grille and lift my veil for your mother; to show her my face, basically. Good grief, it seems you don't know me! I would have opened my belly for her! For her first of all, her above all, who bore you in her womb! (*Pause.*) For her, sure, sooner than for the great Bernini who will make my marble entrails thrill to the cherub's lance. (*Smile.*) The sculptor never suspected that the little angel was you . . . my baby, my lance, my javelin, stabbing me in the heart and beyond . . . deeper, lower, in the castle's remotest chamber. . . . (*Blissful smile.*)

SYLVIA LECLERCQ. Poor thing, what a passion! Shoving the Word in up to her. . . . (*For reasons of technique, the therapist is given to using crude language with certain patients. Today she holds back, flashing a half-mocking, half-complicit grin at La Madre, who doesn't notice, immersed in her sensations.*)

ANGELA. I was thinking, Joanes darling, I'd willingly give the habit to your sister doña Juana, who stayed here with your mother until the last day. And also to that little angel her sister Isabel, "who is as pretty and plump as can be." Doña Juana very much resembles you. . . . (*Pause.*) I'd love to have her with me. By the way, which of us two loves you more, do you think? "Doña Juana has a husband and other children to love, and poor Laurencia has nothing else on earth but this *padre.* . . ."¹⁵ (*Laughs out loud. Pause.*) So, since I couldn't give birth to you, or suckle you, all my care went into feeding you. Remember, Eliseus my soul, how often I nagged you to eat properly . . . (*silly voice*) to put some weight on, to make sure María de San José plied you with tasty dishes? Even if they were cooked by her, who I didn't much like. I took huge pleasure in feeding your mother, as well as your angel of a little sister, Isabel, who is with us at present. "How plump she's getting, and charming";¹⁶ I love her almost as much as I love your mother, since I can't love you more than I do already. (*Knowing smile.*) I give her ripe melon to eat, it's the best I can do, since breastfeeding is not given to all—but shush, that psychoanalyst is still eavesdropping. (*Smile fades.*) My temperament is strange: the less notice you take of what I think, the freer I feel about expressing my desires and opinions. God bless you. . . . (*Long silence, cheeks reddening.*) Ah, it breaks my heart to hear that you are unwell, my father, my son. . . . A rash, it seems, doubtless due to the heat. That reminds me (*tragic voice*) . . . I must tell you about a temptation I had, which persists, concerning you. And I wonder whether you yourself do not neglect the whole truth at times. (*Touching voice.*) Do you think I'm jealous? Well, what if I am?

* * *

Perhaps La Madre is a normal woman after all. Though Sylvia Leclercq already thinks so, she's somewhat taken aback by such goings-on beneath the rough woolen habit. Two hundred years before Diderot's *The Nun*, a scandal in its day. But on closer inspection, is Teresa indulging in a carnal freedom forbidden by her religion, or is she, on the contrary, activating the interior (as La Madre would say) message of that religion? It's an unconscious message as far as Sylvia is concerned, which acquits desire of guilt, provided the desire is for the father. Well then, let it be proclaimed, let it happen in words rather than deeds! And if matters should get so muddled that sin does ensue, the weight can still be lifted through the senses and in words, over and over again. Isn't it more enjoyable that way? The *jouissance* of everything and nothing, from words to flesh and back again. Physical frustration heightens the power of fantasies, while fantasies sharpen sensation to the max. There's no possession as satisfying as abstention. This could be the delights of masochism, or alternatively an inversion of sadism into an objectless exhilaration, in the omnipotence of narcissism; Sylvia Leclercq is not sure what to think anymore. She is disposed—almost—to admire, while concealing her Voltairean smile.

> LAURENCIA. May God pardon the "butterflies." . . . (*Pause.*) I am talking about our Carmelites in Seville, lucky enough to enjoy my Eliseus. It's a great hardship for me. (*Reads.*) "I can't help envying them, but it is a great joy for me that they are so diligently seeking to provide some relief for Paul, and so inconspicuously."[17] I like women, too, I won't deny it. Oh, I understand, Eliseus my son, I even approve. Up to a point. God alone knows which point . . .

Sylvia is practically rubbing her hands. What a windfall! This deathbed is a positive psychotherapist's couch.

> ANGELA. Are you taking revenge on me, adored Pablo? (*Sighs, reads.*) The time left to you after my death—a long time, never fear—"will bring you to lose a little of your simplicity, which I certainly understand to be that of a saint."[18] (*Humbly.*) But be on your guard! The sisters are young, and the thought of you spending the summer in Seville is alarming. (*Touching voice.*) Needless to say you'll be working against our enemies, like those Jesuits who are giving us a hard time. I used to call them "ravens," to amuse you; and what about the "cats" and the "wolves"—the more malicious of our discalced brothers, hard to believe, but they exist, and they were after you; not to mention the "night owls," those dismal calced nuns who can't stop conspiring . . . and of course Methuselah, the apostolic nuncio . . . always the same ones . . . among so many others determined to scupper us! (*Irritated chuckle.*) I wrote to you extensively at the time on these urgent topics, in order to guide you, of course. And now, at the end of my allotted span, I only have two counsels for you. (*Reads.*) *Primo*, "One gains a great deal from being attached to the Society of Jesus": a rule not to be forgotten. *Secundo*, "Believe that I understand woman's nature better than you." That's a fact. The devil likes nothing better than to make a woman's least whims appear attainable.[19]
> (*Silence from Father Gratian.*)
> LA MADRE. Why won't you speak to me? (*Pleading voice.*) Say something? It pains me to remind you of the rumors that hurt me so greatly . . . and against which I defended you with all my might. It's only natural, being your daughter and your mother at once. . . . No need to thank me . . . not that you are thanking me, for that matter. Anyhow, I washed the opprobrium off you with all the friendly

solicitude of the wretched sinner I am.... (*Pause.*) At least I hope so, it's not definite, the future is highly uncertain, and needless to say I'm more afraid for yours than for mine. (*Threatening voice.*) You engaged in carnal relations with the nuns ... you spent the night in such-and-such a convent, you were spotted naked in another ... oh, I know.... (*Tragic voice.*) Our enemies make the most of imagination, just to cause us harm.... Just to prevent my reforms.... (*Hopeless voice, cough, nausea.*) But please be careful all the same.

La Madre's blood pressure shoots up, irrigates her brain. A final apoplexy? Teresita and Ana de San Bartolomé jump nervously to their feet. But the old lady has not done with score-settling on earth.

LA MADRE, *in a menacing voice.* How am I supposed to forget, here on my deathbed, how in ... November 1576 ... I warned you against a strange woman who wanted you to visit her at home, with the excuse of a nervous illness.... (*Pause.*) I'm still convinced it wasn't so much a case of melancholy as of meddling by the devil, because she was obviously possessed. He wanted to see if he could fool you in some way, now that he'd fooled her. (*Normal voice.*) So by no means go to her house! Remember what happened to Santa Marina, who lived disguised as a monk, and was accused of fathering a child! That would be the final straw.[20] (*Arms crossed on chest, strangled voice.*) It's no time for you to be undergoing such an ordeal. In my humble opinion, dear father, dear Eliseus ... if my words are not enough to push you back onto the right path, think of the papal nuncio, Felipe Sega, the bishop of Piacenza.... (*Voice cracks.*) The most inveterate adversary of our reform, who does not bear you in his heart and would pounce on any scandal as grist for his mill, you know it.... (*Long sigh.*)
(*Pure tears trickle from the dying woman's closed eyes. There's no spasm of weeping, her eyes are simply melting, exhausted by visualizing so many scenes of love and turning themselves away from such profanity.*)
SYLVIA LECLERCQ, *entering for the last time, she crosses the stage unseen by Teresita and Ana, praying on their knees beside the bed. La Madre is watering her garden.* Maybe she's the voluptuous type without realizing it, wrapped in that innocence tailor-made for transgression, sure to be forgiven by the Holy, Roman, and Apostolic Church. She takes her pleasures gently, I see, and gives herself down to the last drop, with just enough guilt to spark desire again and again, interminably.
LA MADRE. Lord, I cannot hope for better days than those I spent with my Paul. But for charity, *mi padre*, do not read out my letters in public.... (*With distress.*)

Don't you understand anything? I never wanted anyone to hear me when I spoke with God, I wanted to be with Him in solitude. Well, it's the same thing with you, my dear Paul.

(*Silence, prolonged silence from her Eliseus.*)

LA MADRE. You're in hiding, you don't dare face the nuncio I advised you so strongly to visit. . . . (*Suddenly anxious.*) "My Paul is very foolish to have so many scruples,"[21] if your reverence will permit me not to mince words for once. (*Silly voice.*) For the devil never sleeps, my baby! You, with all your ducking and weaving, your indecision about whether to attend Mass—your obsessional moods, as the Leclercq woman would say—have you, or have you not, been excommunicated by Sega? Oh, stop it! I'm fed up with hearing how depressed you are. (*With sudden violence.*) What would you have said if you'd had to live like Fr. John of the Cross? You are impassioned, agreed, but you could do with more tactfulness and insight. Although you rarely preach, according to you, watch what you say all the same. (*Silly voice.*) My son, my baby. . . . "He looks healthy and well fed." [22] "Even a few hours without knowing about you seem to be a very long time."[23]

(*Still no sign from Gratian.*)

LA MADRE. Right, you let me down when I need you most, and I pardon you for it, because we can only follow the path of perfection in hardship. (*Another coughing fit.*) Allow me, dear friend, to tell you one last time that I am sorry for your "mental fatigue." As I once wrote you: "Learn to be your own master, avoid extremes, and profit from the experience of others [Sepa ser señor de sí para irse a la mano y escarmentar en cabeza ajena]. This is how you serve God, and try to see the need we all have for you to be in good health."[24] (*Long sigh. Pause.*) No, I haven't forgotten what I owe you: you convinced me of Christ's humanity, of which I was not exactly ignorant, but you enabled me to imitate Mary Magdalene for real. (*Coughing, choking.*) Women have a special capacity to love an eternal Spouse, a king-man, a man. . . . Not to die of love, but to suffer from it so as to do things better. I wrote in the account of my *Life* that nothing meant more to me than to attract souls to a higher blessing.[25] That was too general, too abstract, I was being defensive, as the Leclercq woman would rightly say; I think I am about to embrace her logic. And so what? You turned me into a Mary Magdalene, Eliseus, and I found the power to attract, with you and beyond you, in order to serve that higher blessing. . . . (*Dry eyes, long silence.*)

(*No sign from Gratian.*)

LA MADRE. I know you'll remain attached to the memory of me, that's something, my Paul. I mean to say, Glory to God! (*Reading, in sensitive, almost emotive tones.*)

"She told me all about her life, her mind, and her plans," that's what you'll write about me, isn't it? It was the first day we spent together, apart from Mass and mealtimes, of course; the first time we talked about ourselves. "I so submitted to her"—now, that's laying it on a bit thick, Pablo my sweet—"that from then on I never undertook anything important without benefit of her counsel." That's true enough. (*Smothered laugh, voice suddenly dreamy.*) You are destined to write a great deal, in the future, and you will always pray for three hours a day, because you are a saintly man, in a way. . . . (*Pause.*) *The Flaming Lamp*, am I right? There's a title little Seneca would have loved. It's perhaps the book of yours that cleaves most closely to our doctrine. . . . That's right, I said "our." All of your writings evoke your own life, that's only to be expected. Researchers will detect a faint trace of me in your mystical theology, your way of perfection . . . it's not hard to find. . . . After all, you were dead set on getting me canonized. Apparently that's a sign of fidelity. (*Broad smile.*) I want to believe it, and so I will. . . . (*Shaken by simultaneous coughing and laughing fits. Uncontrollable laughter. Tears. Long silence.*) (*She is very cold, shivering in every fiber of her being.*)

Take my hand, Father. . . . Just for a moment. . . . For friendship's sake, I'm on my way to the Spouse, I'm in transit. . . . Hold my hand, in the name of Christ's sacred humanity. . . . (*Flat voice, almost cold.*) No, what are you doing, I didn't ask you to cut it off, just to hold it. . . . You make me laugh . . . no, of course I don't feel any pain, not by this stage. You amuse me, you often did. . . . (*Quick sigh.*) You're still chopping me up . . . you're not listening . . . did you ever listen to me . . . who listens to anyone. . . . There's another fine myth, this business of listening. One hears voices, sure enough, but from there to listening. . . . (*Serious voice.*) Stop it, really, you're hurting me now, for the love of God . . . I suppose you want some relics out of me, what utter nonsense. . . . (*Drawn-out groan, then talks at speed.*) You found my body whole and uncorrupted . . . well, obviously, under that heap of limestone. . . . You conveyed it stealthily to Saint Joseph's at Avila, you set it up as an object of devotion. . . . A great comfort to the dear little nuns. . . . My sisters placed the coffin in the chapter house, on a stretcher, with curtains that could be pulled aside for visitors to gawp, and afterward closed again. . . . Ah, that casket, lined in violet taffeta with silk and silver braids, the outside covered in black velvet with ornaments of gold and silk, gilded nails, locks, rings, and handles, and two escutcheons of gold and silver, bearing the symbol of the order and the name of Jesus, and on an embroidered cloth the words *Mother Teresa of Jesus*. . . . (*Knowing smile.*) I gave off a lovely fragrance . . . I should hope so, what with my four waters every day, and the flesh that becomes Word, or the other way around, goes without saying. . . . (*Reading.*) "The clothing smelled bad once removed from the body, and I had it burned. While it was on the body, it smelled sweet." (*Lips. Pause.*)

(*No sign from Gratian.*)

TERESA, *in a faint voice.* That's what you wrote . . . and the Jesuit priest Ribera would quote your words in the first biography he wrote of me, by the grace of God. . . . (*Reading, fast.*) You also mentioned your surprise at the firmness of my breasts . . . is that so? And then you cut off my left hand, as a gift for the Carmelites of Lisbon, and added in the margin of your memoir: "When I cut off her hand, I also cut off a little finger and kept it with me and from that day to this, glory be to God, I have not suffered any illness, and when I was taken captive by the Turks they took it from me and I bought it back for ten *reals* and some gold rings I ordered to be made using some small rubies that were on the finger."[26] My baby, you'll always be a baby, Eliseus . . . but you still don't miss a trick, do you? A relic can also be a splendid bargaining chip. (*Sigh, broad smile.*) And that wasn't the end of it, you were so proud to have got me home to Avila in the dead of night, firmly sewn into a canvas bag that you flung over the back of a mule. It was a kidnapping, another journey. . . . (*Smile.*) You wanted to be buried next to me. The dukes of Alba objected that I belonged to them, which was only to be expected: Hernando de Toledo, the duke's nephew, thought the world of me. So he went to the Holy See about it and Pope Sixtus V ruled that I be taken back to Alba . . . that was in August 1586. (*Grave voice.*) What a crowd was there . . . an admiring crowd, of course, which would have torn me to bits, so I was kept behind the grille as a precaution. My detached left arm was brown and creased as a date, thin and slightly hairy; after they changed the cloths that wrapped it, the old cloths were touted as relics, too. . . . Ribera was right to predict that I would be chopped up further, into a thousand pieces. . . . What a racket! The new prioress of Alba de Tormes, Catalina de San Angel, demands my heart, to keep in her cell. . . . Saint Joseph's gets a clavicle and a ring finger . . . My right foot and a bit of my upper jaw end up in Rome. . . . (*Faint voice.*) How profitable I am, from the Beyond! . . . Who'd have thought it? (*Long silence.*) Hold my hand, Father . . . it's all nonsense. . . . After all, the sacred wedding takes place in the soul, doesn't it? That's what all the learned fathers worth their salt used to tell me. . . .

SYLVIA LECLERCQ, *who can't resist popping up again.* What a fetishist, really! Father Gratian collecting the organs of the phallic mother! A gore movie, I do declare. The little finger, the hand, the arm—left or right? . . . Who cares, a writer's arm, that's good enough for anyone. (*Exit. The audience boos the intruder who can't stop bothering a dying woman. La Madre pays no attention, absorbed in her Eliseus. But she's reached the end of her tether.*)

LA MADRE, *losing her temper.* Enough, for pity's sake! Eliseus, kindly put a stop to this cult of the corpse, this carnage. . . . (*Pursing mouth and wrinkling nose with vehement revulsion.*) At last! Oh. . . . You no longer dare do it yourself, so you ask Fr. Nazianze to chop off my left arm for the chapter house in Pastrana—I don't believe it! What's stopping you all of a sudden? Are you feeling the pangs of remorse, Father? Is your love growing humanistic? Oh no, not you! An arm is a lot more unwieldy than a finger or a hand, I do sympathize. . . . Ribera, with dark irony or sincere outrage, marvels at how "easily, with no more effort than it takes to slice a melon or some fresh cheese, Nazianze cut off the arm at the shoulder." Oh dear, how tedious men are. . . . I'm tired . . . forgive me, dear Eliseus. . . . (*Weary, fed up. Brief silence. Then speaking fast.*) Poor Fr. Nazianze, he confessed that this act had been the greatest sacrifice he had ever made for our Lord as a token of obedience. . . . What a notion! "Sacrifice," indeed—sacrificing me into the bargain! Now for the best part, which is that my hand will wind up in the possession of General Franco . . . taking pride of place on his bedside table, and all through his long agony! He's anointed me a "saint of the race." What I've had to put with from men. Poor things . . . I'm so tired, so tired, my Pablo . . . my father . . . tired of you, too . . . of everything . . . of nothing . . . my poor sweet. . . . Whatever is the point of that hideous butchery? It's not even mystically correct! Yes, make a note of that expression if you please: mystically incorrect, that's it. . . . I don't know whether to laugh or cry. What's your position on this, Lord? (*Tears flow from wide-open eyes, she is hardly breathing.*)

(*Still no response from Gratian. Nothing from the Voice, either. A long silence falls.*)

LA MADRE, *reading.* Speaking of Eliseus . . . it's a strange thing that the affection I have for him causes me no embarrassment, as though he were not a person.[27]

(*Laurencia falls asleep.*)

SYLVIA LECLERCQ. That's saying something! If he's not a person, Gratian is something more than God's servant; is he God Himself? A splinter of the divine? She loves Gratian in the way she believes the Church wants her to love Jesus—her beaten Father, her manly double, her Lord. "Not a person." And also a twin, perhaps; her male clone, her creature, her work? (*Such is the psychologist's opinion, as she leans against the wall in a corner of the stage, watching the saint doze off. She doesn't say it aloud.*)

★ ★ ★

ACT 2, SCENE 2

LA MADRE

HIS VOICE

TERESITA

ANA DE SAN BARTOLOMÉ

HIS VOICE. "Eat, daughter, and bear up as best you can. What you suffer grieves me, but it suits you now."[28]

LA MADRE. Who goes there? Eliseus?

HIS VOICE. Father Gratian is far away as you know, and you won't see him for a while. He has gone to cross swords with Nicolo Doria.

LA MADRE. In Hell?

HIS VOICE. No. Your Eliseus is not the holiest of men, which won't be news to you, whatever you may have said or written. . . . But he redeemed himself, and he did a lot, on balance, for the creation of your order. Peace be with his soul!

LA MADRE. In Purgatory, then?

HIS VOICE. Steady on! You're far too hasty and intemperate, I am always having to tell you. In his own way, and it's an honorable way, he will remain true to you. Consider: he goes to Rome to plead the cause of your reforms. Embarking for Naples, he falls into the hands of the Turks. Crosses are tattooed on the soles of his feet while he is the pasha's captive. An exceptional destiny, so no need for regrets. Finally he is ransomed by Clement VIII, enters the Carmel, and holds your relics close for the rest of his life.

LA MADRE. Wretched am I, a wretched sinner! (*Normal voice.*) I thought I was Laurencia, or Angela, or goodness knows who. I thought I was married to my Paul as I was married to the Lord. Did I ignore His Majesty's voice? Did I forget to be that other person I became for You and with You. . . . (*Still normal voice.*) The Teresa of Jesus who is in love with the one and only Third Person, His Majesty?

HIS VOICE. My Will is that the great favors come through the hands of the sacred humanity. As I have told you numberless times, that is the gate you must enter through.[29]

LA MADRE. And that's how I understood You, Lord. Your Majesty never said that there is a great difference in the ways one may be . . . a master; (*reading, still in a normal voice*) or that the master "is never so far from his pupil that he has to shout."[30] (*Pause.*) I feared confessors who feared the devil more than I feared the devil. (*Calmly.*) It was Master Gratian who immersed me in Your humanity.

HIS VOICE. Daughter, it is written in Exodus that the people saw the signs, rather than merely hearkening to the "words which the Lord had spoken";[31] but you have done more. You don't merely see My Voice, you feel it in your whole body. More than a visible or audible presence, I am a sensory presence for you.

LA MADRE. "I am the voice of one crying in the wilderness."[32] *Ego phonè, ego vox....* Now I'm talking like a scholar, like John the Baptist. Too proud, again? (*Normal voice.*) And I am the wilderness, and I am the voice that gropes in darkness . . . I don't understand why this is, but that I don't understand gives me great delight.[33]

HIS VOICE. Listen, daughter, there is something demonic about a voice that rises within. A Greek philosopher said so before me and without me, and he was right. Because the voice that calls you out of yourself usually deflects you from what you are doing; it never urges you to act.

LA MADRE, *ardently*, My Lord, Voice of His Majesty, You never turned me away from action.

HIS VOICE. That is what I like about you, daughter. In you, the voices don't die away as the Word grows, they only fan out through all the senses, as Jesus's Voice did in John. But who understood this? It took sixteen centuries for you to come along and persuade the Church that this metamorphosis is always, still, possible. You and Ignatius Loyola, don't forget!

LA MADRE, *greedily*. Nobody receives the Voice of His Majesty . . . without knowing true pleasures and refreshments, *gustos*, from God.

HIS VOICE. What do you mean?

LA MADRE, *in a meditative, quiet voice*. The Lord gives me to understand. El Señor me da a entender. The Lord gives us freedom. Licencia nos da el Señor. As he gives us, when we think of the Passion, greater anguish and torments than the evangelists record.[34] When I speak of refreshment, I am speaking of "a gentle refreshment—strong, deeply impressed, delightful, and quiet."[35]

HIS VOICE. Show some humility, daughter. You are not the first to embark on this path. "The senses rebound in thought," wrote Meister Eckhart; he and his disciples were familiar with "the essential foundation"[36] and "learned ignorance" that were nonetheless open to be "touched" and "tasting of eternity itself."

LA MADRE. I didn't know, my Spouse. I am determined to be different from all those bookish, saintly men. For Your call does not keep me in "indefiniteness," as the honorable doctors past and future like to say.[37] You authorized me not to turn absolutely away from all that is familiar. (*Pause. Eyes, squarely in shot.*) And there's nothing indeterminate about this familiarity, to my mind. It is delectable through and through. . . . (*Smile that fades at once.*)

(*The Voice does not reply.*)

LA MADRE, *in a conversational tone.* That being the case, Your word and Your call are not for me reduced to a "vocal utterance."[38] I appreciate them, I seek them out. You know it. But more importantly I register them as a brazier burning inside my body. Because I don't neglect other sensations, on the contrary I savor them, Lord. . . . Where your humble servant is concerned, I must say that sensations often take the upper hand, I mean the lower, well, in short, they take over! (*Red cheeks despite the livid features; then meditative voice, closed eyes, peacefulness.*) For aren't all sensations destined to be reabsorbed into the movement of imaginative thought that is distinct from intellectual understanding?

HIS VOICE. The flesh is feminine, my beloved child, Christ himself was aware of it. To the best of my knowledge, in his case the Father's Voice was not merely a "giving-to-understand," and was indisputably a "giving-to-feel," as it is for you, my daughter.

LA MADRE. I am born all over again when you call, my Spouse, and my rebirth is not just vocal, not a brute cry, let alone an understanding. I am reborn in You through all my intermingled senses joined into one, mouth, skin, nostrils, eardrums, eyes, the whole garden awash with Your waters. (*Reading, serene voice.*) Didn't you say to me that "turning away from corporeal things must be good, certainly, since such spiritual persons advise it. . . . [But] the most sacred humanity of Christ must not be counted in a balance with other corporeal things"?[39] (*The Voice does not respond.*)

LA MADRE. You are silent. Is Your Majesty's Voice deserting me because It considers any corporeal thing likely to hinder contemplation of It? (*Anxious voice.*) But to withdraw completely from the body of Christ, or to count His divine Body among what causes us nothing but misery, no, I can't accept it.[40] (*Reading.*) We can compare His Voice to "a food that many persons eat."[41] The epileptic, anorexic novice I once was, plagued by such nervous anxiety that everything frightened her, gradually relaxed and grew stronger, according to the academics García-Albea and Vercelletto, as well as that nice psychologist Leclercq. She acquired her manly courage by receiving from His Majesty the kiss a Bride demands. How good it tasted, Lord! (*Replete, satisfied voice.*) One sees how beneficial it is, and one's taste has so adapted to this sweetness that one would rather die than to taste any other food. . . . (*Pause.*) Because anything else would only take away the delicious taste Your food left behind. (*Exhalation.*) Here an abundance of water was given to this unloved woman who was wounded . . . [42] and thus I can live in Your world, separate from the world. Because I clearly heard You say: "You will grow very foolish, daughter, if you look at the world's laws."[43] (*Nostalgic voice.*)

That was You, wasn't it, Majesty? Where are You? You won't talk to me anymore. Say, Lord, where has Your admirable, friendly company gone to . . . ?

(*The Voice remains silent.*)

LA MADRE. "*Dilatasti cor meum*,"[44] so sang the Psalmist, but it's not my heart, it's another, still more interior part that dilates and expands in me. . . . (*Pause.*) It must be the center of the soul. . . . (*Long pause.*) Or the center of the body? (*Shrewd smile.*) Or maybe both?[45] I hope it's not an illusion crafted by the devil, to feel that Your Voice impresses itself by dilating through me. . . . When Your Majesty inhabits me like that, everyone complains of what a ignoramus I am. All but the disciples of John of Avila, and the Jesuits. . . . (*Pause.*) Mind you, on reflection, it was the disciples of Loyola who got me to meditate on the sacred humanity of Jesus—at the time when I'm afraid I was adrift in some fairly hazy orisons, Osuna-style. (*Knowing smile. Pause.*) Answer me, Majesty, don't desert me! (*Silence.*)

LA MADRE. My nuptials with dear Eliseus, my father turned son . . . my fetus . . . my achievement . . . could well have been the devil's work, if I hadn't known that the fire came not from me but from You, Lord. (*Tragic voice.*) Not one word? . . . Perhaps Your silence, Majesty, suggests that Laurencia or Angela once shut herself all alone in a room with Eliseus? That she didn't realize that the light which married them came from His Voice? (*Pause.*) Are you suggesting I've forgotten that the carnal furnace itself, the furnace of desire, is consubstantial with His Voice? . . . (*Tragic but feeble voice.*) That it doesn't come from me or from you, Eliseus, but it does make us other, both of us, because it comes from the Other. . . . Perhaps I was foolish to the point of imagining. . . . Oh, it's nothing but gossip . . . my Gratian decked out in garlands and crowns like a heavenly King. . . . I did, "I saw my Eliseus there, certainly not in any way black, but with a strange beauty. On his head was what resembled a garland of precious stones, and many maidens went before him with branches in their hands singing songs of praise to God. I didn't do anything but open my eyes so as to distract myself, and this wasn't enough to take away my attention. It seemed to me there was music from small birds and angels in which the soul rejoiced; although I didn't hear it, but the soul was experiencing that delight."[46] (*Pause.*) A Christ. . . . (*Pause.*) A sovereign. . . . (*Pause.*)

HIS VOICE, *at last!* You took a risk, the pair of you, unhappy sinners. But you managed to thwart the consequences, in the end. I choose to consider that you thwarted them, and would inevitably have done so sooner or later, because it was My Will that you should. . . . So there you are. It's over now, go in peace, both of you.

La Madre lies motionless for a long while. Exhausted by her efforts, glad to have been accompanied by His Voice one last time, is she still thinking, feeling, or living at all? There's no way of telling, because Teresa has completely merged with her interior castle. There she holds open the doors of possible and impossible dwelling places.

She wants to let go into meaningless words, to speak in tongues ... Delirium is her Pentecost, and she pulls herself together. . . . This transit toward His Majesty is going to be interminable.

LA MADRE, *regaining her breath and her senses.* They say the "babbling talk" of lovers does not say anything about the events of the world. (*Knowing smile.*) I expect they're right, because they are philosophers, whereas I am just a woman, and a wretched one at that. Certainly, lovers' babble has nothing to tell, not about worldly events.[47] (*Another shrewd smile.*) But my own babblings, inflamed to the point of madness by the fire that carried me to Pablo, made me tell everything I knew about . . . about what? (*Stops smiling.*) About my wanting to do what is in me . . . me, outside myself . . . outside the world within the world. . . . (*Opens eyes, seeking to rest them upon an absent interlocutor. Sylvia Leclercq hides, unseen, behind a column.*)

HIS VOICE. What are you talking about now, you stubborn creature?

LA MADRE, *reading.* "Oh, Lord, how we Christians fail to know you!"[48] To do what is in me, "do what lies within your power,"[49] that's what living is. (*Pleading voice.*) That is the reconciliation of Martha with Mary Magdalene. Does it surprise you that a contemplative like me should identify with Martha? (*Pause.*) Because Martha is not a contemplative in the way of the Magdalene, that's official. You know better than I do, Majesty, that contemplative women are not immune to the call of the flesh. (*Pause. Reading.*) If Martha had been like them, who would have prepared food for His Majesty? Who would have served Him? Who would have eaten at table with Him? Contemplation makes one forgetful of self and of all things, and progress is fast.[50] Others such as Martha, however, are led by God into the active life. (*Still reading, gravely.*) The Lord, fostering them little by little, gives them determination and strength. . . .[51]

TERESA, *palms joined in prayer.* By straying with my Eliseus, while also listening to the Voice of the Lord—Oh God, would that I heard it more often!—I was attempting to reunite Mary Magdalene and Martha. (*Pause.*) It seemed to me that, since the Lord is corporeal and likewise His Voice, the Creator was surely to be sought in His creature. . . . [52](*Quavering voice.*) To be precise, I knew this to be true, but thanks to my folly with Eliseus I experienced it body and soul, in this world, by trying to accomplish the work of a Martha reconciled with Mary. (*Lifts hands and holds them open before face.*) A contemplative soul is left floating in the air, as they say; it seems it has no support no matter how much it may think it is full of God. (*Normal voice.*) Well then, the humanity of Christ's body provides that support. . . . Ah, but that humanity attracts the desires, in other words the fires of the Spirit, which weaker souls are daunted by. . . . (*Pause.*) And such souls are quick to conceive fears . . . flee from the pleasures . . . and reject that extreme sweetness . . . which I so often could not tear myself away from, no more than could Saint Francis, Saint Bernard, or Saint Catherine of Siena.[53] (*Expression of happiness.*) Most of the others prefer to ascend or be elevated, and that is doubt-less excellent for the souls most advanced in spirituality, but it is not continual. (*Happy expression fades.*) Pardon me these comparisons, Majesty, I often have trouble being humble, in spite of my best efforts. And yet I fear that others are far more deficient in humility than I am, if they're not content with so fine an object as the humanity of Christ. And, of course, "a woman in this state of prayer is distressed by the natural hindrance there is to her entering the world."[54] . . . She is distressed, I am distressed, do You hear? . . .

(*His Voice remains silent. Here Teresa believes she can hear it smiling at her.*)

LA MADRE, *surer than ever of His Voice.* Jesus was not an angel . . . (*shrewd smile*) . . . so far as I know! (*Reading.*) We are not angels either, we have a body.[55] I always go back to that. . . . Is that called an obsession, you psychologist over there? Lauren-cia and Angela under the habit of Teresa of Avila, Pablo beneath the appearance of Fr. Gratian. . . . (*In a frankly serene voice, still reading.*) Being human, it is very beneficial for us to consider God in human form, suffering because desiring, for as long as we are in this life. . . . (*Voice breaks, blood trickles from right corner of mouth.*) To desire to be angels while we are on earth—and as much on earth as I was—is foolishness. (*Pause.*) Ordinarily, thought needs to have some support. . . . (*Pause.*) Jesus Christ is an excellent friend, in His sacred humanity.[56] (*Broad smile.*)

(*La Madre has finished her plea.*)

TERESITA. She's going to sleep.

ANA DE SAN BARTOLOMÉ. She has seen the Lord.

(*Teresa's visage radiates complete peace. Is there nothing left to wait for?*)

LA MADRE. What's that I hear? His Voice again? No, it's not the same carnal timbre, the voice that guides me tentatively, caressingly, upliftingly. . . . (*Pause.*) So it's not the Lord, not yet. Who, then? Could it be you, my little Seneca? I miss you so much! Even though we don't agree on everything, you and I. What did you say? That you personally don't need support? You push on to the end of the night? (*In a greedy voice.*) Me too, I try in my own way, in my own night . . . No, don't take that for an exaggeration, Father, I pray you, in reality my words fall short because the experience is unexplainable.[57] You know that better than anyone. . . . It seems to be like gibberish, *algarabía.*[58] . . . A taste in the mouth . . . I know, we never finished discussing it; we were both of us rather against it, though, weren't we, my big Seneca? (*Imploringly.*) And what if that were Paradise? An adjustment of just souls? We never stopped trying to be just, did we? You less than me, perhaps, or vice versa. . . . (*Reading.*) For "the soul of a just person is nothing else but a paradise where the Lord says He finds His delight."[59] So what happens when in addition to this, two souls strive to offer delights to the Lord. . . . What do you think? Speak up, won't you, John dear? Come on, force that thin adolescent voice of yours. . . . (*Pause.*) I daresay you've scorched your vocal cords as well, then, today. . . . (*Short laugh.*) All I can hear is an ashen sound, I'm dying, you know. (*Cheerful laugh.*)

Saint John of the Cross. Spanish school, seventeenth century. Toledo, Museo de Santa Cruz.
© Art Archive at Art Resource, New York.

Chapter 32

ACT 3

Her "Little Seneca"

> A great fear and tumult . . . and in a moment . . . all remains calm,
> and this soul . . . has no need of any other master.
>
> Teresa of Avila, *The Interior Castle*

TERESA OF AVILA, with her carers

JOHN OF THE CROSS

MOTHER MARIE

BLANCHE DE LA FORCE

THE CARMELITES OF COMPIÈGNE

BOSSUET, writer, prelate, bishop of Meaux

SYLVIA LECLERCQ, psychologist

VOICE OF LEIBNIZ

VOICE OF SPINOZA

ACT 3, SCENE 1

JOHN OF THE CROSS

TERESA OF AVILA

MOTHER MARIE

BLANCHE DE LA FORCE

THE CARMELITES OF COMPIÈGNE

The scene takes place in the ground-floor parlor of the Convent of the Incarnation in Avila. This is where, according to legend, the levitation of Teresa of Avila and John of the Cross occurred. The two future saints are seated in the very chairs concerned (today on display to the public). Instead of the bluish light of preceding scenes, a fiery glow bathes the room.

JOHN OF THE CROSS. Without support and with support,
> Living without light, in darkness,
> I am wholly being consumed.[1]

TERESA OF AVILA, *after a pause.* "We belong to the party of the Crucified One." Somos de la banda del Crucificado.[2] Your paternity employs the same language as I, but not with the same meaning. To you, everything is wound and oblivion; to me, everything is union and delight. Is that too perfunctory, or exaggerated?

JOHN OF THE CROSS. Surely our first care is to devote ourselves to the dark night of the senses. To detach the exterior senses and pare the natural exuberance of the appetites.[3]

TERESA. Since our first meeting in Medina in 1567—when you, Father, were still a young student in Salamanca—I recognized in you the spiritual authority we needed, by God's grace. (*Shifting her chair away from his.*) I also realized straight away that your paternity would not be easy to deal with. You wanted to become a Carthusian, but I quickly made you see that you could be one, to perfection, with me. Do you remember what you replied? "I give you my word, on condition I don't have to wait too long."

JOHN OF THE CROSS, *after a silence.* "For, the farther the soul progresses in spirituality, the more it ceases from the operation of the faculties in particular acts, since it becomes more and more occupied in one act that is general and pure."[4] "The soul no longer enjoys that food of sense, as we have said; it needs not this but another food, which is more delicate, more interior, and partaking less of the nature of sense,"[5] full of "peace and rest of interior quiet." (*He is motionless, eyes fixed not on her but on the glowing red space.*)

TERESA. I expounded on these delicate matters long before you did, my little Seneca. Recall that by 1567 I had already written the book of my *Life* and *The Way of Perfection.* (*No longer at death's door, voice calm and authoritative.*) It's true that God accorded me the spiritual marriage in November 1572, and your arrival six months earlier did have something to do with it; still, I was already prepared, I had been ready ever since my re-conversion. I know you don't dispute it, but I'd rather set the record straight once more before I die, seeing how absorbed you are by that flame . . . (*Gazing at the brazier herself.*) You didn't write anything before my *Interior Castle*, and that's a fact. (*Shifting her chair back nearer to his.*) The life of the spirit—which I taught you—arises from the most intimate part of the soul. It burns, and how! I am a connoisseur of fire, contrary to what you might expect from the voluble female you suspect me to be. Water is my element, I can't help that, but it doesn't prevent me from acceding to the soaring of the flame. You have often witnessed it yourself. For the spark that suddenly begins to blaze and shoots up like something extremely delicate to the higher plane that pleases the Lord is of the same nature as the fire that remains beneath. "It seems to be a flight, for I don't know what else to compare it to."[6]

JOHN OF THE CROSS. "Withdrawn from pleasure and contentment."[7] (*Pause.*) Nothing! Nothing! I would give up all I am for the sake of Christ! "Love is begotten in a heart that has no love."[8]

> O living flame of love
> That tenderly wounds my soul
> In its deepest center! Since
> Now You are not oppressive,
> Now Consummate! If it be Your will:
> Tear through the veil of this sweet encounter!
> O sweet cautery,
> O delightful wound![9]

(*Silence.*)

TERESA, *in a soft voice, eyes turned inward.* Expiation, are you summoning me to expiation? I know . . . I've tried everything . . . it'll never be enough. . . . But I insist on it right up to the final pages of the *Castle*: "What I conclude with, Sisters, is that we shouldn't build castles in the air," or towers without a foundation; and remember that there is no foundation during this short life other than to "offer the Lord interiorly and exteriorly the sacrifice we can."[10] What generations to come will retain of our experience as Carmelites is the acerbic taste of a noble atonement, isn't that right, Father? Are you thinking, like me, of the Carmelites of Compiègne, in the *Dialogues* screenplay by Bernanos?

(*John remains silent. La Madre glimpses the shadow of Mother Marie sweeping over the walls of Avila.*)

MOTHER MARIE. There is no horror but in crime, and in the sacrifice of innocent lives the horror is expunged, and the crime itself restored to the order of divine charity. . . .[11]

JOHN OF THE CROSS. O sweet cautery!

The two friends hear the court pronounce the death sentence on sixteen Carmelites for holding counterrevolutionary meetings. Then they watch the nuns climb down from the tumbril at the foot of the guillotine in the place de la Révolution. Young Blanche de la Force advances calmly, her face shows no fear. Suddenly she breaks into song: "Deo Patri sit Gloria, et Filio, qui a mortuis surrexit, ac Paraclito, in saeculorum saecula." Blanche becomes lost among the crowd, along with the rest of the sisters.

JOHN OF THE CROSS. *Solus soli.*

TERESA, *after a silence.* The feminist philosopher Edith Stein, who became Saint Teresa Benedicta of the Cross, remembered them too, inevitably, as she offered herself up for God. "Come, we go for our people," she told her sister Rosa, on August 2, 1942, as the Gestapo hustled them out of the Carmel of Echt, in Holland, where they had taken refuge.[12] She refused all privileges, unwilling to be an exception to her people's fate or take advantage of having been baptized. . . . Like the Carmelites of Compiègne, she was thinking of you, Father, when she chose this self-sacrifice. . . . I'm sure of it . . . more of you than of me, anyway. There will be periods like that, in the history of men and women, when chastisement will be salutary. "With his stripes we are healed," the prophet Isaiah said.[13] The concentration of evil will be such that martyrs will be needed to testify that the relationship between Heaven and earth has broken down. . . . Had I lived then, and had they sewn a yellow star onto my sleeve, I would have behaved exactly like Sister Teresa Benedicta, don't you think? . . . I hope I would have taken that decision, or done something similar like joining the Resistance or the maquis. . . . Not really the Carmelite style, I grant. But who knows? I'm asking you, as an expert in martyrdoms. . . .

(*A large photograph of Edith Stein floats above the walls of Avila.*)

TERESA, *voice breaks, then steadies.* Look at that smile. . . . The strength, the steadfastness that supported her along the road to Auschwitz. . . . She must have known she'd enlisted in the struggle between Christ and Antichrist. Why, on Palm Sunday 1939, she gave her prioress a note requesting to be given up as an offering. (*Reads.*) "Dear Mother, permit me to offer myself up to the sacred heart of Jesus as the expiatory victim for true peace, so that the reign of the Antichrist might collapse if possible without another world war, and a new order may be established. I would like to do it today, for we are at the eleventh hour. I know I am nothing, but Jesus wishes it, and He will surely call many others in these days."[14]

All for the love of God, indeed . . . "the love that gives itself unstintingly," as she wrote in a little biography of me, *Love for Love's Sake*, while she was still only a postulant at the Carmel of Cologne, so you see . . . I could have written those words, couldn't I? . . . I feel fulfilled, dear John, I can say this to you, at having been the inspiration for such a soul, who harbors divine grace within her so absolutely. . . . Do you think I'm committing the sin of pride, out of stupid vanity— that this is too much *honra* for the wretched creature that I am? (*Sidelong glance at the photograph of Edith Stein as a young philosophy student, passing swiftly over the Avilan fortress.*)

(*Silence from John.*)

TERESA, *in a melancholic and then assured voice.* I think so too, you know I do, my sweet Seneca, I have often atoned, for far more than you can imagine, although it doesn't stop me sensing the Guest inside of me, that's just how it is. . . . Must one offer oneself up as a holocaust to appease the wrath of God, as Bernanos has the Carmelite prioress decide, during the Terror of 1794? Did the Lamb of God want Sister Teresa Benedicta to become another mystic Lamb, to be immolated by the Nazis, so that the profound joy and inner gaiety with which she submitted to His will at the blackest moment of that black night could burst back over the world to save even the most hardened sinner, and perhaps redeem the criminal himself? Do you know? She will write that "the mania for suffering caused by a perverse lust for pain differs completely from the desire to suffer in expiation,"[15] and I believe her, of course. Although my path was a different one, and different also to yours, dear friend, for all your clear complicities. Sacrifice, suffering, obedience, and profound humility, of course . . . the fact of sin demands them. . . . But martyrdom? . . . *Hombre como Cristo?* What do you say? God loved me as something other than a Lamb, He loved me as a Bride and was content to demand works, works, and more works from me. . . . He bathed me and inflamed me and I wanted to enkindle you all with celestial fire . . . I wanted to become a perpetual spur to virtue . . . I mean, to love. . . . [16] You can be Stein's Science of the Cross, and I, the Hidden Spring. . . .[17] Don't pull that face. . . . All right, it's not so simple! We are converging, though. Saint Teresa Benedicta will experience our reunion in herself. . . . We'll come together in her, do you see? It diverts me to argue with you today, my good friend, just for the pleasure of getting closer to you, I know you understand. . . . In a nutshell, you'll be most read in times of war, and I in times of peace . . . if such a thing exists. . . . (*Moves her chair nearer, he doesn't budge, doesn't look at her.*) In the Love of the Other, it does. (*Tranquil face, pensive smile.*)

JOHN OF THE CROSS, *immobile in his love and as if absent, surrendered to his dark night.* O delightful wound!

(*Silence.*)

TERESA, *shrinks back, straightens up and presses her head against the back of her chair.* Here it comes again, that feeling I always had in your company, Father: dare I tell you aloud, by now? I am frightened by the spell you cast. How grateful I was to your paternity for founding the first discalced male monastery in Valladolid in 1568! But I know you felt snubbed when I wrote more about Prior Antonio de Jesús than about you, in relation to the foundation at Medina del Campo, and didn't even mention you in connection with Granada. And yet you are everywhere in my pages: that wounded deer, for instance, slaking her thirst in the living waters;[18] or that poor little butterfly so full of apprehension that everything alarms it and makes it take flight before the Lord has a chance to fortify it, enlarge it, and render it capable.[19] It's partly me, but very much you: you'll be recognized in those figures one day. Excuse me for prophesying, I do it sometimes, I'm sorry, it's embarrassing, you know how your Madre is. . . . But how can I refer to you but through secret analogies, when the sweet perfection of your suffering body often impressed upon my soul your own lovely pains and froze me with fright: you can understand my trepidation, can't you, dear John? Oh, and those death's-heads, those skulls in Pastrana! When all's said and done it's the Trinity that separates us, Father. I don't feel it in quite the way you do, and your paternity doesn't die of it the way I do.

JOHN OF THE CROSS. "I know that the stream proceeding from these two
Is preceded by neither of them
Although it is night."[20]

(*Pause.*)

"A lone young shepherd lived in pain[21]
Withdrawn from pleasure and contentment."

(*Pause.*)

Even in darkest night.

(*Silence.*)

TERESA. Look here, my brother! Although I am a woman and haven't studied Latin, I try to comprehend the Mystery you describe so well. (*Reads.*) "I was reflecting today upon how, since they were so united, the Son alone could have taken human flesh . . . these are grandeurs which make the soul again desire to be free from this body that hinders their enjoyment."[22] That's what you're saying, too, yes or no?

JOHN OF THE CROSS. "In the beginning the Word
     Was; He lived in God . . .
     The Word is called Son;
     He was born of the Beginning . . .
     As the lover in the beloved
     Each lived in the other . . .
     And the Love that unites them
     Is one with them,
     Their equal, excellent as
     The One and the Other:
     Three Persons, and one Beloved
     Among all three.
     One love in them all
     Makes them one Lover . . .
     Thus it is a boundless
     Love that unites them . . .
     And the more love is one
     The more it is love."[23]

TERESA, *fast.* Father and Son, united in equality and excellence: I see that. The more love is one, the more infinite it is; I'm with you there, too. But what equality, what excellence? And how does this infinity become concretely plural among the Three Persons, and then in our souls? (*Pause.*) Oh, Father, please don't scold me for splitting hairs; unworthy woman I am, and fleshly with it, I don't want to make a mistake. As you know, I would go "to the ends of the earth as long as it were out of obedience."[24]

JOHN OF THE CROSS. "They were meant for the Son
     And He alone rejoiced in them. . . .
     My Son, only your
     Company contents Me."[25]

TERESA, *settling back into her chair, which will not levitate.* Well said! Gospel truth! And yet it would seem that I took the opposite path to yours. One day, "I was given understanding of how the Father receives within our soul the most holy Body of Christ."[26] Have you tried it, my great Seneca? (*Thoughtfully.*) Your vision is pure and intellectual, I know, you refrain from detailing ecstasies and raptures, you prefer only to explain the words, or rather your own stanzas, as befits a learned man. (*Knowing smile.*) You have no time for physical apprehensions and manifestations. (*Pause.*) Whereas me, I am a scruffy sparrow rather than a golden eagle. . . . I try to be inseparable from Jesus's humanity, inside my flesh and its retinue of visions, revelations, words. . . . Your unsullied way is one of darkness, death, and desolation. A wholesale negation that peters out exhausted in a purified tranquility, a terrible, pitch-black peace. Like you I started off with pain, loss and separation. (*Pause.*) In my banishment as I moved toward the Spouse, ecstasy emptied me of myself. (*Long pause.*)

(*Silence from John. Wary tenderness.*)

TERESA, *in an anxious voice.* Do you think, Father, that I allot too little space for the Holy Spirit? That I only mention it when a great scholar like yourself steers me back onto the straight and narrow? (*Pause, short laugh.*) Oh, but I said that in the *Life* . . . that's the meaning of the dove . . . of course![27]

(*Silence from John.*)

TERESA, *fast.* I can see you coming, with your pure-man's objections to the base woman I am! That Christocentric Teresa, not theocentric enough—that's what people will say, and I expect them to. Still, I often wrote and here repeat that when the Persons of the Trinity "take human flesh" in my soul, I felt a kind of obstacle to seeing three of them (*parece me hacía algún impedimento ver tres Personas*):[28] Not easy, for I am a creature, and a sinner.

(*Silence from John.*)

TERESA. Quite quickly, however, the Lord filled me with His presence. "In emptying my soul of all that is creature and detaching myself for the love of God, the same Lord will fill it with Himself."[29] (*In a greedy voice.*) That's right, the Lord, *Cristo como hombre*, man and God, Son and Father, both inseparable and all of them deep inside me. But you're the opposite, you only countenance the carnal figures of God—kisses, splendors, or what have you—to beseech them, to moan and groan over them, and then run away. Whereas I have our Guest *dentro de mí.* (*Normal voice.*) That's the difference between us, my ideal father. For you, it gets cleansed in the fires of agreeable tortures, is that right? That's what you feel?

(*Heavy silence from John.*)

(*Teresa stares at him for a while. Concerned tenderness. Silence.*)

JOHN OF THE CROSS. "Where have You hidden,
>   Beloved, and left me moaning?
>   You fled like the stag
>   And after wounding me;
>   I went out calling You, and You were gone."[30]

TERESA, *pulling back again, not looking at John anymore. Hands crossed over her breast, like the blue-cloaked Virgin image bequeathed by her mother, La Madre looks inside herself.* I'm not saying it's not like that, but here again the Trinity is at stake, and my Trinity is as bodily, delectable and obliging as the Spouse when He does me the favor of lodging within. . . . If I tell you that Christ is inside of me, it goes without saying that only divinity penetrates there, but naturally, if I may put it that way. . . . The humanity alone of the Son could never enter into our souls, many learned fathers have told me so, and I agree. And yet since the Three Persons are united and inside us, I understand—and this is where our experiences differ, Father, with all due respect—I understand how this offering from the Son, the only Person to have become incarnate, is pleasing.[31] . . . Yes, pleasing to the Father who receives it. (*Pause.*) But inside my soul . . . deep inside my soul. . . . (*Reading with her soul the text from the* Testimonies *as it scrolls past on the Virgin's blue veil.*) . . . Pleasing deep inside my soul. . . . Do you understand? This offering enables the Father Himself to enjoy, down here on earth, the pleasure of His Son. Both together. Deep inside me. The Father rejoices in His Son within my soul. I mean that the delights of the filial sacrifice are permitted to the Father and to the Son and to the Spirit, and that these three divine Persons are inside us. . . . (*Pause.*)

(*John keeps his eyes fastened on the flame.*)

TERESA, *exhaling deeply.* Ah, dear Seneca, I'm sorry to repeat myself so often, but within us such great mysteries lie! At the moment of Communion, our interior is more than bodily when pleasure involves both body and soul. Does that make it any less spiritual? (*Pause.*) For me, the two go together. (*Long silence, then slight smile.*) No matter if the officiating priest is in sin: the reception of the *jouissance* of the Three Persons inside depends rather on the soul receiving the sacrament. If the sun doesn't shine on a piece of pitch as it does on glass, the fault is not with the sun but with the pitch.[32] (*Imploring tone.*) I myself have no hopes of conquering Heaven or avoiding Hell, I want to live here and now, lowly smear of pitch that I am, like a pane of glass penetrated by Christ made man, inseparable from the Holy Trinity. By my love, in the delightful friendship of His sacred humanity, spirit and body together, I try to achieve what you seek in your hopeless pursuit: "And He was gone." It's the living God, dwelling in my soul, who grants me the favor of such a powerful energy. "Esto no es como otras visiones, porque lleve fuerza con la fe."[33]

(*Silence.*)

"Look, look, she's going up again, she's off the ground, she's flying!" Ana de San Bartolomé and Teresita scramble for a better look from the parlor door.

"And Father John of the Cross, too!" Catalina de la Concepción and María Bautista have joined them.

(*Silence.*)

JOHN OF THE CROSS. I take what you are saying, Madre, but not completely. What you do in your relish is to gobble down sacred history until your mouth bleeds with it: look at the state you're in! You're dying, I realize that—but throughout your life this kind of symptom, or worse, has always waylaid you. I am well informed of it, and was even a witness on some occasions. (*Pause.*) Once you nearly choked on the Lord's blood . . . or was the blood yours? (*In a cold, level voice.*) You seem blind to the difference, when it comes to union with Him as you engage in it. Is that what you've been trying to tell me, yet again? (*John of the Cross lands his chair on the ground in front of Teresa, the better to fulfill his confessor's vocation.*) (*Long silence from Teresa.*)

JOHN OF THE CROSS. To make myself clear, tell me, are you capable of distinguishing between sensuality on the one hand and the taint of the sensual on the other? I'm asking you, Mother, and I'm not asking lightly. We both agree that nature takes pleasure in spiritual things. "Since both the spiritual and the sensory part of the soul receive gratification from that refreshment, each part experiences delight according to its own nature and properties. The spirit, the superior part of the soul, experiences renewal and satisfaction in God; and the sense, the lower part, feels sensory gratification and delight because it is ignorant of how to get anything else, and hence takes whatever is nearest, which is the impure sensory satisfaction. It may happen that while a soul is with God in deep spiritual prayer, it will conversely passively experience sensual rebellions, movements, and acts in the senses, not without its own great displeasure. This frequently happens at the time of Communion. Since the soul receives joy and gladness in this act of love—for the Lord grants the grace and gives himself for this reason—the sensory part also takes its share, as we said, according to its mode. Since, after all, these two parts form one *suppositum*, each one usually shares according to its mode in what the other receives. As the philosopher says: 'Whatever is received is received according to the mode of the receiver.'[34] Because in the initial stages of the spiritual life, and even more advanced ones, the sensory part of the soul is imperfect, God's spirit is frequently received in this sensory part with this same imperfection. Once the sensory part is reformed through the purgation of the dark night, it no longer has these infirmities. Then the spiritual part of the soul, rather than the sensory part, receives God's spirit, and the soul thus receives everything according to the mode of the spirit."[35]

TERESA, *eyes lowered, she continues to gaze inside her soul.* The sensual also takes delight in spiritual things, Father, and I do not find that spirit and sense are so divorced from one another. Nor does merit consist only of gratification, it also means action, suffering, and love, all at once and together. "Look at my life: you will find no joy there other than that of Mount Thabor." Of the Transfiguration. For incontinence of love is not dirty, Father; it is an excess that leads us down the true path, the path of suffering: I can't forget that.[36] And I understood that you intended to reel me back toward your reason, your purity, when you offered me just half a wafer at Communion; you must remember that occasion, one which religious commentators will pick over avidly for ever and ever, amen. . . . (*Short laugh.*) You were already playing the psychoanalyst, my dear Seneca, trying to cure passion by means of frustration, weren't you, go on! (*Jovial laugh.*) But surely the Discalced Rule I restored aims at the same result? I discovered it long before I met you, after all. (*Vehemently.*) And yet deep down in my soul I never thought it necessary to lay on the penance with a trowel, as your men do in Pastrana, and you too, in your own burning way. . . . The Rule, no more and no less: that seems enough to me. "The rule that heals all," as a woman will write four centuries hence, without the least inkling of my existence. . . .[37]

JOHN OF THE CROSS. I am a denying spirit, whereas you say yes to everything. (*Silence.*)

TERESA. To everything, but also to nothing, Father. (*Eyes, head-on.*) On that day I mentioned, even if you'd given me nothing but a crumb of Host, or none at all, I to whom the Lord had already given so much would have felt just as replenished by the mere fact of knowing He exists. (*Eyes, looking upward.*) Therefore the presence of His Majesty—even in a tiny speck of matter on my tongue—is more than sufficient to unite me to the Beloved, in a way you cannot imagine, Father, with all due respect. (*Lips.*)

JOHN OF THE CROSS. O guiding night! O night more lovely than the dawn! O night that has united the Lover with his beloved, transforming the beloved in her Lover.[38]

TERESA, *losing her temper.* So tell me, Father. When you say: "transforming the beloved in her Lover," you're talking about your soul, of course, but don't you also mean yourself, Brother John, here before me in flesh and blood? Yourself in the feminine? Or am I mistaken, being so lowly. . . . *Yo que soy ruin.*[39] (*Lips.*)

(Silence from John.)

TERESA, *eyes head-on.* Shall I have the impertinence to repeat, Father, that your mournful felicity frightens me? *(Reading.)* Of course, like Christ . . . you are suspended in the void . . . your heart racked by love and forever unsatisfied. How far I am, I the sinner, from that heart burning to obtain something or other . . . but loathing any food he sees![40] I am the unworthy servant of your Lord, chosen by His Majesty to be filled with the divine essence. . . .

JOHN OF THE CROSS, *edging his chair back a little, pinched face, then expressionless.* "Not that which is most delectable, but that which is most unpleasing; not that which gives most pleasure, but rather that which gives least."[41] *(John of the Cross begins to take flight, trying to escape La Madre's appetites.)*

TERESA. Your naked faith, my son, your *desnuda fe* is unsparing toward naked flesh.[42] *(Pause.)* Here, I'll offer you this insight, Father, the modest opinion of a woman. *(Eyes upward, then down.)* The only naked faith is that which transits through naked flesh, that's what I've realized. . . . Only transits, mind you . . . Can you understand that, my little Seneca? *(Broken voice.)* . . . But what an incandescent transport in that baring of the flesh! *(Flies off in her turn.)*

(Silence from John.)

TERESA, *vehemently.* Yes, my soul's union with the Three Persons is a matrimonial one, dear Father—that *is* the divine mystery. Edith Stein says about human marriage in her *Science of the Cross*, listen: "Its actual reality has its highest reason for existence in that it can give expression to a divine mystery"—or perhaps it's the other way around?[43] *(Long silence.)* For my part, I can't see how that can be possible unless the soul is wedded to the sacred humanity of the Son of God. The Lord necessarily wants to make His presence felt: "Quiere dar a sentir esta presencia . . . para conocer que allí está Dios."[44] And God the Father, along with the Holy Ghost, are necessarily present at the nuptials. . . . That is their place, and this union gives it to them, gives rise to them. . . .

(Silence from John.)

TERESA. Won't you answer, my little Seneca? Say, do you really hold the people of Israel to be the Bride? In the Song of Songs, of course. But the Bride of the Trinitary God? Of the Holy Spirit, I mean, as well as of the Father and the Son; of the Three Persons in their distinctness and yet substantial oneness? I can't affirm this incontrovertibly when I listen to you . . . and yet it's of the essence, for me. It's a question of bodies, do you understand? Of course you do, forgive my choice of words, dear John. . . . In the long run people will realize, I know they will, that our religion—Christianity, of course, what else—that Christianity was founded

on the loss of a body. Michel de Certeau will spell it out; he'll be very fond of us both, believe it or not. The loss of Christ's body, of course, but duplicated—are you listening—by the loss of the body of Israel. . . . It's obvious, surely. . . . Well, the disappearance of both kinds of body, the Christic and the Jewish, was perhaps necessary: logically there had to be a detachment from both "nation" and "genealogy," as they will be called, if the religion was to become universal and spiritual. In the Jewish tradition, you know, living bodies are always shifting and moving around. . . . Among us, the party of the Crucified One, it's different, as I hardly need tell you: we start off depriving ourselves of the body and then, based on that absence, we keep trying to "form a body," to incorporate ourselves. Don't you think? You and me too, we make ourselves a body out of words, not in the same way as each other, but still. Add in the ecclesiastical body, the doctrinal corpus, all of that . . . delightful experiences, I grant you. . . . The Word becomes flesh and back again, a risky operation for the likes of us, and not given to all: you tend to overlook the flesh, and I the word. . . . Where was I? Oh yes, the Trinity. Well, there it is, the Bride can't help but wed all three of them! And like the Sulamitess finds her Solomon, I find Him in the actual reality of marriage. "Draw me, we will run after thee." That's your sentiment too, Father. So let's continue. Read with me what follows: "The king hath brought me into his chambers; we will be glad and rejoice in thee, we will remember thy love more than wine."[45]
(*Long silence.*)

TERESA, *heavy sigh, before resuming, convinced and convincing.* Heaven opens its gates to us in this life, that's what I'm trying to say. Your business, the *trato* as you call it, is an affair of faith, that is, of knowledge. But it's not because the contemplation I dwell in is an affair of the heart that the soul does not unite fully with God. (*Short silence. Normal voice.*) Then, in the surrender to God's will, "the soul wants neither death nor life": "Tiene tanta fuerza este rendimiento a ella, que la muerte ni la vida se quiere, si no es por poco tiempo cuando desea ver a Dios."[46]
(*Beaming smile.*) We concur on this point, my son, don't we?

JOHN OF THE CROSS, *clearing his throat, hesitating a moment, then speaking fast.* There's no longer any need to question God as in the olden days, under the Ancient Law. (*Without looking at her, his eyes seem to be listening.*) Listen to Christ: God has no more to reveal. The Word no longer speaks, and instead the Spirit of Truth makes itself understood. (*Closes eyes.*) Understanding . . . understanding . . . understanding. . . . (*Gazing in rapture at the ceiling, with ramrod body.*)

TERESA. In my own way I, too, manage to attain a measure of understanding . . . reaching the Spirit of truth itself . . . fire and splendor. . . . "Neither death nor life are objects of desire anymore," do you hear me? And if my intercession could lead a single soul to love Him more, it would matter more to me than being in glory. "Y si pudiese ser parte que siquiera un alma le amase más y alabase por mi intercesión, que aunque fuese por poco tiempo, me parece importa más que estar en la gloria."[47]

Therefore do the virgins love thee . . .

The Song of Songs, which is Solomon's.

Let him kiss me with the kisses of his mouth . . .[48]

You'll say, my great friend, that I lack "understanding of the vernacular meaning of the Latin," and you have a point. But I feel great joy every time I read the Song of Songs, a great spiritual consolation, for "my soul is stirred and recollected more than by devotional books written in the language I understand."[49]

✳ ✳ ✳

A deafening noise interrupts the holy dialogue. The monastery door is being battered by fists, sticks, and musket butts; will it hold firm?

The stage goes dark for the duration of the protracted assault.

When the lights come up again, but only dimly, the moribund woman is back in bed.

TERESA, *agitated*. Owls, Carmelites of the observation, cats, wolves, discalced monks. . . . I mean, mitigated ones. . . . All of them, anyway, they're coming, they're after Brother John! Help, Sisters, help! (*La Madre rears up in bed, fearfully. She fears the martyrdom planned by the enemies of her discalced reforms for this peerlessly chaste and pure priest. Or does she really fear John's judgment of her?*)

ANA DE SAN BARTOLOMÉ, *never having had much notion of time, now confuses one major crisis with another. After all, there have been so many.* No, Mother, it's the *alguaciles* trying to break down the door. But don't worry, the sisters are reinforcing it with heavy joists. We'll look after you!

ACT 3, SCENE 2

TERESA OF AVILA

TERESITA

JOHN OF THE CROSS

HIS COMPANION
BOSSUET, bishop, writer, the "Eagle of Meaux"
SYLVIA LECLERCQ, psychologist

The stage goes momentarily dark. Teresa is still in conversation with John, now present only in the forms of his voice and his portrait, an anonymous work of the Spanish school.

> JOHN OF THE CROSS, *voice receding, reciting his works.* "The interior bodily sense— namely, the imagination and the fancy; this we must likewise void of all the imaginary apprehensions and forms that may belong to it by nature. . . . "[50]

Now the flame returns, henceforth to remain on stage. Teresa is back at the Incarnation, alone, this time in her prioress's chair. She converses with John's spirit; there is no longer any bodily evidence of him.

> TERESA, *in an anxious voice.* They'll reproach me, I'm sure, for not mentioning him enough in my writings. His body was not at all attractive. Unlike his eyes. And his mind. It's true Fr. Antonio de Jesús takes up more space in my *Foundations*, and God knows he was no genius, nor an *hombre* in the strong sense, well, I know my meaning. Brother John practically forced us to overlook him, such was his urge to self-annihilation. . . . (*Pause.*) He nearly caught us out that way. . . . I wouldn't let him . . . I went all the way to our good Philip II, to rescue him from the mitigated lot . . . and succeeded, thanks be to God. (*Pause.*) There's nobody like him for making me feel obscurely unworthy and infinitely guilty. . . . (*Pathetic voice.*) Under the steady gaze of his burning eyes, I stop being a crystal, I become once more that black pitch I've never ceased to be, as I know better than anyone, with or without the Lord's voice, between ourselves. (*The dying woman, appeased, has recovered the critical lucidity that is the hallmark of her writings. Casts circular glances around her.*)
>
> TERESITA, *mothering her beloved aunt.* Don't beat yourself up so on your deathbed, Auntie: after all, the asceticism of John of the Cross was hardly yours, while you lived. . . .
>
> TERESA, *exhaling.* Never fear, darling, I can look after myself, and even John got the sharp end of my tongue when he deserved it. I must say . . . (*coughing*) over and above the obliviousness to his person that he more or less deliberately instilled in us . . . (*eyes looking right, pause*) the great purifier aroused in me a dash of, what's

the word, impatience. (*Eyes looking left, pause. She is no longer uttering a word, but knows her little niece can read her thoughts and only wishes to do her some good.*) Oh, it was just a game between us, he wasn't fooled . . . a piece of mock cruelty, don't get me wrong. . . . (*Circular glances, sighs.*) Just for a laugh at his expense, and at mine too, of course. I'd found the sweet key to revenge, you see! (*Looks at her fixedly for a while.*) When in distress . . . and to shake up any who wallow in it just to show off . . . there's nothing more effective than to be happy. (*Pause.*) And to laugh. Do you think that's easy? (*Pause.*) But not everyone has the knack. . . . Try it and see. It's enough to disarm the Inquisition itself. Even the "chief angel," as I used to call him in my letters to Gratian, you know, the grand inquisitor . . . that's right, Gaspar de Quiroga, bishop of Cuenca, archbishop of Toledo, well, even he came around to my reforms. As I was saying. . . . One of his nieces became a Carmelite. . . . But to bend such a model of perfection as dear Seneca, that's a whole other matter. . . . It can be done. . . . Well, we'd better wait and see (*Wry smile.*). Death himself may get nothing for his pains, I'll let you know from the Beyond once I have passed over. . . . (*Stops smiling.*). Does it seem to be taking a long time, little one? I think so too. How am I supposed to be afraid of the Reaper, as the wicked call him, when he is what I desire? One stage in my long desire for the Other . . . hardly anything . . . I'm nearly there. . . . (*Deep sigh.*)

The din made by the *alguaciles* can still be heard.

ANA DE SAN BARTOLOMÉ, *upset at her inability to make La Madre's last moments quiet and peaceful.* What a hellish racket!

TERESA, *gaily.* Wrong, my girl, it's not the *alguaciles* but the commotion stirred up by the *Vejamen,* that some will call my *Satirical Critique*! (*Smiling.*) You know, that mock-colloquium, remember? That parody of a homage rendered to me by Julián de Ávila, Francisco de Salcedo, my brother Lorenzo, and John of the Cross himself, in the parlor at Saint Joseph's, before a rapt audience of sisters. . . . (*Broadening grin.*) We're going to have more fun before I take my final leave, come along, cheer up. . . . (*Mock-serious expression.*) Bishop Álvaro de Mendoza had requested them to send me their thoughts upon that edifying instruction I received from the Lord one day of grace in prayer: "Seek yourself in Me." (*Stops smiling.*) The gentlemen's muddled remarks were positively comic: it still tickles me to think of their precious colloquium and my own barbs in response! (*Smiling again; the faithful nurses can't hear the words, and can only imagine what's passing through her mind.*) Good Lord, I had no idea at the time—five years ago, it must be—that one's dying agonies could also be a sort of *satirical critique*. Yes, indeed, a teasing yet gracious exchange with others very similar to my progress toward God, as you'd confirm, my daughters, would you not? . . . I'm much obliged. (*Normal voice, fast.*) Who mentioned Hell? Not I. Nor Heaven, of course, not even Purgatory, it's nothing but a *vejamen*, believe me. (*Coughing, tears.*) Because I don't know who I am, but I know that in seeking myself in the Other within me, I am a double self. I should add that those are Montaigne's terms, the expression of a writer who is younger than me and not precisely on my side, as will soon be a matter of public record. "And there is as much difference between us and ourselves as there is between us and other people."[51] Yet that man is not so far from me, I assure you. . . . Will anyone have the insight to notice? . . . Too bad . . . I am double, I say, and uncertain, endlessly seeking myself; but not shy or distraught, and with good reason! Because the Me in which the Lord invites me to seek myself ("Seek yourself in Me"), the Lord's Me, the Other Me, is nothing less than recollected deep inside of me, for God's sake!

Teresa is wearing her teasing smile again. Her attendants read it as ecstasy, as though La Madre were practically knocking on Heaven's door.

TERESA, *waving her arms.* So I loosed a volley of grapeshot in the direction of those fine, chin-stroking gentlemen, though leavened needless to say by my customary pinch of amused affection. (*Wrinkled nose.*) It was aimed at John of the Cross first and foremost, since the dear friar had contributed the longest commentary of all, as befits a highbrow scholar from Salamanca. (*Lips.*) What's more he was addressing me, a poor unlettered woman, the way the Jesuits always do, with such haughty condescension . . . such. . . . Oh, you know. (*Lips again.*) Between strict paternalists and patronizing persecutors, no contest! I've never hesitated for a moment, do you hear me, girls? (*Wavering voice.*) A tenderly strict paternalist is indispensable, and will be needed for a long time to come, mark my words. (*Does this please or frighten her? Looks up and straight ahead.*)

The dying nun continues to argue in her head with John. He is the only one at her side during these final instants before the Other.

TERESA, *reading, fast.* Why seek God as if we were dead, or when we are dead, my little Seneca? And why do you do no more than seek, unremittingly, wearing yourself out with it? While always claiming that there's nothing more to

question? Why, let's rejoice, now that the Word has been revealed! The Sulami-
tess was good at bliss, even though she was always chasing after her elusive
Spouse. . . . In the union I obtained by means of prayer, God's grace bestowed
on the soul means that the soul has found Him, once and for all. (*Deep breath.
Open palms stretched upward.*) His actual presence actually inhabits me inside
. . . since how long ago? As long as I'm alive I seek, but I seek inside me, because
I've already found Him. I've said *yes* to the Other in me, and His Voice knows it.
He is in me, I am Him, I am she who says *yes*. A woman called Molly Bloom will
do likewise, more drolly. Did Joyce, a Catholic Irishman, think of me when he
set that scene in the Spanish landscape of Gibraltar? (*Pause. Stares at the flame.
Closes eyes. Brief rest.*)

TERESA, *with a beaming smile, reading.* "Yes and how he kissed me under the Moorish wall and I thought well as well him as another and then I asked him with my
eyes to ask again yes and then he asked me would I yes my mountain flower and
first I put my arms around him yes and drew him down to me so he could feel
my breasts all perfume yes and his heart was going like mad and yes I said yes I
will Yes."[52] (*Smiling more brightly still.*) No, that's not me, Father, it's all right, just
a vision that resembles me. I can see the future now . . . having got this far, why
not. . . . Do you consider me excessively carnal? Others have done. A bishop even
wrote to me about it, but which one? I haven't a clue, I get them mixed up, all
those dour, po-faced prelates. (*Pause.*) "God deliver me from people so spiritual
that they want to turn everything into perfect contemplation, no matter what."[53]
I have always felt the greatest envy of you, I've told you so: *le tengo una envidia
grandísima.*[54] Good father, good brother John, you should expect irreverence
from me. . . . (*Wrinkled nose.*) . . . for I already spoke of you in my Dwelling Places.
(*No sign from John. La Madre's gaze alone outlines and enlarges her friend's
portrait.*)

TERESA. Yes, it's not just deer and butterflies, you are present too. . . . (*Reading.*) That
man I was speaking of, who was "so desirous of serving His Majesty at his own
cost, without these great delights, and so anxious to suffer that he complained
to our Lord because He bestowed the favours on him." And had it lain in his
power, that is, in your power, my little Seneca, had you been graced with the enjoyment of His favours, you would have declined them![55] (*Lips.*) Goodness me!
I wouldn't! I am talking about the delights God gives us to taste in contemplation,
not about the visions themselves—you're entitled to despise those, and I myself
am doubtful about them. But the contemplation that emerges out of suffering
to overwhelm us with graces! Why deny ourselves the sweet fruits of spiritual

marriage? I know, you've told me often enough, that the dark night for you is "deprivation of the soul's taste or appetite for things"; "llamamos aquí noche a la privación del gusto en el apetito de todas las cosas."[56] Nevertheless, dear John, to not expand is to shrink. And where love is true, it "cannot possibly be content with remaining always the same."[57] (*Pause.*)

TERESA, *startled and fearful.* Shall I tell you? It was manifested to me, with "a knowledge admirable and clear" how the sacred Humanity of Christ "was taken into the bosom of the Father."[58] Divinity . . . extraordinary glory. . . . (*Trembling voice. Lips.*) . . . And that's not all. Since we are concerned with the Holy Trinity, do you think I've forgotten the Blessed Virgin, in other words, the woman I am? Not at all. Listen: "The Lord placed Himself in my arms as in the painting of the fifth agony."[59] You see? And stop looking at me with those vacant eyes. Christ is held in the Father's bosom, the Virgin's arms, and mine. . . . Same thing. . . . Don't worry, these are merely intellectual visions, the only sort you allow. But they're so vivid that they resemble imaginative ones. . . . (*Pause.*) . . . I'm going too far, aren't I? I'm being too greedy again? (*Throws herself backward as if to picture John more clearly.*)

When the body speaks, seeing images is unavoidable, dear John, but I do not really perceive them with the eyes of the body, in fact they are no more than intellectual visions. . . . In a way, yes, there's such a thing as "sensation freed from the trammel of the senses."[60] Those aren't my words, they belong to Marcel Proust, do you know that writer? An expert in accursed races, men, women, and in-betweens, in hawthorn and rose windows and felt time. . . . Of course I can tell from here, I'm a visionary, don't look at me like that, my great Seneca . . . you understand perfectly well. . . . "My imagination, which was my only means of enjoying beauty."[61] . . . Those words could have been written by me, too bad, Marcel will do it for me. Better than anyone. And that's why the imagination is "the organ that serves the eternal," do you follow us, the two of us, that eternal young man and myself? . . . Deep down you agree with us, Father, but you concur in your own erudite, demanding way. . . . (*Normal voice.*) Does that make you feel better? . . . It's true, I am very spiritual also. (*Pause. Hint of a smile.*) (*Close-up on John's portrait.*)

TERESA. I'd have had to master mathematics in order to please you, and yet, I can't help it, poor little me pleased His Majesty himself from time to time. I'm a pretentious woman and I repent of it. Not your style, I know. (*Closes eyes and reopens them.*) You see, Father, I don't let go of you all the same, I love you more than you think, for look, even on my deathbed I am prolonging our so-called colloquium,

the *vejamen*—remember? (*Normal voice.*) I cannot do otherwise, having this radiant Other at the core of me while you are constantly scurrying after it, poor
little wounded deer, unhappy, racked priest whom I love with all my heart. (*Long
silence.*) I understand, mind you: you're nothing but a wretched man, which
when all is said and done is even more frustrating than being a wretched woman.
The truth is you'll never be the Other's Bride, whereas I am confident that I am.
That's how it is, get used to it. (*Lips.*) I enjoyed having that place, acquired since
my prayer over the Song of Songs, and I'm not budging from it, hardened sinner that I am. But thank you kindly for having so clearly explained to me, in the
course of your fraternal contribution to the *vejamen*, matters I hadn't asked you
about! (*Teasing voice.*) You disparage the understanding, and yet you wouldn't
stop commenting every sentence, interminably, where I, lowly creature, did
nothing but feel. . . . Forgive me, Father, I don't need convincing, as you know,
that you alone are perfection. Me, I'm nothing but a trifler, I own. The Lord will
judge; I'm on my way there now. (*Listening expression.*)
(*Long silence.*)

TERESA. You say that David assures us . . . of what? That the death of the just man
is precious in God's eyes. . . . Speak about yourself, Seneca my dear, I'm a mere
woman, and a hard-hearted one at that. . . . Is it really in my power to tear the
fabric of mortal life, as you put it so well? Perhaps. . . . But only in the Seventh
Dwelling Places. . . . Run away, you say? No, I feel that I'm closing in on the jewel,
la joya, within.

JOHN OF THE CROSS'S VOICE, *with the face of an El Greco Christ. Solus soli.*

TERESA, *vehemently again.* Quite so, I was about to say. "For it is not knowing much,
but realizing and relishing things interiorly, that contents and satisfies the soul."[62]
It may be that I am closer to these words of Loyola's than you are, my friend. Ignatius does not refer to prayer, as we know, even if his spiritual graces are not so very
different from your "substantial words of the soul," are they?[63] And he is warier of
the devil than I am, I agree. But. . . . (*Broken voice, silence.*) but when he has a vision
of the Blessed Trinity "in the form of a lyre or harp," amid uncontainable tears
and sighs, and when. . . .[64] (*Pause.*) When Jesus appears to him in "white," in His
humanity as I see it, and again when He dazzles him like a sun . . . and leaves him
nothing but the relish for the interior *loquela*, the uninterrupted voice. . . . (*Her
breathing and pulse accelerate.*) . . . Well, I feel for it, it moves my soul, wounded
with love, that seeks solitude with the help of the Holy Spirit. . . .[65]

JOHN OF THE CROSS'S VOICE, *still with his El Greco face. Solus soli.* There is nothing nuptial in Ignatius Loyola!

TERESA, *with a broad grin.* Fortunately not! Man or woman, alone with the One
and Only . . . what else do you think marriage is, my great Seneca!

(*The flame turns bright red as La Madre's innocent laugh rings out.*)

TERESA, *suddenly anxious.* I smell burning, daughters, can you smell it? Is it me
that's on fire? That wouldn't be surprising since His Majesty threatened me with
Hell once before, but it was a stinking tube, a space without space where to be
was impossible. A place that John of the Cross alone—who else—managed to
survive and escape from. He must be a saint, that Seneca, as the hole where the
mitigated friars locked him up was so infernal that it was a miracle he got out
alive. A miracle, I tell you! (*Still excitable.*) Oh no, it's not me that's on fire! I do
not consume myself, I can't compete with John on that score, God bless him. It
smells of charred paper; are they maybe burning my letters to the papal nuncio,
the dreaded Nicolás Ormaneto? Or those I wrote to Pius V? To the Carmelite
principal, Ángel de Salazar? To the nuns at the Convent of the Incarnation? How
many thousands of letters and notes have I written . . . a collection not everyone
regards as a treasure trove, naturally, plenty of people would sooner destroy it.
How well I remember. . . . (*Pause. Wide smile.*) I who have a short memory. . . .
(*Smile wider still, with an edge of sarcasm.*) It was the Dominican priest Diego de
Yanguas, a reader of superior capacities, who when he heard that I had written
down my meditations upon the Song of Songs commanded me to torch them on
the spot, and of course I hastened to obey. (*Pause. Hides face behind crossed hands.*)
What a silly I was . . . never suspecting what fearful dangers lurk inside that book
for a woman. . . . (*Uncovers face. Sighs, smiles.*) But what's this I see? (*Worldly.*)
No, not you, my dear John! (*Long pause. Stops smiling.*) . . . So you're playing the
wafer trick on me again? Terminally, this time? I didn't expect that, hats off, I'm
impressed! I should have known it was too much to ask; you couldn't fail to burn
them. All my letters, up in smoke? Incredible. So driven to abolish yourself that
you divest yourself of everything, even of me, especially of me. . . . We are so like
and so unlike, aren't we; day and night. Day is afraid of night. Night is indifferent
to day. . . . And yet they are indissociable, one cannot be without the other. . . .

(*The flame licks into the cell, two shadows move over the white wall: Brother John
and a companion, who is holding a small bag.*)

COMPANION. Look, Brother John, I have just found this *taleguilla* whose contents
might interest you.

JOHN OF THE CROSS, *absorbed in being perfect.* Interest *me*?

COMPANION. I said "might." This bag contains the letters of the late Mother Teresa
of Avila, may she rest in peace.

JOHN OF THE CROSS, *turning slowly but decisively to toss the bag into the fire.* Burn them!

(*After uttering the above words in dispassionate tones, "Little Seneca" glides serenely into the furnace invading the cell. From there we hear* JOHN OF THE CROSS'S VOICE *reciting.*)

> "Without a place and with a place
> to rest—living darkly with no ray
> of light—I burn my self away."[66]

(*John's companion murmurs the words after him and follows his master into the furnace. The recitation can still be heard.*)

JOHN OF THE CROSS'S VOICE. "In order to arrive at having pleasure in everything, Desire to have pleasure in nothing."[67]

(*Pause.*)

JOHN OF THE CROSS'S VOICE. "O living flame of love."

(*We hear Teresa laughing.*)

Sylvia Leclercq sees the shadow of Bossuet approach against the quivering, dark red firelight.[68] The silhouette of the bishop of Meaux advances, carrying the *Funeral Orations* in one hand and the *Instructions upon States of Prayer* in the other.

BOSSUET. "It is an odd weakness of mankind, that while death surrounds us in its myriad forms, it is never present to our minds." But since "we must only be lofty where St. Teresa is concerned," bear in mind that Heaven above "has a plan to repair the house he has given us. When he destroys it and casts it down in order to make it anew, we must move out. Yet he himself offers us his palace, and within it, gives us rooms." "And yet it was never so for this creature, Teresa, who dwelt on earth as though she were already in Heaven."[69]

SYLVIA LECLERCQ, *occupying La Madre's shadowy place stage right, speaking in a drained voice.* Here's a surprise Fénelon will appreciate, not to mention Madame de Guyon. . . .[70] I might have known the Eagle of Meaux would be here; he was never very keen on intimate, Quietist, or amalgamated-type scenes, but he made an exception for Teresa. Sylvia Leclercq "in the footsteps of Bossuet," who'd have thought it? Ah, he's no longer the *bos suetus aratro*, the "ox accustomed to the plough" of the Jesuit school. . . . The old theologian has aged as well, he's got excema and gallstones and who knows what else. . . . But he will still go down fighting, weapons in hand, Saint-Simon tells us, and might have added: "like Teresa."

BOSSUET, *in a metallic, slightly breathless voice.* "Our society is in heaven above," nostra autem conversatio in coelis est. . . . And the hope of which the world speaks is but an agreeable illusion, *somnium vigilantium.* . . . If I don't dare to affirm it, who will? I am a Cartesian, but not to the last ditch. *Primo*: Hope equals the "sleep of vigilance," of course, except. . . . Except when hope comes from the Lord. In that circumstance its words are assured, and consequently the hope in Him is likewise assured, *ergo* it is certain. . . . *Secondo: Contra spem in spem.* . . . This is the anchor of our souls, something the true Christian does not possess, but is looking for. (*Puts down the two tomes he was carrying and takes the* Panegyrics *proffered by Leclercq, riffles through while holding forth in a firm, steady voice.*) And this "infinite munificence" was lavished on Teresa in life, while she yet inhabited her mortal coil. . . . *Tertio*: Such is indeed the grand spectacle to which the Church invites us. . . .

SYLVIA LECLERCQ. Nicely put, "munificence" and "grand spectacle" are appropriate. (*Hand over mouth, she has finally been awed by the infallible rhetorician*).

BOSSUET. "St. Teresa lives among angels, convinced that she is with her Spouse," and thus fulfillment succeeds to yearning. . . . "A divine sickness," undoubtedly, one whose power increases day by day? But there remains the "link, gentlemen, which is charity. . . . It elevates Teresa above the throng. . . . She speeds toward it, driven by ardent, impetuous desires . . . which prove unequal to severing the bonds of mortal flesh, against which she now declares a holy war. . . . For all true Christians should feel like travelers on a journey." They must feel, yes, feel. . . .

SYLVIA LECLERCQ, *hand over mouth again, disconcerted by her sudden admiration for the bishop.* That's right, go on. . . .

BOSSUET, *imperturbably. Qui non gemit peregrinus, non gaudebit civis.* . . . Saint Augustine had some splendid turns of phrase, madam. "He who does not lament the journey will not rejoice on reaching the city." And Saint Teresa becomes "ever freer, more disengaged from perpetual agitation." "The harder she finds it to cast off her body, the more detached from that body she becomes."

SYLVIA LECLERCQ, *admiringly.* Is that in relation to John of the Cross? How unexpected, from you! Might you be an unjustly neglected author?

BOSSUET, *ignoring the compliment, enthused by his panegyric.* One can scarcely credit the way she built her monasteries, that girl. . . .

SYLVIA LECLERCQ, *thoughtfully, almost inaudibly, hugging the* Orations *and the* Instructions. Bossuet the Academician turns out to be a pragmatist with his own brand of mysticism, quite unlike his image. But he couldn't have been any less, if he was to prevent a schism with Rome. Courted by the dauphin, the king, society ladies like Maintenon, Montespan, Sévigné; patron of men like La Bruyère, associating with the likes of Pascal, Molière, La Rochefoucauld, Leibniz.... Yet he still remembers his conversation with our Teresa. "That girl," he calls her. Their conversation is in Heaven above, apparently, albeit that Heaven exists down here on earth, according to La Madre? Intermittently, but still. A weird space it is, Monseigneur. Go take a look.... (*She tries to detain the Eagle of Meaux but he returns the* Panegyrics *to her and vanishes, holding a Cross, into the darkness stealing across the stage.*)

ACT 3, SCENE 3

The voices of TERESA and SYLVIA and the virtual characters of LEIBNIZ[71] and SPINOZA.[72]

The stage is empty. A huge diamond stands in place of La Madre's body, shot through with rays of light and cascading waters that bathe the facets of cut stone and also circulate inside it. The fire that consumed Teresa's letters to John of the Cross has left its red-gold color in the air. From time to time three shadows move through the permeable walls of the liquid jewel; one resembles the Teresa of the portrait attributed to Velázquez, another is Leibniz, and the third, Spinoza. There is also a mathematical formula, to wit:

$$\frac{\pi}{4} = 1 - \frac{1}{3} + \frac{1}{5} - \frac{1}{7} \cdots$$

We hear a high-pitched choir of Carmelites singing the *Veni Creator*, as well as the voice of Sylvia Leclercq and La Madre's mature tones; her body has been removed. This castle without walls stands in for it. The portrait of Teresa the writer is animated, miming the stage directions and accompanying the saint's voice.

TERESA'S VOICE. "A great gush of water could not reach us if it didn't have a source somewhere; it is understood clearly that there is Someone in the interior depths who shoots these arrows and gives life to this life, and that there is a Sun in the interior of the soul from which a brilliant light proceeds and is sent to the faculties. The soul ... does not move from that center nor is its peace lost."[73] It's true, the center exists and is at peace, and that's why I can be so fluid ... and vagabond, if I wish it. . . . (*Subtle smile.*) Who am I? "You who seeks yourself in Me," or "Me who seeks myself in You?" Who speaks? Is Teresa I, You, or She? "We are entirely made up of bits and pieces, woven together so diversely and so shapelessly that each one of them pulls its own way at every moment."[74] (*Eyes glance right, left, close.*) "These interior matters are so obscure for our minds. . . . Whoever reads this must have patience, for I have to have it in order to write about what I don't know. Indeed, sometimes I take up the paper like a simpleton, for I don't know what to say."[75] (*Wrinkles nose.*)

TERESA'S VOICE, *coming from the immense diamond revolving on the stage.* My castle is not an accumulation of images, it's an imaginary discourse: ask Michel de Certeau if you don't believe me! I am indeterminate, fluid, permeable, radiating light from my center: ask Mercedes Allendesalazar. . . . "I want to make one or more comparisons for you."[76] "Turn your eyes toward the center, which is the room or royal chamber where the King stays, and think of how a palmetto has many leaves surrounding and covering the tasty part that can be eaten. . . . The sun that is in this royal chamber shines in all parts. It is very important for any soul that practices prayer, whether little or much, not to hold itself back and stay in one corner. Let it walk through these dwelling places which are up above, down below, and to the sides, since God has given it such great dignity. Don't force it to stay a long time in one room alone. Oh, but if it is in the room of self-knowledge![77] (*Momentarily short of breath, coughing.*) "God help me with what I have undertaken! . . . Let's consider . . . two founts with two water troughs. . . . I am so fond of this element. . . . With one the water comes from far away through many aqueducts . . . with the other the source of the water is right there. . . . The water coming from the aqueducts is comparable, in my opinion, to the consolations drawn from meditation . . . thoughts . . . tiring the intellect. . . . With this other fount, the water comes from its own source which is God . . . with the greatest peace and quiet and sweetness in the very interior part of ourselves. . . . This water overflows through all the dwelling places and faculties until reaching the body. That is why I said that it begins in God and ends in ourselves. . . . The whole exterior man enjoys this spiritual delight and sweetness."[78]

(*After trying in vain to help her drink, Teresita refreshes Teresa's face with a moist cloth.*)

SYLVIA LECLERCQ'S VOICE. "*Transumanar*," why, she talks like Dante:

> "To represent transhumanise in words
> Impossible were; the example, then, suffice
> Him for whom Grace the experience reserves."[79]

TERESA'S VOICE. "The King is in His palace," just as the soul is. The King, the soul, it-you-I? It's all the same. Interchangeable, permutable, reversible. "In those other dwelling places there is much tumult and there are many poisonous creatures and the noise is heard"—all this being the drives, as Dr. Freud will tell us. And yet "no one enters that center dwelling place and makes the soul leave. . . . The passions are now conquered." This is sublimation. "Our entire body may ache; but if the head is sound, the head will not ache just because the body aches."[80] The mind and the word "must have amounted to much more than is apparent from [their] sound."[81] (*Turns head leftward, with calm face.*) It is not an imaginative vision, even if the soul, unable to express it in words, perceives it here by means of sight. And yet the sight is neither with the eyes of the body nor with those of the soul. . . . The three Persons of the Trinity are perceived in an intellectual, yes, intellectual vision, like a certainty of truth in the midst of fiery brightness, like a magnificent splendor coming straight to the mind.[82] I am a point inhabited by infinity, the infinite contracted into a dot, a dot dilated to infinity. Infinitesimal Teresa: a curious phenomenon, don't you think? (*She opens her eyes again, unseeing eyes, as when she bent them on the portrait of Velázquez. La Madre is listening to herself.*)

(*Silence.*)

LEIBNIZ, *in the voice of an anonymous man.* "To me, infinities are not totalities and infinitely small values are not magnitudes. My metaphysics banishes them. I regard infinitesimal quantities as useful unities." "My fundamental meditations turn on two things, namely, on *unity* and on *infinity*." "Each monad is a living mirror, or a mirror endowed with an internal action, and that it represents the universe according to its point of view and is regulated as completely as is the universe itself." "Everything is taken account of, even idle words . . . the just will be like suns . . . neither our senses nor our mind has ever tasted anything approaching the happiness that God prepares for those who love him." "Imaginary numbers have the following admirable property, that in calculus they enclose nothing absurd or contradictory and yet by the nature of things they cannot be represented *seu in concretis*."[83] The same goes for the infinitesimal: it is a *fiction*, and not a true difference. God is "the realm of possible realities."

SYLVIA LECLERCQ'S VOICE. "The infinity-point obeys the laws of transition and continuity: nothing is equivalent to anything else, and apparent coincidences really conceal an infinitely small distance. Thus the infinity-point does not form a structure but instead posits functions and relationships that proceed by approximation. A difference, never to be made good, persists between the number marked π and the set of terms able to express it:

$$\left(\frac{\pi}{4} = 1 - \frac{1}{3} + \frac{1}{5} - \frac{1}{7} + \cdots\right)$$

The unit has been dislocated. The sign-number, a unifying mirror, shatters, and notation resumes beyond its scope. The resulting differential, equivalent to the sixteenth-century nominalists' syncategorical (*in fieri*) infinite smallness, is not a unity that can be added to other unities to form a whole, but rather the slippage of infinity itself within the closed enunciation."[84]

LEIBNIZ, *in the voice of an anonymous man.* "Teresa of Avila had this fine thought, that the soul ought to conceive things as if there were only God and itself in the world." How this limpid, fecund insight gives us to understand immortality! "This thought gives rise to an idea which is significant even in philosophy, and I have made good use of it in one of my hypotheses."[85]

TERESA'S VOICE. Might I be a soul, then, a woman co-present ad infinitum? Might I be an ancestor of infinitesimal calculus?[86] Little me?

SPINOZA, *in the voice of the anonymous man.* "God loves himself with an infinite intellectual love."[87]

TERESA'S VOICE. God loves Himself? Himself, myself, yourself? I *are* the Trinity. I was writing the sensual mathematics of sacred humanity!

SYLVIA LECLERCQ'S VOICE. "Paradise and its plenitude of grace, the Trinity in person, are unveiled in the Intellection of love. The more I love, the more I understand. The more I understand, the more pleasure I feel, and the more I love." Not my words, but those of Philippe Sollers in his introduction to Dante's *Paradiso*.[88]

TERESA'S VOICE. "The image may be very helpful—to you especially—for since we women have no learning, all of this imagining is necessary that we may understand that within us lies something incomparably more precious than what we see outside ourselves." (*Coughs, trickle of blood.*) You say women are hollow inside? You have no inkling of what a Guest we harbor![89] You smile, I see: so who might this Guest be? The Father? The phallus? Animal lust? Hysterical excitability? All of the above, and of necessity sublime? Call it what you please, call it desire for the Other if you want to. Personally I'll stick with Guest, for the moment.... "Nor is that happiness and delight experienced, as are earthly consolations, in the heart. I mean there is no similarity at the beginning, for afterward the delight fills everything; this water overflows through all the dwelling places and faculties until reaching the body. That is why I said it begins in God and ends in ourselves."[90] Clear as day, is it not? Are you with me, my Seneca? (*No reply.*)

TERESA'S VOICE, *meditatively.* Some minds are orderly, and some are "so scattered they are like wild horses no one can stop." I'm thinking of myself, of course . . . you guessed it. . . . Always restless and on the go . . . "and perhaps they were no more than two steps from the fount of living water, of which the Savior said to the Samaritan woman, 'whoever drinks of it will never thirst.' How right and true!"[91] (*Voice weakening, trembling of the arms, legs, head.*) Between ourselves, I prefer Saint Augustine above other spiritual masters because he was once a sinner,[92] a runaway horse. O rushing storm, euphoric tempest that "comes from regions other than those of which [the devil] can be lord"![93] And how can we be sure? Why, because the soul derives benefits from it, by confronting the ringing Voice of His Majesty, or the superego if you prefer, the ideal Father who imparts the Law—that of both Testaments at once, needless to say. Poor butterfly-soul, "that went about so apprehensive that everything frightened it and made it fly. . . . The Lord has now fortified, enlarged, and made the soul capable."[94] (*Long silence. The crimson light turns violet.*) The soul does not leave the wondrous company of His Majesty and never ventures out of its interior mansion, as a consequence of which it is somehow divided, like Martha and Mary Magdalene: perpetual calm and repose on the one hand, problems and worries on the other. (*Exhales.*) Although the degree of clarity is not the same, because the vision of the Divine Presence is rarely as vivid as it is on the occasion of its first manifestation, when God elects to grant His gift, "*quiere Dios hacerle este regalo.*"[95] (*Breathing faster.*) The light has changed color, it will accompany me to the very end of this final road. Its variations still illuminate, even today, the anguish I felt when I discovered that the movement of thought, or more precisely the imagination, was not the same thing as understanding.

(*Pause. Bright lights diffracting the sparkle of the diamond.*)

TERESA'S VOICE, *doubtful, quizzical.* The understanding is one of the soul's faculties, and is apt to be flighty. Flighty, yes, that's the word, like a *tortolito.* . . . The understanding is like an inexperienced novice, or a smitten turtledove; it takes flight in so abstract a fashion that nothing embodies it. The imagination, for its part, cannot be confused with it, but takes from it the cue to soar up; since God alone can hold it fast, one is misled into thinking it detached from the body. "I have seen . . . that the faculties of my soul were occupied and recollected in God while my mind on the other hand was distracted. This distraction puzzled me. . . . The pain is felt when suspension does not accompany the prayer. . . . But it would be very bad if I were to abandon everything on account of this obstacle. And so it isn't good for us to be disturbed by our thoughts, nor should we be concerned. . . . Let us be patient and endure them for the love of God since we are likewise subject to eating and sleeping without being able to avoid it, which is quite a trial."[96] (*Touches her arms, breast, stomach, then relaxes, exhausted.*) Attached or detached? To the flesh or to the Lord? To each of them alternately and together? I love the imagination when it takes flight from the body, with the body, when it dives deep into our entrails and carries them away with it. I can feel it splitting from the senses, becoming purified in the Lord. And I prefer it to that other flighty thought, unsupported and disembodied—abstract thought. "Porque, como el entendimiento es una de las potencias del alma, hacíaseme recia cosa estar tan tortolito a veces, y lo ordinario vuela el pensamiento de presto, que sólo Dios puede atarle, cuando nos ata a Sí de manera que parece estamos en alguna manera desatados de este cuerpo. Yo veía, a mi parecer, las potencias del alma empleadas en Dios y estar recogidas con Él, y por otra parte el pensamiento alborotado: traíame tonta."[97]

(*Exhalation, accelerated heartbeat, repose.*)

TERESA'S VOICE, *getting feebler, but firm, without trembling*. Gratian maintains it's a typical female fallacy to confuse imagination with the movement of thought. Ribera, by contrast, lets me develop my intuition about the existence of an imagination in which thought is fulfilled ad infinitum. One day Sylvia Leclercq will write that I am at the heart of the mystery of a sublimation that "journeys itself" between the instincts and the senses. But I say: a castle compartmented by transparent membranes, translucent walls, between the teeming of poisonous vermin below and the flashing of the central jewel. Between what seems to be me, and the God inside me. (*Unseeing eyes, as in the Velázquez.*) Ah, Sisters, only imagination can bring us close to that desire for the Other within, while at the same time releasing us from that hot brazier. I am leaving you now, so you'll just have to read me. One final word before I depart. You mustn't be afraid to play, to play with that thought in motion. Our worries and our fears don't come from movement, but from a want of light. Inside us a whole world exists, and just as it's not in our power to halt the movements of the heavens, swirling at prodigious speeds, neither can we stop our racing minds.[98]

SYLVIA LECLERCQ'S VOICE. Dante Alighieri, *Paradiso*, I, verses seven to nine: "Because in drawing near to its desire / Our intellect ingulphs itself so far, / That after it the memory cannot go."[99] Is Teresa the Spanish Dante, as Meister Eckhart was the German Dante?

TERESA'S VOICE, *her face in the painting eclipses the polyhedron*. Let's play, Sisters! Play, my girls! To deliver yourselves unto the King and be delivered from Him, endlessly, for there is no stopping this game, this *vejamen*, these death throes. . . . Am I lucid? Let me elucidate. "My soul is completely taken up in its quiet, love, desires, and clear knowledge";[100] "*y claro conocimiento*," oh, yes. Listen: someone who doesn't know how to set up the chessboard will be a bad player, and if he doesn't know to check the opponent's king, how will he ever checkmate it? You will frown to hear me talk of games again, because no games are allowed in this monastery. Look what kind of a Mother God gave you, skilled at such a vain pursuit! . . . But this game is allowed sometimes. And very soon it will be allowed more often, if we practice enough to checkmate this divine King! After that He'll never be able to escape, and indeed He won't want to. (*Perceptibly relaxing, cheerful smile.*)

TERESA'S VOICE, *while Bernini's* Transverberation *is refracted by the jewel*. In chess, the queen has many advantages over the king, and is supported by all the other pieces. Well, there's no queen like humility for forcing the divine King to surrender. Humility drew Him from heaven into the Virgin's womb; and with it, by one hair, we will draw Him to our souls. (*Beaming smile.*) People say, "Here is a very contemplative soul," and immediately expect him to possess all the virtues of a soul elevated to great contemplation. The person concerned aspires to this and more. But he is misguided from the outset, because he didn't know how to set up the game. "He thought it was enough to know the pieces in order to checkmate the King. But that was impossible, for this King doesn't give Himself but to those who give themselves entirely to Him."[101]

(*In a serene voice.*) "La dama es la que más guerra le puede hacer en este juego, y todas las otras piezas ayudan. No hay dama que así le haga rendir como la humildad. Esta le trajo del cielo en las entrañas de la Virgen, y con ella le traeremos nosotras de un cabello a nuestras almas. Y creed que quien más tuviere, más le tendrá, y quien menos, menos. Porque no puedo yo entender cómo haya ni pueda haber humildad sin amor, ni amor sin humildad, ni es posible estar estas dos virtudes sin gran desasimiento de todo lo criado."

As Teresa's voice inundates the stage, we watch the slow rotation of the watery gemstone of her dwelling places.

Chapter 33

ACT 4

The Analyst's Farewell

The distillation and centralization of the ego. Everything is in that.

Charles Baudelaire, *My Heart Laid Bare*

SYLVIA LECLERCQ

The diamond of the previous act retreats into the background, where it refracts the anonymous portrait of Teresa of Avila commonly attributed to Velázquez. The left side of the stage represents Sylvia Leclercq's office. There are a couch, an armchair, and a desk. The analyst is writing. Her voice follows the rhythms of her thoughts, and sometimes the movements of her hand. She is bidding La Madre farewell, from the first to the third person.

SYLVIA LECLERCQ. It's infectious, this journeying to the far depths of private dwelling places, like a sort of self-analysis.... (*Mocking smile.*) I'll never see the end of it.... Just when I thought I'd done with all that ... I managed to send Marianne off to Cuenca and to reconcile her with her father.... The way of perfection is full of surprises, once you set off on it. I might have guessed, in light of the trajectory from beloved fatherhood to loving fatherhood.... (*Hands on temples, affectionate, moved expression. Neutral voice.*).

I never dreamed of my father again, after that teenage nightmare in which I had him run over by a train, inverted Oedipus *oblige*, it's all in the pink pages of the Larousse of psychoanalysis.... One kills one's Laius as best one can these days, preferably by night and at high velocity. Corny as anything. Modern daughters won't be pushed around, and the fathers, or some of them, play along. . . . (*Silence. Hands folded over the white pages. Adopts dreamy voice.*) But for the last week . . . Holy Week, in fact . . . some coincidence . . . Dr. Thomas Leclercq has visited me in dreams, no face, just a presence, and his voice. Singing. All those years of analysis, all those years of clinical practice, and I never gave a thought to Dad's singing. . . . With his decent tenor voice and knowledge of opera and musical culture in general, my doctor of a dad was great company. He really livened up our family meals—though not to the point of leaving his daughter with any recollection of his favorite tunes. (*Still speaking in a dreamy voice, opens a notebook, gropes for a pen.*) For me, his charming amateurism was secondary; his scholarly erudition when in serious "doctor" mode obliterated his fondness for singing in my mind . . . though I do remember how it provoked Mom's pitying condescension, of course. She was a sensible woman, Mme Blandine Leclercq, doctor's wife, schoolteacher, almost a proto-feminist in her way. . . . (*Hesitant voice, screwed-up eyes.*) In my defense, I should say that Dad stopped singing early on, at least I think he did . . . when I graduated from kindergarten, pretty early in my life, anyway. Yes, it was around then. . . . If I remember right. . . .

There was trouble at the hospital, conflicts with some big cheese, possibly a marital crisis into the bargain; I didn't want to know, I cleared off in a hurry, like the self-reliant adolescent I wanted to be. . . . Yes, there must have been some kind of a crisis, because that's when Blandine began hanging out at literary soirees, whatever was hip, launch parties at trendy bookstores for celebrated authors who'd sign your copy. I recall a rapid-fire succession of au pairs who cooked supper for me, because Dad was overwhelmed with work. Doctors are on call day and night, you see, yes, I did see. . . . So, no more singing in the shower. . . . (*Childish smile.*)

That's it: he used to sing in the shower! (*Delighted silence, big smile, hardly awkward at all.*) That's it, that's the tune that has been filling my head at night, all week long. . . . (*Writes.*) . . . so bright and bracing . . . I knew it by heart. . . . I still do, I know the words, I'm asleep, I'm dreaming, I mouth them along with Dad, an unknown joy comes over me, it doesn't wake me up though, it awakens me, I'm dreaming awake, I'm singing with him, a cherub's youthful voice, it's mine it's his. . . . (*Long silence.*)

And then in the morning it's gone, so frustrating, I hardly attend to my patients, I even forget to think about my saint, I rummage through the dream, it gets more and more infuriating, I'm fed up, I turn my memory upside-down:

nothing, not a quaver. And it's the same the next night. . . . So I decide to get up in the middle of the vocal dream, I'll write it down while it's still there in my throat, my lungs, my mouth, my memory, my smile. . . . But I can't, the dream squeezes me in its arms, I am held, held prisoner, all I can do is sing along with Dad, glued to my pillow, unable to raise my head. . . . No worries, this time I'm sure I've got it, the confounded tune he used to warble under the shower while I drank my cocoa and left for school, with a peck for Blandine and a "See you tonight, Dad! Maybe? Okay, 'bye, then. . . ." But when I wake up, nothing. The bird has flown again. A phantom bird, no doubt: Did that song even exist? It's a dream of course, my long cohabitation with Teresa can lead to anything, an unnameable hallucination, there you go, call yourself an analyst but that hoodlum Oedipus can sure play tricks on you. (*Pause. Raises eyes to ceiling, cocks head, listens intently. Picks up pen once more.*)

It must have been in Latin, couldn't have been anything else, since Thomas was brought up in a religious boarding school, after his mother died giving birth to him. . . . I've spent hours of analysis on that little point, at least. My grandfather couldn't think of anything better than to entrust him to the Jesuits. And they eventually expelled him for reading smutty books, as well as revolutionary ones, it was the period of colonial wars. . . . Well, Dad always put on the same complacent smirk when rehashing these daring exploits to Mom and me, over and over again, for the nth time, the only feats to his name. . . . I haven't forgotten that, either. But the singing? . . . Definitely in Latin. Yes. (*Radiant face, writing faster.*)

I've got it. Thanks to that patient this morning, in Holy Week mode, going on about the father and the son in this litany that compulsively linked "father and son" as if we were in church, I thought at one point, it's coming back to me, that's it . . . *Gloria.* . . . No, it wasn't a *Gloria.* I'm burning, it's on the tip of my tongue. . . . I only did two years of Latin, and Dad never bothered passing on much of his Jesuit humanities ("Outdated claptrap, all of it. What's left is an oath for doctors with or without borders, which is: love your neighbor and minister to ailing humanity. There you have it, the one and only universal principle that makes sense. As for the decor, well, that's what museums are for, aren't they?") All the same I knew it wasn't a *Gloria*, no, no, it was . . . Bach's *Magnificat*! BWV 243 in D Major! Of course! I can't get over it! Everybody knows the tune and the lyrics these days, thanks to CDs, MP3, and the rest. Part of the "immaterial human heritage." (*Scratches head. Glance of complicity at Teresa's diffracted portrait.*) How much did I love him, my Dad, to have forgotten those incendiary words, those vibrations that shook his whole being at the beginning of every day, that primed him to set off gaily to work, while Mom seethed: "Listen to that, it's his 'Marseillaise' he's belting out, his 'Internationale,' his 'Hymn to Joy' . . . hopeless! Your father will never change his spots, whatever he says." *Depooo—suit, depoooo—suit poteee— ntes de seeee—de et exaltaaaaaa—aaaa—aaaa—vit huumiiles. . . .*

F♯ F♯ . . . . ED C♯BAG♯ AF♯ B♯
De—po . . . . *su—it*
C♯ C♯ . . . . BA G♯F♯E♯D♯ E♯G♯B D
De—po . . . . *su—it*
C♯ A♯C♯A G♯C♯G♯ F♯DF♯ E♯C♯
po—ten . . . . *tes*
C♯ C♯BAC♯ BAG♯B AG♯F♯A G♯F♯E♯D♯ C♯
de se . . . . *de*
G♯ A F♯ D♯ C♯BA BAG♯B E DC♯B
Et ex—al-ta . . . .
C♯BAC♯ F♯ EDC♯ DC♯BC♯ DC♯DE
. . . .
F♯EF♯G♯ A E D C♯ B A A . . . .
. . . . *vit hu—mi—les*

The stately notes would spiral through the early-morning air, carrying me with them as they rose toward unimaginable expanses that I could barely discern at that age, but I could tell how they uplifted my father until I felt exultant too, sounds pulsing through my lungs, my blood, like a happy cascade of laughter . . . (*Lays down the pen, closes the book, leans chin on clasped hands. Silence. Then, in neutral voice.*) Have I come to the end, at long last, of my analysis of father-hood, my Oedipus complex to be exact . . . as demanded by the Psychoanalytic Society of Paris . . . by rescuing my father from oblivion and making my peace with his voice, over and above his function, his function as a medic of course, as well as the inevitable paternal function . . . all this thanks to my roommate? (*Forced smile.*) Well, it'll do for now, and for a long time to come, I hope. I can say goodbye to Teresa now, withdrawing into my father's youthful voice. . . . Of course I don't intend to say a word to Jérôme Tristan, who's bound to retort to the effect that I'm not well, or positively in regression. Nor to Bruno, he'd only try to convert me to Buddhism. Nor to Andrew, who would make the most of this opportunity to tease the "poor thing" I become when he wants to impose himself, however sweetly. Maybe I'll teach Paul the "Deposuit": his singing is as pitch-perfect as his emotions. Just him. There's no one as sensitive as Paul to what these kinds of melody, words, voices, are all about . . . the way they don't say what they're saying. . . . Sounds that must have lulled me constantly, from birth to when I was about six years old. "*Depoooo . . . suit, depoooo . . . suit poteeee . . . ntes de seeee . . . de . . . Et exaltaaaaa-aaaaa-aaaa . . . vit huuumiiiles. . . .*"

F♯ F♯ . . . . ED C♯BAG♯ AF♯ B♯
De—po . . . .*su – it*
C♯ C♯ . . . . BA G♯F♯E♯D♯ E♯G♯B D
De—po . . . .*su—it*
C♯ A♯C♯A G♯C♯G♯ F♯DF♯ E♯C♯
po—ten . . . .*tes*
C♯ C♯BAC♯ BAG♯B AG♯F♯A G♯F♯E♯D♯ C♯
de se . . . .*de*
G♯ A F♯ D♯ C♯BA BAG♯B E DC♯B
Et ex—al- ta . . . .
C♯BAC♯ F♯ EDC♯ DC♯BC♯ DC♯DE
. . . .
F♯EF♯G♯ A E D C♯ B A A . . . .
. . . .*vit hu—mi – les*

(*Pause.*)

SYLVIA LECLERCQ, *against a faintly heard fragment of Bach's* "Magnificat," *performed by a clear tenor voice.* "He hath put down the mighty from their seat, and hath exalted the humble. . . ." To think how often I must have heard it since, that soaring "Deposuit," looping through clouds and lights! That "heritage hit," as my mother used to call it, among what is called "our sort". . . . (*Sigh.*) But it's never given me the thrill I got from agnostic Thomas when he sang it a cappella. The thrill that led me all unsuspecting to Teresa, who led me back to him. With this dream, the circle is closed. Well then: farewell!

She does not put down the pen, or close the notebook: her hand falls still over the lines.

"*Depoooo . . . suit, depoooo . . . suit poteeee . . . ntes de seeee . . . de . . . et exaltaaaaa-aaaaa-aaaa . . . vit huumiiiles. . . .*"

* * *

Here the front of the stage grows dark, so that we can barely make out the form of Sylvia Leclercq, once more writing at her desk. Spotlights pick out the portrait of Teresa in her diamond. Slides are projected over it from time to time, showing rapid glimpses of Luis de Morales's *Virgin and Child*; Bernini's *Transfixion*; Zurbarán's *Saint Francis*, housed in Lyon; El Greco's *Christ in the Garden of Olives*, in Lille; the royal monastery San Lorenzo del Escorial, by the architects Juan Batista de Toledo and Juan de Herrera; Rubens' *Rape of the Daughters of Leucippe*, in Munich; and the vault of the Church of Saint Ignatius in Rome, painted by Andrea Pozzo. Over these images, only Sylvia's monologue is heard.

SYLVIA LECLERCQ, *in a clear voice*. Is Teresa more analytical than Freud, or differently than Freud? Hope nobody's listening, just kidding, shhh! Enough dreaming, it's time to draw up the balance, since I was with her during her last hours. (*Long silence. Glances at Teresa's portrait.*) She constructed her dialogues from beyond the grave as she built her interior castle: temptations and struggles, associates who were sometimes helpful, sometimes loved, too, and the busy affairs of the world in parallel to the deepening of the intimate sphere, diaphanous, shifting, sensitive, and lucid ... and this intimacy reveals itself only through metaphors and little stories. (*Reads.*)

Teresa moved in spaces that were undistinguishably interior and exterior; they were manifest in a profusion of expressions that resorted to arresting figurations, appealed to meaning, and imposed rules. The "region of the dissimilar," the abode of sin, the deformity of dissemblance, entailed a genuine loss of being for the creatures God made in His own image; this is because the creatures concerned, failing to comprehend the honor, let themselves sink from resemblance into dissemblance. This is where my Carmelite's pen comes along to transform the *regio dissimilitudinis* into a polymorphous world, a shifting, soothing polytopy.

(*Fast.*) It starts with the discovery that body and soul suffer if—and only if—they do not want to know that they are in love with a good, in other words loving, Being. So much for the Christic background: clear, but inadequate. From that point on what's required is to amplify the scenario of the Song of Songs. To generate an infinite number of dwelling places that are not recondite crannies, but multiple crossing points in continual expansion: a blooming of words, representations, and sensations. This could have been represented by a flower, yet like her rocky land of Castile, the more-than-feminine Madre is aquatic and mineral, she must necessarily have architecture. (*Subtle smile.*)

The subject in love and her loving Beloved spread through it, phase by phase, so that the access to the love union (itself not in doubt) is built station by infinitesimal station, the portals to intrapsychic and interactive serenity. The most harrowing ordeals become experiences to be savored, as the lover increasingly appropriates them by the grace of a simultaneously imagistic and controlled verbal representation. And the time wasted in erotic and infantile trauma becomes reversed into infinitely malleable psychic spaces, because they enclose the infinity of love given and received. The interior castle is the product of all this. However, La Madre doesn't shut herself inside; she opens it to the world, because this castle is none other than the volume of her personal experience certified to be shareable—with her sisters, with you and me, in another infinite multiplication. (*Quick glance at Teresa's diamond.*) Could this spatial burgeoning of dwelling places also be a challenge to Hell, the placeless place that terrified her so? The final liquidation of the unbreathable, unrepresentable trauma in which desires and defenses, thoughts, images, and sensations are annulled, leaving only comatose victims, sickening bestiality, cadaverous misery? (*Exhales.*) Her writing is a potion of youth, too, chasing aggressive anxieties away. No more depressions or somatic illnesses; adieu sadomasochistic hatefatuations! (*With a mischievous smile, hands mime the clearing of the air.*)

Teresa is not after a fortified, defensive retreat but a narcissistic, ideal, sublime place of reassurance where you are invited to dissolve into perfume, to intoxicate yourself, but gently and in peace. That's right, perfume, a solid distilled, a sublimation, in other words: she says so explicitly, or almost, I'm coming to that.

(*Talking fast.*) The alchemy she develops in her inimitable style begins with the urge to tell. Nothing new in that, Confession relies on the same thing, as do plenty of spiritual exercises; the young Thomas Aquinas hazarded the notion that theology per se was basically a *narrativus signorum*, a narrating of signs.[1] But Teresa does more than follow their lead: she comes up with fresh words to unfold the temporal phases of her amorous adventure with the Other into space, across spaces. Her baroque spirit whispered to her that only the "image," itself generated by talking and "communication" between lovers, can provoke a "narrative."

Listen. (*Normal voice, underlining the emphases.*)

"What you can do as a help in this matter is try to carry about *an image or painting* of this Lord that is to your liking, not so as to carry it about on your heart and never look at it but so as to speak often with Him; for He will inspire you with what to say. Since you speak with other persons, *why must words fail you when you speak with God?* Don't believe they will; at least I will not believe they will if you acquire the habit. Otherwise, the failure to communicate with a person causes both estrangement [porque si no, el no tratar con una persona cause extrañeza] and a failure to know how to speak with him. For it seems then that we do not know him, even if he may be a relative; *family ties and friendship are lost through a lack of communication.*"[2]

$$\star \; \star \; \star$$

SYLVIA LECLERCQ. Begin, then, by imagining the image of the person you love, and that will encourage you to speak with them, and thence to communicate with the good Being and ultimately partake of Him, logically and inevitably.

The images involved are first of all representations, fantasies that are not always present to the eye, but given to thought, which is visual, and to all the senses. From this derives an apology of mental imagery, with its power to contain the lover's need to be loved and acknowledged as lovable. Here is the cornerstone of belief. We are like blind people in the presence of an interlocutor: "They understand and believe this, but they do not see the other [entiende y cree que está allí, mas no la ve]."[3] They sense the presence: *I sense, therefore I am.* Rather than debating with the Lutherans, what Teresa is doing is rehabilitating a therapy of the imagination, calling it to the rescue of blind reassurance. For she knows from experience that the imaginary is vital to the survival of a subject who only exists insofar as she or he is in love. I am capable of imagining the amorous bond, of communicating with it and about it; I can create/recreate it by my powers of representation; by constantly expressing it in signs, or signifying it, I come to possess it; and therefore I believe in it—more and more. (*Glances at the possible Velázquez portrait.*) Can I say that I *am*? There are many ways one may be. My being has been indefinitely transferred into the Other.

Listen again. (*Normal voice, underlining the emphases.*)

"I could only think about Jesus Christ as He was as man, but *never in such a way that I could picture Him* within myself no matter how much I read about His beauty or how many images I saw of Him. . . . I was like those who are *blind or in darkness* . . . they know with certainty that the other is there (I mean that they understand and believe this, but they do not see the other); such was the case with me when I thought of our Lord. This was the reason *I liked images so much.* Unfortunate are those who through their own fault lose this great good.

It indeed appears they do not love the Lord, for if they loved Him they would rejoice greatly to see a portrait of Him, just as here on earth it really gives joy to see the one whom you deeply love."[4]

Finally the image becomes interiorized, as wordless, nonvisual sensations. Neither "belief" nor "reasoning," this new way of "understanding" is frightening, because it imposes the lover's companionship very very deep inside (*en lo muy muy interior*), in the manner of an inevitable, indelible truth.[5]

At this stage of the spatialization of subjective time, according to Teresa, the "knowledge" identical to "belief" is experienced as a "favor." However, in a crowning twist of genius, the nun grasped that these states of reassurance by osmosis with the Ideal are imaginary "locutions" (*hablas*), and therefore "illusions" (*antojos*).[6] The explorer nevertheless recommends us to entertain these fantastic exchanges in order to combat the devil, who is not, for Teresa, an absolute evil so much as *resistance* itself, opposed to *imaginative experience*. The *tournament* the writer has described creates the amorous union at the same time as it creates the interior space—the space that will be crossed repeatedly, without end.

The great enemy, then (*smile of complicity*) is nothing other than the deficiency of imagination and desire: the lack of figurable representations that makes us settle for harmful, unhealthy drives. Here is a devil whose power Teresa knows too well—*son semblable, son frère*, perhaps.* [*A reference to the famous address to the reader in *Les Feurs du Mal*: "Hypocrite lecteur,—mon semblable,—mon frère!"—Trans.] It tips one into comitial excitability, undermining the containing capacity of thoughts and images. It is futile to resist these imaginary fissures, these feeble, fearful, terrifying fantasies. My message is that it is possible to transform them: plunge yourself into the abundant figurations of my lovers' spaces, read how by amassing them I come into possession of the Other in me, how I change and grow. For is it not foolishness (*desatino*) to believe we could ever enter Heaven without entering into ourselves first?[7]

(*Pause.*)

SYLVIA LECLERCQ, *puffs, and resumes at speed.* And though the building thus erected constitutes a shelter, it is steeped in the inconstancy of the baroque: its safety is but a fleeting spark, "*centella de seguridad.*"[8] A bolt of lightning, a whirlwind, interior rapids: Teresa's writing, reflective and caressing, surges along nonetheless with the speed of Love in Angelus Silesius: "Love is the quickest thing and of itself can fly / To topmost Heaven in but the twinkling of an eye."[9]

Saint Teresa of Avila in Glory. Tapestry woven by the first Carmelites in Avignon (twelfth century). © Fine Arts Museum, Budapest.

And just as opposites coexist, when they are not actually interchangeable, in the works of Rubens, Guarino Guarini, Andrea Pozzo, or Tiepolo, so God and the Devil rub shoulders in the tornado traced by La Madre's pen: why do we cry "'The devil! The devil!' when we can say 'God! God!'and make the devil tremble," she writes defiantly, and earlier, "His Majesty favor me so that I may understand, . . . and a fig for all the devils [*una higa para todos los demonios*]."[10] Teresa has no compunction about firing obscene insults at the paternal superego of her more disapproving confessors! Against them, her love upholds her legitimate right, as the Lord's Bride, identified with His Royal Majesty, not to fear anything or anyone: "I fear those who have such great fear of the devil more than I fear the devil himself, for he can't do anything to me. Whereas these others, especially if they are confessors, cause severe disturbance: I have undergone some years of such great trial that I am amazed now at how I was able to suffer it. Blessed be the Lord who has so truly helped me!"[11] (*Breathes out. Stares at the diamond.*)

The Apotheosis of Saint Teresa (1722). Fresco by Giambattista Tiepolo (1696–1770). Church of the Scalzi, Venice, Italy/De Agostini Picture Library/F. Ferruzzi/ Bridgeman Art Library.

Step by step the imagery of resistance to the erotic brazier gives way before the profusion of another imagery, orchestrating its success. The amorous subject triumphs over the soul unable to represent to itself the trials joining the lover to her Beloved; the castle-building narrative excludes from its halls disgraced souls who stray from the enchanted imaginary, like the prodigal son who once thought he could leave his father's house and live off the husks of swine. A soul in love and proud of it, Teresa stakes out a double space (*anxious voice*): "outside this castle," an alien exteriority inhabited by the kind of person who eats pig-swill, is contrasted with one's "own house," which has everything a person could need, and "especially, has a guest who will make him lord over all goods."[12]

The Ecstasy of Saint Teresa. Giuseppe Bazzani, oil on canvas (1745–1750).
© Fine Arts Museum, Budapest.

Could the imprecision of the phrase *manjar de puercos* (pig feed) suggest that people who are incapable of inhabiting themselves and fully enjoying the riches of the imagination are eaters of pork? A diet that offends Jews and Marranos, not to say . . . the hidden interiority of my Teresa, always in search of some secret faith, some protected clandestinity. Like the faith of her ancestors, perhaps? Of course the prodigal son was uncritically welcomed back by his adoring father, and Teresa herself addressed her experience *en lo muy muy interior* to everyone, for universal dissemination.

(*Silence. In the background we hear the voice of Dr. Thomas Leclercq, softly humming the "Deposuit."*)

SYLVIA LECLERCQ, *fast, reading and underlining*. Clearly, this publicity for an amorous imagination that converts suffering into a gemstone and crystallizes masochism into self-overcoming, without letting itself be affected by the exaltation it rests upon, has nothing in common with the Freudian scalpel. Because the interpretation of *transference/countertransference* proceeds by means of *subtraction*, whereas Teresa *amplifies in order to magnify*; only thus can she render secure the inner being of the loved lover. Freud operates *per via di levare*, he writes, like a sculptor using the chisel of free association to chip away the patient's defenses and uncover the infantile impasses of the capacity for loving and thinking. In aid of this dismantling he is armed with the discovery of the unconscious, based on the Oedipus: killing of the Father and identification with his ideality and power, incestuous desire for the Mother, the accidents of which exhort from our psychic bisexuality the emergence of speaking-thinking-loving beings.

Teresa, for her part, proceeds like the painter of a baroque cupola: applying layer upon layer, *per via di porre*, adding twist upon high-wire twist to her tale— inviting her sisters and readers to dreams and hallucinations of amorous success, a success warranted by the grace of the Trinity and the indisputable devotion of Mary and Joseph, the parental couple.[13] Pointing out all the while what a fiction it was, a necessary game of infinite communication; but since the experience creates a saving neo-reality, it is the Truth. What's more, this amorous intoxication does not display as a liberty taken with the transcendence underwritten by the paternal function and mellowed by the Marian cult, not at all! It merely, if I can put it that way, advances, with extravagant ease, through the fundaments of Christian ethics.

(*Silence. Head in hands.*)

SYLVIA LECLERCQ, *enunciating slowly, underlining*. To sum up, if Teresa's lucidity unwraps the stages and components of amorous passion . . . she does not aim to be delivered from it, as promised by the adventure of analysis; on the contrary, she wants to enjoy it the more, and so demonstrate the ineluctable logic of the biblical and evangelical premise. While Freud *questions* and *dismantles* the patient's defenses in order to leave the subject free to reconstruct his amorous and rational bonds, Teresa, on the contrary—in her infinite traversal of the Oedipus complex—never suspects that God is *a question*. For the Beloved is a strange Archimedes' lever that sends one precisely inside oneself, where the Other dwells. It enables one to let go of the bristling array of defenses and fears, and thus to discover, along with the enigmas of love, *well-being itself*, the *good and supreme Being*. She would agree with Leibniz that "since we are beings, being is innate in us";[14] she went on to prove it by erecting the inner dwelling places of a being that only *is* if he or she is in love. While beating the Lord at chess, it doesn't occur to Teresa for one second that the game could be possible without His august and loving Fatherhood; after all, the player's desire reaches its acme in the avowal that she longs to have a child from Him, to become the Mother of God, Sovereign in her own right. Divine. (*Long silence.*) Reading her, listening to her, it seems the Other in me is not infernal, like the unconscious. It is forcibly uncertain, or prey to the devil. But it is definitively lovable if I can find it in me to listen to it, articulate it, and write it, as a lover/loved.

And yet, after this long trek in Teresa's company, I maintain (*measured, poised, confident voice, occasionally emphatic*) that Freud, while embarking on a completely different course, could not be ignorant of the advantages of the interior dwelling places discovered by La Madre. What "substance" was the dauntless Viennese sculptor chiseling into, if not that enigmatic transference/countertransference that he never really theorized, leaving that task to the female psychoanalysts who were the first disciples of Melanie Klein? Alert to the double Judeo-Christian alliance concealed at the heart of the Spanish sixteenth century,[15] Teresa amplified in her own way the diabolical resistances we each oppose to the flourishing of our amorous representations, themselves founded on a no less amplified *need to believe*, which succeeds to the oceanic dependence on the maternal container and the primal identification with the Father of personal prehistory.[16]

As a writer she shines a light on these fundamental logics, while not averse to pinpointing the abuse or distortion of them by those polar opposites to the Lord (to the ideal of the Self) constituted by the twin tyrants of the sex drive and the moralizing superego. But the holy woman would never question the Other's love and her love for the Other: how could she conceive of a viable way of being if not in love with the ideal Father?

(*Sylvia falls silent. We hear Dr. Leclercq's muffled voice tackling the complex nota-tion of* "Exaltavit humiles.")

SYLVIA LECLERCQ. In my view—but keep this to yourself (*here her voice becomes intimate, hushed, singular*)—our dear, great Sigmund was not far from think-ing, though he stopped short of formulating it, the same as what Teresa celebrat-ed in all her writings. What did he lay onto the couch, if it wasn't love? Love, again, is what's transferred in the attention we pay to our patients' words, drives, and affects. Freud's philosophy was explicitly based on the Enlightenment, his interpretative method was without doubt Kabbalistically and Talmudically Jewish, but his unconscious was baroque. (*Sidelong glance at the diamond.*) Ba-roque—as in inconstant, mobile, playful, reinvented on the go—is the word for the amorous principle upon which he founded psychoanalysis, and over which he lingered in his scrutiny of the history of myths, religions, arts and letters; the principle Teresa crosses back and forth, with cheerful faith, never underestimat-ing the demons of excitation unto death. Teresa reigns as the high priestess of the continent of idealization that inaugurates the transference that precedes the cure, into which the psychoanalyst will hack with the blows of his chisel, ice ax, hammer, or pen. . . .

(*She closes her notebook, rises from the chair, walks toward the door—then turns back and sits down again, picking up the pen in a mood of contented, tran-quil solitude.*)

Can I convince you that by remitting the truth of the amorous bond, and by extension of the transferential bond, to an unconscious that is equally in love and yet infantile, no analytical interpretation can expel this "delusion" of love from the field of that (interminable) analysis? Not only does the constant of the loving bond persist under the guise of some "future of delusion," notably religious delu-sion, which Freud regards as regrettable yet insurmountable; the permanence of the Teresian problematic of love manifests itself even at the termination of the cure, which, for all its dissipation of illusions, merely leads to the creation of . . . new and no less amorous bonds. These new transferences, better apprised of the impasses of the subject's former traumas and hatefatuations, embark all over again—at best more soberly, but never desisting—upon the quest for *jouissance* in the intimacy, forever to be reconquered, of an interior castle forever to be re-built, by the latest self with its latest set of narratives.

SYLVIA LECLERCQ, *in a calm voice, eyes drawn to the divan.* In order to remain psychically alive, or alive *tout court*, I can't do other than try to re-inhabit my inner dwelling places—with someone new this time—while realizing, courtesy of my analysis, that it will once more be in vain, or almost. But as the baroque poet said, "Everything is mutable in this world. We must snatch love as we can."[17] (*Broad smile.*)

Teresa, already a potential saint when on her deathbed, has not quite reached this point. Her brand of baroque differs from that of artists who solemnly assert, in the face of the One, the power of a nonessential, theatrical, "performing" humanity. The baroque illusion—triumph of the as-if, celebration of the inconstancy of objective reality (the very stage sets are to be cast into the flames, like Don Juan)—assumes an extravagant superiority nonetheless, negating every value and form of otherness. The baroque artist lays no claim to inner authenticity; he is praised for shape-shifting alone, for his dexterity with whirling masquerades and the opulent play of simulacra. (*Amused glance at the divan.*)

None of this with Teresa; La Madre was never content to approach delusion as an illusion. Being a mystic, she was afraid the crumbling of fantasy would reduce her to the condition of a worm in the nonspace of Hell; so she distilled the imaginary into the joy of love and a life founded on love, like an alembic distills spirits. (*Exhales, looks at Teresa's diamond.*)

Like me, and after much weeping, La Madre no longer weeps as the end draws near. Now her tears pour forth of themselves, with abandon, with the certainty of happiness. The fruits of a once terrified imagination (before it tamed the plenitude of love), tears remain, to her valedictory eyes, illusions, deceits, *engaños*. They are the devil's work. And if God Himself sometimes has a hand in them, for our gratification, we shouldn't indulge all the same.

Hear what she says (*in a normal voice, underlining*): "I mark danger everywhere and in something as good as tears *I think there can be deception*; you are wondering if *I may be the one who is deceived*. And it could be that I am. But believe me, I do not speak without having seen that these *false tears can be experienced* by some persons; although not by me, for *I am not at all tender*. Rather, I have *a heart so hard* that sometimes I am distressed; although *when the inner fire is intense the heart, however hard, distills like an alembic.* . . . Let the tears come when God sends them and without any effort on our part to induce them. These tears from God will irrigate this dry earth, and they are a great help in producing fruit. The less attention we pay to them, the more there are. . . ."[18] (*Meditative silence.*)

"And suddenly it seemed that day to day was added, as if He who has the power had with another sun the heaven adorned." (*Sylvia recites the unknown lines that have swum into her mind. It's not Hell any more, nor is it Purgatory,*

so could this be Paradise? If Teresa hasn't earned a place in Heaven, who has?)
"*Transumanar.* . . . To represent transhumanize in words impossible were." Teresa, transhuman? No, not that chess-playing woman. Transfinite, rather . . . an infinitesimal human. . . . "She, who saw me as I saw myself. . . . Here do the higher creatures see the footprints of the Eternal Power. . . . Here vigor failed the lofty fantasy: but now was turning my desire and will, even as a wheel that equally is moved, the love which moves the sun and the other stars."[19] (*Rubs her eyes, comes back to her roommate.*)

The loving heart, Teresa fashion, is hard as diamonds, meaning it cannot be liquefied anymore: it endures the toughest test, it is rock solid. (*In a voice of farewell.*) But it is no less subtle for that. It distills into scents, penetrates castle walls, traverses the spaces and elements it imbues. And then it takes wing, spinning and fluttering with the Other's voice, that necessarily loving voice. Pulverizing the rectilinear power of the Lord Himself into cloudy cascades of justice implored, of sublimated desires. (*With a final glance at Teresa's portrait.*) A vibrating voice, arpeggios and triplets, mounting and descending, a-flutter, *à la volette* [Repeated phrase in eponymous traditional French children's song.—Trans.], again and again, exultant:

F♯ F♯ . . . . ED C♯BAG♯ AF♯ B♯
De—po. . . . . *su—it*
C♯ C♯ . . . . BA G♯F♯E♯D♯ E♯G♯B D
De—po . . . . *su—it*
C♯ A♯C♯A G♯C♯G♯ F♯DF♯ E♯C♯
po—ten . . . . *tes*
C♯ C♯BAC♯ BAG♯B AG♯F♯A G♯F♯E♯D♯ C♯
de se . . . . *de*
G♯ A F♯ D♯ C♯BA BAG♯B E DC♯B
Et ex—al-ta . . . .
C♯BAC♯ F♯ EDC♯ DC♯BC♯ DC♯DE

. . . .
F♯EF♯G♯ A ED C♯ B A A . . . .
. . . . *vit hu—mi—les*

Just like my father's voice. (*In the background, a snatch of Bach's "Magnificat."*)

Part 8

Postscript

Chapter 34

LETTER TO DENIS DIDEROT ON THE INFINITESIMAL SUBVERSION OF A NUN

> God, through whom we discern that certain things we had deemed essential
> to ourselves are truly foreign to us, while those we had deemed foreign to
> us are essential.
>
> Saint Augustine, *Soliloquies*

> Divine understanding . . . the domain of possible realities.
>
> Leibniz to Antoine Arnauld

Dear Mister Philosopher,

You began *The Nun* as a farce, because there was no question of publishing such a thing in 1760. (You'd have been off to the Bastille—worse than the jail at Vincennes where the *Letter on the Blind* put you!) And you ended it in tears, or rather not at all, because the text published in 1796, as it has come down to us, is unfinished.

Your *Nun* has been on my mind throughout my journey with Teresa. Please don't take this admission for a piece of persiflage. I am incapable of that, and besides, I should never dare to be ironical with you!

Still, I must confess that I first approached Teresa somewhat lightly and unthinkingly. Not to raise a laugh, as you did with your story of the nun from Longchamp, but to challenge a kind of UFO, a baroque relic. I, too, was rapidly swept off my feet by a story that overturned my assumptions and sent me into analysis. "Whatever next?" drawls my friend and colleague Marianne Baruch, but she didn't come out unscathed herself from this excursion into the heart of belief. Andrew teases me nonstop, rather sullenly, while my learned colleague Jérôme Tristan smirks discreetly: "You have to be ready for anything, with mysticism"—it's his department, after all.

Impressed by the "old religious vice," the sagacious Mallarmé felt that the tendency toward the secular (likened to atheistic "insignificance") "doesn't quite have a meaning."[1] While I agree with the poet on this, it doesn't prevent me from being an atheist, just as you are, my dear Philosopher. You start off as a theologian and a canon, but you won't even be a deist by the end, unlike your friends-foes Voltaire and Rousseau. Irked by Jean-Jacques' philosophical moralism, lacking the caustic temper of the Sage of Ferney, you are sensual, violent, something of a "comedian," passionate about science, curious about women, and smitten by Sophie Volland. You flaunt a brutal, streetwise—cynical?—sort of carefreeness: your thoughts are strumpets, you say, you are regarded as a "materialist," but I wonder about that. I think of you, and it's a compliment, as the carnivalesque type.

Your partiality to the fair sex—which was surely one reason to defect from the career in the Church for which you were destined by your father, the worthy cutler Didier Diderot, and by the Jesuits whose brilliant pupil you were—does not stop you from feeling profoundly ambivalent toward women. The lyricism of the writer, the volatile delicacy of the man, these flatter me: "When we write of women, we must needs dip our pen in the rainbow and throw upon the paper the dust of butterflies' wings." But I also sympathize with the alarm aroused in you by the unknowable matrix: "The symbol of women in general is that of the Apocalypse, on whose forehead was written MYSTERY," and with your perplexity in the face of female genius: "When women have genius, I think their brand is more original than our own."[2]

Of all those in whose company, during that legendary era of Enlightenment, you wakened humanity from its dream of transcendence to lead it toward the best and the worst, it is you I feel closest to. I feel close to *Jacques the Fatalist*, *The Indiscreet Jewels*, *Rameau's Nephew*, the *Letter on the Blind*. I feel close to your atheism, as redoubtable today as ever it was, which deeply and openly guides your liberty. From Paris to St. Petersburg, it was like a bracing wind that blew away the obscurantist miasmas battening like parasites on women's bodies and the beliefs that exploited the quiverings of desire. It was your atheism that first rumbled the tortured sacristies and the torturing boudoirs, whose victims were unconscious of their sexual slavery. Because your atheism did not bow to any cult; it gaily honored the one sovereignty that means anything, the impudence of speaking out.

A DELUSION WITHOUT SOLUTION

In *The Nun*, you showed scant consideration for the feelings of the faithful.[3] The story of young Marie-Suzanne Simonin, first confined in a convent and then debauched by a hysterical prioress who exploits her innocence, is more than a scathing satire on religious delirium; it also shows how ferocious repression and erotic *passage à l'acte* are the two inseparable faces of a culture that sets such excessive store by ideals because it is obsessed by the violence of the instincts.

Lambasting the unnatural life of Christian religion, you denounce the hypocrisy that goes on to infiltrate lay culture as well. Marie-Suzanne's "inflexible" parents, for instance, invoke among others the "knowledge" of the Abbé Blin (a doctor at the Sorbonne) and the authority of the bishop of Aleppo, who receives the poor girl into the Church on a day that is "one of the saddest ever." Family conformity and spiritual dogma are for you the twin aspects of a social code that forces the young girl to take vows of chastity, poverty, and obedience in order to expiate her mother's adultery, of which she is the product. To cap it all, her legal father is a lawyer! This "morality tale" would have made for hilarious vaudeville, had it not continued with the punitive enclosure of the girl and then, inside a supposedly liberating convent, with the lewd embraces forced on the novice by a mother superior with a contorted face and a warped, disjointed mind.

On the one hand, Longchamp:

A rope was placed around my neck, and with one hand I was made to hold a flaming torch, with the other a scourge. One of the nuns took hold of the other end of the rope and pulled me along between the two lines, and the procession made its way towards a little inner oratory dedicated to St. Mary. They had come singing softly; now they walked in silence. When I had reached the oratory, lit by two lamps, I was ordered to ask both God and the community to forgive me for the scandal I had caused. The nun who had led me there said the words I had to repeat, and I repeated them all. Then the rope was removed, I was stripped down to the waist, they took my hair, which was hanging down over my shoulders, and pulled it to one side of my neck, they placed in my right hand the scourge I had been carrying in my left, and they started reciting the Miserere.[4]

On the other, Arpajon:

At such times, if a nun does the slightest thing wrong, the Mother Superior summons her to her cell, deals with her harshly, and orders her to get undressed and to give herself twenty strokes with her scourge; the nun obeys, gets undressed, picks up her scourge, and mortifies her flesh, but no sooner has she given herself a few strokes than the Mother Superior, overwhelmed with pity, snatches the instrument of penitence from her and starts crying; how dreadful it is for her to have to punish people! She kisses her on the forehead, eyes, mouth, and shoulders, caresses her, and sings her praises . . . She kisses her again, lifts her up, puts her clothes back on for her, says the sweetest things to her, gives her permission not to attend the services, and sends her back to her cell. It is very difficult being with women like that, as you never know what they are going to like or dislike, what you need to avoid doing or what you need to do. . . . I went inside with her; she accompanied me with her arm round my waist. . . . "I utterly adore you, and once these bores have all left, I shall gather together the sisters and you'll sing a little tune for us, won't you?"[5]

Here are the two sides of a single madness, "the folly of the cross," as you write, which "flies in the face of our natural inclinations" by inciting human beings to "hide away," even though "God made man sociable"; locking them up into "madhouses" and giving free rein *in fine* to "animal functions" through the very savagery by which these are supposed to be curbed.

Your indictment, Mister Philosopher, is earnest, detailed, and uncompromising: you are up in arms, a militant.

Are convents so essential to the constitution of a state? Did Jesus Christ institute monks and nuns? Can the Church really not do without them? . . . Can these vows, which *fly in the face of our natural inclinations*, ever be properly observed by anyone other than a few abnormal creatures in whom the seeds of passion have withered and whom we should rightly consider as monsters, if the current state of our knowledge allowed us to understand the internal structure of man as easily and as well as we understand his external form? . . . Where does *nature*, revolted by a constraint for which it is not intended, smash the obstacles put in its way, become enraged, and *throw the whole animal system into incurable disarray*? . . . Where is the dwelling place of coercion, disgust, and hysteria? Where is the home of servitude and despotism? Where is undying hatred? *Where are the passions nurtured in silence?* . . . "To make a vow of poverty is to swear to be an idler and a thief. To make a vow of chastity is to swear to God constantly to break the wisest and most important of His laws. To make a vow of obedience is to renounce *man's inalienable prerogative: freedom*. If you keep these vows, you are a criminal; if you do not keep them, you are guilty of perjury before God. To live the cloistered life, you have to be either a fanatic or a hypocrite."[6]

As you write this—understandable—indictment, you are in tears. Diderot, in tears? It's hardly posterity's vision of him. We prefer to picture the philosopher patting Catherine the Great on the thigh, she who would later purchase his library . . . Are you weeping for your little sister, Marie-Angélique, who died a lunatic at the age of twenty-eight in an Ursuline convent, whom you haven't forgotten, since you named your beloved daughter after her? Or are they tears of outrage, like the way I feel about fundamentalism, before the religious obscurantism that oppresses "our natural inclinations"? Or are your tears even more a surprise to you because you are so well aware that in the human animal, a speaking being, the capacity to make meaning has long ago "flown in the face" of any "natural inclination," for there is a specific—hence natural—human capacity to clash with nature by dint of language, of thought?

You are discovering that this clash breeds delusions, in which wonders rub shoulders with follies; an inextricable jumble, a merry-go-round of bodies and souls whose perils and charms you brilliantly expose in the character of *He*, Rameau's nephew, for example (to the delight of the gloomy Hegel), ten years after *The Nun*. Here follies cohabit with thought, sure enough; they make this noncharacter live, create, and decline, this literally polyphonous third person, *He*, the spasmodic artist, the *Nephew*. But they don't spare his interlocutor either, *I*, which is to say you, the philosopher. The humans who lived before you or the Enlightenment ascribed such inconceivable oddities to either the devil or God: "God, through whom we discern that certain things we had deemed essential to ourselves are truly foreign to us, while those we had deemed foreign to us are essential," wrote Saint Augustine.[7] But what if the demonic and the divine were the same thing? What if your "tale" of *The Nun* led you to locate them, not in the Beyond but in "human nature" itself, which has become so dreadfully foreign? These possibilities are hinted at in your dialogue with that *Nephew* into whom you poured so much of yourself . . .

In the tragic story of Mademoiselle Simonin, the impulse that will lead you to the *Nephew* is still incipient; libertarian revolt prevails throughout. While following the martyrdom of your heroine the reader cannot help distinguishing the bright light of thought, championed by free spirits, from the cringing delirium propagated by fanatics, and the goodness of nature from the evil loosed against it—even though your artful love of masks can't resist confusing the issue. Matters will be harder and often impossible to sort out when you venture into the subtler crannies of culture, where flesh overlaps with word, and vice versa, as they do in the character of Rameau's nephew.

And yet, my dear Denis Diderot, I think you already came up against that overlapping at the time of *The Nun*, and that's why your story made you cry. One of your cherished "strumpet thoughts" must have come over you: that the deadly excesses of religion, like its deliciously sensual enslavements, don't come out of nowhere, and they don't come from the people who use them to justify their liberticidal power. Their egregiousness amplifies and exploits the "clash" inherent in the "natural inclinations" of the human beast, in whom nature chafes with culture—because those two, nature and culture, are always yoked together, however awkwardly, in the speaking animal.

Such is my hypothesis, justified to my mind by the *Nephew*. Now, if you'll permit me, I will carry it forward.

Was the end of your novel really lost, as some witnesses allege? Or did you condense the end of the story into a sketchy outline because, overcome by emotion on the heels of a mocking laugh, you found yourself simply unable to finish? "What ails you? What a state you are in!" exclaimed Monsieur d'Alainville, a friend of Grimm's and yours, when he found you plunged in grief, your face wet with tears. "What ails me?" you replied. "I am undone by a tale I'm telling myself."[8] This "tale" you were "telling yourself" would have no conclusion. The end of the Enlightenment went awry with the Terror. Today's ending seems interminable, and no less problematic.

PERSIFLAGE: FAITH OR WRITING?

And yet it all started off as a farce. That year, 1758, the charming marquis of Croismare was sorely missed by his friends. You had met the gentleman at the salon of Madame d'Épinay. He was a paragon of lively good humor, "devoted to numberless pleasures in succession," as your friend Grimm described him. One day he decides to move for a time to his Normandy estate, where his affairs require attention. But he fails to return, having caught a serious case of religion! It was then that you, Denis Diderot, hatched the idea (with the help of some co-conspirators, including Grimm) of an amusing prank, otherwise known as a wicked, perfidious piece of jiggery-pokery: to write to the marquis of Croismare some letters purporting to be from a genuine nun of Longchamp, Marguerite Delamarre. This lady had gone to court to have her vows annulled, claiming she had been forced into the nunnery by her parents. The marquis, although he did not know the plaintiff personally, had tried in vain to intercede for her with the councillors of the great chamber of the Paris parlement.

According to the fake letters, the nun had now run away from the convent and was begging for help from the marquis, who fell straight into the trap. The hoaxers split their sides. Eager to succor a nun in distress, the newly reverent Croismare offered her a chambermaid post in his household. This forced you to contrive the death of the supposed heroine of the correspondence, so as to relieve your friend without letting the deception be known. Soon afterward you decided to assemble the letters into a narrative, revised in 1780, but still unpublished: private copies circulated from hand to hand. The joke came to light, and Monsieur de Croismare took it with great good humor. The text did not appear as a novel until 1796, twelve years after your death. There was a general consensus to forget about the persiflage of its origins, but this stratagem nonetheless forms the backdrop to the drama ("a tale I'm telling myself") and confers an elusive dash of unreality and indeterminacy to the tragedy it recounts. A very French way, isn't it, of tackling the secrets of religion, not to say the mystery of God, at the same time as attacking head-on the evils of superstition!

On rereading, I find myself thinking that you wept over the novel you were attempting to synthesize from your prank, not only out of compassion for the unhappy victims of the "folly of the cross," as you call it in your role as encyclopedist and man of the Enlightenment, but also because the fine novelist you are was so stricken by the transference of your feelings upon those of your heroine Marie-Suzanne Simonin that, parallel to your indignation before her ordeals at the hands of religion, you succumbed to the blessings—sorry, the snares—of this magical thing, faith. Here are the words you put into her mouth:

> It was then that I came to feel that Christianity was superior to all the other religions in the world. What profound wisdom there was in what benighted philosophy calls the folly of the cross! In the state I was in, how would the image of a happy and glorious law-giver have helped me? I saw that innocent man, his side pierced, his head crowned with thorns, his hands and feet pierced with nails, and dying in agony, and I said to myself: "This is my God, and yet I dare to feel sorry for myself!" . . . I clung to this idea and felt a renewed sense of consolation in my heart.[9]

Such were, too, your own last words, according to posterity or wicked tongues. Distinctly over-the-top for an atheist!

Here's the nub: you, who taught me that "the first step toward philosophy is incredulity,"[10] didn't hesitate to make a character sing the praises of the Christian faith, even though she had been ill-treated by it! Is this another ironical pirouette, should it be taken with a pinch of salt, are you teasing us? Or are you rehearsing, slyly, vicariously, what it would be like to feel enthralled by that "profound wisdom," to submit to its attachments, to practice its dialectics? To comprehend its logic while condemning its abuses?

Maybe this was not more than a "strumpet thought" among others, one you discarded, before capsizing at the end. There was more urgent business to attend to in those effervescent days, after all. But I wonder: by limiting yourself to diagnosing how religion oppresses "good nature," didn't you deny yourself the chance to deploy the complexities of your discernment, to plumb the "mysteries" of that mystification after having denounced its aberrations?

You did, however, in your correspondence with Sophie Volland, undertake to plumb a different mystery—that of the Apocalypse whose name is "Woman." And still another after that, the enigma of the asocial individual, the eccentric parasite, the nephew of the great Rameau. Religion, seduction, hysteria, art . . . As mystifications and delusions go, you are not exempt: by rewriting your mocking farce in the form of a narrative, you stepped right into that region of mystification that could not fail to "clash" with your personal continent, that further illusion of which you are the master: literature. The imaginary, the fantasized, the written. How does it connect with religion? What links are there between religion, literature, the female body, and the artistic body? Between desire, seduction, and manipulation? Between feminine and masculine? Between art and parasitism? Truth and falsehood? Such are the abysses of philosophy. And how about between dominion over others, elevation of others, abuse of others? Between the powers of language, rhetoric, faith, and the Word? Such are the abysses of culture, of freedom, of the Enlightenment.

In a bid to cast light on your tale, scholars have pored over the original "correspondence" with the pious, deceived Monsieur de Croismare; but there is another, missing *correspondence* that remains unwritten and whose absence drove you to tears: that of the canon you once were with the philosopher you became. Is it because the ill-being of others—or your own?—wounds you so much that you prefer to act rather than to delve into its labyrinth of impasses and delights? "I would rather dry the tears of those who are unhappy than share the joy of the rest," you wrote to Sophie Volland. And to Madame d'Épinay: "I belong to the unhappy; it would seem fate sends them into my path; I cannot fail a single one of them, I haven't the strength; they rob me of my time, my talent, my fortune, my very friends . . ."[11]

How I understand! Barring the talent and the fortune, I could write the very same words—why else would I be so attached to the MPH? But I'm not with you all the way. The Diderot who bursts into tears, undone by his *Nun*, makes me doubt his luminous encyclopedist's certainties elsewhere.

Did you really believe in that benign "nature without artifice" touted by the Enlightenment? At the time of writing those mischievous letters to Croismare, you were also beginning work on the *Nephew*. And in that book, over and above its notoriously baroque, corrosive, seething critique of buffoons and braggarts, musical feuds and anarchic enthusiasms, what is it but good old "human nature" that gets blown to smithereens in the convulsion of passions, mimeses, unbearable truths, impossible filiations, tempests of the senses and sensations, in short, in the absence of any point of reference amid the strange, the infinite comedy of language and languages? All of this—the crucible of persiflage, of the literary laboratory, of imaginative power, of the hatefatuation of the sexes—surrounds *The Nun*, shattering the hypocrisy of sanctimonious God-botherers, beyond the control of the very institution of faith. You make no effort to contain it. You simply make it exist, in laughter, in tears, in style.

Do not think I am turning my back on your *Nun*. Your writing, lightened or indeed denatured by the silliness of the prank that brought her into being (you revel in those sorts of ambiguities, you cultivate them in all of your works), gradually pulls free from that "self-delusion . . . ruled by . . . instincts" that Nietzsche thought was characteristic of Christianity and, I might add, of its repressed substitutes.[12] Epistolary satire (or persiflage) and the novel that attempts to reason through it (*The Nun*) seem to me to have been engendered by the selfsame "clash" between *nature* and *meaning* that you sought to demystify in faith itself, overshooting your immediate target, the abusive enclosure of young women. As though at the very moment your work was engaged in extirpating the religious, it became apparent to you that it was "inoperable" of that religion. Thus the esthete Swann, that *inoperable* "celibate of art," as Proust wrote in the voice of the Christlike narrator of *In Search of Lost Time*;[13] thus too the Sade–Pascal duo, encompassing a peculiarly French genius, according to Philippe Sollers.[14] The need to believe is inoperable of desire, desire for meaning, whirlwind of the thinking flesh: that is what flew into your face, Mister Philosopher, and reduced you to tears, just when you were hoping to wind up *The Nun* in a hurry.

THE MISSING LINK OF EUROPEAN CULTURE

Your libertarian verve, the incisive violence of the French body and sense of humor, the upheavals of a history that was preparing to guillotine the king and overthrow the Church, all these impelled you to strike a ringing, well-aimed blow against obscurantism. After you, and largely thanks to you, religion (especially Catholicism) lost much of its aura of absolute revelation and institutional impregnability. This happened first in France—often accompanied by "revolutionary" atrocities whose tragic balance sheet not been fully reckoned yet—and little by little spread elsewhere in the world by means of the awesome, unstoppable march of secularization. Here I include religious pluralisms of every stripe, spiritualist mystifications, sectarian outpourings, and the "black tide of occultism" that so revolted Freud.

Is Christianity irrevocably discredited?

Many people are worried about this. Some question secularism, others dread the comeback of clericalism and its twin, anticlericalism. I know of some who try to deal with the problem by going back to the source, such as biblical inspiration, obviously: these read the alliance of the crucified Jesus with His Father as the accomplishment of the Jewish *Akedah*, not so much an "imperfect" to be "voided" as a truth forever present in the evangelical pronouncement, in the truth and presence of its accomplishment. As an epochal gesture this re-sourcing claimed to settle the old intra-Hebraic quarrel between Old and New Testaments, by re-founding the Pauline separation into a fresh unity of Jews and Christians. Is it a response to the tragedy of the Shoah and to the current threats posed by the "clash of religions"? Some people content themselves with a return to Latin. Others begin to listen to their contemporaries . . . And so on.

The atheist that I am holds her breath while asking herself these questions. And I dream that Teresa's experience could add to the movement for a salutary re-foundation a new reading of this revitalization of European culture that was ushered in by the much-maligned Counter-Reformation, of which Teresa was the more or less clandestine inspiration—alongside Ignatius Loyola and John of the Cross, but very differently from them.

This renovation, launched in part by La Madre's exemplary experience, makes me see that Christianity did not come to a halt in the Middle Ages; it was not killed off by the Renaissance, the Reformation, and humanism, contrary to what is often said. Mingling the message of the Song of Songs with the Passion on the Cross and infusing them through the bodies of the Renaissance and right into the entrepreneurial pragmatism of modern times, strongly marking the artistic sensibilities of the seventeenth and eighteenth centuries, but stuck in the tribunal of moral values, Christianity let itself be cowed by the libertarian energies of the Enlightenment and sidelined by the technical and multicultural acceleration of history. It flourished, however, under unexpected forms that might not always welcome the association: in your novels, Diderot, *Jacques the Fatalist* and *Rameau's Nephew*; in Mozart's *Magic Flute*, for instance; even in the care for human uniqueness professed by the European Union today. Does that surprise you? Good, I'm flattered! To issues of love, the Bible, and the Gospels I would attach everything that, without sinking into modern nihilism, patiently breaks down and recomposes the desire to believe with all one's body and soul. Everything that stays close to myths and rituals, monotheistic or otherwise, and revisits those bold condensations that restore humanity—disoriented by the threat of global disaster—to its own "monumental" history: a history made of the self-transcendence speaking beings have labeled the "divine," the "unconscious," "being," and "time," not to say "lost time."

Less than two centuries after Teresa's death you could not have perceived, dear Denis Diderot, this renovation within continuity achieved by a strange nun living at the very heart of the ontotheological continent you were determined to blow up, with swimming eyes. As an impatient, libertarian protester, committed to the efficiency that would benefit the humble and the wronged, you proceeded in plebeian fashion by dint of "epistemological breaks." Was that how it had to be in order for me, Sylvia Leclercq, beyond any real, imaginary, or symbolic guillotine, to find my way back to Teresa? After you, yet upstream from you? I don't know, but that's how it is.

Others, in ever greater numbers, would align themselves with what they took to be your fight against obscurantism, and continued the desecration with the help of a cudgel: this, those poor unprotected believers believed, was indispensable for lancing the boil of superstition and subjection. But they had overlooked the fertile twists, the vicious benefits, the ineffable traps of the desire for meaning: morbid fancies, instinctual eruptions, hopes and despairs, physical and psychic manipulations.

You've got it, Mister Philosopher: being the person I am, my cohabitation with that roommate is the paradoxical, but inevitable, result of your *Nun*. I began by rebelling, in step with you, against the physical and psychic oppressions effected by religions and ideologies, the latter being more or less secretly modeled on the former; I shared your revulsion at monastic claustration; I felt the empathy that made you weep over the fate of the victims of so many enforced, but often voluntary, delusions.

Over time, however, I found myself parting ways with you. Or rather I attempted to shine your light, in my own way, into the murky chambers of the female soul that intrigued you so much in Marie-Suzanne Simonin. Into what Freud called the "psychic apparatus," of both sexes: the recondite places where torture is distilled into secondary benefits, into a "surplus" of *jouissance*, and where the need to believe constitutes the foundations of a culture, with or without apparent malaise.

I wonder if you'd ever accept—as Freudians do, like me, who cannot share your enlightened optimism on this point—that delusion, with all its dangers, is a constitutive part or the now immersed face of a civilization seemingly melting away under the overheated blast of technology.

I have tried to channel your imagination, passion, and empathetic compassion for your nun in another direction in my own exploration of the interior dwelling places of

Teresa of Avila. My heroine was not spared the woes of the good sister of Long-champ and Arpajon, but she forged ahead right through them, first toward ecstasy, then into writing and action, and finally into sainthood. I spoke of the "interior dwelling places of Teresa of Avila," but they are not only hers. They do not harbor only the pioneering audacity of an elite soul of the sixteenth century, or the ravings of certain Catholic women in any century; perhaps (following Leibniz, with deficient humility once more) Teresa's inner mansions could be relevant to all kinds of passionate souls? Not because they share the same faith, but because such souls speak and think and *are* in time in a particular way. "There is a great difference in the ways one may be," the Carmelite wrote.

To get to the bottom of religious experience a slow, interminable effort remained and remains to be made, and it always will. Your *Nun* initiated the process with an almighty thwack at pious hypocrisy, but it was received with bland applause, reducing your text to an institutional operation: you were not seen to be interested in religion itself, let alone in God, you were merely attacking religious "power" in relation to personal and private life. There was a reaction of denial, a refusal to dig further! And yet your polyphonous adventure, your polymorphous oeuvre meant so much more. Is it by chance that you are the only Enlightenment philosopher cited by Freud? Your *Nun* pulled open the secret drawers of faith. Pieces like "First Satire," *Rameau's Nephew* (my own favorite), "Conversation of a Father with His Children," and "Conversation of a Philosopher with the Maréchale of —," attempted to explore religion's links with the law, filiation, and parenthood. Delving into the exquisite refinements and treasures of perversity lodged within bodies and souls with, around, and despite the realities of servitude and despotism, you continued to construct the bridge that leaps from Teresa's ecstasies (via Bernini, Tintoretto, and Tiepolo) to the passions of those modern monsters, the men and women of today, balanced aloft on the stilts of incorporated time, à la Proust, or dispersed into kalei-doscopic shards à la Picasso.

Teresa leads me through that labyrinth where the present has no meaning unless it recollects the inaugural moment and re-engenders it; where the now is only of interest insofar as it continually re-founds what came before, like Teresa does when she places Solomon's Bride inside the body of a woman praying to Jesus. This woman passes the baton to Bernini, who passes it on to Molly Bloom. Let us walk a little further in La Madre's company. I am trying to work through the tangled mazes you abhorred with a patience I hope to make as incisive as your own sardonic passion. Wounding or tiresome I may be, and yet somewhat appeased, I hope. And if so, it will be thanks to your preparatory spadework.

NEITHER RHENO-FLEMISH, NOR A QUIETIST

Did I say patience? Am I not rather caught, with this great Teresa, in the turmoil of a *transference*—that again, always that!—which I am trying to assume with whatever vigilance I still have? Behind my curiosity about this saint, what really fascinates me is the dynamic of the loving bond itself. It preexists this or that individual along with whatever objects of transference may present themselves in the course of the person's lifetime, for it is by the grace of the transference upon my parents, which founded my psychic life, that *I* think and therefore *I* am. "I have found out that you were less dear to me than my passion," wrote the Portuguese nun to the French officer who had forsaken her.[15] You will understand, Mister Philosopher, that if I am not content with thinking up equations but ask myself: "What causes me to think?" then I am still preoccupied by that foundational passion. So I am not about to close down my dialogue with my roommate, Maître, and now you know why you are its last witness here. How could I interrogate the original transference without moving backward through the battles you fought on behalf of the freedom of bodies and souls, the struggles you bequeathed to us, which are now mine? Who am I? Who is she? What is she looking for?

Who are you, Teresa? A garden irrigated by four waters, a fluid castle open to infinity with seven permeable "dwelling places," an inexhaustible writer, a dauntless warrior, a languid lover sighing for "more!" under Bernini's caress? A pitiful epileptic or a woman of power? A Carmelite cloistered in hopeless delusion or a modern, more than modern, subject? Do I really have an answer, at the end of this long sojourn side by side?

After following you as best I could through your life and death, through the firmament of ideas where you hover with the opus that is your jewel, that last question remains open.

Is it because you were a woman, or because you were Teresa de Cepeda y Ahumada, then Teresa of Jesus, then Saint Teresa of Avila—who I watched being born, vibrating, and passing away, with your epoch and against it—that you built yourself a soul, as it used to be called, that matched your body but did not fit the Aristotelo-Thomist model of the *interior man* and the *exterior man*? That equally contradicted the rationalist, sensualist model mounted by Fénelon and Madame Guyon?

The history of Christianity is actually littered with sophisticated anatomies of the soul, vertiginous palaces of the inner life. Might I run through some of them with you, Mister Philosopher, as a way of clarifying my disagreement? I'll use the bits and pieces to enhance my Teresian "installation," like the Beguines decorating their offerings to

the Sacred Heart with shreds of grass and scraps of floral fabric. Or like contemporary female artists who eschew synthesis and prefer to pile up the fragments of their
untenable identities. A nod at the scholastics, a glance at the Rhenish philosophers,
an allusion to quietism, all to be submitted for your inspection. It's my patchwork
sampler, my polychrome canvas, my MoMA-worthy "mobile." So that the dwelling
places of my saint are sure to stand out while remaining connected, I tighten my
gestures, quicken my paint drippings, gather time into the space of a condensation.
Teresa of Avila's revolution can only be assessed in relation to that mutation of mystical subjectivity, those variations on the "kingdom" of which modernity knows nothing,
but in which I tried to steep myself while traveling through the works of the woman
from Castile.

As you know, my dear Philosopher, after Saint Paul and Saint Augustine, scholasticism came up with a topology of inner space in which the *higher part* comprised
man's rational faculties, and the *lower part* the sensitive faculties.

The Rheno-Flemish mystics modified the structure established by Aristotle and
Aquinas by adding to this bilevel schema a new "higher part": the locus of mysticism itself, the site of the "essence" of the soul, above the median level of rationality
and the base level of the sensitive. Transcending the operative powers (*intellect, will,
imagination*), irreducible to the actual *capabilities* of any given subject, the *indivisible
essence of the soul* is deployed in a rigorously ontological context. This summit of
man's interiority is described by Meister Eckhart as the "innermost source" in which
"I spring out in the Holy Spirit, where there is one life and one being and one work."[16]

The soul sits at rest on this crowning point to "merit" an "interior nativity," in
other words an overcoming of the "self" by means of the rebirth of the "subject" as
Other, in the modern interpretation. "Be quiet, let God speak and work within": this
is the method advocated by Johannes Tauler, Eckhart's disciple, to enable the soul
within which the (re)birth occurs to become "a child of God."[17] An essential, noetic,
abstract, imperceptible union, "without images or instruments," "a learned ignorance," *ignota cognitio*, this "depth"—or rather pinnacle—of the soul in Rheno-Flemish
mysticism is thus an ontological reality, the transcendence of *being* over *doing*.

And yet the consciousness of the feeling and thinking subject is by no means
abolished here. Meister Eckhart's experience is more like a "flickering" between the
three hierarchically separated levels of *essence, reason,* and *sense*.[18] Mysticism only
sacralizes the noblest part of the soul, the *essence,* and this can only be attained in the
seclusion of silence, causing the rebirth of subjectivity through its immersion in Being;
its power is none other than the pure silence of noetic alteration. The "vain pursuit"
of faith in Saint John of the Cross has affinities with this noetic alteration described by

Tauler: "There is no doubt that Almighty God has appointed a special place for Himself in the soul which is the very essence itself, or *Mens*, whence the higher powers emerge. This spirit or *Mens* is of such great dignity that no creature has or ever could rise to the height necessary to understand it."

★ ★ ★

Teresa was not unaware of this noetic ambition, for her whole reformation of the Carmel, with its stress on austere enclosure, silence, and purity, alluded and adhered to it. But my roommate went further: her life, her writings, and her deeds embody and testify to a different mystical model.

If more evidence is needed of the impossibility of reducing Teresa's procedure to the Rheno-Flemish model, suffice it to say that the sensualist-rationalist tendency, opposed to the mystics of the North, acknowledged a debt to the saint's experience. This current, launched by Francis de Sales in his *Treatise on the Love of God*,[19] hit the zenith with Fénelon[20] and Madame Guyon.[21]

In one of your marvelously intransigent fugues, my dear Philosopher, you yourself conflated "*la Guyon,*" her verbose *Spiritual Torrents*, and Fénelon, with . . . Teresa! You begin by expounding rapturously on the fickle female of the species. Then, having immortalized Jeanne Guyon, you automatically associate her with my saint. So La Guyon writes with unrivaled eloquence in her book *Torrents*? You go on to declare: "Saint Theresa has said of devils, 'How luckless they are: they do not love!' Quietism is the hypocrisy of the perverse man, the true religion of the tender woman."[22] Indeed. But Teresa a "tender woman"? Never! Next, carried away by enthusiasm, unless it's persiflage again, you commend Fénelon as a "safe" man: "There was, however, a man of such honesty of character and such rare simplicity of morals that a gentlewoman could safely forget herself beside him and melt into God. But this man was unique and called Fénelon." Right! Enough of that, let's get back to the female genius. "Women are subject to epidemic attacks of ferocity." Although: "Oh, women, what extraordinary children you are!"

With that, were you edging nearer to Teresa? Not in my opinion. Dare I say that the philosopher lacks something indispensable for following the Carmelite in her cruelty, her infantilism, her raptures, her foundations? You don't know what to do with those exaltations in which the soul becomes one with the Other, because the atheist in you is condemned to diminish the singularity of innerness and to lock himself out from the mansions of the soul by his refusal to countenance the Other's very existence. I'm not asking you to believe in it, to subscribe to it, or even to make use of it. I'm asking you to make your object of incredulity—God—into an object of interpretation.

It was impossible: you were blocked by the same rationalistic sensualism that had already produced a new mystical model, itself sense-based and psychologistic, with which you rather sympathized. It made you "shiver" in the company of Guyon-Fénelon, and you redressed it on the reason side or tilted it toward the side of emancipation to castigate the iniquities of an oppressive obscurantism. But it debarred you from the subtle paths of perceptible—and imperceptible—perfection that are opened up by the experience of faith.

What if your *Nun* were not only the fruit of a revolt against the abuses of religious institutions but also and equally an ultimate consequence of the rationalistic sensualism that abrogates, along with the "God question," the true complexity of the "castle of the soul"? First by belittling it, then by ignoring its intrinsic logic, and finally by annulling it? You perceive the threat, Mister Philosopher, and fight it by creating the polyphonic and carnivalesque characters of your novels, you entrust the imagination with the job of *musiquer* (setting to music, the term used by *He* in the *Nephew*) the psychic life.[23] But you're not sure that all this is enough, and you have no desire to finish the novel of *The Nun* now that you've released her from religion. The "benighted philosophy" of the "folly of the cross," as Suzanne puts it in her letters to the marquis, is, I suspect, somewhat yours as well—for haven't you elected to remain blind to the voyage of souls toward the God question?

I am not suggesting that you personally, Maître, closed the God question in favor of another question, not entirely divorced from it but not to be reduced to it either: the question of subjection and how to get rid of it. I am only saying that this closure has a history, which involves you, and that the history of mysticism itself participates in it. But since my wager is to reopen the God question in the thinking that crystallized in the enlightened Encyclopedia and culminated, as I see it, with Freud, I can only do this by way of your good self, replaying your revolts and querying your silences.

It's well known that you found Christianity a doleful affair, compared with the zest for life, sensual gaiety, and civic pugnacity you valued so highly in pagan antiquity and transposed to the dimension of mankind. And yet I hear you tell your Maréchale that all deities, including pagan ones, belong in the madhouse: grist to my psychologist's mill, as you can imagine.

"In no century and with no nation have religious opinions been the basis of national morals. *The gods* adored by the ancient Greeks and Romans, the most virtuous of people, were *the merest scum: a Jupiter who should have been burnt alive: a Venus fit for a reformatory: a Mercury who ought to be in a jail.*"

But while you shared Freud's abrasive unbelief, you feared that delusion could not be so easily eradicated. "Do you think man can get along without superstition?" asks the Maréchale de —. "I do not entertain this hope, because desire for it has not blinded me to its hollowness: but I take it away from no one else." At the same time you doubted that the Christian message had been heard: "But are there any Christians? I have never seen one."[24] Echoing Hobbes, you rightly contended that religion is a superstition that is allowed, and superstition a religion that is not allowed.[25] Being a reasonable fellow, more influenced by your English contemporaries than by the Hebrews of yore, you felt that religious abuses are best remedied by sound legislation, devised in the public interest. It is impossible, you tell the Maréchale, to subject

a nation to a rule which suits only a few melancholiacs, who have imposed it on their characters. It is with religious as with monastic institutions; they relax with time. They are lunacies which cannot hold out against the constant impulse of nature, which brings us back under her law. See to it that private good be so closely united to public good that a citizen can hardly harm society without harming himself. Promise virtue its reward, as you have promised wickedness its punishment. Let virtue lead to high offices of state, without distinction of faith, wherever virtue is to be found. Then you need only count on a small number of wicked men, who are involved in vice by a perversity of nature which nothing can correct. No. Temptation is too near: hell too far off. Look for nothing worth the attention of a *wise law-giver*.[26]

But your affinity with religious—and with Freud's—experience is never more glaring than when you equate the Creator and His Laws with the good father and his selective authority. With feigned ingenuousness you remind the Maréchale of the story of the young Mexican and the old man. The Mexican (yourself, perhaps?) doesn't believe that anybody lives across the sea, until one day, blown by a storm, he lands there and finds to his relief a venerable old man on the beach. He falls to his knees. "'Get up,' said the old man; 'you have denied my existence?'" Of course, he pardons the Mexican for his ignorance. This allows you to make a point to the Maréchale to the effect that fatherly forgiveness trumps the punishment that "real" religion metes out—according to her (surely un-Christian) preconceptions.

Law or mercy? To this intra-Hebraic crossroads where the God question leads, you will return very analytically, dear Denis Diderot, with regard to yourself and your father. We know that as an impudent thirty-something you went to your father's house to ask for his permission to marry Anne-Toinette Champion, a modest lace vendor. He refused and had you locked up in a monastery, you escaped, laid low in

Paris and married your sweetheart—only to find her a bore. Well, it was in that same family home at Place Chambeau, in Langres, that the prodigal son, having disobeyed the paternal injunction to become a churchman, mused with his father over the need for a Law and how to become free of it. You attributed to this father, the underwriter of the Law, not so much the authorization to defy it as the shrewdness to be wisely unconventional. I am thinking of your "Conversation of a Father with His Children": "When it was my turn to bid him goodnight, I embraced him and said into his ear: 'Strictly speaking, Father, there is no law for the wise.' 'Pray keep your voice down.' 'All laws being subject to exceptions, it is for the sage to judge in which cases to bow to them and in which to ignore them.' 'I should not mind,' said he, 'if there were one or two citizens like yourself in the town; but I should not live there were they all to think likewise.'"[27]

I rather fear, Sage of the ideal polis whose citizens do not all think likewise, that your philosophy has not been followed to the letter. I'm afraid your unconditional fans tend not to know or to forget about your writings and your tears, this time at the death of the cutler, a paragon of piety and justice: "I feel an infinite sadness," wrote the inconsolable son who was not by his father's side when the time came.

All in all you are a tolerant atheist, Mister Philosopher, and it doesn't come amiss to repeat it, even if your oh-so-reasonable sensibility makes Teresian interiority a closed book to you. I like to think that if I met you today, more than two hundred years after your demise, you would have persevered with your nun's story, and our paths might have crossed. Personally, I'm sure of it.

Let us return then to that other mystical model, distinct from the Rheno-Flemish school. This developed through the rationalist-sensualists, aiming to integrate the Cartesian subject while adapting it to lived experience, and bewitching the French—or rather, French women. To my mind, this model was not in keeping with Teresa's project either. Descartes' *ego cogito* gradually infiltrated Christian mysticism to eclipse the *ego amo* and *ego affectus est* of the Christian subject; it was Julia Kristeva and her *Tales of Love* that made me understand this long ago, when, disappointed in my unfinished thesis on Duras, I attended her classes at Jussieu. Briefly, faith ordered by reason is accompanied in Francis de Sales by a mutation of love that finds peace in knowledge. Pascal himself insists, in his *Discourse on the Passion of Love*, on the role of reason in love, and presents the latter as a clear-sighted vision of truth rather than a form of blindness.

Paradoxically, the desacralization of mystical experience begins with this second would-be mystical current or "model," with its inflexion of *being* toward *doing*. The desacralization is lasting, even or especially when the praying person resists *doing* with all his or her might in order to find refuge in *non-action*. How can this be? The faculties (*intellect, will, imagination*) are henceforth located on the higher planes of both the *Rheno-Flemish trichotomy* and the *Aristotelo-Thomist dichotomy*; as a result, the *mind* is split from the *senses*, that is from *feeling* or sentiment, relegated to the lower plane of *human reason*. The two activities nonetheless overlap and encroach to produce an amazingly complicated map of the soul, a jumble of components, degrees, and postures, but this "vertiginous carousel with its proliferating subdivisions" has nothing in common with Teresa's dwelling places, as we will see.[28]

Among the rational sensualists, my dear Denis Diderot, the *essential soul* of Rheno-Flemish thought is invoked only to be redistributed through a rational and sensitive topography. This entails a psychologization of experience that in turn leads Fénelon, the Swan of Cambrai, in his *Explication of the Maxims of the Saints*, to define the "supreme peak" of the loving union of the soul with God in negative, sentimental fashion as the *absence* of any intellectual discourse or inclinations of the will based on the exercise of reason.[29] The concept of Being remains, of course, but only as a *posited reference* (henceforth *separate* from the "subject," or more exactly of the psychological "self," which becomes merely the *sign* of it) in a supradiscursive regime of rational faculties. In fact, this attempt to make mystical doctrines compatible with scholastic theology signals the impossibility of preserving any *mysticism of the essence* within rational and sensualist parameters.

For the subject of the Cartesian *cogito* wrecked the ontological ambition of the Rheno-Flemish mystics,[30] which now became inaccessible to such anti-mystics as Bossuet, who devoted himself to "tempering by means of holy interpretations" the notions of the "great exaggerators," mystics who have no idea of what they're talking about.[31] This did not prevent the Eagle of Meaux from standing up for Teresa in his own terms, as we've seen, and he also had kind words for Saint Francis of Assisi, Saint Bernard, Saint Catherine, and a few others. Nothing is simple in this area, Maître: I can't keep up myself, which is saying something. Let's press on. The ontological ambition would also be inaccessible, in a different way, to Pierre Poitiers and to Fénelon, even though these claimed to be the greatest defenders of mysticism in all the seventeenth century. The first declared that the union of the human soul with the divine essence should be understood as merely a "metaphor," while the second depicted the essential mystical union in terms of a simple affective bond whereby the soul unites with God in pure, disinterested love. Thus the way was paved for sensualist materialism to sound the knell of the mysticism of Being in favor of the mystique of the psychological ego.

May I put more clearly, in light of this, the objection I raised before with regard to Jeanne and Teresa? When, with touching quietist "abandonment" and in the dignified perfection of "pure love," Jeanne Guyon seeks to identify with Teresa of Avila, a serious misunderstanding has occurred. "Not being able to find in [myself] anything that can be named. . . ."[32] You well know, Maître, as a declared admirer of *Spiritual Torrents*, that Jeanne's encounter with nothing failed to stem her outpourings on the vicissitudes of her sensory ego. The saint of the Counter-Reformation, for her part, was equally conversant with the psychological maze of earthly affections, their frustrations and glories, somatic consequences, narcissistic or depressive recesses, and manic excitements—all taking turns to cram or vacate the psyche of Madame Guyon, according to her torrential text. The main difference between the two women was that Teresa's "abandonment" of herself to the infantile was merely a transition, to be elucidated and then situated in the co-presence of emptiness and infinity.

With La Madre we find none of the apotheosis of "Nothingness" so central to Guyon's approach, which betrays an obvious narcissistic regression to the infant's impotence / omnipotence binomial. Teresa would never say, "I suffer as gaily as a child." She would never offer an apology of the "abjection" that advocates "pollution" and presupposes the *abolition of sin* by the quietists. Where Jeanne Guyon *annihilates herself* in an Other reduced to an unnameable Nothing—symmetrical counterpart of the mercilessly judgmental paternal divinity—Teresa *exults at being* the infinitesimal presence of the Other, an atom forming part of infinite Love itself: the infinitely present, rewarding Love that embraces her viscerally (*entrañarse*)[33] and allows itself to be checkmated, no less, in a game she plays to infinity and with energy to match.

Teresa, contrary to *La Guyon*, as you call her, merges with the divine placed at the luminous center of her dwelling places, whose depiction she refines by way of savors (*gustos*), ways, and foundations that forever lead her to new encounters. Outside the self or inside it, nothing but intrepid alterations of her emptied-out identity, which is, by the same token, not so much verbose as polymorphous, plural, pragmatic. Her manner of inhabiting her dwelling places, her multiple interior-exterior topologies, lead into a rebirth of the subject who writes "fictions," which I receive as strings of alterations of the new Self into the Other: wars on the self, or transcendences of the self, through the deepening of elucidated desires and at the same time through the amplification of historical action. This nonsymmetrical reversibility between the "other Self" and the Other (Teresa and her Voices), just as between the Subject and the World, which characterizes Teresa's experience, was for a long time misunderstood, indeed persecuted, before it was recognized and recommended by the Tridentine revolution. In reaction to the narrowness of both Protestantism and humanism, the Jesuits encouraged Teresa's oscillation (which was also theirs) between interiority and spirituality, seclusion and the world, Being and Subject, religion and politics. Having cast themselves as the soldiers of a new logic, they quickly recognized themselves in the ecstatic foundress as she recognized herself in them, amid suspicions, tensions, and conflicts—for the blessings of dialectics are infinite.

So you see, dear Maître, why I am so interested in a nun who might have been like yours but did not merely resemble her, or rather, resembled her not at all. Neither Rheno-Flemish nor a Fénelonian, Teresa operated a change in the mystic soul whose enigmas we, would-be modern subjects trapped between secularism and fundamentalism, have barely begun to plumb.

When she raised the erotic body into the sphere of essential union with the Other-Being, she was not merely revaluing the flesh (which so tormented Marie-Suzanne Simonin) as the ultimate site of the experience of the divine. Rheno-Flemish mystics like Meister Eckhart had already done this, albeit intermittently. Fénelon and Guyon were to bring the desiring body back to the quiet of a child in its mother's lap—mistaking narcissistic exaltation for serenity.

Likewise Teresa did more than just ennoble "lust" by defensively making the Spouse into its sole object, and dispensing her personal seductiveness to a number of His servants of both sexes along the way.

Even if she often got lost in the psychological labyrinth of those male and female attractions, Eros and Agape together, drives and idealizations combined, Teresa was not content, either, to rehabilitate an Aristotle of *touch* in order to sketch the outlines of a new *Ethics*: one that had remained embryonic in the Greek philosopher's writings and that it is our task to develop, over and over again, in a modern world that doesn't bottle up its desires.

She achieved more.

Body and soul, the Teresa-subject is torn apart and reassembled in and by the violent desire to both feel *and* think the Other, both at once. This desire, resting on the tactile contiguity of bodies, is recognized by its violence and endlessly alleviated through its elucidations. The touch of another, elevated into the principle of the Other, consecrates what is foreign to one as an intimate, indelible component of psychic and physical vitality from now on. Touch is at once the ultimate survival instrument of animals, betraying the persistence of animality in the human *zoe*, and tact—a supremely human quality, an acute attention brought to bear on the tolerable, a psychic flexibility. The Teresa-subject confers ontological status on the desiring body, while at the same time ascribing to it—via the ambivalence bestiality/tact—a certain polyphony, polysemy, with all the malleability of the many dwelling places of this new soul. You can see how such topologies are not chunks of a sunken continent, nor ruins awaiting an Infinity of abandonment, far from it: they are the points of impact of infinite desire, locations touched by and in desire's unending motion.

Your daughter Angélique would not have scorned my saint, since she once said, as you reported to Sophie Volland, "On fait de l'âme quand on fait de la chair": "you make soul by making flesh."[34] In *D'Alembert's Dream* (1769), you expounded something more than a materialistic doctrine. Could it actually be an experience?

TERESA, NOW

Teresa's extraordinary innovation consists in this incorporation of the infinite, which, working backward, against the grain, returns the body to the infinite web of bonds. I could scarcely have gotten you to appreciate the magnitude of such a revolution, dear Maître, had Leibniz not perceived it first. The polyvalent soul-body ensemble, constructed and written with Teresa and thanks to her, is only possible so long as it refuses to be merely the *sign* of an Other-Being, affixed to it from outside (as we find in Fénelon-Guyon). *This* is possible if—and only if—the body-soul ensemble is experienced as a point in which the infinity of the Other-Being *insists* on impressing itself. If, and only if, the speaking subject, body-and-soul, *is* an *infinity-point*; and, conversely, if the infiniteness of the Other-Being "presents" itself in the point that *I* am. Indeed, Teresa the Bible reader (perhaps reluctant to admit it, and never acknowledging her Marrano genealogy) specifies that "He" is "graven."

The "mystical marriage" and other inordinate formulations, such as "I am transformed into God," among countless equally extravagant metaphors-metamorphoses, herald this modulation of the subject that *consists* in and with Infinity—though Teresa herself disowns it at times as a piece of pure "folly." I am not a "sign" that "suggests" an external Being (whether Creator or Savior, loving or judging). I form part of Him, I participate in Him, I seek myself in Him, I *am Him*, for all that I do not equate with Him. *I*, the subject, belong to a symbolic sequence where nothing is a mensuration of the whole part by part. As an *infinity-point*, I obey a different logic: I follow laws of transition and continuity where nothing equates with anything else and every coincidence conceals an infinitely small distance. An irreducible gap always obtains between Being and the broad ensemble of "subjects," "singularities," "numbers" able to express it, among which *I* disseminate myself by writing and doing. I belong to a geometry that is no longer algebraic, but analytical. I am a site of the limitless signifier.

In this my dynamic of perpetual transit, knowledge (*connaissance*), as in joint birth (*co-naissance*), is not a totalization so much as an exhaustive process of subtraction whereby the infinite moves closer to an always retreating term. Why do you talk of "lack," "suffering," "persecution"? I've escaped your algebraic world of "selves" orphaned of the Whole, because *I* am *the very impact of the Infinite*, ad infinitum.

But, let's be clear, this infinity at work in the infinity-point that I am never reaches fullness: that is how I avoid misidentifying the Nothingness that so beguiles you and brings you peace, or so you say. My All, which is Nothing, has nothing to do with the full Whole. Because if lack there is, it's that very plenitude that is incomplete: the Whole is limited by being a non-infinity, a privatory concept, a "lack," if you prefer. Whereas my tiny point—my nothing—contains infinity.

Such is, then, the Teresa-subject (or her soul, she would say), provided we consider that "subject" as an infinity forever developed across points; as a subject neither external nor internal to the Other-Being, but instead deictic/anaphoric: *Ecce* (Behold); *Haec* (This). Its function is demonstrative, to designate—and de-sign— infinite plurality. A sign is normally independent of its referent, but that's not the case in the anaphoric economy: the "sign" (*I*) and the "referent" (*other*) are a single dif- ferentiated continuity. One should not conceive this subject as a Cartesian number value, conferring space and time on the entity that thinks it. On the contrary, let us imagine it as the infinitesimal, giving back to the number its infinity-point, and there- fore without space or time. If nowhere and no-time coincide with eternity, then the infinitesimal subject, constructed according to infinitesimal logic, can only be a set of plural, contingent transitions and continuities. Its *co-naissance* or joint emergence in narrative elucidation cannot take the form of *connaissance*, knowledge, in the Cartesian sense of calculus or algebra; it can only appear as a game. In Teresa's terms, a "fiction."

Thus the Teresa-subject does not end up "absorbed" into the divine, like Jeanne Guyon, who compares herself to "a drop of water lost and dissipated in the sea." You will find no trace in La Madre of that "pure love" that aspires to be "work without effort," "passive night," "the privation of all things," "demise," "disap- proval"; instead Teresa rejoices while reflecting, and vice versa; the infinity-point she has become freights an indomitable energy, it's a big bang in female form. Nor do feelings take precedence over language: spoken-and-written words together entertain the felt at the very instant of its emergence, to confer real existence upon it. Raptures are preceded and followed by words that are always redolent of biblical, evangelical, or biographical signifiers—precisely because those signifiers are not, or are no longer, rational signs referring to external realities, but rather "fictions" that touch the Other-Being and are themselves touched by that infinity, those meta-morphoses of *I* into Other. Since the monad is coiled inside infinity, it is by infinity that it is penetrated, and it will never resort to Nothingness as a retreat for injured affections or a bandage for melancholic annihilation.

There is no "communication of silences," either. Only a constant preoccupation with narrating *dissemblance*—that region of human sin and deformity, according to Saint Bernard—in order to open it up to mystical marriage, boost the exercise of con-templation, and metabolize both into political action. Teresa knew all about words and silences and made good use of them in writing and founding. Her way of perfec-tion did not, however, seek after taciturn quietude to fill in as an artificial mother. She was the Mother. This is how her sacred femininity was crystallized, the same in every particular as the sacred humanity of the Spouse, and recognizing nothing of the sexual female body but its gaping excitability, the avid seduction that Her Majesty the female Subject deploys so actively. Incommensurate with any "numerical" unity or "me-like" identity whatsoever, it is rather a perpetual becoming, forever in progress, forever en route. This contact of the *subject* with *infinity*, in the region of dissem-blance itself, is the source of its *jouissance*, as it is of the libidinal energy, supervised writing, and historical action that account for such a genuine, noninfantile serenity— not to be confused with passive quietude, whose narcissistic fulfillment springs from the satisfaction of the infant's need to be mothered.

Although the subject aspires toward the Other-Being, which insists and consists in it, the two cannot be equated: as a *signifying differential* of infinity, *I* am never filled or fulfilled, and such an awareness of my dissemblance protects me from madness at the same time as it guarantees my limitless singularity. My "identity," like any other "unity," is thereby dislocated and the Subject that I am is constantly in process, driven to act in view of what is as yet unaccomplished and may be accomplished later, or never. I do not aspire to any "performance" or "efficiency," for no sequence of unities or actions adds up with others to form a Whole, whether an "oeuvre" or a "program." Not that I reject them, either, far from it. There is nothing but the soft slide of infinity, modulating the word (*la parole*, by definition finite), and transfiguring the experi-enced affects—henceforth ek-static, and, in keeping with this logic, necessarily so—of my body (by definition mortal).

You will have perceived, Mister Philosopher, that the Teresa I am attempting to share with you is the Teresa read and understood by Leibniz. We are moving away from your *Nun*; but not so much, perhaps, from that medical vignette of yours that Freud appreciated so much: "A woman dominated by hysteria experiences some-thing infernal or divine. Sometimes she makes me shudder; I have seen and heard her carrying within herself the fury of a wild beast! How much she felt! How wonderfully she expressed it!"[35] I am confident of following your diagnosis, except I also listen to, and hear, precisely what this "wild beast" is feeling and expressing. I strive to plumb the "hysteria" you evoke, that region where the felt and the expressed, fierce bestiality and pure divinity, live side by side. Because the human adventure, at the intersection of desire and meaning, is simultaneously linked to and distant from the two shores between which you frame us, the two metaphors tradition has bequeathed for thinking about thinking. Teresa's autoanalysis, extraordinary for how deeply it goes into what she "felt and expressed," indicates a way through obscurantism that differs from yours as it does from that of the French Enlightenment. I boldly claim that my interpretation, undoubtedly less caustic than yours, is more profound, while operating on a continuum with your unbelief: such is my conviction, at this point at any rate.

LOVE IN QUESTION

I don't take myself for an infinity-point, believe me; I just do the best I can here in the MPH, which is to say, not much. The good old home is in full-blown crisis these days, "as is its wont," Marianne points out. Funds are low, nobody wants to be a psychiatrist anymore, there's a shortage of nurses, and our crowded premises are overflowing with patients suffering from unspeakable pathologies, according to the insane reports and other assessments thrown at us by demented technocrats at the helm of a society that would rather not know madness exists.

"Listen, honey, the cloister is what you choose when you're at your wits' end to defend yourself from the primal scene! And from the revulsion it arouses in the hysterical subject, male or female, toward their own excitement—unless it's toward their frigidity, the other side of the same coin. And what do they replace it with? A fantasy proximity to the ideal Love Object, Daddy and Mummy fused into one big Whole, with a capital W! That's the lush paradise of pure spirituality for you, where lurks the phobia of sex fed by sexual hunger! Religious vocation is in love with the phallus, or if you like it overidealizes the paternal superego in whose name the cloistered guy or gal is prepared to undergo maximum frustration. And more, in case of affinity. I gather that even the masochistic orgy of penance takes less of a physical form, these days. It's kept on the moral level! That's allowed! Not to say highly promising, liable to take you beyond perversion into full-blown psychosis."

Marianne has come to the end of her analysis and has enrolled for further study at the Parisian Psychoanalytic Society. Her views on vocations and cloistered confinements ring with beginner's self-assurance. She plows on:

"Mind you, the cloistered *woman*—your Teresa was a woman, riiight—can easily accept her subordination to one or several bossy mother superiors, just to tickle her latent homosexuality, not half as unconscious as one might think. Next thing you know, the path of these handmaids of the ideal Phallus is paved with pleasures that are out of this world. In fact, once they run out of excitement they jettison the Word itself, which likely panics them by becoming flesh, and these halo-hunters take refuge in the Void: pure love, cult of silence, take or leave a whiff of Buddhism. Did you see yesterday's *Monde*? Apparently more and more monks and nuns are raring to drop Our Father who art in Heaven and even the Name of the Father, and move to India instead. Faith is getting with the decentralization program at long last. All roads lead to India, you're behind the times, sweetheart!"

The new Marianne is unrecognizable: energetic, outspoken, confident, briskly efficient. Shall I get her to have lunch with Bruno? That would be a scream. She's given up the cigs and scruffy jeans; today she's modeling a shimmery silk ensemble. I don't take her up. My smile can only be read as agreement.

"Still, I think you're doing the right thing, getting stuck into your saint like that. So I changed my mind. Can I? You're too kind. Because what I said about vocations, enclosures, and co doesn't just apply to a handful of visionaries. That lot, who survive by stopping time, only succeed in aggravating the soul distress we find in milder form—let's be thankful for small mercies—in our own everyday hysterics, do you see? Actually, I don't understand why the PPS insists on saying hysteria is on the wane and that most cases count as borderline. First of all, it's not true; second of all, they're not mutually exclusive. Take what I just said about the disgusted hysteric, male or female, hiding from the primal scene, and apply it to a Marie or a Chloe, model wives and mothers who wipe their brats' noses and get depressed at the office and dream of a higher love, or even better—it's forbidden to forbid—a romance with Patrick Bruel or Brad Pitt or some TV anchor, yeah? When it comes to the eternal call of infinite love, the possibilities are infinite . . . QED! You're so right to devote yourself as you do. I applaud you from the bottom of my heart."

She blows me a kiss, sashays away, leaves me.

Marianne is triumphant, and I applaud with her. Just one damper on my side: Is there any hope of Marie or Chloe setting down their soul distress on paper and "elucidating it through narrative," as my learned colleagues would say? Our patients, Marianne's and mine, are probably too image-soaked to indulge in that kind of old-fangled pursuit. As for those who surrender to the sexual night of hackneyed autofiction, that's part of the program: no comparison with my exigent Carmelite.

Fortunately, Paul, who really does love me, arrives to rescue us from certainties and hypotheses that lead nowhere, as I'm prepared to admit. He's holding an open book, it's my copy of Diderot, he's reading as he walks in and doesn't stop. He's letting me know he wants to share in what I'm reading. He must have picked it up off my desk, my door is always open; he often borrows books of mine and as often returns them, with the utmost tact. After a sidelong, hostile glance at the departing Dr. Marianne Baruch, who was surely "bothering Sylvia," as he unceremoniously calls me, he starts reading out loud from *The Nun*.

> I am overwhelmed by tiredness, I am surrounded by terror, and rest escapes me. I have just reread at leisure these memoires that I wrote in haste, and I have realized that, though it was utterly unintentional, I had in each line shown myself to be as unhappy as I really was, but also much nicer than I really am. Could it be that we believe men to be less sensitive to the depiction of our suffering than to the image of our charms, and do we hope that it is much easier to seduce them than it is to touch their hearts? I do not know them well enough and I have not studied myself enough to know the answer. But if the Marquis, who is credited with being a man of exquisite taste, were to persuade himself that I am appealing not to his charity but to his lust, what would he think of me? This thought worries me. In fact he would be quite wrong to attribute to me personally an impulse that is characteristic of all women. I am a woman, perhaps a little flirtatious for all I know. But it is natural and unaffected.[36]

Paul lifts his head and looks at me.

"Have you any idea what she means?"

I don't respond, that's my role.

"A natural, unaffected woman? What's that?"

Silence from me again.

"'A woman dominated by hysteria experiences something infernal or divine.' What do you make of that, Sylvia? Shall I go on? 'Saint Teresa has said of devils, How luckless they are! They do not love.'"[37] Paul carries on reading out his latest discoveries in the Pléiade edition of Diderot.

Now I'm in a fix. I can't tell him about the conviction I have lately reached, which is that devils are inseparable from love, and that love, that is, God, goes hand in hand with its best enemy, the demonic, and that it's impossible to free oneself from demons without freeing oneself from God, and hence from love. This doesn't mean we must, or even can, eradicate love, whether diabolical or divine; that would be to castrate ourselves of our inner being and turn us away from the exterior world; it would deprive us of discovering, acting, wandering, journeying through the self. No, it means that it is possible to move through love indefinitely, infinitely, to make of love one's infinity-point. An eclipse, a bedazzlement. Teresa, again. A serenity. Very hard to put into words. I try saying something:

"There's no better Catholic than the devil."

My allusion to Baudelaire falls flat, as expected.[38] But that's also a part of my role: to plant a seed for later, or never.

Paul's not up to it yet. All of a sudden he's not interested in me anymore. He carefully places the book on my desk and saunters off with an air of insouciance, crooning: "Depoooosuit . . ." He's got perfect pitch, that boy! Suffering from psychomotor disharmony (another definition from his compensated autistic file), he needs love to screen his anxieties. He's got to think of himself as a lady-killer, he has to charm the girls, as many girls as possible, in hopes of finding the very best, though even if he found her he'd keep on looking. He dreams about the idea, he plays on it, a lot; he very seldom tries it out. I wouldn't be surprised if one day he took off from the MPH in pursuit of love and Love in an Indian ashram, a Jerusalem synagogue, a Roman church, a Venetian back street, a Chinese pagoda, why not? I wouldn't be the one to stop him.

I wouldn't stop anybody who felt that kind of need. Which includes each and every one of us when we feel excluded, forsaken, penniless, disabled, forgotten, erased, when we send the past to hell, or make a clean sweep of it, when we are sick of the nothingness of Nothingness . . .

Even me, I still dream of love, at my age! Not very often, of course, and only for a laugh.

And not today.

Today, writing to you, Mister Philosopher, after saying goodbye to Teresa, my love, I am faithless and lawless. Utterly available. Ready to listen to Paul with his perfect pitch, to Élise with her lavender flowers, and to all the rest. Ready to disappear into their sorrows and joys. A therapy, that's what love is. Freud stretched it out on the couch, not without reading you first, and I'm continuing the experiment. God is Love, and we listen to Him. A different kind of humanity began to take shape with and after you, Mister Philosopher, as it did with and after my Teresa. Checkmate to God, to Love? For sure, but not right now. Otherwise, hello Apocalypse, Ground Zero, reproductive cloning, synthetic wombs, the works! Please, not that. I too stretch Love out and operate on it, and I do so inside myself as well, of course. Delicately, laughingly, yes, and starting over, playing it out in that eternal and infinite recurrence. I try. "And will we checkmate this divine King?" "¿Daremos mate a ese rey divino?"

We'd be wrong to think "it was enough to know the pieces." But this King (Love, in other words) "doesn't give Himself but to those who give themselves entirely to Him." "Pensó bastaba conocer las piezas para dar mate, y es imposible, que no se da este Rey sino a quien se le da del todo."[39]

We are not done rereading Teresa, are we, Mister Philosopher? If I have moved you to meditate afresh upon those dwelling places I recently revisited, I will have accomplished what I set out to do.

Yours in respectful complicity,
Sylvia Leclercq

Notes

1. PRESENT BY DEFAULT

1. Gian Lorenzo Bernini (1598–1680), *The Transverberation*, in the Cornaro Chapel, Santa Maria della Vittoria, Rome.
2. Mary of Magdala has already foreshadowed the loss, absence, and reinvention of the body of love in the mystical experience: "I know not where they have laid him." She says to Jesus, mistaking him for a gardener, "If thou have borne him hence, tell me where thou hast laid him, and I will take him away." Jesus says to her, "Mary"; she answers, "Rabboni," meaning "master" (John 20:13–16).
3. *Life*, 29:11–14, *CW* 1:251–3.
4. VI *D*, 2:4, *CW* 2:368.
5. IV *D*, 2:2, *CW* 2:323.
6. Jacques Lacan, *Encore, The Seminar of Jacques Lacan*, trans. B. Fink, book 20, *On Feminine Sexuality, The Limits of Love and Knowledge 1972–1973* (London: Norton, 1999).
7. Stendhal, *A Roman Journal*, trans. and ed. Haakon Chevalier (New York: Orion, 1957), 133: "St Teresa is represented in the ecstasy of divine love. It is the most vivid and the most natural expression. . . . What divine artistry! What delight!"
8. *Life*, 6:4, *CW* 1:78–9.
9. Colette, *The Vagabond*, trans. Enid McLeod (London: Secker & Warburg, 1974), 158: "Femelle j'étais et femelle je me retrouve, pour en souffrir et pour en jouir."
10. Francisco de Osuna: ca. 1492–ca. 1540.
11. Sigmund Freud, *The Schreber Case*, trans. Andrew Webber (New York: Penguin, 2003).
12. *Life*, 16:1–6, *CW* 1:147–50.
13. Michel de Certeau, *The Mystic Fable*, trans. Michael B. Smith, vol. 1, *The Sixteenth and Seventeenth Centuries* (Chicago: University of Chicago Press, 1992), 23.
14. *Life*, 40:8, *CW* 1:357.
15. *Life*, 26:5, *CW* 1:226.
16. Bernardino de Laredo: 1492–1540.
17. *Life*, 23:15, *CW* 1:207.
18. Pedro de Alcántara: 1499–1562.

19. John of the Cross, *Ascent of Mount Carmel*, book 1, part 3, section 1, trans. and ed. E. Allison Peers (Tunbridge Wells, Kent: Burns & Oates, 1983), 21.

20. Council of Trent, 1545–1563.

21. IV *D*, 1:7–14, *CW* 2:319–22.

22. IV *D*, 1:11, *CW* 2:321.

23. *Letter* 237, to María de San José, March 28, 1578, *CL* 2:46.

24. *Critique*, *CW* 3:357.

25. Socrates: 460–399 B.C.E.

26. Plato: ca. 428–ca. 347 B.C.E.

27. Michel de Montaigne, *The Essays: A Selection*, trans. and ed. M. A. Screech (London: Penguin, 2004), book 2:12, 590: "I find it unacceptable that the power of God should be limited in this way by the rules of human language."

28. René Descartes, *Discourse on Method* (1637).

29. Arthur Rimbaud: 1854–1891.

30. Baruch Spinoza: 1633–1677.

31. G. W. Leibniz, *Discourse on Metaphysics and Related Writings*, ed. and trans. R. N. D. Martin and Stuart Brown (Manchester: Manchester University Press, 1988), 77.

32. Letter from Leibniz to André Morell (1696), translated from French by Lloyd Strickland (2007), www.leibniz-translations.com/morell1696.htm. [It quotes as its source the following: G. W. Leibniz, *Sämtliche schriften und briefe series I*, ed. Deutsche Akademie der Wissenschaften, 13:398. This book seems to be in German, with only excerpts translated.] Cf. M. Leroy, *Discours de métaphysique et correspondance avec Arnaud de G. W. Leibniz*, (Paris: Grua/ Presses Universitaires de France, 1948), 103.

33. Cf. J. K. Huysmans, *En Route* (Sawtry, U.K.: Dedalus, 2002), 221: "the virile soul of a monk."

34. John of the Cross: 1542–1591.

2. MYSTICAL SEDUCTION

1. Julia Kristeva, "Le bonheur des Béguines," in *Le jardin clos de l'âme. L'imaginaire des religieuses dans les Pays-Bas du Sud depuis le XIIIᵉ siècle*, ed. Paul Vanderbroeck (Brussels: Société des expositions, Palais des Beaux-Arts, February–May 1994).

2. See Gershom Scholem, *Major Trends in Jewish Mysticism*, 3rd ed. (New York: Schocken, 1995); *Zohar: The Book of Splendor* (New York: Schocken, 1995).

3. See Émile Boutroux, "Le mysticisme," *Bulletin de l'institut général psychologique*, 31 (1902); André Lalande, *Vocabulaire technique et critique de la philosophie*, ed. Félix Alcan (Paris: Presses Universitaires de France, 1926), 496.

4. Jacques Lacan, *Écrits*, trans. Bruce Fink (New York: Norton, 2006).

5. Denys the Areopagite (or Pseudo-Dionysius), *Complete Works*, trans. Colm Luibheid and Paul Rorem (Mahwah, N.J.: Paulist, 1987).

6. Plotinus: 204/5–270.

7. Aristotle: 384–322 B.C.E.

8. Exod. 3:1–6.

9. Ezek. 10:1–22.

10. *Sefer Yetzirah*, short treatise of some 1,600 words, third to twelfth century.

11. Judah Halevi: 1075–1141.

12. Moses Maimonides: 1135–1204.

13. Saadia ben Joseph of Fayum: 882–942. Author of *Commentary on* Sefer Yetzira, ca. 931.

14. Solomon Ibn Gabirol: 1020–1058.

15. Plato: 428–348 B.C.E.

16. Philo of Alexandria: ca. 10–45 B.C.E.

17. Bahya Ibn Paquda: tenth or eleventh century.

18. Abraham Abulafia: 1240–1291.

19. Moisés de León: second half of the thirteenth century.

20. Cf. André Néher, "La philosophie juive médiévale," in *Histoire de la philosophie*, ed. Y. Belaval (Paris: Gallimard, Pléiade Collection, 1969).

21. *Le Zohar*, trans. Jean de Pauly (Paris: Ernest Leroux, 1908); *The Zohar*, ed. H. Sperling and M. Simon, 5 vols. (London: Soncino, 1949).

22. Cf. Julia Kristeva, *Time and Sense: Proust and the Experience of Literature*, trans. Ross Guberman (New York: Columbia University Press, 1998), 148–9, 325.

23. Louis Massignon, *Al Hallaj: Mystic and Martyr*, trans. Herbert Mason (Princeton: Princeton University Press, 1994); Anne-Marie Schimmel, *Mystical Dimensions of Islam* (Chapel Hill: University of North Carolina Press, 1978).

24. Ibn al-Arabi: d. 1240 in Damascus.

25. Ibn al-Farid: d. 1235.

26. Jalal al-Din Rumi: d. 1273.

27. Al-Ghazali: 1058–1111.

28. Al-Hallaj: 857–922.

29. Cf. Noël J. Coulson, *A History of Islamic Law* (Edinburgh: Edinburgh University Press, 1964).

30. Al-Kindi: 800–873.

31. Albert the Great: 1200–1280.

32. Origen: 185–253.

33. Gregory of Nyssa: 335–394.

34. De Certeau, *The Mystic Fable*: "Since the thirteenth century (courtly love, etc.), a gradual religious demythification seems to be accompanied by a progressive mythification of love. The One has changed its site. It is no longer God but the other, and in a masculine literature, woman" (4); "for reasons that need clarifying, the woman's experience held up better against the cluttered ruins of symbolic systems, which were theological and masculine, and which thought of presence as the coming of a Logos" (6).

35. Thomas Aquinas: 1225–1274.

36. Jan van Ruysbroek: 1293–1381.

37. Hadewijch of Antwerp: ca. 1200–1260.

38. Ps. 42:7: "Deep calleth unto deep."

39. *Homo quidam nobilis*: "A certain nobleman went into a far country to receive for himself a kingdom, and to return" (Luke 19:12), commented on by Meister Eckhart, *Von dem edeln Menschen*. See *The Complete Mystical Works of Meister Eckhart*, trans. and ed. Maurice O'C. Walshe (New York: Crossroad, 2009), 544; for the short quotations, 422–4, 543–4.

40. Angelus Silesius: 1624–1677.

41. Henry Suso: ca. 1296–1365.

42. Johannes Tauler: ca. 1300–1361.

43. Nicholas Krebs of Cusa: 1401–1464.

44. Jakob Böhme: 1575–1624.

45. G. W. F. Hegel: 1770–1831.

46. Angelus Silesius, *Selections from* The Cherubinic Wanderer, trans. J. E. Crawford Flitch (Westport, Conn.: Hyperion, 1978), 148: "*The Mystical Abandonment.* Abandonment ensnareth God: / But the Abandonment supreme, / Which few there can comprehend, / Is to abandon even Him."

47. Hildegarde of Bingen: 1098–1179.

48. Angela of Foligno: 1248–1309.

49. Catherine of Siena: 1347–1380.

50. Francis of Assisi: 1182–1226.

51. Martin Luther: 1483–1546.

52. Henri de Lubac, *Corpus Mysticum: The Eucharist and the Church in the Middle Ages*, trans. Gemma Simmonds et al. (London: SCM, 2006), 256: "Of the three terms: historical body, sacramental body and ecclesial body that it was a case of putting into order amongst each other, the caesura was originally placed between the first and second, whereas it subsequently came to be placed between the second and the third."

53. Cf. de Certeau, *The Mystic Fable*: "After the middle of the twelfth century, the expression [*corpus mysticum*] no longer designated the Eucharist, as it had previously, but the Church. Conversely, 'corpus verum' no longer designated the Church but the Eucharist. . . . The Church, the social 'body' of Christ, is henceforth the (hidden) signified of a sacramental 'body' held to be a visible signifier . . . the showing of a presence beneath the 'species' (or appearances) of the consecrated bread and wine. . . . The sacrament ('sumere Christum') and the Church ('sumi a Christo') were joined . . . in the mode of the Church-Eucharist pair . . . of a visible community . . . and a secret action (*ergon*) or 'mystery' . . ." (82–3). "The mystical term is therefore a mediating one between the historical 'body' that becomes 'similar to a Code that is the law' and the 'mystery,' the sacramental body . . . recast in the philosophical formality . . . as one 'thing' which is visible, designating another, which is invisible. The visibility of that object replaces the communal celebration, which is a community operation. . . . The mystical third is no more than the object of an intention. It is something that needs to be made manifest . . . constructed, on the basis of two clear, authoritative 'documents': the scriptural corpus and the Eucharistic ostension." "A mystical Church body would have to be 'invented,' in the same sense in which there was to be an invention of the New World. That endeavor was the Reformation. It was gradually divided into two tendencies: one (Protestant) giving a privileged status to the scriptural corpus, the other (Catholic) to the sacrament" (84). "Furthermore, despite the ups and downs of the papal states, from the Lateran Council until the reformism following the Council of Trent (1545–1563), that pastoral (centered on the only body that could symbolize and sustain the restoration/institution of a visible Church) would have great stability. . . . One trait is of special interest in the question of the apparition of mystical science: the progressive concentration of these debates around *seeing*" (87–9).

54. Lateran Council III: 1179.

55. Lateran Council IV: 1215.

56. Council of Trent: 1545–1563.

57. Antonio Vivaldi: 1678–1741.

58. Jacopo Robusti, Il Tintoretto: 1519–1594.

59. Martin Heidegger, "What Is Metaphysics?" *Basic Writings*, rev. and expanded ed., ed. David Farrell Krell (London: Routledge, 1993), 108.

60. Immanuel Kant, *Critique of Pure Reason*, trans. J. M. D. Meiklejohn, part second, I, 3, *Canon of Pure Reason* (1781; London: Dent/Everyman's Library, 1945), 458–9.

3. DREAMING, MUSIC, OCEAN

1. Koran, Sura LVII.
2. Alfred Rosenberg:1893–1946. See *The Myth of the Twentieth Century*, trans. V. Biro (1931; Torrance, Calif.: Noontide, 1983).
3. Marcel Duchamp: 1887–1968.
4. David Bakan, *Sigmund Freud and the Jewish Mystical Tradition* (New York: Dover, 2005).
5. Letter to R. Rolland, July 20, 1929, in Ernst L. Freud, ed., *Letters of Sigmund Freud, 1873–1939* (London: Hogarth, 1970), 389.
6. Wilhelm Fliess: 1858–1928.
7. Letter to W. Fliess, in Jeffrey Moussaieff Masson, trans. and ed., *The Complete Letters of Sigmund Freud to Wilhelm Fliess, 1887–1904* (Cambridge, Mass.: Belknap, 1985), 398.
8. Sigmund Freud, *Civilization and Its Discontents*, trans. David McLintock (London: Penguin, 2002), 10.
9. Letter from Romain Rolland to Freud, December 5, 1927, in Francis Doré and Marie-Laurie Prévost, eds., *Selected Letters of Romain Rolland* (New Delhi: Indira Gandhi National Centre for the Arts and Oxford University Press, 1990), 87.
10. "Black mud": Quoted in Carl Jung, *Memories, Dreams, and Reflections*, Waukegan: Fontana, 1992, p. 150.
11. Sigmund Freud, *New Introductory Lectures on Psychoanalysis*, trans. J. Strachey (London: Pelican, 1977), 60.
12. Sigmund Freud, *The Future of an Illusion*, trans. J. A. Underwood and Shaun Whiteside (London: Penguin, 2005), 71–2.
13. William McGuire, ed. *The Freud/Jung Letters*, trans. Ralph Manheim (London: Picador, 1979), 146.
14. Letter to Anon., in *Letters of Sigmund Freud, 1873–1939*, 435.
15. Cf. Paul-Laurent Assoun, "Résurgences et dérives de la mystique," in *Nouvelle revue de psychanalyse*, no. 22 (Fall 1980).
16. Freud, *New Introductory Lectures*, 112.

4. *HOMO VIATOR*

1. See Marcelle Auclair, *Thérèse d'Avila, Œuvres complètes*, 2 vols. (Paris: Desclée de Brouwer, 1964); Thérèse d'Avila, *Œuvres complètes*, (Paris: Éditions du Cerf, 1995).
2. Meister Eckhart, *The Complete Mystical Works of Meister Eckhart*, trans. and ed. Maurice O'C. Walshe (New York: Crossroad, 2009), 422, 424.
3. "Yearning" or "craving" are attempts to render the Freudian term *Sehnsucht*: "nostalgia," "longing," "ardent desire," not necessarily addressing the past, but rather the absence of the love object.
4. *Life*, 3:5, *CW* 1:63.
5. Jean Baruzi, *Saint Jean de la Croix* (Paris: Presses Universitaires de France, 1924; Éditions Salvator, 1999).
6. Teresa of Avila, *Poems*, "Aspirations Toward Eternal Life," *CW* 3:375.
7. *Testimonies*, 58:4, *CW* 1:418.
8. VI *D*, 9:2, *CW* 2:411–12.
9. Letter 177, to don Lorenzo de Cepeda, January 17, 1577, *CL* 1:476–77.

5. PRAYER, WRITING, POLITICS

1. *Life*, 10:7, *CW* 1:108.
2. *Soliloquies*, 15:3, *CW* 1:459.
3. Ibid., 17:2, *CW* 1:461.
4. *Letter* 219, to Gaspar de Salazar, December 7, 1577, *CL* 1:583.
5. Theopathy: from "*pathon ta theia*" (cf. Pseudo-Dionysius the Areopagite, *Divine Names* 2 n, 9), or "to suffer God" as the supreme perfection.
6. Chrétien de Troyes: poet and troubadour, late twelfth century.
7. *Life*, 11:5, *CW* 1:112.
8. *Life*, 10:7, *CW* 1:108.
9. V *D*, 2:7, 2:343.
10. Donald W. Winnicott, "Mind and Its Relation to the Psyche-Soma" (1949), in *Collected Papers, Through Paediatrics to Psycho-Analysis*, (London: Tavistock, 1958), 243–54.
11. *Life*, 20:9 *CW* 1:176.
12. *Testimonies*, 3:1, *CW* 1:382.
13. *Letter* 24, to don Lorenzo de Cepeda, January 17, 1570, *CL* 1:83.
14. Cf. Friedrich Nietzsche, *The Anti-Christ*, trans. H. L. Mencken (1920; Tucson: Sharp, 1999).
15. *Life*, 20:9–10, *CW* 1:176.
16. *Testimonies*, 3:5–6, *CW* 1:383.
17. "*Mantener la tela*": "It was the custom at the joust for one group of supporters to hold up a banner bearing the colors of the group's favorite knight." *Notes to the Life*, *CW*, 1:474. Cf. M. Alonso, *Enciclopedia del idioma* (Madrid: Aguilar, 1968), 3: 3909.
18. *Life*, 18:10–13, *CW* 1:161–2.
19. *Life*, 18:14, *CW* 1:163.
20. "¡Ay, qué vida tan amarga / Do no se goza el Señor!" These two lines at the start of verse 5 in this poem reminds us of Plotinus's "Leave everything!" (*aphele panta*), associated with Aristotle's contemplation (*theoria*) and understood as a "denuding" or detachment, as well as a *surpassing* of all representation (*aphairesis*), and *Gelassenheit* (abandonment) in Angelus Silesius's sense; see *Selections from* The Cherubinic Wanderer, trans. J. E. Crawford Flitch (Westport, Conn.: Hyperion, 1978), 1, 22.
21. *Poems*, "Aspirations Toward Eternal Life," *CW* 3:375.
22. *Life*, 20–21, *CW* 1:172–90.

6. HOW TO WRITE SENSIBLE EXPERIENCE

1. The Spanish title *Libro de la Vida* (*Book of the Life*), was given by the Augustinian friar Luis de León: "The book of the life of Mother Teresa of Jesus and account of some of the graces she received from God, written by her own hand by order of her confessor for whom it was intended." The autograph manuscript is stored in the library of the Escorial Palace, at the original request of Philip II. It goes by the title: "Book of Mother Teresa of Jesus written in her own hand with the approval of Fr. Domingo Báñez, her confessor, the Prime Chair at Salamanca."
2. The first draft of *The Way of Perfection* was completed in 1564 and reworked in subsequent years. Teresa revised the text in 1569, and it was ready for publication by 1579 under this title,

chosen by her. However it was not to appear until 1583, after her death, in a highly "corrected" version. It was republished by Fr. Gratian in 1585. In 1588, at last, Luis de León oversaw the release of the original as revised by Teresa.

3. Chapters 1–20 of the *Foundations* were written in 1573; the next, 21–27, date from 1580; and 28–31 were completed in 1583. Ana de Jesús and Jerome Gratian were responsible for the first publication, in 1610, of the "Book of the Foundations of the Discalced Carmelite sisters, written by the Mother Foundress Teresa of Jesus."

4. *Life*, 13:15, *CW* 1:129–30.

5. VI *D*, 5:3, *CW* 2:387.

6. *Life*, 11:9–10, *CW* 1:114–15.

7. *Life*, 11:16, *CW* 1:118.

8. *Way*, 19:4, *CW* 2:108.

9. *Life*, 11:6, *CW* 1:112–13.

10. *Life*, 11:7, *CW* 1:113.

11. Dominique de Courcelles, *Langage mystique et avènement de la modernité* (Paris: Champion, 2003), 189–294.

12. Estéban García-Albea, *Teresa de Jesús, una ilustre epiléptica o una explicación epilogenética de los éxtasis de la Santa* (Madrid: Huerga y Fierro, 2002); Pierre Vercelletto, *Expérience et état mystique. La maladie de sainte Thérèse d'Avila* (Paris: Éditions La Bruyère, 2000).

13. Edmund Husserl, *Ideas: General Introduction to Pure Phenomenology*, §70, trans. W. R. Boyce Gibson (London: George Allen & Unwin, 1931), 201.

14. *Life*, 20:2–4, *CW* 1:173–74.

15. *Life*, 16:4, *CW* 1:149.

16. Charles Baudelaire, *Artificial Paradises*, trans. Stacy Diamond (1860; New York: Citadel, 1998): "You endow the tree with your passions and desires; its capriciously swaying limbs become your own, so that soon you yourself are the tree" (51); "cause and effect, subject and object, mesmerizer and somnambulist" (25).

17. J.-L. Chrétien, *L'appel et la réponse* (Paris: Éditions de Minuit, 1992), 125.

18. *Way*, 19:3–5, *CW* 2:107–9.

19. *Way*, 19:4, *CW* 2:108.

20. *Way*, 19:6–7, *CW* 2:110.

21. *Way*, 19:8, *CW* 2:111.

22. *Way*, 19:13, *CW* 2:113.

23. *Way*, 19:9–10, *CW* 2:111.

24. *Way*, 19:10–12, *CW* 2:112.

25. IV *D*, 2:2, *CW* 2:323.

26. *The Rubaiyat of Omar Khayyam*, trans. Edward Henry Whinfield, 1883; http://therubaiyat.com/whinfield (accessed May 14, 2011).

27. Dante, *The Divine Comedy*, trans. Henry W. Longfellow, *Paradiso*, canto 19 (London: Capella, 2006), 337.

28. Pierre Ronsard, "To His Mistress," trans. A. S. Kline, 2004; http://poetryintranslation.com (accessed May 14, 2011).

29. William Shakespeare, *A Midsummer Night's Dream*, act 2, scene 1.

30. Charles Baudelaire, "To Her Who Is Too Gay," in *Selected Poems of Charles Baudelaire*, trans. Geoffrey Wagner (New York: Grove, 1974).

31. Rainer Maria Rilke, "Epitaph," trans. Erik Bendix, http://movingmoment.com/poetry/Rilke's Epitaph.htm (May 14, 2011).

32. Philippe Sollers, *Fleurs. Le grand roman de l'érotisme floral* (Paris: Hermann Littérature, 2006).

7. THE IMAGINARY OF AN UNFINDABLE SENSE

1. Aristotle, *Metaphysics*, ed. and trans. John Warrington (London: Dent, 1956), 346: "Now thought does think itself, because it shares in the intelligibility of its object. It becomes intelligible by contact with the intelligible, so that thought and object of thought are one."

2. In Jewish mysticism, the contemplation of God's Throne-Chariot (*Merkabah*) is the goal of a long journey through the *Hekhalot* or celestial palaces/temples (cf. the treatises on the Great Hekhalot, or *Hekhalot Rabbati*, the Small or *Hekhalot Zutarti*, etc.). This ascent toward the seven heavenly abodes forms part of the synagogal liturgy and features in a more secret scholarly language, the Shi'ur Qomah.

3. See Maimonides, *A Guide for the Perplexed*, trans. M. Friedlaender (New York: Dutton, 1904).

4. Cf. St. Augustine, *De Trinitate* [*The Trinity*] (399–419), trans. Edmund Hill (New York: New City Press, 1991).

5. I *D*, 1–3, *CW* 2:283–4.

6. *D, Epilogue*: JHS, *CW* 2:451.

7. Bernardino de Laredo: 1482–1540.

8. Luis de la Palma: 1560–1641.

9. Ignatius Loyola, *Spiritual Exercises*, Second Annotation: "For it is not knowing much, but realizing and relishing things interiorly [*mas el sentir y gustar de las cosas internamente*], that contents and satisfies the soul."

10. Jerónimo Nadal: 1507–1581. See his "Oraison pour ceux de la compagnie Mon. N. 4," quoted in Victoriano Larrañaga, *Sainte Thérèse d'Avila, Saint Ignace de Loyola: Convergences* (Paris: Pierre Téqui Éditeur, 1998), 125.

11. I *D*, 2:5, *CW* 2:290.

12. I *D*, 2:8, *CW* 2:291.

13. IV *D*, 2:1–2, *CW* 2:323.

14. IV *D*, 2:2–4, *CW* 2:323–24.

15. IV *D*, 2:6, *CW* 2:324.

16. IV *D*, 3:2, *CW* 2:328.

17. VII *D*, 2:11, *CW* 2:438.

18. VI *D*, 2:6, *CW* 2:369.

19. Cf. Francisco de Osuna, *The Third Spiritual Alphabet*, trans. and with an introduction by Mary E. Giles (Mahwah, N.J.: Paulist, 1981).

20. IV *D*, 3:2, *CW* 2:327–28.

21. VI *D*, 4:4, *CW* 2:380.

22. VI *D*, 6:10, *CW* 2:395.

23. VII *D*, 1:3, *CW* 2:428.

24. VI *D*, 2:6, *CW* 2:369.

25. I *D*, 2:7, *CW* 2:290.

26. *Testimonies*, 26, *CW* 1:399.

27. V *D*, 2:2–5, *CW* 2:341–3. Compare with the reading of this passage by Michel de Goedt, "La prière de l'école de Thérèse d'Avila aujourd'hui," in *Recherches et expériences spirituelles, Conférences* (Paris: Cathedral of Notre-Dame de Paris, 1982).

28. *Letter* 237, to María de San José, March 28, 1578, *CL* 2:46.

29. VI *D*, 5:1, *CW* 2:386.

30. VII *D*, 2:1–3, *CW* 2:432–33.

31. The practice of "fiction" in Teresa can be approached in the light of Jean Ladrière's interpretations of "the language of the spirituals," or mystics, marked by the linguistic theories of D. D. Evans and J. L. Austin (Jean Ladrière, "Le langage des spirituels" [1975], in *L'Articulation du sens* [Paris: Éditions du Cerf, 1984]). Descriptive at the same time as engaging the affective and sensory experience of both speaker and hearer, the language of such spirituals is posited as a "self-implicating act," consisting in "rendering what is uttered actually the case in it; in this sense, one can say that the act of faith is the effectuation of its content" (79). Further, "there is a genuine continuity between the language of the spirituals and their experience; experience is prolonged in and by the word [*parole*], while the latter enriches experience by endowing it with structure and intelligibility" (80). Therefore if any truth is contained in this powerfully analogical, allegorical, and symbolic language, its credibility "can only be established by means of a detour, regardless of the language in which it is proposed." This "detour" being defined as "a genuine affinity with the person speaking," the "spiritual language consequently becomes a "language of affinity" (82–83) (my translation—LSF).

32. VI *D*, 5:2–3, *CW* 2:386–87.

33. VII *D*, 2: 3–6, *CW* 2:434–35.

34. Yirmiyahu Yovel, *The Other Within: The Marranos. Split Identity and Emerging Modernity* (Princeton: Princeton University Press, 2008); *The Mystic and the Wanderer: Conversos in the Culture of Golden Age Spain*, forthcoming (in Hebrew).

8. EVERYTHING SO CONSTRAINED ME

1. Teresa is reported to have said to Juan de la Miseria: "Dios te perdone, fray Juan, que ya que me pintaste, me has pintado fea y legañosa." Esteban García-Albea, "La epilepsia extática de Teresa de Jesús," *Revista de neurología* 37, no. 9 (2003): 880.

2. *Found.*, 17:6, *CW* 3:180–81.

3. Marcelle Auclair, *La vie de sainte Thérèse d'Avila* (Paris: Seuil, 1950); Rosa Rossi, *Esperienza interiore e storia nell'autobiografia di Teresa d'Avila* (Bari: Adriatica Editrice, 1977); Dominique de Courcelles, *Thérèse d'Avila, femme d'écriture et de pouvoir dans l'Espagne du Siècle d'Or* (Grenoble: J. Million, 1993); Mercedes Allende salazar, *Thérèse d'Avila, l'image au feminine* (Paris: Seuil, 2002); Alison Weber, *Teresa of Avila and the Rhetoric of Feminism* (Princeton: Princeton University Press, 1996); Gillian T. W. Ahlgren, *Entering Teresa of Avila's Interior Castle* (New York: Paulist, 2005); Mary Frohlich, *The Intersubjectivity of the Mystic: A Study of Teresa of Avila's Interior Castle* (Atlanta: Scholars Press, 1994); Michel de Certeau, *The Mystic Fable*, op. cit.; Denis Vasse, *L'Autre du désir et le Dieu de la foi* (Paris: Seuil, 1991); Jean-Noël Vuarnet, *Le Dieu des femmes* (Paris: Editions de l'Herne, 1989); Américo Castro, *Teresa la santa y otros ensayos* (Madrid: Alianza, 1982); and *De la edad conflictiva. Crisis de la cultura española en el siglo XVII* (1961; repr. Madrid: Taurus, 1972); Antonio Márquez, *Los alumbrados* (Madrid: Taurus, 1972); Marcel Bataillon, *Erasme et l'Espagne* (Geneva: Droz, 1998).

4. Joseph Pérez, *Thérèse d'Avila* (Paris: Fayard, 2007), esp. 155, on the incorruption of the corpse.

5. *Life*, 3:2, *CW* 1:61.

6. *Life*, 2:6, *CW* 1:59.

7. *Life*, Prologue, *CW* 1:53.

8. *Life*, 1:1–3, *CW* 1:54–55.

9. *Found.*, 31:46, *CW* 3:306.

10. See Bartolomé Bennassar, *Le Siècle d'Or de l'Espagne* (Paris: Robert Laffont, 1982).

11. Jorge Manrique: 1440–1479. See *"Coplas* on the Death of His Father,"* trans. Thomas Walsh, in *Hispanic Anthology* (New York: Putnam's, 1920).

12. *Life*, 3:4, *CW* 1:62.

13. St. Jerome, Letter 22, "To Eustochium," in *Nicene and Post-Nicene Fathers*, trans. W. H. Fremantle, G. Lewis, and W. G. Martley, Second Series, vol. 6, ed. Philip Schaff and Henry Wace (Buffalo, N.Y.: Christian Literature, 1893); http://newadvent.org (accessed November 15, 2012).

14. Francisco Goya: 1746–1828. Found in *Album* C.88.

15. *Way*, 36:6–7, *CW* 2:179–80.

16. *Way*, 36:4, *CW* 2:179.

17. *Way*, 36:6, *CW* 2:180.

18. *Life*, 2:3, *CW* 1:58.

19. *Life*, 2:3–5, *CW* 1:58–59.

20. *Life*, 3:7, *CW* 1:63.

21. *Life*, 31:20, *CW* 1:273.

22. *Way*, 12:7, *CW* 2:84.

23. *Life*, 4:1, *CW* 1:64.

24. *Life*, 31:23, 25, *CW* 1:274–75.

9. HER LOVESICKNESS

1. *Life*, 4:2, *CW* 1:65.

2. *Life*, 4:9, *CW* 1:69.

3. Francisco de Osuna, *The Third Spiritual Alphabet*, trans. and with an introduction by Mary E. Giles (Mahwah, N.J.: Paulist, 1981), 165, 562, 356, 359.

4. Ibid., 356–59.

5. *Life*, 8:3, *CW* 1:95.

6. *Life*, 7:1, *CW* 1:82.

7. *Life*, 4:9, *CW* 1:69.

8. *Life*, 5:7, *CW* 1:74.

9. *Life*, 5:8, *CW* 1:74.

10. Jean-Martin Charcot, "The Faith-Cure," *New Review*, 7 (January 1893): 73–108: "It is striking to find that several of these thaumaturges suffered from the very malady whose manifestations they would henceforth cure: St. Francis of Assisi and St. Teresa, whose shrines are among those where miracles most frequently occur, were undeniable hysterics themselves" (*unfindable*: LSF trans.).

11. *Life*, 5:9, *CW* 1:75.

12. Josef Breuer (Josef Breuer and Sigmund Freud, *Studies on Hysteria*, trans. and ed. James Strachey [New York: Basic Books, 2000], 232): "Among hysterics may be found people of the clearest intellect, strongest will, greatest character and highest critical power. No amount of genuine, solid mental endowment is excluded by hysteria, although actual achievements are often made impossible by the illness. After all, the patron saint of hysterics, St. Theresa, was a woman of genius with great practical capacity." On the subject of female sexuality, sainthood, and hysteria, see also Cristina Mazzoni, *Saint Hysteria: Neurosis, Mysticism and Gender in European Culture* (Ithaca: Cornell University Press, 1996).

13. García-Albea, *Teresa de Jesús*.

14. Pierre Vercelletto, *Expérience et état mystique. La maladie de sainte Thérèse d'Avila* (Paris: Editions La Bruyère, 2000).

15. *Life*, 6:1–2, *CW* 1:76–77.

16. *Life*, 5:10–11, *CW* 1:75–76.

17. *Life*, 7:10, *CW* 1:87.

18. *Life*, 7:1, *CW* 1:82.

19. *Life*, 7:5, *CW* 1:85.

20. Francisco Gómez de Quevedo y Villegas: 1580–1645.

21. *Life*, 7:2, *CW* 1:83.

22. *Life*, 7:13, *CW* 1:88–89.

23. *Life*, 1:3, *CW* 1:55.

24. *Life*, 7:14, *CW* 1:89.

25. Ibid.

26. *Life*, 5:3, *CW* 1:71.

27. *Life*, 5:6, *CW* 1:73.

28. Ibid.

29. *Life*, 31:20–22, *CW* 1:274.

30. *Way*, 12:7, *CW* 2:84.

31. *Meditations*, 2:23–24, *CW* 2:232–33.

32. *Life*, 2:2, *CW* 1:57.

33. *Life*, 2:3–4, *CW* 1:58.

34. *Life*, 7:6–7, *CW* 1:85–86.

35. *Life*, 7:6, *CW* 1:85–86.

36. *Life*, 7:8, *CW* 1:86.

37. *Life*, 6:6–8, *CW* 1:80–81.

10. THE IDEAL FATHER AND THE HOST

1. *Life*, 7:12, *CW* 1:89.

2. *Life*, 15:10, *CW* 1:144.

3. *Life*, 25:21, *CW* 1:222–23.

4. VI *D*, 2:6–7, *CW* 2:369.

5. VI *D*, 3:1, *CW* 2:370–71.

6. See Caroline W. Bynum, *Holy Feast and Holy Fast: The Religious Significance of Food to Medieval Women* (Berkeley: University of California Press, 1988).
7. *Life*, 29:4, *CW* 1:247.
8. VII *D*, 2:6, *CW* 2:435.
9. *Medit.*, 5:4, *CW* 2:249.
10. *Medit.*, 5:5, *CW* 2:249.
11. *Medit.*, 1:9–10, *CW* 2:220–21.
12. *Way*, 7:8, *CW* 2:70.
13. *Testimonies*, 31, *CW* 1:402.
14. Ibid.

11. BOMBS AND RAMPARTS

1. Élisabeth Reynaud, *Thérèse d'Avila ou le divin plaisir* (Paris: Fayard, 1997).
2. Miguel de Unamuno: 1864–1936.
3. Piero della Francesca: 1415/1420–1492.
4. "Low Food" is a translation of Madeleine Ferrières's title: *Nourritures canailles* (Paris: Seuil, 2007).
5. Francisco de Borja: 1510–1572.
6. *Life*, 8:12, *CW* 1:100.
7. Ibid.
8. *Life*, 8:3, *CW* 1:95.

12. "*CRISTO COMO HOMBRE*"

1. *Life*, 9:1, *CW* 1:100–1.
2. *Life*, 9:4, *CW* 1:101.
3. *Life*, 9:6, *CW* 1:102.
4. Matthias Grünewald: 1475–1528.
5. *Life*, 10:1, *CW* 1:105.
6. *Life*, 9:9, *CW* 1:104.
7. St. Augustine, *Confessions* 11.27.
8. *Life*, 9:8, *CW* 1:103.
9. *Life*, 9:6, *CW* 1:102.
10. *Way*, 26:9, *CW* 2:136: "Lo que podéis hacer para ayuda de esto, procurad traer una imagen o retrato de este Señor que sea a vuestro gusto; no para traerle en el seno y nunca le mirar, sino para hablar muchas veces con Él, que Él os dará qué le decir. Como habláis con otras personas, ¿por qué os han más de faltar palabras para hablar con Dios?"
11. Plato, *The Banquet*, ca. 375 B.C.E.
12. *Life*, 10:2, *CW* 1:105.
13. *Life*, 27:2, *CW* 1:228.
14. *Life*, 29:7, *CW* 1:249.
15. *Life*, 10:1, *CW* 1:105.
16. Ibid.

13. IMAGE, VISION, AND RAPTURE

1. *Life*, 4:7, *CW* 1:67.
2. *Life*, 29:9, *CW* 1:250.
3. *Life*, 20:3, *CW* 1:173.
4. *Way*, 22:3, *CW* 2:123.
5. *Life*, 29:13–14, *CW* 1:252–53.
6. *Testimonies*, 14, *CW* 1:392–93.
7. VI *D*, 4:5–6, *CW* 2:380.
8. VI *D*, 4:6, *CW* 2:381.
9. VI *D*, 4:7, *CW* 2:381.
10. VI *D*, 4:8, *CW* 2:382.
11. VI *D*, 4:9, *CW* 2:382.
12. *Life*, 26:5, *CW* 1:226.
13. VI *D*, 4:8, *CW* 2:381–82.
14. VI *D*, 8:2, *CW* 2:405.
15. VI *D*, 8:3, *CW* 2:406–7.
16. VI *D*, 9:4, *CW* 2:411–12.
17. *Life*, 4:7, *CW* 1:68.
18. Ibid.
19. VII *D*, 2:4, *CW* 2:434.
20. IV *D*, 1:8, *CW* 2:319.
21. Mercedes Allendesalazar, *Thérèse d'Avila, l'image au féminin* (Paris: Seuil, 2002).

14. "THE SOUL ISN'T IN POSSESSION OF ITS SENSES . . ."

1. *Life*, 18:2, *CW* 1:158.
2. *Life*, 18:1, *CW* 1:157.
3. *Life*, 18:2, *CW* 1:158.
4. *Life*, 18:4, *CW* 1:158.
5. *Life*, 18:12–14, *CW* 1:162–63.
6. *Life*, 19:2, *CW* 1:164.
7. *Life*, 14:8, *CW* 1:137.
8. *Life*, 19:9, *CW* 1:168.
9. Giovanni Battista Tiepolo: 1696–1770.
10. *Life*, 20:24, *CW* 1:182–83.
11. *Life*, 20:25, *CW* 1:183.
12. *Life*, 20:24, *CW* 1:183.
13. *Life*, 20:15, *CW* 1:178–79.
14. *Life*, 20:12, *CW* 1:177.
15. Ibid.
16. *Life*, 18:1, *CW* 1:157–58.
17. *Life*, 18:12–13, *CW* 1:162.
18. *Life*, 18:10, *CW* 1:161.

19. *Life*, 20:3–4, *CW* 1:173.
20. *Life*, 20:5, *CW* 1:174.
21. *Life*, 20:7–8, *CW* 1:175.
22. *Life*, 20:9, *CW* 1:176.
23. *Life*, 20:12, *CW* 1:177.

15. A CLINICAL LUCIDITY

1. Marguerite Duras, *The Vice-Consul*, trans. Eileen Ellenbogen (London: Hamish Hamilton, 1968), 61. The first part of the quote was mistranslated by Ellenbogen.
2. Marguerite Duras, *Destroy, She Said*, trans. Barbara Bray (New York: Grove, 1994).
3. Marguerite Duras, *Hiroshima mon amour* and *Une aussi longue absence*, trans. Richard Seaver and Barbara Wright (London: Calder & Boyars, 1966), 65: "All I could see were the similarities between this dead body and mine . . . screaming at me."
4. Marcel Proust, "The Prisoner," in *In Search of Lost Time*, trans. and with an introduction and notes by Peter Collier, ed. Christopher Prendergast (London: Penguin, 2002), 5:357.
5. Marcel Proust, *Time Regained*, trans. Stephen Hudson (London: Chatto and Windus, 1949), chap. 2: "A material of its own, a new one, of a special transparency and sonority, compact, fresh and pink" (215); "Ideas are substitutes for sorrows" (260).
6. Maurice Barrès: 1862–1923.
7. See Julia Kristeva, *Time and Sense: Proust and the Experience of Literature*, trans. Ross Guberman (New York: Columbia University Press, 1998), 106–8, 245.
8. *Way*, 28:10, *CW* 2:144.
9. Colette, *Le pur et l'impur*, in *Œuvres* (Paris: Gallimard, 1991), 3:565: "Ce qui me manque, je m'en passe."
10. Colette, *Mes apprentissages*, in *Œuvres*, 3:1053: "Ce bon gros amour . . ."
11. Colette, *Retreat from Love*, trans. and with an introduction by Margaret Crosland (London: Peter Owen, 1974), 27.
12. Colette, *La naissance du jour*, in *Œuvres*, 3:290: "On possède dans l'abstention, et seulement dans l'abstention . . . pûreté de ceux qui se prodiguent."
13. Fyodor Dostoyevsky, *The Devils*, trans. and with an introduction by David Magarshack (London: Penguin, 1971), 586–87.
14. Fyodor Dostoyevsky, letter to A. N. Maikov, Florence, May 15/27, 1869, in Joseph Frank and David I. Goldstein, eds., *Selected Letters of Fyodor Dostoyevsky* (New Brunswick: Rutgers University Press, 1987), 311: "The main reason [for not writing] was despondency."
15. Gérard Labrunie (Gérard de Nerval), "El desdichado," trans. Richmond Lattimore, in *The Anchor Anthology of French Poetry*, ed. Angel Flores (New York: Anchor, 2000), 9: "Twice have I forced the crossing of the Acheron / and played on Orpheus's lyre in alternate complaint / Mélusine's cries against the moaning of the Saint."
16. *Life*, 20:18, *CW* 1:180.
17. *Life*, 20:19, *CW* 1:180.
18. *Life*, 20:22, *CW* 1:181.
19. *Life*, 29:11, *CW* 1:251.
20. *Life*, 10:1, *CW* 1:105.

21. *Life*, 29:8, *CW* 1:250.
22. *Life*, 4:9, *CW* 1:68.
23. *Life*, 4:9, *CW* 1:68–69.
24. *Way*, 38:9, *CW* 2:188.

16. THE MINX AND THE SAGE

1. *Life*, 23:7, *CW* 1:203.
2. Colette, *Les Vrilles de la vigne*, in *Œuvres* (Paris: Gallimard, 1991), 1:961: "Je voudrais dire, dire, dire, tout ce que je sais, tout ce que je pense, tout ce que je devine, tout ce qui m'enchante, et me blesse, et m'étonne" (my translation—LSF).
3. *Life*, 30:16, *CW* 1:261.
4. *Life*, 30:19, *CW* 1:262.
5. *Life*, 29:4, *CW* 1:247.
6. *Life*, 31:12, *CW* 1:269.
7. *Life*, 31:13, *CW* 1:269.
8. *Life*, 31:16, *CW* 1:270.
9. *Way*, 12:1, *CW* 2:81.
10. *Way*, 40:9, *CW* 2:195.

17. BETTER TO HIDE . . . ?

1. Cf. Joseph Pérez, *L'Espagne de Philippe II* (Paris: Fayard, 1999), 140 et seq.
2. Miguel de Cervantes, *Don Quixote* (1885; Project Gutenberg) first part, chap. 1, trans. John Ormsby, www.gutenberg.org/cache/epub/996/pg996.html. Release date July 27, 2004. Accessed November 11, 2012.
3. Juan de Ávila: 1499–1569.
4. Luis de Granada: 1504–1588.
5. Fernando de Valdés: 1483–1568.
6. Melchor Cano: 1509–1560.
7. Martin Luther : 1483–1546.
8. Juan de Valdés: 1498 (?).
9. Francisco Jiménez de Cisneros: 1436–1517.
10. Benito Arias Montano: 1527–1598.
11. Christophe Plantin: 1520–1589.
12. *Life*, 24:2, *CW* 1:209.
13. *Life*, 19:4, *CW* 1:166.
14. *Life*, 18:4, *CW* 1:159.
15. *Life*, 40:8, *CW* 1:357.
16. *Life*, 18:4, *CW* 1:159.
17. *Life*, 9:2, *CW* 1:101.
18. *Life*, 27:2, *CW* 1:228.
19. *Life*, 27:3, *CW* 1:228–29.
20. *Life*, 27:5, 7, *CW* 1:229–30 (adapted).

21. *Life*, 27:8–10, *CW* 1:230–32.

22. *Life*, 28:1, *CW* 1:237.

23. *Life*, 28:3, *CW* 1:237–38.

24. *Life*, 28:4–5, *CW* 1:238–39.

25. Rosa Rossi, *Thérèse d'Avila* (Paris: Cerf, 1989), 67: "S'unir, se transformer en Dieu [to be united, to be transformed into God]."

26. V D, 1:12, *CW* 2:340.

27. VI D, 4:4, *CW* 2:380.

28. I D, 1:3, *CW* 2:284.

29. VII D, 2:3, *CW* 2:434.

30. *Life*, 28:9, *CW* 1:241.

31. *Life*, 29:3, *CW* 1:247.

32. *Life*, 28:8, *CW* 1:240.

33. *Life*, 40:1, *CW* 1:354.

18. . . . OR "TO DO WHAT LIES WITHIN MY POWER"?

1. *Letter* 5, to padre García de Toledo, 1565, *CL* 1:41.

2. *Way*, 7:8, *CW* 2:70 (amended).

3. VII D, 2:10, *CW* 2:437.

4. *Life*, 10:7, *CW* 1:108.

5. *Life*, 23:1, *CW* 1:200–1.

6. *Life*, 23:3, *CW* 1:201.

7. *Letter* 269, to padre Pablo Hernández, S.J., October 4, 1578, *CL* 2:122.

8. *Way*, 19:8–10, *CW* 2:111.

9. *Way*, 19:10, *CW* 2:111–12.

10. Phil. 1:23–24.

11. *Way*, 19:12, *CW* 2:112.

12. *Life*, 24:5, *CW* 1:211.

13. *Life*, 24:6, *CW* 1:211–12.

14. *Life*, 26:3, *CW* 1:225.

15. *Life*, 28:14, *CW* 1:244.

16. *Life*, 38:14, *CW* 1:334–35.

17. On St. Teresa's relationship with the Jesuits, see Victoriano Larrañaga, *La espiritualidad de San Ignacio de Loyola. Estudio comparativo con la de Santa Teresa de Jesús* (Madrid: A.C.N. de P. Casa de San Pablo, 1944). For the French translation, see *Sainte Thérèse d'Avila, Saint Ignace de Loyola: Convergences* (Paris: SJ Pierre Téqui, 1998).

18. *Letter* 336, to Isabel Osorio, April 8, 1580, *CL* 2:295.

19. *Letter* 378, to doña Ana Enríquez, March 4, 1581, *CL* 2:401.

20. *Way*, 31:5, *CW* 2:155.

21. Ibid.

22. VI D, 9:2, *CW* 2:411.

23. *Way*, 19:15, *CW* 2:113.

24. Ibid.

25. VI D, 9:2, *CW* 2:411.

19. FROM HELL TO FOUNDATION   ·

1. *Life*, 32:3, *CW* 1:277.
2. V *D*, 3:10, *CW* 2:352.
3. *Way*, Prologue, *CW* 2:40.
4. *Life*, 22:10, *CW* 1:195.
5. *Letter* 402, to Jerome Gratian, July 14, 1581, *CL* 2:445.
6. *Life*, 32:1–3, *CW* 1:276–77.
7. On Paul Claudel's attitude to St. Teresa, see Paul Claudel, *Journal*, vol. 1 (Paris: Gallimard, 1968), 306–11.

21. SAINT JOSEPH, THE VIRGIN MARY, AND HIS MAJESTY

1. The *deewan* of the Persian mystic and teacher Mansur al-Hallaj (858–922) have not been translated into English in their entirety. This fragment is my rendering of Louis Massignon's 1955 translation in Husayn Mansür Hallaj, *Dîwân* (Paris: Seuil, 1981), 114 (LSF).
2. *Life*, 40:1, *CW* 1:354.
3. *Life*, 32:11, *CW* 1:280–81.
4. *Life*, 33:2, *CW* 1:285.
5. I *D*, 1:5, *CW* 2:285.
6. *Life*, 39:8, *CW* 1:345–46.
7. *Testimonies*, 3:10, *CW* 1:384.
8. *Life*, 37:7, *CW* 1:326.
9. *Life*, 40:4, *CW* 1:355–56.
10. *Letter* 24, to Lorenzo de Cepeda, January 17, 1570, *CL* 1:83.
11. *Life*, 33:5, *CW* 1:286–87.
12. *Life*, 33:7–8, *CW* 1:288.
13. *Life*, 33:9, *CW* 1:288–89.
14. *Life*, 33:10, *CW* 1:289.
15. *Life*, 38:15, *CW* 1:335.
16. *Life*, 40:13–14, *CW* 1:359.
17. *Life*, 33:11, *CW* 1:289–90 (sentence order rearranged to comply with original).
18. *Life*, 33:12, *CW* 1:290.
19. *Life*, 33:14–15, *CW* 1:291–92.
20. Ibid.

22. THE MATERNAL VOCATION

1. Quoted by Marcelle Auclair, *Thérèse d'Avila, Œuvres complètes* (Paris: Desclée de Brouwer, 1964), 111.
2. *Letter* 41, to María de Mendoza, March 7, 1572, *CL* 1:119.
3. *Testimonies*, 3:6, *CW* 1:383.
4. *Letter* 2, to Lorenzo de Cepeda, Quito, December 23, 1561, *CW* 1:32–33.
5. *Life*, 34:1–4, *CW* 1:293–95.
6. *Life*, 38:4, *CW* 1:331.

7. *Life*, 34:4, *CW* 1:295.
8. *Testimonies*, 2:4, *CW* 1:381.
9. *Life*, 34:7, *CW* 1:296.
10. *Life*, 37:5, *CW* 1:325.
11. Miguel de Cervantes, *Don Quixote* (1885; Project Gutenberg), second part, chap. 54, trans. John Ormsby, www.gutenberg.org/cache/epub/996/pg996.html. Release date July 27, 2004. Accessed November 11, 2012.
12. *Life*, 36:18, *CW* 1:317.
13. *Life*, 36:6–7, *CW* 1:311–12.
14. *Life*, 36:11–13, *CW* 1:314–15.
15. *Life*, 36:14, *CW* 1:316.
16. *Life*, 36:15, *CW* 1:316.
17. *Life*, 36:16, *CW* 1:317.
18. *Life*, 36:22, *CW* 1:319–20.
19. *Life*, 33:15, *CW* 1:292.
20. *Life*, 36:24, *CW* 1:320.
21. *Life*, 39:26, *CW* 1:353.
22. *Way*, 31:9–10, *CW* 2:156–57.
23. *Testimonies*, 15, *CW* 1:393.
24. Ibid.
25. The verb *entrañar* in Spanish connotes intimacy, love, affection; it means to "embrace with passionate strength." It also has a very "visceral" dimension, as *entrañas* are "entrails," and the verb *entrañarse* suggests a total, intimate union with a person. The Spanish mystics used this term to describe union with Christ. Thus fray Luis de León: "Nomb. de Crist. en el del Hijo. Entonces entra en nuestra alma su mismo espíritu, que entrando se entraña en ella y produce en ella luego su gracia."
26. *Soliloquies*, 17:3–5, *CW* 1:462–63.
27. V D, 2:5, *CW* 2:343.
28. *Life*, 36:29, *CW* 1:321–22.
29. *Life*, 38:1, *CW* 1:329–30.

23. CONSTITUTING TIME

1. *The Constitutions*: 1567.
2. *The Way of Perfection*: 1566–1567.
3. *The Book of Her Foundations*: 1568–1582.
4. Ignatius Loyola: 1491–1556.
5. Michel de Montaigne: 1533–1592.
6. *Way*, 1:2, *CW* 2:41.
7. *Life*, 35:2, *CW* 1:303.
8. *Const.*, 1, *CW* 3:319.
9. *Const.*, 3, *CW* 3:319.
10. *Const.*, 15, *CW* 3:323.
11. *Const.*, 10, *CW* 3:321–22.
12. *Const.*, 11–14, *CW* 3:322–23.

13. *Way*, 9:2, *CW* 2:74.

14. *Way*, 4:7, *CW* 2:55.

15. *Const.*, 28, *CW* 3:328.

16. *Way*, 7:4, *CW* 2:67.

17. *Const.*, 26, *CW* 3:327.

18. *Const.*, 26–7, *CW* 3:327–28.

19. *Const.*, 8, *CW* 3:321.

20. *Const.*, 22, *CW* 3:326.

21. *Way*, 4:4, *CW* 2:54.

22. *Way*, 6:1–7, *CW* 2:62–64.

23. *Way*, 4:2, *CW* 2:53.

24. *Way*, 24:4, *CW* 2:129.

25. Ibid.

26. *Way*, 24:5–6, *CW* 2:130.

27. *Way*, 24:2, *CW* 2:129.

28. *Way*, 31:10, *CW* 2:157.

29. *Way*, 36:9, *CW* 2:181.

30. *Life*, 25:3, *CW* 1:214.

31. *Way*, 31:10, *CW* 2:157.

32. *Way*, 19:2, *CW* 2:107.

33. *Way*, 19:3–4, *CW* 2:108.

34. Ibid.

35. *Way*, 12:1, *CW* 2:81–82.

36. *Way*, 11:5, *CW* 2:81.

37. *Life*, 25:14, *CW* 1:220.

38. *Life*, 25:10, *CW* 1:217.

39. *Letters* 124 and 155, *CL* 1:333, 154.

40. VI *D*, 4:4–5, *CW* 2:380.

41. *Life*, 25:15, *CW* 1:220.

42. *Life*, 25:20, *CW* 1:222.

43. *Life*, 39:17–18, *CW* 1:349–50.

44. *Critique*, "*Búscate en mí*," *CW* 3:359.

45. *Found.*, 1:1, *CW* 3:99.

46. Monteverdi: 1567–1643.

47. Petrarch: 1304–1374.

48. Giulio Strozzi: 1583–ca. 1660.

24. *TUTTI A CAVALLO*

1. Miguel de Cervantes, *Don Quixote* (1885; Project Gutenberg), second part, chap. 4, trans. John Ormsby, www.gutenberg.org/cache/epub/996/pg996.html. Release date July 27, 2004. Accessed November 11, 2012.

2. *Testimonies*, 5, *CW* 1:386.

3. Letter from Juan de Ávila, April 2, 1568; see Rosa Rossi, *Thérèse d'Avila* (Paris: Cerf, 1989), 76.

4. *Letter* 8, to Luisa de la Cerda, May 27, 1568, *CL* 1:49.

5. *Letter* 9, to Luisa de la Cerda, June 9, 1568, *CL* 1:52.

6. *Letter* 10, to Luisa de la Cerda, June 23, 1568, *CL* 1:53.

7. *Letter* 14, to Luisa de la Cerda, November 2, 1568, *CL* 1:62.

8. *Letter* 13, to Francisco de Salcedo, late September 1658, *CL* 1:60.

9. *Life*, 37:5, *CW* 1:325.

10. *Life*, 20:27, *CW* 1:183.

11. *Found.*, 18:1, *CW* 2:3:185–86.

12. *Testimonies*, 12:4, *CW* 1:390.

13. *Letter* 38, to Luisa de la Cerda, November 7, 1571, *CL* 1:110.

14. *Testimonies*, 31, *CW* 1:402.

15. *Testimonies*, 30, *CW* 1:401.

16. *Letter* 219, to Gaspar de Salazar, December 7, 1577, *CL* 1:583.

17. *Life*, 14:11, *CW* 1:138.

18. Ibid.

19. *Life*, 25:13, *CW* 1:219.

20. V *D*, 3:10, *CW* 2:352.

21. Ibid., 3:11.

22. VI *D*, 2:6, *CW* 2:369.

23. VI *D*, 2:4, *CW* 2:368.

24. VI *D*, 2:7, *CW* 2:369.

25. VI *D*, 6:6, *CW* 2:393.

26. Ibid.

27. VI *D*, 6:9, *CW* II 395.

28. VI *D*, 6:8, *CW* 2:394.

29. VI *D*, 6:10–11, *CW* 2:395–96.

30. VI *D*, 6:10, *CW* 2:395.

31. Ibid.; see also the reference to "*algarabía*" in *Life*, 14:8, *CW* 1:137: "It is more difficult to speak about these things than to speak Arabic."

32. *Testimonies*, 33, *CW* 1:404.

33. *Testimonies*, 36:1–2, *CW* 1:405–6.

34. *Testimonies*, 36:3, *CW* 1:406.

35. Dante, *The Divine Comedy*, trans. Henry W. Longfellow, *Paradiso*, canto 33 (London: Capella, 2006), 381.

36. *Way*, 19:9–10, *CW* 2:111–12.

37. *Letter* 88, to María Bautista, August 28, 1575, *CL* 1:221 et seq.

38. *Letter* 105, to María Bautista, April 29, 1576, *CL* 1:268.

39. *Letter* 104, to María Bautista, February 19, 1576, *CL* 1:263–64.

40. *Letter* 106, to Ambrosio Mariano, May 9, 1576, *CL* 1:272–75.

41. *Visitation*, 2, *CW* 3:337.

42. *Visitation*, 3, *CW* 3:337.

43. *Visitation*, 1, *CW* 3:337.

44. *Critique*, *CW* 3:359.

45. *Letter* 219, to Gaspar de Salazar, December 7, 1577, *CL* 1:582.

46. *Letter* 218, to King Philip II, December 4, 1577, *CL* 1:580.

47. *Letter* 226, to Teutonio de Braganza, January 16, 1578, *CL* 2:15.

48. *Letter* 247, to Jerome Gratian, May 22, 1578, *CL* 2:75.

49. *Letter* 258, to Jerome Gratian, August 19, 1578, *CL* 2:103.

50. See Rossi, *Thérèse d'Avila*, 168, concerning the attacks on Baltasar Alvarez.

51. *Letter* 228, to Juan Suárez, February 10, 1578, *CL* 2:21–22.

52. *Letter* 261, to Jerome Gratian, end of August 1578, *CL* 2:108.

53. *Letter* 283, to Hernando de Pantoja, and *Letter* 284, to the Discalced Carmelite nuns, both January 31, 1579, *CL* 2:153–60.

54. Cf. Joseph Pérez, *Thérèse d'Avila* (Paris: Fayard, 2007), 283, letter to Teresa of Avila from the "Great Angel."

55. *Letter* 408, to Jerome Gratian, September 17, 1581, *CL* 2:457.

56. *Letter* 410, to Jerome Gratian, October 26, 1581, *CL* 2:464.

57. *Letter* 426, to Jerome Gratian, early December, 1581, *CL* 2:500.

58. *Letter* 465, to Jerome Gratian, September 1, 1582, *CL* 2:582.

25. THE MYSTIC AND THE JESTER

1. Miguel de Cervantes, *Don Quixote* (1885; Project Gutenberg), first part, chap. 1, trans. John Ormsby, www.gutenberg.org/cache/epub/996/pg996.html. Release date July 27, 2004. Accessed November 11, 2012.

2. Dominique Barbier, *Don Quichottisme et psychiatrie* (Toulouse: Privat, 1987).

26. A FATHER IS BEATEN TO DEATH

1. Sigmund Freud, "A Child Is Being Beaten" (1919), *Penguin Freud Library*, vol. 10, *On Psychopathology*, trans. James Strachey, ed. Angela Richards (London: Penguin, 1993), 159–94.

2. Sigmund Freud, *Totem and Taboo*, trans. James Strachey (London: Routledge and Kegan Paul, 1999), 1912.

3. "*Urfantasien.*" Cf. "Un cas de paranoïa qui contredisait la théorie psychanalytique de cette affection" (1915), in *Revue Française de Psychanalyse* 8, no. 1 (1935): 2–11.

4. John 14:7–12.

5. Cf. Friedrich Nietzsche, *The Anti-Christ*, trans. H. L. Mencken, (1920; Tucson: Sharp, 1999).

6. *Testimonies*, 52, *CW* 1:414.

7. *Testimonies*, 29, *CW* 1:401.

8. Cf. Gilles Deleuze, "Coldness and Cruelty," in *Masochism*, trans. Charles Stivale (New York: Zone, 1989).

9. Cf. Julia Kristeva, "The Two-Faced Oedipus," in *Colette*, trans. Jane Marie Todd, European Perspectives: A Series in Social Thought and Cultural Criticism (New York: Columbia University Press, 2005), 408–19.

10. Charles Baudelaire, "Recueillements," in *Les fleurs du mal*. "Sous le fouet du Plaisir, ce bourreau sans merci" is rendered most literally in William Aggeler's translation (*The Flowers of Evil*, Fresno, Calif.: Academy Library Guild, 1954): "under the scourge / Of Pleasure, that merciless torturer."

11. John of the Cross, "Spiritual Canticle" and "More Stanzas Applied to Spiritual Things on

Christ and the Soul," in *The Collected Works of St. John of the Cross*, trans. Kieran Kavanaugh and Otilio Rodriguez (Washington, D.C.: Institute of Carmelite Studies, 1973), 712, 723.

12. Pierre Klossowski, *Such a Deathly Desire*, trans. Russell Ford (State University of New York Press, 2007), 67: "a transgression of language by language"; see also *Roberte ce soir and the Revocation of the Edict of Nantes*, trans. Austryn Wainhouse (Urbana, Ill.: Dalkey Archive Press, 2002).

13. Mark 15:34.

14. Paul of Tarsus: "Christ died for us" (Rom. 5:8); "Christ died for our sins" (1 Cor. 15:3).

15. Deleuze, "Coldness and Cruelty," 116.

16. G. W. F. Hegel, *Lectures on the Philosophy of Religion*, ed. Peter Hodgson (Oxford: 2006), 3:219.

17. Nietzsche, *Anti-Christ*, 5.

18. Cf. "Le hiatus comme ultime Parole de Dieu," in André-Marie Ponnou-Delaffon, *La théologie de Baltasar* (Les Plans sur Bex, Switzerland: Parole et Silence, 2005), 129–32; and Urs von Balthasar, *La gloire et la croix*, vol. 3, part 2, *La Nouvelle Alliance* (Paris: Aubier, 1975).

19. Meister Eckhart, *The Complete Mystical Works of Meister Eckhart*, trans. and ed. Maurice O'C. Walshe (New York: Crossroad, 2009), 424.

20. Benedict de Spinoza, *The Ethics* (1677), part V, proposition 35, translated from the Latin by R. H. M. Elwes, projectgutenberg.org/files/3800/3800-h/3800-h.htm. Released February 1, 2003. Accessed April 3, 2012.

21. Philippe Sollers, *Guerres secrètes* (Paris: Carnets Nord, 2007): "D'après la révolution opérée par la Contre-Réforme . . ."

27. A RUNAWAY GIRL

1. Louise Bourgeois, "Entretien entre Louise Bourgeois, Suzanne Pagé, Béatrice Parent," in Louise Bourgeois, *Sculptures, environnements, dessins, 1938–1995*, catalog of Musée d'Art Moderne, Paris, 1995 (my translation—LSF); various quotations also taken from Louise Bourgeois, *Destruction of the Father/Reconstruction of the Father: Writings and Interviews, 1923–1997*, ed. Hans-Ulrich Obrist and Marie-Laure Bernadac (Cambridge, Mass.: MIT Press, 1998).

2. Christopher Marlowe, *Hero and Leander*, I, 167–68, in *Complete Works* (Cambridge: Cambridge University Press, 1973), 2:435.

3. Julia Kristeva, *The Female Genius*, II: *Melanie Klein*, trans. Ross Guberman (New York: Columbia University Press, 2004).

4. Julia Kristeva, *Murder in Byzantium*, trans. C. Jon Delogu (New York: Columbia University Press, 2005).

5. John of the Cross, *Ascent of Mount Carmel*, book 2, chap. 31, trans. and ed. E. Allison Peers (Tunbridge Wells, U.K.: Burns & Oates, 1983), 205: "It is as if Our Lord were to say formally to the soul: 'Be thou good'; it would then substantially be good."

6. *Life*, 15:8, *CW* 1:143–44.

7. William Blake, *Complete Writings* (Oxford: Oxford University Press, 1972), 71: "To Nobodaddy."

8. Robert Storr, Paulo Herkenhoff, and Allan Schwartzman, *Louise Bourgeois* (London: Phaidon, 2003), 24.

9. Cf. Marcel Proust, "Time Regained," in *In Search of Lost Time*, trans. and with an introduction and notes by Peter Collier, ed. Christopher Prendergast (London: Penguin, 2002), 6:292–321.

28. "GIVE ME TRIALS, LORD; GIVE ME PERSECUTIONS"

1. *Letter* 253, to Juana de Ahumada, August 8, 1578, *CL* 2:89.
2. *Way*, 12:1, *CW* 2:81.
3. *Medit.*, 7:8, *CW* 2:259.
4. Ibid.
5. *Testimonies*, 46, *CW* 1:412; Seville, second half of 1575. Michel de Goedt writes: "Christ treated her as a spouse and a sovereign, and granted her the freedom to make use of his own property, the most precious good of all, his Passion" ("La prière de l'école de Thérèse d'Avila aujourd'hui," in *Recherches et expériences spirituelles*, lectures edited by the Cathedral of Notre-Dame de Paris, 1982). Note that in Spanish, the terms chosen by the writer are laden with sensuality. Thus *señorío* means "mastery over something," as though one were a *seigneur*, lord or owner. "Power," "conquest," "taming,"—*señorío* is the "dominion" I exercise over you as much as the "demesne belonging to a feudal lord." Likewise, *alivio* denotes "the relief or cure for an illness," the "alleviation of fatigue, of bodily sickness, of spiritual affliction"; the result of an "elimination of a burden or trouble." *Alivio* conveys "easing," "abatement," "solace."
6. *Medit.*, 7:1, *CW* 2:256.
7. For the testimonies gathered as evidence for the beatification and canonization of St. Teresa, see Gillian Alghren, *Teresa of Avila and the Politics of Sanctity* (Ithaca: Cornell University Press, 1998), 154 et seq.
8. *Way*, 7:8, *CW* 2:70: "I would not want you to be like women."
9. *Way*, 38:8, *CW* 2:181 (paraphrased): "And so as to reign more sublimely it understands that the above-mentioned way [suffering] is the true way."
10. For the cucumber anecdote, see Marcelle Auclair, *La vie de sainte Thérèse d'Avila* (Paris: Seuil, 1950), 140.
11. *Letter* 92, to Jerome Gratian, October 1575, *CL* 1:233.
12. Ibid., 234.
13. *Letter* 248, to Mother María de San José, June 4, 1578, *CL* 2:80.
14. *Found.*, 7:4, *CW* 3:135–36. The original passage in its entirety runs as follows: "Si no bastaren palabras, sean castigos; si no bastaren pequeños, sean grandes; si no bastare un mes de tenerlas encarceladas, sean cuatro: que no pueden hacer mayor bien a sus almas. Porque, como queda dicho y lo torno a decir (porque importa para las mismas entenderlo, aunque alguna vez, o veces, no puedan más consigo), como no es locura confirmada de suerte que disculpe para la culpa, aunque algunas veces lo sea, no es siempre, y queda el alma en mucho peligro; sino estando—como digo—la razón tan quitada que la haga fuerza, hace lo que, cuando no podía más, hacía o decía. Gran misericordia es de Dios a los que da este mal, sujetarse a quien los gobierne, porque aquí está todo su bien, por este peligro que he dicho. Y, por amor de Dios, si alguna leyere esto, mire que le importa por ventura la salvación."
15. *Way*, 19:4, *CW* 2:108.
16. *Const.*, 24, *CW* 3:327.
17. *Const.*, 26, *CW* 3:327.
18. *Const.*, 44, *CW* 3:448.
19. *Way*, 19:9, *CW* 2:111.
20. *Way*, 19: 9–11, *CW* 2:111–12.
21. *Const.*, 44, *CW* 3:448.

22. *Letter* 161, to Mariano de San Benito, December 12, 1576, *CL* 1:430–31.

23. *Testimonies*, 53:1, *CW* 1:415.

24. *Testimonies*, 54, *CW* 1:416.

25. *Letter* 108, to Jerome Gratian, June 15, 1576, *CL* 1:280.

26. *Life*, 21:11, *CW* 1:190.

27. *Way*, 15:1, *CW* 2:91.

28. *Letter* 182, to Lorenzo de Cepeda, February 10, 1577, *CL* 1:494.

29. *Life*, 13:4, *CW* 1:124.

30. *Life*, 13:7, *CW* 1:126.

31. *Life*, 13:5, *CW* 1:125.

32. *Way*, 39:3, *CW* 2:190.

33. *Found.*, 28:21–34, *CW* 3:258–63.

34. *Testimonies*, 19, *CW* 1:394.

35. *Testimonies*, 17, *CW* 1:394.

36. *Life*, 22:15, *CW* 1:199.

37. *Life*, 22:16, *CW* 1:199.

38. *Life*, 22:10, *CW* 1:195.

29. "WITH THE EARS OF THE SOUL"

1. See Julia Kristeva, "The Semiotic and the Symbolic," in *Revolution in Poetic Language*, trans. Margaret Waller (New York: Columbia University Press, 1984), 19–106.

2. *Testimonies*, 58, *CW* 1:423.

3. Sigmund Freud, *Totem and Taboo*, trans. James Strachey (London: Routledge and Kegan Paul, 1999), 153.

4. VI *D*, 2:6, *CW* 2:369.

5. VI *D*, 2:7, *CW* 2:369.

6. VI *D*, 3:12, *CW* 2:375.

7. *Life*, 20:12–14, *CW* 1:177–78.

8. Melanie Klein, *Collected Writings of Melanie Klein*, vol. 1, *Love, Guilt and Reparation: And Other Works 1921–1945* (London: Hogarth, 1975); Julia Kristeva, *The Female Genius*, II: *Melanie Klein*, trans. Ross Guberman (New York: Columbia University Press, 2004).

9. *Life*, 20:16. English version, *CW* 1:179: "In this pain the soul is purified and fashioned or purged like gold in the crucible so that the enameled gifts might be placed there in a better way, and in this prayer it is purged of what otherwise it would have to be purged of in purgatory."

10. *Life*, 20:18, *CW* 1:180.

11. VI *D*, 9:4, *CW* 2:412.

12. VI *D*, 3:5, *CW* 2:372.

13. VI *D*, 3:7, *CW* 2:373.

14. VI *D*, 9:5–7, *CW* 2:412.

15. *Testimonies*, 52, *CW* 1:414–15.

16. *Way*, 11:2, *CW* 2:80.

17. *Way*, 11:3, *CW* 2:80.

18. *Way*, 11:4, *CW* 2:81.

19. *Life*, 7:11, *CW* 1:88.

20. *Life*, 7:10, *CW* 1:87. For Teresa's encouragement of her father's faith and growing closeness to him at the end of his life, see *Life*, 7:10–16.

21. *Life*, 22:3, *CW* 1:192.

22. *Life*, 22:6, 8, *CW* 1:193–95.

23. *Way*, 19:2, 4, *CW* 2:107, 108.

24. VI *D*, 3:5, *CW* 2:372.

25. VI *D*, 3:6, *CW* 2:373.

26. *Testimonies*, 51, *CW* 1:414.

27. Denis Diderot, *Elements of Physiology*, from "Notes for *Elements of Physiology*, probably in preparation for a larger work on the nature of man," quoted in Jim Herrick, *Against the Faith* (New York: Prometheus, 1985), 84. (Passage from the "Conclusion" not included in Diderot, *Interpreter of Nature: Selected Writings*, ed. J. Kemp [New York: Lawrence and Wishart, 1963], the only place that seems to contain the *Elements* in English.)

28. *Way*, 31:9, *CW* 2:157.

29. *Way*, 24:4, *CW* 2:129.

30. *Life*, 14:5, *CW* 1:135.

31. VII *D*, 2:7, *CW* 2:435–36.

32. VII *D*, 2:9–10, *CW* 2:436–37. (Translation modified.)

33. I *D*, 1:5, *CW* 2:285.

30. ACT 1: HER WOMEN

1. V *D*, 1:4, *CW* 2:336–37.

2. I *D*, 2:7, *CW* 2:290.

3. *Way*, 28:10, *CW* 2:144.

4. IV *D*, 2:2, *CW* 2:323.

5. *Testimonies*, 58, *CW* 1:424.

6. VII *D*, 3:2, *CW* 2:438.

7. *Found.*, 12, *CW* 3:156–60.

8. *Found.*, 12:6, *CW* 3:158–59.

9. *Found.*, 5:10, *CW* 3:120.

10. *Life*, 40:8, *CW* 1:357.

11. *Life*, 24:4, *CW* 1:211.

12. *Life*, 30:3, *CW* 1:254.

13. Cf. Rosa Rossi, *Thérèse d'Avila* (Paris: Cerf, 1989), 177: Teresa and Ana de San Bartolomé.

14. *Way*, 7:7, *CW* 2:69.

15. *Way*, 10:5, *CW* 2:69.

16. *Life*, 10:8, *CW* 1:109.

17. *Letter* 135, to Ambrosio Mariano, October 21, 1576, *CL* 1:361.

18. *Way*, 4:13, *CW* 2:57.

19. *Way*, 7:8, *CW* 2:70.

20. *Found.*, 17, *CW* 3:179–85.

21. *Letter* 58, to Domingo Báñez, January 1574, *CL* 1:148.

22. *Letter* 109, to María de San José, June 16, 1576, *CL* 1:285.

23. *Letter* 112, to María de San José, July 2, 1576, *CL* 1:291.

24. *Letter* 126, to María de San José, September 22, 1576, *CL* 1:337.

25. *Letter* 132, to María de San José, October 13, 1576, *CL* 1:351.

26. *Letter* 137, to María de San José, October 1576, *CL* 1:373.

27. *Letter* 146, to María de San José, November 8, 1576, *CL* 1:392.

28. *Letter* 152, to María de San José, November 26, 1576, *CL* 1:409.

29. *Letter* 152, to María de San José, November 26, 1576, *CL* 1:411.

30. *Letter* 198, to María de San José, June 28, 1577, *CL* 1:542.

31. *Letter* 331, to María de San José, February 8–9, 1580, *CL* 2:282.

32. *Letter* 173, to María de San José, January 3, 1577, *CL* 1:460.

33. *Letter* 186, to María de San José, February 28, 1577, *CL* 1:511.

34. *Letter* 330, to María de San José, February 1, 1580, *CL* 2:273.

35. *Letter* 311, to Jerome Gratian, October 14, 1579, *CL* 2:226.

36. Ibid.

37. *Letter* 88, to María Bautista, August 28, 1575, *CL* 1:224.

38. Ibid., *CL* 1:223.

39. Dante, rhyme 67: "Però nol fan che non san quel che sono; camera di perdon sano uom non serra, ché'l perdonare e bel vincer di guerra." The envoi of his canzone of exile, beginning "Tre donne intorno al cor mi son venute" (1304). Trans. Barbara Reynolds, in Reynolds, *Dante: The Poet, the Political Thinker, the Man* (London: IB Tauris, 2006), 96.

40. *Letter* 307, to Jerome Gratian, July 25, 1579, *CL* 2:218.

41. Samuel Beckett, *Waiting for Godot* and *Not I*, in *Collected Shorter Plays* (London: Grove Press, 1994).

42. I *D*, 1:5, *CW* 2:285.

43. *Foundations*, 10:14, *CW* 3:150.

44. *Way*, 4:16, *CW* 2:58.

45. *Letter* 177, to Lorenzo de Cepeda, January 17, 1577, *CL* 1:474–75.

46. *Sol.*, 14:4, *CW* 1:458.

47. *Life*, 21:6, *CW* 1:187.

48. *Found.*, 20:4, *CW* 3:198.

49. *Found.*, 20:3, *CW* 3:198.

50. *Letter* 342, to duchess of Alba, May 8, 1580, *CL* 2:310.

51. *Letter* 94, to Inés Nieto, October 31, 1575, *CL* 1:237.

52. *Letter* 278, to the duchess of Alba, December 2, 1578, *CL* 2:147.

53. Exod. 5:1; 6:8. See also Exod. 9:1: "Thus saith the Lord God of the Hebrews, Let my people go, so they may serve me."

54. Maria Theresa of Naples and Sicily (1772–1807) was the last Holy Roman Empress and first empress of Austria, wife of Francis I of Habsburg-Lorraine, first emperor of Austria. Granddaughter of Habsburg ruler Maria Theresa of Austria, who was the mother of the Holy Roman Emperor, Joseph II.

55. VI *D*, 6:3, *CW* 2:392 (adapted).

56. John of the Cross, "The Dark Night," in *The Collected Works of St. John of the Cross*, trans. Kieran Kavanaugh and Otilio Rodriguez (Washington, D.C.: Institute of Carmelite Studies, 1973), 712.

31. ACT 2: HER ELISEUS

1. *Testimonies*, 34, *CW* 1:404.
2. *Letter* 159, to Jerome Gratian, December 7, 1576, *CL* 1:423.
3. Ibid.
4. *Letter* 162, to Jerome Gratian, December 13, 1576, *CL* 1:436.
5. *Letter* 170, to Jerome Gratian, late December 1576, *CL* 1:450.
6. *Letter* 242, to Jerome Gratian, April 26, 1578, *CL* 2:62–63.
7. *Letter* 297, to Jerome Gratian, June 10, 1579, *CL* 2:195.
8. IV *D*, 1:7, *CW* 2:319.
9. *Found.*, 23:13, *CW* 3:222.
10. *Letter* 141, November 1576, *CL* 1:379.
11. *Letter* 81, to Isabel de Santo Domingo, May 12, 1575, *CL* 1:202.
12. *Letter* 246, to Jerome Gratian, May 14, 1578, *CL* 2:72.
13. *Letter* 145, to Jerome Gratian, November 4, 1576, *CL* 1:390.
14. *Letter* 124, to Jerome Gratian, September 20, 1576, *CL* 1:328.
15. Ibid., *CL* 1:328–29.
16. Ibid., *CL* 1:333.
17. *Letter* 147, to Jerome Gratian, November 11, 1576, *CL* 1:394.
18. *Letter* 141, to Jerome Gratian, November 1546(?), *CL* 1:378.
19. *Letter* 92, to Jerome Gratian, October 1575, *CL* 1:233–34.
20. *Letter* 149, to Jerome Gratian, November 1576, *CL* 1:400.
21. *Letter* 261, to Jerome Gratian, late August 1578, *CL* 2:108.
22. *Letter* 196, to María de San José, May 28, 1577, *CL* 1:538.
23. *Letter* 108, to Jerome Gratian, June 15, 1576, *CL* 1:279.
24. *Letter* 311, to Jerome Gratian, October 14, 1579, *CL* 2:225.
25. *Life*, 18:8, *CW* 1:160.
26. Jérôme Gratien, Glanes, *Quelques brèves additions de la main du père Jérôme Gratien à la première biographie de Thérèse d'Avila par le père Francisco de Ribera*, presented by Fr. Pierre Sérouet (Laval: Carmel de Laval, 1998).
27. *Letter* 98, to María Bautista, December 30, 1575, *CL* 1:245.
28. *Testimonies*, 22:2, *CW* 1:397.
29. *Life*, 22:6, *CW* 1:194.
30. *Way*, 24:3, 5, *CW* 2:129, 130.
31. Exod. 4:30.
32. John 1:23.
33. *Medit.*, 1:1, *CW* 2:216.
34. *Medit.*, 1:8, *CW* 2:219 (adapted).
35. *Life*, 25:11, *CW* 1:217.
36. See Mino Bergamo, *L'anatomie de l'âme: De François de Sales à Fénelon* (Grenoble: Jérôme Millon, 1997), 135 sq: "essential foundation," "fond essentiel."
37. Martin Heidegger, *Being and Time: A Translation of* Sein und Zeit, trans. Joan Stambaugh (New York: State University of New York Press, 1996), vol. 2, chap. 2, §57, p. 253: "The caller, too, remains in a striking indefiniteness . . . leaves not the slightest possibility of making the call familiar."

38. Heidegger, *Being and Time*, vol. 2, chap. 2, §55, p. 251: "Vocal utterance is not essential to discourse . . . a 'voice' of conscience, . . . which can factically never be found, but 'voice' is understood as giving-to-understand."

39. *Life*, 22:8, *CW* 1:194–95.

40. *Life*, 22:1, *CW* 1:191 (adapted).

41. *Life*, 22:16, *CW* 1:199.

42. VII D, 3:13, *CW* 2:442.

43. *Testimonies*, 5, *CW* 1:386.

44. Ps. 119:32: "Dilatasti . . ."

45. IV D, 2:5, *CW* 2:324.

46. *Testimonies*, 39, *CW* 1:409.

47. Heidegger, *Being and Time*, vol. 2, chap. 2, § 56, p. 252: "The call [like the babbling voice] does not say anything . . . has nothing to tell." Cf. Jean-Louis Chrétien, *The Call and the Response*, trans. Stephen E. Lewis (New York: Fordham University Press, 2004).

48. VI D, 9:6, *CW* 2:412.

49. *Way*, 7:8, *CW* 2:70.

50. *Way*, 17:5, *CW* 2:100.

51. *Life*, 22:15, *CW* 1:199.

52. *Life*, 22:8, *CW* 1:195.

53. *Life*, 22:7–10, *CW* 1:194–96.

54. VI D, 6:3, *CW* 2:392.

55. *Life*, 22:10, *CW* 1:195.

56. Ibid.

57. VI D, 11:3, *CW* 2:422.

58. VI D, 6:10, *CW* 2:395.

59. I D, 1:1, *CW* 2:283.

32. ACT 3: HER "LITTLE SENECA"

1. John of the Cross, "Commentary Applied to Spiritual Things," in *The Collected Works of St. John of the Cross*, trans. Kieran Kavanaugh and Otilio Rodriguez (Washington, D.C.: Institute of Carmelite Studies, 1973), 734.

2. *Letter* 194, to Ambrosio Mariano, May 9, 1577, *CL* 1:33.

3. John of the Cross, *Ascent of Mount Carmel*, book 2, chapter 12, trans. and ed. E. Allison Peers (Tunbridge Wells, Kent: Burns & Oates, 1983), 103: "all the detachment of the exterior senses . . ."

4. Ibid., 106.

5. Ibid.

6. *Testimonies*, 59:11, *CW* 1:428–29.

7. John of the Cross, "More Stanzas Applied to Spiritual Things on Christ and the Soul," in *Collected Works*, 722.

8. John of the Cross, Letter 33, October–November 1591, in *Collected Works*, 706.

9. John of the Cross, "The Living Flame of Love," in *Collected Works*, 717.

10. VII D, 4:15, *CW* 2:450.

11. Francis Poulenc, *Dialogues of the Carmelites*, libretto, original text and English translation (Melville, N.Y.: Ricordi and Belwin Mills, 1957, 1959). (This cannot be consulted; trans. LSF.)

12. Sacra congregatio pro causis sanctorum, *Positio super causae introductione servae Dei Teresiae Benedictae a Cruce (in saeculo Edith Stein) monialis professae ordinis carmelitarum discalceatorum (1891–1942)*, Rome, 1983, 322.

13. Isa. 53:5.

14. Edith Stein, *Getsamtausgabe, 3 (1933–1942)* (Freiburg: Herder, 2000–2001), 373, quoted by Cécile Rastouin, *Edith Stein. Enquête sur la source* (Paris: Cerf, 2007). Edith Stein's *Collected Works* have been issued by the Institute of Carmelite Studies (Washington D.C.: ICS, 1992/2003) in an eleven-volume series involving various translators and editors.

15. Stein, *The Hidden Life*, in *Collected Works*, vol. 4, 92.

16. VII D, 4:14, *CW* 2:450.

17. Allusion to Edith Stein's works, *The Science of the Cross* (*Collected Works*, vol. 6), dealing with John of the Cross, and *The Hidden Life* (*Collected Works*, vol. 4), hagiographic meditations and spiritual texts.

18. VII D, 3:13, *CW* 2:442.

19. VII D, 3:12, *CW* 2:442.

20. John of the Cross, "Song of the Soul that Rejoices in Knowing God Through Faith," stanza 8, in *Collected Works*, 724.

21. John of the Cross, "More Stanzas Applied to Spiritual Things on Christ and the Soul," in *Collected Works*, 722.

22. *Testimonies*, 42, *CW* 1:410–11.

23. John of the Cross, "First Romance: On the Gospel. Regarding the Most Blessed Trinity," in *Collected Works*, 724–25.

24. *Letter* 297, to Jerome Gratian, June 10, 1579, *CL* 2:195.

25. John of the Cross, "Romance 2," in *Collected Works*, 726.

26. *Testimonies*, 52, *CW* 1:414.

27. *Life*, 38:9–11, *CW* 1:333–34.

28. *Testimonies*, 14, *CW* 1:392.

29. VII D, 2:7, *CW* 2:435–36.

30. John of the Cross, "Spiritual Canticle," in *Collected Works*, 712. With regard to John of the Cross and Teresa of Avila, see the work of Fr. Michel de Goedt: *Le Christ de Thérèse de Jésus* (Paris: Desclée-Fleurus, 1993), 169–82; and *Le Christ de Jean de la Croix*, (Paris: Desclée, 1993).

31. *Testimonies*, 52, *CW* 1:414.

32. Ibid.

33. *Testimonies*, 49, *CW* 1:413.

34. Thomas Aquinas, "Quidquid recipitur ad modum recipientis recipitur," *Summa Theologiae* 1a, q. 75, a. 5; 3a, q. 5.

35. John of the Cross, *Dark Night of the Soul*, book 1:4.

36. *Testimonies*, 31, *CW* 1:402.

37. Colette, *Mes apprentissages*, in *Œuvres* (Paris: Gallimard, 1991), 3:1039 : "*la règle qui guérit de tout.*"

38. John of the Cross, "The Dark Night," in *Collected Works*, 712.

39. Marcelle Auclair, *La vie de sainte Thérèse d'Avila* (Paris: Seuil, 1950), 188.

40. John of the Cross, "A Gloss," in *Collected Works*, 736: "Like a fevered man's / Who loathes any food he sees."

41. John of the Cross, *Ascent of Mount Carmel*, book 1, chapter 13, 58.

42. "Naked faith": John of the Cross, ibid., book 1, chapter 2: "Luego entra el alma en la segunda Noche, quedándose sola en desnuda fe." The English version drops the adjective: "The soul at once enters into the second night, and abides alone in faith." (John of the Cross, *Ascent of Mount Carmel*, book 1, chapter 2, 20).

43. Edith Stein, *The Science of the Cross*, in *Collected Works*, 6:228: "The actual reality . . ."

44. *Testimonies*, 65 (Spanish *Relaciones*, 6): 9, *CW* 1:438.

45. Song of Solomon 1:4.

46. *Testimonies*, 65 (Spanish 6): 9, *CW* 1:438: "This surrender to the will of God is so powerful that the soul wants neither death nor life, unless for a short time when it longs to die to see God."

47. Ibid.: "And if through my intercession I could play a part in getting a soul to love and praise God more, even if it be just for a short time, I think that would matter to me more than being in glory."

48. Song of Sol. 1:3; 1:2.

49. *Medit.*, Prologue, *CW* 2:215.

50. John of the Cross, *Ascent of Mount Carmel*, book 2, chapter 12, 103–4.

51. Michel de Montaigne, *The Essays: A Selection*, trans. and ed. M. A. Screech (London: Penguin, 2004), book 2:1, 131.

52. James Joyce, *Ulysses* (London: Penguin, 2000), 933.

53. *Critique*, "On Father Fray John of the Cross's Reply," *CW* 3:361.

54. *Letter* 260, to Jerome Gratian, August 1578, *CL* 2:107.

55. VI *D*, 9:17, *CW* 2:4.

56. John of the Cross, *Ascent of Mount Carmel*, book 1, chapter 3, 21.

57. VII *D*, 4:9, *CW* 2:447.

58. *Life*, 38:17, *CW* 1:336.

59. *Testimonies*, 53:3, *CW* 1:416.

60. Marcel Proust, *Jean Santeuil*, trans. Gerard Hopkins (New York: Simon & Schuster, 1956), 1:409.

61. Marcel Proust, "Time Regained," in *In Search of Lost Time*, trans. and with an introduction and notes by Peter Collier, ed. Christopher Prendergast (London: Penguin, 2002), 141.

62. Ignatius Loyola, *Spiritual Exercises*, 2: "Porque no el mucho saber harta y satisface al ánima, mas el sentir y gustar de las cosas internamente." See also the final prayer of the person doing the retreat, called "Application of the Senses," in Victoriano Larrañaga, *Sainte Thérèse d'Avila, Saint Ignace de Loyola: Convergences* (Paris: Pierre Téqui Éditeur, 1998), 121.

63. John of the Cross, *Ascent of Mount Carmel*, Book 2, chapters 28:2 and 31:1 (regarding the sensorial conversion of the word/call), 195, 205: "Substantial words are others which also come to the spirit formally . . . these cause in the substance of the soul that substance and virtue which they signify. . . . It is as if Our Lord were to say formally to the soul: 'Be thou good'; it would then substantially be good. . . . Or as if it feared greatly and He said to it: 'Fear thou not'; it would at once feel within itself great fortitude and tranquility."

64. Ignatius Loyola, *The Autobiography of Saint Ignatius*, ed. J. F. X. O'Conor (New York: Benziger, 1900), 54: original Spanish "*en tres teclas*," three clavecin keys. See also Larrañaga, *Convergences*, 56.

65. VI *D*, 1:1, *CW* 2:359.

66. John of the Cross, "Without a Place and With a Place," in *The Poems of John of the Cross*, trans. and ed. Willis Barnstone (New York: Norton, new edition, 1972), 83.

67. John of the Cross, *Ascent of Mount Carmel,* Book 1, chapter 13:11, 59.

68. Jacques Bénigne Bossuet (1627–1704), prelate, author, and preacher, Bishop of Meaux.

69. Extracts from Bossuet's "Sermon on Death," trans. Christopher O. Blum, available online: thomasmorecollege.edu/wp-content/uploads/2009/07/Bossuet-Sermon-on-Death.pdf, accessed February 2014; from Bossuet's *Œuvres Oratoires*, ed. Abbé J. Lebarq, IV (Paris: Desclée, 1926), 262–81. The quotations from the "Panegyric of St. Teresa" (declaimed before Anne of Austria in Metz, October 15, 1657) are translated by LSF.

70. See also Julia Kristeva, "A pure silence: The perfection of Jeanne Guyon," in *Tales of Love*, trans. Leon S. Roudiez (New York: Columbia University Press, 1987), 297–318.

71. G. W. Leibniz: 1646–1716.

72. Baruch Spinoza.

73. VII *D*, 2:6, *CW* 2:435.

74. Montaigne, *Essays*, book 2:1, 131.

75. I *D*, 2:7, *CW* 2:290.

76. VII *D*, 2:10, *CW* 2:437.

77. I *D*, 2:8, *CW* 2:291.

78. IV *D*, 2:1–4, *CW* 2:322–24.

79. Dante, *The Divine Comedy*, trans. Henry W. Longfellow, *Paradiso*, canto 1, 70–72 (London: Capella, 2006), 289.

80. VII *D*, 2:11, *CW* 2:437.

81. VII *D*, 2:7, *CW* 2:435.

82. VII *D*, 1:6, *CW* 2:430.

83. G. W. Leibniz, letter to Bernard Le Bovier de Fontenelle, 1704 (my translation—LSF): "To me, infinities are not totalities . . ."; *Leibniz and the Two Sophies: The Philosophical Correspondence*, ed. and trans. Lloyd Strickland (Toronto: Iter/Centre for Reformation and Renaissance Studies, 2011), 151: "My fundamental meditations . . ."; *Philosophical Papers and Letters, A Selection,* ed. and trans. Leroy E. Loemker, vol. 2, *The Principles of Nature and of Grace, Based on Reason* (1714; Chicago: University of Chicago Press, 1956), 1035: "Each monad is a living mirror . . ."; *Discourse on Metaphysics*, trans. D. Garber and R. Ariew (Indianapolis: Hackett, 1991), 41: "Everything is taken account of . . ."; *Leibnizens Mathematische Schriften*, ed.C. I. Gerhardt (Halle 1855–1863), (my translation—LSF): "Imaginary numbers . . ."

84. Julia Kristeva, "L'engendrement de la formule," in *Semiotike* (Paris: Seuil, 1969), 296–300: "L'infini-point obéit aux lois de transition et de continuité: rien n'équivaut à rien, et toute coïncidence cache en fait une distance infiniment petite. L'infini-point ne forme donc pas de structure, il pose des fonctions, des relations qui procèdent par approximation. Jamais comblée, une différence reste entre le nombre marqué ainsi π et l'ensemble des termes susceptibles de l'exprimer. L'unité est disloquée. Le nombre-signe, miroir unifiant, se brise, et la notation s'engage au-delà de lui. La différentielle qui en résulte, et qui équivaut à l'infiniment petit syn-catégorique (*in fieri*) des nominalistes du XIVe siècle, n'est pas une unité qui s'ajouterait à d'autres pour faire un tout, mais le glissement même de l'infini dans l'énoncé clos."

85. Leibniz, letter to Morell, December 10, 1696. Cf. M. Leroy, *Discours de métaphysique et correspondance avec Arnaud de G. W. Leibniz*, (Paris: Grua/Presses Universitaires de France, 1948), 103.

See also Michel Serres, *Le Système de Gottfried Wilhelm Leibniz* (Paris: Presses Universitaires de France, 1968).

86. Alain Badiou, "La subversion infinitésimale," in *Cahiers pour l'analyse* 9 (1968).

87. Benedict de Spinoza, *The Ethics* (Project Gutenberg), part V, proposition 35, translated from the Latin by R. H. M. Elwes, projectgutenberg.org/files/3800/3800-h/3800-h.htm, released February 1, 2003, accessed April 3, 2012.

88. Philippe Sollers, "Le temps de Dante," in *La Divine Comédie* (Paris: Gallimard, 2002), 13.

89. *Way*, 28:10, *CW* 2:144.

90. IV *D*, 2:4, *CW* 2:324.

91. *Way*, 19:2, *CW* 2:107.

92. *Life*, 9:7, *CW* 1:103.

93. VI *D*, 2:6, *CW* 2:369.

94. VII *D*, 3:12, *CW* 2:442.

95. VII *D*, 1:9, *CW* 2:431.

96. IV *D*, 1:8, 11, *CW* 2:319–20, 321.

97. IV *D*, 1:8.

98. IV *D*, 1:9–13, *CW* 2:320–21.

99. Dante, *The Divine Comedy (Paradiso)*, canto 1, 7–9.

100. IV *D*, 1:10, *CW* 2:321.

101. *Way*, 16:1–4, *CW* 2:94–95. Cf. *Obras completas de Santa Teresa de Avila*, chap. 24, 557–58.

33. ACT 4: THE ANALYST'S FAREWELL

1. Cf. Thomas Aquinas, *Scriptum super Sentensiis*, Prologue, 1.5: "Oportet . . . quod modus istius scientiae sit narrativus signorum, quae ad confirmationem fidei faciunt."

2. *Way*, 26:9, *CW* 2:136.

3. *Life*, 9:6, *CW* 1:102.

4. Ibid.

5. VII *D*, 1:7, *CW* 2:430.

6. VI *D*, 3:1, *CW* 2:370–71.

7. II *D*, 11, *CW* 2:303.

8. VI *D*, 3:8, *CW* 2:374.

9. Angelus Silesius, *Selections from* The Cherubinic Wanderer, trans. J. E. Crawford Flitch (Westport, Conn.: Hyperion, 1978), 178.

10. *Life*, 25:22, *CW* 1:223. The "fig for all the devils" is an allusion to the female sex.

11. Ibid.

12. II *D*, 4, *CW* 2:299–300.

13. Sigmund Freud, *Selected Papers on Hysteria and Other Psychoneuroses*, trans. A. A. Brill (New York: Journal of Nervous and Mental Disease Publishing, 1912), 178: "*Per via di levare*" (as in sculpture and psychoanalysis) is opposed to "*per via di porre*" (as in painting).

14. G. W. Leibniz, *New Essays Concerning the Human Understanding*, trans. and ed. P. Remnant and J. Bennett, book 1, "Of Innate Notions," chapter 3, §3 (Cambridge: Cambridge University Press, 1996), xc [102].

15. On the "double alliance," see Antoine Guggenheim, *Jésus-Christ, grand prêtre de l'ancienne et la nouvelle alliance: Étude du commentaire de saint Thomas d'Aquin sur l'"Épitre aux Hébreux"* (Paris: Parole et Silence, 2004).

16. Sigmund Freud, *Complete Psychological Works*, vol. 19, *The Ego and the Id and Other Works*, trans. James Strachey (London; Vintage 2001), 31: "His identification with the father in his own personal prehistory." See also Julia Kristeva, *Tales of Love*, translated by Leon S. Roudiez (New York: Columbia University Press, 1987); and *This Incredible Need to Believe*, trans. B. Bie Brahic (New York: Columbia University Press, 2009).

17. The "baroque poet, " Annibal de Lortigue (1570–1640): "*Toute chose est muable au monde. Il faut aimer à la volée . . .*"

18. VI *D*, 6:8–9, *CW* 2:394–95.

19. Dante, *The Divine Comedy*, trans. Henry W. Longfellow, *Paradiso*, canto 1 (London: Capella, 2006), 61–63, 70–71, 85, 106–7; and canto 32, 142–45, 289, 383.

34. LETTER TO DENIS DIDEROT

1. Stéphane Mallarmé, "The Same," in *Divagations*, trans. with an introduction by Barbara Johnson (Cambridge, Mass.: Belknap, 2007), 251.

2. Denis Diderot, "On Women," trans. Edgar Feuchtwanger, www.keele.ac.uk. Accessed August 2012.

3. Denis Diderot, *The Nun*, trans. Russell Goulbourne (Oxford: Oxford University Press, 2005), 6, 14. The text was originally circulated in handwritten copies of *La correspondance littéraire*, exclusively read by a handful of enlightened North European royals. The novel appeared posthumously in 1796. The philosopher's previous convictions deterred him from publishing it during his lifetime.

4. Ibid., 81.

5. Ibid., 92–93.

6. Ibid., 74–75.

7. Augustine, *Soliloquies*.

8. For M. d'Alainville's visit, see Diderot, *Œuvres Complètes* (Paris: Gallimard, 1951), 1385 (my translation—LSF).

9. Diderot, *The Nun*, 65.

10. For the last words attributed to Diderot ("The first step towards philosophy is incredulity"), see Jim Herrick, *Against the Faith* (New York: Prometheus, 1985), 84.

11. Diderot to Sophie Volland, August 8, 1762 (my translation—LSF). This is not among the letters featured in Diderot's *Letters to Sophie Volland: A Selection*, trans. and selected by Peter France (Oxford: Oxford University Press, 1972). Letter to Mme d'Epinay, 1767 (my translation—LSF). See *Correspondance de Diderot*, ed. G. Roth and J. Varloot (Paris: Minuit, 1955–1970), vol. 7, 156.

12. Friedrich Nietzsche, *The Anti-Christ*, trans. H. L. Mencken, (1920; Tucson: Sharp, 1999), 113.

13. Marcel Proust, "Time Regained," in *In Search of Lost Time*, trans. and with an introduction and notes by Peter Collier, ed. Christopher Prendergast (London: Penguin, 2002), 6:157: "sterile celibates of art."

14. Philippe Sollers, "Ma France," *Revue des deux mondes*, April 2006. Cf. "Pascal et Sade."

15. Mariana Alcoforado, *The Letters of a Portuguese Nun*, trans. Edgar Prestage (London: David Nutt, 1893), letter 5, p. 93.

16. Meister Eckhart: 1260–1327. See "German Sermon 6," in *The Essential Sermons, Commentaries, Treatises, and Defense*, trans. Edmund Colledge and Bernard McGinn (Mahwah, NJ: Paulist,1981), 187.

17. Tauler: 1300–1361.

18. Mino Bergamo, "La topologie mystique," in *L'anatomie de l'âme: De François de Sales à Fénelon* (Grenoble: Jérôme Millon, 1997), 149 sq., 166 sq., 193 et seq.

19. Francis de Sales: 1567–1622.

20. Fénelon (François Salignac de la Mothe): 1651–1715.

21. Jeanne Guyon: 1648–1717.

22. Diderot, "On Women."

23. Denis Diderot, *Rameau's Nephew, D'Alembert's Dream*, trans. with introduction by Leonard Tancock (Harmondsworth: Penguin, 1966), 105: "set to music."

24. Diderot, *Dialogues*, "Conversation of a Philosopher with the Maréchale de —," trans. Francis Birrell (London: Routledge, 1927), 172, 177–78, 173, 175–76.

25. Thomas Hobbes, *Leviathan* (1651; Seattle: Pacific Publishing Studio, 2011), chap. 6, p. 30: "Publiquely allowed, RELIGION; not allowed, superstition."

26. Diderot, *Dialogues*, 183.

27. Diderot, "Entretien d'un père avec ses enfants, ou du danger de se mettre au-dessus des lois," in *Œuvres complètes de Diderot*, vol. 5, 2 (Paris: Édition Assézat-Tourneux, Garnier Frères, 1875–1877), 308 (trans.— LSF).

28. Bergamo, *L'anatomie de l'âme*, 67: "carrousel vertigineux et proliférant de subdivisions."

29. Fénelon, archbishop of Cambrai, was nicknamed the Swan of Cambrai in allusion to his disagreements with Bossuet, known as the Eagle of Meaux.

30. Bergamo, *L'anatomie de l'âme*, 160 et seq.

31. J. B. Bossuet, *Correspondance*, ed. C. Urbain and E. Levesque (Paris: Hachette, 1909), 6: 424: the mystics as "great exaggerators" (October 10, 1694).

32. Jeanne Guyon, *Spiritual Torrents*, trans. A. W. Marston (1875), online at passtheword.org/DIALOGS-FROM-THE-PAST/spiritualtorrents.htm. Accessed January 12, 2013.

33. See chap. 22, note 25 on *entrañarse*.

34. Letter to Sophie Volland, August 10, 1769. *Correspondance de Diderot*, ed. R. Versini (Paris: Laffont, 1999), 960.

35. Diderot, *On Women*.

36. Diderot, *The Nun*, 152.

37. Diderot, *On Women*.

38. Rosemary Lloyd, trans. and ed., *Selected Letters of Charles Baudelaire: The Conquest of Solitude* (Chicago: University of Chicago Press, 1986), 176: "Is there, can one say, any one more Catholic than the devil?"

39. *Way*, 16:1, 4, *CW* 2:94, 95.

Sources

The works of St. Teresa of Avila are quoted from the following translation issued by the Institute of Carmelite Studies:

The Collected Works of St. Teresa of Avila. trans. Kieran Kavanaugh and Otilio Rodríguez. 3 vols. Washington, D.C.: ICS, 1976–1985.

The Collected Letters of St. Teresa of Avila. trans. Kieran Kavanaugh. 2 vols. Washington, D.C.: ICS, 2001–2007.

Within quoted matter, emphases are of the author of the present work. [Occasionally, when the ICS translation does not follow the Spanish as faithfully as is needed for the purposes of the present work, I have put an alternative version in square brackets, followed by the Spanish.—Trans.]

The original in Spanish was consulted online at: *Obras completas de Santa Teresa de Jesús* (es.catholic.net/santoral/147/2519/articulo.php?id=2059).